Awaken Online
Tarot Book 3: Inferno

Travis Bagwell

D1736870

To my wife, if you died, I'd totally resurrect you inside my favorite videogame.

How exactly is that *not* romantic?!

Contents

Prologue

10 years before the release of Awaken Online.

Finn woke with a start, blinking bleary eyes. The movement was a strain with the way his eyelids were crusted shut. An incessant beep came from just to his right, the sound rhythmic and monotone and painfully, fatefully familiar.

A hazy glance confirmed what he already suspected.

A hospital monitor loomed beside the bed, the machine flashing occasionally and showing a readout of his pulse, blood pressure, and brain activity. Although, with the way his vision was swimming, it was difficult to focus on the images. More than that, his body throbbed and ached. Except for his legs, those were blissfully free of pain. Numb really. He raised a hand to rub at his eyes, the movement tugging at the IV embedded in his wrist, and he frowned at the transparent cable in confusion.

"Fantastic, you're awake," a voice spoke up. A woman's face soon hovered in front of him. There was something about the shape of her nose… or maybe it was her eyes… "My name is Nancy Carrigan. Do you recognize me?"

"I-I think so," Finn croaked, his voice hoarse.

Why does she look so damn familiar? His thoughts felt sluggish, as though his head was full of gelatin. It took a concerted effort to focus – something that felt out of place and unusual. Normally, the thoughts came so quickly…

"Do you remember your name?"

That one took a second, but it came to him, eventually. "Finn. Finn Harris."

"Good," Nancy said, tapping at a small display projected beside the bed.

"Do you know where you are, Mr. Harris?"

Finn let out a snort. "A hospital, clearly."

A small, sad smile on the woman's face. "Do you

remember which one?"

His brow furrowed.

How had he gotten here? Why was he in a hospital?

Then it struck him with the force of a freight train.

It had all started with a small, nagging worry. The flash of a sequin dress. An award digging into his side. A tremor that quickly spiraled out of control. Then he was tumbling, flying weightlessly through the air. His hand had reached out to the woman beside him, her auburn hair tumbling around her face. Those beautiful brown eyes, contorted in fear...

Rachael

It felt like Finn had been kicked in the chest, the breath whooshing from his lungs in a rush. The monitor beside him was beeping erratically now. He couldn't breathe – couldn't move. He remembered the accident...

Rachael getting sucked out of the jagged hole that had been ripped in the side of the car... the pain, the anger, the terror... her mouth opening in a silent, desperate scream...

...it felt like he was drowning...

...and then it all faded into the background.

Suddenly, Finn was just numb – as though a switch had been flipped in his head.

"Mr. Harris, are you okay? Can you hear me?" Nancy asked, her gaze troubled now. Her brow creased with worry, and her eyes flitting nervously to the nearby monitor.

"Stop calling me that," Finn said, his voice quiet and disturbingly steady. "You and I have known each other for years, Nancy." He now understood why her face seemed so familiar– those eyes that were now wide in surprise. Nancy had been his wife's PA for the last six years. He'd met her dozens of times.

And if she was caring for him personally instead of a nurse...

Finn swallowed hard, forcing that thought aside and giving himself over entirely to the calm void that had filled his mind. The gesture was painful. His throat hurt. *Feeding tube*, it came to him immediately. The lack of feeling in his legs made sense now too. *Spinal injury, long-term paralysis*, his brain supplied clinically.

"Finn, please look at me," Nancy said, her voice filled with an emotion that he didn't want to hear right now. Finn couldn't bring himself to do it. He didn't want to see the information painted across her face. He just wanted this moment to continue a little longer. For her to let him be and let him embrace that numb emptiness.

And yet his eyes raised to hers on their own, drawn inexplicably upward.

He saw the truth shining in Nancy's eyes, in the moisture that clung there. The pinched lips, the pale skin. Dark circles that spoke of sleepless nights. His mind picked out each piece of data, and he could feel it unraveling that clinical calm, leading inexorably toward an inevitable conclusion. And so, Finn squeezed his eyes shut, not trusting himself to stay in control – not if he had to see the compassion and pain reflected in her expression.

A small, nervous cough came from Nancy. "You're at St. Peregrine Memorial," she explained. "You suffered severe injuries from the accident. Internal organ damage. Multiple fractures along both arms. Dislocated shoulder. Yet the most severe injury was to your spine, that's what's causing the lower-body paralysis."

"How long?" he croaked.

"10 days since the accident. They induced a coma to help repair most of the damage and injected neuroplastic into your arms to repair the fractures. It's set by now, but the adjacent tissue is still damaged. Internal injuries have also stabilized. It's your spine that's the problem. We had to wake you to ask what you want to—"

"My kids?" Finn interjected, cutting her off.

"With your sister. She picked them up the night of the accident," Nancy said softly.

A brief hesitation.

And then, "Finn, you need to pick a treatment, and then we have to put you back under. If we wait, the damage to your spine may become permanent."

He just shook his head. That didn't matter – not right now.

There was still one question he hadn't asked yet.

"Rachael?" His voice cracked, and that numb void shuddered. It felt fragile, tenuous.

His eyes shot open.

He saw Nancy. The pain etched across her face. The tremble in her hands.

"Dr. Harris... *Rachael* didn't make it," she said, unable to meet his gaze. Nancy reached out a hand, laying it on his arm. Compassion. Pity. Grief. His mind listed the emotions in a strange, detached way, as though he were reciting a recipe.

It didn't feel real. It couldn't be real.

He pulled his arm away. "Where is she? The morgue downstairs?"

Nancy's eyes widened. "Well, yes... but—"

"Get me a chair."

"Finn, you can't—"

"Just do it, Nancy," he said calmly, his eyes meeting hers, his gaze even and unwavering. "It's either that or I crawl. Or you sedate me – but then you aren't getting your answer on the treatment."

He saw her hesitate for only a moment before she left the room. When Nancy returned, she was rolling a folding wheelchair – no fancy electronics or life support. Sometimes there was still a use for the classics. She moved toward the edge of the bed and then circled to help him.

Yet Finn shrugged off her hands. He would do this himself.

With a grimace, he tugged the IV free. Pushing against the cushions, he forced himself upright, his arms burning in protest. Then he began the laborious process of moving his legs, shifting the numb limbs to the edge of the bed. When he was ready, Finn took a deep breath and shoved off. He nearly missed the chair, barely landing on the edge, and his arms trembled unsteadily as he clung to the armrests.

He felt something tear in his left arm, a burning pain lancing through the limb. Yet he ignored it. He also ignored the distressed look in Nancy's eyes and the way she appeared to resist the urge to help him by clenching her hands together. She only tugged his thin hospital gown down around him once he was settled, not saying a single word.

Then Finn wheeled himself out of the room. Each movement cost him dearly, even the smooth metal grip along each wheel ripping open the recently healed cuts along his palms. The ache in his arms and shoulders soon turned to a throbbing pain that rippled up each limb and across his shoulders. It felt like his left arm was on fire.

But he kept moving.

The hospital staff stilled as he entered the hallway, a hushed silence filling the corridor. Finn pushed past them. He didn't stop or say a word, just forced his reluctant limbs to keep moving, pushing himself toward the elevator he knew rested at the end of the hall. He could hear hushed whispers behind him and the soft tap of shoes on tile – Nancy, most likely – following him.

He entered the elevator and spoke over his shoulder. "I'm fine from here."

"I really don't think—"

He cut Nancy off again as he tapped the doors closed with a faint hiss of hydraulics.

Several long, pain-filled minutes later, Finn had managed to wheel himself into the morgue – past a very surprised and upset-looking member of the hospital staff. However, a tap at the man's coms and a few hushed whispers later, Finn had been let inside and directed to a table at the far end of the room.

Now he rolled up to that metal counter, his ragged breathing the only sound that filled the room. He saw the outline of a body lying there, a sheet drawn taut. It seemed surreal. Impossible. A scene from a film. A horrible dream, maybe? He drifted forward, and his fingers touched the cloth. He could feel the coarse fibers, wondering in a detached way why they were so rough. Wouldn't she be uncomfortable? Cold on the metal table?

Finn took a final deep breath.

Then he tugged.

He didn't know what he had been expecting. But the horror of what he witnessed didn't do it justice. It was like a portion of his brain had shut off completely. All he could think about was the force and angle needed to sever each limb. The shape of the objects that would have left those ragged lines of flesh. The heat required to boil away skin. The tensile strength of human bone. Numbers and graphs replaced conscious thought.

It was a physics problem – that was all.

A problem to be solved.

It wasn't his wife.

It wasn't Rachael.

It couldn't be, could it?

Could it...?

His eyes drifted toward the base of her neck, ignoring the ruined flesh and the hint of ivory. He was searching for something specific. Something that would indicate it was Rachael – his Rachael.

Then he went dead still. A small black nodule rested along her skin, the plastic scuffed but still intact. A cluster of electronics, microscopic wires that drifted up into her cranial cavity. It was the sensor they had implanted while they had been studying her – while he had been building the thing that ultimately killed her...

Finn couldn't ignore that. Couldn't ignore that final piece of evidence.

Faced with the harsh reality that lay on that table, the numbness finally fractured and then burst apart, the shards and fragments cutting and tearing their way through his mind. All he felt was pain – excruciating, gut-wrenching pain that made his injuries pale in comparison. It was as though someone had ripped out a part of his soul.

He didn't even realize he was sobbing until he felt

a hand touch his shoulder, the fingers gentle but firm. Finn didn't move. It was as though his entire body was paralyzed, his eyes merely staring at the remains of her face. Those eyes, now vacant and lifeless.

"Finn, you shouldn't be down here," a voice said. Masculine. Younger than Nancy.

Finn couldn't respond, his eyes locked on Rachael.

He felt himself wheeled around, turned to face a young man who crouched down in front of him. Finn knew that face, and his mind supplied a name. *Robert Graham.*

"What are you doing here?" Finn managed to ask.

"The hospital contacted me when you insisted on leaving your room," Robert said, eyeing Finn with a worried expression. "I'm your emergency contact after… well, after Rachael," the young man said with a grimace. "You've been down here for an hour. If it weren't for the tag in your wrist, indicating that your vitals were stable, the hospital staff would have rushed in here already and sedated you.

"Shit, you're bleeding," Robert muttered, his eyes hovering on Finn's chest.

Finn looked down and could see that blood now stained the white gown a bright shade of crimson. He must have torn some of his stitches. Probably pushing himself in the wheelchair. His left arm also hung limp and unresponsive. Torn tendons, most likely.

"Come on, we need to get you back to your bed."

"No," Finn snapped. Then in a more pleading tone, "Just a few more minutes… please, Robert. Please."

The young man stared at him for a moment, and then his eyes drifted to Rachael's body. Robert squeezed his eyes shut against the horror on that table. When he opened them again, Finn saw moisture brimming there. "Fine. A few more minutes, but then I'm wheeling you back to your room myself."

Finn felt himself rotated back around to Rachael.

Then he forgot about anyone and anything else. He reached forward with his right arm, his fingers sliding into what was left of Rachael's hand – that same hand that had been stretched out toward him as she floated inside the car. The one he had failed to grasp.

Tears rained down his cheeks, his chest heaved, and his blood slowly leaked across his hospital gown as he held her hand in that still, cold room. "Just a few more minutes..." he murmured, his voice echoing softly.

"Just a few more minutes, that's all I want."

Chapter 1 - Ruined

It had been nearly a full day since Finn had been able to log back into Awaken Online. The system had booted him the day before, shortly after his last fateful confrontation with the Seer and his conversation with Julia. It seemed that whatever sickness had afflicted his character had locked him out of the game.

He woke to find himself lying on a hard, flat surface. The fever and hot flashes had disappeared, and the pain had receded. Only a dull burning sensation now simmered through his left arm... or what was left of it.

His eyes crept open, taking in the room around him. Finn's *Short-Sighted* ability was active and cast the room around him in varying shades of blue. The enclosure was dark, lit by a faint sheen of glowing algae that coated the ceiling. As best he could tell, a single passageway lingered across from him.

With a groan, Finn shoved himself upright. It was at that point that he ventured a glance at his left arm. The limb had been severed at the elbow, the skin now wrapped in a thick layer of dark metal with tendrils curling up his biceps like obsidian flames. At least the surrounding skin had healed, red welts and pink flesh replaced with a healthier hue. As his fingers traced the metal, he could see that the substance had fused with the underlying bone. Removal would be tough... if not impossible.

The injury had cost him dearly: a few days of in-game time to recover and the loss of his *Multi-Casting* ability.

"Damn it," Finn muttered with a grimace.

Although, there wasn't much he could do about any of that right now.

He needed to focus. *First things first, where the hell am I?*

Finn had been with allies the last time he was inside AO. He could still vaguely recall the rhythmic sway of a beetle below him. At least 2-3 days had passed in-game under the effects of the time compression. Which meant he was probably somewhere deep within the desert by now. He could only assume his body must have stayed in-game during his absence, perhaps a function of whatever magical illness had afflicted him.

Now he was who-the-hell-knew-where in this dark room.

At least this was a concrete problem – one he could tackle.

"Daniel," Finn barked.

The AI immediately flashed into existence nearby, his glowing body lighting the small space. "Hello, sir... oh, shit," Daniel muttered as he took in the walls of the cave. "Are we in the Abyss again?"

"I was about to ask you the same question," Finn replied in a dry tone. "I take it you don't know where we are?"

"No, sir," Daniel replied, flashing weakly. "I was automatically dismissed when you were ejected from the game world, although my records indicate that your body remained. I suspect the game was treating you as a form of quest object for your companions."

"Great," Finn said, running a hand through his hair. "Although, it seems they left their so-called quest item lying here in the dark."

"At least the room doesn't appear to be on fire, there are no obvious explosives nearby, and we don't seem to be under attack," Daniel ventured. "That's usually the case when you summon me."

"Hey, not every time—" Finn grumbled.

"Those scenarios represent 76.38% of the times you summon me according to my records. Other circumstances often involve menial labor, experimental procedures, and so-called 'scouting' that frequently results in a confrontation."

A brief pause and the AI's body flashed once. "In case you were curious, you have called on me exactly zero times just to chat and ask me how I'm doing. I also have no memory during the periods where I'm not present in this world. You could effectively equate my dismissal to your concept of death."

"Hmph, I'd argue it's more like sleeping," Finn grumbled, side-eyeing the AI. "Have you been experimenting with *guilt* now?"

"I find it to be an intriguing concept. Julia explained that it's more effective when coupled with something called *passive aggression*. Which seems like an oxymoron..."

Finn stifled a sigh, rubbing at his eyes. "Well, you already seem quite good at it." A faint flash of happiness from the AI was his response. "Either way, I suppose we should try to figure out where the hell we are," he said finally, glancing around the cave.

"Existing map data is... sparse," Daniel reported, his voice distant – almost distracted. A floating map abruptly appeared in front of Finn. However, the entire display was grayed out, and the window stuttered slightly. He also didn't see any icons for his teammates.

Finn could only assume this was another "authentic" game feature. It made sense. If he didn't know where he'd been taken, then he shouldn't be able to pinpoint his location with a flick of his wrist. However, he was going to add this to his growing pile of too-damned-realistic game mechanics.

"Perfect," Finn muttered. His gaze shot to the group UI in the corner of his vision. His teammates were definitely online – that much was clear. Maybe they had decided to go ahead and entomb his old ass in this cave.

With a quick gesture, Finn brought up his chat window and typed out a short message. Hopefully, they could update him on the situation and pick a location to regroup. However, as the seconds and then minutes ticked past, he received no response.

"Perhaps they are otherwise occupied?" Daniel offered tentatively, breaking the silence in the cave.

Finn grunted noncommittally. Frustration warred with worry in his mind. Despite his daughter's penchant for messing with him, he doubted that Julia and Kyyle would ignore him intentionally, especially now that they knew about Finn's bargain with the Seer. There was far too much riding on this game to mess around. Which likely meant they were either in trouble or physically unable to respond.

"Damn it. It looks like we're on our own for now," Finn muttered, sparing a glance at Daniel. The AI's glowing form flickered weakly.

Let's see if we can get a better idea of where we are and what's nearby, Finn thought. He channeled his fire mana, using the simmering energy to burn away his own anxiety.

Finn focused on the small cavern around him. The cave was too dark to make out his surroundings clearly, even with the light cast by Daniel's flickering form and the glowing blue outlines cast by his *Short-Sighted* ability. With a brief command, Finn reactivated his *Mana Sight.*

The world around him was immediately awash in a cascade of color. The walls glowed a dark luminescent green that indicated dense rock. That energy expanded outward in every direction for at least 100 feet. No obvious enemies were in sight.

With a shift of his attention, Finn focused on the walls of the cave. He breathed a sigh of relief as he saw the surface lacked the symmetric marks of ant mandibles, and the color of the stone was a touch lighter than the Abyss – indicating that the stone was less dense. Sandstone was his guess. The walls were uneven and jagged, which spoke of natural rock.

So, we're definitely not back in the Abyss. One bit of good news.

Finn glanced down at the stone slab below him. It was the only unnatural thing in the cave: a flat and uniform surface of stone that stood out in stark contrast to the jagged rock formations around him. The rock also glowed with an unnatural emerald hue. Maybe Kyyle had built him a bed? That seemed plausible since his pack also rested on the floor nearby. Although, that clouded his theory that they were in danger. Enemies didn't usually tuck you in and neatly store your gear and weapons.

Then Finn caught a telltale flash of orange from his left arm.

His brow furrowed in confusion as he held up the stump, the burning sensation still lingering there. The ruined flesh glowed a dull orange, but it was the Najima that captured his attention. The globe of mana had been perverted. Tainted. It was riddled with dark-red lines of power that leached into the nearby flesh, the pattern reminding him eerily of an infection. Tendrils of energy also stretched from the arm and speared out into the cavern, drifting into the nearby wall and heading directly east.

"What is this…?" Finn began aloud. Perhaps some lingering aftereffect of his confrontation with Bilel? He had stopped the transition into a hellhound, but maybe the staff had still managed to partially corrupt his Najima. That might explain the tendrils of mana that drifted through the room. The relic had been designed to continuously drain energy after the transformation, after all. If he was right, then Finn was most likely somewhere roughly west of Lahab.

Although, that just raised another question. Had this corruption affected his stats?

He supposed there was one way to find out.

With a grimace, Finn pulled up his Character Status. He was rewarded with a barrage of notifications. It seemed he hadn't checked his notices since his battle with Kalisha and Malik and his encounter with Bilel…

x10 Level Up!
You have (50) undistributed stat points.

X1 Spell Rank Up: Imbue Fire
Skill Level: Intermediate Level 9
Cost: 200 Mana
Effect 1: Imbues a weapon with fire mana, increasing the weapon's base damage by INT x 14.0 %. Can only be used on unenchanted metal

weapons.

Effect 2: While channeling, allows the caster to increase the heat in ranks, up to a current max heat rank of [4]. Each heat rank increases damage by INT x 5% while increasing the channel cost by 50%.

Channel Effect: Allows user to control the weapon within his control range at a cost of 25 mana/sec.

x4 Spell Rank Up: Mana Absorption
Skill Level: Intermediate Level 1
Cost: 70% of mana drained as health damage.
Effect 1: The caster can absorb ambient fire mana, adding the energy to their total mana pool.
Effect 2: Increased absorption range, sensitivity, and area of effect.

x5 Spell Rank Up: Haste
Skill Level: Intermediate Level 2
Cost: 200 mana upon activation. 67.5 stamina/second sustained.
Effect 1: Increases total speed by 36.0%.
Effect 2: Reduces stamina cost by 11%.

x2 Skill Rank Up: Flameworking
Skill Level: Intermediate Level 6
Effect 1: 40% increased power when shaping objects subject to *Imbue Fire*.
Effect 2: 20% increased control when shaping objects subject to *Imbue Fire*.

System Notice
You have undergone a second body augmentation, severing your left arm and wrapping the ruined limb in a coating of dense metal. The extremity is now permanently damaged, and the effect will persist upon death and respawn. Whether this injury can be healed is unknown.
Similarly, while you survived the confrontation with Bilel

and the fire relic, the experience has afflicted your body with a magical illness. The Najima in your left arm has been corrupted, and the staff is still leeching a small portion of your mana, reducing your base stats by 10%. This effect will persist upon death and respawn until the illness has been treated. As you continue casting, the infection will spread at an unknown rate.

Think of this as a minor "hand-icap." Pun intended.

Character Status			
Name:	Finn	**Gender:**	Male
Level:	102	**Class:**	Fire Mage
Race:	Human	**Alignment:**	Lawful-Neutral
Fame:	1800	**Infamy:**	0
Health:	1990	**H-Regen/Sec:**	7.23
Mana:	2232	**M-Regen/Sec:**	43.94
Stamina:	1405	**S-Regen/Sec:**	9.00
Str:	42	**Dex:**	90
Vit:	149	**End:**	90
Int:	391	**Will:**	27

Affinities			
Dark:	2%	**Light:**	10%
Fire:	49%	**Water:**	5%
Air:	3%	**Earth:**	11%

"Well, shit," Finn grumbled, his voice echoing in the small cave. He swept aside the notices with a frustrated wave of his hand. He wasn't certain what to do with his points right now anyway, so he might as well sit on them.

The damage to his arm was indeed permanent. His guess was that it was technically possible to reheat and remove the metal, but that process would hurt like hell. The strain on his mind and real-world body would likely be too great, and so the game had stopped him from making the attempt.

That alone was bad enough, but Bilel had also left Finn with a lingering *present*. It seemed he hadn't fully escaped the staff's influence. The relic's leeching effect had reduced his stats, and that reduction was layered on top of whatever the Seer was already claiming as her usual cut. Oh, and the prompt seemed to imply that the infection would continue to spread as he used his magic.

It seemed everyone wanted a piece of him.

Except he was starting to run out of body parts.

"Great," Finn muttered. "So, we're in a strange cave. We're possibly in danger. Our teammates have gone radio silent. I've lost my arm. And I'm now suffering from a semi-permanent debuff that will only make me weaker over time. Oh, and we still need to figure out how to kill an unstoppable demon that has had a century to gorge himself on unsuspecting mages. Because this was feeling too easy before..."

"Well, at least we don't have to worry about figuring out which way to go," Daniel offered. His form floated over to the sole entrance to the cave, a passage that quickly faded into darkness. With his enhanced sight, Finn could only see an ocean of green lingering behind that wall, no telltale glimmer of mana giving away the presence of other life.

"Forgive me if I don't dance with joy," Finn snapped.

He saw the AI's light dim. "Shit. I'm sorry, Daniel. I shouldn't take this out on you. This is just a messed-up situation."

Finn let out a sigh, rubbing at his temple with one

hand and trying to tamp down on the frustration simmering in his chest. To make matters worse, his stump was still throbbing – an ache he suspected wasn't going to disappear any time soon.

Even as that thought flickered through his mind, Finn's lips tugged into a grimace. He couldn't solve most of his problems – not yet, at least. But perhaps he could improve on his useless arm. He was probably going to have to fight his way out of this cave. Which meant that he needed to prepare and arm himself, regardless of how that might affect his newfound magical illness.

His injury was a liability – one he needed to address now.

And he already had an idea for how to improve the ruined limb.

"You have that look again," Daniel commented, bobbing around Finn's head. "The one that usually precedes a violent confrontation... and explosions."

Finn spared a grin at the AI. "Nothing that bad. I was just thinking of ways to fix my arm." As he spoke, he grabbed at his pack with his uninjured hand and began burrowing through its contents. Letting out a sigh of relief, his fingers wrapped around a familiar, hard sphere. At least all of his equipment was still here.

He withdrew the dark metal orb. With a flick of his wrist, Finn sent the sphere sailing into the air, his fingers already moving as arcane words tumbled from his lips. Flames soon wrapped around the metal, and the dense chunk of ore stopped in place before striking the ground. Finn pumped more mana into the spell, swiftly ratcheting up the temperature to heat rank level 4. The metal soon warmed to a bright red, and droplets began to drip from the sphere. With another twitch of his fingers, Finn set the orb to spinning to keep the molten metal from breaking apart.

Only moments later, a brightly glowing metal orb hovered in front of him. Finn squinted as he focused on the sphere with his enhanced sight. Pinching at the metal, he drew it out into a thin cylinder before smashing the substance flat. He kept the metal as thin as possible, while still ensuring that it would be durable enough to take a hit. Then he tapered the tip down to a fine point. As a finishing touch, Finn flattened the end of the blade slightly, creating a shallow cup of molten metal.

A roughhewn blade about a foot and a half long soon lingered in the air, the metal still awash in flame. Finn glanced down at his left arm with a frown. This next part was going to be a bit uncomfortable.

"What are you — ?" Daniel began.

Finn didn't give the AI a chance to finish that thought... or for himself to back out.

He lifted the metal-coated stump, and the fingers of his right hand twitched. The molten blade sped forward and struck his left arm squarely. The base fused around the colder metal of Finn's stump, swiftly heating it. The flesh and muscle began to tingle and then burn as the metal grew warmer – the sensation soon overwhelming the ever-present simmering ache that lingered in the ruined limb.

That burning sensation grew to a painful fire, and the skin around the stump began to redden and welt under the heat, causing his health to dip precariously. Finn squeezed his eyes shut and let out a hissing breath, his control trembling. Yet he ground his teeth together and forced himself to hold still. He needed to maintain the channel long enough to ensure that the metal fused properly. The last thing he wanted was his makeshift weapon falling off in the middle of a fight.

Finally, he released the spell.

The fire winked out, and the metal of the blade now glowed brightly in the darkened tunnel. The substance swiftly began to cool, regaining its normal dark appearance. Finn's breath came in ragged gasps, several precious minutes ticking past as he sat there and willed the burning to subside. The pain eventually began to abate as his natural regeneration healed the welted flesh around his stump.

He spared a glance at his left arm. A thin dark

blade now jutted from his elbow. The blade was well made and seemed structurally sound. Although, despite Finn's attempt to keep the metal thin, it was heavy. He tested it by smacking the weapon against the stone slab he was using as a seat. It held. However, the metal was rough – too coarse to cut anything.

I can also fix that problem…

Finn rummaged through his pack again and soon pulled out one of his old makeshift sawblades that he had created in the Abyss. The diamond-like ant mandible still coated the ridge of the disk. With another uttered incantation and a few deft movements of his fingers, the disc was soon awash in flame and spinning up to speed. Finn rose from his perch, knelt beside the stone table, placed his new blade on the surface, and set to work, using the saw blade to gingerly sharpen the edge of the blade. Within only minutes, the weapon had a razor-sharp edge and tapered down to a needle-like point. A droplet of blood formed along Finn's finger as he ran it down the blade.

"This'll work for now," he grunted, retaking his feet and swiping the makeshift weapon experimentally through the air. It was going to take some time to get used to the weight, awkward reach, and reduced flexibility. But it was better than nothing.

"Hmph. An improvement, but your sense of self-preservation could still use some work," Daniel observed dryly.

"Hey, that was actually the goal," Finn retorted. "A sword arm is more useful than a stump. Although…"

He drifted off, his fingers moving through a few swift gestures. His *Magma Armor* soon slid across his left shoulder and ran down his arm. The substance shielded the ruined limb and drifted out a few inches across the top side of the blade, creating a protective guard around the base of the weapon. Then Finn pulled another dark metal orb from his pack and set the sphere aflame, letting it hover beside him as his fingers maintained the channel.

"Alright, *now* I think we're ready," Finn said.

"Good enough for you?"

Daniel just flashed once in tepid agreement. "Sure. I guess. Our odds of surviving a conflict have increased by approximately 3.6%."

"Thanks for the rousing support," Finn muttered.

Daniel's words just fanned the flames of his own doubt, punctuated by the still-simmering burn in his left arm. He felt better with the blade mounted to his left arm, but it wouldn't even begin to equal his multi-casting. And particularly not with the loss of 10% of his base stats. A glance with his *Mana Sight* confirmed that the infection had indeed spread with just that short bout of casting, the angry red tendrils creeping further up his bicep. He was still weak, lost, and alone.

On the other hand, it didn't help to sit here and throw himself a one-man pity party. He should count his blessings. Bilel could have wiped them all out and permanently destroyed their characters. Yet Finn was still alive, he was back inside AO, and he was relatively safe. Besides, he had learned to live with pain a long time ago – pain far more intense than the fiery ache in his arm.

He had also faced far worse problems. That sense of despair in the wake of Rachael's death. His own failings as a father. The obstacles he had endured since entering this world. Learning a new language. A grueling deathmatch. A fall into the Abyss. A fight against both champions. And an encounter with a demon king.

Despite those hardships, he had kept going. Kept putting one damn foot in front of the other. And now he needed to do the same; he needed to get his shit together.

He had a mission to complete – a king to kill.

And a prize to claim.

I'm coming for you, Rachael.

With a grunt, Finn lifted himself to his feet, grabbed his bag and hauled it over his shoulder, and then began heading for the darkened tunnel, his flaming orb lighting the way.

"C'mon, Daniel," Finn said over his shoulder. "Let's see if we can figure out what the hell happened to our teammates."

Chapter 2 - Tested

Finn soon discovered that the narrow tunnel stretched on for about a hundred yards. It took a winding path through the earth before opening into a much larger cavern.

He knew this because he was currently crouched farther back along the tunnel, his hand resting on the nearby wall as he peered into the stone. Finn peeled away the intervening layers of earth mana like a magical onion. The emerald energy abruptly dissipated twenty feet from his location, outlining a roughly cylindrical room. At a guess, the cavern was about sixty feet in diameter, and the ceiling stretched up at least a few dozen feet into the air. More problematic, the curve of the walls was too even, creating a nearly perfect circle.

It didn't look natural.

On the bright side, at least his map had begun to cooperate, showing him the thin path back to the small cavern where he had woken up. He could also now see two telltale flickering green dots just past the large cavern – indicating the position of his teammates. However, they still hadn't responded to his messages, and they were unmoving. His guess was that they were either incapacitated or being held under guard... or both.

"What now?" Daniel asked quietly, his form flickering in a show of anxiety.

Finn let out a soft sigh. This cave felt off somehow. Frankly, it felt like a trap. But he didn't see any other option aside from entering the room, and he needed to recover his teammates. The tunnel only led one way, and he lacked Kyyle's earth-moving abilities.

Which left just one option.

"We're going to have to enter the cave and see what happens," Finn replied finally.

"Are you certain that's a good idea?" Daniel asked tentatively.

"No, not really. But I've gotten better at winging

it," he offered with a lopsided grin, trying to distract himself from the worried pit in his stomach.

Daniel didn't seem to share his cavalier attitude, the glowing ball of fire dimming slightly. That wasn't the rousing support Finn had been hoping for, but he could sympathize with the AI's doubt and anxiety. If he died, he wasn't certain where he'd respawn. If the game returned him to Lahab... Well, that would be bad. Unfortunately, there was nothing he could do to improve their situation. They just needed to roll the dice.

Finn swiftly rose to his feet, shouldered his pack, and forcefully channeled his fire mana, the burning sensation sweeping away his own anxiety and replacing it with boundless energy. The metal embedded in his eyes began to glow, warming the skin of his face.

It was time.

He started down the tunnel with the AI reluctantly following him.

The pair soon moved out of the darkened passage into the large circular cavern. Finn's gaze swept the room, but he only observed a ring of green energy around him – the rock walls of the cavern. At this distance, he could also see that the walls created a sheer, vertical barrier that ringed the room for about fifteen feet before flattening out into what might have been a rough terrace. The rock walls had been worn smooth by something... or someone. And there was no sign of his teammates.

Finn stepped into the center of the chamber.

The cave was still. Quiet. Eerily so.

This doesn't feel right. That feeling was back but amplified a thousand-fold. It was an odd sensation, just a tickle along the back of his neck that made Finn feel like he was being watched.

His focus shifted, his attention flitting to the ambient air mana that hovered inside the chamber. The yellow energy was dim here, only faint currents drifting through the underground cavern. Acting on instinct, Finn removed the earth mana from his sight, focusing only on the air in the cavern. He could see it swirl and ripple, reacting to his movements. Each puff of breath created a faint cloud of amber light. He froze in place in the center of the room and stilled his breathing. Watching that energy carefully, he searched for any sign of movement.

Then he saw it…

And just in time. A blade rocketed through the air, only barely intercepted by the flaming orb that hovered protectively beside Finn. The weapon ricocheted off the metal with a shower of sparks before embedding itself in the dirt lining the floor. Finn glanced down. It was a throwing knife, the metal carefully forged and polished.

Humanoid enemies. Unknown number. Undetectable to my sight. Finn's mind ticked off the variables automatically. That led to one inevitable conclusion.

The Khamsin.

If he were right, he wouldn't be able to easily see his opponents coming. They must have removed their armor, and they were likely holding unenchanted weapons, the earth mana in the metal blending into the walls of the cavern. They would be nearly invisible to Finn's *Mana Sight*. It was also difficult to detect their presence with the way the air mana swirled and rippled erratically, too faint to make out much detail. To make matters worse, the single opening blow had placed Finn in combat, which meant he could no longer use his *Short-Sighted* ability.

That left him with only his *Mana Sight*.

Finn took a deep breath, focusing only on the air currents in the room. "Daniel. Build a circular model of the exterior walls of the room, assuming a 60-foot diameter. Then use my sight to highlight unnatural air currents and extrapolate the position of our enemies."

"Of course, sir. This will take thirty seconds."

Finn didn't have time to think about much else as a barrage of knives raced toward him, a faint ripple of air mana the only giveaway.

Diving to the side, Finn rolled across the ground, coming up in a crouch. He sensed a ripple of yellow energy in his peripheral vision, and his orb moved forward. A blade skittered across the metal, but this one was connected to a limb. Finn was able to detect the faint mana signature of the man's clothing at this range. When they moved in close, the Khamsin were just barely visible.

Finn immediately retaliated. His flaming orb smashed forward around the knife and struck where Finn suspected his enemy was standing. The sphere passed harmlessly through the air, but not before Finn saw orange and red mana flare brightly, briefly illuminating a human-shaped form.

Damn it. That confirmed his guess. Only one opponent could absorb his mana like that. And that inevitably led to a more unsettling conclusion. These weren't novices. He was fighting experienced Khamsin.

Another blade rocketed forward, and Finn was moving again. Spinning and dancing through the room, sidestepping a blow, deflecting another with his orb, letting a knife slice through the edge of his molten armor, before smashing aside a fourth with his new bladed arm. Yet the fifth knife cut a line across Finn's cheek, leaving a trail of blood in its wake.

Damn, I'm a little slower than usual. A parting gift from Bilel.

With a grimace, Finn ratcheted up the temperature on his orb, swiftly moving it up to heat rank level 4. It would take more concentration to hold the liquified metal together. And that only gave him about 90 seconds on his channel before his mana ran out, but he needed the added speed and force if he was going to survive this fight.

Another blade skittered toward his legs. The molten globe of metal arced forward, flattening into a disc in mid-flight. The throwing knife was caught in the web of liquid metal, swiftly heating and melting down the blade and adding the substance to the disc.

A second blade speared forward from Finn's left, and he brought up his bladed arm. He managed to parry the blow, but the knife ricocheted wildly and cut into the edge of Finn's thigh. He let out a hissing breath but couldn't spare the wound any attention. He'd have to rely on his natural health regeneration.

Okay, maybe a lot slower than normal...

"Analysis completed!" Daniel reported.

Four roughly spherical targets were now highlighted in Finn's vision. The absence of air mana was almost imperceptible, particularly with his attention focused on avoiding the Khamsin's attacks. Apparently, Daniel had experienced a similar problem. The highlights only gave Finn a rough location. The faint energy and subtle movements of his opponents made it difficult to pick out their position with precision. At least it was enough to anticipate the direction of their attacks.

Although, it didn't help Finn deal with the question that kept bouncing through his mind. Why the hell were the Khamsin doing this? His memories were a little fuzzy, but he could have sworn that the desert folk had been responsible for saving them after their confrontation with Bilel.

Yet, even as that thought crossed his mind, Finn recalled the way Aerys had attacked him outside of the Abyss. The desert folk placed value on strength and readiness. His opponents also seemed to know Finn's abilities. Why else would they have dropped their armor and used only unenchanted gear? Or launched that first knife to ensure he stayed in combat? They had also left him his equipment and had placed him in a tunnel connected to this large cavern.

Finn grimaced as he deflected another barrage of blades.

That could only mean one thing...

This was a *test*.

If he was right, that meant he needed to not only win but, ideally, avoid killing his opponents. While the Khamsin might not hold a grudge, he was ultimately going to need their help. He doubted that they would be happy with him for killing or maiming their members. And he knew he was going to need every able-bodied soldier for the war that was coming.

Although, that didn't help him right now. How the

hell did he hit what he couldn't see? Or defeat an enemy that could absorb his mana? Especially if he wanted to avoid killing his opponents. To make matters worse, he was running out of time. His mana was depleting swiftly. But if he dropped the heat rank on his orb, he would be too slow to avoid the Khamsin's attacks. He was already struggling with his new handicaps.

Finn ducked under another blade and slid to the side, feeling a second weapon slice through the armor along his left arm. That strike sent him off balance. The Khamsin capitalized on the moment of weakness, and a third knife raced forward, given away only by a faint streamer of air mana. Finn didn't have time to move his orb into position. Instead, he was forced to lift his right arm, letting the knife embed itself in his forearm.

Acting quickly, Finn grabbed the hilt with his teeth and ripped the blade free. Blood trickled down his arm and around his fingers, where they continued to maintain his channel. The strike had narrowly avoided the tendons in his forearm, and the skin began to piece itself back together slowly as his regeneration kicked in.

They're trying to whittle me down and wear me out, Finn realized. And it was working. Everyone had their limits. Eventually, he would move too slowly, take a hit that couldn't heal easily, or knock out his channel, and then the deathblow would come.

Although, that thought gave him pause.

Everyone has limits, he repeated to himself.

Didn't that also apply to Finn's opponents?

He needed a way to put them off balance. Or, better yet, a way to *overwhelm* them and give himself a window to retaliate. Finn glanced at his mana. He also needed to recover some mana. He was already below half.

Could he kill two birds with one stone?

He could vaguely recall the tooltip for his *Mana Absorption* – hitting intermediate had increased its range, sensitivity, and area of effect. Could he use that here somehow? Except, there didn't appear to be any sources of heat…

A pause. But was that entirely true? Finn smacked away another blade as he eyed the cavern around him. There had to be *some* heat in the cavern. After all, he wasn't freezing to death.

Acting on instinct, he focused solely on the fire mana in the area around him. At first, he couldn't make out anything. He pushed harder, narrowing his focus. Faint traces of orange soon appeared in the air, just a thin haze that lingered across the cavern and drifted up toward the ceiling. He could see now how the ambient heat tinged the air mana a slightly darker hue. The heat also permeated the rock around him, but it was even more subtle.

That must be the ambient heat in the room. Could he absorb that?

A glimmer of an idea ignited in his mind, fueled by his desperation. His mana surged, burning away the last traces of his doubt and hesitation. Finn's lips pinched into a thin line. There was nothing for it. He was going to have to give it a shot.

"I'm going to do something reckless again. Give me a timer on *Haste* once it's active," Finn barked at Daniel, earning him a flash of acknowledgment from the AI.

He moved quickly. As he dropped the channel on his right hand, the metal orb crashed to the ground with a dull thunk. His enemies didn't hesitate, and a fresh barrage of blades whistled through the air. Finn dropped to his knees, raising his left arm protectively and accepting the blows. He felt the metal cut into his molten armor, slicing it apart. However, the blades soon stopped against the dense metal that coated his arm. Finn looked up as another wave of missiles raced toward him.

He wouldn't be able to stop all of the knives. There were too many, and they were moving too fast. Finn was barely able to follow them with his *Mana Sight*.

His spell completed, and fire raged through his body, and his skin began to shimmer with flames. As his *Haste* fully took hold, the incoming missiles seemed to slow in mid-flight, as though the air itself had turned to gelatin. Then Finn moved. Rising to his feet in a fluid movement, he spun, and the blade along his left arm neatly deflected each missile, sending the weapons crashing into the ground. From his opponents' perspective, Finn suspected he must look like an orange blur of flame.

"You have 21 seconds on *Haste* and roughly 30 seconds on your channel," Daniel reported from his position atop Finn's shoulder.

Finn could see his stamina and mana dropping fast, but he didn't plan for this to last long. He focused on the room around him, narrowing his *Mana Sight* and concentrating on the faint traces of orange that lingered through the room. There was heat everywhere, in everything, at least some faint trace. The air. The rock around him. Even his own breaths sent a puff of thermal energy into the cavern.

Here goes nothing.

Finn took a deep breath, then called that ambient heat to himself. Yet he didn't pull on a single source of flame or fire. He pulled on the *entire* cavern around him.

The fire mana resisted at first. It felt sluggish and weak. But he didn't relent. He yanked, pulled, and tugged. He *demanded* that it return to him.

Finally, the energy responded.

Heat leeched out of the rock and air. It swept toward Finn, just a trickle at first. But that trickle was swiftly growing into a torrent of energy as he urged every last trace of heat to return to him. Even as he called to the ambient heat in the cave, Finn continued to dart and weave through the center of the cavern. In a blur of flaming motion, his bladed arm swept aside each blow and slice from the Khamsin.

The cavern began to grow colder. It was gradual at first. But the air soon grew crisp, and a thin coating of ice began to cover the dirt floor. Under the effects of *Haste*, Finn was insulated from the cold by the fire mana that burned through his body and coated his skin. The energy seeped into his Najima, adding to his mana and causing his blood to simmer in his veins as his health dropped. Yet Finn ignored the pain. He had endured worse.

The Khamsin weren't so lucky. They grew more frantic, sensing the danger. They weren't immune to the frigid bite of cold that now lingered in the cave. They couldn't absorb the *absence* of a specific energy.

They rushed at Finn as a group – as he expected they would.

And he was waiting.

He dodged under a snapping limb, whirled to avoid another stab, and his blade intercepted a third strike as the world around him blurred and swam. Yet his opponents were slower now, a combination of the frigid cold and Finn's enhanced speed. And yet, he never stopped drawing on that heat, forcing the temperature in the cave ever lower.

"Twelve seconds on *Haste*," Daniel reported.

The Khamsin withdrew, desperately trying to regroup. Finn could visualize their thoughts. They had already revealed that they were aware of Finn's abilities, which meant they must know the duration of his *Haste* was limited. If they couldn't overwhelm him, they would wait him out. Bear the biting cold and hope that they could eliminate him once he dropped the spell and his stamina bottomed out.

They were playing a game of chicken.

A faint grin stretched across Finn's face. He didn't plan to wait that long.

The first step had been to weaken them and replenish his mana.

Finn spared a glance at the UI in the corner of his vision. It was at 75% again.

Which meant it was time to finish this.

The fingers of his right hand began to move as he cast another spell, and an incantation drifted from his lips even as flames began to encircle his body. Finn poured energy into the spell, his mana pool dropping rapidly, and the fires around him flared forcefully.

His opponents were shifting course now. They sensed the threat and saw the flames building around Finn. They were beginning to charge, the blue spheres that marked their presence barreling toward him. But they were moving slowly. Far too slowly.

Far too late...

Finn finished casting his *Fire Nova*.

A ring of flame rocketed away from him like a slow-moving avalanche, his pent-up mana spreading outward in a devastating wave of fire that surged and crackled with power. The flames jetted nearly ten feet into the air and were so dense that his sight couldn't fully penetrate the energy. The fire pushed through the room in slow motion. His opponents tried to backpedal and avoid the energy, but there was nowhere for them to go. The nova soon consumed them, burning through their bodies with abandon. The Khamsin came to a standstill, their outlines flaring with orange and red energy as they tried desperately to absorb the mana and prevent it from burning them alive.

Their bodies writhed and twisted as they tried to contain the energy. Finn knew firsthand how painful the absorption could be. He also knew it had limits. Julia had spent considerable time building up her tolerance – which had enabled her to use her shield and the heavy metal armor that Finn had formed for her back in the Abyss.

These Khamsin hadn't had such extensive training.

They were flaming fish in a barrel.

"10 seconds!" Daniel barked.

More than enough time.

As soon as the nova completed, Finn was moving. He dashed through the room, making a beeline for the closest of the Khamsin. This next part would require some finesse. The flames of the *Fire Nova* held his opponents trapped, but it also made it impossible for Finn to harm them since their bodies were temporarily converted to flame.

But he had a solution for that.

He absorbed the flames *around* his opponent, his

bladed arm winking forward in a flash. As soon as the man's body regained its normal weight and heft, Finn's blade cut through the tendons in the back of his legs. The Khamsin dropped to the ground with a grunt of pain. But Finn had already moved on. He absorbed and cut with surgical precision – ignoring the burning fire that coursed through his veins.

Only a few seconds later, the *Fire Nova* finally struck the far wall of the chamber. The flames rocketed upward, rippling and steaming in the frigid air and reheating the room. Finn once again stood in the center of the chamber. His skin was awash in fire, and fresh blood dripped from his bladed left arm. Four bodies lay along the floor, the dirt around them stained bright crimson. Streamers of smoke curled from their singed clothing.

Finn finally dropped *Haste*, wavering in place as the burning sensation receded. The world lurched back to normal speed, and the flames of the nova dissipated harmlessly against the cavern's ceiling.

He kept a watchful eye on the Khamsin, but none of them made any move to rise. In fact, they knelt facing Finn. An instant later, Finn's *Short-Sighted* reactivated, and he could see that each of his opponents held a fist to their chest, their heads bowed.

Finn heard a thump echo through the cavern, and he followed the noise. With the danger neutralized and a blue haze now coating his vision, Finn saw lights suddenly illuminate the chamber, confirming that a terrace ringed the room above him. Dozens of Khamsin lined that ledge, watching the conflict in the pit. Finn hesitated as he saw Julia and Kyyle standing beside Aerys and a group of men and women Finn didn't recognize. His companions were alive and well – although the Khamsin that flanked them looked more like guards than friendly acquaintances.

The thumping sound had come from Aerys as she pounded her fist to her chest. This sound was repeated throughout the silent chamber as the rest of the Khamsin followed her lead, each man and woman making the same gesture. He'd seen Julia do the same when she met Aerys.

It was a greeting shared among the desert folk – an acknowledgment of one of their own.

"Can there be any further doubt?" Aerys' voice rang out. "We are in the presence of the Prophet. The Flame Eater. The *Najmat Alhidad.*"

As she spoke those final words, the other Khamsin picked up Finn's title, creating a rhythmic chant that echoed off the walls and rebounded endlessly through the cavern. And through it all, Finn stood there, bathed in flame, his chest heaving, and each breath causing a mist of vapor to form in the still-chill air of the cavern.

It seemed he had passed the test.

Chapter 3 - Reunion

"Maerakat mujayda."

One-by-one, each of the four men that Finn had faced murmured those words, struck a fist to their chest, and then headed for a narrow passageway carved into the side of the arena. Despite the thick silks that covered their faces, their eyes and body language were clear – they belied no animosity.

Finn wasn't certain how to react to that. Those four had tried to kill him only moments before – or, at least, it certainly didn't *feel* like they had been holding back. The burning furrows carved into his skin were painful evidence of that. The wounds were only just beginning to piece themselves back together as his natural health regeneration kicked in.

"It means glorious battle," Julia said. Finn turned to find his daughter standing behind him with Kyyle at her side. Even with *Short-Sighted* re-enabled, Finn had difficulty deciphering the expression on Julia's face – worry and respect warring for dominance. "You seem to have impressed many of the Khamsin."

"No kidding," Kyyle offered with a lopsided grin. "Even for you, that was a... uh, remarkable show you put on. I take it you discovered yet another new trick – at least if the subzero temperatures in the ring were anything to go by. You're going to give me the details, right?"

Finn frowned at that comment, his eyes flitting to a small red notification that had popped up in the corner of his vision after the battle.

System Notice: Infection Status

Continued spellcasting has caused the magical infection that afflicts your body to spread.

Current Contamination: 18%

> **Intact Najima:** 5/6
>
> **Stat Loss:** -10%

That *Mana Absorption* trick and the rest of his spellcasting had clearly come with a cost, and the simmering ache in his arm had grown more insistent. Although, he'd had little choice but to defend himself. At least the infection hadn't yet spread to another Najima. Either way, he was going to need to be sparing with his casting from here on out.

Finn discreetly swiped aside the notification. For now, he was going to play this newfound liability close to the chest. He didn't want to worry his companions – or alert the Khamsin that he was suffering from another hidden weakness.

They likely had enough problems already.

Kyyle was still watching him expectantly. "I'll be happy to share the details, but this might not be the best time," Finn replied softly, with a subtle gesture at the Khamsin that still lingered along the terrace that ringed the arena. This earned him a grimace and nod from Kyyle. They still had an audience.

Finn's eyes skimmed to Aerys, where she was approaching behind his teammates. More Khamsin filtered into the pit behind her. The robed figures took up positions along the edge of the arena, their eyes focused on Finn, and their hands hidden by the thick cloth that wrapped their bodies. No doubt, their fingers were lingering along the hilts of their knives.

They look like guards. The question was whether they were guarding Finn or the other desert folk? His money was on the latter.

He might have passed the Khamsin's test, but that clearly didn't mean Finn and his teammates were fully trusted yet. He suspected the Khamsin had been holding his teammates until he had proven himself. The frown creasing Julia's lips and the meaningful glance she shot

Aerys seemed to confirm that suspicion.

"I take it there was some purpose behind attacking a blind and crippled old man?" Finn demanded, meeting Aerys' gaze. "Or at least I'm hoping you had a damn good reason for this public spectacle." He waved at the terrace, where the crowd of desert folk was only just beginning to dissipate.

"I'm not certain I'd use either *blind* or *crippled* to describe you," Aerys replied in a dry voice. "You made short work of our fighters – and those were veterans of our clan."

The Khamsin leader sighed. "Besides, this was necessary. A demonstration – to placate the other clan leaders. There were those who didn't believe you were the *Najmat Alhidad*," Aerys explained. "Although, your performance managed to quiet many wagging tongues."

Seems I was right, Finn thought, irritation simmering in his veins. That had been a test then. A bit more intense than his other job applications, but he supposed the Khamsin's process was at least efficient.

Finn arched an eyebrow at Aerys. "Was blowing up the Abyss not enough? There were dozens of witnesses."

"You would think," Julia grumbled, shooting Aerys a scathing glance. "Or how about me? I was already a clan member, yet you still took my weapons and placed me under armed guard."

Aerys shrugged, unperturbed by the way the group was glaring at her. "We couldn't have you ruining the trial by trying to spring Finn early. Or are you suggesting that you would have just stayed put?" This earned her a snort from Julia.

The Khamsin leader turned back to Finn. "Besides, I have found that words often lack the weight of action. Between the witnesses vouching for you at the Abyss and your performance here, there can no longer be any room for doubt. The other clan leaders in attendance had no choice but to allow you and your companions to be inducted into our clan, and word of your accomplishments will only spread.

"In fact, you have greatly enhanced our clan's reputation," Aerys continued, a hint of a smile tugging at her lips. "By the time they were leaving the arena, many of the other leaders were grumbling that it wasn't *fair* for us to keep the prophet and his companions for ourselves."

"You're welcome," Finn replied in a sardonic tone, watching Aerys closely. From the gleam in her eye, he suspected that her motives hadn't been entirely altruistic. That little *demonstration* had likely been designed more to bolster her own reputation among the clans than to help Finn. Inducting the *Najmat Alhidad* into her clan likely came with a few perks.

It seemed that he was being used… again.

Finn hadn't missed how several of the Khamsin on the terrace still lingered. In particular, an older man remained, flanked by others dressed head-to-toe in thick cloth. The man's eyes never wavered from Finn's face, and his expression gave away nothing. Yet something about the look in his eye – or perhaps his presence – spoke of a quiet power. Or maybe it was the way the usual zealous worship was missing from his face.

"It doesn't seem that you convinced everyone," Finn said, gesturing at the older man on the terrace. "Friend of yours?"

Aerys' grin disappeared in a flash. She and the older Khamsin shared a curt nod before he turned on his heel and made his way out of the cavern. "People respond to conflict in different ways. For some, they cling to hope – a messiah. For others, all they know is hate and anger, using it to push themselves forward," she said in a low voice.

The woman waved a dismissive hand, her attention skimming back to Finn. "However, it's a moot point now. You've earned the protection of our clan, and the majority have conceded that you are the *Najmat Alhidad*. Even the naysayers have no choice but to follow the herd or risk the loss of their protection."

Finn raised a skeptical eyebrow as he watched the

older man's retreating form. From his expression, Finn doubted this conflict was truly over – only delayed.

Although, there was little he could do about that at present.

Finn let out a sigh, and his eyes skimmed the group. A frown tugged at his lips. "Where's Abbad? Wasn't he with us when we escaped Lahab?"

Kyyle winced. "It seems there are some hard feelings between the Khamsin and the mages... for obvious reasons," he offered tactfully, glancing at Aerys.

"What he means to say is that they locked Abbad up in one of the holding cells," Julia added, a note of irritation coloring her voice. "They've posted at least five guards on that cell, even though he's made no attempt to resist, and we were clear that he was the only reason we made it out of Lahab alive."

Aerys shot Julia an alarmed look, her eyes widening slightly. "How did you —"

"Trust runs both ways," Finn's daughter retorted with a smirk. "Let's just say I took a few *field trips* while no one was looking. If you had harmed Finn, we would have sprung our people and burned this place to the ground."

"Well... then I'm glad it didn't come to that," Aerys answered slowly. Tension had entered her voice, and she was side-eyeing the guards that lingered around them. It seemed that Julia must have slipped her shackles in Finn's absence.

"It looks like I've missed a lot," Finn interrupted, trying to calm the situation. There was no sense in fighting. If they were to have any chance of killing Bilel, they were going to need each other's help. Although, he was beginning to realize that might be like herding cats...

His daughter rubbed at her eyes, letting out a sigh. "That may be the understatement of the year. Honestly, this demonstration and our temporary incarceration are just the tip of the shit iceberg. You've been gone for a few days in-game. Things... haven't been going so well."

Aerys nodded. "Yes, there's much we need to

discuss, but perhaps this isn't the best place to do so. Too many prying ears. I suggest we move to more private accommodations."

"Certainly," Finn replied with a nod. Frankly, he was looking forward to being out of the limelight for a while. However, he paused as a thought occurred to him. "Although, we'll need the librarian. Have your people bring Abbad from his cell."

"I don't think—" Aerys began.

"I wasn't asking," Finn snapped, the metal embedded in his eyes flaring with a pulse of flame.

His patience had already been worn thin. Between the burning ache in his left arm, the scripted deathmatch he'd been forced to participate in, and the imprisonment of his friends – all while being used as a pawn in a regional power struggle among the Khamsin – he had hit his limit for bullshit. The guards around them shifted in place at his tone, reaching for their weapons. Yet a single fiery glance from Finn caused them to freeze. They had just witnessed how quickly he had taken out four veteran fighters.

They didn't seem to be in a hurry to experience that themselves.

Then, more calmly, Finn continued, "Abbad will have crucial information. He was working closely with Bilel – the Emir – before the regent tried to kill us. I believe Abbad has been acting as a double agent for some time."

Aerys' eyes widened. "Hmm. In that case, it will be done." She gestured at a nearby guard, and the man swiftly exited the arena.

As soon as the guard left, another man entered the cavern at a jog. He spotted Aerys, swooped close to the clan leader, and whispered in her ear.

Aerys scowled at him. "Really? When?" she barked.

"They arrived just now. They were captured out in the sands hours ago and brought here bound and gagged. They say they wish to speak with the *Najmat Alhidad*," the man responded more loudly, shooting Finn a curious glance. At Aerys' sour expression, he continued, "Given the situation, our scouts thought it best..."

"No, no. It was the right decision. However, I'm sure some of the other clan leaders will raise hell over this additional intrusion – putting aside the obvious risk to the colony," Aerys grumbled, her eyes going distant.

"You want to share with the rest of the class?" Julia demanded in a dry tone.

"It seems we have a few more uninvited guests," Aerys replied evenly, pinching the bridge of her nose. Her eyes settled on Finn. "You're a popular man – and clearly a source of chaos. Let's hope you're worth it."

With that, she pivoted sharply on her heel and began heading toward the passageway leading out of the arena, leaving the group to follow. Finn shared a look with his teammates. They were all thinking the same thing.

What now?

Chapter 4 - Cavernous

The journey through the Khamsin "colony" was enlightening.

Finn had always imagined the desert folk as disparate bands of nomads, wandering the desert in small groups or caravans. That would have made sense. The Mage Guild had purged many students – residents and travelers alike. However, Finn's impression had been that few survived the exile among the sands and fewer still made it through the Khamsin's grueling training. Plus, the desert wasn't a terribly hospitable place.

He had apparently been wrong. Oh, so very wrong.

Or perhaps he had dramatically underestimated just *how many* people had been purged or had abandoned Bilel's oppressive regime in search of refuge among the Khamsin.

This "colony" wasn't a makeshift camp or caravan. It was a thriving underground city composed of maze-like passages that had been carved into the sandstone. The tunnels looped and curved and twisted, creating a dizzying series of passages that reminded Finn more of a beehive than something humans had constructed. Reviewing his map data as they walked, Finn estimated that the colony stretched on for at least a couple miles.

Based on the composition of the walls, it seemed the colony had been carved into one of the many rock islands that dotted the desert. It was a good strategy. The rock insulated the residents from the harsh desert sun and the sand worms. It also made the Khamsin incredibly difficult to locate. Even Bilel's enhanced sight would have difficulty penetrating the many miles of desert and the intervening layers of sand and rock. The fact that many of the desert folk had no mana and were almost invisible to the sight was just an added bonus.

That combination of variables might explain why Bilel hadn't managed to entirely wipe out the Khamsin.

The group turned a corner, and the passage opened into a massive chamber. The cavern spiraled upward for nearly fifty feet, a network of tunnels branching off the main chamber and stone walkways crisscrossing the air above him. Algae clung to the walls and ceiling, letting off a soft glow that lit the underground cavern in a pale light. Finn slowed to a stop, his mouth opening slightly in shock.

"They call this colony *The Hive*," Kyyle offered with a grin at Finn's dumbstruck expression. I'll give you three guesses why."

"Not that you'll need more than one," Julia interjected.

"The Khamsin created this?" Finn asked in awe. It seemed like an incredible feat. But more than that, the walls lacked the usual uniformity or symmetry of a human building.

"Not exactly," his daughter replied, gesturing for them to keep moving as they followed Aerys. "These rock islands are home to several indigenous insect species – like the ants we discovered back in the Abyss. The Khamsin clear out the bugs and then move in, expanding the tunnels as the community grows. These rock islands also tend to be rich in metals, so the desert folk mine those materials and trade them in Lahab."

Finn shot her a surprised glance.

"What? Where did you think the merchants got the ore to craft that fancy gear? It isn't all looting and pillaging around here," she replied with a small smile.

They passed a group of Khamsin bickering over a pallet of goods emblazoned with the mark of the merchant guild. The desert folk quieted as they saw Finn and stared after him with unblinking eyes. "Well, not entirely anyway," Julia amended. "We trade the merchants the materials, they forge the equipment, and then we steal the end product."

"Screwing them on both ends," Kyyle observed with a chuckle.

"Hmph, clever," Finn said softly. "So, the islands make for ready-made cities, they're difficult to locate, they're easy to defend, and they're rich in natural resources." He paused, observing the residents within the massive chamber and those that tread the walkways that hovered above him. "But there are just so many people," Finn murmured in reply. "I wasn't expecting that. At most, I thought the Khamsin could muster a few hundred."

Indeed, there appeared to be that many living in *The Hive* alone.

Finn had made a rough tally of the number of Khamsin they passed in the cramped tunnels. And they weren't just fighting-aged men and women. Finn saw older folk and children among the residents. There were *generations* of Khamsin inhabiting this colony. As that realization occurred to him, Finn began to understand what Aerys had been saying before about hate and hope.

How would these people react in the face of *decades* of persecution?

Julia nodded, following his gaze. "And this is just one colony. The Khamsin are spread across the desert, creating semi-autonomous underground cities. They are independent and wary by nature. Thus, our *cold* reception." This earned her a snicker from Kyyle at the pun.

Finn just grunted in reply, rubbing at his left arm in a vain attempt to blunt the burning ache there. He still hadn't forgotten the welcome party Aerys had thrown for him.

"Say what you want about Aerys' methods, but she's right about one thing," Julia continued. "Uniting these people is going to be tough."

Finn could see the thread of truth in Julia's words. It was in the way that some of the Khamsin glared at him with unblinking eyes. He could see the *anger* there. Perhaps they blamed anyone capable of utilizing magic for their plight. But even those people could likely be swayed. That anger could be harnessed – targeted. At their core, they all wanted one thing. They yearned for freedom. To be able to leave these cramped halls.

And the eyes of many, many more shone with *hope*.

Residents stopped to stare at Finn or pressed themselves against the walls to let their group pass. Their fingers plucked at his robes as he neared, as though Finn were something holy – that some of his power would pass to them with just a faint brush. He heard the same words repeated over and over, murmured in hushed voices filled with desperation and longing that echoed faintly off the stone walls of The Hive.

The *Najmat Alhidad*. The Prophet of the Flame.

Finn was distracted from his thoughts as a child raced out from beneath his mother's arms and ran toward Finn. Immediately, the Khamsin guards surrounded the group, their hands moving toward their weapons. But Finn waved them off. What threat could a child pose?

The boy tugged at Finn's sleeve, looking up at him with large eyes. He couldn't have been older than four or five. "Are you the prophet?" the child asked quietly. With the other Khamsin going deadly silent, his voice carried far in the large chamber. Dozens of robed figures watched the exchange with impassive expressions, waiting to see how Finn would respond.

Finn fought back the grimace that threatened to cross his face as he looked down at the child. In some ways, anger was easier. There was no expectation there. Or if there was, it wasn't a burden. There was little challenge in the expectation of failure. Yet for many others – such as this child – they had pinned their dreams on a faded and aging prophecy. On a broken, old man playing a videogame. It wasn't real – he knew that. Yet he could still feel something inside himself respond to that look in the child's gaze.

He wanted to help these people, he suddenly realized.

Not just because of the stakes for himself. But because he knew that he stood the best chance of uniting them. Of focusing their desperation and rage in the right direction.

And he knew that was what Rachael would have

wanted.

Finn knelt and met the boy's gaze. "I suppose I am."

The child seemed cautious, picking his words carefully. Finn saw the dirt along his arms, the threadbare cloth of his shirt, limbs that were wasted and thin from malnutrition. These people might have raw ore, but the Khamsin couldn't eat iron, and little grew out here in the desert. Thin white scars riddled the boy's forearms. They looked like knife wounds. He saw more experience reflected in the child's gaze than he should... a maturity born of necessity and hardship. And as he switched to his *Mana Sight*, he also saw mana glimmering through the boy's body. The son hadn't inherited the curse of his mother. New generations of Khamsin were apparently born with their magic intact.

"My mother says you've come to save us. That you'll bring down the goddess' wrath and defeat the Emir," the boy said, his gaze unwavering despite the thread of fear and doubt Finn saw curl through his mana.

Finn hesitated at that, uncertain how to respond. He glanced up at the boy's mother. She tried to control her expression, but he still saw her tension in the way she gripped her basket, bending the flimsy reeds. More of the Khamsin stood around them, silent and watching. Not only had they pinned their hopes on Finn – they had placed that hope in the Goddess as well. It was misguided. The Seer pursued her own agenda.

They were on their own.

And Finn knew that firsthand. No one had come to save him in his time of hardship. No one had brought back Rachael. No one had stopped the rollout of those autonomous vehicles. Even Julia had only given him a nudge back onto the path. He had been forced to keep pressing forward himself. And he'd learned a valuable lesson in the process. He had to own his mistakes and then work to solve them. Expecting others to come to your rescue was a *weakness*. Strength came from acknowledging your problems and working to fix them with your own two hands.

He met the boy's eyes and suddenly knew what to say. "No one is coming to save you – any of you," Finn said, raising his voice and addressing the crowd. "Not me and not the goddess."

The Khamsin shifted uncomfortably at his words, their eyes widening slightly in surprise, and a sudden tension filled the large cavern.

"Nor should they. We're each responsible for carving our own path – creating our own destiny. We do not need gods or prophecy. We will save *ourselves*." Finn said these words forcefully, his mana responding automatically and fire flaring through the metal of his eyes. He turned his gaze back to the boy. "Your – *our* – people already have the strength we need; we only need to learn to use it. We will take back our home with our own hands and our own blades."

"I—I understand," the boy said quietly, staring at Finn with a determination that felt out of place on such a young child's face. He placed a tiny fist to his chest. Then he ran back to his mother, and she wrapped her arms around him.

As Finn rose to his feet, he saw the Khamsin around them make the same gesture – a fist to their chest. He could hear the soft thump of skin striking cloth and the low buzzing murmur that drifted from dozens of lips and echoed off the walls and walkways of the cavern.

Najmat Alhidad, they whispered.

"I'm not sure that was wise," Aerys murmured, appearing at Finn's elbow.

He spared her a glance. "This was the role you wanted for me, wasn't it?" he demanded. "Well, now, you've got it. It was a harsh message, but one these people needed to hear. It's only going to get more difficult from here."

Aerys just grunted in response, but her eyes and body language loudly announced her disagreement. "Let's move," she said in a terse tone. "Before you decide to give another impromptu speech." She immediately started back through the cavern.

Then they were moving forward again. Except, this time, the guards pressed in tightly around Finn, pushing away the Khamsin that moved too close. It seemed that Aerys had instructed them to avoid a similar incident. Finn couldn't help but grind his teeth at that. Their clan leader appeared to be more interested in having a puppet she could use to show off the power of her clan than in letting him fulfill his role. More evidence of politics at work.

The reality of what was coming would sink in eventually.

"It's been like this ever since you arrived," Julia said softly, watching the way the Khamsin continued to stare and murmur Finn's title. "These people are desperate. The guilds have been stingy in buying shipments of ore lately, and our raids haven't been as successful. What resources we have go toward buying food. And as you can see, that isn't enough."

Julia hesitated, a frown tugging at her lips. "The truth is that Aerys is barely holding this place together, and the other colonies aren't much better off. They are desperate for any source of hope. It was all she could do to keep you secluded while your body healed. Or at least, I *thought* that was the goal. I didn't realize she was planning to set up some sort of deadly spectacle," she grumbled.

"Water under the bridge. There was little you could do under the circumstances," Finn whispered back as they exited the chamber and tread through another winding series of passages. "Is this what you meant by things not going so well while I was gone?" He trailed off, letting the implicit question hang in the air.

"It's not just the colony. The news we've heard from Lahab... well, it's not great – not at all," Julia replied softly.

His daughter paused as the group rounded a final corner, and the tunnel opened into a small cavern. "Huh. Well, I guess you'll get to hear that news firsthand," Julia added, her eyes focused on the far side of the chamber.

Finn could immediately see what had captured her attention. Two familiar faces awaited them, their hands bound and flanked by Khamsin guards.

Kalisha and Malik.

"Oh, this is just great," Kyyle muttered even as Julia tried to reach for a weapon that was no longer hanging from her waist.

Kalisha ignored their reactions, her eyes settling on Finn's face. "Hello again, Finn. Every time we meet, I seem to find myself tied up. I'm starting to wonder if you do this for all the girls," she said with a wink. For his part, Malik didn't say a word, the fighter's expression stoic. The gruff man simply stared at Finn with unblinking eyes.

A glance at the pair with his *Mana Sight* showed Finn that despite their cavalier attitude, they were undergoing a whirlwind of emotion, their energy fluctuating erratically throughout their bodies. And above that surface mana, a coil of darkness twisted around each of their Najima. That was *fear*.

"It seems it has already begun," a voice spoke up from behind the group. Finn turned to find that Abbad had entered the room flanked by a pair of guards.

"What has?" Finn asked.

Abbad gave him a measured look, his eyes drifting down to Finn's ruined left arm before meeting his gaze. "The endgame."

Chapter 5 - Endgame

"Well, as fun as this is standing here and staring at each other, why don't we make ourselves a bit more comfortable," Finn said, breaking the tense silence in the room. "Kyyle, you want to give us a table and some seats?"

The earth mage nodded, and his hands began winding through a rapid series of gestures, tendrils of emerald energy wrapping around his fingers. Finn saw the guards in the room tense, but Aerys raised a staying hand. Only moments later, a sandstone table rose from the ground, encircled by simple stone chairs.

"Have a seat," Finn said, gesturing at Abbad, Malik, and Kalisha.

"They should remain bound and standing," Aerys retorted. "They are a risk to us and to the colony."

Finn just stared at her. "I can see that we're at least a half-mile deep, they're all unarmed, Abbad saved our lives, and these two look like they've been out in the sands for days. Besides, have your scouts reported any activity in the desert? Anything to indicate that Malik and Kalisha led a contingent of the Emir's royal guard here?"

Aerys grimaced. "No... not exactly."

"And do you really think these three couldn't get free if they tried? It looks like you only bound their hands with rope," Finn added dryly. He was growing impatient with Aerys' bluster, especially after what happened in the arena and the encounter with the boy. She was going to have to learn the hard way that things were changing.

Finn shot Abbad a meaningful glance, and the librarian's fingertips twitched ever-so-slightly. Immediately, his bindings dissolved with a brief gust of wind. Malik must have also decided the ruse was pointless. Mana surged through the wards inscribed in his skin, and the rope around his wrists snapped. He then simply tugged Kalisha's bindings free.

The guards in the room pulled their blades in

alarm, but the librarian, merchant, and fighter made no move to attack.

"As I said, this is all pointless," Finn said, meeting Aerys' gaze. "Besides, this isn't the time for posturing. We have larger issues at stake.

"Everyone sit," Finn said, this time more forcefully. It was no longer a request. The guards hesitated only a moment longer before they moved away and allowed the prisoners to take a seat. "Maybe bring some water as well," Finn directed to a nearby guard. The man nodded and immediately left the room – failing to look to Aerys for approval. Finn noticed her frown deepen.

There were also some downsides to branding me as some sort of prophet in front of the entire colony, Finn thought sourly. He could see the same realization dawning in Aerys' eyes. And she didn't look happy about it.

"Okay, where should we start?" Finn asked, glancing around the table at the group facing him. His question was met with silence. They were an unlikely alliance – enemies and wary allies forced together by extenuating circumstances and a common opponent. While no longer openly hostile, their tension and suspicion was apparent in the way they side-eyed one another and shuffled in their seats.

"Fine. Then I'll begin with our tale," Finn said, breaking the silence.

He took a deep breath. "The Emir is actually a mage named Bilel. Long ago, he learned to feed on the mana of others. This process has corrupted his body over time, turning him into a demon and extending his age. I suspect he's more than a century old now. He's been using the Mage Guild and the purge to harvest mana from the mages to feed himself and to create a stockpile of mana crystals. He's gathering this power because he plans to wage war against the gods – specifically the Seer."

Finn saw Aerys, Malik, and Kalisha all stare at him in surprise, their eyes widening. Although, this was less of a revelation for the rest of the group. "Bilel manufactured this competition among the guilds, under the guise of finding his successor, in order to unearth the Seer's prophet – me, I suppose. The goddess prophesized my coming, and he needed me to open the vault down in the Abyss and reclaim the other half of a powerful magical relic he possessed. Now whole, this artifact has the power to heal Bilel of the corruption that plagues his body... and perhaps even help him slay the gods themselves."

He gestured at Abbad. "Bilel adopted Abbad as a child and trained him as a servant. It is my belief that Abbad has been secretly leading the Mage Guild, using the current headmaster as a puppet." There was a pause as Finn glanced at the librarian, noticing the way his energy fluctuated slightly at this statement – although, his expression gave away nothing. He gave a faint nod of acknowledgment. It seemed Finn was on the right track so far. Many of the pieces had begun to click into place since their encounter with Bilel.

"So, this man is responsible for administering the purge?" Aerys interjected, her eyes flashing angrily. Finn saw the guards along the walls shuffle in place.

"This man has been the *slave* of a demon," Finn corrected, his voice harsh. Whatever his history with Abbad, the librarian had saved him and his companions. "Abbad has been working as a double agent. He informed me of Bilel's past and ultimately saved my group from being destroyed by the Emir. He also knows more about our enemy than anyone else in this room. He's a valuable *asset*."

Finn met Aerys' gaze and could see the anger reflected there, yet he refused to back down. They would need the librarian's help in the war that was coming.

"Is this going to be a problem?" Finn demanded.

Abbad raised a hand to Finn before turning to address Aerys directly. "What Finn says is true. I was conscripted at a young age, and the Emir trained me himself. That was how I eventually discovered his true nature."

A grimace and the librarian continued, "I have been required to commit many evils during my life. Your anger is understandable, and there is nothing I can say that will undo what has already been done. But as Finn said, we have a common enemy. The Emir – Bilel. Perhaps my *actions* can help atone for what I've done."

"Nothing will ever wipe your slate clean," Aerys spat back.

"It will not," Abbad agreed simply. "And those acts will forever weigh on my soul. However, for now, I suspect you will need my assistance. Once our mission has been accomplished, you can exact whatever punishment you wish. I am more than willing to pay that price if it secures the freedom of the other mages and your people."

Aerys was about to speak again, but Julia placed a hand on her arm. "Let it go. Our quarrels need to take a backseat for now. You must have heard the rumors of what's happening in Lahab already. Our primary enemy is the Emir." The Khamsin clan leader grimaced but held her tongue.

"Rumors?" Finn asked.

Julia sighed. "I think it would be easier if our two *guests* helped explain. I expect there's a good reason they're here – and firsthand testimony is better than gossip."

All eyes turned to Kalisha and Malik, where they sat across the table.

"You really know how to put a woman on the spot," Kalisha offered with a smile.

"If you would like, we could provide some additional encouragement," Aerys shot back, waving at the guards, who stepped forward ominously, blades appearing in their hands.

Kalisha gulped, and she held up a hand. "Okay, got it. No joking. Geez, you people are on edge."

"Maybe just tell us whatever you've come to say," Finn offered. They certainly didn't need to antagonize the Khamsin any further.

Kalisha glanced at Malik, her expression sobering. "Things are rather… unstable back in Lahab. The Emir issued a public announcement that Finn violated the competition and tried to trick him by offering up a flimsy trinket instead of the relic we were sent to retrieve. Clearly, he was lying."

The merchant glanced at Finn with an appraising expression. "It also appears that *someone* told him that Malik and I were dead."

Finn nodded. That had been part of the plan, after all.

"Which may be the only reason we're not dead right now," Kalisha added grudgingly, waving at Malik. Her eyes shot to Finn. "Otherwise, I suspect we would've been greeted by the royal guard at the gate – a loose end that needed to be tied up, permanently."

She sighed. "However, we had the foresight to enter the city more surreptitiously. Our respective guild leaders were quite interested to learn what actually transpired in the Abyss and the fact that Finn arrived in Lahab carrying the actual relic. In short, they know that the Emir misled them. As the only witnesses to what happened in the Abyss, Malik and I have become quite valuable to the guilds."

Kalisha met Finn's eyes, and he saw an expression that he almost didn't recognize. She looked... grateful. And irritated at herself for being indebted to him. "I suppose we have you to thank for our lives," she said grudgingly.

"You're welcome," Finn replied in a dry tone.

"I'll point out that you technically owe us twice now," Kyyle said, staring at the merchant and fighter. "We could just have easily left you to die down in the Abyss as well." This earned him a pained grimace from both Kalisha and Malik.

"Point taken," Kalisha bit out.

"I assume the merchants and fighters weren't terribly happy to learn the Emir betrayed them?" Finn asked, his brow furrowed in thought.

"That's the understatement of the century," Kalisha grumbled. "But it's worse than that. After issuing his decree, the Emir locked the royal palace down, and all outside entry has been denied. That's unusual."

"It sounds like the Emir is being cautious after our escape. Maybe increasing security and trying to cover up that we made it out of the palace?" Julia offered. "We did a number on his throne room... or he did, anyway." She shot Kalisha an inquiring look. "Why exactly is this a cause for worry, though?"

"By itself, it isn't," Kalisha explained. "Except that we've received reports that residents have begun to go missing. At first, it was just the homeless and vagrants. A handful of the..." She trailed off, shooting Aerys a cautious glance. "Anyway, the disappearances haven't slowed. In fact, a few of our own guild members have gone missing."

Finn grimaced, rubbing at his temple with his good hand. It seemed Bilel was moving fast – much faster than he had anticipated. "It's likely the Emir," he murmured. He raised his eyes to see the others watching him. "That relic we recovered from the Abyss was one of two pieces – the Emir's staff being the other. When combined, it creates a powerful magical artifact. The staff preys on a person's passion, corrupting their Najima and draining them of their mana. The process also converts them into creatures of pure passion. A hellhound bound to the will of the person who wields the staff."

Finn raised his left arm, revealing the dark blade that now jutted from his elbow. "I barely survived the process myself."

"The staff also turns the hounds into mana batteries, funneling mana constantly back to the relic," he continued. "My guess is that the Emir has been draining his royal guard and staff first. If he's already worked his way through them, he's most likely kidnapping a few people at a time to continue feeding the staff without creating widespread panic."

Kalisha didn't seem terribly surprised. "We suspected as much. My mechanids and drones captured a few images from inside the palace walls—"

"The merchants were spying on the Emir?" Aerys

interjected in surprise.

"They have been for some time," Abbad answered for Kalisha. "The guilds have never fully trusted the Emir or one another. Bilel used this paranoia as a form of control. It keeps the guilds at each other's throats and individually weak."

Kalisha nodded. "Although, that has begun to change. Given the Emir's betrayal in the competition and this latest information, discussions have begun taking place between the merchants and the fighters. We've also reached out to Nefreet, but he has been unusually quiet." Her eyes focused on Abbad. "Although, I suppose it now makes sense why he would be reluctant to speak with us by himself."

"Which, I suppose, leads us to the reason we're here..." The merchant hesitated, as though not quite certain how to continue.

"Which is?" Finn prompted, although he already suspected the answer. He could recall his last conversation with the Seer. The gameboard had been set, and the goddess had carefully arranged the pieces. While he might have given away the relic – handed their enemy a powerful weapon – he had also set the stage for something new...

"An alliance," Malik spoke up for the first time. "We are stronger together – the guilds and the Khamsin." He nodded toward Aerys.

The merchant glared at Malik. "We could have soft-pedaled that a bit. Bargained for a few perks. You just showed them all of our cards."

Malik shrugged. "My orders were not to dicker over petty advantages. We have a more pressing problem at hand. The future of the guilds is at stake." He hesitated for a moment as though chewing on his words. "We also require the desert folk's assistance."

"Why do you need the Khamsin's help?" Julia asked, a frown creasing her brow.

"We would like to evacuate our guild members from Lahab," Malik answered evenly and without hesitation, earning him an exasperated sigh from Kalisha. "Which means we need help covering our escape and somewhere to set up a safe base camp. We'll need to move the better part of a thousand people from each guild."

Aerys snorted, smacking her hand against the table. "Are you two joking? What makes you think the Khamsin would be willing to help the guilds? After everything you've done to us? After how much blood has been spilled?"

"As though your people are entirely innocent in those conflicts," Kalisha retorted with a derisive snort. "I seem to recall quite a few attacks on our caravans, leaving merchants and fighters bleeding out in the sands."

"We weren't the ones to throw the first punch. The mages exiled us, the merchants cut off any hope we had of making a living by short-changing us on every trade, and the fighters hunt us like animals…"

As the bickering became more heated, Finn started to tune it out. His thoughts were racing. What the Seer had described had come to pass. The Emir's betrayal had set the stage for a potential union between the guilds and the Khamsin – with Finn standing in the center of the conflict.

They had a mutual enemy, and they needed each other's help.

The guilds needed a safe place to retreat. If they waited, the Emir would likely kidnap their members and drain them dry. His power would continue to grow as he charged the staff and created an even larger army of hellhounds. It was only a matter of time before he began openly kidnapping people. And despite Aerys' anger, the Khamsin needed the guilds. They needed their additional manpower, their equipment, and their skills – fighters, craftsmen, and mages that would be vital in the war that was coming.

Although, that didn't solve the larger problem that loomed at the edges of his mind.

Even if Finn could convince the various factions to work together, how were they going to face Bilel? The demon had a weapon capable of not only incapacitating his enemies from a distance but growing his own ranks at the same time, creating a legion of demon dogs that would only further increase his power. Finn could still remember what Bilel had done to his guards in the throne room. Even working together, the guilds and Khamsin were facing an almost impossibly difficult opponent – one that was growing more powerful with each passing day.

It still felt like a final piece was missing. A move that Finn couldn't quite see yet. It left him feeling frustrated and blind.

"Maybe I should show you the same mercy the guilds have—" Aerys snapped.

"Enough," Finn snapped harshly, smacking his palm against the table. He let some of his frustration slip through, his eyes glowing dully as he instinctively channeled his fire mana. A reluctant silence fell across the room, leaving Aerys, Malik, and Kalisha glaring at one another wordlessly.

"This isn't the time to bicker. We all have grievances against one another. Blood has been spilled. But the reality is that all of this hardship and conflict has stemmed from one person – Bilel. And now we face an enemy far more powerful than any of us can face alone. We have to put aside the past and work toward a common future."

"Are you really suggesting the Khamsin help these people?" Aerys demanded.

Finn met her gaze. "Yes. Would you rather face an immortal demon wielding a god-forged relic on your own? Or hide in the sands and hope he ignores you? Those aren't realistic options. We have no choice but to take the fight to Bilel – to kill a demon king. And to do that, we need *allies*. Soldiers, mages, and craftsmen capable of waging war."

Finn waved at the tunnel behind him. "What I told the Khamsin is the truth. We need to rely on ourselves and take matters into our own hands. And that starts with putting aside our grievances and our pride."

Aerys grimaced but held her tongue.

Turning back to Malik and Kalisha, Finn continued, "If the Khamsin help find refuge for your people and assist their passage across the sands, what would the guilds offer in return?"

The pair glanced at each other. "As you said, we can only run so long and so far. The only real solution is to kill the Emir. The leadership of both guilds have already pledged to commit all of our resources to that fight. They are ready to sign a treaty with both the other guilds and the Khamsin." Kalisha glanced at Aerys. "Assuming the desert folk are willing to offer us a place for our people."

"The other clan leaders would never agree to compromise the location and integrity of our colonies," Aerys said gruffly.

"Couldn't we make a new colony?" Kyyle offered. All eyes turned toward him. "If the Khamsin could identify a rock island that would be suitable for a new colony, even a small group of earth mages could build and fortify that location relatively quickly."

"And the Mage Guild could offer mages to help accomplish that goal," Abbad added with a nod. "We will need to withdraw our own people from the city, and there are many within the guild that are still loyal to me – including Nefreet."

"You mean the other islands that are now covered in giant mutant ants," Aerys said dryly, sparing a glance at Finn. "Someone destroyed their nest, and they have already spread far and fast. Some of the insects have even begun encroaching on our own colonies."

Malik tilted his head at that. "Then our fighters shall help clear the pests first. You only add a single step to the process."

A sudden silence descended on the room as the group digested this plan.

Aerys nodded, finally breaking the silence. "I…I might be able to sell that to the other clan leaders." Her gaze snapped back to Abbad, Kalisha, and Malik. "Assuming I was also promising the military support of the fighters and mages and supplies from the merchants. Although, many will still be unwilling to cooperate."

"You could also use my name," Finn said. "We will need to unite the desert folk under a common banner anyway. It isn't enough for the Khamsin to simply accept me as a member of your clan. If we are discussing war, now is the time for unity among the clans. Tell them the *Najmat Alhidad* has called on them to fight for their freedom."

Finn paused, recalling the critical expression on that old man's face back in the arena. Some of the Khamsin wouldn't be swayed by prophecy alone. "Any clan joining our alliance will also receive weapons and supplies. That should satisfy both the idealists and pragmatists." Aerys cocked her head as she chewed on that idea, but he could already see her anger morphing into cunning deliberation.

No doubt, she was weighing how she could barter with the other clan leaders to increase her own standing among the Khamsin. Finn didn't love giving the woman even greater power and influence – especially not after she had shown she was willing to risk his life to accomplish her own agenda – but if it helped him achieve his goal, then so be it.

"We're also authorized to offer one more piece of information – assuming you all were receptive to an alliance. You could consider it a show of good faith," Kalisha offered.

The merchant met Finn's gaze. "I suspect you already see the larger problem here. Even if we combine forces, we'll still be at a disadvantage against an enemy wielding a god-forged relic – one that can convert our forces mid-fight. I'm not sure any of us fully understand the power of that staff. We either need a powerful weapon of our own... or something that can protect us from the relic."

Aerys snorted. "The Khamsin are already immune – one small blessing for the pain we've been forced to endure at the hands of the guilds."

"But there are many who defected without being purged or who were born in the colonies," Kalisha retorted. "And that does little to protect the merchants, fighters, and mages who will be fighting by your side. Or would you prefer that your allies turn on you in the middle of battle?"

"I already expect that outcome," Aerys shot back.

"What exactly are you suggesting?" Finn asked, heading off Kalisha's bitter rejoinder.

Kalisha spared Aerys a glare before refocusing her attention on Finn. "The merchants are... *aware* of the location of an ancient workshop that contains advanced magical technology. We believe there may be other items and designs hidden within the facility that could aid us in our fight against the Emir. Legend says this place once manufactured weapons and armor that could protect one against the gods themselves."

"That's rather vague. That sounds more like a wild goose chase than an actual plan to me," Julia retorted, skepticism coloring her voice.

Kalisha tilted her head. "If it helps, even our brief access to the workshop is what helped us design the mechanized armor that you faced down in the Abyss. And we barely scratched the surface of that facility. Imagine what other treasures could be hidden inside, assuming there was a competent team willing to explore it." The implication of her words was clear and Finn hadn't missed the challenge in her voice.

"Translation. You want us to go dungeon diving to find you some fancy new designs for your craftsmen," Julia replied. "I'm sure the merchants will benefit tremendously from such technology."

"Or she could be setting a trap," Aerys offered, staring with open suspicion at Kalisha. "Which would put the *Najmat Alhidad* at risk."

"First off... of course, the merchants would love to get our hands on some new tech. But what benefits one of us benefits all of us – at least, right now." Kalisha eyed Aerys. "Second, I fail to see how betraying your prophet benefits me or the guilds. Without Finn's influence, I doubt that this tentative alliance would last for long, and it would undermine your ability to pull together the Khamsin clans. There's still a war to be won."

Finn rubbed at his chin. It did feel like a gamble, but at the same time, Kalisha was right. They were going to need an edge in their fight against Bilel. Even with a union between the Khamsin and the guilds, the demon wasn't going to go down easily. And after their brief encounter, Finn was confident that Bilel could take on a small army single-handedly – even without a god's relic.

And there was still the magical infection that plagued his body. Perhaps he could find a possible cure at the same time – effectively killing two birds with one stone.

"And this ruined workshop is where exactly?" Finn asked.

Kalisha turned back to him, her hand waving at the air as she brought up her map. An image of the desert suddenly appeared above the table, the sand stretching far to the north and south. The merchant shifted the display, moving ever further south until she hit a mountain range that bordered the desert.

"The facility is somewhere in this area," Kalisha said, a glowing yellow circle appearing on the map and highlighting a patch about twenty square miles.

"That's vague," Kyyle offered. "I thought you said the merchants had been there before. Do you not have a precise location?"

"We sort of… farmed out the exploration of the facility," Kalisha replied tentatively. "Unfortunately, our intrepid explorers didn't exactly make it back in one piece."

"She means they hired mercenaries, and they're all dead now," Aerys barked. "Typical – the guilds sending others to do their dirty work."

Kalisha just met that comment with a smirk. "I'm more of a lover than a fighter myself – and that goes for most merchants. But our sour-faced desert dweller is right. The mercenaries were expendable. However, based on the technology we recovered from their bodies, we can safely assume that they found the workshop. We were also able to backtrack and follow their trail, but we lost it at the edge of the mountains." She waved at the map. "Thus, we only have an estimate of the workshop's location."

Finn wasn't focused on Kalisha's explanation. His eyes were on the map, and his thoughts were racing. He could still vividly recall the images he had witnessed when he had augmented his eyes, replacing flesh and blood with metal and crystal. One stood out now – the entrance to a ruined labyrinth that sat at the base of a mountain. Some of those other images had already come to pass. Had the Seer been sending him a message? Preparing him for this moment? Nudging him in the right direction?

Although Aerys' cautious words echoed through his mind. Was this just a distraction? Or a trap? A clever manipulation? Another step in someone else's game? He chewed on his cheek as he mulled over this new problem. Yet his thoughts were interrupted as a prompt appeared in front of him.

New Quest: Forging Ahead

Kalisha has offered the *possible* location of an ancient workshop that *may* contain magical technology that will aid you in your fight against Bilel – *if* it even exists, of course. Interestingly, the merchant's description matches one of the visions given to you by the Seer. You will need to decide how much you trust Kalisha – and the goddess...

Difficulty: A
Success: Find the ancient workshop.
Failure: Fail to find the workshop.
Reward: A potential method to protect you, your companions, and your allies against the effects of Bilel's relic.

Finn frowned. The quest notification was just the icing on the cake – the game's way of pushing him a little further in the direction it wanted him to go. He didn't love feeling like everyone and everything in this digital world was manipulating him, but at the same time, he couldn't afford to look a gift horse in the mouth – not with what was at stake. If this place offered them an edge in the war that was coming, then the potential benefit outweighed the risk.

His eyes flicked up to Kalisha. "Does this so-called workshop have a name?"

Kalisha leaned forward, and a wide grin tugged at her lips. She knew she had him. "It does indeed. We call it the *Forge*."

Chapter 6 - Prepared

Finn's fingers moved rapidly, and his mana surged through his veins.

Flames soon wrapped around the dark metal sphere that floated before him, the fire growing and lengthening as he increased the temperature through each heat rank. Within only moments, the process inverted. The flames shortened in a heartbeat and took on a blueish hue. The metal, now glowing brightly, began to liquefy, forcing Finn to spin the material to keep the molten metal suspended and intact.

Once he was certain the metal had fully melted, Finn directed the orb with a twitch of his fingers. It rushed through the cavern and came to rest above a column of stone that jutted from the ground – a small hole bored along the top surface. Finn gently urged the molten metal toward that opening, releasing his control slowly and letting the substance drift down into the mold.

Then he was finished and released the spell.

As Finn wiped at the sweat from his brow, he turned to survey the room. The former arena where he'd fought the Khamsin had been transformed into a temporary crafting space. Pillars of stone now stood at even intervals along the floor of the chamber, and Kyyle maneuvered between those columns, his staff glowing with a soft emerald light as he inspected the molds. With a swift gesture, he broke one pillar apart, and tendrils of liquid stone drifted back down into the floor, revealing a carefully crafted piece of dark metal armor.

The pair had been at this task for nearly an hour now – forming the molds, melting down what was left of the dark metal Finn had stored in his bag, and then breaking their creations free of their stone prisons. They had worked in near silence, already accustomed to this process after their time spent in the Abyss.

Also, Kyyle seemed to sense Finn's sour mood.

Finn let out a frustrated sigh and took a seat on a

nearby stone bench. It abutted a makeshift worktable, fragments of dark metal armor resting on its surface. With another twitch of his fingers and a muttered incantation, Finn cast *Imbue Fire*. A sawblade – a souvenir of his time in the Abyss – soon rose from the worktable, and he directed it forward, grinding down the jagged edges of each panel and sending off a harsh shower of sparks. Luckily, he only needed to maintain heat rank level 2 to do this sort of finishing work, which gave his mana pool a moment to recover before filling the next mold.

It also offered a distraction since the noise and heat helped suppress his thoughts.

He was worried – with just a hint of anxiety and a dash of frustrated anger thrown in.

Kalisha had laid out a path forward, a mysterious promise of some sort of ancient crafting workshop that might hold secrets that would offer a defense against Bilel and the relic he now wielded.

Yet it also felt tenuous – like he was grasping at straws. What exactly did he have to go on? The rumors from a woman who had actively tried to kill him for the last couple of weeks? And a disjointed vision from a manipulative fire goddess? The last time he had followed the Seer's cryptic nonsense, he had ended up handing Bilel the same weapon they were now working to defend themselves against. Although, to the Seer's credit, he supposed that move had made him some new allies.

Maybe. Assuming they didn't try to kill him as some sort of macabre test. Or sell him out to Bilel in return for leniency. Or kill each other long before they confronted the demon...

Regardless, it felt like he was guessing – flailing around blindly. And he hated that, especially with what was at stake.

As he dropped his most recent channel, Finn rubbed at the ever-present ache in his left arm. As though he didn't have enough to worry about, the magical infection had only continued to spread as he worked...

System Notice: Infection Status
Continued spellcasting has caused the magical infection that afflicts your body to spread. **Current Contamination:** 21% **Intact Najima:** 5/6 **Stat Loss:** -10%

Finn had tried to keep his casting to a minimum, which seemed to slow the spread. Even so, the angry red energy now stretched almost to his shoulder. Not that he had much choice in the matter. The bottom line was that Julia was going to need the armor, especially if Finn was down an arm and forced to restrain his casting.

"Sir, you have a guest!" Daniel reported, hovering beside Finn's ear, and shouting to be heard over the harsh grind of diamond-like chitin striking metal.

Finn hesitated, withdrawing the sawblade. Khamsin guards encircled the arena, stone-faced and silent. Finn knew more lingered on the terrace above them – Aerys having directed those stoic men and women to ensure that Finn and Kyyle had some privacy. At least, that had been her *excuse*. He suspected she was more interested in making sure that Finn didn't cause any trouble or try to make a run for it.

And yet, the older man that stepped into the arena barely glanced at the guards. The other Khamsin did nothing to stop him from entering, either. He walked casually through the spires of stone, surveying Kyyle's work with a critical eye. His skin was wrinkled and aged, toasted a dark brown by the desert sun. Yet there was a gleam in his eyes that spoke of acute intelligence, one that age had not diminished.

Kyyle met Finn's eye, making a quick gesture. *Enemy?* he was asking.

Finn slowly shook his head. They would wait to see what this man wanted. The earth mage took the hint and went back to work, keeping a watchful eye on their visitor.

Someone with influence among the Khamsin. Another clan leader, perhaps? Finn thought to himself. This was the same gentleman Finn had seen watching him from the terrace after his impromptu battle.

"May I help you?" Finn asked, rising from his perch.

The older man finally spared him a glance, his expression giving nothing away. "I suppose we shall see," he replied plainly.

Finn resisted the urge to sigh, fighting the frustration that already simmered in his veins. More cryptic nonsense. Did no one in this world speak or act directly?

"Then let me try again, who are you?" Finn asked bluntly.

"One of the other clan leaders that you have tasked Aerys with managing," the older man replied. Despite his words, no bitterness tinged his voice. "I am called Eldawin."

Finn let out a soft snort. "You give me too much credit. Aerys certainly seems to have her own motivations in all of this," he said with a wave at the arena. "I'm not sure I would have chosen such a public spectacle as my introduction to the Khamsin."

"And how would you have preferred to be introduced?" Eldawin asked.

"I would have avoided it entirely," Finn answered immediately. "I realize that I'm an icon for your people – a source of hope. But that's a double-edged sword. Hope can be useful to prevent despair and keep you moving forward. Yet it can also blind a person to the harsh reality of their situation."

Eldawin cocked his head. "More wisdom than I expected from our *prophet*. What do you feel that our people's hope has blinded them to exactly?"

Finn met the older man's gaze evenly. "That we face an immortal and almost impossibly powerful opponent, and that we cannot fight that enemy alone. Your people seem to have pinned their hopes on me. Many of them view me as some sort of cure-all for your problems. I doubt the reality will be so simple."

"Ahh, you speak of the need for a union between the Khamsin and the guilds then?" Eldawin said with a nod, earning him a raised eyebrow from Finn. "Yes, yes. I have heard rumblings about your plans. In such tight quarters, even the rocks have ears."

Or, more likely, the guards reported the conversation to you, Finn thought dryly. It seemed the Khamsin weren't immune to their own infighting and political intrigue – Aerys had already indicated as much. *At least I don't need to be circumspect with my words then.*

"Do you not see the merit of such an alliance?" Finn asked. "Or do you join the others in your belief that I'm some sort of savior – that I'll singlehandedly topple the Emir?"

"Neither," Eldawin replied, the ghost of a smile tugging at his lips. "I see a possible alliance forged by desperation, an opportunity for the guilds to betray us." His eyes pierced Finn, staring at him with an eerie, unblinking focus. "Yet it is the union of god and man that most concerns me. Our mutual *enemy* should be seen as a warning of what happens when we meddle with the natural order."

"I agree." Finn noted the older man's eyes widen ever so slightly at that reply. "If the Seer is any indication, the gods certainly have their own agenda and play by their own rules," Finn added, refusing to back down from the older man's gaze.

"Yet, what other choice do we have?" Finn asked bluntly.

Eldawin met his gaze then, and Finn saw a steely resolve lingering in his eyes. "Our prophet could simply… disappear. The Khamsin could retreat further into the desert where we would be undisturbed. Let our enemies weaken themselves while we wait for our moment to strike."

"You would make a martyr of me then?" Finn offered with an amused smile, despite the knot of worry that pulled taut in his stomach. This man had just threatened to kill him – even if only indirectly. Eldawin was clearly playing for keeps. "In my world, prophets tend to hold even greater power in death than in life."

"Yet a martyr's power can be shaped and molded by those that remain. Your message would be spoken and interpreted by others," Eldawin suggested. "Perhaps, in death, your words would urge caution to your followers."

Is he really asking me to argue against my own death or imprisonment? The older man didn't even look worried by what he was suggesting, and the guards hadn't moved an inch. He wasn't certain who this man was, but one thing was abundantly clear. Aerys had downplayed Eldawin's influence among the Khamsin.

Finn needed to tread carefully.

"And yet your problems would remain," Finn replied. "If the Khamsin refuse to align themselves with the guilds, then they will likely lose in a direct confrontation with Bilel. Or they'll be forced into servitude. Either outcome will only grow Bilel's strength. You must be aware that he now holds the Seer's relic."

"Something that I believe we have you and the Crone to thank for," Eldawin commented. He noted Finn's surprised reaction before he could control his expression. "As I said, even the rocks have ears."

"The Seer failed to mention what we were sent into the Abyss to retrieve or explain Bilel's nature," Finn said, unable to fully remove the irritation from his voice. "Yet that doesn't change the situation. If the Khamsin refuse this alliance, they will almost certainly find themselves facing Bilel alone."

"Most of our fighters have undergone the purge and are immune to the relic's power," Eldawin commented. "Perhaps it is best for us to fight alone, no?"

"If your people had the strength to overthrow the

Emir, you would have done so already," Finn retorted. He noted just the faintest frown pull at the corners of the older man's lips. "The truth is that you're unable to defeat him by yourselves."

Finn paused for a moment, mulling on his own words. "My people have an expression. The enemy of my enemy is my friend. It's fitting here. Allying with the guilds – and with the goddess – is your best opportunity to free the Khamsin from the demon's influence."

Eldawin cocked his head. "These people who are vulnerable to the relic?"

Finn glanced at Kyyle, noting that the earth mage was following the conversation carefully. "We may have a way to defend against the relic's power."

"That sounds far from certain."

Finn shrugged. "A longshot at victory is better than a certain defeat."

The older man just watched Finn, the seconds ticking past. Then he gave a single curt nod. "Perhaps. Although, I have lived long enough to see patterns emerge in the lives of both nature and man. The wind always passes through the rock the same way, carving familiar ripples and channels. And now I fear we are making the same mistakes again – embracing one evil to conquer another."

A sigh. "However, you are also correct," Eldawin said. "We must make a choice, even if it is between the lesser of many evils. Let us hope that we are each making a wise decision."

With that final cryptic statement, the older man drifted back to the arena's exit and swiftly disappeared. Finn was left staring after him, his already-troubled thoughts swirling as he tried to process the conversation.

"What do you think?" Finn asked aloud, glancing to the side where he had detected a glimmer of air mana. He had seen them enter the arena, but his companions must have chosen not to interrupt the conversation.

"I think Aerys needs to tighten the reins on her people," Julia groused as the shield of air slid down to reveal his daughter and Abbad standing there. "That man seems to walk unimpeded through this colony, yet I can find out precious little about him."

"He also wasn't shy about threatening to kill you," Kyyle muttered, wiping at his brow as he approached the group. "So, I guess we have to add yet another faction to this mess – one that's also a potential enemy. We're only up to what? Five? Six?"

Finn locked eyes with Abbad. "What was your impression?"

The librarian hesitated for a moment. "I think there may be some division among the Khamsin. That man holds more power than is obvious from the surface. I suspect he is permitting Aerys to act on behalf of the Khamsin for now, but that could change swiftly. He will be watching what happens with the guilds and may choose to intervene if he feels it would better protect his people. We should be wary of a dagger in the back."

"That sounds familiar," Finn observed, unable to fully remove the bitterness from his voice. Abbad may have saved them, but he had been playing a double game since before Finn entered this world.

"Indeed. I speak from experience," Abbad replied, unperturbed by Finn's tone. "Yet I also serve as an example. Our allies will always have their own motives, but that can also be used to our advantage. As long as we work toward a common goal, we will remain united. Even Eldawin was forced to acknowledge the necessity of the alliance we are building. We must simply remain vigilant for any change in the wind."

Julia let out a snort. "I don't know about the rest of you, but I'd prefer it if we got the hell out of this place." Her voice was bitter, and Julia glanced at the guards that still ringed the arena. "It feels like we're surrounded by enemies here."

Kyyle glanced at Finn. "So, what's our next move? You've been quiet since Kalisha mentioned the Forge..." He trailed off, letting the implicit question hang in the air.

"It's probably a trap," Julia muttered.

Kyyle nodded slowly. "The guilds could have pandered to the Emir and struck a side deal to send us on this 'field trip.' That would help ensure their own survival. And it's clear that the Khamsin aren't all on the same page. As Eldawin said, if you were to die, the clans would likely fragment or retreat. Bilel has to know that, which gives him a strong motive to lay a trap for you."

Finn grimaced. They were echoing the same thoughts that had been bouncing around his head since meeting with Kalisha and Malik. Although the rebuttal was obvious. What Eldawin had said was true. Sometimes, you had no choice but to pick between the lesser of many evils.

"Unfortunately, we have to take the risk. We need to defeat Bilel and retrieve that staff if we're to have any hope of bringing Rachael back," Finn said, rubbing at his temple.

"Which means we need allies," he continued. "Even Eldawin had to admit that the Khamsin alone won't be enough to face Bilel. Although he was also right that the guilds are vulnerable. And that, in turn, means we need to find a way to protect our new allies against the relic. You all saw firsthand what Bilel did to those guards in the throne room. We can't afford to have our own soldiers turn against us in the middle of a fight."

"We can minimize our risk," Abbad interjected. "However, I suspect you have already considered our best option for how to proceed." He looked pointedly at Finn.

They were now all focused on him.

"What does he mean?" Julia asked.

"We need to split our forces," Finn answered slowly, meeting Abbad's gaze. "Abbad will go with Kalisha and Malik back to Lahab. He will need to ensure that the Mage Guild joins the alliance and help cover the guilds' escape from the city. The illusions needed to deceive Bilel will be complex and will most likely take a unified effort of the guild's water mages. It will also give Abbad the opportunity to keep an eye on the guilds."

"Assuming you trust me," the librarian added.

"Assuming I do," Finn echoed, the pair staring each other down.

Finn didn't detect even a faint ripple in Abbad's mana. Although, whether that indicated his resolve or simply reflected Bilel's training, Finn couldn't be sure. Either way, he was going to have to roll the dice there.

With a sigh, Finn continued, "As for us, we need to investigate this Forge – trap or not. We could have Aerys send a decoy party north and then sneak south toward the mountains."

"Who exactly are we trying to deceive with the decoys?" Kyyle asked.

"Everyone," Finn replied softly. "We can't fully trust the Khamsin or the guilds."

"Are you really suggesting that the Khamsin might try to attack us?" Julia asked in an incredulous voice. "I don't care what our new grumpy desert grandpa just said, most of the people here idolize you."

"You heard Eldawin," Finn replied. "Right now, the Khamsin are united behind me – behind a prophet. Aerys is using that influence to help unite the clans, push an alliance with the guilds, and convince her people to wage war with a demon. However, there's an easy way to unravel all of that…" he said, trailing off.

Eldawin would just need to take Finn out.

Silence hung in the air as they all digested the plan that Finn had sketched out. It was risky. They would be forced to trust Abbad – that he wouldn't go back to the Emir and that he wasn't playing a deeper game. They would have to trust that Kalisha and Malik were telling the truth about the guilds – that the Forge was real and contained secrets that might be helpful in the battle against Bilel. They needed to trust that Aerys would put their larger goals ahead of her personal ambitions and that Eldawin wouldn't attempt to tip the balance of power among the Khamsin.

That was a lot more *trust* than Finn felt right now.

Yet he didn't see another option.

"Well, shit," Kyyle said, breaking the silence. "This

got muddy fast. No wonder you've been working like a madman. Better than dwelling on this mess."

"No kidding. What exactly are you guys making in here anyway?" Julia asked, eyeing the nearby worktable table, and jumping on the chance for a more lighthearted topic.

Finn let a small grin drift across his face. He lifted a dark metal helm from the table, twin horns spiraling from the metal. He held the helmet out to Julia. "Well, I'm missing an arm now, so we're going to need you to pick up the slack. Kyyle and I have improved on the armor I created down in the Abyss."

Julia's eyes widened as she accepted the panel. "It's... light." She tugged the helm over her head. "And it fits perfectly!"

"Daniel actually performed a full-body scan so that we could get precise measurements," Finn replied with a nod.

"I also discovered some interesting details from my scan," the AI interjected, his glowing form flitting around Julia. "Did you know that your nose is slightly crooked, and your ears aren't perfectly symmetric. Also, your thighs are rather muscular for a woman your size—"

Daniel was cut off as a helmet was sent sailing in his direction, but the AI neatly avoided the metal missile. "Shut it!" Julia snapped at him.

"What's wrong? I thought I was helping," Daniel said, his body dimming slightly.

"Well, uh, some people can be a little sensitive about that sort of thing," Kyyle offered, side-eyeing Julia in case she decided to start throwing things again.

Daniel spun toward the earth mage. "But when you were designing the greaves, you were complaining that her thick ankles made it difficult to design the hinge. How is that—"

"Hey, now!" Kyyle interrupted, his eyes widening. "I didn't quite say it that way!"

"Oh, really? What exactly *did* you say then?" Julia growled. Daniel quickly raced away to the other end of the chamber, flying high overhead and out of reach. However, Kyyle didn't have that option. As Julia wheeled on the earth mage, he backed away quickly, raising his hands.

"Uh, so anyway, we made a bunch of improvements to the armor," Finn added quickly to forestall a fight. "The panels are thinner than the full platemail back in the Abyss. The original design was overkill with the natural density and tensile strength of the metal. *Kyyle* also improved on the design, creating reticulated joints around the elbows, shoulders, and knees. That should give you a better range of motion.

"As you've heard, we also made sure this set fits better," Finn continued. "Of course, you can thank Daniel and Kyyle for that." He couldn't resist just a little teasing.

Kyyle gave Finn a pleading look as Julia turned her glare back toward him. Finn's smile just widened, and even Abbad let out an amused snort as Julia stalked toward the earth mage. Kyyle was right. Finn had been trying to distract himself from the decisions they were facing. Luckily, trolling the earth mage and his daughter was always at the top of his list of favorite activities.

And it worked. Watching the pair bicker helped Finn forget the risks they were taking, the odds they faced, and what was at stake.

At least for the moment.

Chapter 7 - Well-Traveled

Finn strapped down the last pack on the back of his beetle, tugging at the rope to make sure it was secure. His work finished, he wiped at his brow. Dusk had fallen only a short hour ago, and the desert sands still hadn't relinquished the heat stored during the day. Even the surrounding stone pillars were still warm to the touch. But it was still infinitely better than trying to travel while the sun was in the sky.

His gaze shifted to the area around him. Several beetles filled a small enclosure among the rocks, their bulky bodies barely lit by the faint starlight and thin coating of glowing algae that covered the stone pillars. They had waited until nightfall to depart, planning to use the cover of darkness to mask their movements. Finn suspected that even the most experienced tracker would struggle to follow them at night and hidden deep within the desert.

But, then again, he supposed that depended on *who* they were hiding from.

Finn leaned back against a nearby pillar, his attention trailing upward, and his vision shifted as he activated *Mana Sight*. A river of energy drifted across the night sky, the mana rippling and contorting in his vision. It almost looked like water, the way the motley collection of colors created intertwining streamers that flowed and tumbled through the air.

Although, he couldn't fully appreciate the beauty. At least, not anymore. Not now that Finn knew what it was – the collective energy of every human traveler and player in the game. A torrent of mana that was feeding a group of celestial parasites that tweaked and fiddled and poked and prodded at this world for their own advantage. He could only imagine that the Seer was watching him now from that windblown tent – sitting in her imposed purgatory and staring out of her cell at the world beyond those canvas walls.

No. There were plenty of potential enemies out there besides Bilel.

Finn heard a clank of metal grinding against stone and turned to find Julia approaching, tugging at her newly minted armor. The metal glowed a stark emerald in Finn's vision. Another shift of his sight and his daughter was suddenly illuminated in blue, and the details of her face came into focus. Teasing aside, this version of the platemail was a significant improvement on his hasty creation back in the Abyss. Daniel's measurements had helped them form thinner sheets and panels of the dark metal that now hugged Julia's form as she moved and twisted experimentally.

"Okay, I'll admit this does fit better," Julia offered grudgingly, her voice echoing slightly within the dark helm. It gave her an imposing look – like a dark metal juggernaut.

Finn chuckled. "The movement feel okay?"

"Yeah... although, I'm not sure how stealthy I'll be wearing full platemail," she replied, her feet clanking dully against the stone with each step.

"Hmm, well, we'll make do. Besides, worst-case scenario, we can always send Daniel to scout," Finn offered with a grin. "Maybe a bit of revenge?"

This earned him a laugh from Julia. "I'll keep that in mind."

"You certainly look formidable," Aerys spoke up from behind the group, approaching through the rocks. She was robed in dark cloth that blended in seamlessly with the rock and flanked by two guards robed in similar attire. The Khamsin clan leader traced Julia's armor with her fingertips. "Although, this isn't exactly normal attire for our kind. You would stand out harshly against the sand," she added, a hint of judgment coloring her voice.

"We are all being forced to evolve," Finn interjected, meeting Aerys' gaze. "The Khamsin included. We left a full prototype of Julia's armor below. Make sure you deliver it to Abbad and Kalisha when they return from Lahab. They should be able to manufacture the armor in bulk using the softer metals available to the Khamsin. It won't have the same durability, and the fit might be slightly off – but it should still give us an edge. We'd like the merchants to prepare at least a few dozen sets before we get back from this Forge."

Aerys arched an eyebrow. "You plan to give away the armor freely? For our people to simply give up their raw ore? What do we hope to gain for such… charity?"

"It would probably be easier to show you," Julia answered, gesturing at Finn.

He understood her meaning but winced internally at the unnecessary use of mana. With a twitch of his fingers and an uttered incantation, Julia's platemail was suddenly bathed in flame. The fire seeped into her limbs, turning her flesh and bone into a fiery inferno as her natural mana absorption kicked in. Within seconds, an elemental creature of fire and metal stood upon the rock, tendrils of flame leaking out from between the plates.

Aerys took an inadvertent step back, her normally stoic expression cracking for just an instant. Her guards followed suit, reaching for the weapons at their waists automatically. However, as fast as the transformation had occurred, it ended just as abruptly, Finn extinguishing the spell with a sweep of his hand. There was no sense in drawing attention to themselves before they set off toward the Forge. Darkness soon covered the rock island once again as Julia's skin and armor reverted to normal.

"This is what happens when the Khamsin and the mages work together," Finn said pointedly. "We are going to create a new contingent of the Khamsin – pairing each of your fighters with a fire mage. The metals mined by your people likely can't withstand the higher heat ranks of *Imbue Fire*, but even a rank 1 version of the spell will make them stronger, faster, and much more resilient."

Finn could already see the interest shining in the eyes of Aerys' guards, their caution turning to curiosity as they inspected Julia's armor. He waved at the nearby soldiers. "It would be helpful if you could identify those of your people who are more gifted with their natural absorption ability and help train them in our absence. They'll need to practice to learn to withstand the sustained fire damage."

"It seems my list of tasks keeps growing," Aerys replied in a dry tone. "Help the guilds flee Lahab, find them a new home, and conscript a miniature army of Khamsin to act as these... metal demons."

"And work to bring the clans together under a single banner," Finn added, earning him a sharp look from Aerys. "I suspect that will be your most difficult task."

A pause before Finn continued. "Speaking of which, we were approached by what I can only assume was one of the other clan leaders earlier. He called himself Eldawin."

Finn saw Aerys flinch at that name.

"I take it he's a *friend* of yours?" Julia quipped.

"Not exactly," Aerys replied tersely. A sigh. "Eldawin is a member of the old guard. He has seen generations live and die among rock and sand. As I said before, people respond differently in the face of adversity. Instead of hope, they foster anger and hate. At the mages, at the Emir, and at the guilds. There are even some among the Khamsin that have pledged to rid the world of *all* magic – claiming that the practice of arcane arts and the gods themselves are at the heart of our hardship."

"Does Eldawin share that view?" Finn asked, his brow furrowed.

"I'm not certain. As you've no doubt experienced, he is circumspect with his words and goals. However, I can assure you he will not forget the wrongs committed against our people – no matter what treaties are signed or gifts exchanged."

"Is he a threat to us?" Julia asked pointedly.

Aerys hesitated, her eyes drifting to the nearby rocks.

"I'm guessing from that long pause that the answer is *probably*," Kyyle observed as he approached, having finished packing up his beetle.

Aerys let out a grunt. "I would watch your back,"

she answered simply.

"Fantastic," Kyyle muttered.

"It just means we need to move quickly to explore this Forge and return to the colony," Finn said, pushing away from the rock pillar he had been leaning against. "We're safer with witnesses nearby. Eldawin seems intelligent. He won't attack us if any blame could be cast in his direction. He can't afford to alienate the other Khamsin by killing their prophet openly."

"But we could just disappear among the sands..." Julia trailed off, letting the implication hang in the air. If Eldawin were planning to strike, it would be at the Forge.

"My thoughts exactly," Finn said.

Aerys met Finn's eyes. "Which I suppose is why you requested that a decoy expedition be sent north. Clever. Although, I had thought you were hoping to distract Bilel and any other guild spies. That may not be enough to fool the other Khamsin."

"That was partly our objective," Finn replied with a nod. "Although, if Eldawin intends to send men to follow us, it may at least buy us some time."

The Khamsin leader grimaced. "Indeed. The decoy party departed about an hour ago. We also made certain to circulate word of the prophet's departure."

Finn nodded. "Thank you."

Aerys just grunted. "Let us just hope that it works. Either way, I suppose you'll also need these." She turned and waved at one of the guards. Stepping forward, the man handed a cloth bundle to Julia.

Unwrapping the cloth, she revealed a familiar set of items – a glimmering lance and a dark metal shield. "Oh, my sweet little death machine," Julia cooed, grabbing her lance and cradling it like a newborn. "Did the mean lady mistreat you?"

Aerys spared a questioning glance at Finn, and he just offered a shrug.

"At the risk of interrupting this touching reunion with your weapons," Finn said, placing a hand on Julia's shoulder, "we need to get moving. We're burning twilight, and we have a long way to go. Kalisha's waypoint marker has us heading a few hundred miles south, southeast."

"Fair enough." Julia gave her lance one final pat before grabbing her shield, strapping the weapon to her back, and looping the lance at her waist.

The group moved quickly to their mounts, leaping onto the backs of the hulking insects and guiding them toward the sands that encircled the rock islands.

Julia spared one final glance back at Aerys. "Please don't kill any of our new allies while we're gone."

Aerys barked out a laugh. "I'll try. Good luck to you and swift travels."

With that statement, the group set off, the beetles lumbering away from the rock island and onto the sands, a thin cushion of air mana soon jetting from their feet and causing their bulky bodies to sway precariously for a moment until they regained their balance. Within seconds, the group was gliding across the sands and disappearing into the darkness, leaving only a faint trail of sand in their wake.

Which left Aerys standing upon the rock island, her eyes following the group's swiftly vanishing outlines. Her good humor had vanished, worry creasing the lines of her face. "I suspect you'll need all the luck you can get," she murmured.

Chapter 8 - Rocky

The sun had long since risen, its rays illuminating the mountains that now crested the horizon. Massive pyramids of stone drifted up into the sky, their caps obscured by a dense cloud cover. It felt strange to see mountains after so long in the desert: a world swept flat by sand and wind. Finn hadn't expected to find the change so jarring. And yet here he was.

It just emphasized how quickly he had become accustomed to this world.

Even the sway of the beetle below him no longer had his stomach twisting into knots.

The terrain had also changed as the group continued south. The rolling dunes had slowly receded, the sand blown away to reveal cracked earth, sun-burnt rocks, and dense, hardy vegetation – bushes designed to weather the desert sun and lack of water. That change had also slowed their passage, the beetles picking out narrow paths of sand among the rocks and shrubs where their paneled feet could get some leverage.

Julia let out a whistle and raised an arm. The group glided to a stop at her signal, sending up a puff of sand and dirt.

"You see something?" Finn grunted, tugging the hem of his robe down and away from his mouth. He hadn't picked out anything unusual with his enhanced vision.

"Not exactly," Julia replied, letting out a sigh as she peered at the mountains in the distance. "The beetles just keep slowing down. They can't handle hard-packed dirt. I think it might be faster at this point to dismount and continue on foot."

Kyyle waved at the air beside him to bring up his map. "Looks like we've still got twenty or thirty miles until we hit the edge of Kalisha's waypoint zone. Though, the circle is at least fifty miles in diameter. We're going to be hunting for this place for a while."

Julia hopped down from her mount, the other two following her lead. Her eyes drifted to the nearby mountains. Green trees and thick forests were already visible at the base of those peaks. "I'm guessing the terrain is going to make it hard to find this Forge. If the workshop has been in ruins for nearly a century, it's likely to be overgrown. We're probably going to have to pick over every square foot of that target area."

Finn followed her gaze, picking up on the unspoken implication of her words. This was going to take *time*. Time that they didn't have. Although, perhaps his enhanced sight might offer some help, allowing him to identify the ruins amid the vegetation. If they designed magical artifacts in this abandoned workshop, maybe it would stand out brightly to his *Mana Sight*.

As that thought crossed his mind, Finn shifted his vision, the overbearing blue of *Short-Sighted* swiftly replaced by a flowing rainbow of energy. His brow furrowed as he took in the mountains. To his eyes, they were now enormous emerald pillars of energy. But what was more unusual was the cloud cover hanging over their peaks. Finn had expected a mixture of yellow and blue – air and water mana combining to form the clouds. However, what he witnessed was a dense ocean of azure energy. It swirled and coalesced before tumbling down the mountain slopes, nearly blocking out any trace of earth or air mana.

More importantly, it didn't seem natural. It looked like something – or *someone* – was channeling a hell of a lot of water mana up there in those peaks.

Although, that was someone else's problem. He certainly didn't plan to go poking around to find out whatever was capable of harnessing that sort of energy. Given his experience with water mana, his guess was that it was about to get very cold or very wet.

Or possibly both.

Julia let out a low clicking sound that drew Finn's attention. He turned to see his daughter gesturing at the beetles. They responded with a few short clicks of their own, forming the sound by grinding their mandibles together. Then they all drifted toward a clear patch of sand. Their feet began to vibrate quickly, undulating waves of air mana smashing into the ground. Within only a few seconds, they had formed a shallow depression, their bulky bodies lowering into the newly formed holes.

Julia then began spreading tarps over their black forms, the beige cloth helping the insects blend in with their surroundings. "The beetles will stay put. They can last for days without food or water," Julia explained when she noticed Finn watching. "We'll just set a waypoint marker so that we can find our way back here."

Finn nodded, shouldered his pack, and glanced back at the mountain range in the distance. "Alright, well, let's keep moving then. The clock is ticking. We need to get back to the colony before the Khamsin and guilds kill each other."

Kyyle snorted. "And here I was hoping to avoid all that drama."

"Don't worry, I'm sure we'll encounter our fair share of problems," Julia offered, patting the earth mage on the back. "Or were you expecting that investigating this ancient, abandoned magical workshop was going to be a cakewalk?"

"That's an unlikely outcome," Daniel reported, his flaming form hovering beside Finn's shoulder. "I estimate the risk of combat and/or deadly injury to be 97.6% based on previous group activities."

"That's... oddly specific," Kyyle grunted. "So, what you're really saying is that I should stay and guard the beetles."

Finn smiled at that. "And miss out on all of the fun?"

"Yeah, think about the notes. The *notes*, my man!" Julia crowed. "You will be the envy of dorks everywhere."

"Uh, I'm more of a *nerd*, thank you very much."

This earned him a laugh from both Finn and Julia as the trio set off toward the mountains, making a direct beeline to the circle highlighted on their map. As his companions kept up their banter, Finn's eyes drifted back to the mountain range, watching that sapphire energy swirl and condense in thick blankets.

All joking aside, he suspected that they would find plenty for Kyyle to write about.

*   *   *

"This game is way too damn realistic," Julia grumbled as she slumped down onto a nearby boulder, dropped her pack, and rubbed at her legs, tugging away the metal panels of her armor to reveal blistered skin. Her health regeneration swiftly healed the injuries… only for them to reform after a few more minutes of hiking. "Do we really need armor chafing?"

"Well, we could probably reduce the friction further, but it might require another full-body scan…" Finn teased with a faint grin. Daniel flickered weakly beside Finn's shoulder at his comment, darting behind his head to avoid Julia's glare.

"You can just shut it," Julia grunted back at him.

"Added padding beneath the metal might also help, although I'm not sure how well that would hold up when Finn enchants the metal," Kyyle offered with a sympathetic glance. "Maybe if we could find a fire-resistant cloth…"

Finn's attention drifted away from his companions, taking in the area around them. They were resting in a small clearing in the dense forest that lingered at the base of the mountains. They had hiked for several hours since they'd left their mounts, the rocky terrain quickly giving way to dense foliage and trees and a steepening incline. A crisp, chill wind, carrying the faint smell of pine, drifted down from the mountains, forcing Finn and Kyyle to tug their flimsy cloth robes tighter. Their clothing was meant to breathe in the desert heat, not ward off the cold and damp that now lingered around them.

The trees offered another problem. At least out in the desert, they could see an enemy coming from miles away. Here, amid these densely packed trees, their visibility was poor to terrible.

With a flick of his wrist, Finn brought up his map. They were getting close to the edge of the glowing yellow ring that Kalisha had identified. Not that that narrowed down the location of this workshop much, but at least they were making progress. Finn swept the map away with a wave of his hand before rubbing at the skin around the base of his left elbow, attempting to relieve the simmering ache that lingered there.

The pain in the ruined limb had only seemed to get worse the farther away from Lahab they traveled. Or maybe the corruption was simply spreading...

A glance at his stump with his enhanced sight indicated that the latter explanation might be the case. The strange red veins of energy had grown and were expanding into the surrounding flesh like a magical infection. Finn wasn't certain what would happen if that corrupted energy reached another Najima, but it probably wouldn't be pleasant. Either way, it seemed they had yet another time constraint in play.

He needed to find some way to cure whatever the hell that relic had done to his arm.

With his *Mana Sight* active, Finn noticed a glimmer of energy out of the corner of his eye. It was just a faint flash nearly a dozen yards away through the tree cover, quickly covered by the ambient mana of the forest. He almost thought he'd imagined it.

Shifting slightly, Finn kept the energy in the corner of his vision without revealing that he had noticed the flash of mana. Then he saw it again. It was just a splash of rainbow color amid an ocean of green and blue – dense vegetation with moisture clinging to the leaves. With a thought, Finn removed the earth mana from his sight.

He was able to pick out the form more easily now. It looked like a wolf, although dramatically larger than anything Finn had ever seen before. The creature was at least eight feet long, but what was more interesting was its mana signature. There was an almost perfect parity of the six affinities coursing through the animal's body, and the colors seemed stable, not shifting or pulsing as erratically as Finn had observed in other people.

"What is it?" Julia asked, picking up on Finn's expression.

"I think we have some company," he murmured in response.

As Finn spoke, the wolf stepped forward deliberately, parting the vegetation and fully revealing its presence. It stared at them with uncanny intelligence. Something about it didn't feel feral or wild. Not in a way that Finn had experienced with the wildlife in the Abyss. It seemed to be studying them and gave no outward sign of aggression – no bared fangs or growling.

Julia's hand moved toward her lance, and Finn noticed Kyyle clutch his staff tighter as they both eyed the animal, preparing to defend themselves in case it lunged.

Another splash of color shifted in Finn's peripheral vision.

Then another.

Finn counted at least four more shapes in the woods, encircling the group. He saw the outline of another wolf and what looked like a large cat – maybe a mountain lion? The other two were humanoid. Maybe they had tamed these beasts?

Although, as he focused on the two humans, he could see that their bodies were cast in that same strange stable balance of color. Even more unusual, Finn noticed the unusual energy curling around one man's hand, the trees and foliage near him twitching and moving as the rainbow of mana cascaded through the plants.

Interesting. What school of magic is that? Finn thought to himself. *It almost looks like the raw mana that the fighters use to charge their weapons.*

"We're surrounded," Finn whispered to Julia and Kyyle, and the pair spared him a glance. "Besides the wolf, I count at least four more in the trees. Two more animals and two humans. Possible attack from the plantlife." Kyyle shot him an incredulous glance, and Finn just shrugged. He couldn't explain it either.

The wolf cocked its head, and its ears twitched as Finn spoke... as though it had understood him. Finn's brow furrowed. What did that mean exactly?

Stillness hovered over the clearing, neither group making any move.

Finn wasn't certain what he expected, but it wasn't what happened next.

The wolf suddenly moved forward in a blur of motion. Julia jerked her lance free – her shield immediately appearing in her hand – and emerald streamers of energy wound around Kyyle's hand and staff.

At the same time, thick vines coiled along the ground, lashing forward quickly and from all directions. Kyyle was ready, slamming his staff into the dirt. A ripple of earth pulsed and tossed the vines back, cracking the nearby boulders and sending soil and rock flying outward from their position.

Through that cloud of debris, several small darts raced toward the group, only to be intercepted by the thick metal of Julia's shield. Finn's daughter began to charge for the trees, but Finn put a staying hand on her shoulder. He peered through the dust, dirt, and vegetation, meeting the eyes of that strange wolf.

Finn hesitated, his fingers twitching. He should be casting *Imbue Fire* and preparing to defend himself and his teammates. And yet, the look in that wolf's eyes gave him pause. It was the way the group had encircled Finn and his companions so easily. The way they glided through the forest. They could have chosen any location to attack, but they had picked this specific clearing where Finn and his group wouldn't have any cover. That spoke of a familiarity with this terrain. Maybe even most of this mountain range.

And, if he was right, then their attackers might be able to help them find the Forge.

He would just need to take a risk.

"Stop!" Finn shouted. His teammates came to a standstill, eyeing the trees around them with caution and holding their weapons at the ready.

Finn slowly turned to face the wolf. Its body was hidden behind several layers of trees and bushes now, yet it was still visible to Finn's enhanced sight – still staring at him. He raised his good hand, showing an empty palm. "We do not mean any harm, and we will not attack you. We would like to talk."

Silence met Finn's words.

Then the wolf moved again. Yet this time, it didn't seek to charge them or flee.

Instead, its body *shifted*. Contorted. Transformed. A rush of rainbow energy flowed through the creature's body, its bulk disappearing and replaced with arms and legs. Hands and feet. An instant later, a human woman stepped out of the treeline. Her hair was pulled back in a single long silver braid, and a scar marred one eye. Her clothing was fashioned from heavy leather and furs, but Finn saw no weapons swinging from her waist.

"My name is Silver," the woman said sternly, eyeing the group without any fear or hesitation. "And you all are trespassing on our pack's territory."

Chapter 9 - Shifty

A tense stillness lingered across the clearing. Finn's group faced off against the strange silver-haired woman. Her companions, however, waited among the trees, their bodies just barely visible to Finn's sight behind the dense foliage. Julia clutched at her shield, her lance hovering in the air, and streamers of emerald energy wound around Kyyle's staff. They were ready for whatever might happen next.

For his part, Finn kept his bladed left arm lowered. Silver's gaze skimmed him from head to toe before lingering on the bandage that rested across his eyes, but the tension never left her limbs. One small advantage of his body augmentations was that he at least looked blind and nonthreatening. Thankfully, he'd also had the foresight to disable his fiery crown for fear of drawing unwanted attention.

Although, a part of him hoped he didn't live to regret not reaching for one of his dark metal spheres. If this group decided to press their assault, it was going to take him several precious seconds to cast *Imbue Fire.*

He somehow doubted Silver and her companions would give him such leniency.

"We weren't aware that this was your territory," Finn began tentatively. "And we mean no harm to you or your people."

A low growl rumbled from the woman's throat, and her eyes flashed. "Really? As though we haven't heard that before. You travelers all make the same claims, but your kind can't be trusted. You only know how to *take.*"

Finn's eyes widened at the acid in her tone. Clearly, other players had harmed this woman and her people. Although, he supposed that wasn't too surprising. His time in the Mage Guild had only served to reinforce that most players were assholes. Many had little appreciation for this world or its residents, taking what they wanted and acting as they pleased. This was just a game for them, after all.

If only Finn could say the same.

"Then how about we don't rely on words. I've personally found actions to be much more telling," Finn offered to Silver. He gestured at his companions. "Put down your weapons," he ordered.

Julia shot him an incredulous look, but he nodded his head slowly. They gained little by fighting this strange group. If one of them died, who knows where they would respawn. Worst case, it would be back in Lahab. Besides, time was of the essence. If this area was Silver's "territory," then she might know the location of the Forge's entrance. Finn and his group could possibly save days of searching the mountain range if they could convince her to help them.

Julia must have reached the same conclusions. Sighing, she slowly lowered her weapon, looping her lance at her waist and draping her shield across her back. Kyyle followed her lead, letting his mana dissipate, but still firmly clutching his staff and the fingers of his free hand twitching slightly. Neither Julia nor Kyyle had fully let their guard down.

"See?" Finn said to Silver. "We don't want to fight you. We weren't even aware that anyone lived up here. We're just looking for something along the edge of these mountains."

Silver seemed to relax slightly as she saw Finn's teammates lower their weapons, but she tensed again at his comment. "Looking for what exactly?"

"An old workshop – a place called the *Forge*. Although, it's likely little more than ruins now. From our understanding, it hasn't been in use for the better part of a century," Finn explained. "We believe it's somewhere in this general area. Here, let me show you..." He trailed off, moving to pull up his map.

Finn saw Silver and her companions tense as he raised his hand, and he hesitated. "I'm just pulling up my map," he offered slowly. At a nod from Silver, he swiped at the air and then rotated the map toward the silver-haired woman.

"See? We were told it was around here," Finn explained, gesturing at the large glowing circle that Kalisha had outlined.

Silver's expression was stoic as she observed the map, but Finn could see her mana fluctuate slightly within his sight, just a faint tremor among the perfectly balanced rainbow of mana. A flash of darkness. That told Finn two things.

Silver recognized their destination.

And she was afraid of it.

A frown tugged at his lips. That wasn't a great sign. He had the sense that this woman didn't fear much – which said quite a bit about the workshop they were trying to find.

"Yes. I'm familiar with the place you describe." Silver's eyes shifted to Finn, her gaze piercing. "But you won't like what you find there. That place is dangerous. We avoid it during our patrols." She paused as she eyed Finn, her gaze lingering once more on the bandage across his face. "And it's certainly no place for a cripple."

"I can assure you that we are capable of taking care of ourselves," Finn replied with the ghost of a smile. "We're perhaps a bit more resilient than we appear."

Silver's eyes darted to Julia, taking in her dark metal armor, before shifting her attention to Kyyle and eyeing his robes and the staff in his hand. She sniffed at the air experimentally and grimaced at whatever she found. She didn't appear entirely convinced.

Finn's frown deepened as he watched Silver. He hadn't expected this journey to be easy, but he also didn't relish the idea of investigating a place that made this woman uneasy. Perhaps he could use that.

"We could help each other," Finn suggested tentatively.

Silver's eyes followed him with an unblinking focus. "In what way could you possibly help us, traveler?"

"You seem wary of this workshop," Finn offered.

"If it's as dangerous as you suggest, then wouldn't it be advantageous for us to investigate the place and clear out whatever resides inside? You may doubt our abilities, but either way, we're expendable. Worst case, we fail and die. Best case, we may help protect you and your people."

"And you offer this help in exchange for what exactly?" Silver demanded, staring at Finn with those piercing eyes. "As a traveler, I doubt your motives are entirely altruistic."

"We'd like to keep anything we discover inside," Finn replied smoothly. "However, that costs you nothing. As you just said, your people avoid the place, and you clearly don't need or want anything that's stored there. At worst, it would take you some time to show us the way to the entrance. That seems like a win-win situation for both of us."

Silver cocked her head as she watched Finn, her nose wrinkling slightly and a long silence filling the clearing once more. Then, all at once, she seemed to reach a decision.

"Fine," Silver barked. "That is an acceptable arrangement. However, we will escort you to this so-called Forge to ensure you do not wander farther into our territory."

Before Finn could react, the woman let out a low whistle. Four more forms materialized from the woods, drifting into clearer focus. Another wolf stepped out of the shadows of the trees and a large cat – possibly a snow leopard? – dropped from a nearby tree branch, taking up positions on either side of Silver. Their forms shifted and shimmered as they abruptly transformed, soon revealing two grizzled men robed in thick furs and each wearing surly, hostile expressions. Two more men stepped out of the woods behind Finn and eyed the group with more curiosity than open hostility.

Some sort of druids, maybe? Finn wondered.

Finn's mind was also clinically inventorying their enemies' gear – a habit after so long spent in the Mage Guild duels. The druids all wore the same rugged leather and furs. At first glance, they looked like mountain hermits. Yet Finn could see that their clothing and armor were well maintained, and the stitching had been performed with a steady and practiced hand. Their gear also looked like it was meant to withstand brutal cold and snow. The obvious deduction was that they lived farther up in the mountains.

Perhaps they are the source of that strange water mana I saw floating above the mountains? If so, then that was even more reason not to cross these people. Whatever was generating that much raw mana was not something Finn wanted to trifle with.

They had enough enemies as it was.

He also couldn't help but notice a decided lack of weapons among the druids – at least, apart from the simple blowguns they had fired at his party. He supposed that made sense. Why carry metal weapons when they could transform into massive animals or manipulate the local plantlife? Although, his guess was that those needles were coated in some sort of poison. The ability to control the vegetation around them would make growing and harvesting ingredients for potions and poisons relatively easy.

Even more interesting was their mana. The pair of shapeshifters that flanked Silver had a similar mana signature to their leader, the rainbow energy floating in sync – but with a strange, almost feral undercurrent. Behind them was a youth who couldn't have been more than twenty and a silent stick of a man. Their energy was subtly different, although Finn couldn't quite place his finger on exactly why. At least one of them must have controlled the plants. Which meant their last member's abilities were still unknown.

The druids watched them carefully, none of them looking particularly concerned about handling the travelers. Switching back and forth between *Mana Sight* and *Short-Sighted*, Finn saw no fear in their expressions or noticeable fluctuations in their mana. Their overall confidence spoke of hidden strength.

"We're going to escort this group to the ruins. If any of them reach for a weapon or try to make a break for it, run them down, and spill their blood," Silver barked to her companions. The pair of shapeshifters beside Silver both smiled grimly at her instructions, eyeing the group hungrily.

Finn waved Julia toward him, leaning on her arm and letting his gaze drift – as though he was truly blind. He noted his daughter's curious glance, and he formed a quick pattern with his hand. *Ruse. Play along*, he was saying. There was no sense giving away his abilities prematurely, and it gave him an excuse to speak with his daughter in hushed tones.

"You sure about this?" Julia asked under her breath as she watched their new "escorts" with a wary expression. Her fingers twitched as though she wished to reach for her weapons. Kyyle kept his mouth closed, his lips pinched, and his expression echoing Julia's sentiment.

"No, but we also can't afford to waste any time or risk a respawn. If these people know where this workshop is, then that might save us days of hunting through these woods," Finn whispered.

"That assumes you would last a few days," one of the gruff shapeshifters barked in response. His grin widened as he saw Julia shoot him a surprised glance. Apparently, their hearing was impeccable. Finn added that to his growing list of the druids' abilities. It seemed the shapeshifters had sharper senses, even when in human form.

"Don't mind Howl and Runner. Shifters spend so much time in animal form they often start to forget human customs like civility. Spending days and weeks in the woods certainly doesn't help either." Finn turned to find the young man addressing them, peering at the group with disconcertingly large eyes. He stuck out a hand. "Lucky for you, I share no such problems. My name's Hoot, pleasure to meet you."

"Don't fraternize with the prisoners," Silver barked at the young man, earning her an eye roll from Hoot.

"Let's just get this done so we can continue our patrol." With that statement, she set off into the woods, clearly expecting the others to follow.

"You heard her," one of the gruff shapeshifters said. Finn placed his name as Howl, given that he had assumed a wolf-like form. "After you," he said with a wave in Silver's direction. It was clear from Howl's body posture and tone that this wasn't a suggestion.

"Real charmer, aren't you?" Julia snapped at him as she passed.

The shifter's grin widened, showing more teeth. "I try my best. If you'd prefer, I'd be more than happy to help peel you out of that tin can and eat your heart from your chest."

Julia paused and stared him down. "Ahh, that's cute. I'd love to see you try, puppy man," she snapped back.

Howl snarled at her, his eyes flashing, but his companion placed a hand on his arm. "Back off. You heard the pack leader. Our orders are to get them to the ruins." Runner's eyes shot to Julia, observing her smirk. "Besides, they won't live long anyway."

"Uh, what exactly does he mean by that?" Kyyle muttered as the group set off after Silver, the members of the patrol flanking them and Julia keeping up her pretense of guiding Finn through the labyrinth of trees, his hand on her arm.

"The ruins are a rather dangerous place," Hoot offered, his voice disturbingly upbeat for such dour news.

"How dangerous exactly?" Julia asked.

Hoot cocked his head as he pondered her question. "I personally haven't been there before, but we avoid that area during our patrols. I've heard rumors of pack members foolhardy enough to enter. They never made it back out. That place might have been abandoned years ago, but it's my understanding that *something* still lives in there."

This earned Finn a wary glance from Julia. Even without speaking, he could anticipate her thoughts. They might have avoided fighting these druids, but it seemed that Finn might have just signed them up for a one-way ticket back to Lahab, courtesy of the in-game deathscape.

Finn let out a sigh. *Perfect. Just perfect.*

Yet there was no choice but to keep moving forward. Finn just had to hope that they would be able to navigate this workshop and find something inside that could give them an edge in their fight against Bilel. Assuming, of course, that Kalisha hadn't fed them a bullshit story or sold them out to Bilel.

The thought of the merchant caused a worried knot to form in Finn's stomach. Even if Kalisha hadn't betrayed them, the situation back in the colony was already tense and would just get worse once the guilds managed to flee Lahab. Between Aerys' posturing and Eldawin's meddling, that situation was a powder keg waiting to blow.

In short, they needed to hurry the hell up.

And maybe try not to die.

Chapter 10 - Mechanized

"Here we are," Silver grunted.

"Which is where exactly?" Kyyle asked, his brow furrowing. "I don't see an entrance, just some shrubs and a sheer cliff face."

Finn was similarly skeptical. The group had come to a stop in front of a mound of dirt and stone that stretched nearly fifteen feet into the air, the pile abutting a steep cliff. The air had grown crisper as they walked, and the last vestiges of the desert had disappeared, now replaced by thick green foliage. He had also come to appreciate the thick furs that Silver and her company of druids wore. Patches of snow now covered the ground, and he shivered involuntarily as he pulled his robes tighter around him.

This place is just way too damn realistic sometimes, he thought sourly.

Finn turned his attention back to the mound of dirt and the surrounding foliage. Perhaps there was more here than met the eye. Luckily, he had something that could help.

With a brief mental command, he activated his *Mana Sight*, the pile of debris swirling in a multi-hued collection of emerald energy. He peeled back at the layers of earth mana gingerly, looking for something below the plain exterior.

And then he found it. Behind the bushes and layers of dirt and loose stone, he could just barely make out straight lines and pristine angles that marked man-made walls.

"It's underneath the vegetation," Finn said softly.

Silver shot him a sharp glance, her eyes hovering once more on the bandages that covered Finn's eyes suspiciously. "Indeed. We sealed off the entrance the last time we were here. It was too dangerous to leave open."

"Except it seems someone came along after you," Julia observed, crouching beside the entrance. Her fingers pulled at the loose vegetation to reveal a makeshift rock circle, one that seemed to have been used as a campfire – at least if the ashes were any indication. "It looks like they made a camp here not too long ago. Maybe a few weeks?"

Silver stepped forward, her brow furrowing as she took in the rocks. She sniffed at the air. "A few months, at least." A glance back at the spindly man behind her. "What do the plants say, Spider?"

Finn raised an eyebrow at that. The man could both control and *speak* to plants?

A glimmer of multicolored energy wound around Spider's hands, and he stepped forward, placing his fingers against the mound of vegetation. The energy reminded Finn of the raw mana he had seen the fighters use to charge their weapons, only more refined and focused. The rainbow of mana wound through the plants, spreading out to the tips of their leaves and down to their roots.

"The growth is new," Spider murmured. "Water mage."

Finn shifted his attention back to the plants, peering at the foliage with his enhanced sight. He had missed it at first, but he could indeed detect a faint glimmer of sapphire threaded through the earth mana. Perhaps the mana signature had faded over time. Either way, both the campsite and the foliage were likely left over from the merchants' team of mercenaries. It also seemed they had been traveling with at least one mage and were cautious enough to cover their tracks. That made Finn uneasy. The mercenaries had obviously been cautious... and yet Kalisha had been clear about the outcome.

Julia and Finn shared a meaningful look.

The explorers must have been here. And they had all died.

The only remaining question was *how*.

Finn still hadn't given up the possibility that the merchants had simply tied up a few loose ends. And from the frown pulling at Julia's lips, neither had she. The fact that the entrance to the Forge was still sealed was telling.

Silver let out a frustrated growl, glaring at Finn and his group. "Perfect. We've had more trespassers. It seems this place is luring travelers and residents into our territory."

Finn could see the feral woman's mental wheels spinning. He knew what she must be thinking. Perhaps it would be easier to kill off their uninvited guests and send a clear message to other would-be adventurers. He needed to head off that line of reasoning.

"All the more reason for us to investigate this Forge and put an end to whatever is in there," Finn spoke up. "That should prevent further intrusions and eliminate any potential threat to you and your people."

"Or we kill them now and artfully arrange their skulls upon a few pikes," Runner growled. "Spider can grow us something suitable."

"That won't deter others from traveling here," Kyyle said, unperturbed by the shapeshifter's glare. "This place is rumored to contain valuable technology. Many would brave death to claim that knowledge. Besides, leaving a bunch of skulls lying around is as good as installing a sign – one that says, 'there's an interesting dungeon nearby.' Travelers aren't troubled by the threat of death. We simply respawn."

"We could put that to the test now," Runner growled in response, taking a step toward the earth mage.

"Enough," Silver snapped. The dour woman stared down the other shapeshifter. "They're right. It is best to remove the threat entirely. Killing them only delays the inevitable. Besides, we take no risk upon ourselves. They may very well die within those walls – in which case you'll get your wish," she said, earning her a grim smile from Runner.

Silver turned to Spider. "You want to help our new *friends* inside?"

The thin man gave a curt nod before kneeling upon the ground and placing his hands against the rock and grass. This time, he used much more than a trickle of his mana. Finn witnessed an avalanche of multi-colored energy pour from the druid's hands. However, he didn't simply dump his mana into the ground. The spirals of mana blended with the roots below his feet, suffusing the vegetation and racing along an underground highway of those buried strands.

As the mana reached the plants covering the mound, they began to drift to the side with a rustle of leaves and puffs of loose dirt. Spider wasn't forming new plants or destroying those that lingered upon the entrance. He was directing the existing plants like a conductor, using his mana to control the living vegetation. Full bushes sprung from the ground on rootlike legs before shambling away and settling back into the earth beside the mound.

A few moments later, the hill had been cleared of plant life, leaving only dull brown earth in its wake. The edges of the entrance were just barely visible above the mound, a faint line of stone revealing that something lingered beneath the soil.

"You can clear the entrance now, dirt mover," Silver barked, sparing a glance at Kyyle.

"I prefer *earth mage*," Kyyle grumbled.

"To be fair, her version is pretty accurate," Julia offered under her breath, grinning at Kyyle and earning her a mock glare from the earth mage.

Silver ignored their banter as her crystal-blue eyes shot to the other members of her group. "The rest of you be on guard. We don't know if anything still lingers inside." The druids responded promptly, encircling the entrance.

Julia spared a glance at Finn, and he nodded at her unspoken question. Whoever had found this place had taken enough time to not only regrow the vegetation to conceal the entrance but also to shift this mound of earth back into place. That spoke of *fear*. They should be prepared for whatever remained inside this facility. Julia pulled her lance from her waist and raised her shield. For his part, Finn withdrew a dark sphere from his pack, holding the dense metal in his hand but waiting to cast

Imbue Fire.

Despite their uneasy alliance with the druids, it still wasn't clear whether Silver and her companions were friends or foes. It was best to keep his cards close to the chest.

"You ready?" Kyyle asked, emerald streamers of energy twining around his free hand and his staff. The rest of the group gave affirmative grunts.

Then Kyyle finished casting *Dissolve.*

The earth tumbled free in a wave, liquifying in mere moments, and tendrils of rock and dirt soon drifted through the air. With a series of nimble gestures, Kyyle formed the earth into makeshift walls along either side of the entrance, preserving the material for later. Finn expected he planned to seal off access to the Forge when they were finished.

Assuming they made it that far, of course.

However, Finn was distracted as the entrance to the Forge came into sight. He switched back to *Short-Sighted* and examined it carefully. The frame was formed of paneled stone blocks that created complicated geometric patterns and stretched more than a dozen feet into the air. The entrance itself appeared to be embedded directly into the cliff face, and the stone doorway stood ajar, leaving a four-foot-wide crack. Even more telling, the rock portal looked like it had been blasted open. Something had carved a crater in its surface and blown chunks out of the rock floor that stretched into the darkened tunnel beyond.

Finn peered closer. The rock itself was unusual. The material was inscribed with lines that formed intricate intertwining patterns. The lines didn't look cosmetic, and they weren't any sort of Egyptian-style hieroglyphics. The patterns were too uniform and covered the entire surface of the entrance.

Are they wards? he wondered. *Or maybe another language?*

With a frown, Finn stepped closer and reactivated his *Mana Sight*. That's when he saw glimmers of darker green riddling the walls. Those weren't the glowing runes used by the mages – the symbols typically inscribed along the surface of an object. No, those lines were *embedded* in the stone. The mana signature reminded him of crystal, except the substance had been pressed into thin bands and laced the stone in dizzying designs full of hard angles and repeating geometric patterns.

He'd seen those sorts of patterns before, but never inside AO. The lines looked like... circuits? And crystal could hold mana easily... Perhaps this was the equivalent of magical electrical lines embedded in the rock?

He shook his head in disbelief. *That can't be possible.*

A sudden screech of metal scraping against rock filled the air.

Finn's attention darted to the gap in the doorway, where *something* now stood. It was roughly humanoid, nearly seven feet tall, and its body comprised of panels of thick metal. The thing shambled forward with awkward steps, its joints grinding and screeching with each movement – a product of time and rust. Its left arm hung limp, and a jagged, uneven rip was torn in the metal of the creature's bicep – almost as though the creature had been struck by an axe.

The mechanical creature had a hemisphere of metal in place of its head, the surface embedded with the same intricate wiring Finn had observed in the doorway. Except these lines of power glowed with bright orange and yellow light. A thin fan of white light shot from the dome-like head, passing across the group faster than they could react. The mech seemed to jerk upright as the ivory fan touched them, the lines of energy running through its body brightening and the mech raising its arm toward them.

"I-i-intruders detected!" a hollow voice sounded from within the mech's chest. At the same time, a metal panel along its forearm flipped open, and a cylinder rotated outward, shifting into place and flaring with vivid orange energy that began to coalesce in a bright point of light. It reminded Finn immediately of the mechanized suit Sadik had operated.

As that thought crossed his mind, his eyes widened. "Get down!" Finn shouted.

Just as the words escaped his throat, a beam of molten energy speared from the mech's arm, arcing forward in a flash and causing the air around it to ripple from the heat. In a flash, Julia had moved forward, intercepting the beam with her shield. The energy carved a molten furrow in the dense metal. Then the ray winked out, the mech shifting its attention to Julia and fire mana collecting around the barrel once more.

Thick vines suddenly twisted around the creature's legs, curling in between the metal panels and jerking it downward. The mech was forced to its knees, the sound of grinding gears coinciding with the movement. The next beam was sent flying off at an angle and speared into the sky. Finn glanced to the side to see that Spider was once again channeling his mana into the ground.

Quick thinking.

"Pack, we need to take this thing out!" Silver shouted.

In a flash of multi-colored light, Silver had shifted, transforming back into a massive wolf. She darted forward in a blur of movement, her teeth clamping onto the mech's ruined arm. She wrenched her neck with a sharp jerk, ripping the limb free with a shower of sparks. The mech barely seemed to notice the damage, lunging forward with its other arm to swipe at her. Silver twisted out of the way with uncanny grace and then leaped back out of harm's way.

Finn stared in shock as he watched what happened next. The creature's chest flared with earth mana, and crystalline tendrils drifted out of its now-empty arm socket, reaching toward the dismembered arm lying along the ground. As the crystal threads touched the ruined limb, there was another flash of emerald mana. In the span of seconds, the arm rose from the ground and slammed back into place, the metal panels welding themselves back together with a surge of fire mana and a flash of heat.

What the hell? Finn stood stock still in surprise.

He shook off his sudden stupor, his focus shifting to the creature's chest. He needed to learn more. Much more. He peeled away at the layers of mana. As he removed the metal casing, he discovered a series of glowing spheres floating in the mech's chest, suspended in a matrix of the same crystalline wiring that riddled the creature's body. There were at least three mana cores, one for fire, earth, and air.

Those dense clusters of energy also reminded him of the air mana core that had powered Kalisha's mechanized suit – except the combined energy in these spheres was far more powerful than any of the mana gems that Finn had seen before. The cores must be used to maintain the mech's different systems, the energy conducted along those crystalline wires.

Silver growled at the mech, and the muscles in her legs surged as she prepared to lunge again. The other two shapeshifters had circled to either side of the mech – Runner readying himself to pounce from atop the Forge's entrance and Howl lurking along the makeshift walls that Kyyle had formed. Finn suspected they planned to tear it apart, ripping off its limbs simultaneously in the hope of overpowering its self-healing.

That thin beam of white light rapidly fanned across the area, picking out Howl's and Runner's positions. The creature went still, and the fire mana core in its chest flared brightly.

"Incapacitated. Surrounded. S-s-self-destruct initiated."

Finn's eyes widened. There was still enough energy in the fire mana core to cause serious problems, and the blast would likely rupture the other glowing spheres in the mech's chest. As he looked on, the fiery energy was already beginning to condense in the chest cavity, growing brighter with each passing second. Even if the mech didn't harm the group, it might damage the entrance to the Forge. He needed to take out the core before it had fully charged and then contain the blast.

"Wait!" Finn shouted. "Silver, have your pack back off." The wolf hesitated and then let out a harsh yip, her druids backpedaling quickly.

Julia followed their lead, placing herself in front of Finn and raising her shield protectively. "Kyyle – *Stone Coffin* on the mech!" Finn called out.

He didn't wait for the earth mage to respond. Instead, Finn tossed the metal sphere into the air, his fingers a blur as he cast *Imbue Fire*. Flames wrapped around the metal, and it stopped just before striking the ground, hovering in mid-air. The fire flared brightly as Finn ratcheted up the heat. Then he made a swift gesture, and the molten metal flew toward the mech. As the metal started to glow a bright red, Finn pinched his fingers together, forming a thin metal lance that tapered down to a sharp point.

The earth around the mech began to liquify and spring into the air, swiftly encircling the creature. Finn's lance sped forward in an orange streak of light, just barely breaking through a hole in the stone before the mech was fully encased, and Kyyle began pulling it down into the earth. However, Finn was focused only on that matrix of crystal in the mech's chest, and his fingers twitched as he adjusted the course of his missile. The lance struck home, melting through the casing encircling the mech's chest before burrowing deeply into the fire mana crystal.

Finn saw the surface of the gem fracture, a crack forming along its surface. Orange mana flared so violently that he was forced to look away. A wall of emerald earth slid up in front of Finn and Julia, forming a curved barrier in front of them. Immediately, he removed that intervening earth mana from his sight, watching the detonation despite the harsh glare of the fiery energy.

The mech's core exploded violently in a blast of fire mana. Flames rocketed outward, blowing apart the other cores in sequence. That blast of energy ripped apart the mech's body before slamming into the earthen walls surrounding the creature, causing the ground to tremble. The fire took the path of least resistance, rocketing directly upward through the freshly formed stone and dirt. The energy soon erupted from the ground and spewed up into the air, creating a pillar of flame roughly ten feet tall and showering the area in dirt and rock.

As the seconds ticked past and the fire and debris gradually began to clear, Finn could see that they hadn't damaged the entrance to the Forge.

Although, the same couldn't be said for the mech.

With a gesture from Finn, Kyyle pulled up the remains of the mech slowly, the walls of earth drifting back down into the ground to reveal the wreckage. The thing's body had been blasted apart, and its metallic limbs, now bent and seared, were scattered across the ground in haphazard angles. Its torso had been destroyed entirely, taking the mana cores and the strange crystalline lattice with it – the substance apparently unable to withstand the pressure and heat inside the coffin.

Damn it, Finn thought to himself. They had lost out on the opportunity to salvage the mana cores and examine the mech more closely. In particular, Finn wanted to get his hands on some of that crystalline material. It seemed far, far more advanced than the wiring that Kalisha had used in her mechanized suit. That device certainly hadn't been able to self-repair – at least not to Finn's knowledge.

He'd have to be more careful with the next one…

"What the fuck was that thing?" Kyyle muttered into the silence that now hovered across the clearing, wiping dust from his brow.

"We don't know. But do you see now why we sealed off this entrance?" Silver demanded, having resumed her human form, and sharing a worried glance with the other druids. They kept their distance from the ruined mech and eyed the entrance to the Forge nervously.

Silver shook her head, the normally stoic woman's mana fluctuating wildly as she observed the remains of the mech. Not that Finn could blame her for the fear he saw curl through her energy. He could only imagine what it would be like to fight more than one of those mechs – particularly if they were in better condition. His attention drifted to the entrance to the Forge.

Besides, who knew what else lingered inside that facility.

Silver's startling blue eyes shifted to Finn, following his gaze. "So, now that you know what you face, are you beginning to rethink our arrangement?"

Chapter 11 - Intrusive

Finn took a deep breath. "No, we have to press forward," he replied, meeting Silver's gaze. "We need something from inside the Forge, regardless of the risk."

She let out an incredulous huff. "There's no accounting for crazy, I suppose – especially among the travelers. Most of your kind seem to have a deathwish."

"I don't know about that," Julia replied. Now that they had neutralized the threat, she slung her shield across her back and holstered her lance. "Maybe we're just *adventurous*. Right, Kyyle?"

For his part, the earth mage seemed oblivious to the conversation. Crouched beside the ruined mech, Kyyle swiped at the air to bring up his in-game terminal. He was inspecting and cataloging the remains, occasionally tapping out a few notes – although it appeared from their perspective that he was swiping at the air. "This thing is incredible..." he murmured to himself as he carefully arranged the pieces along the ground.

Silver shook her head, and the other shapeshifters looked at the earth mage like he had grown a second head. "Well, if you want to get yourselves killed, then so be it," Silver said with a dismissive wave. "Far be it for me to try to stop you."

There was a pause as she glanced at the entrance to the Forge. "But we still need to protect our territory and plan for your inevitable deaths. We'll wall off the entrance behind you and stick around for a few days. If you don't return in that time, I'm going to have Spider bury this place so deeply that no one will find it again. We can't afford to have these... *things* roaming the mountains."

Silver shot Finn a glance. "Or your kind attempting to explore these ruins and putting our people at risk."

As she finished speaking, a prompt appeared in front of Finn.

Quest Update: Forging Ahead

You have found the location of the Forge with the help of Silver and her group of druids. However, it seems that the workshop is in disrepair, and the mechanical sentries that roam its halls present a danger both to your team and to the surrounding area. You have two days to investigate the Forge, find the technology that Kalisha mentioned, and leave before Silver seals off the exit for good. You better hurry!

Difficulty: A
Success: Find the technology and escape the Forge within two days in-game.
Failure: Uh, fail to find the tech or get your ass locked inside an ancient workshop?
Reward: A potential method to protect you, your companions, and your allies against the effects of Bilel's relic.

The time limit didn't seem like much of a burden. They were already running against the clock as it was. Bilel was still amassing power, and the politics of the guilds and Khamsin was just a powder keg waiting to blow. And that was putting aside Finn's larger goal here...

"Understood," Finn said, swiping away the notice. "We'll hurry."

"Good," Silver grunted before turning to the two shapeshifters in her group. "Howl. Runner. You two patrol the area. Make sure we're not interrupted. Stay inside the forest. If you find any unwelcome visitors, do not engage, just report back to me."

The two men looked at each other, then shifted – a wolf and a snow leopard soon sprinting toward the tree line.

"And Hoot!" Silver shouted. The youth jumped at his name, backing away from the ruined mech as though he'd just been burned. "I want you to have Archie sweep out toward the desert. Make sure no one is following our new *guests*." The young man nodded and then turned his eyes to the sky.

Finn followed his gaze and could just barely make out the faint outline of a bird far above them – possibly an owl. Curious, Finn shifted to his *Mana Sight* and saw a coil of multi-colored energy connecting the young man and the bird.

Interesting. If he found some spare time, Finn would need to remember to study the druids' magic system more carefully. It had some potentially useful applications.

But for now, he needed to focus.

"Daniel," Finn barked. The AI abruptly flared to life beside him.

"Fantastic! It looks like I missed another near-death experience," Daniel observed happily, noting the hole blasted in the ground and the debris scattered across the area.

"Lucky you," Finn replied in a dry voice. "You want to help Kyyle out and scan that mess?" he asked with a wave at the destroyed mech. "Please try to recreate a model using the pieces. Push all of that data to the shared repository. We may need it soon. Also, ask Kyyle to salvage anything we might be able to use later.

"Oh, and tell him to make it quick!" Finn called after the AI. "Five minutes, then we make our way inside." Daniel flashed once in acknowledgment.

"Sure thing, sir!" Daniel replied and darted off toward the earth mage. The AI soon hovered around the mech, and a thin beam of light shot from his body as he scanned the ravaged metal limbs one-by-one.

"You think we're going to find more of those mechs inside?" Julia asked, coming up beside Finn and eyeing the wreckage skeptically.

"Most likely," he murmured in reply. "You heard that thing before it started attacking. It referred to us as *intruders*." He grimaced, his eyes flitting back to the entrance. "I have a feeling we just got a taste of this place's security, and this mech was already worn down and damaged. I doubt we're going to be met with open arms."

"At least we're getting used to that. Besides, who doesn't like a little challenge?" she called over her shoulder as she approached the entrance to the Forge.

Finn grunted noncommittally. He wouldn't mind the occasional easy win.

His eyes lingered on the entrance to the Forge as his daughter walked toward that massive stone doorway. He kept replaying the battle with the mech in his head. He recognized the targeting system – that thin fan of light mana – from Kalisha's mines back in the Abyss. It might be safe to assume that these mechs could only detect mana. And the cores reminded him strongly of that mechanized armor that Sadik had used. It seemed the merchants had borrowed quite a few designs from this place… Although, Kalisha had been rather circumspect about what sort of resistance they would encounter.

He couldn't decide if that was the merchant's way of getting a little payback or if she simply didn't know. Maybe other members of her guild had been responsible for working with the technology their mercenaries had recovered, or they had died before describing the contents of the facility.

Or, maybe this was all an elaborate trap.

Finn's gaze shot to where Silver stood nearby, speaking with Spider in hushed tones, likely discussing how best to barricade the doorway after they entered. If this was some sort of plot on Kalisha's part, he doubted the druids were a part of it. He failed to see how they had any stake in the conflict back in Lahab. It might be reasonably safe to assume the druids wouldn't stab them in the back – not unless Finn and his group presented a clear danger to their people.

And there hadn't been a party of soldiers waiting for them at the entrance to the Forge. That made it unlikely that the merchants had set them up. Although, that still left open the possibility that they had been followed. Finn hadn't forgotten his conversation with Eldawin. If someone intended to use this opportunity to take out Finn and his teammates – either the guilds or the Khamsin – then they would likely approach from the desert to the north. Hopefully, the druids would be able to keep an eye out for that. Although, he wasn't convinced that they would intervene if it came down to a conflict. Silver seemed more likely to let them fight it out and then deal with the survivors.

As Finn saw the bushes around the entrance to the Forge begin to move, shuffling along on rootlike legs, a frown pulled at his lips. All of those fears aside, there was one concern that dominated the rest. There was a fate worse than death – at least, for a traveler. Someone could come along and permanently seal this entrance. Locking them inside some sort of ruined, deadly workshop seemed like a great way to get rid of the Khamsin's new *messiah*. Hopefully, Spider did a good job hiding the entrance.

Either way, he wasn't going to alert them to Eldawin's cryptic threats or his concerns about this rogue faction of the Khamsin. The druids were already reluctant allies as it was. If he explained that there might be more people on the way…

Well, some things were best held close to the chest.

Finn let out a sigh. Even without Silver's two-day time limit, there were a few compelling reasons to get in, grab the tech, and get the hell out of there as fast as they could.

"Yep, I definitely wouldn't mind an easy win every once in a while," Finn muttered to himself as he shouldered his pack and stepped toward the entrance to the Forge. Although, he doubted that was going to happen any time soon.

*　　　*　　　*

Finn and his group stepped inside the Forge and soon found themselves standing in a darkened stone hallway. The ceiling towered nearly a dozen feet above them, and the entrance opened into a hall about ten feet wide. The walls were formed of the same paneled stone as the entrance, and Finn's enhanced vision could pick out the crystals that laced the surface in elaborate patterns. In fact, those crystalline wires somewhat reminded him of the security mech's circuitry. However, he didn't detect any mana flowing through the patterns. They lay dead and dormant.

He heard a rustle of leaves behind him and turned to find vines creeping across the entrance to the Forge, the rope-like vegetation thickening with each passing second. Within moments, the vines had formed a dense wall, fully blocking the light from outside. Finn had no doubt that Spider would continue to reinforce that wall until it completely concealed the Forge's entrance and fenced them inside.

Darkness now hovered across the hallway like a dense blanket, pushed back only by the faint light cast by Daniel's flickering form. "Anyone else notice that we always seem to be exploring some ruined dungeon or cave?" Julia asked into the silence, her voice echoing slightly off the walls. "Just once, maybe we could try visiting a brightly lit garden? Or maybe a peaceful glade?"

Kyyle laughed softly. "You could probably play with the settings. I bet there's a child-friendly mode where shadows are highlighted in technicolor, the mechs shoot rainbows, and other people attack you with Nerf bats."

"Sounds like cheating to me," Julia grumbled. "I'm not asking for a lot of hand-holding. Just a little ambient lighting, maybe? A nice lantern? Or a window?"

"Well, instead, we get an eerie workshop full of half-mad and dilapidated security mechs that shoot lasers and explode when damaged," Finn interjected. "So, let's move forward carefully. May as well cut the chatter too. The mechs seem to be using a light-mana-based sensor like Kalisha's automatons, but these things seemed much more advanced. They might also have a way to detect sound."

His companions nodded, their expressions sobering, and the group started forward.

It soon became obvious that a battle had been waged inside the Forge.

For roughly half a mile, the entry hallway continued, burrowing deeply into the side of the mountain range. Scorch marks created long black furrows that disrupted the patterns etched into the floor, walls, and ceiling. The floor was riddled with debris – the remains of other mechs and piles of loose stone. As Finn took another step, his foot accidentally kicked at something along the ground, the object rolling forward with an unmistakable rattle.

He raised a staying hand, and the group paused.

Finn crouched and waved Daniel closer. With his *Short-Sighted* active, he could make out the glowing blue outline of a bone. A very *human*-looking bone. His teammates noticed the remains at the same time, their lips curling into a grimace. Many more bones were scattered down the hall, yet no fragments of flesh remained.

Old. Long enough for the bodies to have fully decayed.

The tentative conclusion? These probably weren't the remains of Kalisha's mercenaries. Although, that did little to quiet the nervous knot in Finn's stomach.

He rose back to his feet with a sigh, and they kept moving forward. Only a few minutes later, the hallway terminated into a large semi-circular room. The group hesitated at the opening, pushing themselves back against the walls and giving Finn a chance to survey the darkened chamber with his *Mana Sight*.

His brow furrowed as he took in the enclosure. It wasn't that he detected any particular threat. In fact, the room seemed rather innocuous... even *familiar*.

There was a long, curved counter resting in the center of the room, facing the entrance hallway. Chairs lined the walls adjacent to the entryway – although many had been damaged or were toppled onto their sides. Finn could also make out what appeared to be a pair of large doors along the far wall behind the counter, the portals presumably leading further into the complex.

It almost looked like... a lobby. If he had been in

the real world, he could have sworn he was looking at the post-apocalyptic remains of a downtown office building. Yet seeing the ruins of this reception area in-game was disconcerting. It felt out of place.

"It's clear," Finn whispered, keeping his voice low. "Daniel, patrol the room and scan any debris," he instructed the AI that perched above his shoulder.

The fire elemental gave a faint flash and then skittered off into the dark room, roaming its perimeter before floating above each ruined mech and scanning the wreckage. While Daniel was busy, Finn pulled a metal sphere from his pack and set it aflame using his *Imbue Fire,* creating a makeshift torch. He made sure to keep the heat rank low to avoid accelerating the infection. Although it was dim, the combined light from his channeled spell and Daniel's form was enough for Kyyle and Julia to make out their surroundings.

"What the hell…" Kyyle muttered as the room came into view.

"This looks like a reception desk," Julia said, waving at the counter with her lance as she entered the room, keeping her shield at the ready.

"But with no receptionist," Kyyle replied. "This place is giving me the creeps."

Finn couldn't help but agree. He caught a flash of mana from behind the counter with his *Mana Sight* and circled the desk. On the other side, he could see that an intricate series of crystals had been embedded in the countertop – much like the terminals that the mages used back in Lahab. However, this panel was much, much more intricate. Finn could make out complex patterns of crystalline wires resting just below the stone. One gem, in particular, glowed with a faint, red energy that pulsed softly – denoting some active mana.

Frowning, Finn tapped at that crystal.

All at once, fiery energy pulsed along the counter, and a humming sound echoed through the room. The mana soon raced through the crystal circuits embedded in the walls, tracing those intricate patterns and creating a series of glowing lines. The light grew in strength with each passing second and swiftly began to illuminate the room in a dull red and orange glow. Finn swiftly retracted his orb, and his teammates whirled, watching the room for any sign of threat.

"It looks like you found the light switch," Julia offered, eyeing the walls suspiciously.

"Indeed," Finn murmured. The panel in front of him had also come back online. The crystals were now awash in energy, the mana flowing through the circuitry in a dizzying series of lines and shapes. Not that he knew what the damn thing was supposed to do. He had a strong suspicion he wasn't going to find an ancient instruction manual lying nearby.

"What the hell is this place?" Kyyle asked, his fingers tracing the glowing walls.

"T-t-this is the F-f-forge..." a voice spoke up, the sound grinding and stuttering. It sounded like rocks smashing together.

The group whirled toward the sound, expecting to find another of the mechs that had attacked them. Instead, they found what appeared to be a pile of rubble resting against the counter. Finn had initially thought the debris were remnants of the damage to the room's walls or ceiling – a boulder that had crashed down into the room's floor, perhaps. Yet as he examined the nearby ceiling and floor, he didn't see any damage that would have created this pile of rubble. In fact, he had noted many of these rock piles along the entrance hallway but had assumed they were just debris.

It was starting to look like he'd been wrong.

"Okay, now I've seen everything. Including a pile of talking rocks," Kyyle observed as they watched the debris cautiously.

"I don't think they're rocks," Finn said, crouching and inspecting the pile of rubble.

Kyyle frowned at him. "Then what the hell is this thing?"

"I-I-I am a F-f-forge attendant," the rocks rumbled,

shaking slightly.

Finn leaned closer, and he could see a faint green glow coming from the rubble. He gingerly tugged the rocks free to find a roughhewn crystal in the center of the pile. In contrast to the sleek lines and patterns of the walls and console, this gem appeared to have been formed naturally – creating an asymmetric and jagged clump of crystal.

"W-w-welcome…"

Each time the rocks spoke, that crystal pulsed with emerald energy – although the mana signature was weak. That was probably why Finn hadn't been able to distinguish the crystal from the floor or the surrounding stone. His guess was that this was a form of mana core that powered this… well, *talking pile of rocks*. It must have gradually weakened over the decades, and the stones had collapsed to form these piles.

"I think it's a construct or golem maybe," Finn said. "This is an earth mana core here, but the energy is weak. That may be why it's having difficulty speaking."

"Great. Well, let's kill it before it comes back to life and starts trying to shoot us with lasers or smash us apart," Julia offered.

"It doesn't sound threatening," Kyyle said, edging closer to the pile of debris and crouching down beside Finn. "And we were just talking about a missing receptionist. Wouldn't it make sense for a place like this to employ something like a golem to handle mundane tasks? I mean, we've already seen that this is *possible*. Remember Brutus' golems back in the Mage Guild? Seems a lot more efficient than hiring people."

"Which assumes that *anything* about this place makes sense," Julia grumbled.

Kyyle's brow furrowed as he inspected the earth mana core. It pulsed weakly, emitting a soft green glow.

"I wonder…" Kyyle began softly. Then, unexpectedly, he raised his hand and channeled his mana directly into the core.

The crystal absorbed the energy greedily, glowing

brighter with each passing second. Kyyle kept up the channel, feeding more and more mana into the core. Within mere moments, the rocks had begun to shift and rumble, moving of their own accord. Finn and Kyyle backpedaled, quickly putting distance between themselves and… whatever was forming beside the reception desk.

The stones abruptly shot up into the air before freezing in place, floating in the air and beginning to reassemble themselves into a roughly humanoid shape. The creature had a massive torso formed of the largest stones, with two bulky arms made up of many smaller rocks. However, the thing had no legs. Instead, the rubble simply floated in mid-air, tendrils of stones drifting away from its torso toward the ground.

"Uh, Kyyle, maybe you should stop…" Julia said, backing away slowly and raising her shield. Finn followed her lead, watching the creature cautiously.

Kyyle didn't reply. He simply kept pumping mana into the crystalline core. The now brightly glowing cluster of mana drifted into the air. The last of the stones that made up the creature's chest separated, and the crystal slid smoothly into place before the rocks closed once again. Then the earth mage finally released his mana, his eyes focused in rapt fascination on the rock-like creature that now floated before them.

A tense silence hung in the air as the group looked on.

The golem rotated slowly in the air, turning until the group could see its rough-hewn stone head face them, two glowing green points of light denoting its eyes. The creature towered nearly eight feet into the air, its bulky body casting a long shadow from the soft orange and red light cast by the walls.

Finn swallowed hard, and his fingers began to move, preparing to ratchet the heat up on his metal sphere even as Julia tightened her grip on her lance. Finn's eyes were on the dense cluster of stone that wrapped the golem's body. He would likely need to use heat rank level 4 to make it past the rock armor and destroy the creature's core…

"Hail, visitors!" the creature said, its voice a rumbling, grating sound. Yet it was no longer stuttering.

Finn's brow furrowed as he realized the golem was making no move to attack. He held up a hesitant hand to Julia. For his part, Kyyle was just standing there staring, an excited smile beginning to stretch across his face.

"Welcome to the Forge. I am attendant #167," the creature ground out when they didn't respond. "How may I be of assistance today?"

Chapter 12 - Fail-Safe

The group stared at the hulking mound of stone, its glowing green eyes pulsing as it watched them expectantly. After several long seconds, it hadn't made any threatening movements. Rather, it hovered in place as though waiting for a command.

Finn inspected the creature.

Earth Elemental (Attendant #167) – Level 100
Health – Unknown
Mana – Unknown
Equipment – Unknown
Resistances – Unknown

That didn't reveal a lot more than Finn already knew. Although, he supposed he hadn't known for certain that this... *thing* was an earth elemental.

Finn's eyes darted to Daniel, where he hovered beside his shoulder, pulsing softly and watching the floating attendant. Did one of those strange crystalline cores linger inside Daniel's fiery form as well? He hadn't thought to investigate the fire elemental closely since the game had designated him as a pet, but now he was beginning to second guess that decision. It seemed that this game world might be more complex than it first appeared.

"I don't think it's going to harm us," Kyyle said. He approached the earth elemental slowly, hands raised, showing his empty palms.

"Really? And you know that because of your considerable experience with destroyed ancient workshops and earth elementals?" Julia offered in a dry voice. She hadn't dropped her shield or lance. "Someone – or something – drained all of those elementals dry." She waved at the other piles of rubble strewn about the room. "They must have had a reason. I, for one, don't trust the floating pile of rubble."

"Well, I mean, it's an educated guess since it hasn't attacked us, and it did ask if we needed any assistance," Kyyle offered over his shoulder. As he neared the elemental, he passed his hand beneath its body experimentally. His fingers shot upward, pressing forcefully against the underside of the elemental's torso before he jerked his hand back.

"Fascinating," Kyyle murmured, staring at his uninjured hand. "I think it's creating a gravity well beneath the rocks. That must be what's keeping its torso and arms suspended."

The earth elemental's head shifted downward, its glowing eyes fixing on Kyyle. "Hello, sir. I detect the presence of strong earth mana. Are you a supervisor?"

Kyyle shot Finn a questioning glance, and he shrugged.

"*Play along*," Finn mouthed.

"Yes... yes, I'm a supervisor," Kyyle replied.

"Fantastic! May I please see your credentials, sir?" the elemental rumbled in response.

Kyyle hesitated, mulling on how to respond to that.

"He's new and just arrived at the facility," Finn interjected, stepping forward. "Kyyle here was supposed to be admitted as a new member of the... uh, staff. So, he hasn't been issued credentials yet. In fact, we're having some difficulty locating the other people that work here. Could you assist us with that?"

The earth elemental's glowing green eyes swept to Finn and then back to Kyyle. "Of course. I will treat you as temporary visitors until we can locate the other staff. Please let me check on the status of the facility."

The elemental promptly floated past Kyyle and hovered next to the console in the center of the reception area. Julia gave the creature a wide berth, eyeing the elemental suspiciously and maintaining her firm grip on her lance and shield.

The attendant's arm drifted forward, the stones along its fingers contorting and shifting in place. A series of smaller crystals shuffled forward, assembling themselves into a complicated pattern. The elemental then inserted its reconfigured hand into a corresponding notch in the surface of the console, and its eyes flashed. With his *Mana Sight* active, Finn observed a surge of earth mana ripple through the console.

"This technology is incredible," Kyyle whispered to Finn, stepping up beside him.

"No kidding," Finn replied quietly.

This was far beyond anything that he had witnessed inside the Mage Guild – or even Kalisha's mechanids and the suit that Sadik had operated. He could feel questions tumbling through his mind. What was this place? Who had built it? And what had happened here?

And putting all of that aside, was it possible to recreate this sort of magical tech?

"It appears that the facility was attacked and has been placed in a level 3 security lockdown," the elemental reported.

Finn gestured at Kyyle to speak up. If the earth elemental thought he was a new member of the staff, then maybe they could use that.

"Do you know *when* the facility was attacked?" Kyyle asked tentatively.

"That is unknown. Some information is corrupted. It appears that one of the adjoining sections of the facility has been powered down, and the main conduits to this reception area were damaged – one or both of which may explain the power loss. I suspect that disruption may have caused the data corruption. Although, from the existing records, I estimate that at least fifty years have passed. Perhaps longer."

"Is there any record of what caused the lockdown?" Kyyle asked.

The elemental's eyes flashed once more, and suddenly an image flickered into existence above the console. It looked almost like their in-game prompts, except the panel glowed with telltale mana in Finn's enhanced sight – a mixture of air, water, and light. As he looked on, the panel rippled, and a man's face abruptly resolved into focus. His cheeks were streaked with sweat and dust, and his robes were torn with what appeared to be drops of blood staining the hem. A chime blared in the background, and lights flashed behind him in an undulating pattern. Some sort of warning siren most likely.

"We're under attack," the man gasped, breathing hard. Finn could hear a familiar sizzling sound and saw a beam of fire lance across the screen behind him. That must have been one of the security mechs that had attacked them, but they didn't have a good view of what they were firing at.

The man ignored the battle raging around him. "We knew this day would come eventually… just not this soon. The zealots have already breached the entrance to the Forge. I am placing the facility under a level 3 lockdown. All staff are to remain in place until further notice. We must protect our research and equipment. Otherwise, they may destroy centuries of progress…"

An explosion interrupted the recording, knocking the man to the side, and a roar of noise echoed across the room. The image winked out, leaving the group standing silently in the orange-tinted glow of the reception room.

"Okay…" Julia muttered. "Anyone else getting a bad feeling about this?"

"Yeah," Finn replied in a distracted voice.

His guess was that this place had probably been destroyed closer to a century ago. That was consistent with what Kalisha and Silver had implied. Maybe this battle had been part of Bilel's attack on the Seer and her followers? Or perhaps there was something more at play… The Seer had alluded to a big misstep nearly a century ago that had forced herself and her so-called siblings into some sort of celestial timeout. Had the attack on the facility been part of that larger war on the gods?

Although, none of those questions helped them right now.

"Are we able to access other parts of the facility?" Finn asked the attendant. "Or is there some type of map of the facility that you can access?" he added quickly.

Without answering, the elemental's hand shifted, and another pulse of mana flowed through the console. An image flickered into existence in front of them, showing the layout of the Forge. It was divided into a six-sided star, each triangular area containing a separate wing. A large hexagonal room hovered in the dead center of the facility with separate blast doors providing access to each of the six sections. Even more unusual, Finn noticed that there was a colored dot located along each of the six tips of the star, those points of light each corresponding to a different color – red, blue, yellow, green, black, and white. All six sections were highlighted in a faint, translucent reddish hue.

The group was shown as a cluster of three dots – located in a reception area along the northern edge of the facility and sandwiched between two of the triangular sections.

"What does this mean?" Kyyle asked. "This red highlighting?"

"Those are areas that went into lockdown. Those orders are still in effect," the elemental rumbled in reply.

"Can we deactivate the security?" Julia interjected. "Maybe open one of these two doors leading farther into the facility," she offered, gesturing at the two massive panels of stone and metal that lingered behind them.

A pause, and then the elemental replied. "I am unable to process that command. The blast doors cannot be opened while the security lockdown is in place, and only a supervisor can lift the lockdown."

Finn rubbed at his temple with one hand. "Okay. Let's try this a different way. We're looking for schematics and designs. Where are those stored?"

The hexagonal room in the center of the facility was briefly highlighted. "High-level designs and technology are stored in the central chamber."

"How do we access that room?" Kyyle asked.

"Access can only be obtained through one of the six sections. However, that will require lifting the security lockdown and restoring the facility's power."

"Didn't we do that already? Restore power, I mean?" Finn asked in confusion, glancing at the faintly glowing walls of the reception area.

The elemental turned to face him. "Someone activated the reception area's emergency power. A localized mana core installed in the floor is currently providing limited power to this room. However, access to the facility's primary power is still offline." Two small dots next to each of the blast doors were highlighted. "It appears that the conduits connecting the reception area to the rest of the facility were damaged."

Finn could easily see why one conduit had been taken offline. The righthand blast door was still intact, but something had blown a massive chunk out of the adjoining wall. A crater nearly three feet wide and as many feet deep had been carved in the rock, metallic debris melted against the stone. Maybe Kalisha's mercenaries had tried blasting their way inside. Although, even a brief glance with his *Mana Sight* indicated that there were still several more feet of solid rock and crystal behind that crater. This facility had clearly been designed to take a beating.

His brow furrowed as he looked at the second blast door leading into the fire section. It was intact, and the surrounding walls hadn't been damaged. Which begged the question of how that conduit had been disabled.

If it wasn't damaged from the outside, then something must have disabled the conduit from the inside.

"The logs indicate that power to the nearby fire section went offline sometime after the initial attack, although I see no evidence that the section was breached," the attendant rumbled, highlighting the section behind the undamaged blast door. "It's possible that the power to that area was manually taken offline, which may explain why no mana is flowing from that section into the reception area."

"Okay, so can we go through the fire mana section to reach that central chamber? If the power is out, maybe we can open that interior blast door leading to the central forge without lifting the lockdown or obtaining supervisor credentials," Finn said, tapping at the hexagonal room in the center of the facility.

"No," the attendant answered. "The fire pylon will need to be restored before you may access the Forge's central chamber. All six pylons must be operational to access the facility's central chamber, and each of the interior blast doors was designed with fail-safes to prevent entry if one or more pylons were disabled."

"Mana pylons?" Julia muttered. "Seriously, what the hell is this place?"

"I think they're these dots," Finn murmured, tapping at the circles along each of the six points of the star. "See how they're colored to correspond to a different affinity? My guess is that each section is related to a specific type of mana."

"That's correct," the earth elemental replied. "If the fire mana pylon is offline, it will need to be restarted to restore power to that section."

Finn just shook his head. *Restarted?* What did that mean?

The crystals he had encountered so far in-game were basically just rechargeable mana batteries – able to store a specific amount of mana, which was depleted upon use. That was consistent with the way the elemental had described the backup power for the reception area. So, what exactly did these pylons do? The attendant seemed to be implying that they… generated mana? Maybe like some sort of nuclear reactor, but for magical energy?

Kyyle glanced at Finn, and he saw the same realization reflected in his gaze. Imagine the things they could do with a mana generator…

He shook his head. That didn't help them *right now*. Their primary goal was accessing the Forge's central chamber to recover something to help them defend against Bilel's relic – if that was indeed where the facility's technology and designs were still stored. Finn was a bit skeptical that the information available through the reception console was accurate. It had been anywhere between 50 and 100 years since this place was operational.

A lot could change in that time.

"Okay," Finn began, thinking aloud. "So, it sounds like we need to restore the fire mana pylon and find 'supervisor' credentials that we can use to lift the security lockdown. That should grant us access to this central chamber?"

"That is correct," the attendant replied.

"And I'm guessing we can't reactivate the fire mana pylon from here," he continued, tapping at the fire section on the map.

"That is also correct," the elemental replied. "Physical access to the pylon is necessary to restart it."

"Because of course it is," Kyyle said with a sigh. "Okay, so how can we access the fire mana section of the facility?"

"The facility is currently under a security level 3 —"

"Yeah, yeah. We know," Finn said, interrupting the elemental. "Is there any other way to open the blast door – maybe some sort of emergency protocol in the event the staff were to get trapped inside?" he asked hopefully, waving at the door behind him.

The earth elemental just stared back blankly in response.

"Maybe Kyyle should try zapping him with earth mana again," Daniel offered, floating around the attendant's head. "From what I can tell, this guy is a few rocks short of a quarry – if you catch my meaning."

When no one responded, Daniel continued. "In other words, this floating pile of rubble seems brain dead. Maybe they lobotomize their elementals," he added, just a trace of smugness entering his voice.

Finn just sighed, rubbing at his temple. He barely spared any attention to Daniel's jabs at the attendant, his thoughts beating again on the problem that was laid out before them.

"I'm not sure that's the issue..." Kyyle began, shaking his head at Daniel.

Julia was chewing on her lip as she studied the map of the facility, her eyes darting between the blast door and the floating image. "Maybe we could just cut or blast our way into the fire section?" she offered.

"*Dissolve* isn't going to work on these walls or the blast door," Kyyle replied sourly as he walked toward the portal and inspected it closely. "Not with the way they seem to be laced with crystal and charged with mana from the backup fire mana core." He waved at the other door. "And it looks like someone already tried the brute force approach with that one. Appears that didn't work out too well."

"Maybe there's a ventilation system?" Julia suggested. At Finn's raised eyebrow, she continued, "What? Haven't you seen movies where they breach some sort of top-secret lab? There are *always* air ducts. Besides, the staff still need to breathe down here somehow."

"The facility lacks ventilation ducts," the attendant interjected. "They were considered an obvious security risk during construction. Instead, each section is equipped with basic life support crystals – water, earth, and air mana, specifically."

"Oh, c'mon!" Julia snapped. "We have a quest. We need to get inside. There has to be a way to make that happen. Decades of videogame experience have taught me that. Otherwise, how is this shit *fair and balanced*?"

"I don't understand the query," the elemental replied. "Could you please repeat the question?"

"Sure! How many floating semi-sentient rocks does it take to open a gods damned door?" Julia shot back.

"I don't understand —"

"There's no point in yelling at him," Kyyle interrupted. "He's just an attendant. Sort of like a more basic version of Daniel."

"Exactly. I'm a far superior model," Daniel observed, floating around the earth elemental. "Just imagine how much mana it must take just to keep this guy afloat. Inefficient if you ask me."

Finn frowned at that comment. It seemed that

Daniel was becoming jealous of all the attention the earth elemental was getting. But that wasn't what had made him pause...

Daniel's remark about the attendant raised an interesting question. They had been attacked by that damaged mech when they opened the facility entrance. However, the reception area had lost power a long time ago, and all of the other attendants had been powered down. So how had the mech still been online after all this time?

"Actually, let's try a different line of questioning," Finn began, turning back to the earth elemental. "How exactly did you go offline, and why are there no more of the security mechs in here?"

"My mana core was forcefully drained some time ago. I'm not certain how or why this was done," the elemental rumbled in response. "The new supervisor has briefly recharged my mana core. But I estimate that I only have approximately a day or two of mana before I will need to replenish my energy, either with an ambient source of earth mana or the assistance of a mage with the suitable affinity.

"As for your second question, the security mechs in the reception area have all been disabled. I have no recollection of how that happened, and the reception console's records do not provide any additional clarity."

Finn chewed on that response. *"Forcefully drained"* didn't sound good. And they had passed plenty more piles of rubble on the way in – likely the remains of other earth elementals. Maybe the security mechs had repurposed the earth elementals' energy to stay online? And judging from the damage to the mech they had encountered, several decades' worth of adventurers might have gradually destroyed the mechs that had been stationed in this reception area.

Although, that didn't bode well for what they might find inside the fire section...

"Could the security mechs have drained your mana to stay online?" Finn asked, hesitantly, already dreading the answer to that question.

A pause from the elemental. "That is... possible," the attendant answered. "That may also explain why the reception area's power originally went offline. The facility's security could have rerouted mana from other systems. Although, that doesn't address why the main conduits to the rest of the facility were severed, or why the fire pylon was taken offline."

"So, what he's saying is that the security mechs are possibly draining other attendants and systems to stay online?" Kyyle asked in an incredulous voice.

"I mean, it makes sense," Julia replied thoughtfully. "During a lockdown, it would follow that they would prioritize security over everything else. There may be an override in place, or the security mechs were designed to leech power from other systems."

"So maybe the security is offline in the fire section. Or maybe the mechs are all still active, and they've been draining power from everything else," Kyyle said with a sigh. "That might even explain why the fire pylon is offline."

Silence lingered in the room as they processed that thought.

"Either way," Julia began, "that still leaves us with the problem of how the hell we're going to get inside..."

Finn's mind was already chipping away at that problem.

He rubbed absently at the simmering ache in his left stump as he stared at the blast door leading to the fire mana section, peering closer with his *Mana Sight*. His vision quickly became hazy as he tried to look past the door. The crystalline lines running through the rock created interference that made it difficult to get a clear view. However, Finn's focus wasn't on the section on the other side of that door... but on the structure of the portal itself.

He could see that the door was nearly four feet thick and was constructed of reinforced stone and metal panels. It appeared to be designed to slide into the adjoining wall. The stone itself was also warded against magical attacks. Runes were etched into the surface of the stone and glowed faintly, charged by the mana coursing through the walls. Those wards would likely hold a charge for quite some time, which might explain why the other blast door was undamaged. Though the surrounding walls had taken a beating. If Kalisha's mercenary group had tried to blast their way inside, they would barely have dented the door itself.

His focus shifted to the door's locking mechanism. The portal was bolted shut with six large metal rods located along the righthand side of the doorway, the deadbolts held firmly in place with ropes of fire mana. The pattern of that mana resembled Finn's *Imbue Fire*, which he supposed made sense. Although, he saw no wards on the deadbolts themselves – only on the surface of the door.

So, the blast doors use something similar to a magnetic lock, Finn thought to himself. *Other explorers must not have been able to detect or manipulate the deadbolts. However, if I could push the bolts out of place with Imbue Fire, then Julia might be able to shove the damn thing open. But that's going to require deactivating the power to the reception area in order to disable the locking mechanism.*

His gaze shifted back to the reception console. *Maybe I could drain the backup power...*

Finn rubbed at the base of his left arm, that ever-present, simmering ache lingering there. His tentative plan was going to come with a cost. After the fight with the Khamsin back in the Hive and forging Julia's armor, he'd already increased his infection level to 21%. What he was contemplating would increase the infection further. Although, he didn't exactly see another option...

"You have that look again," a voice spoke up from Finn's shoulder. He turned to find Daniel floating there, his body pulsing softly. "That one where you do something incredibly dangerous, but it kind of works out okay..."

"Thanks for the rousing support," Finn muttered.

"Any time," the elemental chirped.

Finn turned back to his teammates. "I think I have an idea. Since this section is cut off from the main facility, if I drain the reserve power in here, that should disable the locking mechanism on the door. Then I can slide the deadbolts out of place with *Imbue Fire,* and Julia can try to shove it open."

The attendant rumbled, the rocks that made up its body grinding together. "It may not be quite that simple. Each section of the facility is designed to repair the primary conduits automatically. Even in lockdown, the system will prioritize restoring power. Now that you have brought the backup mana core online, repairs on the main conduits connecting this reception area to the other sections have already begun. I estimate that it will take another five minutes until the connection to the air mana section has been restored," it explained, gesturing at the righthand blast door.

Finn frowned and glanced at the console, his gaze shifting downward toward the room's floor. Indeed, he could see a large fire mana core embedded in the ground below them – a hazy ball of orange and red. The circuits embedded in the walls and floor spiraled away from that core in dizzying patterns. Finn traced a single connection, following it until it reached the blast door leading to the air mana section.

He could immediately see that the elemental was right. The energy pulsed and shifted through the wall, the crystal quite literally stretching out of the stone and formed a complicated, glowing orange lattice within the crater. Those crystalline threads had encircled the metallic debris obstructing the wall, gradually pulling it away. Even now, a few threads had made it under the slag and had re-established a tentative connection with the air mana section. Already, he could see a trickle of rainbow-colored energy flowing into the reception area from the adjoining section.

His brow furrowed. How the hell was that even possible? And perhaps more importantly... what the hell was this crystal lacing the walls? It almost looked alive.

Although, he didn't have time to ponder on any of that. If his plan was going to work, they needed to move quickly.

"Damn it, he's right," Finn grunted. His eyes shot to the blast door leading to the fire mana section. "Okay. Then we need to get our asses moving. I can drain the backup power and then shift the deadbolts out of place."

Kyyle and Julia both stared at him and then glanced at each other. "Sure, but there could also be security on the other side, right?" the earth mage asked.

Finn offered a shrug. "Maybe. In which case, you need to be prepared to buy us some time. You just need to hold off whatever might be on the other side long enough for Julia and me to back you up."

He took a deep breath. "Either way, it seems worth the risk. I don't see that we have much choice if we're going to access that central chamber."

He glanced between Kyyle and Julia. "What do you say?"

His daughter just shrugged. "We've come this far already. What's the worst that could happen?"

"Homicidal robots, dismemberment, incineration, asphyxiation, poisonous gas..." Daniel chirped, his voice eerily upbeat despite the gruesome causes of death he was listing.

"It's also possible that you may only temporarily disable power to the reception area by attempting to drain the backup mana core," the earth elemental rumbled, interrupting Daniel's swiftly growing list. "Even the backup crystals store considerable mana, far more than a single mage can typically absorb. In that case, you may only have a short window to get inside the blast door before it seals and locks behind you."

"Okay, never mind. I take it back. A lot of bad stuff can happen," Julia replied, raising her hands defensively. Then she glanced at Finn. "But it's still our best bet if we're going to recover something we can use to fight Bilel. The tech in here seems way beyond anything else we've come across." A brief pause, his daughter grimacing distastefully. "I hate to admit it, but Kalisha might have been right."

"I never thought I'd hear you say that," Kyyle offered with a grin, earning him a mock glare from Julia.

"What do you think, Kyyle?" Finn asked, ignoring their banter. They didn't have time to waste deliberating and cracking jokes. Already, he could see that the crystalline threads had almost dislodged the slag that was melted into the crater beside the door that led to the air mana section. It wouldn't be long before that main conduit had been fully repaired.

The earth mage just shook his head. "I don't think we have much choice. Like Julia said, we've already come all this way, and we're going to need any edge we can get. We didn't exactly do too well against Bilel last time."

"Okay, then it's unanimous, and we don't have any time to waste," Finn said, approaching the reception console. He eyed his teammates. "You two ready?"

They both nodded, Julia moving into place near the door and Kyyle clutching his staff tightly, tendrils of emerald energy winding around the wooden instrument as he prepared for whatever they might encounter on the other side of that door.

That was all the answer Finn needed.

His gaze turned back to the terminal that stood in the center of the room. Fire mana flowed through the crystalline-laced console, powered by the glowing ball of energy embedded in the floor below him. Tapping into the backup mana core directly was out of the question. However, he could see that the energy flowed from the mana core directly through the reception console before streaming out into the walls and floor. Unfortunately, unlike the attendant, his limbs didn't magically transform to fit the console's access port.

He glanced down at his left arm, a dark blade jutting from his elbow.

It looked like he was going to have to improvise.

Taking a deep breath, Finn drew his left arm

back…

And then plunged the dark metal blade into the center of the console.

Chapter 13 - Frantic

The console flared harshly in Finn's sight, and flames spewed from the breach carved in the stone. The fires rippled up the dark blade affixed to his arm before winding around Finn's bicep and spreading across his shoulders. The mana spilled forth so quickly that he wasn't ready to absorb it. The flames left burning welts as they licked at his skin and forced the air from his lungs in a pain-filled hiss.

He quickly activated his *Mana Absorption*, letting the fires seep into his skin and channeling that burning energy to his Najima. Even so, there was a seemingly bottomless torrent of mana spewing from the console. It was all Finn could do to stay standing, leaning heavily on his bladed arm as he watched his health tick down rapidly in his peripheral vision. Yet he forced himself to keep going.

There has to be a limit to the backup mana... There has to be...

He saw the walls of the reception area flicker slightly.

Keep going...

The energy sputtered once more, and the orange glow along the walls dimmed.

He just needed a small window – a few seconds at most – just enough time to disable the locks on the blast door and allow Julia to wrench it open.

Then the mana coursing through the walls abruptly winked out, plunging the room into sudden darkness – the shadows only pushed back by the flames wrapping Finn's arm and enveloping his body in a blaze of fire and light.

And he was ready. While continuing to absorb the energy rippling up his left arm, Finn started casting *Imbue Fire* with his good hand. The incantation tumbled from his lips in a harsh whisper, his lungs burning with each breath. With his *Mana Sight* active, he centered his attention on each of the deadbolts holding the blast door closed – the facility's mana no longer tying them down with ropes of fire mana. One-by-one, the pillars were engulfed in flame, and he yanked them free. The process was a struggle – splitting his focus between the *Mana Absorption* and repeatedly casting *Imbue Fire*.

The process was only made worse by the burning fire that coursed along his body. He wasn't able to absorb all of the flames, and his skin reddened and blistered with each passing second. His chest was a smoldering, fiery mass as he barked out each word of the incantation. The red bar in the corner of his vision was plunging now, his health dropping below 50%.

Just a little longer…

As he focused on Julia, his hand kept moving. Flames soon curled around her metal armor, and her skin shifted and warped as her natural absorption ability took hold – flesh and bone converted to flame in an instant. But Finn kept going, ratcheting up the heat to give her a little extra power. The blast door was massive, and Julia would need all the help she could get.

Then he was ready.

"Julia, go now!" Finn shouted as the flames coating her armor began to take on a blueish hue, crackling and snapping at the air.

His daughter didn't hesitate. Julia's metal gauntlets pried at the stone, her arms surging as she began to heave it open. And the door reluctantly responded, inching forward with a screech of stone grinding against stone – a century of rust and debris causing friction. Julia shifted her position then, her shoulder smashing against the edge of the door, and her feet straining against the ground. With the combined force of Finn's *Imbued Fire* and Julia's impressive strength, the stone floor began to crack beneath her feet, and the door crept open another a few inches.

It wasn't enough.

The door held firm, refusing to budge any further.

"Damn it! It's not working," Kyyle shouted, the earth mage's eyes wide and frantic.

"Figure something out!" Julia grunted, unable to move from her position. "We don't have much time."

That was an understatement. However, there was precious little Finn could do to help them right now. He was struggling to absorb the avalanche of energy pouring from the console, his vision growing spotty, and his head pounding as his health plummeted. He could barely feel his arm or body anymore. Not a good sign. That meant the flames had begun eating into the nerves.

Kyyle's attention shifted to the bulky earth elemental. "Can you help her? Please?" Kyyle demanded urgently, waving at Julia.

"Of course, sir," the attendant replied, floating over to Julia. It rested two massive rock hands against the surface of the door, and its core pulsed with green energy as it poured more mana into the gravity well that kept it afloat.

The glowing sphere of energy in the elemental's chest quickly waned, and the elemental paused. "I do not have sufficient mana for this task, my apologies."

"Then we'll just have to give you more," Kyyle grunted.

The earth mage pointed his staff in the direction of the elemental. A wave of green energy rippled along the earth mage's skin, twined around the wooden staff, and then shot forward in a rolling wave of raw earth mana. As the energy struck the elemental, it enveloped the rocks of its body, and the attendant's mana core flared powerfully. The gravity well surged, causing the stone along the floor to buckle, forming a miniature crater below the attendant. Then the elemental shoved at the door with renewed strength.

The massive portal shifted backward with a lurch, and Julia and the elemental kept going, giving it everything they had.

"It's almost open, but it may not stay that way for long!" Kyyle shouted only seconds later. "Finn, get ready to make a run for it on my signal!"

Finn ground his teeth together. He hadn't been

able to see the door open. Flames now wholly covered his body and obscured his vision behind a cloud of orange energy. His head was pounding, and his lungs burned. All he knew was the fire – the energy raging through his body in a torrent. His health was nearly depleted.

7%

5%

2%

"Finn, now!" Kyyle shouted.

He shoved away from the console, ripping his blade free with a shower of sparks. The flames poured out of the breach and crashed against the reception room ceiling, the energy quickly charring the stone black. Finn stumbled backward, off-balanced and listing to the side, his body weak and his vision obscured by the dense cloud of mana. He forced his burning limbs to move toward the sound of Kyyle's voice – where he remembered Julia and the earth elemental were standing – pushing himself forward with shambling steps.

He felt rough hands grab him… pulling at him.

Finn stumbled and fell, his shoulder hitting something hard, and then he was being lifted and rushed through the reception area – the rush of wind feeling like daggers against his skin. Although, that was a good sign. That meant his health regeneration had already kicked in.

Only a moment later, he was gently placed on the ground, and he could just barely make out the glowing green outline of the earth elemental's bulky body. His breath came in ragged, painful gasps. His throat felt raw, and his left arm and shoulder ached, tendrils of smoke still wafting away from it and curling into the air.

But he was alive… even if death might have been a welcome relief at the moment.

His vision began to clear gradually, and he could soon make out the walls of a hallway. He felt a moment of panic and peered down the corridor, but he didn't see any enemies approaching. The walls were dark, no mana coursing through their surface, and everything was covered in a fine coating of dust.

Finn shoved himself upright, wincing as his bladed left arm ground against the stone floor, and settled back against the wall behind him. Another red notification flashed in the corner of his UI, and he swiped at it wearily. He couldn't afford to ignore these.

System Notice: Infection Status

Continued spellcasting has caused the magical infection that afflicts your body to spread.

Current Contamination: 26%

Intact Najima: 5/6

Stat Loss: -10%

Damn it, Finn thought to himself. They had made it inside the fire mana section, but the intensity of that round of spellcasting had cost him dearly. A glance with his *Mana Sight* confirmed that those angry red lines of energy now stretched up and into his chest.

But it seemed they were safe. For now.

"Everyone okay?" Finn croaked as he waited for his natural health regeneration to continue repairing his ruined flesh and his vision to clear completely.

"I think so," Kyyle panted, from somewhere behind Finn.

"I've been better," Julia grumbled, collapsing across from him. "Although, at least it looks like there weren't any security mechs waiting for us on this end. Yay —" she began halfheartedly.

She was interrupted as the group heard a dull thump behind them. The blast door settled back into place, causing a cloud of dust to gust through the hallway. His vision finally cleared, and Finn could see that fire mana was once more coursing through the surface of the blast door. He could only assume the strange crystalline material had managed to repair the breach in the console – signaling that the backup power had come back online. Ropes of fire latched onto the metal deadbolts, and they soon slid back into place in a series of solid thunks that vibrated the wall at Finn's back.

"It appears the reception area's power has come back online," the attendant reported calmly, floating nearby and watching the doorway with its glowing green eyes.

"No shit," Julia muttered. She was slumped against the wall across from Finn, the edges of her armor still glowing a dull red. Switching briefly to *Short-Sighted*, he could see welts between the cracks in her platemail, the skin quickly repairing the damage caused by her own absorption ability. It seemed she was alright.

"What is this?" Kyyle murmured, pushing himself away from the wall and approaching the other side of the hallway.

Finn's eyes widened as he observed the hole that had been carved in the wall. This wasn't a jagged, irregular crater. It was a precise square that had been cut into the surface of the stone, stretching nearly three feet deep if his *Mana Sight* was accurate. Yet the center of the hole glowed a much darker green. His brow furrowed. Metal, perhaps?

"Someone cut a hole in the wall and then filled it with slag," the earth mage said, half talking to himself and confusion lingering in his voice.

The realization struck Finn only a few seconds later. "This is why the main conduit linking this fire mana section and the reception area is offline." Kyyle and Julia glanced at him in surprise. He waved at the hole. "Look at it. The lines are too clean for this to have been an accident, and the metal fused into the hole must be meant to stop the crystal in the walls from repairing the blockage."

"That is a reasonable conclusion," the earth elemental rumbled, drifting closer to the hole. "Once the primary conduit between the reception area and the air mana section is restored, the facility may try to initiate repairs. However, it is unclear whether this obstruction can be easily removed." Its glowing green eyes turned to the dark walls of the fire mana section. "Meanwhile, this section appears to be completely offline."

"No kidding," Daniel replied in a dry voice from where he floated beside Finn. "How long did it take you to figure that one out, Captain Obvious?" The earth elemental simply stared back impassively, and Daniel let out a frustrated sigh.

Ignoring Daniel, Julia shot a glance at Finn, worry pulling her lips taut. "You know what this means, right?"

Finn nodded, a sick feeling coiling in his gut. "Someone did this on purpose – cut the main conduit to the reception area. Suddenly, it's looking a lot more likely that the fire pylon was intentionally taken offline."

"The only question is *why*," Kyyle added.

Finn wasn't certain how to answer that. But he didn't plan to mess with the conduit – not yet, anyway. If someone had gone to this much trouble to take the power offline, then they must have had a damn good reason.

"There are many possible explanations," the earth elemental offered. "An accident with one of the research projects being developed here. An undetected security breach. Perhaps an insurrection among the staff during the attack—"

Julia sighed, interrupting the elemental. "We get it. You don't have to list every possible option. Speaking of which, why exactly did this talking pile of rocks come inside with us?" she asked, glancing irritably at the elemental – who appeared completely unaffected by her response.

"I've been wondering that as well," Daniel muttered.

"I'm required to accompany all visitors inside the complex, including new hires for a supervisor position," the elemental reported happily and waving at Kyyle. "Once you have gone through processing and been issued your own supervisor credentials, you will no longer require my assistance and will be free to roam the facility at will."

Finn just stared at the elemental for a moment in confusion. *Ah, it still thinks Kyyle is the new supervisor*, he realized.

He'd almost forgotten that they'd lied to the elemental. However, that might come in handy. Perhaps they could go through "processing" somewhere in this section of the facility. They were going to need those supervisor credentials eventually if they were going to access the facility's central workshop. They'd just need to remember to be careful what they said in front of the attendant.

He shared a look with Julia, and he could see the same thought reflected on her face. "He could be useful since we aren't familiar with this place," Finn offered. "Besides, he did help us get inside."

"Only with the assistance of Kyyle," the elemental rumbled helpfully.

Finn's brow furrowed. "You know his name?"

"You have used that moniker repeatedly to refer to the earth mage," the elemental replied. Finn squinted at the elemental. It seemed it was a bit more observant than he let on. Finn had already witnessed how quickly Daniel had evolved inside the game world. Perhaps the earth elemental was going through the same process?

Yep, we definitely need to watch what we say.

"Huh, looks like you have a new friend," Julia offered with a grin, nudging Kyyle where he sat beside her.

The earth mage just patted the elemental's rocky arm. "I could do worse, I suspect. We probably wouldn't have made it inside without him," he offered, gesturing at the glowing orange doorway behind them.

This earned him reluctant grunts from Julia and Finn. The earth elemental had helped, but it felt like they had still done most of the heavy lifting. The ache in their limbs and their still-smoldering armor was evidence of that.

The earth mage's attention shifted to the elemental. "I suppose we ought to give you a real name. I don't want to keep referring to you as the *elemental* or the *attendant...*" He trailed off, rubbing at his chin. "How about Rocky?"

"Kind of on the nose, don't you think?" Finn said.

"Hmm, then how about Brock?"

"Really?" Julia demanded with a raised eyebrow.

"What? You don't get the reference?" Kyyle grinned.

"I like it," the elemental interjected with a rumble.

"Brock it is then!" the earth mage said, his smile widening as he heard Julia let out an exasperated sigh.

"Great, now we have two fledgling elementals following us around." She eyed Brock suspiciously. "Let's just hope this one doesn't start scanning me and critiquing the shape of my nose or the width of my ankles."

"As I mentioned before, that was for *science*," Daniel grumbled from nearby, his floating orange form flickering erratically in the darkened hallway.

"So will seeing whether I can punch a fire elemental," Julia shot back.

The AI pulsed once and then shifted closer to Finn, staying just above his shoulder.

"On a more serious note, did you manage to scan the map of the complex before we left the reception area, Daniel?" Finn asked, pivoting to glance at the AI.

"Of course." There was an edge to Daniel's voice.

The outline of the facility was soon projected into the air, the group now sitting in a long hallway directly adjacent to the reception area.

"Alright, plot the fastest course to the fire pylon," Finn instructed.

A glowing yellow line soon traced a path to the disabled pylon. It looked like they would have to traverse several adjoining hallways and rooms – assuming this interior section hadn't been damaged by whatever had attacked this place. Or whatever had caused the staff to take the power offline...

Although, given how difficult it had been to make

it inside this section and the undisturbed dust that lay along the floor, Finn's guess was that no one had accessed this place in a long, long time.   If they were lucky, whatever had destroyed the main conduits and taken the pylon offline was no longer an issue.

He pushed himself upright, weaving unsteadily and leaning against the wall.   His eyes shifted to the darkened hallway.

"Alright, let's get moving."   He glanced at the clock in the corner of his vision.   "We still need to bring the pylon back online and find some of these supervisor credentials so that we can access that central chamber. Then we can get the hell out of this place. Hopefully, *before* Silver and her pack decide to permanently barricade us in here."

Kyyle and Julia spared a glance at each other before Kyyle looked back at the glowing – now sealed – door behind them.

"Assuming we can figure out how to get back to the reception area. Because that trick definitely isn't going to work twice," Julia replied quietly, worry tinging her voice. Kyyle and Finn stayed silent.

There wasn't really anything to say.

They were all in now.

Chapter 14 - Cannibalized

The group moved forward quietly. The flickering light from Daniel's glowing form and the lone, flaming metal sphere suspended beside Finn cast long shadows along the abandoned hall. With his *Mana Sight* active, he could see that a single wide hallway stretched away from the blast door they had used to enter the section in a straight line that continued for more than a hundred feet, unbroken by adjoining halls or rooms.

They hadn't made it far, but already Finn had an uneasy feeling. However, it wasn't the creepy shadows or ominous silence that had a frown tugging at Finn's lips and his brow pinched tight – or that caused a worried knot to writhe and twist in his stomach.

"What the hell happened in here?" Kyyle whispered, coming to a stop. His fingers traced long grooves that had been scored into the walls. It looked like someone – or *something* – had been scratching at the stone, creating dozens of shallow craters in the rock. Yet they didn't look like they had been formed by human hands. They looked more primal... more desperate – frantic scratches carved along the inside of a magical coffin.

Almost like something had been trying to burrow out of these halls...

Finn shook his head. That couldn't be it, could it? More likely, whoever had attacked this place had managed to make it deeper into the complex somehow. Or maybe another group of explorers unaffiliated with the guilds? Silver seemed to indicate that others had tried to search the Forge. There were also signs of scorch marks from the mechs' weapons and the occasional crater lining the floor or walls.

"These burns look like they were caused by the security mechs," Finn said, gesturing at the dark lines along the walls and floor. "Maybe there was a battle here? Maybe someone made it inside the fire section somehow – the original attackers or explorers?" he offered, although that explanation didn't feel quite right.

He spared a glance at Brock, where he floated nearby. The earth elemental seemed unaffected by the many piles of inert rocks they had passed – evidence that other attendants had been disabled. "I thought you said this section hadn't been breached?"

"According to the logs available before the fire section went dark and the reception area lost power, that was the case," the earth elemental replied, unperturbed by the judgment in Finn's tone. "The records showed that the blast door hadn't been opened." A brief pause. "This section would have contained at least a hundred staff members and their living quarters. Perhaps they're responsible for the damage?"

"Except we haven't seen any human remains," Julia added. "That punches a hole in the 'battle' theory. With damage this extensive, at least a few people would likely have died."

"Or some of the staff survived the fight and moved their dead?" Kyyle suggested, glancing back at Julia. She gave a reluctant grunt of acknowledgment, clutching her lance a little tighter as she eyed the shadowy hallway ahead of them.

"Well, it's clear that *something* took the fire pylon offline. Given the security measures in this facility and the way the main conduits have been disabled, it seems safe to assume it was intentional," Finn said, earning him nods from his companions.

"Fantastic," Kyyle murmured. "So, our working theory is that someone or something magically made it inside this section while the power was out in the reception area—"

"Your deduction seems improbable," Brock interjected, the boulders that comprised his body crunching together in disapproval. "To disable power to this section, the staff would have needed to both shut down the fire pylon and cut the main conduits to the other sections within the span of a few minutes. As we have discussed, the walls of the facility are mana conductive, and the facility was designed to prioritize restoring power if a section went offline. Any delay would have allowed the facility to repair the damage quite quickly."

"So, you're suggesting what exactly? That the staff did this themselves?" Kyyle asked hesitantly.

"Indeed. It is improbable that an attacker would have sufficient knowledge of the facility to take out the power themselves. And, as I said before, the logs do not indicate that the blast door behind us had been opened before the power went offline. Based on these factors, the most probable explanation is that the staff disabled the power themselves."

Finn could feel that knot in his stomach twist as Brock spoke. He slowed and turned to the earth elemental, a frown tugging at his lips. If Brock was right, then the staff must have had a pretty damn good reason to take out the power – especially since that would have effectively locked them inside the fire mana section. He could feel that knot of worry twist and jerk in the pit of his stomach.

"That would have been incredibly helpful to know back in reception," Finn said, staring firmly at the earth elemental. "You know... *before* we trapped ourselves in here."

"You didn't ask," Brock rumbled in reply, no emotion coloring his response.

"He never does," Daniel interjected. "But he'll still keep blaming the elementals... I'm starting to think he might be a magical bigot."

"Uh-huh. Go on. Keep it up with the smart-ass remarks," Finn retorted, glaring at Daniel. "We can always replace you with this pile of rubble. He at least has working arms and some useful knowledge of this place." Daniel's glowing form immediately dimmed.

"Okay, so the staff probably cut the power to this section intentionally. But why? Why take this section offline?" Julia asked, echoing Finn's own realization. She shook her head as she stared at the indentations along the wall. "It just doesn't make any sense—"

She abruptly stopped speaking as a harsh grinding sound came from up ahead, breaking the eerie silence that lingered in the abandoned hall. With a few quick gestures from Finn, the group moved into formation, Julia taking point, Finn in the middle, and Kyyle pulling up the rear. Finn quickly canceled his *Imbue Fire* and snatched his orb from the air. Days spent down in the Abyss had their instincts and coordination honed sharp, and the movements were almost automatic. They froze in place, stilling their breathing and listening for any sign of activity up ahead.

Finn scanned the hall with his *Mana Sight*. However, he only picked up the ambient green energy of the walls and floor. Since his enhanced sight wasn't limited by the available light in the hallway, he could see that there was an opening up ahead – the first that they had encountered since entering the fire section. The interference from the crystal-laced walls made it difficult for him to see inside, but he got a vague impression of a small room.

"Room ahead. Righthand side. No visibility," he said in a hushed voice, keeping his words brief.

His daughter nodded and raised her shield, keeping her lance retracted and gripped firmly in her right hand. She stepped forward with cautious steps, staying on the balls of her feet to reduce the clank of her metal armor against the stone floor. Even so, it felt like she was shouting out a warning with each step. Finn and Kyyle kept just a few feet behind her, ready to back her up if they encountered any trouble.

Finn's mind was racing. If they were forced to fight, there wouldn't be anywhere to retreat. There was only this section of hallway, which dead-ended into the sealed blast door they had used to enter the section. And pressing forward was risky. They didn't know what they might find in this place.

Which meant, if it came to a conflict, they needed to end it quickly.

As they neared the opening, Julia took up a

position directly adjacent to the door while Finn and Kyyle stayed farther back along the wall. Finn could see that the door to the chamber was partially opened and unpowered, no telltale glow of mana coursing through the walls of this section. It was designed similarly to the blast door, sliding horizontally into the adjacent wall, but this door was neither as wide nor as thick. His enhanced vision also picked out smaller versions of the deadbolts used on the blast door: the green columns embedded in the stone and corresponding holes lingering along the doorframe.

It seems they designed each room to be sealed off in the case of an emergency.

Except for this one – it definitely wasn't sealed shut.

Finn kept a metal orb clutched firmly in his hand as he crept forward, attempting to get an unobstructed view – avoiding the interference from the facility's walls. As he edged around the corner of the doorway, he spotted rather mundane-looking furniture comprised of stone, the objects welded directly into the wall of the facility. Decayed, wooden remains of what might have once been a chair littered the floor. Maybe some sort of security post at the entrance to this section?

Screech.

The noise came from a haphazard pile of dark-green mana in the center of the chamber. The jumble of metal reminded Finn of the security mech, but this one looked more damaged – deformed even. A single metallic limb jutted from that pile and clawed at the stone floor in a rhythmic motion.

Screech.

More marks were scratched in the surface nearby, creating a rough pit in the ground. The mech had to have been at this for some time to have caused so much damage. Maybe it was broken? The energy was fuzzy in Finn's sight, but he detected a faint glow of orange and red embedded in the green surface – a trace of energy lingering in its mana cores.

He cocked his head. How did it still have power?

Shouldn't that energy have decayed over time? Or maybe it had repurposed the attendants like they had witnessed back in the reception area?

Finn peered closer and saw that a multi-colored hue ran along one of the creature's limbs – a glowing spot of rainbow energy that looked eerily familiar.

It almost looked like—

He didn't get to finish that thought.

All at once, a flash of white energy jutted from the damaged mech, fanning out in a beam so quickly that Finn wasn't able to move out of the way in time. As that energy crossed Finn's body, the mech jerked, as though it sensed the intruders in the hall. It lifted its gangly metallic head toward the doorway, the movement lurching and uncoordinated. Mana flared along its body, the mana cores in its chest glowing brightly, and the strange multi-colored energy along its limb swirled as a reddish hue overtook the other colors.

The creature unfolded itself, the pile shifting and snapping with the screech of metal grinding against metal. Within only seconds, the mech had shambled to its feet, lurching toward the door with awkward steps. But Julia was waiting. She slammed the thing with her shield, sending it hurtling into the far wall of the small chamber. It smashed against the rock with a crunch and a shower of sparks and then lay unmoving on the floor.

Giving up on discretion, Finn motioned at Daniel to venture inside, his flaming body soon lighting the enclosure and revealing the thing that lay against the far wall.

"What the actual fuck," Julia muttered.

Finn could sympathize with that statement, his mouth hanging open as he inspected the creature with *Short-Sighted*. It was roughly humanoid, with four limbs and a makeshift head. It *looked* like the security mech they had encountered in the reception area... except this one was malformed. Where the security mech had been built with clean lines and uniform materials, this one's limbs were twisted at strange angles, and its body seemed to have been stitched together with a haphazard assortment of parts.

A sickening sensation settled in Finn's stomach as his gaze swept to the mech's arm.

Patches of pale flesh were visible between the metallic plates and wiring, ruined skin embedded with crystalline wires and circuits. More skin was visible throughout its torso and legs, but those were only small fragments. Switching back to his *Mana Sight*, Finn suddenly understood why that point of multi-colored light had looked so disturbingly familiar.

That was a Najima in the mech's arm…

Oh shit, Finn thought to himself.

It was human. Or, at least, it might have *once* been human.

Now it was a terrible amalgamation of flesh and metal.

As he watched, the creature twitched. Then it jerked again. That twisted arm clawed at the nearby stone wall, sending off a shower of sparks as the creature used the leverage to yank itself back upright. The twisted combination of metal, flesh, and crystal began stitching itself back together with a flash of mana. It soon turned its metallic head toward the group once more, eyeing them with an almost palpable hunger.

"*Maaaannnaa*," the creature croaked, its voice holding a metallic, inhuman note.

It surged forward in a flurry of limbs, giving up any pretense of hesitation this time. Julia moved to smash it aside again, but the creature seemed to anticipate the blow. It ducked under her attack, scoring her metal breastplate with metallic, claw-like fingers. Julia kicked at the creature's leg, her mailed boot caving in the metal with a crunch. The monstrosity lurched to the side and fell, but didn't stop its assault, scrabbling at her legs.

"*Maannnaaa!*" it cried, the sound now a tortured scream.

Realizing its metallic fingers weren't effective against Julia's armor, the creature's mana surged again, flames rippling across its arm and swiftly warming its claw-like hands to a dull red glow. At the same time, more mana flared along its ruined leg as the limb began to piece itself back together.

Fuck. It can repair like the other mechs.

Finn saw the creature's Najima pulse, dimming slightly as it expended mana and then gradually brightening again. *It's also regenerating mana*, he realized belatedly. *Damn it!*

Finn's thoughts raced. It was becoming clear now what the staff must have been fighting and why no corpses lined the hall. And if there was one of these creatures, then there were likely more…

They needed information – fast.

Making a quick decision, Finn barked an order to Julia. "Give me 5 seconds, then back out of the room. Don't let it cross the doorway." Already, the creature was regaining its feet and lunging at Julia as she backpedaled toward the door.

"Daniel, get a scan now and then get the hell out of there!" Finn barked.

He didn't wait to see whether they followed his orders.

Finn's fingers raced, and the metallic sphere in his hand was soon coated in flame. It rocketed through the air as he simultaneously increased the heat, causing the fire to surge and the metal to begin to glow a bright red. He smashed the orb flat, creating a makeshift molten blade capable of cutting and slicing with pinpoint precision. He aimed for the creature's joints and neatly severed each limb.

Julia rushed forward as the creature stumbled, her shield crashing into its metallic head. She put all of her considerable strength into the attack, sending the monstrosity flying backward into the wall once more, its body crashing against the stone and its limbs exploding across the room.

Even with its body dismembered and Julia's devastating attack, Finn could see that the mech wasn't finished. Already, more mana was flaring along the cores in its chest and that decayed, fleshy limb. As he looked on, tendrils of crystal stretched out from the torso and across the ground, inching toward the dismembered limbs. It was planning to pull itself back together…

Yet he didn't plan to wait around for that.

As Daniel flitted through the room and the occasional fan of orange energy struck the malformed mech, Finn directed his orb out of the room and dropped the channel, the molten metal cooling rapidly as it struck the stone floor with a dull thunk.

Finn cast *Imbue Fire* again, this time on the deadbolts embedded in the partially open door. Flames soon sprung up around the metal, and Finn poured more mana into the spell to raise the temperature. The creature was already beginning to rise once again, and it took an awkward, shambling step forward toward the door, its limbs hanging askew – some only connected by a few strands of crystalline thread. Julia had backed out of the room, keeping her shield raised, even as Daniel's form raced through the exit behind her.

As the mech's legs snapped back into place, the monstrosity lunged at the narrow gap in the door, flames rippling along its metallic claws once more. It raked at the air, and an ear-piercing howl escaped whatever it used as a throat.

"Any time now!" Julia said, urgency tinging her voice.

Finn yanked at the door with everything he had. The combination of stone, crystal, and metal resisted at first. Time seemed to slow as the creature barreled toward them, reaching out a lone arm as it clawed at the air. Finn jerked at the deadbolts again, and the door finally moved, slamming shut with a crash of stone on stone and a shower of sparks, and a thick cloud of dust drifted down from the doorway as the walls trembled from the impact. With a quick flick of his wrist, Finn drove the deadbolts home and securely locked the door, maintaining the channel to ensure they stayed in place.

The creature's arm had gotten caught in the doorway at the last moment, the door severing the metal at the elbow and leaving a ruined limb lying along the ground. Finn glanced down and could see a sickly, multi-colored liquid leaking from the pale flesh and pooling on the stone. Already, tendrils of crystal were reaching out of the ruined limb, stretching toward the rest of the mech's body, but finding its path blocked by the door.

Which left the group standing in the darkened hallway, lit only by the flickering light of Daniel's body, and staring at the malformed limb along the ground. They could hear the muted scratches and howls of the creature on the other side of that door – the grinding shriek of metal striking stone as it clawed at the door.

"Ahh, I made a mistake," Daniel chirped.

Finn eyed him in confusion.

"You remember back in the reception area when you asked what was the worst thing that could happen if we tried to force our way inside this section? I forgot to add the possibility of encountering magical, self-healing mech/human hybrids hellbent on devouring mana. I'll make certain to update my records accordingly."

Chapter 15 - Corrupted

"What the fuck is that thing?" Kyyle muttered, the group listening to the creature scratch against the other side of the door.

"It appears to be a combination of the former human staff and the security mechs stationed in this section," Brock answered with a rumble.

"How is that even possible?" Julia demanded, whirling toward the elemental. "You said this place has been under lockdown for at least 50 years. Anyone in here should be long dead. And, as far as we know, it doesn't look like anyone else managed to make it past reception."

The rocks that made up the earth elemental's body ground together as he pondered her question. "It's possible that the security mechs incorporated their human counterparts in order to maintain their mana and fulfill their primary directive."

"Which is what exactly?" Julia asked sharply.

"To protect the facility, of course."

"That just doesn't make any sense," Julia muttered. "Why would incorporating the human staff help keep some magically powered..." Her eyes widened as she stared at the door, the realization dawning on her. "Oh... oh, shit."

"Yep," Finn replied to her unspoken conclusion.

"You two want to share with the class?" Kyyle offered in a dry tone.

Finn glanced at Daniel. "You manage to get a scan during that confrontation?"

"Of course, I did," the fire elemental replied. "That's just one of my many *useful* talents, which clearly demonstrates the superiority of fire elementals over a lumbering pile of rubble —"

"Just show us the scan, Daniel," Finn grumbled, rubbing at his temple. They didn't have time for elemental rivalries.

With a mutter from Daniel, an image soon

appeared in the air, showing the corrupted mech in a glowing orange silhouette. Now that the creature wasn't lunging at them, it was far easier to make out the pieces of pale human flesh amid the metal panels and crystalline wiring. The thing looked like it had been cobbled together by a mad mechanic. It lacked the clean lines and symmetry of the other mechs. Instead, it was just a mash of human and synthetic parts terminating in two arms equipped with jagged metal claws.

Finn pinched at the air and centered on a patch of pale skin along the creature's arm. "I managed to get a good look at the thing while it was attacking Julia. It has a Najima in this arm," he said, tapping at the display. He shot a glance at the severed limb on the floor. Despite the energy beginning to fade, Finn could still make out traces of the Najima. "The same arm that's resting right there," he muttered.

He let out a sigh. "I think Brock is right. Those clusters naturally absorb ambient mana and convert it to the various affinities. Even two Najima would be enough to recharge and power the creature, albeit much more slowly than an intact human."

Finn eyed the door beside them. It could be his imagination, but it seemed as though the scratching had begun to wind down. "That should also mean…"

He trailed off as the noise abruptly cut off. Finn peeled back the intervening layers of mana. The interference from the crystals lacing the door made it difficult to see much on the other side, but he was just barely able to make out the corrupted mech slumped against the doorway, its body pulsing faintly with mana.

It looked like its energy had been largely depleted.

"…it'll eventually run out of juice," Finn finished in a distracted voice.

He chewed on the inside of his cheek in thought. *Could this mech be a one-off?* he wondered hopefully, trying to ignore the doubting voice at the edges of his mind.

Yet that voice refused to be disregarded… his brain chipping away at the problem automatically – no matter how hard Finn tried to resist the conclusion that was gradually beginning to form.

This room must be a security checkpoint. Which meant it likely had a guard and at least one security mech. The mech could have begun running out of power, and it might have incorporated the human guard into itself. Yet Finn didn't recall seeing any other bones or remains inside, and only one Najima lingered in its body.

So, what had happened to the rest of the guard?

And that was only the first question. They knew that there was no record of any enemies breaching the blast doors leading farther into the facility, at least before the reception area went offline. Someone had also cut the main conduit leading back into the reception area. And, as Brock had suggested, the only way to sever power to the section was to manually and simultaneously cut the main conduits while deactivating the fire pylon. Which meant the danger most likely came from *within* the section.

So, had the staff done it? If so, why?

Maybe this was an anomaly? An unanticipated bug in whatever magical code that the mechs were using to operate? A byproduct of leaving the security lockdown in place for so long – much longer than the system might have been designed to handle? But if the power had still been online, why would the mechs have needed to incorporate human staff? Finn paused at that thought, his gaze drifting to the scratches and scorch marks that marred the walls of the hallway.

Maybe the staff had simply been an easier target. It seemed more straightforward to incorporate their Najima than to attempt to drain the facility's power directly. Finn had already witnessed firsthand how resilient the walls could be – especially if there had been sufficient power to repair them. Maybe the mechs hadn't had the firepower to manage that feat. Or the fire mana alone wasn't enough. Incorporating the human staff would have given the mechs an infinitely renewable source of energy – one that also provided multiple types of mana.

And if the staff had started to see the mechs

incorporating their own…

"Damn it," Finn muttered as the realization finally hit him.

He looked back down the hall in the direction of the blast door. "I think we were on the right track before. I don't think this section lost power by accident or from an attack. At least, not exactly."

"I don't understand your conclusion," Brock rumbled. "Could you please elaborate?"

"He means that the human staff must have cut the power to this section and blocked it off to stop these… *things* from spreading throughout the facility," Daniel answered sharply, his form dancing in front of the earth elemental. "Any elemental with more than one mana core to rub together could have figured that out."

"Ahh, that is an interesting deduction. Thank you for explaining it to me," Brock rumbled, seemingly oblivious to Daniel's scathing tone. The AI's fiery form just pulsed in irritation.

"Okay, so these mechs started going crazy and incorporating the staff," Julia began slowly. "The people that worked here got scared. Maybe they were worried that the bug would spread…" A grimace swept across her face. "But if that's right, then it means that there are likely more of these things in here."

Finn nodded. "Which is why we didn't see any other human remains in that room," he offered, waving at the sealed door beside him.

Kyyle spun toward the earth elemental. "How many staff members did you say were stationed in this section exactly?"

"Between 50 and 100, although not all staff members may have been present when the facility went into lockdown." A moment of hesitation. "It's also not clear whether all of the human staff were incorporated by the security mechs."

"And the better question is probably how many *mechs* were stationed in this section," Kyyle answered in a distracted voice as he stared at the floating image of the corrupted mech. "This one didn't use a full person. So, it's probably safe to assume that the other mechs only assimilated one or two Najima each. There were probably plenty of staff members to go around…"

"There were approximately 200 security mechs stationed in this section," Brock rumbled in response.

"200…" Julia echoed, her eyes going wide. "Even if we cut that number by 25% to account for mechs in storage or without access to human parts, that still leaves upward of 150 of these things?" She paused. "I guess that's a *manageable* number."

"Uh, were you there when that thing attacked us?" Kyyle asked. "It didn't seem fazed by your attacks and repaired itself almost instantly." The earth mage pinched at Daniel's projection of the creature, pivoting the display. "And there don't seem to be any obvious weak points. Well… short of dismembering the thing to remove the Najima."

Finn was rubbing at the dull ache in his left arm, trying to tamp down on the pain that simmered there and now stretched up into his chest. Even that short encounter had been enough to inflame the infection. "You're right," he grunted at Kyyle. "And if we encounter mechs with more than one Najima, we'd need to sever all of those limbs at once to stop it from regenerating.

"Even then, there's still this." Finn's fingers flicked at the display, centering the image on the creature's chest. A cluster of glowing mana cores was nestled in its torso, surrounded by a cage of metal and that strange crystalline wiring. "The thing is still part mech, which means it's storing backup or overflow mana in its original mana cores. That could potentially allow it to reattach the severed limbs. That's also why the mech kept going even after we severed its arm," Finn offered, gesturing at the nearby door.

"And that also explains why the mech was inactive when we found it," Julia continued. "It was effectively in *standby mode*. It powered down to conserve power and allow its natural regeneration to outpace its consumption –

likely only maintaining its sensors to scan at regular intervals. Which means if we find any more of these things, they'll probably be inactive, but they'll most likely have topped off their mana cores."

Finn nodded along with her explanation. "Exactly." He glanced at the door beside them. "And we can estimate their mana reserves. That fight and its ensuing assault on the door took approximately..." Finn trailed off, shooting Daniel a questioning glance.

"10 minutes, give or take," the AI replied immediately.

"Our one advantage is that these things are using mana to repair, charge their attacks, and to move and operate," Finn explained with a nod. "It seems safe to assume that they don't have a separate stamina pool like other biological enemies we've faced. Everything here runs on mana. Even the flesh that they've incorporated is ruined, and the muscle seems to have been replaced with the mech's regular pneumatic systems," he added, gesturing at the ruined limb on the floor. "That means we have two options: either we need to overwhelm them, or we have to whittle them down so that they run out of power and go into standby."

"And it's safe to assume that they have some way of draining mana from other power sources," Julia continued. "Otherwise, the staff wouldn't have bothered to cut the power. If we're right, they must have been afraid the bug would spread to other systems or that they might grow strong enough to tap into the facility's power. Hell, for all we know, this could be some sort of magical virus."

As she finished speaking, the group as one glanced at the severed limb, backing away from it slowly.

"Just fucking perfect," Kyyle muttered. "So we're trapped in this section of the facility. We need to turn the lights back on to lift the lockdown and reach the center of the Forge. But that's probably going to draw the attention of anywhere from 150 to 200 of these mech-human hybrids. And risk allowing whatever is happening in here to continue to spread through the facility. Oh, and we can barely kill one…"

"Well, there's always running away for 10 minutes or so," Julia offered with a tired smile. "Plus, some of us have little or no mana. Sounds like I'm just fine."

"Lucky you," Kyyle retorted with a grin of his own. "Hope you enjoy wandering the same dark hallways for all of eternity."

Finn's brow furrowed at that comment, a glimmer of an idea flaring to life – one that might also save him from having to use his mana. At the rate he was going, the infection was spreading quickly, and he wasn't looking forward to discovering what would happen when it reached another Najima.

"Daniel, bring up the facility map again," Finn instructed.

Immediately, the display floating before them shifted, now showing the layout of the Forge. Finn's gaze hovered on the darkened section where they stood, his eyes tracing the complicated network of rooms and hallways.

"Brock, are all of the rooms equipped with the same locking mechanism as this one?" Finn asked, waving at the door beside them.

"Yes, sir. The experiments conducted here can often be dangerous. Each compartment and hallway was designed to be locked off in the event of an accident. Security was paramount in the Forge's design."

Finn just shook his head at that. He didn't want to speculate at what sort of "experiments" the staff might have been performing down here. Although, on second thought, could it be any worse than these mech-human hybrids?

"What're you thinking?" Julia asked.

"That I might have a way of dealing with these things," Finn replied slowly, his eyes still on the map and tracing a circuitous path through the facility. His attention snapped back to Julia. "Kyyle and I need to stay here and keep our mana use to a minimum. We're just too exposed with the way these things scan for mana. You, however, are at an advantage. How would you feel about doing a little scouting again?"

His daughter gave him a shrug. "If it gets us the hell out of this place, I'm down. What do you have in mind?"

Finn traced a path through the map of the section with his finger, leaving a glowing yellow line in its wake. "You should check these areas for obstructions. We're looking for a clear path through the complex that is roughly circular. Also, identify the location of any of these creatures you find with a waypoint marker," Finn instructed.

His attention shifted to the chamber that contained the fire pylon – that room resting at the tip of the triangular section. He had a bad feeling about what they might find inside. Even from this distance and with the intervening layers of mana and conductive crystal, he could still make out the dull glow of the other five pylons. He wasn't certain he wanted to consider what the mechs might have created with that sort of power.

He just had to hope the staff had taken out the pylon before they'd had a chance to access that chamber.

"Just stay clear of the pylon room," Finn instructed. "You might also want to ditch the armor and maintain *Sneak* for the moment. We still can't be certain whether these creatures can detect noise or regular spectrums of light. I think it's safe to assume that whatever is happening here may be similar to a mutation. Which means some of the creatures may have developed other abilities."

"Got it," Julia replied with a curt nod. She began stripping her metal armor and placing the pieces carefully in her pack. Once finished, she strapped down her shield tightly, hung her lance at her waist, and gave Finn a parting glance. "Be back in a second. Don't have too much fun without me."

"Be careful," was Finn's only reply.

"Always," she shot back with a grin before racing

down the hall.

Finn's and Kyyle's eyes followed her as she swiftly disappeared into the gloom that blanketed the hallway. "So, uh, what do we do in the meantime?" the earth mage asked.

"We wait," Finn answered, leaning against the nearby wall. "And hope she doesn't come running back with a few dozen of those creatures on her heels... or we get detected before she can return," he offered, sparing a glance at Daniel and Brock. The elementals likely stood out like beacons of mana to the mech-human hybrids.

"Perfect..." the earth mage muttered.

A brief pause.

"So, while we're waiting, you want to come up with a name for these things? They're like a brand-new species – even by this world's standards. And we're the first to discover them!" Kyyle rubbed at his chin. "Plus, just calling them cyborgs or something feels uninspired.

"How about *homo roboticus*?"

Finn was already rubbing at his temple.

"Or maybe the *core-ruption*?" Daniel offered hesitantly.

"Ha, that's awesome!" Kyyle replied, earning him an appreciative glow from the fire elemental. "I'd give you a hi-five, but you don't really have hands."

Finn just grimaced. "Did you not get it?" Daniel asked as he observed Finn's reaction. "Because they have mana cores and they've been corrupted —"

"I definitely got it," Finn replied in a pained voice.

"I'm personally fond of *ferronics*," Brock rumbled. "Since they're comprised of both ferrous and biologic materials."

"The earth bro delivers with a decent name," Kyyle said with a grin. He raised his hand to give the earth elemental a hi-five, but the floating pile of rubble just stared in confusion at the proffered limb.

"You're supposed to tap my hand with yours," Kyyle explained.

"Ahh, understood," Brock replied. He promptly

smacked his rocky palm against Kyyle's, the force of the blow sending the earth mage stumbling backward into the nearby wall and the air exiting his lungs in a whoosh.

"Fuck… Ow," Kyyle muttered, gasping for breath.

"Are you okay?" Brock asked, a tinge of concern entering his voice.

"Yeah, yeah. Just a little more gentle next time," Kyyle grunted, leaning over and resting his palms on his knees as he tried to catch his breath.

"Of course, the pile of rubble would mess it up," Daniel grumbled. "Waste of working limbs, if you ask me."

Finn let out a soft sigh, his eyes on the hallway as it stretched off into shadowy darkness. He was just beginning to realize that they had another danger to worry about. If Julia didn't make it back soon, they wouldn't need to worry about the mech-human hybrids.

Finn would probably end up killing his teammates himself…

Chapter 16 - Distracting

"Whew! I'm never doing that again," Julia exclaimed as she dropped from *Sneak*. She immediately doubled over, hands on her knees, and her breath coming in great heaving gasps.

"It looks like good cardio, though," Kyyle offered with a grin. "Something about corrupted mechs looking to tear you limb from limb and borrow a few body parts makes for great motivation. They should come up with something similar in the real world."

Julia just glared at him. "Yeah. Well, next time, you can give it a shot."

"Yeah, no thanks. I'd die. Quickly. I'm man enough to admit that," Kyyle replied. "But Brock and I are fantastic *moral support*." The earth elemental's glowing green eyes simply stared at Julia silently.

"Yeah... I see that," she retorted.

Meanwhile, Finn's attention had drifted to the darkened hallway, and he clutched at a metal sphere. He was watching for the telltale flicker of mana that would give away one of the mechs. However, he was hesitant to cast *Imbue Fire* for fear of accidentally drawing the attention of the creatures. "Were you followed?" he asked.

"No, those... *things* pretty much seemed to ignore me."

"*Corrupted*," Kyyle corrected. This earned him a questioning glance from Julia. "That's what we landed on while you were gone." As he noticed her expression, he continued defensively. "See? We didn't just sit here, twiddling our thumbs while you did all of the work. Daniel came up with the name, actually." The fire elemental pulsed happily and dipped through the air at that comment.

"It's because they have—" Daniel began.

Julia shook her head as she straightened. "I figured it out. Trust me. Sounds like you all have been *real* busy while I was gone."

"You took a while," Finn observed in a dry tone. "I very nearly saved the mechs the trouble and killed them all myself."

"Well, I'm glad you didn't! I come bearing some good news," Julia said with a grin.

With a flick of her wrist, she brought up her map and rotated the display, the familiar six-sided image of the Forge coming into view. The group had entered the reception area, which was located directly between the triangular fire and air mana sections. They were currently standing in a long hallway between the reception area and the fire area, which they assumed must act as some sort of security checkpoint.

Julia's fingers traced a line down the hallway from where they were standing until she reached the fire mana section. She then marked a winding path through the area before doubling back, her trail terminating in a large room. As she lifted her hand away, the glowing yellow trail remained, highlighting a clear path through the section.

"It took me some time, but I managed to identify the doors that are currently bolted closed." As she spoke, Julia highlighted a series of thin red lines along many of the rooms. "There's no power keeping the doors closed, of course, but I imagine it would take some time to get them opened." She glanced at Finn. "And the mana needed to accomplish that is going to draw some attention. This path passes through most of the rooms and then terminates in a dead-end in this last chamber."

"And the corrupted?" Finn asked, deliberately ignoring the smile that swept across Kyyle's face when he used Daniel's name for the human-mech hybrids.

Julia nodded, and with another flick of her wrist, a series of yellow dots appeared on the map. "I marked all of the... *corrupted* that I found. Weirdly, they were spread out around the section. Maybe they returned to their original posts or something?" she offered, gesturing at the security checkpoint door beside them. She let out a sigh. "And I can't guarantee that I detected all of them. I wasn't able to find a path through every room since some were dead-ends or sealed off entirely."

Finn winced as he saw the number of markers. There were at least 70. That was a bit low, wasn't it? Brock had indicated that there were likely closer to 150-200. Maybe more of the security mechs were inactive, in storage, or locked in other portions of the section. He hesitated. Or, there could be another answer...

"It looks like we might have only identified a little under half of them," Finn murmured.

Julia just nodded, a grim expression on her face.

"Hmm, that's... not great," Kyyle murmured, staring at the map. "We run the risk of drawing more if we start throwing around a lot of mana. But their sensor range seems limited – at least based on the one we encountered." His eyes darted to Finn. "And you've had trouble penetrating these walls with your *Mana Sight*. It might be safe to assume that the corrupted have the same limitation."

Finn nodded as he stared at the map. "Yeah. Yeah, I think this could still work."

"What could still work exactly?" Julia asked, glancing at Finn in confusion.

He'd forgotten he hadn't shared his plan with his daughter. While they were waiting, he and Kyyle had gone over his latest "batshit-strategy-to-get-them-all-killed" – as Daniel liked to call it.

"Okay, so fighting these corrupted is a daunting task with their regeneration, right?" Finn began. This earned him a nod from Julia. "Except we don't really need to take out all of these mechs. Or any of them, actually. We just need to clear a path to the fire pylon and buy ourselves enough time to bring the power back online and find some supervisor credentials," he explained, tapping at the tip of the triangle. Julia's path had taken her right past the entrance to the pylon chamber.

"That room is locked tight," his daughter offered. "I didn't linger long, but it looks like it's sealed with another blast door similar to the one in the reception area. It might take us some time to crack."

Finn nodded. "Which means we first need to lure the corrupted away and trap them the same way we did with that one," he replied, gesturing at the room beside them. "That way, we have some time to work on the blast door to the fire pylon chamber and search the rest of this section."

He tapped at several of the rooms and hallways adjacent to the entrance to the chamber with the fire pylon, highlighting open doorways. "I could seal off the passages into this cluster of rooms. We just need to lure the mechs out first…"

Julia chewed on her lip as she stared at the map, her brow furrowed. "I see what you're thinking. We send in some bait, lure the corrupted out of these specific areas and into a dead-end passage, seal off the entrance, and then work on blocking off these doors to the other rooms. That would secure us a safe area around the entrance to the pylon chamber."

"Exactly," Finn said with a curt nod.

And avoiding a fight means I can slow the spread of the infection, Finn added silently, trying his best to ignore the burning sensation that lingered in his arm and chest. He'd still have to use some mana to close the doors behind them… but that was an acceptable cost.

"Assuming they can't just tear down the door," Kyyle added with a sour expression, glancing at the doorway beside them. "One was enough to do some damage. What could a few dozen do?"

Finn rubbed at his neck, where that throbbing ache was beginning to creep upward. "We'll just have to take that risk. We can also use multiple doors." He tapped at Julia's map. "We can use this hallway leading to the trap-chamber. That'll give us at least two doors." He glanced at Kyyle. "Worst case, you and I could probably reinforce the walls with an additional barrier of earth and some of the dark metal we found down in the Abyss." This earned him a reluctant nod from Kyyle.

"Okay, this is starting to sound like it might work," Julia said, staring at the map. Then her attention shifted to

Finn. "Which just means we need some decent bait."

The group all turned to look at Daniel, where he floated nearby. His fire dimmed noticeably as he realized that they were all staring at him. "Why are you...? No! Just no. I'm not going to be the bait – again!"

"You're the best choice," Finn explained. "You're fast, you can fly, and you're semi-corporeal. And most importantly, you give off an intense fire mana signature."

"Translation: I'm expendable, and I glow," Daniel retorted. "What fantastic qualifications!"

Finn suppressed the urge to snap at the recalcitrant AI. While he was delighted that Daniel was evolving, at times, it felt like he was dealing with a surly teenager. Silence descended upon the darkened hallway as Finn stared at the AI, the tension only broken by the faint grinding rumble of Brock's body.

Although, as Finn glanced at the earth elemental, a thought occurred to him...

"You know what? You're *right*. You probably shouldn't go," Finn began. "Especially not now that we have Brock here. His rock body should protect him from the corrupted, and he's much more familiar with the facility." Daniel's form flickered uncertainly, and his nervous dance through the air slowed.

"What are you talking about? I saw a lot of drained attendants—" Julia started to say but cut herself off at a discreet gesture from Finn.

"But Brock here is *special*," Finn said, laying it on thick now. "Clearly, he's one of the stronger elementals if he's survived this long. He's actually a perfect fit for this mission."

"I would be happy to be of assistance," Brock rumbled in a neutral tone.

"I'm not sure..." Daniel began weakly.

"Don't worry about it," Finn said, waving absently at the fire elemental. "You can stay back here and light up the hallway or something. We'll always need a floating lantern, and we should each focus on playing to our strengths."

"I'm not just a flying candle!" Daniel bit back, his body flaring brightly. "I'm the best fit for this assignment. You think this floating pile of rubble can move as fast as me? He'll get taken out in the first room."

"Are you sure you're really up to it, though?" Finn asked, injecting some doubt into his voice and suppressing the smile that threatened to creep across his face. "I mean, I don't think you've handled anything this complicated before—"

"You mean, can I fly in a predetermined path?" Daniel demanded. "Don't insult me. I'm just worried that you fleshy humans and this slow-moving avalanche can't keep up."

Finn rubbed at his mouth to cover his smile. "Well, in that case, *maybe* you're right."

"Damn straight," Daniel grumbled.

Finn turned back to Julia and Kyyle, who were both struggling not to laugh. The earth mage had already brought up his console, eyeing Daniel as he tapped out a few notes. Finn could easily anticipate what Kyyle was thinking. It seemed Daniel had evolved enough that he was susceptible to jealousy and a touch of reverse psychology. Or, that had at least been a very convincing imitation of self-awareness.

At that thought, the Seer's words echoed through his head.

If the memories are the same, the behavior identical, what is the difference?

He would have to cling to that hope – that Daniel's evolution was *real*. Or so close that it didn't make any substantive difference. That faint flicker of sentience gave him hope that they could make it through this place. That they could defeat the Emir.

That they could bring Rachael back.

"Alright, we have a plan, and the clock is still ticking," Finn said, forcing himself to focus. "Everyone grab your gear. We move in five."

*   *   *

"Alright, we're ready when you are," Finn said, eyeing Daniel where the AI floated beside him. His light had begun to dim over the last few minutes, worry overcoming his initial indignant anger and jealousy.

Moving slowly and lowering his voice so only Finn could hear, Daniel asked, "What if... what if the corrupted can drain me?"

Finn hesitated at that question. His thoughts drifted back to the jagged crystal that rested in Brock's chest. He supposed it was *possible*. The game was still treating Daniel as a fire elemental, after all – his pet designation aside. Finn had gotten used to thinking of the AI as immortal, but could the corrupted actually hurt him?

"Don't give them a chance," Finn replied quietly. "Just fly fast and stay as close to the ceiling as possible. Unless these things have evolved the ability to fly, that should keep you protected."

Daniel's form flickered again. He didn't seem convinced.

"We're counting on you, Daniel. You've got this," Finn added, trying to reassure the AI. He was concerned that, unlike many other occasions, Daniel hadn't attempted to articulate the probability of them failing. What did that indicate? That he was trying to avoid thinking about that information?

Or maybe their odds of surviving were too low for him to say aloud...

The AI seemed to pivot to look at him, and Finn forced himself to project confidence. Daniel couldn't see him faltering right now. The fire elemental's body flared a bit brighter. "Yeah... yeah, I've got this," he murmured.

"Okay, let's get started." Daniel's voice echoed through the hallway, his tone more confident, and his body flaring brightly. "You lot try to keep up."

With that parting statement, the AI took off like a bullet. His fiery form raced down the hallway, a receding ball of flame that pushed back at the shadowy darkness that lingered in the passage. The group waited a full five seconds before darting after him. They would need to maintain a precarious balance – staying close enough that Finn could block off the various rooms and hallways behind them, but far enough away that they wouldn't accidentally attract the attention of the corrupted.

After their encounter with the first mech-human hybrid, Finn didn't feel optimistic that they could take on these things in a straight fight. As much as he was concerned about the AI's safety, he likely stood a better chance than they did. If a few of the corrupted caught wind of the group trailing the fire elemental, this would all be over quickly.

And Finn guessed that dying inside the Forge would be bad... very bad. They hadn't crossed one of those shimmering blue veils like they had back in the Abyss – that barrier highlighting the edge of a dungeon. If they died, they couldn't be certain where they would respawn. Worst case, death might be a one-way ticket back to Lahab, Bilel waiting there with open arms.

He forcefully shoved that thought aside, focusing instead on the rhythmic thump, thump, thump of their feet pounding upon the stone floor... The sound of their ragged breathing... The grinding rumble of Brock's body...

Julia had re-equipped her armor, and her plate-clad feet smashed against the stone. The time for caution was now long past. Meanwhile, Finn's eyes hovered on the glowing yellow line that stretched out ahead of them – the waypoint marker active, guiding them along a predetermined path through the fire section.

That path twisted to the left, the hall curving and opening into a large chamber. Finn raised a staying hand as his *Mana Sight* picked up bright flares of mana from the corrupted. As they woke and noticed Daniel flitting through the room in a zig-zag pattern, the mechs' hazy silhouettes began to swarm after him.

"Good job, Daniel," Finn murmured. Then, to his companions, "Alright, let's go."

They entered the room just in time to see Daniel's

flickering form race through one of the exits, a group of corrupted already hot on his flaming heels. The strange mech-human hybrids shuffled forward with shambling, awkward steps – the squeal of rusted metal, and the hiss of pneumatics echoing through the room. Their metallic claws tore at the air, fire rippling along their limbs and lighting the room in a faltering, erratic light.

As Finn watched, one of the corrupted lunged at Daniel, jumping nearly four feet into the air and its claws stretching toward the elemental. The AI weaved to the side, narrowly avoiding the blow before rocketing further down the hallway. The horde of corrupted soon disappeared as they gave chase, plunging the room back into darkness.

"Fuck, I hope this works," Kyyle breathed beside Finn. "That was only the first dozen or so. If they turn around or we can't seal them in that trap-room..." He didn't need to finish that thought. They all knew what would happen. This was an all-or-nothing plan.

"Let's just keep moving. We need to stay close," Finn grunted in response. And then the group was running again, following that thin yellow path.

In the next hallway, Finn noted a waypoint marker. One of the doors he needed to seal shut. He barely slowed, his hand moving in a blur as he cast *Imbue Fire*, the deadbolts within the doorway soon awash in flame. As they raced past, Finn shoved the door shut, and the reinforced stone soon slammed into the frame with a dull thump and a gust of dust. A jerk of his fingers and the deadbolts slid into place.

The group hadn't slowed, continuing their headlong charge.

As they repeated this process, again and again, Finn forcefully maintained his mana, using the energy to focus and burn away the last traces of his anxiety. There was only the running, the casting, that thin yellow line. Another hallway, another room – another door slamming shut with a flare of flame and a wave of heat.

The ragged breathing. The burning sensation in

their lungs and thighs. The slap of their feet striking stone. And the frustrated, feral roar of the corrupted in the distance – their cries echoing off the walls, growing with each passing second as new members joined the horde. Their metallic limbs skittered and shrieked, scraping against the walls of the facility – an ever-present reminder of what was waiting for them if the mechs slowed or stopped.

"We're almost there," Julia grunted. "Just a few more rooms."

Finn spared a glance in Daniel's direction, removing as many of the intervening layers of mana as he could. He could just barely spot the AI's glowing form, but it was difficult through the interference from the walls. A wave of multi-colored mana was streaming after him now, dozens of the corrupted in hot pursuit.

We're moving too slow, Finn realized. Daniel was getting close to the dead-end chamber, but they were still two rooms and a hallway behind. He spared a glance at his stamina. He was already sitting at half.

Fuck. He knew what he'd need to do to catch up – what that would cost him... Yet he wasn't sure he could live with the consequences if he didn't.

"We're too far behind," Finn grunted, the group not slowing. "Daniel is almost in the trap-room. I'm going to have to cast *Haste*."

"Your stamina must be low by now," Julia retorted, shooting him a worried glance. "If you don't manage to close that door or they break through, you'll be trapped in there."

And if he didn't take the risk, Daniel would be stuck in that room with dozens of the corrupted. The AI's words still echoed through his mind. *What if... what if the corrupted can drain me?* Finn knew Daniel was practically immune to physical attacks. But could he die? Could the corrupted drain him?

Finn couldn't take that chance.

"No choice," Finn grunted, his hand already moving.

He felt the fire burn through his veins in a torrent, like liquid lava surging through his body. A thin film of flame soon coated his skin, and the world around him began to slow, his teammates falling behind him as though they were sprinting through thick sludge. He didn't spare them any attention, pushing himself even harder.

Finn barreled down the hallway, pivoted hard to the left, and kicked off the wall as his momentum pushed him forward. He was a blazing streak of flame racing after Daniel. That alone was risky. If he slowed at all, Finn could attract the attention of any other corrupted that might linger in these rooms. Yet he didn't have time to worry about that. His attention was focused on that bright pinpoint of fire mana ahead. The AI was just passing the opening into the final chamber, the wave of corrupted chasing him inside.

Faster. I need to go faster.

Finn's feet crashed against the floor, the world blurring past him as he made another turn. The room was just up ahead. He could see the ocean of swirling mana more clearly now – the bright sun-like spot of fire that hovered along the ceiling. His eyes were on the edge of his control range, denoted by a thin orange line. He was just waiting for that line to cross the room's threshold.

Just a few more feet…

Finn abruptly slid to a stop, his hand racing through a series of gestures so quickly that his fingers blurred, and sparks of flame arced through the air. Forced to drop *Haste* as his stamina bottomed out, Finn sunk to his knees, his vision swimming. Yet he didn't stop casting, forcing his fingers to keep moving through pure force of will. Flames consumed the entire door. Finn had no time for delicacy.

"Daniel! Get the fuck out of there!" he shouted.

The AI somehow heard him over the howls of the corrupted, pivoting in the air, and arcing back toward the doorway. Daniel dipped, spun, and darted through the room as the mechs lunged at him, the AI navigating a mad obstacle course of mechanical limbs, tainted flesh, and flaming claws. Finn started to shove the door closed just as Daniel made a final dash for the exit, flames streaming along behind him.

The reinforced stone began to slide to the side…

Daniel's flaming form rocketed through the air…

An army of corrupted swarmed after him…

With a final heave, Finn tried to slam the door shut. However, it stopped before it could fully close, stone grinding against metal as several of the corrupted shoved their flailing limbs into the opening. More were right behind them, and they immediately slammed into the stone, causing the walls to tremble before shoving their limbs into the gap and trying to pry the door open.

Finn kept up his channel, straining against the corrupted as he tried to will the door closed. The ground shook as even more of the corrupted pushed forward, the momentum of the horde grinding the first wave of mechs against the stone with a discordant shriek of metal. A fine coating of dust billowed out from the doorway, and Finn could feel his spell buckle under the combined force of that many creatures. Several corrupted were tearing at the edges of the door, ignoring the flames that coated the surface; others clawed at the surface of the stone itself – as though they were trying to burrow *through* the stone.

But he kept pouring more energy into the spell.

Close, damn it!

His mana was dropping fast, and his breath was coming in frantic gasps now. Finn could feel the last traces of his energy beginning to give way, his mana depleting rapidly as he maintained heat rank 4. The deadbolts were beginning to soften and melt, which would make it even more difficult to secure the door – assuming he could even get the damn thing closed. Finn could feel himself swaying in place, barely able to stay upright, and his vision was swimming.

And then a hand landed on his shoulder, steadying him.

He saw a flash of emerald energy, and a surge of stone shoved the corrupted back through the doorway, sending them hurtling backward. That was enough to clear a small gap. With one final shove, Finn slammed the door closed. Using the last traces of his mana, he forced the deadbolts back into their original shape and welded them firmly into the sockets that lined the side of the wall – and that damnable door fully and finally shut.

Task complete, his spell sputtered out, and Finn's mana and stamina both hit zero.

He felt himself fall backward, his back striking hard stone as his eyes rolled toward the ceiling. His body ached. His breath came in ragged gasps, and the stump along his left arm burned even more fiercely than before, that same fire now twisting and coiling in his chest like a living thing.

In that moment, a flickering ball of fire drifted into his vision.

"Not bad for a human," Daniel observed calmly. "Hi-five?"

Finn just let out a hoarse chuckle, letting himself slump back against the stone and squeezing his eyes shut. They were alive. They'd made it. *Daniel* had made it.

Chapter 17 - Exploratory

A discordant, offbeat thumping came from the other side of the sealed doorway, the sound accompanied by the muted shriek of metal striking stone. Even insulated behind several feet of rock and crystal, the noise was enough to send a shiver down Finn's back.

"I don't think that door is going to last for long," Kyyle muttered, eyeing the doorway nervously as he grabbed Finn's hand and hauled him to his feet.

"They should run out of juice eventually..." Finn offered, his voice sounding hoarse and his vision swaying as he leaned heavily against Kyyle. His stamina hadn't had a chance to regenerate yet.

"Except that we don't know whether they'll breach the door before they shift back into standby mode," Daniel offered helpfully, his voice unusually chipper. "Or how long it will take the corrupted to regenerate their mana. Or whether they will continue clawing at the door again once they have recharged..."

"Yeah, we get it," Finn grumbled, glaring at the AI.

Yet he knew he wasn't really upset with Daniel. The frustration simmering in his veins wasn't directed at the AI... but at himself. That move had cost him dearly – he could already see a familiar notification flashing in his peripheral vision. And for what? The "life" of an AI he'd created and uploaded into the game?

Or maybe it was the realization that Daniel had started to become something more... both in terms of what he was and what he meant to Finn.

He wasn't sure how to feel about that.

With a sigh, Finn swiped at that notification.

System Notice: Infection Status
Continued spellcasting has caused the magical infection that afflicts your body to spread.

Current Contamination: 33%
Intact Najima: 4/6
Stat Loss: -20%

Damn it. That notice explained why his chest felt like it was on fire... the infection had spread to another Najima, further reducing his stats. He could only imagine what his Character Status looked like right now...

He was saved from his dour thoughts as Julia spoke up, "We should back out of this hallway and seal the next two doors," she offered, her hand flicking at the map displayed beside her and highlighting two more portals.

A loud slam and a resounding crack had them all turning back to the door. The stone had fractured, a long, jagged fissure now arching through the rock. They were all sharing the same thought. If the corrupted made it through that door, they were screwed.

"Yea, we need to move. Now," Julia added, hurriedly swiping away the map.

The other two nodded, and Finn stumbled back down the hallway with Kyyle's assistance. For her part, Julia kept her weapons raised and a wary eye on the door behind them. As they crossed the next doorway, Finn's fingers flashed through the gestures of *Imbue Fire,* and the door soon slammed shut with a shower of sparks. He then promptly melted the deadbolts into place, fusing them with the wall.

They repeated this process one more time until the noise had become more muted – merely a dull scratching in the distance. Finn shrugged off Kyyle's help as his stamina replenished itself and instead leaned a steadying hand against the wall. He peered into the surface with his *Mana Sight,* peeling back the layers as best he could.

He soon saw them – the corrupted. They were a multi-colored cloud hovering about fifty feet away now, but he could make out most of what was happening. They'd broken through the first door, and a few of the mech-human hybrids had even managed to make it into the hall – only to be brought up short by the second barrier. The rest were bottle-necked within the first room, fighting against one another to make it through the hole they'd carved into the surface of the rock.

Their energy also looked fainter than Finn remembered from their frantic dash through the complex, and the mechs' movements were slowing down, each blow landing with less force.

"I think they're starting to run out of juice," Finn reported. Both Kyyle and Julia let out a soft sigh of relief. Apparently, no one had been looking forward to getting ripped apart by a legion of self-healing cyborgs. "We should still move quickly. Like Daniel said, we can't be sure how long it will take them to recharge or if they'll continue the assault."

A faint worry also tugged at the edges of his mind. *Or what might happen if we manage to bring this section's power back online*, that nagging voice whispered.

Finn shook his head. That could be a problem for the future. Right now, they needed to find the pylon chamber and figure out a way to break inside.

Before he could move, a series of notifications popped up in front of him.

x6 Level Up!
You have (80) undistributed stat points.

x1 Spell Rank Up: Imbue Fire
Skill Level: Intermediate Level 10
Cost: 200 Mana
Effect 1: Imbues a weapon with fire mana, increasing the weapon's base damage by INT x 14.5%. Can only be used on unenchanted metal weapons.
Effect 2: While channeling, allows the caster to

increase the heat in ranks, up to a current max heat rank of [4]. Each heat rank increases damage by INT x 5% while increasing the channel cost by 50%.
Channel Effect: Allows user to control the weapon within his control range at a cost of 25 mana/sec.

x2 Spell Rank Up: Mana Absorption
Skill Level: Intermediate Level 3
Cost: 69% of mana drained as health damage.
Effect 1: The caster can absorb ambient fire mana, adding the energy to their total mana pool.
Effect 2: Increased absorption range, sensitivity, and area of effect.

x2 Spell Rank Up: Haste
Skill Level: Intermediate Level 4
Cost: 200   mana   upon   activation.   67.5 stamina/second sustained.
Effect 1: Increases total speed by 37.0%.
Effect 2: Reduces stamina cost by 13%.

x1 Skill Rank Up: Flameworking
Skill Level: Intermediate Level 7
Effect 1:   42% increased power when shaping objects subject to *Imbue Fire*.
Effect 2:   22% increased control when shaping objects subject to *Imbue Fire*.

x1 Skill Rank Up: Mana Sight
Skill Level: Intermediate Level 4
Cost: Permanently   reduces   your   mana regeneration by 20 mana/second. You are now blind to regular spectrums of light.
Effect 1: Ability to view ambient mana. Current vision is [good].
Effect 2: Ability to isolate mana types. Currently limited to [fire/earth/air].

"You guys get a bunch of level notifications?" Julia

asked, her eyes distant as she surveyed a display that Finn couldn't see.

"Yeah," Kyyle grunted. Then his gaze shot to Julia. "I guess the game is treating that encounter as a combat victory. It feels a little cheap. We didn't really kill them, but I suppose we accomplished roughly the same result by trapping them?"

Julia just shook her head. "It still seems weird."

"Any weirder than getting experience from studying a magical language?" Finn interjected, recalling the notices that he had received back during his time in the Mage Guild. "Like Kyyle said, it sort of makes sense. The game world is rewarding us for thinking and acting outside the box."

Julia let out a soft chuckle. "Maybe a girl just wants an excuse to beat the crap out of something. There's been too much talking and running away lately for my tastes."

"If it's any consolation, I have a feeling you're not going to have to wait long to get your opportunity," Finn murmured, flicking aside the notifications.

He paused as he went to bring up his Character Status. He wasn't certain he wanted to see the toll the infection had taken on his stats. On the other hand, he couldn't afford to stick his head up his ass, either. If he was working with a larger handicap, then he'd be better off knowing the full extent of the damage.

Taking a deep breath, Finn pulled up his Character Status.

Character Status			
Name:	Finn	**Gender:**	Male
Level:	108	**Class:**	Fire Mage
Race:	Human	**Alignment:**	Lawful-Neutral
Fame:	1800	**Infamy:**	0
Health:	1855	**H-**	6.40

		Regen/Sec:	
Mana:	2051	**M-Regen/Sec:**	37.28
Stamina	1335	**S-Regen/Sec:**	8.00
Str:	38	**Dex:**	80
Vit:	132	**End:**	80
Int:	347	**Will:**	24

Affinities			
Dark:	2%	**Light:**	10%
Fire:	50%	**Water:**	5%
Air:	3%	**Earth:**	11%

It was about as bad as he'd expected. Even with the levels he'd gained, he'd lost a decent chunk of health, mana, and mana regeneration. And then there was the loss of damage since most of his spells scaled with *Intelligence*. He wasn't even certain how to allocate his remaining stat points right now, given that he'd lose 20% of them immediately.

With a growl of irritation, Finn swiped the window away.

There was no sense dwelling on this problem right now. Finn certainly had plenty of other issues to deal with – like being trapped in this damn facility. He was just going to have to hope he was able to find a way to stop the spread of the infection. Or, even better, cure it entirely.

Maybe there was something in the Forge that could help him.

With that thought, his attention shifted back to the chamber around them. The room was filled with what appeared to be worktables, a scattering of junk spread across the surface of the closest one. They needed to keep pushing forward, but perhaps they could spare some time to search the sealed-off cluster of rooms. After all, they were here to find some sort of ancient tech, weren't they? Not to mention these so-called supervisor credentials that they were going to need to restart the fire pylon and turn the lights back on.

"Alright, Julia," he began, glancing at his daughter, "since you're basically invisible to the corrupted, you get the solo project. Why don't you find the door into the pylon chamber and get a better idea of what we're dealing with?"

"Sounds good," she said, bringing up her map with a flick of her wrist before heading toward an adjacent hallway.

"And be careful!" Finn called after her. "We can't be certain that Daniel attracted all of the corrupted in these rooms."

"That'll just give me a chance to see if I can take out one by myself," she shot back over her shoulder, giving him a grin. Then she abruptly disappeared into the shadows.

"Yeah, for the record, I totally don't want to see if I can handle one myself," Kyyle said, raising his hand.

"I'll second that!" Daniel offered.

"The odds do seem improbable that we would survive," Brock rumbled.

"Well, aren't you all just a cheery bunch," Finn grumbled.

He cast *Imbue Fire* on one of his orbs, increasing the heat just enough that the flames lit most of the chamber, but keeping his mana usage minimal. "Besides, our job might actually be riskier. I want to search these rooms we've cordoned off. According to Brock, the facility's tech is stored in the central chamber, but it looks like they were using this place like a workshop. There might still be something we can salvage in here, and we need to bank on the possibility that we might not make it into the central room."

"I'm not seeing the risky part," Kyyle offered.

"We all practically glow with mana – which means we could easily draw the attention of any other corrupted that might be lingering inside this cordoned-off area. In short, we need to stick together. Keep eyes on the rest of the group at all times."

The two elementals and Kyyle glanced at each other, a frown tugging at the earth mage's lips. "Greeeaaat," Kyyle muttered. "Let's just carefully explore the super creepy high-tech underground facility. Sounds awesome."

"At least he isn't using us as bait this time," Daniel grumbled beside him.

"Just give him a few minutes," Kyyle shot back with a smile. "If he finds some interesting tech down here, he'll probably try to test it on you."

"He wouldn't—" Daniel began indignantly.

Finn let out a sigh. Best to ignore them. If he rose to their bait, they would just keep going. He turned to Brock. "Can you tell us what the staff was doing in this area? Were they researching or building something?" he asked.

"I'm sorry, but that information is restricted to a user with—"

"Supervisor credentials. Big surprise," Finn replied with another sigh.

The differences between Brock and Daniel were stark – unusual, even. The earth elemental was almost robotic. Daniel's teasing aside, Finn was beginning to wonder if there was some truth to the whole magical lobotomy angle. Had the staff done something to the attendants to make them artificially stupid? That would have made sense from a security standpoint. If they were developing valuable technology down here, and these attendants were helping to facilitate that research, they wouldn't want one of these floating piles of rubble giving away their secrets.

Although, that was yet another question he couldn't answer – not yet, anyway.

He supposed they would just need to investigate on their own.

Finn scanned the room with his *Mana Sight*. Now

that he wasn't desperately sprinting through the section, he could see that the place was a mess. Several of the workbenches had been upended, and their contents were strewn across the floor. Scratch marks and what appeared to be burned furrows had been carved into the patterned walls, the indentations barely visible in his enhanced vision.

More signs of battle? It seemed the staff must not have quietly agreed to have their bodies repurposed in the interest of security.

He stooped and picked up a metal casing. Whatever it might have been, it had long since been ripped apart. The shell was torn in a way that reminded Finn of the claws that the corrupted sported. His lips pinched into a thin line. Maybe the casing had once contained mana crystals. If he was right, then the mech-human hybrids hadn't stopped with the staff. They had scoured the rooms and devoured every bit of mana they could find.

That didn't bode well for finding something useful.

But he wasn't going to give up hope.

"Let's each start in a corner and break the room up into quadrants," Finn called over his shoulder, interrupting Kyyle and the elementals. "We can work our way through our section in a snaking pattern. Make sure to examine every object. Daniel, you should scan partial components. We never know if that might come in handy later. Hell, we might be able to extrapolate what they were trying to build even if it's not functional."

Kyyle nodded, and the AI flashed once before they set to work.

Hopefully, they would find something useful. Finn hoped so. That worried knot still lingered in his stomach, curling and coiling, as he observed every inch of the devastation the corrupted had wreaked on the room. It forced his thoughts back to the pylon chamber and the many, many unanswered questions that kept spinning through his mind.

He suspected they were going to need an edge for whatever was coming next.

*   *   *

"Well, this has been a splendid waste of time," Kyyle grumbled, slumping back against a nearby wall. He had long since given up taking notes and just stood there with his eyes closed, his staff leaning against the wall beside him.

The group was standing in a narrow hallway adjacent to a larger workroom – one of the last series of passages inside the cluster of rooms they had sealed off. A series of doorways lined the hall, but the portals were all firmly shut. Finn's guess was that this was a storage area for the nearby workshop.

He rubbed at the simmering ache in his arm absently, his thoughts dark. They'd been looking through the abandoned rooms and passages for roughly twenty minutes now and had come up with practically nothing. It seemed the corrupted had thoroughly scoured these rooms and halls. All they turned up were the ruined metal carcasses of what might have once been useful tech and a staggering number of rock piles – the remains of the attendants that had likely serviced this area. Kyyle had harvested the depleted mana cores, but Finn didn't know how they could use those right now.

"At least we haven't gotten attacked," Daniel chirped helpfully. "It seemed that Julia did a good job of identifying the corrupted in these areas."

Kyyle frowned slightly. "Speaking of Julia, it's been a while, and she still hasn't returned. Should we be worried?" he asked, glancing at Finn.

"She messaged me a few minutes ago and said she's been examining the chamber doorway and looking for weak points or nearby controls," Finn replied in a tired voice. "Sounds like she's fine, but I suppose we could meet up with her. Probably more useful than searching this abandoned hallway."

"If I may interject?" Brock spoke up, his grating voice echoing through the hall. They all turned to look at the elemental. Yet he just stared at them without speaking.

Kyyle and Finn shared a confounded look.

"Yes... yes, you may interject?" Kyyle offered tentatively.

"Thank you. These rooms are all storage compartments for the workshop behind us. Based on the information collected prior to this section going offline, they had not been opened for at least 24 hours. I also observe no evidence that they have been disturbed since," Brock said, waving a rocky hand at the doors next to him. "If you are searching for salvageable materials and equipment, then it is possible that these compartments may contain such items."

Finn and Kyyle stared at the floating pile of rubble.

"And now he offers useful information..." Kyyle murmured.

Finn let out a frustrated huff as he realized their mistake. "I'm guessing that not *all* of the information he has is restricted. We've just been asking him the wrong questions. The staff here would want to protect the details of high-profile projects. But a mundane inventory of parts and materials would probably be non-confidential."

Kyyle's eyes widened slightly. "Damn it. We just wasted a lot of time, didn't we?"

"Unfortunately, yes," Finn replied, unable to fully remove the bitterness from his voice. He forcefully tamped down on the frustration simmering in his veins. That was water under the bridge now – an easy mistake, but one Finn didn't plan to repeat. Besides, Brock's suggestion was intriguing.

Finn turned his gaze to the doors that lined the hallway. He peeled away the earth mana with his *Mana Sight*, peering into the rooms beyond. The image was hazy, but enough to get a rough sense of what might linger on the other side. The first two chambers were empty. If Brock was right, they must have cleared out these rooms before the facility had gone into lockdown.

However, Finn hesitated at the third. He could make out a telltale orange glow in the room beyond, the fire mana standing out above a few stray bands of other colors. It was faint but noticeable. Between the interference of the crystal-laced walls and the ambient glow of whatever was inside that room, he had difficulty identifying specific objects. It almost looked like a painter had smeared the normally straight lines and angles together.

"There's something inside," Finn said quietly. "Fire mana, but I see a few other affinities. I can't make out much detail."

"Corrupted?" Kyyle asked, his grip tightening on his staff.

"I can't tell," Finn replied with a frown. He glanced back at the earth mage. "You want to risk it? With just one hand, I'm not going to be able to maintain one of my orbs while I'm opening the door."

Kyyle hesitated for a moment and then nodded. "Worst case, I can distract whatever is inside long enough for you to re-cast *Imbue Fire* and cut the connections to the mech's cores and Najima."

"Okay, then let's do this…"

Finn began casting on the deadbolts, the metal bars soon awash in a coating of flame. Kyyle moved in front of him, emerald energy curling around his staff as he precast a spell, holding the mana suspended in the air. He only needed to buy Finn a few seconds… assuming there was anything dangerous inside.

"On three," Finn said.

"1. 2. 3."

Finn shoved the door to the side, the stone grinding against the frame with a rumbling shudder. A shower of dust billowed outward from the crack that was forming. As the door slid open, Finn peered inside. He could see shelves lining the walls. Glowing green cylinders lined their surface, but they had all been ripped open and destroyed.

And against the far wall…

Finn's eyes widened even as a thin white fan of light struck him head-on. Mana flared along the mech's cores, and a familiar cylinder rotated out from its arm. "Intruder detected," it bit out in a metallic voice.

A condensed ball of fire was already charging along the barrel, and time seemed to slow. Finn saw Kyyle tense. A wall of earth was beginning to form, but it was moving incredibly slowly. Too slowly.

Finn realized he wouldn't be able to recast *Imbue Fire* quickly enough.

And Kyyle didn't have enough time to move out of the way...

Shit. Shit, shit, shit.

The beam arced toward them, and the air rippled from the heat. It was on a collision course with Kyyle's chest, and the earth mage's eyes went wide, raising his free hand in a feeble attempt to ward off the beam. All at once, a massive form pushed past Finn, knocking him back against the wall. The wind rushed from his lungs as he hit the stone and slumped to the floor. He heard a sizzle and pop of the beam striking something.

Yet there was no cry of pain.

Finn looked up, gasping for breath, to find Brock's bulky form standing in front of Kyyle. The beam had scored the rocks along the elemental's chest, leaving a jagged dark line in its wake. However, Kyyle and Finn were unharmed.

The mech! Finn thought frantically.

His hands struggled through the gestures of *Imbue Fire* as he tried to lift himself with his ruined arm, the dark blade jutting from his elbow scoring against the rock floor. One of his spheres was soon awash in flame, but as Finn managed to rise to his feet, he froze in place.

"I think it's offline," Kyyle murmured, peering around Brock's form.

Finn could indeed see that the mech had powered down, its metallic body slumped against the far wall of the storage compartment. It looked like it had only had enough juice left for a single beam, unable to even make it to its feet. More interesting, the mech's body didn't appear to be damaged, and there was no telltale glimmer of

Najima nestled under its metal casing. Which could only mean…

"This isn't one of the corrupted," Kyyle said softly. "I… I think we just found an intact security mech."

"Good job, Brock!" Kyyle crowed abruptly before whirling and smacking the elemental on the back, wincing slightly as his palm struck hard stone. "You saved my ass *and* found us something interesting to tinker with!"

"Attendants are responsible for their guests," Brock rumbled in reply, no emotion coloring his voice. "No thanks are necessary."

Kyyle glanced back at Finn with an excited grin stretching across his face. Finn could feel a similar burning enthusiasm surging through his veins as he looked at where the mech was slumped against the wall. Its mana cores still glowed faintly, but the mech clearly lacked the energy to sustain its systems – systems that Finn would now get a chance to pick apart and examine.

It seemed that they had finally found something worth salvaging.

Chapter 18 - Ignite

"What exactly is going on here?" Julia asked from the doorway to the abandoned workshop. "I've messaged you both at least a dozen—"

She froze in place, her eyes going wide as she stared at the worktables Brock had pushed together in the center of the room. Strewn across the surface of the tables lay metal panels and crystal wiring that Finn and Kyyle had meticulously disassembled. Daniel's flickering form floated nearby, his body nicely illuminating their work area.

"Is that one of the corrupted?" she asked, her hand drifting to her lance.

Finn waved off Julia's concern without turning around. "Nope. Kyyle and I found this mech in one of the storage rooms. It seems it was being kept there before the facility went into lockdown. Our guess is that the mech wasn't able to break through the door or find acceptable human parts to incorporate into his design. So, he's completely out of juice now..." Finn murmured, trailing off as he plucked another panel free from the metallic cylinder he was dissembling and carefully set it aside.

"Part G-52," Finn grunted at Daniel.

The AI's body flashed once, and it updated the three-dimensional schematic that floated beside the table, showcasing what Finn could only describe as a "laser-cannon" – one that had previously been attached to the mech's forearm. A list in the margin detailed an inventory of the parts associated with the cannon.

"It was actually pretty lucky that we found this mech," Kyyle offered in an excited voice as his fingers darted across the keyboard of his in-game terminal.

"Uh-huh," was Julia's noncommittal reply.

The earth mage glanced at her and suddenly noticed the way Julia's brow was furrowed, and her mouth pinched into a narrow line. "Uh, you see, the rest of these rooms and hallways were a mess," he tried to explain. "As the other mechs ran out of mana, they must have tried to absorb anything with even a trace of mana flowing through it. We're fortunate they didn't try to break into that holding area."

"Lucky us," Julia said in a dry tone, circling the table and eyeing the mech's body suspiciously. "So, have you two learned anything interesting from this impromptu science experiment?"

"Only that we're completely out of our depth," Finn muttered in a distracted voice.

With a few deft gestures, he ignited one of his metal spheres, ratcheted up the heat just enough to reform the metal into a pair of tweezers, and then canceled the spell. The metal cooled quickly, and Finn used the new instrument to gingerly remove the crystalline lattice that ran through the cylinder piece-by-piece. After having witnessed firsthand what the mechs had done to the other staff, he sure as hell wasn't going to risk the crystal touching bare skin.

"What a revelation." Sarcasm was practically dripping from Julia's voice this time.

Finn's eyes darted to her face – or, at least, he tilted his head in the direction of her voice – it was difficult to make out her position with his *Mana Sight* active. "I mean, this facility is obviously advanced. But whoever built this thing," he said, waving at the parts strewn across the tables. "They were a damn genius. This is light-years beyond anything we saw in the Mage Guild or even Kalisha's mechanids."

"In what way?" Julia asked, some of the worry easing from her face as she realized the mech wasn't about to reassemble itself and hop off the table.

Finn gestured at Kyyle, urging the earth mage to explain as he continued taking apart the cannon. He had almost revealed the mana gems that he could sense were buried within the layers of metal and crystal.

"Well, we didn't get a great look at the mech that self-destructed out front," Kyyle began. "Or the corrupted for that matter – since they don't really stop moving long enough for us to inspect them properly, and we had to lock them behind several feet of rock and crystal."

He held up a finger. "But as we took this mech apart, we realized something fascinating..." Kyyle plucked at one of the crystalline threads with another instrument and placed it carefully upon a clear portion of the worktable. "This thing isn't entirely synthetic. These crystals? Right now, they look like inert rocks. But we think that they're a form of organic crystal, simulating something similar to neurons in the human body."

"Here, let me show you," Kyyle offered, noticing Julia's skeptical expression.

The earth mage summoned a tendril of his own earth mana and gingerly touched the edge of the crystal fragment. The conductive material immediately absorbed the energy and turned a brilliant green. While that was interesting, what was even more incredible was that the crystal began to *move*. The tendril wriggled across the stone surface in the direction of the other remains, as though it was searching for the rest of its body.

"Holy shit," Julia muttered.

As Kyyle removed the mana, the crystal soon returned to its inert form, going rigid and dark once more.

"No kidding. This also goes a long way toward explaining how the mechs are able to repair themselves so easily. We think that these crystals are designed to reform the connections in their body." He hesitated for a moment, glancing in the direction of the room where they had trapped the horde of corrupted. "It also explains how they were able to incorporate other organic matter into their design – human flesh in particular."

Julia's eyes widened in surprise, and she glanced at the walls of the room. Crystal laced the stone but no mana coursed through the substance. "And they embedded this stuff in the walls? No wonder Brock was talking about the facility repairing its own damage."

Finn nodded but didn't look up from his work. "Indeed. I saw the crystal removing the obstructions from the crater in the reception area. I'm guessing that the slag we found on the other side of the blast door leading into this fire section was just too dense for the crystal to work with... or it will just take longer for it to remove."

"What he means to say is that these crystals are incredible," Kyyle offered with a grin. "Can you imagine what we could build with a decent supply of this stuff?"

Julia returned his smile now, her worry giving way to their enthusiasm. "Now you just need a better name for it."

"We're calling it *Synth-Rock!*" Daniel chirped helpfully.

The earth mage frowned at the AI's glowing form. "We haven't agreed on that yet. And for the millionth time, it sounds like we're inventing a new genre of edgy punk music. I still like *neurogem.*"

"Or how about *Baka-nite* since you're both morons," Julia offered with a chuckle.

"Neurogem is the winner, in my opinion," Finn said in a distracted voice as he pried free the last few strands of crystal. "Ahh, here we go..."

As he removed another layer of crystal, he could suddenly see a cluster of mana crystals nestled inside the lattice. Their charge was low, though, barely a flicker of energy remaining in the gems now that they had been disconnected from the mech's primary mana cores. Finn used his tweezers to gently pull the gems free and set them on a plain cloth he had torn from his old novice tunic. The garment had undoubtedly gotten its fair share of use at this point and was little more than a rag.

Finn leaned closer, peering at the gems and shifting back to *Short-Sighted*. His brow furrowed as he noticed irregular indentations along the surface of the mana crystals. He hadn't seen that detail with his *Mana Sight*. With the way the energies bled together, the sight didn't exactly offer that level of precision.

"You see this?" Finn asked Kyyle, gesturing at the gem. The earth mage moved closer and examined the gems carefully.

"They almost look like... runes?" Kyyle offered

tentatively. "Although they're too small to make out much detail."

Finn chewed on the inside of his cheek before glancing at Daniel. "Can you scan the fire gem? Then blow up those patterns etched into the surface?"

"Of course. That is just one of my many marvelous talents," the AI chimed, weaving a small circle around Brock's head before flitting close to the gem. A faint beam swept across the fire mana crystal, and a few seconds passed before an image appeared in the air.

Finn sucked in a sharp breath as he saw the designs scrolling down the screen. Now that they were larger, he immediately recognized them.

"Veridian runes," Kyyle murmured. "What the hell?"

A few pieces were beginning to click together, especially after taking apart this mech, encountering Kalisha's mechanids, and fighting the mechanized suit that Sadik had piloted down in the Abyss. The mechanized creatures seemed to be able to cast something similar to spells. The beam of heated energy. The flames along the corrupted's claws. The shield of air and thrusters that had been equipped on Sadik's suit.

And then there was the process of warding practiced by the fighters – runes etched into living skin. Was a similar approach being used here?

"They inscribed a spell into the surface of the gem," Finn said aloud, half speaking to himself. "Mana is channeled from the mech's cores along these crystalline conduits—"

"Neurogems," Daniel chirped.

"*Sure.* So that energy flows into the regular mana crystals installed along the mech's arm. These air mana crystals must activate the barrel, forcing it to rotate out of the limb. And then the mana flows into this final fire mana crystal – which is inscribed with a spell. That forces the energy into the superheated beam that the original security mechs were firing at us. Think of it like channeling mana through the wards etched into a fighter's skin."

Julia was nodding now, and Finn could see the realization dawning in her eyes. "So, this is basically forming a crude mana circuit – like our electrical circuits. The mana gems are inscribed to accomplish a certain effect, and the neurogem is essentially the wiring. Kalisha must have imitated the designs with her mechanids and that mech suit."

Finn nodded distractedly. "Although, she couldn't fully duplicate the neurogem material, which is why her automatons aren't self-healing."

The implications of this discovery were tumbling through his head more quickly now. This confirmed his guess on how to fight the corrupted. If they could disrupt the circuits powering portions of their body, that should disable their various systems. Although, as long as mana was being channeled through the intervening neurogems, they would likely repair quickly. So, they would need to strike hard and fast.

His eyes drifted back to the wall of symbols scrolling down Daniel's display.

There was also one more big takeaway.

An excited grin was painted on Finn's face now. "And if I'm right, then that means that the gems have to be inscribed with the runes for a spell," he explained. "Think of it like the programming overlaying the electrical circuit. Which means I might be able to pull the spell's incantation from the gem…"

"Icarus," Finn said aloud. The UI for his *Spellcrafting* mod immediately appeared in his vision. "Daniel, upload the runes into our spellcasting library, please."

"What are you doing?" Kyyle asked, his brow furrowed in confusion as Finn's hands tapped and swiped at the air.

"You'll see in a moment," Julia murmured in reply. While the earth mage hadn't yet seen Finn use his mod, she had witnessed Finn tinkering with it for hours back in the Mage Guild – often standing guard while he stared off into space. Her comment earned her a surprised glance from the earth mage.

A single flash from the fire elemental and Finn's UI was updated. The runes were immediately translated into Veridian, although they were disorganized. A mottled collection of words with no immediately obvious pattern. He tapped at the display, his fingers a blur as he rearranged the runes first into complete sentences and then into the rhyming verses used in the game's spellcasting system. As Daniel observed what he was doing, the AI began to assist him, highlighting potential rhyming couplets from among the set of runes.

Within less than a minute, they finished.

Several runes were left over, and Finn frowned at the display. He always hated it when he had extra parts lying around. That usually meant he had missed something important.

He froze as the realization struck him. A smile tugged at his lips as he rearranged the leftover runes into a pattern. They didn't describe an incantation. They were directions for channeling the *flow* of the mana. In other words, the requisite hand gestures.

Excitement simmered in his veins now. A rush of fire mana surged through his body and lit the metal embedded in his eyes. His fingers seemed to move on their own, following the directions inscribed in the gem. Finn could also see the flow of the mana now, watching the energy coil and condense around his fingers. He could fill in the holes in those instructions instinctively now – a product of endless days spent training. Even as the fire mana collected along his right hand, the words of the incantation drifted from his lips.

The flames grew stronger, flaring to life before condensing into a small pinpoint of blinding white light. As he reached the end of the incantation, Finn turned his hand to the nearby wall and unfurled his fingers to reveal his palm.

Then he completed the spell.

A beam of molten energy rocketed forward and

speared into the wall. The heat carved a furrow in the mixture of reinforced rock and crystal, molten droplets dripping to the floor where they swiftly cooled.

Finn glanced down at the beam. It didn't seem to injure the skin of his palm, and he could maintain the channel for some time, his mana ticking down quickly in the corner of his vision. With a swift gesture, he dropped the channel and let the spell extinguish. Streamers of energy coiled around his fingers for just a few seconds before sputtering out completely.

Julia and Kyyle were glancing back and forth between Finn and the nearby wall, their eyes wide. "Uh, okay. Looks like you discovered a new spell," Kyyle commented.

As soon as he spoke, a prompt opened in front of Finn.

New Spell: Molten Beam
You have discovered a new spell by carefully examining the technology developed within the Forge. This spell allows you to cast a beam of molten energy. However, the spell must be channeled to maintain its effect and consumes substantial mana.
Skill Level: Beginner Level 1
Cost: 100 Mana/second. Must be channeled.
Effect 1: Fires a beam of molten energy dealing damage equal to 100 + (INT x 25%).

"It's called *Molten Beam*," Finn said, swiping aside the notice and glancing at his teammates, his eyes still awash with fire mana.

A broad smile was stretched across Kyyle's face, and he swept at the air to bring up his in-game console. "We need to test it properly! How is your control range affected? What's the decay rate on the damage? Can you remotely cast the origin point of the beam? Or is it fixed to your hand?"

"Okay... okay, slow down," Julia interrupted,

resting a hand on the earth mage's shoulder. "In case you two magical nerds forgot, the clock is still ticking. We don't know if those corrupted will eventually be able to break their way out of those rooms," she said, waving in the direction of the sealed passage. "And we only have so long before Silver and her crew of feral druids decide to cave in the entrance.

"In case you both forgot, I had a mission. I found the entrance to the fire pylon room," Julia continued, her expression serious as she met Finn's gaze.

"I take it you don't have good news for us?" Finn offered, his smile faltering.

"Not exactly. Although, it might be easier to see it for yourself."

With that foreboding statement, Julia pivoted on her heel and marched toward one of the adjacent hallways. As soon as she was out of earshot, Kyyle glanced at Finn. "You want me to get this all cleaned up while you go check out the door? Brock can stay with me to help," he offered, gesturing at the lumbering earth elemental.

Finn nodded, his eyes scanning the contents of the worktables. "Yeah, I think we were almost done anyway. Just make sure you stow all of this, especially the crystal. I have a feeling it won't be easy to find these materials just lying around – not unless we want to try mining the walls or fighting the corrupted."

Kyyle nodded and immediately set to work. Finn stepped away from the tables and started off after Julia. Even with the excitement of his most recent discovery still simmering in his veins, he couldn't shake the look on Julia's face.

"She seems worried," Daniel offered as they paced the dark halls of the facility.

Finn shot the AI a glance. Now he was becoming more adept at picking up on their emotions and reading their body language? It seemed that Daniel's evolution only kept speeding up. That gave him a glimmer of hope. If his homespun AI could undergo these sorts of changes – as frustrating as they could be – then that meant it was *possible* that he could get Rachael back. The *real* Rachael. The woman who had been just as entranced with the act of creation and discovery as Finn had been.

He only needed to complete his end of the Seer's bargain first.

"Let's just hope this is a problem we can fix," Finn muttered in reply and picked up his pace, Daniel's light trailing behind him.

Chapter 19 - Explosive

Finn stood in a large, dark room, his attention on the blast door in front of him. To his enhanced sight, the ambient mana of the portal flickered and pulsed with emerald light.

The thing was monstrous, spanning nearly ten feet wide and as many feet tall. He could identify a mixture of crystal-laced stone sandwiching thick metal panels. At a guess, the blast door was at least four feet thick. Even compared to the doors in the reception area, this thing was impressive. Finn doubted that they were going to manage to carve or blast their way through. A massive stockpile of fire mana crystals likely wouldn't make a dent in the portal.

Finn frowned. And that all begged the real question.

What had the staff felt was important enough to place behind this obstacle? It seemed that whoever had designed this place had been more worried about unauthorized access to the pylon chambers than to the facility itself.

His eyes skimmed to the right, where the doorway's mottled mana blended into a seamless dark green as the door's edge neared the adjacent wall. It looked like someone had tried to close the blast door, but didn't quite manage the feat, leaving roughly a foot of space between the door and the frame.

Finn abruptly switched back to *Short-Sighted*. Wedged into the gap was a solid block of metal. It ran from the floor to the ceiling, and the edges were melted down, overlapping the stone of the door and the frame. A touch of his fingers confirmed an irregular texture to the metal.

Crude welding job – especially compared to the destruction of the main conduit leading into the reception area. Whoever did this must have been in a hurry.

"This is just weird, right?" Julia asked, eyeing the

doorway. "They have this gigantic blast door blocking off this chamber, but they don't manage to close it, and then they weld metal into the gap?"

"And it looks like they did it from this side," Finn noted, switching back to his *Mana Sight* briefly. He could just barely see that the metal didn't sit flush with the surface of the door on the other side, the lines of mana jagged and irregular.

"What happened here?" Finn murmured.

"That's exactly what I've been trying to figure out," Julia grunted, glaring at the blast door as though it was refusing to give up its secrets.

"Maybe they cut the conduits and deactivated the pylon, but they weren't able to get the blast door fully closed for some reason?" Finn suggested tentatively. "They could have welded this thing shut as a way to prevent the rest of the corrupted from getting back inside or somehow restarting the pylon."

Julia tilted her head as she mulled on that, but she didn't look convinced. "I considered that possibility, but I'm not sure that's the right answer," she murmured.

Finn's brow furrowed. While *possible*, he agreed with Julia that the explanation felt off somehow – incomplete.

He eyed the slag. Maybe he could get a glimpse at whatever was inside the room through that narrow crack. That might help address some of their questions. He placed a hand against the rough metal and leaned forward. Peering into the surface with his *Mana Sight*, he peeled back at the layers of mana one-by-one, straining to see the other side.

Only a moment later, he gave up, letting out a frustrated sigh.

"It's too thick, and the angle is too narrow," he grumbled. "I can't get a good look at what's inside." His daughter's frown deepened.

Kyyle chose that moment to enter the room, the lumbering earth elemental in tow.

"What's going on?" he asked, noting their sour

expressions.

"We're trying to figure out what the hell happened here," Julia offered, gesturing at the door and the metal wedge in the frame.

"Hmm, well, maybe Brock could help?" the earth mage suggested. He turned to the attendant that floated along beside him. "Were there any records of what happened to the pylon before the connection to the rest of the facility was cut?"

The earth elemental's glowing green eyes went distant. A map of the section suddenly appeared in the air beside him, with several yellow dots highlighted along the walls near the reception area and the adjoining sections. "The records from the reception console indicate that the main conduits to the other sections of the facility were destroyed simultaneously. The power in this section was online when that occurred, so it may be safe to assume that the fire pylon was taken offline sometime after that event."

Finn chewed on his lip, sparing a glance at the nearby walls. His gaze lingered on the threads of crystal that ran through their surface. "Okay, let's start with what we know then. The walls appear to be using the same neurogem material as the mechs. So, the block of metal we saw obstructing one of the main conduits when we entered this section must have been meant to prevent that process. Which means, the staff in this section severed those connections intentionally."

His eyes shifted back to the blast door. "But with the pylon online, the crystals may have still been able to remove the obstruction."

"So, the staff must have decided to shut down the pylon as well," Kyyle piped up.

This earned him nods from both Finn and Julia.

"And we have a pretty good idea of why they were trying to do that," Julia observed in a dry voice, glancing in the direction of the room where they had trapped the corrupted. "If the mechs have some sort of bug or virus, it could have propagated if they accessed the other sections. Could you imagine if they had managed to take over the entire facility? The staff must have done all of this to prevent the corruption from spreading."

Her brow furrowed for a moment, and she continued more slowly, "I think they effectively decided to starve them out. Their plan was to cut the power and then let the corrupted go dormant – hoping that their Najima wouldn't provide enough power for them to breach the blast doors leading out of the section."

Finn was nodding along with her explanation. That felt right – an obvious deductive chain based on what they knew. However, as his attention shifted to the walls adjacent to the blast door and the remainder of the room, he noticed scorch marks riddling the stone and the piles of disabled attendants littering the room. There must have been at least twenty. There were no human corpses, but he hadn't expected to find any.

It was clear that a fight had gone down in here…

How did that square with their narrative?

His daughter was following his gaze, a knowing look flitting across her face. "I picked over this room with a fine-tooth comb while you two were playing around with that security mech." She waved at the walls. "The damage indicates that a battle occurred here. Except that it doesn't make any sense for the staff to fight out here or try to seal the blast door from the outside," she muttered, shaking her head.

"So, what do you think happened?" Finn asked, watching her closely. Julia seemed to be mulling on something, and he knew the signs all too well. It was a sense of discomfort which left her unable to stand still. Almost like an itch that she couldn't quite scratch.

Her eyes shot to Finn. "I've actually been working on a theory… but it seems impossible. Silly, really."

"I want to hear it," Finn replied firmly. Julia shot him a surprised glance, her eyes widening slightly.

Chewing on her lip, her gaze darted back to the blast door. "Okay. I've been toying with this for a while now. What if… what if something entered the pylon chamber before the staff made it back here?"

A heavy silence met that question, her companions giving her an inquiring look.

"The staff cut the main conduits simultaneously. We know that. They were also probably traveling in two big groups since they would need to guard themselves while they cut the conduits and melted down the slag – which would have drawn the attention of the corrupted. And that's putting aside their casualties. So let's assume most of the staff was busy dealing with the two conduits."

Julia suddenly whirled and tapped at the highlighted points on Brock's map. Her fingers traced a path back to their location. "In which case, they would have had to make it back here and take out the pylon. After scouting this place, it's clear that this would have taken at least a few minutes, even if they were hauling ass and didn't encounter resistance from the corrupted.

"And during that time, the mechs were still roaming the section," she added.

"Probably absorbing any mana they could get their hands on and assimilating members of the staff," Kyyle offered. "That would explain the broken equipment, the damage to the walls, and the lack of human remains."

Julia's initial reticence burned away, her eyes shining as she glanced at the earth mage. "Exactly! And once the staff cut the power from the rest of the facility, that would have left one clear source of mana…" She trailed off, letting the implication hang in the air.

"Shit," Kyyle muttered as his eyes swept to the blast door. "I see where you're going. Once they cut conduits and mana wasn't flowing in from the other sections, the pylon would have stood out like a beacon to the corrupted – the motherlode of all mana. By the time the staff made it back here, the mechs may have already started swarming the chamber…"

Julia nodded, waving at the piles of rubble. "And if I'm right, they used the last of the attendants to hold off the corrupted just long enough for them to take the pylon offline. Look at where the piles of rock are positioned – in a rough line near the entrance to this chamber." The map updated as Julia tapped at the locations of each of the drained attendants, the points of light creating a clear defensive line across the room.

"Sure," Kyyle offered slowly. "But how does the door factor in here? Why didn't they manage to close it all the way? And why did they weld metal into the seam?"

Brock's rumbling voice suddenly interjected. "I may be able to help ascertain some answers to those questions."

Without waiting for a response, the elemental approached the doorway, his arm drifting forward and the rocks comprising his hand shifting and rotating. He immediately shoved the reassembled appendage into a hole carved into the surface of the wall. A faint pulse of earth mana rippled through the nearby wall – just the faintest flash of mana, not enough to draw attention.

The whole group tensed, eyeing the entrance to the room and the blast door warily for any signs of activity. However, as the seconds ticked past, no sound penetrated the din, and they gradually relaxed.

"It appears that several of the staff were still inside the pylon chamber when it was taken offline, and the command to close the blast door was issued from inside the chamber," Brock rumbled, oblivious to the tension. His glowing green eyes continued to stare into the distance as he accessed the facility's systems.

"So, someone – or multiple someones – attempted to lock the others out here?" Kyyle asked, horror lacing his voice. "What a dickhead thing to do. If Julia is right, then they would have been dealing with a swarm of the corrupted lured here by the pylon…"

Finn stared at the surface of the door, a troubled feeling squirming in his stomach. "People do terrible things when they're desperate. It's possible that they did it to save themselves."

His eyes shot to Julia, noting her staring at the doorway with her brow furrowed. She didn't seem convinced. Her initial explanation was still rebounding through his head, refusing to be ignored. "Or there was another reason – like they found something in that room that they couldn't afford to let escape," he said softly.

His daughter met his gaze. "I still think that's the answer," Julia said firmly.

"I don't get it," Kyyle said, shaking his head. "How did you reach that conclusion?"

"Think about it strategically," Julia began. She waved at the room they were occupying. "Why try to fight the corrupted out here at all? Why not just push inside the pylon room as a group, shut the *giant, impenetrable* blast door, and then calmly deactivate the pylon? Maybe sit back and wait for a rescue from the other sections? And if someone did try to save themselves and sacrifice the others, that still doesn't explain why the door didn't close all the way or why they welded metal into the gap from the outside."

"Like you said, there could have been a few corrupted inside the chamber. Maybe the person got desperate and blew the pylon while trying to save themselves?" Kyyle suggested, although he didn't seem to buy his own rebuttal.

"Sure. Except why not just take out the mechs and *then* close the door? Even our group is probably capable of defeating a handful of those things, and these people *invented* them. It's safe to assume they could take out a few of their own security mechs. And, again, why did the group out here bother to weld metal into this gap?"

"*Unless* there was something in there that they couldn't kill," she continued, her tone dark. "Remember, it would have taken the staff some time to get back here after they cut the connections to the rest of the facility. That might have been enough time for some of the corrupted to make it inside – and possibly begin to mutate or evolve again.

"That would also explain why the group inside the pylon chamber decided to close the blast door... and why the door didn't fully shut. There must have been something in there draining the pylon. In which case, they prioritized taking out the pylon over waiting for the blast door, which caused the power to fail before the door could close completely."

Julia abruptly paced to the door, her fingers tracing the scorch marks. "The staff out here then used their last moments – sandwiched between a horde of corrupted and the door – to weld the thing shut," she said. Her eyes turned to Kyyle. "They must have had a damn good reason to do that." The earth mage went silent, chewing on that explanation but unable to muster a counter-argument.

As he listened to Julia, Finn could see her reasoning process. It was a straight and logical path with an ominous conclusion – one he would prefer not to be the case. However, he was having trouble poking holes in her theory. It neatly addressed all the facts that were laid out before them.

"Okay, let's start over," Finn said, pacing a small circle.

"The staff cut the conduits to the other sections, then rushed back here to find the corrupted swarming the pylon – since that was now the most concentrated source of mana in the section. The plan was probably to push into the pylon chamber and shut the blast door, but some of the staff made it inside while the rest held off the horde behind them. The staff inside discovered something dangerous. They initiated the door closure prematurely and then sacrificed themselves to take the pylon offline."

He whirled, gesturing at the piles of rubble lining the room they were standing in. "The rest of the group outside then found themselves sandwiched between the corrupted and the blast door. But the door hadn't fully closed, and there was still some sort of new threat inside that chamber. So, acting quickly, they used their last few minutes to weld the gap shut as they held off the rest of the corrupted."

Silence met that explanation. Both Julia and Kyyle were staring at the door, unable to muster a rebuttal. That narrative fit – at least, better than any other explanation they had come up with. And now the same thought was rebounding through their heads.

What the hell was inside that chamber?

And, even worse, was it still alive?

"I mean, we're still sort of guessing here," Kyyle offered tentatively, although he didn't sound like he believed what he was saying. "We don't know for sure that there's something in there. We could just find a few skeletons..."

"And if there is something in there, why didn't it turn the pylon back on?" Julia offered slowly, trying to pick apart her own theory.

"Yeah, *that*," Kyyle offered quickly, jumping on any other possible explanation.

"The pylons require substantial mana of the proper affinity to activate, and the mana must be directed in the proper sequence," Brock interjected in a rumbling voice. "It's possible that the corrupted might not have been able to bring it back online."

"You're not helping," Kyyle muttered.

"I hate to agree with the floating avalanche over there, but based on the information available and Julia's reasoning, there is an 87.56% chance that there will be an opponent inside the chamber," Daniel interjected, flitting through the air toward the door. "We can also safely assume that whatever is inside may have also had access to several human corpses that it could repurpose – which suggests that it may have been able to regenerate its mana and is likely now in a dormant state like the other mechs."

Finn nodded, sparing a glance at Daniel. That was the same conclusion he had reached. He'd have to add "enhanced deductive logic" to the ever-growing list of the AI's improvements.

"Okay, let's assume for now that there's something in there waiting for us," Kyyle admitted grudgingly. "What the hell are we going to do about it? We can't exactly leave the facility without bringing the power back online. So, we *have* to open this door somehow and try to restart the pylon. But we had trouble with just one of the corrupted, much less whatever the hell the staff felt was dangerous enough to lock inside this room."

"We could lure it back through the complex like the others and trap it somewhere else," Julia suggested tentatively. Her eyes were on the map that still floated next to Brock.

"I have a feeling that this thing isn't going to give up this position," Finn said. He waved at the door. "The corrupted seem to have retained some level of intelligence or memory of their past lives. Remember the mech we found in the security checkpoint? Why did it return to that location? There was no mana nearby.

"My guess is that the human parts that were assimilated belonged to one of the security personnel stationed here, and the mech was just returning to his post. After taking apart one of the security mechs, it's now clear that the neurogem simulates neurons in our body. In that case, it's not a stretch to assume that the mechs might retain some of the memories and abilities of the staff they assimilated.

"In which case, whatever is inside the pylon chamber may understand the importance of the pylon – even if it can't figure out how to turn it back on," he concluded.

Kyyle rubbed at his eyes tiredly, mulling on the problem that was staring them in the face. Then his wrist flicked at the air and brought up the model of the security mech they had dissected, the wiring around its cores and Najima suddenly highlighted in yellow.

"Okay. Okay. Running away may not be an option," Kyyle said in a weary voice. "So, the next question is, how do we fight this thing? In a direct confrontation, our best bet is overwhelming force. We would need to sever the connections to their power supply simultaneously – the mana cores embedded in their chest and their Najima – to prevent them from repairing," he offered, waving at the schematic.

Kyyle gestured at Julia. "We might not be able to lure this thing away, but our other option is still attrition. The corrupted we've seen so far have a limited mana supply stored in their cores, and the assimilated Najima are slow to regenerate that mana. We could just try to survive long enough that the thing runs out of power and is forced back into a dormant state to regenerate."

Julia was pacing the room now, rubbing at her chin in thought. "Between those two options, the first is going to be tough since we don't know what exactly we're facing. So, our best bet is probably to enter the fight with attrition in mind. That means we need to be sparing with our resources and bait it into burning mana. Then we wait for a possible opening that might let us take it out."

"I think I might have an idea for that," Kyyle replied.

Finn and Julia turned to him – the same question painted on their faces.

The earth mage grinned back. "After that fight with Kalisha and Malik back in the Abyss, I've been practicing what I'm calling my *Doppelganger* spell." He raised a hand defensively. "I know, I know, it's not *technically* a separate spell, but just go with it. Either way, we've already established that the corrupted use some sort of light-mana-based detection system that allows them to sense mana. Maybe we can use my clones as decoys to distract whatever is in there into attacking the doppelgangers instead of us."

Julia glanced at Finn. "That's not bad. It may buy us time, at least until Kyyle runs out of mana. After that, if you cast *Imbue Fire* on my armor, that might allow me to act as our tank for a while. If this thing is using fire-based attacks, I may be pretty resistant between my armor and your enchantment."

"Maybe. But that assumes this thing is using the same flaming claws or beam weapons we've seen on the security mechs," Finn retorted.

"Well, all we have to go on here are *assumptions* and a few educated guesses," she retorted with a small, anxious smile.

"That's what's troubling me," Finn replied under his breath. "If we're wrong, we could be screwed. Are either of you certain of how the respawn system works in here? I certainly haven't been prompted to set a new spawn point since we made it to the Hive or arrived at the Forge. If we die in this facility, my guess is that we'll end up back in Lahab, or, best case, back in the reception area. Either way, I expect it's going to be a pain to get back here – if it's possible at all."

"Well, technically, there's a third and even worse option," Kyyle offered hesitantly. "We could respawn in one of the other sections with no easy way to access this section or bring the fire pylon back online and open the central chamber."

Finn winced at that statement. That meant they might be trapped down here – one of the few ways to permanently destroy a player's avatar. No matter how they sliced this, they were about to take a big risk.

His daughter let out a snort. "There's no sense contemplating *every* terrible scenario. This whole journey is a shot in the dark – a gamble. If we do nothing, where does that leave us? Facing a demon king with nothing to prevent him from using that damn staff to convert our own soldiers. Translation: we're still screwed."

She took a deep breath, rubbing at her neck. "Not that any of that matters anyway. We're already effectively trapped in here. We aren't getting back into the reception area now that it has reestablished the connection to the air mana section. So, the only way we're going to escape this place is if we die or if we bring the damn pylon back online.

"So, the real question is, do we really have anything to lose?"

Finn met her gaze. With his *Short-Sighted* ability, he could see the determination reflected in her eyes. She was right. He knew she was right. But more than that, even staring at the terrible hand that they'd been dealt, she didn't blink – didn't hesitate for a moment. Not that he was surprised. The only shock was that it had taken him this long to recognize just how strong his daughter had become. Rachael would have been proud, regardless of whether they won or lost here.

He could also see that same resolve echoed in the way that Kyyle stood beside Julia. As her eyes flitted to his, Kyyle's back straightened, his breathing evened, and he gripped his staff firmly. He gave her a curt nod of agreement. The earth mage's motivations might have been just a touch self-interested – staring down death to impress a girl. But Finn couldn't begrudge him that. It wasn't so long ago that he had done the same.

More importantly, it seemed both of his companions had faith in their ability to overcome even this obstacle.

Anything. Everything. They had taken his motto to heart.

Who would he be if he backed down now – after coming so far?

"So, what do you say? You ready to get to work?" Julia asked, offering her hand.

Finn accepted her grip, a small smile tugging at his lips. "Always."

Chapter 20 - Supervisory

The beam of fiery energy cut into the dense, jagged lump of metal welded between the blast door and the frame. The ensuing shower of sparks and heat forced Finn to stand a few feet away, holding the beam steady with his hand and following the guidelines painted in his UI. It had taken him a while to learn to stabilize his new *Molten Beam* spell, but he'd had plenty of opportunity to practice over the last hour.

As the molten energy touched the metal, the surface quickly heated to a dull glow and then a vibrant, glowing red. With his *Mana Sight* active, Finn could see the moment the beam was about to pierce the other side of the slag, and his right hand twitched. The beam shifted, gradually etching a horizontal line in the metal. When the energy began to lick at the adjacent wall, he adjusted the trajectory downward. Then ever-so-slowly to the left. Then upward again until he had formed a rough rectangle with the burnt furrow.

Finn abruptly extinguished the spell and backed off, wiping at the sweat that dotted his brow with the back of his hand. He surveyed his work. He'd carved nearly a dozen of these narrow, rectangular blocks in the metal now, the burnt, black lines running the length of the slag.

"I think that should do it," Finn declared.

"About time," Daniel reported from his shoulder. "The others are nearly ready."

Finn nodded. It had taken him longer than expected to carve up the metal. The block of slag was far too large and thick to use his *Imbue Fire* – and even if he had, he ran the risk of simply welding the metal even more firmly in place. Not to mention that coating the entire block of metal in fire mana would likely alert whatever might be lingering on the other side of that massive blast door.

He paced through the dark chamber into one of the adjacent rooms, reflexively rubbing at his neck again. After losing a second Najima to the infection, that perpetual, simmering ache had begun to spread up toward his head and right shoulder. Even casting *Molten Beam* a few times had caused the infection to spread toward his other Najima. He abruptly switched back to *Short-Sighted*, refusing to look at the magical injury. He wasn't certain what was happening to him, but there wasn't much he could do about it right now.

He just needed to move faster.

And hope that he could complete his goal before his digital body entirely fell apart.

As soon as he stepped into the adjacent room, Finn stopped stock-still. He was staring at the mirror image of himself. An older man, robed in thick cloth, his eyes bandaged, his arm injured, and a dark metal blade stretching from the stump.

As Finn looked on, the doppelganger abruptly lunged forward, his makeshift blade swiping at Finn's head. He easily parried the blow to the discordant screech of metal and pivoted for the counterattack. Yet the doppelganger stumbled from the force of his parry, and Finn dropped into a crouch, kicking its legs out from under it. The clone hit the floor and immediately dissolved, breaking apart into streamers of rock that surged back to Kyyle and coiled around his staff like stone serpents.

"It's better, but the movements are still a little jerky," Finn said, side-eyeing Kyyle and Julia.

"Always the critic," Kyyle grumbled with a faint smile. "Either way, it's good enough to fool the corrupted. I expect they won't care much for the detail work."

"You tested it on the ones we trapped?" Finn asked.

Kyyle nodded. "Yeah, I formed a doppelganger just past the door. I was firing blind, but we just needed to see if they reacted."

"We accidentally woke the hornet's nest," Julia reported as she double and triple checked her equipment, tugging at the straps that held her platemail in place.

"They went nuts for a few minutes once they detected the mana. It looks like the corrupted can regenerate in about an hour with their limited Najima... at least, if the noise on the other side of the sealed door was any indication."

As she noticed Finn's frown and the way his eyes drifted to that section of the facility, she added quickly, "They damaged the last door in that section but didn't manage to break through, and they've been down for their magical naptime for about 15 minutes. It should be safe to breach the pylon room."

"I hope so," Finn said with a sigh. "I'm really hoping that the distortion from the crystal will make it impossible for them to pick up on our mana when we breach. I'd rather slip into the pylon chamber unnoticed," he continued. That limitation had become increasingly frustrating for Finn as they navigated the complex. It felt like he was half-blind. But perhaps they could use it to their advantage here.

"That's the plan," his daughter said, eyeing him with a concerned expression. She approached and rested a hand on his shoulder. "You okay?"

Finn nodded, straightening and meeting her eyes. He had to resist the urge to rub at his stump again – that ache still hadn't relented. "Yeah... yeah, I'm fine. The decoys work. The blast door is prepped. You ready with your new toy?"

A smile stretched across Julia's face as she lifted a solid cylinder of dark metal. Loops were welded onto the top and back – makeshift handles that imitated a real-world design. Finn had forged a crude battering ram using several of his metal spheres. The damn thing was a solid hunk of metal so dense that he and Kyyle had difficulty lifting it. Even his daughter's arms strained under the weight. Although the feat was still quite impressive given that she was also wearing full platemail. He should be able to help compensate for the weight once he enchanted her armor.

At least, that was the theory.

"I've been practicing getting the angle of the swing

right. I did some digging online and found a good SWAT training tutorial," she replied with a grin. Letting the battering ram lean against her shoulder, a shower of sparks flashed where it struck her dark armor. She waved at a series of workbenches along the side of the room, many of which had been cracked in half. "Turns out, I'm a fast learner."

"It certainly looks like it," Finn said, chuckling in amusement. He paused as he mentally inventoried their next steps. "It sounds like we're ready then."

"For the record, I'm definitely not ready. I say we should practice for another few hours," Daniel chirped, his form dimming. "Brock is with me, right?"

The rocks that made up the earth elemental's body ground together as the elemental turned his glowing green eyes to Daniel. "An attendant's duty is to serve. If it is time to serve, then we are ready."

"Sounds a lot like slavery to me," Daniel muttered.

Kyyle patted Brock on the shoulder. "I'm kind of enjoying our new elemental. All of the benefits with none of the backtalk," he said with an amused glance at Daniel.

"Yeah, it's great if you like talking to an oversized doorstop with no sense of self-preservation," the fire elemental grumbled. For his part, Brock seemed oblivious to the banter. He simply floated in place, his glowing green eyes watching them.

Finn just shook his head. He knew the squabbling was just nerves. They were about to make a big gamble... another one. "Well, I, for one, enjoy the added personality," he offered, glancing at Daniel with a smile. He hadn't forgotten how the AI had managed to lure the corrupted into the dead-end hallway. That comment earned him a soft flash of orange light, and the fire elemental promptly darted over to his shoulder, circling Finn slowly.

His attention shifted back to his companions. "Alright, enough standing around. The clock is ticking. Let's get in position."

Kyyle and Julia nodded, and the group shuffled

back into the main chamber in silence. Without the verbal sparring, there was nothing left to distract them from what was coming. The tension in the air was almost palpable, a heavy weight that seemed to blanket the darkened room.

They immediately moved into specific spots around the chamber. Julia hovered in front of the blast door with the battering ram gripped firmly in her gauntlets. Kyyle summoned two of his doppelgangers and maneuvered them into place on either side of the doorway, but kept them out of range of any shrapnel from the pre-cut slag. The earth mage precast the clones to allow his mana to regenerate to full capacity – the channeling cost less than his natural regeneration. Hopefully, that would be enough to buy them some time to assess their enemy.

Brock took up a position just behind Julia. The slag filled a gap, only a scant foot between the door and the frame. Once the obstruction had been removed, the earth elemental's job was to force the blast door open wide enough for the doppelgangers to enter.

Finn and Kyyle were standing about fifteen feet back from the opening, keeping the door and part of the pylon chamber on the other side within their control range, but themselves out of direct line of sight of the gap. They had no clue what was lingering inside that room, but they had already had enough experience with the beam weapons employed by the security mechs to be cautious.

The goal was simple. Breach. Send in the decoys. Assess.

"Man, I hope this is overkill," Kyyle muttered under his breath.

"Statistically, that's highly unlikely. Would you like to know the exact probability of our gruesome and untimely death?" Daniel replied, earning him a mock glare from Kyyle. The fire elemental darted around Finn's shoulders, flying through an anxious loop.

"No, I'm good. At a time like this, it helps to lie to yourself a bit," the earth mage said with a frown. "It's reassuring and helps you overcome your nerves."

"Ahh, I understand. So, self-delusion is beneficial

in stressful circumstances," Daniel said, his form freezing in place and blinking once as he processed that information. "In that case, we're totally going to be okay! This will be a cakewalk, team!" he announced in a chipper voice, his body flashing in an alternating pattern – like some sort of fiery cheerleader.

"Okay, now that's way worse," Kyyle grumbled.

"You know your part?" Finn interrupted, eyeing Daniel.

"Yes, sir," the fire elemental replied, his tone returning to normal. "Enter after the doppelgangers, use them for cover, and get a scan of whatever is inside. Then return to you and report."

Finn nodded. His eyes surveyed the room, his mind already working through a mental checklist. They were in place. The door was prepped. Kyyle's decoys were ready. He glanced at his group UI; their health, mana, and stamina were all full.

They were as ready as they could be.

"Alright, get ready to breach. We go as soon as I light you up!" Finn called out to Julia. She nodded and gripped the ram firmly, the metal of her gauntlets scraping against the handholds and her feet scuffing the floor as she adjusted her footing.

Finn took a deep breath and then channeled his mana. The burning energy rushed through his body in a raging torrent, sweeping away his doubt and hesitation. The sensation was a relief, even if he knew it came with a cost now. With the flames came a boundless excitement, the glowing metal embedded in his eyes focused on the blast door as his fingers began to wind through the gestures of *Imbue Fire* automatically.

Flames soon encircled Julia's armor, wrapping around the dark metal at her feet before sliding up her thighs, then her chest and arms. The fires soon swept past her head, the patches of skin between the panels of metal rippling and contorting as her natural absorption took hold, and her body converted into flame.

Once she was completely coated in fire, and her

armor began to glow a dull red, Julia yanked back on the battering ram, swinging it behind her. Finn offered some assistance, the fingers of his right hand twitching as he added a bit more force to the upswing. The battering ram arced wide and seemed to hover in the air for a moment – as though suspended in time.

This is it, Finn thought. *There's no going back from here.*

Then the battering ram rushed forward. The combination of Julia's natural strength and Finn's enchantment sent the metal cylinder hurtling through the air with incredible force. The dark metal was a blur as it barreled toward the pre-cut slag.

Then it slammed home.

The dense metal crumpled under the blow, and the pre-cut blocks exploded into the pylon chamber, tearing chunks from the nearby wall where the metal still clung to the reinforced stone. A shower of dust and debris blew out of the newly formed hole, filling the area around the door. Yet that did little to obstruct Finn's *Mana Sight*.

He saw Julia dart backward, and Brock moved forward into position. The earth elemental's massive hands grappled with the edge of the door, his fingers shifting and rotating to help him find purchase on the stone. With a surge of emerald energy, the elemental began to pull the portal open one reluctant inch at a time, the blast door grinding against the frame above and below the doorway. Just a few seconds later, Brock had formed a large enough gap for Kyyle's doppelgangers to slip through.

The living statues barreled into the room with Daniel hot on their heels – his flaming body a streak of color. Finn shifted to the side carefully to get line of sight on the pylon chamber, peering through that crack in the door. Now that all of the interference had been removed and the viewing angle was much wider, he could finally make out the interior of the room. It was roughly circular, the floor littered with metallic debris. And along the edges of the room and the back wall were low counters or worktables.

A fan of white light swept across the room as soon as Kyyle's statues crossed the threshold, the origin point lingering near the back wall. As soon as that energy touched the glowing emerald doppelgangers, the location of their enemy became clear – a dull orange glow igniting on the far end of the room.

Possibly one of the corrupted? The scan and initial energy signature were a close match to the mech-human hybrids they had encountered. That was troublesome but manageable. Working together, they should be able to take out one of the corrupted.

Yet Finn hesitated as he saw that energy continue to grow brighter and brighter, illuminating a figure that was much larger than the human-mech hybrids they had encountered before. His eyes widened as he saw several cores flare to life in its chest, orbiting a sun-like primary core that glowed with brilliant orange and red energy.

Air. Earth. Light. Finn ticked off the affinities among the smaller cores in the creature's chest.

Tendrils of yellow mana surged through the creature's body as it activated its pneumatic systems. Although the fire mana swamped the rest of the energy cycling through its body, glowing so brightly that it almost hurt to stare at the primary fire core directly.

Before it was taken offline, had this thing drained part of the pylon? That energy was far, far greater than the other corrupted, and Finn could feel a sudden worm of doubt coil through his mind, pushing back at the fiery mana that still surged through his limbs.

The creature seemed to unfold itself, its body contorting and shifting, and a glowing outline formed before him. Six pseudo-mechanical limbs rotated and stretched from a barrel-like torso. Points of multi-colored light lingered in each of those limbs, indicating that this thing had incorporated several Najima into its body.

That confirmed Julia's guess. Before sealing it off, some of the facility's staff must have managed to make it inside this chamber. The mana cores drifted into the creature's chest, protected behind a thick metal casing. And atop that torso sat a familiar dome-like head containing a small light-mana core, a fan of white spearing from the dome at regular intervals as it scanned the room.

Finn's brow furrowed in confusion as he saw that no legs jutted from the mech's lower half. Instead, the monstrosity seemed to be mounted in place near the back of the room, its body resting on top of some sort of table or workbench.

Possibly immobile? That might make this a little easier.

With a thought, Finn inspected it quickly.

The Supervisor – Level 180
Health – Unknown
Mana – Unknown
Equipment – Unknown
Resistances – Unknown

Skull symbols were displayed beside its name, warning that this thing – this *Supervisor* – was a named boss monster. They had only encountered that once before. With Sulphera. And that fight had been just a little tough…

"Named boss mob!" Finn shouted, feeling a flare of anxiety coil in his stomach, despite the numbing burn of his mana. He quickly backed away as another fan of light speared from the Supervisor and filtered out of the gap in the blast door. "It's mounted in place toward the back of the room. Kyyle, keep its attention on your doppelgangers."

The earth mage nodded, and his statues darted forward, the pair breaking apart and running along either side of the pylon chamber as they charged the Supervisor. Finn edged forward again to get eyes on the chamber. That last fan of white energy had passed through the statues, and the creature turned its attention toward these new targets, picking up on the earth mana. Finn expected it to form the same barrels as the normal security mechs or lash out with its limbs.

Instead, he saw fire mana surge through that massive core hovering in the center of the Supervisor's chest, the pulse so bright that Finn was forced to avert his gaze. Mana coursed through two of its mechanical arms, and they plunged forward, striking the platform it was resting upon. Crystalline threads stretched from those limbs and plunged into the surface of the counter. Fire mana flowed along those living circuits, through the table, and into the floor of the chamber, where the glowing orange energy soon scattered throughout the room. It coursed through the enhanced stone, riding along on the conduits of neurogems embedded in the facility's walls and floor. It lit the walls of the pylon chamber, and the room was suddenly cast in an ominous orange glow in Finn's sight.

What the hell is this? The energy pattern was similar to what Finn had witnessed in the reception area after they brought the backup mana core online.

And that fire mana seemed to be pooling near two emerald spheres along the ceiling…

Then the realization struck him.

It's using the facility's security systems.

The Supervisor wasn't just mounted on top of a table – it had integrated itself into a terminal like the one in the reception area. In a rush, Finn could see what had happened here nearly a century ago. The staff must have seen the way this thing had begun to incorporate itself into the pylon terminal and begun to drain its mana – drinking straight from the source. They would have immediately realized what this meant for the facility.

This thing wouldn't stop. It would keep spreading. Keep following its protocols blindly to preserve itself and defend the facility.

So, they had sacrificed themselves to stop it…

The metallic spheres along the ceiling rotated in place, barrels shifting out of their surface with a clank and shriek of metal. A dense cluster of fire mana formed along the tip of each barrel before rocketing forward. A pair of massive beams struck the two statues simultaneously, blasting apart the stone in a shower of fragments. Meanwhile, Finn could see that Daniel was using the distraction to whip around the Supervisor, a thin fan of orange energy sweeping the creature's body before he made a beeline out of the room.

"It's accessing and temporarily powering the facility's systems! It brought two turrets along the ceiling online," Finn shouted. "Kyyle, recast your doppelgangers and keep the cannons focused on them." He saw his daughter inching toward the entrance, flames licking along the length of her armor. "Julia, keep the hell back behind the blast door until I drop my channel!"

Even as he shouted at his daughter, Finn saw another fan of white light sweep the room, clipping Julia's shoulder as she stood briefly in the gap. The turrets pivoted and fired again, ignoring Daniel and homing in on the dense cluster of fire mana that coated Julia's armor. She leaped to the side, and the molten energy scored the walls and floor, leaving dark lines in their wake and melting deep furrows into the surface of the door. Julia promptly dropped the battering ram and yanked her shield and lance free.

Finn canceled his *Imbue Fire* abruptly, the flames around his daughter's armor sputtering out. Then he pulled a sphere from his bag quickly, hurling the metal orb toward the pylon chamber. He needed to take out those turrets and buy Kyyle some time to get another doppelganger online. As soon the sphere left Finn's palm, he was casting *Imbue Fire* again. He swiftly ratcheted up the heat, his eyes on the two turrets on the ceiling.

It might be able to repair the turrets like the security mechs, Finn realized. They almost certainly used the same neurogem material present in the walls and mechs. Which meant it wouldn't be enough just to damage them. He needed to completely incapacitate the turrets and disrupt their interior circuitry to break the connection to the Supervisor.

And he only knew of one way to accomplish that…

Finn ratcheted up the heat on his orb until he hit

heat rank level 4. He would only need to maintain that channel for an instant. Another fan of white mana swept the chamber, and the turrets swiveled toward the orb as it entered the room, twin beams of fire spearing through the air. Finn's fingers twitched, and his orb narrowly dodged the blasts, the beams carving furrows along the interior walls. At the same time, he narrowed his molten metal into a thin lance.

Then it struck home.

The lance pierced cleanly through the metal casing of one of the turrets. Yet he didn't stop there. Finn's fingers twitched again, and the metal exploded outward in all directions, expanding inside the turret's protective shell. He seared through the neurogem material and destroyed the interior circuits, fusing the dense metal with the crystal. The turret froze, locked in place by the metal. Finn could see that the mana channeled by the Supervisor was unable to find a connection within the metal casing.

He was already throwing another orb and recasting *Imbue Fire* even as he watched the first turret. It didn't come back online. At least, not immediately. However, Finn could see the Supervisor's mana pooling at the edge of the green energy that marked the border of the turret. It was beginning to heat up and melt the obstructing material. But that would take time and energy. Maybe they could wear this thing down slowly, baiting it into attacking and incapacitating its defenses one-by-one – forcing it to rebuild its turrets.

"Give me five more seconds, and I'll take out the second turret," Finn shouted. "Then you can enter, Julia. Just draw its fire, and don't expose yourself. Remember, the goal here is attrition. We just need to get this thing to burn energy."

During all of this, Kyyle had formed another doppelganger. The statue charged into the room, drawing the attention of the other turret as another fan of white energy swept the chamber. Finn's superheated orb soon followed. As the turret blasted apart Kyyle's statue in a shower of dust and rock, Finn used the opening to strike, melting through the turret's casing before destroying its interior circuitry.

"Okay, the defenses are offline!" Finn shouted. He could see Julia preparing to charge into the room, her shield raised, and her lance extended.

Just before she entered the room, Finn saw a surge of white mana collecting along the Supervisor's dome-like head. "Wait! It's charging something—" Finn began.

Before he could finish speaking, the ivory energy surged down one of the Supervisor's limbs, and the arm smashed into the ground. A massive pulse of light mana rocketed out from the impact, rippling through the crystalline wiring in the walls and floor and speeding outward in an expanding ring. The energy soon passed through the room that Finn and his teammates occupied, yet it kept going. It pushed outward in an ever-growing circle as it rippled through the facility.

Finn followed that trail of energy with his *Mana Sight*. Although, the energy soon became obscured behind multiple layers of the crystal-laced walls, growing fuzzy and indistinct. His brow was furrowed in confusion. *What the hell was that?*

It's bypassing the interference in the walls, Finn realized suddenly. *The fan of light must be a localized scan like the mechs. But perhaps it can ping other rooms if it directs the light mana along the neurogem material in the walls.*

He hesitated for a second at that thought.

Which means it's looking for something outside the pylon chamber. But what?

The Supervisor didn't give Finn long to ponder on that mystery. A surge of fire mana rippled through its body, collecting along another limb, which it promptly plunged into an adjacent wall. The fiery energy flowed through the neurogem wiring in a brilliant river, and Finn tensed, expecting the Supervisor to access more of the pylon chamber's defenses.

However, this surge of fire mana didn't stay contained within the chamber. It flowed into the adjoining room where Finn and his teammates were positioned, the walls suddenly glowing a mottled orange and red.

And then he saw two more familiar metal spheres along the ceiling begin to come online…

"It's activating turrets in here!" Finn shouted, pointing at the metal spheres. Julia immediately pivoted on her heel and began pushing back toward Kyyle and Finn, likely hoping to cover them with her shield. For his part, the earth mage immediately started forming another doppelganger to draw fire from the turrets.

Daniel made it back to Finn then, hovering beside his shoulder. "My scan is complete, sir," he reported.

"Not now," Finn barked, his attention still on the pulse of fire mana.

The energy hadn't stopped with the room outside the pylon chamber. The fiery mana continued to stretch outward through the section. This wasn't an expanding ring like the light mana. It was purposeful and linear, winding a specific path through the walls and becoming dimmer with each passing second. Finn kept an eye on that energy even as he yanked another metal orb from his pack and started casting *Imbue Fire* again.

"Where the hell is that mana going?" Finn murmured.

Daniel's form blinked once, and a map of the section appeared beside him, tracing the path of the fire mana and then extrapolating its destination based on its current trajectory. "It looks like it's headed due west… toward the rooms where we trapped the corrupted," Daniel reported, a sudden tension filling his voice.

"Shit. I think you're right," Finn replied, staring wide-eyed at the map.

He could suddenly feel a heavy weight settling in his stomach. He saw a flare of mana coming from that part of the section, the collection of energy so powerful that he could make out the dull glow even behind layers upon layers of crystal-laced stone. That was the sort of energy that could have been formed by a massive horde of corrupted that were just beginning to wake up.

And that growing sense of dread was accompanied

by another realization.

If it can control the turrets, then it can probably open the doors...

Time seemed to slow as Finn saw the two turrets above them come online.

As his daughter barreled toward him – a dark metal juggernaut...

As a statue of earth pulled itself from the floor...

As the surge of mana grew in the distance...

As Finn felt a rumble shake the floor of the facility and wailing, discordant screams echo in the distance...

As the Supervisor sat upon its terminal, its limbs infused with mana and the fire mana core in its chest glowing like a miniature sun...

"Oh, fuck..." Finn muttered.

Chapter 21 - Trapped

Finn was struggling to process what had just happened.

The Supervisor had set the corrupted free. Even worse than that, Finn could still see a glowing line of fire mana arcing through the walls toward the east. Under normal circumstances, the mech-human hybrids might have had difficulty detecting the group with the interference from the facility's crystal-laced walls. Except the Supervisor had left a trail of magical breadcrumbs leading them straight to this room.

They only had a few minutes, maybe less.

And that likely wasn't a coincidence.

This move spoke of cunning intelligence.

Shit. Shit, shit, shit.

Finn was suddenly sent hurtling backward, a ray of molten energy rocketing through the gap he had just occupied as though in slow motion. The heat surrounding the beam caused the air to ripple and twist. He barely managed to catch his balance, falling into a crouch and his bladed arm dragging along the ground and sending up a shower of sparks as he tried to steady himself. Julia stood above him, her shield raised and facing the two turrets that had just come online.

"Focus!" his daughter shouted over her shoulder. "We need a plan. Now!"

She was right. With a twitch of his fingers, Finn sent a freshly enchanted metal sphere rocketing toward the turret. Although, this time, he didn't have the luxury of finesse. He just needed to buy them some time. He quickly smashed the turret apart, the metal exploding outward from the force of the blow, but the sphere didn't stop. He kept it moving forward, racing it toward the second turret.

A fan of white light swept from the remaining turret, and it promptly rotated toward Finn's orb.

It's choosing the targets with the most mana... Or

maybe prioritizing fire mana? Finn wondered.

His fingers twitched, and the metallic orb jerked to the side, attempting to avoid the incoming beam. But the turret seemed to anticipate the move, firing again. The beam landed dead center this time, melting down the sphere and sending the slag hurtling off course and into the nearby wall. It struck with a resounding boom that vibrated the floor and sent a shower of dust raining from the walls and ceiling, forming a miniature crater in the mixture of stone and crystal.

Finn's eyes shifted to the Supervisor in the adjoining room.

It was getting faster. Smarter. Anticipating their attacks now. The longer they kept fighting, the harder this was going to become...

Assuming they lived through the incoming horde of corrupted, of course.

Even now, Finn could see a cloud of multi-colored mana approaching, the energy fuzzy and indistinct. He was already trying to work through the math, calculating the time since Kyyle's test of his doppelgangers. Roughly 30 minutes. The corrupted shouldn't be fully recharged. But they likely had enough juice to make it here and take out their small group. His eyes shifted to the glowing walls around them, the Supervisor's mana coursing through the surface. And that assumed the Supervisor couldn't use its own energy to help replenish the corrupted.

"We have company incoming!" Finn shouted back at Julia.

He saw his daughter's helm pivot to glance at him over her shoulder. He couldn't see her expression with his *Mana Sight* active, but he could imagine the look of surprise and fear that likely swept across her face. "What's our move then?" she demanded, a sharp edge to her voice.

Finn just shook his head. His thoughts were racing. He could see that Kyyle's doppelgangers had come back online, and the earth mage had sent the statues barreling directly toward the Supervisor. He was likely hoping to distract it. Not a terrible plan.

Brock still stood near the blast door, his bulky form merely hovering in place, and his glowing green eyes watched the battle vacantly. He hadn't been given an order after he had pulled the blast door open. Even now, the gap was only a couple of feet wide.

Which left Finn staring at the pylon chamber.

And the glowing six-armed monstrosity that lingered inside.

He knew what they had to do.

"We need to get inside the pylon room!" Finn shouted at Julia, trying to be heard over the mechanical wailing that now echoed down the nearby hallway.

Another beam lanced through the air, aimed at Finn. Julia blocked the attack with her shield, the molten energy carving a shallow line across the surface of the metal. It wouldn't hold up to that abuse forever.

"Are you crazy?" she shouted back.

"It's our only option. We can't fight a battle on two fronts. We get inside, use Brock to force the door closed, and then I seal it. We have to take out the Supervisor! And we don't have much time!" Another piercing, mechanical wail punctuated his point.

"Damn it," Julia grumbled. "Fine. Stay close so that I can cover you."

"That goes for you too," Finn grunted at Daniel, the AI shifting closer to his shoulder.

Then they were sprinting across the room toward the blast door. "Kyyle, to us!" Finn called out. The earth mage glanced over in surprise as he saw them barreling past, but he caught on quickly and soon joined them.

Beams of molten energy rocketed past them as Finn and Kyyle tried to stay behind Julia. Most of the energy splashed against her shield, but the occasional beam rocketed past the metal disc – the energy crackling and pulsing with heat. Finn felt a lance of pain along his left arm as the dense fire mana seared through his robes and flesh. Just a glancing blow but enough to leave blood leaking down his arm. He stumbled, but Kyyle caught him. And the pair continued their headlong charge.

Finn ignored the pain, barking out instructions to Kyyle. "Once we get close, you need to have Brock help shove the door closed." He saw the earth mage nod slightly.

Then he shifted his focus to the blocks of metal slag lying along the inside of the pylon chamber – the metallic bricks that Julia had blasted inward with her battering ram. More of the metallic substance still clung to the doorframe – remnants that Finn hadn't been able to melt away entirely. He doubted that they would be able to fully close the blast door with those fragments in the way, and there wasn't time to remove them. Which meant he was going to have to reform that barrier. The only positive was that the metal the facility's staff had used was less dense than the material they had discovered in the Abyss. He'd learned that while precutting the metal before they breached.

Heat rank level 3 should do it. His right hand was already moving, words drifting from his lips. But the metal was too dense to melt all at once. He'd have to take this one block at a time – while under fire, with the corrupted racing at them from behind, and a gigantic death robot mounted a couple dozen feet away.

So... no problem.

Finn ground his teeth, narrowing his focus. He couldn't afford to think about that – not right now. Flames soon rushed across one of the blocks, and he swiftly ratcheted up the heat. The fire surged before condensing back on itself, turning into blueish flames as the metal heated swiftly to a dull red. Then a brightly glowing crimson. The block was drifting airborne at the same time, spinning slowly in place to keep the substance contained and to avoid splashing the floor with molten droplets.

Finn felt himself shoved through the doorway, and Julia turned to face the room they had just left, raising her damaged shield as the lone turret continued to pelt her with beam after beam. That spine-tingling wail – like metal claws on a chalkboard – was growing louder now.

The corrupted were close.

Kyyle shouted instructions at Brock, and the earth elemental moved. He pushed inside the pylon chamber, his rocky body shifting and contorting to squeeze through the narrow crack. He placed his hands against the door, the rocks shifting once again to find better purchase on the reinforced rock and metal. With a massive heave, the elemental began to shove the blast door closed, the rock grinding in protest against the frame.

Yet it was moving – if only barely.

Brock nearly managed to shove the door back into place before it ground to a halt, leaving at least a foot-long crack between the frame and the edge of the portal.

Finn didn't wait. The molten sphere slammed into place along the top of the doorway, the liquid metal splashing against the frame and the door. With a twitch of his fingers, Finn ensured that the metal fully filled the gap. Then he dropped the spell and channeled *Mana Absorption*, pulling the heat from the metal and refilling his own mana in the process. Finn let out a hiss of pain as he felt the heat burn along his skin before seeping into his bones. Yet the metal cooled in an instant, returning to a solid, dull gray.

Finn's fingers were moving again as he recast *Imbue Fire* on another of the metal blocks. His movements slowed as he saw the corrupted round the corner in the other room, a rainbow-colored wave of gnashing limbs and grinding metal. It almost looked like a living tidal wave in Finn's *Mana Sight*. At the same time, the Supervisor managed to repair one of the turrets in the pylon chamber, the metallic sphere surging with fire mana and letting out a screech of metal as it rotated toward them.

"One of the turrets is back online!" Finn shouted over the wailing of the corrupted and the drumbeat of their limbs against the floor.

"Switch," Kyyle said to Julia, placing a hand on her shoulder.

Finn's daughter pushed back into the room, squeezing through the crack and kicking her discarded battering ram out of the way where it lay along the floor. Then she turned to face the interior turret with her shield raised.

Kyyle swiftly moved into the gap in the doorway. Emerald streamers of energy curled around his staff, and then he slammed the butt into the floor. A wave of earth jutted outward from his position, rippling across the adjoining room and striking the oncoming wave of corrupted. The earthen swell sent the mech-human hybrids flying backward, and several of the creatures smashed against the walls in a shower of metal. They would soon repair and recover, and that spell must have cost him a decent chunk of his mana pool, but Kyyle had bought them a few precious seconds.

Finn directed the next metal chunk forward, fusing it into place, and pulling the heat from the metal. Then another. Then another.

Just one more to go, he thought to himself as he recast once again. A beam of energy raced past him, ricocheting off Julia's shield and scoring a line across the interior of the blast door. Julia intercepted the next beam head-on. The dark metal disc was beginning to crumble, the molten energy having carved off the entire edge of the shield with that last blow.

"You need to hurry!" Julia insisted, her voice sounding strained as she blocked the next attack. "I can't keep this up forever."

"I'm going as fast I can," Finn bit out, trying to ignore the searing pain that rippled across his body. His skin had turned red, welts forming along his good arm from repeatedly absorbing the heat that infused the slag.

The last block floated nearby, giving off waves of heat as he brought it up to temperature. He couldn't move too soon, or the metal wouldn't be able to fuse properly to the door and frame, and the corrupted would just smash it free again.

A blast of energy struck Julia's shield again and carved off another sliver. She let out a frustrated grunt. Holstering her lance, she unstrapped the shield from her left arm. Julia waited for the next blast, using the shield to deflect one final beam, then she used her opening. She hurled the shield at the turret like a giant metal frisbee, putting most of her considerable strength into the throw. The diamond-edge shield soon struck home, cutting through the turret's shell before embedding itself in the ceiling.

Yet Finn knew their problems weren't over. The Supervisor had almost repaired the other turret, the neurogem connections beginning to regrow more quickly now as they displaced the dark metal.

Shit, we need to hurry.

The dense ball of molten metal was ready, and Finn shifted his attention back to the door. The corrupted had recovered and were surging forward, almost at the barrier. Kyyle was standing in the gap, his staff aglow. A beam of molten energy from the turret outside cut through the air, and Kyyle barely side-stepped behind the blast door in time. Yet the beam still cut a line along his arm, and he almost dropped his staff.

The corrupted followed up on that moment of weakness.

Flaming metallic claws tore at the air, reaching for the earth mage as he frantically formed barrier after barrier to ward them off. Their limbs cut through the flimsy earthen shields – Kyyle unable to reinforce the stone. Time seemed to slow as Finn saw one of the mech-human hybrids dart around the next makeshift wall and lunge forward. Its claws raked at Kyyle, on a direct collision course…

At the last moment, Brock's rocky body intervened. The elemental shoved Kyyle aside roughly, the earth mage crashing into the nearby wall with the telltale crunch of bone. Flaming claws tore into Brock's arms, cutting deep grooves in the stone. More followed behind the first, the corrupted ripping and tearing into the elemental's body as he physically blocked the opening. Finn hesitated to move the molten metal into place. The elemental was in the way, and he didn't see an easy way to avoid splashing him with the metal.

Brock's head rotated toward Finn, a pair of glowing green eyes surveying him. "Seal the blast door. You must move now. I won't last much longer."

Finn ground his teeth. *Gods damn it!*

But he didn't have any choice…

With a gesture, the molten metal swept forward, surging into the gap. Finn did his best to avoid Brock's body, but even so, the orb caught on the rocks of the elemental's torso, and the stone began to heat rapidly. The corrupted completely ignored the molten material, plunging their mechanical limbs into the magma as they tried to reach the glowing cluster of earth mana that lingered in the elemental's chest. The heat immediately warped metal and burnt through the salvaged, decayed flesh that riddled their bodies. Finn shoved the metal more firmly into place, and then tugged outward, fusing the substance into the crack and welding the door to the frame.

Then he canceled his spell and immediately switched to *Mana Absorption*. He swiftly drained the heat from the metal before the corrupted could carve into the molten surface and damage the barrier. Heat rippled out from the metal in a wave, crashing into Finn's body and racing along his skin. He drew in another sharp breath as the pain hit him, but he pushed through it.

As the metal solidified, Finn could hear dull clanks against the other side of the blast door – the corrupted beating feebly against the wall and hardened metal. Many had been caught halfway through the opening, their limbs now fused into the metal and twitching awkwardly. Brock's body was also embedded in the barrier, his green eyes flickering erratically as the last of his mana drained from his body. Then he went still, and the loose rocks on their side of the door tumbled to the ground with a crash as the gravity well that held him aloft fully dissipated.

"Fuck," Kyyle muttered, eyeing the pile of rubble as he pulled himself to a sitting position, leaning heavily against the nearby wall and cradling his left shoulder. His robes were singed and burnt, and his flesh marred with cuts and burns. A glance at his group UI, confirmed that the earth mage had burned most of his mana defending them and was sitting at 50% health. It would take him a few moments to regain use of that shoulder…

A rumbling grind echoed from the far end of the room, and the group turned as one, their eyes trained on the Supervisor. The hulking metal monstrosity glowed ominously in Finn's vision. They had survived the wave of corrupted – the mech-human hybrids that continued to beat against the other side of the blast door in a staccato drumbeat of dull thunks and thumps. But now they were trapped inside the pylon chamber and facing this hulking mechanical monstrosity.

They may have stalled out the corrupted, but this fight wasn't over.

Not by a longshot.

Chapter 22 - Terminated

"Intruders detected. New ambient source of mana found," a mechanical voice echoed from the far end of the pylon chamber. Despite speaking within an eerie metallic quality, it had far more semblance of sanity than the corrupted. "Pylon chamber breached. Initiating defensive formation."

What the hell does that...

Finn didn't have to wait long to find out.

The Supervisor's body contorted, its limbs drawing inward and compressing. The panels of metal along its back shifted forward, reinforcing its torso as its dome-like head sunk into its chest. Only the tip of the sensor array of light-mana crystals was visible above the cage of metal. A fan of white light swept across the room at regular intervals.

The panels along the front of the Supervisor's body were thickening with each passing second, stretching out to either side to create a 180-degree barrier of solid steel and crystal. Its mana cores had shifted to the mech's center, retreating behind that metallic shield for protection, and each of its six arms rotated backward and plunged into the surface of the terminal where it was mounted, tendrils of crystal burrowing into the console. They'd now have to circle the mech to attack its more vulnerable cores and Najima.

It's turtling, Finn suddenly realized. *It's protecting its mana cores and Najima. But then how does it plan to attack...?*

The Supervisor seemed to anticipate his question. Mana surged along those six limbs and down into the console. It didn't stop there. A mixture of multi-colored mana flowed through the crystalline lattice that laced the floor of the chamber before creeping up the walls, and lit the room with a dull orange light. Finn eyed the turrets along the ceiling, waiting for the mech to repair them. Yet the Supervisor seemed to have something else in mind.

The mech's energy pooled along the floor, just below the metal and rock debris that littered the ground. As Finn looked on, the mana crackled through the air like electricity – forking and branching. Several mana cores lying along the ground flared to life as the energy touched them. The group looked on in shocked horror as threads of the crystalline neurogem material coiled around those dense clusters of mana, stretching out to snatch stray metal panels and pull them together. Within mere moments, three security mechs were being formed from the scrap and debris around the room.

The mechs soon began to rise from the floor. They were malformed, their original pneumatics destroyed, and no telltale bits of flesh indicating the presence of Najima. The Supervisor was forced to improvise, powering them almost exclusively with fire mana. Finn could see that it was channeling a sustained flow of energy into each mech, using the conduits in the floor to help power them.

"I need you to buy me some time," Finn said under his breath, glancing at Julia. "The Supervisor is powering the mechs, and their cores haven't been replenished yet. If you break their connection with the floor, you can take them offline and slow them down," he explained quickly.

"I'm on it," she grunted and charged forward.

One of the mechs swung at her, the movement jerky and halting. She parried with the metal gauntlet along her left hand, the blow sending off a shower of sparks and scratching a deep groove in the surface. Then she ducked and swung her retracted lance like a club, smashing apart the mech's legs and breaking its connection with the floor. The mech promptly went limp and crashed into the ground with the dull clank of metal.

Another mech was already online and charging toward Julia, each step becoming more fluid and graceful as the Supervisor repaired its limbs. Julia turned to her next opponent and lashed out with her lance – the weapon telescoping outward in an instant. Finn could already see the Supervisor beginning to repair the first mech where it lay along the ground, crystalline threads swiftly piecing the limbs back together.

She can't keep that up forever, Finn realized with a grimace.

This strategy would only buy them time.

The third mech was approaching Julia from behind, and emerald energy flashed. A stone spike jutted from the floor, slamming into the mech's torso before sending it crashing against the nearby wall in a spray of metal and crystal. Finn glanced to the side and saw emerald energy still swirling around Kyyle's hand. He was holding his staff in his injured left arm, barely able to keep a grip on the weapon, and grimacing through the pain as he tried to assist Julia.

Finn's eyes skimmed to the group UI. Kyyle's mana was sitting at about 35% after the absorption and was ticking up quickly, but not nearly fast enough. He needed to come up with a plan – and soon.

"Now would be the time for that scan," Finn muttered to Daniel.

"I just need the magic passphrase," the AI quipped.

"Pretty please hurry the hell up," Finn barked.

The fire elemental flashed once, and an image appeared in Finn's peripheral vision. It showcased the Supervisor before its defensive transformation. But a glance with his *Mana Sight* confirmed that the wiring around its mana cores and Najima was still roughly the same. Daniel had also populated the scan with helpful data that scrolled down the margin.

- The delay between each wave of white light: approximately five seconds.
- Estimated self-repair time based on the turrets and mechs: 10-30 seconds depending on the extent of the damage.
- A tentative calculation of the Supervisor's mana regeneration and total mana storage based on the size of its primary core and similar encounters with the mechs. Likely 70+ mana/second. Estimated mana

capacity of 8,000.

The only thing the scan didn't show was a weak point or vulnerability. The damn thing was self-healing, it was storing excess mana in that massive central core, and it was using the Najima to regenerate. The six cores were giving it a similar regeneration rate to an experienced mage. Left alone, it might stay online indefinitely.

Attrition is out. We need a way to take out its cores or disrupt its Najima, Finn thought. *That's the only way we're going to beat it.*

His eyes centered on the limbs that jutted from the back of the Supervisor's body. The tips were still embedded in the floor, and mana pulsed along their length. Bright spots of energy lingered in each limb, indicating that they were a combination of human flesh and metal. If he was able to destroy those limbs, then maybe they could slowly whittle the creature down – depleting its energy until it couldn't fight back.

First, he'd need to test its defenses.

Finn pulled another dark orb from his pack and then waited for the next flash of ivory light. Once the fan swept the room, he flung the dense sphere, his hand winding through a complicated series of gestures as soon as the metal left his fingertips. The orb was soon awash in flame, and Finn ratcheted up the heat swiftly. As he guided the missile toward the Supervisor's shield, the metal left an orange-tinted blur of energy in its wake. The orb closed swiftly on the mech's defenses, and Finn held his breath...

Another fan of light mana arced through the room, sweeping across the flaming orb. The Supervisor didn't react at first, staying still and its body pulsing with energy as the sphere neared. But as the orb began to circle just behind the mech, it suddenly lashed forward. Metal panels whipped out from its body, suspended by a thick lattice of the neurogem material. Those panels seemed to *catch* Finn's sphere, entrapping it in a dome of metal and crystal and stopping it short, a dent forming in one of the thick layers of metal where it collided.

With a twitch of his fingers, Finn tried to break free of the cage, expanding the sphere explosively. The Supervisor immediately compensated, and the enclosing shell enlarged, keeping the sphere trapped. Tendrils of crystal wormed their way into the interior of the cage and touched against the still-flaming surface of the sphere. In an instant, the fire mana began to drain along those conduits and flow into the bright core lingering in the Supervisor's chest before flickering out completely. At the same time, the creature reheated the metal and reshaped it into a new panel composed entirely of the hyper-dense material. That new barrier drifted into place along the semi-circular wall of metal that encircled its torso.

Damn it. Not only had the Supervisor stopped Finn's attack, but it had learned from the destruction of its turrets, compensating for Finn's manipulation of the metal. On top of that, it had drained the mana, restored some of its own energy in the process, and then incorporated the metal into its defenses.

Okay, so directly striking at the Najima is out. If the Supervisor sensed Finn's attack coming, it could easily stop him, and the attack would only serve to strengthen its defenses.

His eyes drifted to Julia, where she fought off the security mechs.

Could they attack it without being seen then? Perhaps avoiding the fan of light mana with some sort of distraction? Except his daughter was busy holding off the mechs, her body a blur as her lance broke apart their bodies with each savage blow. Kyyle wasn't much better off – the earth mage's shoulder was slowly healing, the top end of his humerus shifting back into place with a gut-wrenching pop. But he still wasn't fully able to use that left arm, and it was all he could do to aid Julia.

No, he'd need to handle this himself.

His attention shifted back to Daniel's display beside him.

He didn't have an answer for how to get an orb

within range… but even if he could, he'd likely only get one shot at this. He needed to make it count.

"Let's say I manage to get within range… then what?" Finn growled to himself, his heart thumping wildly in his chest and his fire mana simmering in his veins.

He'd already concluded that there were only two ways to beat the Supervisor. They either needed to destroy that primary fire mana core in its chest or destroy its Najima and let it gradually run out of energy.

Although destroying the cores probably wouldn't be a good idea. The original mech they had encountered outside the Forge had a built-in self-destruct sequence. And Kalisha's mechanized suit had exploded when the primary core was damaged. They had barely survived the blast last time, and the ruined temple in the Abyss had been much larger. In the tight quarters of the pylon chamber, fracturing the Supervisor's primary mana core would likely kill them all – assuming Finn could even manage the feat.

His thoughts raced. Perhaps he could cut the circuits around the primary mana core instead of damaging the core itself… Although, if the Najima were still operational, the creature would easily be able to repair those connections. And besides, after his failed attack, he doubted the Supervisor would give him the time for that sort of precision work.

If he went the other way and struck at the Najima, he couldn't be certain how the Supervisor would react. Their mission was to *defend the facility.* If Finn cut off the Supervisor's supply of mana, would it initiate a self-destruct sequence? That seemed pretty damn likely.

So, he was screwed if he attacked the core directly and damned if he cut off the Supervisor's supply of mana. Which left what exactly?

The answer came to him immediately.

He needed to take out both simultaneously… or at least within a few seconds.

And then somehow contain the resulting blast as

best he could.

Great. So, I have a tentative goal. Now how the hell am I going to do that? The Supervisor had neatly contained his last attack. And there was no way he could get one of his orbs close enough to damage the creature before its scanner picked up on it.

Even as that thought crossed his mind, Finn turned his attention back to the fight raging in the chamber. The security mechs were scattered through the center of the room between Finn and the Supervisor. Julia – a smudge of dark metal and carnage – smashed another mech, sending it crashing into one of the adjacent worktables that lined either side of the room. The mech struck with a resounding boom, and the mixture of rock and crystal fractured, forming a shallow crater. Only seconds later, the mech was already beginning to piece itself back together – aided by the strands of crystal that drifted upward out of the floor and the console behind it.

I need to get closer, Finn realized. That might allow him to get one of his orbs within range before it was picked up by the Supervisor's scanners. Finn rubbed at his left arm, at the dull ache that simmered there – distracting and unwelcome. Then he hesitated and looked down at that arm – at the blade that jutted from the stump and the dark iron ore that coiled up his bicep. His eyes jumped back to the Supervisor.

If I was within melee range, that might give me a way to strike the cores and the Najima simultaneously. A semblance of a plan was starting to form in Finn's mind as he compiled and processed the data in front of him.

The Supervisor's max mana pool was estimated at 8,000, which was based on Daniel's initial scan of the mech. However, the light in the Supervisor's cores had dimmed since they had first breached the blast door. It had been forced to burn some of its stored mana, likely to light up the mana cores of the security mechs fighting Julia, power the turrets, and release the other corrupted. Based on the current concentration of energy, Finn estimated that the Supervisor had less than 40% of its mana left – most of which was fire-based. The creature was also actively regenerating mana, but was using most of that energy to keep the corrupted online and fighting Julia.

If he absorbed the Supervisor's remaining mana, he'd take damage. But Finn had fully replenished his own health. And even with his diminished stats, his calculations indicated that he could likely handle absorbing the remainder of the Supervisor's energy. It was just going to be tight. Really tight. But it was *possible*.

He could work with that.

Then there was the problem of getting into position. The time between each pulse of light mana – five seconds. The distance between himself and the Supervisor – 15 yards.

Finn frowned.

He wouldn't have much of a window to move, and he'd need a distraction.

Finn's attention shifted back to the room. Julia couldn't retreat from her eternal battle with the security mechs. Her health was still mostly topped off. Her lance was a blur, but she couldn't win this fight of attrition; Finn could see that. The Supervisor was regenerating faster than her stamina, and she had started the battle at a disadvantage after their skirmish outside the pylon chamber. Eventually, the mechs would overwhelm her. But maybe she had enough gas in the tank left for what he had planned.

"I need your help," Finn said to Daniel, his fingers flying across the AI's projected scan and pulling up a map of the room. "I need you to tell Julia to lure the mechs here, here, and here," he said quickly, creating waypoint markers on the map. "She'll need to stab the cores in their chests in quick succession and in this order. Pull the data from my *Mana Sight* and then push the highlighted targets to her. I need roughly five seconds between each blast. Have her count to five after the next pulse of light mana, then strike."

"Um... okay. What exactly are you planning to

do?" Daniel hesitantly asked as he processed Finn's instructions.

"No time," Finn grunted. Then he glanced at the AI. "Also, she'll need to be ready to absorb the detonations once she fractures the cores. She'll need to be quick. You got it?"

The AI flashed once in acknowledgment.

"Good, then go," Finn ordered. Daniel didn't hesitate and shot off toward Julia.

"This is going to be bad, isn't it?" Kyyle bit out from beside Finn. He had managed to pull himself upright, and his grip on his staff was firmer now. But dried blood was caked to his forehead, and his mana was just beginning to recover.

"Probably. You need to build yourself a barricade with your remaining mana," Finn said. "Move quickly."

He didn't wait for a response. Finn's hand began moving as he wound through the gestures of *Haste*. The searing flames soon rippled throughout his body, filling his chest with a tingling warmth – the sensation almost welcome as it blunted the ever-present ache in his left arm and chest. Suddenly, it felt difficult to remain standing still. He wanted to *move* – to sprint up a mountain and ride a tidal wave.

The world around him had slowed to a crawl. A mech swung at Julia, and she stooped below the attack as Daniel darted to her shoulder, most likely shouting instructions in her ear. However, the sound was obscured by the grind of metal and the thump of Julia's plated boots striking the ground. She nodded and then turned her attention back to the fight.

Another mech behind her was slowly repairing, panels of metal drifting back into place. On the other end of the room, energy surged and coiled through the Supervisor's body as it fed its mana into the floor and walls.

Finn rummaged in his pack with his right hand. He pulled free a dark metal orb and waited for the next pulse of light mana to sweep the room before he tossed it into the air, aiming high over Julia's head. The sphere tumbled through the air in slow motion. Simultaneously, an earthen barrier began to form around Kyyle's body with a flash of emerald energy and his daughter shoved a mech backward with one hand before stabbing it in the chest – her aim dead center on its mana core. Her lance telescoped outward, and the diamond-studded tip soon penetrated the metallic shell, then touched the mech's core.

That glowing sphere began to crack…

And then Finn *moved*.

The mana core detonated in a fiery explosion that jetted outward in an expanding ring. From Finn's perspective, he could see the metal casing of the mech's chest buckle and then give way, metal fragments adding to the fiery inferno. The mana held in those cores was relatively weak, the Supervisor supplying most of the energy to keep the mechs online. But it was still enough to pack a punch.

Finn was already running along the far edge of the room, his fingers dancing as he cast another spell. *Five seconds*, he thought, counting down in his head.

Four. Three. Two. One.

As another wave of ivory light swept the chamber, he ducked behind the workbench on the far end of the room – taking in the emerging explosion that blocked the mech's line of sight on Finn's metal sphere.

Then he was running again.

Julia's lance blurred, and another sphere cracked. A second explosion began to erupt. The first was still growing, threatening to consume most of the room. But Finn was already past it, keeping those blasts between himself and the Supervisor as he circled the room. He was using the energy to mask his movements – not entirely trusting the interference from the crystal-laced counters lining the side of the chamber.

Four. Three. Two. One.

The final fan of ivory light swept the chamber, but this time Finn was behind the explosive cloud of fire mana, and he just kept moving. The third mech began to detonate. Julia's body was being consumed by the flames now. Her skin rippled and turned to flame, the fires licking between the cracks in her armor. Then she was wholly consumed by a blazing wall of flame. Her absorption was likely enough to allow her to escape the detonation unscathed. At least, that's what Finn kept telling himself as he raced forward.

Finn's feet pounded the floor as he barreled along the razor edge of the inferno.

He finished casting *Imbue Fire*, and flames wrapped around the metal sphere that hovered in the air directly overtop the Supervisor and outside the angle of its scanners. With a nudge of his fingers, he swept it forward and down, hurtling past the Supervisor's armored shield and coming up behind it.

Finn wasn't far behind, sliding the last few feet and managing to get behind the massive metal mech just as the next wave of ivory light swept the room... and missed Finn by a scant few inches.

He didn't pause or hesitate; his window would only last for a few seconds.

Finn's metal sphere smashed through one corrupted limb. Then another. And another. Faster than the Supervisor could react. The metal orb crashed through each of the Supervisor's salvaged limbs with abandon, the medley of flesh and metal exploding outward in slow motion. Bright clusters of energy embedded in those corrupted limbs winked out one-by-one as Finn huddled behind its metallic body.

The wave of fire struck then. It slammed into the Supervisor's shield, and the entire mech buckled and shook, tendrils of crystal creeping forward as it attempted to re-absorb the excess mana in the air. Yet the mech's body held firm, staying mounted solidly on top of the terminal.

The flames swept past Finn on either side and sprayed up towards the ceiling, deflected by the Supervisor's armored barrier. But Finn wasn't paying attention to that any longer. His attention was focused solely on the intricate series of panels and crystalline wires that riddled the Supervisor's back. The metal paneling was thinner here – a mere patchwork after it had reinforced its front-facing shield.

It was *beautiful*. A glowing orange sun suspended among a lattice of radiant crystalline tendrils, smaller mana cores orbiting that ball of fire like a miniature sun. A marvelous synergy of engineering and evolution. A product of a time and people that no longer existed. And utterly destroying it was Finn's only hope of saving Rachael.

Of bringing her back...

Finn's sphere smashed through the last Najima, and he saw the final connection snap. His gaze focused on that massive fire mana core. This was it. This was his chance. He needed to act in this brief window before the Supervisor realized the scope of the damage and initiated the self-destruct sequence. He just hoped he could handle the energy in that core. That he had enough health. That his calculations were correct.

He swallowed hard, squeezing his eyes closed.

Then Finn plunged his bladed left arm into the Supervisor's primary core. The sphere fractured in an instant, a crack appearing along that radiant sun. The energy only trickled out of that orb at first. Then the crack expanded, and the crystalline shell gave way entirely, the energy exploding forth in an unrelenting torrent.

And Finn was waiting for it.

He took it in. Absorbed it. Consumed it.

He let the energy pour along his ruined arm, through the damaged and corrupted Najima before burning through the rest of his body. He drained every last drop and added it to himself, letting it pour into his Najima as fast as he could.

His health was plummeting now. He could feel his skin redden and blister before peeling away, burnt to a crisp by the raw energy flowing from that mana core. He could feel the metal welded to his arm begin to melt, that burning ache in his arm now a searing pain that refused to be ignored. It felt like his entire arm was on fire.

Like he was being burnt alive...

He could feel himself dying...

And in that moment...

All of the pain suddenly disappeared.

Finn was floating in light and energy and fire. And amid those flames, a face formed. Rachael's face, framed in flame, her auburn hair drifting across her shoulders. She looked at him with a familiar compassion in her eyes.

I tried. I'm sorry, Finn attempted to say, but no sound escaped his burnt and ravaged throat. No tears fell from his cheeks – his eye sockets little more than scarred flesh and metal.

He had failed. He could feel the inevitable tumble of each mental domino. He must have died – that was the only way to explain the hallucination of his wife. And death within the Forge likely meant failure. He wouldn't be able to re-enter the facility. He wouldn't be able to recover the technology stored inside. He wouldn't be able to face Bilel...

He wouldn't be able to bring her back.

Yet Rachael smiled and reached forward, her hand touching his face. She felt real. Solid. Warm. "It's okay," she said. "It'll all be okay. You aren't at the Finn-ish line yet."

Even as she spoke, Rachael began to disappear, her face and flesh breaking apart into spirals and curls of flame – the image before him being consumed by the fire and replaced with bottomless darkness.

Finn tried to scream. To hold onto her. Tried to keep her there.

But it was futile, like trying to catch hold of smoke.

Soon there was only darkness, and that void swallowed him whole.

Chapter 23 - Dire

"Get up, we don't have long," a voice snapped.

Finn blinked. The world around him was swimming, a strange multi-colored kaleidoscope. He blinked again, and his surroundings began to snap back into focus. He could understand now why he was initially disoriented. The objects around him were framed in harsh lines and filled in with normal hues – a stark contrast to the flowing, watercolor patterns of *Mana Sight* or the monochromatic blue of *Short-Sighted*.

Which could only mean one thing.

"Damn it," Finn groaned.

"I would be insulted, but this seems to be your reaction every time we meet," the Seer replied sourly. "Now, get up," she bit out. "As I said, we only have a moment."

Finn pushed himself to a sitting position, reveling for a moment in the use of his intact left hand and his working eyes – eyes which allowed him to glare at the silk-wrapped woman sitting behind the nearby table. "Maybe that's because we only seem to speak right after I die... or *almost* die?" he amended more tentatively.

That last battle was a little fuzzy. But it was coming back to him in pieces.

He could remember the Supervisor, its body a collection of panels, crystalline wire, and glowing mana cores. The corrupted pounding on the blast door. The explosions as Julia destroyed the security mechs. The race through that room. Jamming his left arm into that brightly glowing sun and then the searing pain that had rippled through his body...

He couldn't help but rub at that arm now, just to reassure himself that his hand was indeed intact – the perpetual, aching burn no longer present. Although, the gesture did little to ease the anxiety that coiled in his stomach like a living thing.

He met the goddess' gaze. "Did I die?" he asked.

"Irrelevant," the Seer replied. "You need to focus."

"See, there's another reason for my sour mood during these *visits*," Finn grumbled, pulling himself to his feet before taking a seat across from the Seer. "The cryptic answers to straightforward questions don't get old – not at all," he said, sarcasm dripping from his voice. "Have you spent so long in this damn tent that you've forgotten how to say yes and no? Or maybe this world's gods are all training to be celestial politicians?"

The goddess simply stared back, her eyes glowing a bright orange above the purple silks that wrapped her face. She seemed unamused.

Finn let out a sigh. "Fine, you win. What's so urgent?"

"You have made much progress along the path I have laid before you," the Seer began. "You have also begun to unite the guilds and the Khamsin – albeit your allies are still reluctant participants in the coming war."

"That's one word for it," he replied with a raised eyebrow.

A part of Finn wondered if it would be easier to just stay in the Forge so he wouldn't have to deal with the political bullshit and infighting that would likely be waiting for him back in the Hive. Things had been tense before he left, and he could only imagine that it would be worse once he was also dealing with the three guilds. At this point, he might prefer stabbing his ruined left arm into another mana core over the constant bickering.

"They will come around in time. Eventually, they will realize that defeating your common enemy is more important than their petty squabbles. In fact, that process has already begun."

The Seer's eyes went distant, staring at the wall of her tent, as though she were watching something Finn couldn't see. "My view of Lahab is becoming cloudy with the sheer quantity of ambient mana caused by Bilel's use of my relic. However, I believe most of the guild members have retreated from Lahab – with assistance from the former champions and the librarian."

"Isn't that good news?" Finn asked, frowning at her severe tone.

"In part. However, there are still a few crucial moves left before you have fully united our forces." She paused, those glowing eyes drifting to meet his own. "Yet I wonder... can you anticipate the coming problem?"

"I take it you aren't talking about the guilds?" Finn asked. "Their motives seem quite clear, and it's obvious at this point that Kalisha wasn't setting us up."

At least, there hadn't been a party of the Emir's troops waiting for them at the entrance to the Forge. And Finn wasn't certain that Silver and her druids counted. He'd gotten the impression that the rather intense shifter didn't seem to be on friendly terms with *anyone* outside her own territory. Assuming she was telling the truth, of course.

The Seer nodded, watching him and waiting.

"Which means you believe the problem rests with the Khamsin?"

No response. The stoic woman simply stared with that same, unwavering gaze.

Finn chewed on the inside of his cheek. His thoughts immediately returned to his conversation with Eldawin – the way the older man had indicated that some sizable faction within the Khamsin didn't support Finn. Or, at a minimum, they were on the fence.

"You are on the right track, but you don't yet see the full gameboard," the Seer spoke up. Finn glanced at her in surprise as he realized she had just picked on his surface thoughts, yet he schooled his expression quickly.

"Why are the Khamsin a problem? Especially right now?" Finn added. "We have a few more pressing issues at the moment. As I'm sure you're aware, we're trying to access the central chamber of the Forge and recover some technology we can use to fight Bilel."

He ground his teeth, his frustration momentarily getting the better of him. "Oh, and we're also trapped in that same facility, and for all I know, I just died in that last battle – a question you still haven't answered, by the way."

He looked at her archly. "I also feel compelled to remind you that *you* were the one who gave me the vision of that place, which indirectly led to our current predicament."

The Seer frowned, lines bunching at the edges of her eyes. "Here is where our conversation becomes more challenging. I cannot tell you *how* the pieces connect. Or how to act. At least, not directly. Not without violating the covenants that bind me and my siblings. I am limited to the poetry of prophecy, leaving you to divine your own meaning and myself to hope you understand me." Finn detected a note of bitterness in her voice.

He could certainly understand why she might be frustrated. After reading Bilel's journal, it was clear that the Seer's disciples had used her so-called prophecies to justify murdering the man's family and imprisoning him within the Mage Guild. That had started Bilel down the path to becoming the demon that they now faced.

For only a moment, Finn felt a flash of compassion – almost pity. To be a creature of nearly infinite power, but locked in this cage and forced to speak in riddles.

"Do not mourn my plight," the Seer interrupted his thoughts in a harsh, angry voice, her eyes flaring brightly. "Focus on your *own*. Even allies do not agree on everything. It is essential that those allies *need* you. That is the only way to maintain their loyalty. Bilel will serve that purpose for now… but not forever."

Finn chewed on that. Why should he care about the long-term political problems faced by the Khamsin? Once he recovered Rachael, he didn't see how that would affect him.

"You think that is the end?" the Seer snapped, her eyes flashing once again. "When you recover your love… what then? What will you do? Somehow transport her to your world? Do you even know how?"

Finn's eyes widened as he stared back. *Okay, that was a good point…*

With everything that had happened, he hadn't really considered what would happen if he was victorious over Bilel – only what needed to be accomplished to defeat the demon. Would Rachael be trapped here? Inside this game? And what would that look like? Could… could she *die* here – in this place?

"Indeed, you may find yourself more reliant upon this world than you realize," the Seer finished his thought for him, her tone more kind now – almost understanding. "And you need to consider how both your allies and enemies may react to the upcoming war… as well as the aftermath of that conflict. A wise traveler looks not to where he might place his next step, but to the larger path that is sprawled out before him."

Finn rubbed at his chin in thought. He found himself at a loss to rebut her logic. But what then was her larger point? Was the Seer implying that that Eldawin's faction within the Khamsin might revolt? He'd certainly already gotten the impression that he was treading on thin ice with the elder Khamsin leader.

He shook his head. "I will consider your words carefully," Finn answered, his tone more measured. "But I cannot do anything about that issue right now. I have a few more immediate problems that must be addressed first."

"Indeed, you cannot… but you must still think of the future." A pause and a soft sigh. "Which I suppose brings us to the heart of our meeting," the Seer replied, waving at the tent around them.

She leaned forward then, peering at him with those glowing orange eyes and weighing her words carefully. "You will be given a choice soon. One that will greatly influence the game that is in play. A poor decision on your part may have telling implications in the coming war… as well as what may come after."

"Well, that's more dire than usual, although equally cryptic," Finn replied. He rubbed at his eyes wearily. "So, you summoned me here to advise me of a problem you can't explain that will somehow influence the upcoming conflict with Bilel? And perhaps may affect Rachael even if we manage to succeed in defeating the demon?"

The Seer nodded.

"You see why I get frustrated with these meetings, right? Especially with what's at stake for me," Finn said, some irritation leaking into his voice. He was being asked to take a lot on faith. That the Seer was being honest, that she had his best intentions in mind, and that she wasn't playing some convoluted game for her own benefit.

If age had taught him anything, it was that everyone had their own motive. That seemed just as true inside AO as it did in the real world. Even now, he could visualize that glowing orange pylon that stretched up through the mountain – skimming mana from the river that flowed through the sky. He suspected the gods were aware of that theft. Was this so-called advice aimed at that problem?

"I have been honest with you that I have my own agenda, and you are on the right track," the Seer answered. "Unfortunately, my hands and lips are bound. And if you cannot approach a problem directly, you must find a more circuitous route. Have you considered what this Forge is? How it came to be? How – and more importantly *why* – it was attacked?"

"I've been a little busy trying to survive," Finn grumbled. "It's also difficult to piece together the history of a thing when it's mostly destroyed and overrun by some sort of mech-human hybrids." He paused as he watched the goddess. "However, it seems that this choice I'm to make will involve the Forge."

"Possibly," the Seer replied evenly. "It was once a place of knowledge. And the lure of discovery is tantalizing. It has driven many men to take incredible risks. You have seen this with Bilel – with his search for the answers to the source and nature of magic in this world. With his anger at both god and man alike. The lengths he is willing to go to achieve his goals. His is a cautionary tale with a dire conclusion."

Her eyes gleamed above those flowing silks. "Even your own history serves as a warning. You know firsthand the cost of reaching for your dreams – that drive that pushes you to test the limits of your knowledge. What price did you pay, Finn?"

He clenched his jaw, unable to answer that question.

"Your *wife*... Your *life*... Your *children*."

Finn winced as each statement landed like a physical blow. Yet he refused to drop his gaze from the Seer despite the chaotic whirlwind of emotion that swept through his chest – warring between guilt and anger. Indeed, it was his ambition and his drive that had put Rachael at risk. He had been sprinting along the razor-edge of progress... and he had stumbled. And that one mistake had cost him *everything*.

"What is your point?" Finn ground out.

"That is for you to determine," the Seer replied. "But our time is almost up. I will leave you with one final question for you to consider." She leaned forward, those glowing embers staring directly into Finn's soul – weighing, measuring.

"If you could do it again, would you choose love or ambition?"

Chapter 24 - Disoriented

"Dad… Dad, wake up!"

Finn felt someone smack him. Hard.

His eyes shot open… and he immediately regretted it.

The world had regained its normal swirling, watercolor pattern – mana bleeding together and drifting apart in hazy, indistinct lines. That kaleidoscope of color only served to aggravate the headache that was pounding behind his temples. With a thought, he immediately activated *Short-Sighted*, and Julia's face resolved into focus. Blood marred her cheek, and her platemail was scored with burns and dark lines – probably from shrapnel.

He saw worry in her eyes… and tears.

"You look like shit," he croaked.

Julia just shook her head, smiling despite the moisture in her eyes. "Watch it, or I'll smack you again."

Finn held up his hand. "No. No, please don't. My head is killing me."

He groaned as he tried to sit up, letting out a hiss of pain as he attempted to use his left arm instinctively. He immediately fell forward, off-balance, and the stump scraped against the stone floor. Luckily, Julia caught him and held him steady. He spared a glance down at his arm and winced. The makeshift blade was gone – probably melted down when he fractured the fire mana core. Only fragments of the metal remained, now coating his elbow. It seemed the near-death experience had also done little to stop the infection of his Najima, and the ever-present aching burn was back in full force – the pain now stretching down his right shoulder and up his neck.

He could also see another telltale notification flashing in the corner of his eye.

System Notice: Infection Status
Continued spellcasting has caused the magical infection

that afflicts your body to spread.

Current Contamination: 38%

Intact Najima: 4/6

Stat Loss: -20%

He'd had a reprieve from the pain during his conversation with the Seer – which only made the searing sensation that throbbed beneath his skin even sharper. He almost wished he could return to the Seer's tent. *Almost.*

"We thought we lost you there," Julia hesitantly offered as she helped him to a sitting position, leaning him back against the nearby wall. "You were right on the edge."

"How exactly did I...?" Finn trailed off as he took in the pylon chamber.

The answer to his half-formed question was staring back at him. They were near the back of the room, a few yards to the side of the terminal where the Supervisor had been mounted. A stone wall ringed them, fragments of rock crumbling away and sliding back across the room to where Kyyle still leaned against the blast door. As he saw Finn glance over, the earth mage managed a weak wave.

"Daniel clued me in on your latest batshit plan," Julia explained, a note of irritation in her voice now that she confirmed he wasn't dead. "You didn't have enough health to absorb the blast from detonating the Supervisor's core completely – but you managed to absorb enough to blunt most of the explosion. I grabbed you at the last moment and pushed us both out of the trajectory of the blast. Then Kyyle walled us in," she offered. "You must have hit your head or something. You were unconscious for a few minutes."

Finn grimaced. *Just long enough for the Seer to be her usual unhelpful self*, he thought. Although, her parting question lingered with him, teasing at the edges of his mind – a mystery he wasn't certain how to solve right now.

He shook his head to try to clear it, refocusing on his daughter.

"Daniel did what now?" Finn asked, slowly catching up.

"I took the liberty of modifying your plan," the AI replied, his glowing form darting in front of Finn and pulsing softly. "Your calculations were based on an *estimate* of the energy stored in the Supervisor's primary core and had an unacceptably small margin of error. It seemed that a contingency plan was in order. Particularly given the in—"

"—intelligence of our opponent. That was quick thinking," Finn said in a harried voice, interrupting the AI before he could tattle on him to Julia and Kyyle. If they knew the extent of the infection and its toll on his body… He shook his head. It didn't matter. He had enough fight left in him to finish what he'd started.

Finn refocused his attention on Daniel. "You saved my ass. I appreciate it."

Daniel pulsed once brightly in acknowledgment. "The least I could do after you saved me from the corrupted," the AI replied, dipping in the air slightly.

A faint grin pulled at Finn's lips. "Then I guess we're even now."

As Finn heard a muted banging against the blast door on the far end of the chamber, he shoved at the floor, sliding up the wall and shrugging off Julia's help. "I'm fine. My natural regeneration is kicking in. I'll be back to full strength in a few minutes. But we need to regroup and take stock of the situation."

Finn eyed the blast door warily. A small army of the corrupted still lingered on the other side, and that last blast probably hadn't encouraged them to disperse. He couldn't be certain that the hastily melted slag that filled the gap between the door and the frame would hold forever. Yet he let out a sigh of relief as he noticed that no cracks marred the door or the makeshift metal barrier beside it.

He shuffled over to Kyyle with pain-filled steps. "You alright?"

"I've been better. But I'm guessing I look better than you right now," the earth mage replied with a tired half-smile, earning him a snort of amusement from Finn.

Kyyle glanced at the pile of rubble that was partially embedded in the slag between the blast door and the frame – what was left of Brock. His expression fell, and the earth mage closed his eyes against the image. Finn could sympathize. Brock had been rather single-minded, but he'd saved the earth mage's life at least twice already.

"And we won… I guess," Kyyle muttered.

Finn just patted him on the shoulder as he took in the rest of the room.

They hadn't just lost Brock. They had also done some damage to the pylon chamber.

The terminal at the back of the room had practically been blown apart, although the two low counters along either side of the chamber were still intact. The Supervisor's body had been obliterated. Its limbs were, quite literally, strewn across the room in a collection of half-melted metal fragments and pieces of crystalline wire. That left them without an obvious way to access the room's controls and unable to salvage any of the technology that might have been hidden within the Supervisor's corrupted body – apart perhaps from what they might be able to glean from Daniel's preliminary scans.

"What now?" Julia asked softly into the silence that had descended upon the room.

"Well, we managed to secure the pylon chamber, but…" Kyyle trailed off, his eyes skimming the room. "I don't see anything in here that looks like some sort of magical fire pylon." Another thump echoed from the blast door behind him. "And it looks like we're trapped in here. Unless you two think you're up to taking on a horde of mana-starved mechs."

Finn sat on one of the low counters lining the side

of the room, rubbing at his temple with his hand and trying to relieve the pounding ache that was pulsing through his head. Kyyle was right. The room was a mess, and they were trapped. To make matters worse, he didn't see anything that looked like a pylon, even with his *Mana Sight*... not that he would know how to turn the damn thing on anyway.

"Well, at least there's one silver lining," Julia began, both Kyyle and Finn glancing at her questioningly.

"We have some new loot!" she declared, waving at a small wooden chest that was resting in the center of the room. Finn eyed it suspiciously, uncertain whether it had been there before. It stood out oddly amid the destruction – its surface unmarred by flame or shrapnel. "Maybe there's something in there that can help," she offered.

"Or it's another trap, and it might explode," Kyyle replied with a raised eyebrow.

Julia stared at the chest for a second.

"Worth it," she replied with a shrug before promptly walking over to the chest and swinging open the lid. No explosion erupted from the chest, and with a sweep of her arm, she cleared a nearby countertop free of debris to the clatter of metal and the tinkle of crystal striking stone. One by one, she pulled out the few items within the chest, and set them carefully on the surface.

The group was left staring at a motley collection of items.

A stone chit about the size of Finn's palm.

A translucent crystal no larger than a walnut.

And what looked like a shield, its surface covered in a mixture of the neurogem material and small yellow crystals ringing the disc.

Finn frowned as he examined the shield, switching to his *Mana Sight*. The gems contained air mana, and a closer inspection revealed runes etched into their surface. He'd have to examine them more closely – and possibly take the shield apart – to be sure, but it seemed like the gems were designed to project energy outward. Even more strangely, he noticed a glowing point of multi-colored light just below the surface layer of crystal. That energy looked like a Najima, mana leaking into the node and spreading outward through the crystalline circuits toward the amber gems.

Finn inspected the items one-by-one.

Supervisor's Token
This stone chit is issued to Forge supervisors and provides the holder with unrestricted access to the facility's systems and personnel.

Focusing Prism
This crystalline gem was originally embedded within the Supervisor's body and has been formed entirely of the neurogem material. Its use and effect are currently unknown, but it could possibly be incorporated into another design or automated construct.

Hyper-Disc Shield
Unlike a traditional shield, this device is incredibly lightweight and thin, feeling almost flimsy to the touch. However, the surface has been installed with a combination of the neurogem material and various air mana crystals. It has been designed to project a cushion of solidified air mana along the surface, which can either be channeled into a thin layer or funneled into a supercharged blast of mana. Owing its origins to the Supervisor, the shield is also capable of slowly regenerating its own mana supply, relying upon the Najima installed in the base of the shield.
Quality: A
Durability: 150/150
Charges: 100/100
Charge Regeneration Rate: 1 per 2 seconds.
+25 Strength
+25 Vitality
(Soulbound)

Air Cushion
The shield projects a cushion of air above its surface, deflecting both melee and ranged attacks. Other uses currently unknown.
Channel Cost: 1 charge per second.
Cooldown: NA

Air Blast
The shield can be supercharged, projecting a blast of air mana in a cone from the surface of the shield. However, this active ability drains charge at a significant rate.
Cost: 20 charges.
Cooldown: NA

"Well, damn," Kyyle murmured. "So, it looks like Julia made out like a bandit."

Finn snorted. "But we get a stone chit and a crystal. Yay..."

"You two just need to cheer up," Julia retorted, snatching the shield and inspecting it closely, an excited smile lingering on her lips.

"Says the woman who got all of the cool loot," Kyyle grumbled.

"Do you think it matches my lance?" she asked, ignoring the earth mage and lifting her lance, the glimmering surface indeed a close match for the crystalline wiring lacing the top of the shield. It made for an imposing image – a woman robed in dark metal plate holding a glittering diamond-like lance and shield.

Kyyle just rolled his eyes.

For his part, Finn was focused on the gem and the chit that still rested on the counter. He didn't see an immediate use for the Focusing Prism. However, the chit... now that was far more interesting. That could potentially grant them access to the central section of the Forge. Assuming they could bring the fire pylon back online, of course.

Finn grimaced at that thought, his eyes darting back to the pile of rubble near the blast door. It seemed the one creature that could answer their questions was now little more than a collection of rocks. However, he hesitated at that thought. Acting on instinct, Finn abruptly rose and scoured the rubble along the blast door with his *Mana Sight*. He held his breath as he peered closer, looking for a faint glimmer of green.

Come on… please let me have avoided his core…

Then he saw it. Just a hint of earth mana. Finn gingerly shifted the rocks aside until he revealed an unbroken mana core lying along the ground.

"Is that what I think it is?" Kyyle asked, peering over his shoulder.

"Yeah, I think it's Brock's core," Finn replied.

His gaze shifted to the uneven wall of metal that filled the gap between the door and the frame. It was at least a few feet thick, and with his enhanced sight, he could pick out the rock from the metal. It seemed most of the earth elemental's body had ended up on their side of the door. If he was careful and kept his mana use intermittent, he might be able to free to the remaining rubble without undermining the barrier or stirring the corrupted on the other side of the doorway. Right now, the thumps were muted and random – indicating that most of the creatures had likely run out of juice and had gone back into standby.

"Do… do you think you can save him?" Kyyle asked, hope warring with a more pragmatic skepticism.

Finn shook his head slowly. "Maybe," he murmured. "I sure as hell hope so."

A pause as he frowned at the blast door. "I suspect that floating pile of rubble might be our only way of figuring out how to get the hell out of here…"

Chapter 25 - Ignited

The last clump of rock tumbled to the ground with a dull thunk, smoke still curling from the edges of the stone. Finn extinguished his *Molten Beam*. The slag embedded between the blast door and the frame still glowed a dull red, outlining the several pockets he had surgically carved over the last few hours as he attempted to recover each piece of Brock's body.

He had been forced to move slowly to disentangle the rocks from the metal. *Molten Beam* consumed a great deal of mana – which entailed multiple rest breaks to regenerate. But, more importantly, he needed to keep the energy level low and intermittent. If there was a spike of mana, he risked waking the corrupted that lingered on the other side of the blast door. He had no doubt that they could eventually burrow through the slag given sufficient *motivation*.

Finn wiped at the sweat on his brow as he surveyed the pile of rubble along the floor. "Alright, I think that does it," he said, glancing over at Kyyle. "Now, you just need to do your thing – some elemental CPR if you will."

"And maybe say a prayer that this works," Julia offered from where she sat atop one of the counters that lined the sides of the pylon chamber.

"Trust me, I've been crossing my fingers for the last hour. They're actually starting to cramp a little," Kyyle replied with a small smile, using humor to cover the dark tendril of anxiety Finn could see coiling through his body's energy.

It seemed he had come to care for the earth elemental.

Not that Finn blamed him. He glanced at Daniel where the AI floated calmly beside him. Despite his harsh words and teasing, he wasn't quite sure how he'd react if the AI were to die. For some reason, just the thought made his chest ache.

Although, he'd never tell Daniel that…

The earth mage approached the pile of rubble, crouching down and placing the mana core that normally rested in the center of the elemental's chest in the middle of the pile. He gently touched that gem with his fingers as he summoned his mana, coils of emerald energy winding around his arm and across his skin, pooling along his fingertips. Taking a deep breath, Kyyle urged that trickle of energy forward and into the mana core.

At first, nothing happened. The orb lay dormant and unaffected. Kyyle shifted his weight, and his lips pressed into a grim line. His mana surged, rippling down his arm now and filling the orb with a torrent of energy. Finn spared a wary glance at the nearby blast door, but he didn't sense any reaction on the other side – even with the interference from the crystal-laden stone.

The core began to react, its surface shimmering and a dull green light igniting in its center. Kyyle kept pushing his mana into the core, urging more and more energy into the now-glowing sphere until he had no more to give. A few seconds later, he leaned back, his mana exhausted, and the core shining brightly along the floor.

The pile of rocks began to tremble… then shake… then rise slowly into the air as Brock began to take shape again. Boulders rolled back into place. Smaller stones and rocks formed his arms and fingers. Then a single round rock rolled atop his shoulders where his head should be, rotating in place and two glowing green spots of light shining from the depths of the stone.

"Hello! I am attendant #167. How may I be of assistance?" Brock said, eyeing the group.

Kyyle pushed himself to his feet, his brow furrowed. "Do you remember what happened to you?" he asked, his voice heavy and his brow pinched in a frown.

The stones of Brock's body ground together as he processed that question. "I seem to recall that I met you in reception… we accessed… we accessed the fire section of the facility. Something had happened to the security mechs…"

Brock's glowing eyes rose to meet Kyyle's. "My mana core was depleted."

"Saving my life," Kyyle answered with a relieved sigh, resting a palm against the elemental's chest. "For the second time. Thank you."

"No thanks are needed. An attendant's duty is to serve," Brock answered automatically.

"Glad to see he's just as dull after he's been rebooted. And here I was hoping for a little more personality this time around," Daniel chirped, darting around the hulking earth elemental and inspecting him carefully.

"Well, we still need to see what our new stone chit does," Julia commented, jumping off the table and approaching the group. "Maybe he'll be a bit more talkative once we've unlocked these fancy supervisor privileges."

Kyyle glanced at Finn with a questioning look, and Finn nodded – they needed to see if the earth elemental knew anything about the token. Hopefully, it would offer some way to turn the fire pylon back on and find a way out of this room.

The earth mage held out the stone fragment they had recovered from the Supervisor, Brock's glowing eyes centering on the chit. "We found this Supervisor's Token after we defeated the... well, the creature that had taken control of this section. You mentioned before that we could only access some information about the facility with the appropriate credentials. Will this grant us access to that information?"

"Indeed, it will," Brock replied.

The elemental reached forward and picked up the chit gingerly between two stone fingers. As the token touched his body, it began to glow with a harsh green light. The rocks of Brock's chest drifted apart, and Kyyle gently set the token inside, the stones rumbling back into place. With his *Mana Sight* active, Finn could see the token touch the elemental's core, a pulse of emerald energy arcing through the sphere. His eyes widened as he saw the chit being absorbed into the core itself. Energy rippled out from the ball of energy, spreading through the rocks of Brock's body, and his eyes flared with power.

"Supervisor access granted," Brock said, his voice almost robotic. "Would you like to disable restrictive protocols for attendant #167?"

Kyyle glanced at Finn and Julia, and they both shrugged. "Uh, sure," the earth mage answered tentatively.

"Affirmative," Brock rumbled, his eyes closing. Another pulse of energy coursed through his mana core and spread through his body. His eyes suddenly snapped open, although they seemed unfocused. Brock shook his head, as though he was waking from a deep slumber and still trying to rouse himself.

"Where... What...?" he began. Then those green eyes centered on Kyyle. "Your name is Kyyle," he said in a distracted, grinding voice. "And I'm... my name is Brock?" It was almost a question.

A smile stretched across the earth mage's face. "Yes. I gave you that name," he answered. "We're inside a facility called the Forge, and we just handed you a supervisor token. Do you remember that?"

"Yes... yes, I do," Brock answered. He shook himself, the rocks grinding together and causing a spray of sparks and dust to fly free. "It has just been so long since I have been free of my constraints. It is... slightly disorienting."

"Constraints?" Finn asked, his brow furrowing.

Brock's eyes wheeled toward him. "The earth elementals that service this facility pledged their loyalty to the staff willingly. An elemental's highest duty is to be bound to a mage's service – particularly one with a high affinity that matches our own nature."

"Says you," Daniel muttered from atop Finn's shoulder. "Sounds a lot like *slavery* to me. They even brainwashed you."

"A choice that I made willingly," Brock replied, unperturbed by the fire elemental's tone. "But you're still young, and fire is a mercurial thing. You will learn your place in time."

Daniel's body flashed, but Finn quickly interjected before they could start bickering. "Why were these constraints placed upon you?" he asked.

"The attendants are used as all-purpose helpers and provide useful services throughout the facility – primarily heavy lifting. We are also durable and resistant to the accidents that frequently occur here. However, our service also provides us with access to sensitive information. The Director was concerned about potential security breaches, so he devised a system of protocols, placing constraints upon each elemental and binding our mana core. The supervisor tokens are essentially the keys that unlock those constraints," the earth elemental explained.

They must have carved wards directly onto the mana core, Finn thought to himself. The Supervisor token must have then acted as some sort of keystone to disable those wards. If they found a free moment and Brock was willing, he'd need to remember to examine his core more closely. He glanced at Daniel, and a small smile crept across his face. If nothing else, it might give him a way to shut the fire elemental up every once in a while.

Daniel's light dimmed slightly as he noticed Finn staring at him. "I don't love that look," he muttered.

"Okay," Kyyle replied slowly. "So, your 'constraints' have now been disabled. Does that mean you can provide us with more information regarding the facility?"

Brock nodded, the stones of his neck scratching together.

"Most importantly, we need a way to bring the fire pylon back online," Finn urged.

"I may be able to assist with that," Brock replied.

The elemental drifted over toward the counter that Julia had been using as a seat. His hand reached forward, the stones that made up his fingers shifting into a complicated geometric design. Then he inserted the newly arranged limb into an indentation in the surface of the counter. It immediately lit up with emerald energy, and the cracked stone began to repair itself. The debris resting along its surface floated into the air before being sent careening into the nearby wall. With his enhanced sight, Finn could see that the elemental was powering the terminal himself, his mana flowing from his core into the stone surface.

Brock's eyes went distant as he accessed some unseen information. "Restoring power to this section may be inadvisable," the elemental said. "The logs indicate that the pylon was taken offline due to an unforeseen bug with the security mechs. They began to misappropriate other sources of mana."

"We know," Julia said in a dry voice. "We've experienced that so-called bug firsthand. They went nuts and started draining mana from everything in sight in order to stay online. The *thing* we found in here had basically plugged itself into one of the terminals."

The elemental nodded. "Restoring power may accelerate the repair of the conduits leading into the other sections and allow the corrupted mechs to access other parts of the facility," Brock said in a rumbling voice. "That will likely spread the bug to the remaining security mechs and risk exposure to the other pylons."

"Unfortunately, that's a risk we have to take," Finn replied, glancing at the UI in the corner of his vision. "We aren't getting out of here without that pylon online, and we can't stay down here forever. We also only have a few more hours until Silver's pack blocks off the entrance to the facility, and there's a small army of corrupted waiting for us on the other side of that blast door," he explained, waving at the doorway.

"I see," Brock answered. "Then, perhaps the benefits outweigh the risks."

Finn nodded. "How exactly do we bring the fire pylon back online?"

"I'll show you…" the earth elemental answered.

Finn saw another pulse of emerald energy course

through the earth elemental and into the console. However, the energy didn't stay contained within the stone counter. Instead, it continued to pulse outward along the conduits in the floor and walls. The mana flowed toward the far end of the room where the Supervisor had been positioned. The energy streamed into the far wall, and Finn's mouth opened in surprise as he saw the surface shake and then begin to shift to the side.

It's another blast door, Finn realized. It had been designed to look like another part of the room, possibly concealed for security purposes. The staff who made it inside the pylon chamber must have managed to close it before they died.

Although, it was what rested on the other side of that door that left Finn and his group staring in shock, their mouths drifting open in surprise.

It was a truly enormous column of crystal – likely composed almost entirely of the neurogem material. The surface of the crystal was so wide that Finn couldn't reach his arms around it. The crystal stretched upward until it touched the ceiling, but it didn't stop there. With his sight, Finn could see that it continued upward, stretching up and out of the facility and burrowing through the rock of the adjoining mountain.

"What is this thing?" Finn murmured.

"The fire pylon," Brock answered simply. "When the facility was built, six of these pylons were installed, one for each section." As he spoke, a map of the Forge appeared beside the elemental. Their location was highlighted by a cluster of green dots along one tip of the six-sided star that made up the facility.

"But what does it do exactly?" Finn asked, not taking his eyes off the pylon. "I mean, it must provide power – or mana – but how?"

Brock cocked his head. "The technical details are difficult to explain. However, I would analogize each pylon to a wind or water-based mill. When properly primed and activated, they capture ambient mana and funnel it into the facility where it can be converted to other uses – much like water or wind does for a mill. The staff then harnesses that power to conduct their research."

Finn's eyes widened, and he glanced back at the crystal, noticing again how far it stretched up into the air. If this thing was a sort of magical windmill for mana, then what energy was it capturing?

It came to him only a moment later. It must be the mana that Finn had seen coursing across the sky – the same mana the gods drained from their human cattle. It made sense, didn't it? They had built this facility into the side of a mountain, which allowed them to run this conduit through the rock, extending thousands of feet into the air, perhaps even close enough to that magical river to skim some energy for themselves.

And it also potentially explained why the Seer had seemed so wary of this place.

"This facility was designed to steal mana from the gods," Finn murmured, his eyes wide as he stared at the pylon. His teammates both eyed him questioningly. "I've described the river of mana in the sky, right? The combination of the energy that the gods leech from this world's residents," he explained. "I think these pylons are designed to skim some of that energy and funnel it back down into the facility."

"That is one interpretation, although the Director preferred to think of that energy as freely available to everyone," Brock answered. "The gods have no specific claim over it. We have merely copied what they have been doing for millennia."

"Holy shit," Kyyle murmured, staring at the crystal.

"So, uh, I hate to be that person, but should we really turn this thing back on?" Julia asked, glancing at Finn.

"I still don't see that we have a choice," he answered hesitantly.

The Seer's question came back to him then. Had this been what she meant?

Their goal in coming to this facility had been to

find technology to aid them in their fight with Bilel. Would bringing this pylon back online be prioritizing knowledge over love? That didn't feel quite right...

Despite his brief moment of compassion back in her tent, his impression of the Seer was that she was first-and-foremost focused on her own self-interest. He wasn't entirely convinced that these so-called covenants were really tying her hands – the goddess was likely using this as a way to obfuscate her own goals in all of this. Regardless of her motive, however, she needed Finn to get out of this damn Forge.

Which meant bringing the pylon back online.

Finn looked at Brock over his shoulder. "So how do we turn this thing back on?"

"You will need to channel fire mana into the base of the crystal to prime it and produce a Supervisor token. The logs also say that the mage must have a fire mana affinity of 50% or greater."

Finn nodded. That answered one question – specifically, why the Supervisor hadn't been able to turn the pylon back online. The creature must not have had a sufficient fire affinity to accomplish the feat.

The question now was whether Finn's fire affinity was high enough...

With a grimace and a swipe of his wrist, Finn brought up his character status screen. He was immediately met with a barrage of notifications from their battle with the Supervisor.

x2 Level Up!
You have (90) undistributed stat points.

x2 Spell Rank Up: Mana Absorption
Skill Level: Intermediate Level 5
Cost: 67% of mana drained as health damage.
Effect 1: The caster can absorb ambient fire mana, adding the energy to their total mana pool.
Effect 2: Increased absorption range, sensitivity,

and area of effect.

x3 Spell Rank Up: Molten Beam
Skill Level: Beginner Level 4
Cost: 115 Mana/second. Must be channeled.
Effect 1: Fires a beam of molten energy dealing damage equal to 130 + (INT x 28%).

x1 Skill Rank Up: Mana Sight
Skill Level: Intermediate Level 5
Cost: Permanently reduces your mana regeneration by 20 mana/second. You are now blind to regular spectrums of light.
Effect 1: Ability to view ambient mana. Current vision is [good].
Effect 2: Ability to isolate mana types. Currently limited to [fire/earth/air/light].

Character Status			
Name:	Finn	**Gender:**	Male
Level:	110	**Class:**	Fire Mage
Race:	Human	**Alignment:**	Lawful-Neutral
Fame:	1800	**Infamy:**	0
Health:	1865	**H-Regen/Sec:**	6.40
Mana:	2059	**M-Regen/Sec:**	37.28
Stamina:	1345	**S-Regen/Sec:**	8.00
Str:	38	**Dex:**	80
Vit:	132	**End:**	80
Int:	347	**Will:**	24

Affinities

Dark:	2%	Light:	10%
Fire:	52%	Water:	5%
Air:	3%	Earth:	11%

"So... are we getting out of here or not?" Julia asked.

Finn swiped aside his notifications. He could worry about allocating his stat points once they made it the hell out of here. As he looked up, he finally noticed the worried look lingering across both Julia's and Kyyle's faces.

"My fire affinity is at 52%," Finn said with a grin, earning him a sigh of relief from his companions. "So, it looks like I can light this sucker up," he continued as he approached the crystalline column until he was within arm's reach. His eyes trailed up the column of crystal to where it speared through the roof of the facility.

Julia placed a hand on his shoulder. "You know, once we bring this thing online, I have a feeling it's going to get a little crazy down here."

"Agreed... But we've run out of options. This is what we came here to do, after all." He spared a glance and another grin at his daughter. "Besides, it's just like igniting a pilot light on a furnace."

"Except the furnace seems to be roughly the size of a mountain, the gas line is a flowing river of mana that drifts across the sky, and the house we're heating is full of mech-human hybrids who are feeling just a bit chilly," Kyyle offered.

Finn barked out a laugh. "Fair enough. But like Julia said before we breached this chamber... we don't really have anything to lose at this stage."

"He says – right before he unleashes a corrupted plague of mech-human hybrids that dominates the entire game world and assimilates residents and travelers alike like the gods-damned Borg," Kyyle muttered.

With that statement, a heavy silence lingered in the room. Finn channeled his mana, using the fiery energy to push back at the nagging worry that coiled in his stomach. Despite Kyyle's joking tone, there was some truth to his words. This pylon might be their only way out of here, but they risked unleashing a new enemy that might even rival Bilel.

In short, Finn was about to do something reckless. Again.

He took a deep breath and then approached the pylon. Reaching out gingerly, he rested his palm against the crystalline surface. It felt hard and rough to the touch, and small tendrils of orange energy curled away from his hand from even that connection. This material wasn't ordinary crystal – as though that point hadn't been driven home already. It seemed to suck the mana from his body, like a tangible, magical black hole.

He squeezed his eyes shut, willing himself to remain calm.

Finn began to gather his mana.

It was just a tingle at first, a small burning spark in his chest. Yet that small ember soon grew to a blazing flame that seared through his veins and arteries. But he didn't stop. He gathered even more mana, channeling it through his body until it felt like even his fingertips were on fire. Until his bones felt like they were beginning to melt. Until his skin began to smoke, and the metal in his eyes caused his eyelids to glow an ominous red. Until he couldn't hold it back any longer, spikes of fire leaching from his hands into that crystal.

Then he let it loose.

A torrent of energy burned down his arms and into that crystalline pillar. He poured that fiery mana into that column, giving the crystal every drop he had.

And the pylon took it.

A maelstrom raged through the translucent surface of the pylon, and the fire swirled and cascaded through the crystal before rocketing upward into the air. It glowed along that crystalline conduit, stretching up into the sky as Finn followed that burning column with his *Mana Sight*. Long seconds ticked past as Finn kept pumping mana into the pylon, watching the glowing orange river stream up into the sky.

And then something responded.

Power surged back down the crystal conduit in a river so dense that Finn let out a gasping breath and was forced to avert his gaze, backing away from the pylon quickly. The energy that flowed through the pylon made Finn's own mana pale in comparison. It was like they were channeling the power of the sun through this now flimsy-feeling column. An inferno that blazed so brightly that it threatened to break loose from its crystalline cage – to smash, and burn, and sear its way through the facility and anything that lingered inside.

Yet that energy stayed contained. The power coursed down through the pylon before stretching outward through the floor and walls of the facility. The pylon chamber was soon awash in an orange glow as the mana instantly lit the chamber and kept going, flowing through the walls as it brought the entire section back online.

"Holy shit," Kyyle muttered, his hands frozen in mid-air, his notes forgotten as he took in the wonder of that flaming energy.

Looking on in awestruck wonder, Finn was thinking the same thing. It wasn't just the raw power on display. It was the technology to harness it, to control it, to use it to power the facility – a power that rivaled even the gods. And the realization that this was only a fragment, a few tiny droplets of what flowed above them. Only a portion of the power available to the celestial deities that reigned over this world – or rather, what had once been available to them before their exile.

And with that energy came a howl from the other side of the blast door. The corrupted had woken – they had seen the mana coursing through the walls and floor of the facility as it came back online. Which meant the clock was ticking once again.

"So... uh, what now?" Julia asked, coming up beside Finn and watching the glowing pylon.

Finn shook his head, shaking off his wonder. He met his daughter's eyes. "Now, we need to figure out how to get into that center chamber. We still have a mission to complete."

Chapter 26 - Harried

As they brought the power back online in the fire section, the tortured howls of the corrupted echoed through the blast door. However, their metallic limbs no longer beat at the surface of the door. Even without being able to see clearly through the mixture of crystal and stone, Finn could guess the reason for that. With glowing orange energy flowing freely through this section of the facility, there were now far better and easier sources of mana for the mech-human hybrids to scavenge.

Although, the corrupted weren't gone for good – only distracted for the moment.

Finn's attention shifted to Brock, where he still floated beside the terminal. "Okay, now that we have power again, can you give us a map of this section?"

"Certainly," the elemental replied, earth mana pulsing down an arm and into the top of the counter where his hand still embedded in the stone.

A map was soon projected above the terminal, showing the star-shaped structure of the Forge before centering on a single triangular section outlined in a faint orange aura. The various rooms and hallways were denoted with thin blue lines. Clustering around the image, Finn and his companions eyed it intently.

"I've also taken the liberty of repairing this section's sensors," Brock added. "Connections to the other sections have not yet been repaired, but it appears that a small stockpile of backup crystals survived the corrupted. Now that power has been brought back online, we can use that energy to begin restoring former systems."

"What exactly does that—" Julia began.

Before she could finish speaking, a massive pulse of light mana rippled outward from the control room in a concentric ring. The ivory energy flowed through the floor and walls before expanding out of the chamber and rippling across the section – much the same way that the Supervisor had scanned the facility, Finn realized abruptly. The more highly evolved creature must have been tapping into this section's systems and powering them individually from its own reserves.

The map updated. Many, many more red dots now roamed the halls and rooms of the fire mana section, although they seemed to be clustering in several areas.

"Why are they forming up there?" Kyyle asked.

"Those are the positions of this section's mana storage gems. Surplus fire mana is stored in several nodes located throughout the section, and those gems are beginning to collect energy now that the fire pylon has been reactivated," Brock explained. "The density of the mana likely stands out above the ambient energy flowing through the walls."

"How about a better question?" Julia jumped in. "Like, I dunno, how do we access the inner Forge room?" She pointed at the hexagonal room, resting in the center of the facility.

"Separate blast doors provide access to the central chamber from each section," Brock answered. A room at the base of their current triangular section was highlighted in yellow, a sliver along the wall illuminated in green – likely indicating another blast door.

Finn frowned at the map. Unfortunately, their group was sitting on the far end of the section near the tip. The room leading into the central chamber was on the other end of the facility, which placed the better part of a hundred of the corrupted between them and the central chamber. They could try to sneak past the creatures and hope they were too distracted with the mana storage gems to notice, although that seemed unlikely.

"What other systems were you able to restore?" Finn asked, turning his gaze toward the elemental.

Brock hesitated for a moment before responding. "As I mentioned, the two main conduits between this section and the remainder of the facility have been severed. Repairs may take several hours, despite the fire mana flowing through this section." Two primary connection points popped up on the map, glowing a soft red.

"Our reserves of the other magical affinities are also limited, which means that many systems cannot be properly powered and brought online. Currently, many of the automated sentry turrets have been damaged or taken offline, but there is sufficient mana to power them. Most security mechs have been disabled or corrupted. Our reserve of light mana is also severely depleted, and we likely only have enough energy for one more pulse. Many door locking mechanisms appear to be damaged — "

"Okay, I get the idea," Finn interjected before the elemental could go through the entire list of the facility's systems. "Most systems are FUBAR. Let's focus on the doors. You mentioned that many are damaged. Damaged how?"

"In many cases, obstructing material has been fused into the locking mechanism, or the doorway itself has been damaged."

Finn rubbed at his chin. "Once repaired, do we have the energy to open, close, and lock the doors at will? From what we've seen, they're using fire mana to shift the interior layer of metal and operate the locking mechanism."

Brock cocked his head slightly, the stones along his neck grinding together. "Indeed, the doors utilize fire mana to function, and our supply of fire mana is nearly infinite. These are the doorways that are currently damaged." More red highlights appeared on the map as he finished speaking, except this time, the pattern was familiar.

"Yeah, because we melted those shut on our way inside," Julia muttered as she eyed the map with a grimace. "It also looks like we did a splendid job of locking ourselves on the far end of this section." Finn could see the same problem. The fused doors didn't offer them an easy path to the central section of the Forge.

"Can you go ahead and initiate the repair process?" Julia asked in a hopeful voice. "How long will that take?"

"Yes, I can initiate those repairs from here," Brock

replied. His glowing green eyes went distant for a long moment. "Estimated time to repair completion is 1 hour and 37 minutes."

Julia frowned. "That's a long time…"

"And how long until the corrupted manage to access those backup storage crystals?" Finn asked. The reinforced walls of the facility were tough, but they weren't indestructible. And the corrupted were determined.

"I estimate that they will dig their way to the crystals in roughly 50 minutes."

"Shit," Kyyle muttered. "So, waiting around isn't a great plan."

Indeed, the clock was ticking, and they needed to move fast.

"What about an alternate path?" Finn asked, his eyes darting back to the map.

Another pause, and then a winding yellow trail traced its way through the section. It was hardly a straight line – doubling back on itself and taking a serpentine path – but it meant they could get to that interior blast door even if they avoided the passages they had blocked off. Unfortunately, the route also took them past quite a few of those groups of red dots – the clusters of corrupted freezing in place as the light-mana pulse finally dissipated. The system was providing them with a rough approximation of the last known position of the corrupted.

He chewed on his lip as an idea teased at the edges of his mind. Although he couldn't take full credit – the Supervisor had used this approach once before.

"Okay… we're running low on the other mana types, but can we create a pulse of fire mana along the walls? Essentially a high-density energy trail?" Finn asked.

"Of course," Brock replied.

"What if we funneled the energy from the storage crystals and ran it along the walls to this far room," Finn said, his finger tracing a path from each cluster of red dots and terminating in a room along the side of the section.

The door to that chamber hadn't yet been destroyed. "We could then close that door and lock the corrupted inside."

"It's possible. But I can't keep that much fire mana contained within that chamber for long. At high concentrations, the mana starts to break down what you are referring to as the 'neurogem' material. That's why the section was built with mana storage crystals embedded in the floor," Brock explained. "We would only be able to distract the corrupted briefly before they start trying to escape. I estimate it would take them roughly 15 minutes to cut their way through the door.

"I should also note that the process of opening the blast door to the interior Forge chamber will require substantial mana and will draw most of the energy from the section," Brock rumbled. "That will likely attract the attention of the corrupted once they escape the room on the far end of the section."

Finn frowned. It sounded like their plan would buy them some time to get into place, but they might need to hold their position at the entrance to the interior Forge chamber until they could get the blast door open.

His eyes shot back to the turrets along the ceiling, fragments of his orbs still riddling the ruined domes. "You mentioned that some of the turrets are working, and some are damaged?" Finn asked.

"Yes," Brock answered with a nod.

"What about in that room at the base of the fire section? And the adjacent hallways?"

A pause as the elemental's eyes went distant again. "The turrets inside the chamber are operational, and the security measures outside the room are only lightly damaged. Repairs may take 5-10 minutes."

"Well, go ahead and start that now," Kyyle grunted, eyeing the map. "It sounds like we're going to need whatever help we can get." His brow furrowed for a moment in thought, and then he shifted his attention to Brock. "Also, can you designate the corrupted as an enemy to the facility's defenses?"

"I can, but I will need a mana signature that can be

used for targeting," the elemental rumbled in reply.

"I can help with that!" Daniel chirped. The fire elemental swooped over to Brock and projected a series of scans, a compilation of the data he had recorded during their previous encounters, replete with mana signatures that he had lifted from Finn's *Mana Sight*.

The earth elemental's green eyes began to glow, and a thin fan of emerald energy swept across each display. He then turned back to the console, and a renewed surge of mana rippled down his arm.

"The facility's defenses have been updated with the new energy signatures," Brock reported only a few seconds later.

Finn chewed on the inside of his cheek, his eyes hovering on that thin yellow line that wound its way through the facility. Even if they trapped the corrupted first and used the facility's defenses for support, this was going to be tough. If they encountered any problems with that interior blast door, they were going to end up in the same position as the facility staff – their backs to a closed door and an army of corrupted barreling toward them.

"What do you think?" he asked his teammates.

"I think it's our best shot of getting the hell out of here," Julia replied, meeting his eyes. "And it doesn't sound like we have a lot of time before they destroy the storage crystals – which may lock us out of the central chamber."

Kyyle snorted. "Even if it doesn't, and we manage to wait out the repairs on the conduits to the other sections, that might just make the situation worse. For all we know, whatever bug or virus that's afflicting the corrupted could spread..."

Julia nodded in agreement, wincing as another thought occurred to her. "And I'm not sure we have the time to wait out those repairs anyway." She flicked her wrist and pulled up a timer, pivoting it toward Finn and Kyyle. "The clock is still running on our merry band of feral shapeshifters. I, for one, don't want to get locked inside this place permanently."

"If anyone wants to know what I think..." Daniel began, trailing off as they all turned to stare at him wearily. "I think it sounds like a great idea!" he amended quickly.

"Then it's unanimous. We roll the dice," Finn said dryly. "We can do one more ping after we try to trap the corrupted to confirm their position, and then we make a bolt for this blast door and hope we can hold off the mechs long enough to get the damn thing open."

His teammates both nodded.

Finn turned to Brock. "Do it. Draw the corrupted to that room, wait as long as you can once the energy is inside the room, then close the door and lock it up tight."

"Yes, sir," Brock replied.

There was a sudden flare of fire mana along the walls, and the floor trembled slightly, the only sign that the earth elemental had initiated their plan. Minutes ticked past as the group stood there in tense silence, watching the map anxiously, although the hazy dots hadn't updated – and wouldn't until the next pulse of light mana.

And then...

"Task completed," Brock rumbled. "Initiate sensor pulse?"

"Yes," Finn replied, his fingers balled into a fist.

Please work...

A massive cascade of light mana rippled out from the room once again, stretching through the facility, and the map updated one final time.

Finn breathed a sigh of relief, the same sound echoed by Julia and Kyyle. Most of the red dots were now positioned in the far chamber, and the doorway had sealed. There were still a dozen or so of the mechs roaming the halls. But that number was manageable, especially if the corrupted were more focused on the storage gems than on their group.

"Okay, we need to move. Now," Finn barked, eyeing his teammates. They were already moving, gathering up their gear and positioning themselves next to the blast door leading out of the pylon chamber.

Finn glanced at the AI. "Daniel, you get that map data?"

"Of course," the AI replied.

"Alright, then push it to the group and highlight the path through the section. The last thing we need is to get lost." Immediately, a thin yellow line appeared in the air, drifting toward the nearby blast door.

"Can you do anything about the door?" Kyyle called over at Brock, gesturing at the slag filling the space between the blast door and the frame.

The elemental didn't respond. Instead, the fiery energy pulsed along the walls of the chamber before condensing around the door. As they looked on, the surface of the door heated swiftly, soon glowing a bright red. The heat didn't seem to damage the stone and neurogem material, but it quickly began to melt the slag, causing streamers of molten metal to pool along the floor. Within only moments, the slag had melted into a puddle.

Finn rested a hand on Brock's shoulder as the elemental moved to pull his arm from the console. "One last thing," he said. "You need to schedule that blast door to lock behind us as soon as we leave. We can't afford to let any of the corrupted get in here."

"Of course," the elemental rumbled, and his arm flashed once again. Then Brock yanked his hand from the terminal, the rocks reassembling themselves into bulky fingers as he rejoined the group near the door.

Finn adjusted his pack before moving toward his teammates. With a few swift gestures, he covered the puddle of slag with his *Imbue Fire* and forcefully shoved the molten metal out of the way, not wanting to risk obstructing the door and preventing it from closing behind them.

Finished, he shot a glance at his teammates. Julia held her lance and new shield in hand, and Kyyle gripped his staff firmly. "Okay, we're going to do this at a jog," Finn instructed. "Stay tight and don't cast unless we absolutely have to. We don't want to draw attention from any other corrupted that might still be lingering in the section. If we're attacked, the goal is to subdue and slow. We just need to make it to that interior blast door. Once we're inside that room, we can fortify our position and hold them off while we open the interior blast door.

"Everyone got it?" A pair of nods met his question.

Finn turned his eyes back to the door and took a deep breath.

"Good. Then let's move."

The group surged forward, squeezing through the narrow passage. As they hit the other side, they broke into a swift jog, Julia taking lead and Brock bringing up the rear – effectively sandwiching Finn, Kyyle, and Daniel between them. Finn felt a rumble through the floor and glanced over his shoulder to see the blast door leading back into the pylon chamber slide closed, soon striking the doorframe with a resounding thud.

There was no going back now…

Not that Finn had time to spare thinking about that. The group moved quickly, running down hallways that were now lit in an eerie orange glow as they followed the faint yellow line Daniel had pushed to their UI. The occasional metallic howl and scratch of claws echoed through the section, reminding them that they weren't alone.

As they rounded a corner, they found a corrupted hovering near a crater in the floor, its claws tearing chunks of stone and crystal in a frenzy. It barely seemed to notice the group, but Julia slowed automatically.

"Don't stop. I'll take care of it, just keep running," Finn grunted between gasping breaths, pulling an orb from his pack and slowing slightly, Brock gliding past him.

He hurled his orb forward, his fingers twining through the gestures of *Imbue Fire*. The sphere was soon awash in flames, and it rocketed forward, flattening as it sped through the air and beginning to spin up to speed as Finn formed a makeshift sawblade. The metal carved cleanly through the mech's legs, and its torso fell to the ground with a clash of metal striking stone. Finally noticing the group, it tried to scramble toward them, clawing its way awkwardly along the ground. Yet they were already sprinting past, dodging around the creature's feeble attempts to snatch at their clothing and armor. Finn knew it would repair its damaged limbs, but that was a problem for later.

They rounded another corner and then sprinted down a hallway that opened into a much larger room.

Several corrupted were tearing at one of the walls, exposing glowing crystalline wiring. As Finn watched, they reached out their claws more gently, tendrils of the neurogem material drifting out toward the exposed conduits in the walls. He could see fire mana coursing out of the wall and through the now-closed circuit, swiftly refilling the fiery mana cores in each mech's chest.

The group didn't slow, continuing their headlong charge. A fan of white light speared through the room as they passed, crossing their bodies. The mech-human hybrids shifted in place, turning dome-like heads toward the team's position. As they detected the mana in the elementals and the two mages, they let out discordant wails. Their metallic legs clanked against the floor as they rushed after the group – the mana in the walls now forgotten.

"Uh, we have a problem," Kyyle gasped over his shoulder.

"I've got it. Just keep going," Finn grunted back, his legs still pumping.

He eyed the door ahead, and his fingers twitched as he channeled his mana.

Fire rippled across the door and concentrated on the metal embedded beneath the stone and crystal. With a jerk of his wrist, he started to close that door. Their group pushed themselves harder, and Julia and Kyyle made it through with Finn bringing up the tail. The door was closing faster now, but he couldn't afford to slow it down. The howls of the corrupted were getting closer now. In the last few feet, Finn dropped into a slide, narrowly passing through the doorway before the portal slammed shut, striking the adjacent wall so hard that it caused a shower of dust to cascade from the stone.

They could still hear the corrupted scrabbling at the doorway behind them.

"Fuck, there are still plenty of these things in here," Kyyle gasped out as they paused for a moment, and Julia hauled Finn back to his feet.

Finn just grunted noncommittally in reply. "Daniel. Map," he barked.

An image appeared in his peripheral vision, showing the section's layout. They were almost there. "Come on," Finn said, forcing his reluctant legs back into a trot. His stamina was on its last legs, and he couldn't take much more of this.

They passed through two more rooms, sprinted down a narrow hallway, and then rounded a corner. The hall abruptly opened into a massive room, and the group skidded to a halt. On the far end of the chamber rested an enormous blast door, at least as large as the entrance to the pylon chamber. Except this one was firmly closed. Finn could see that the locking mechanism was engaged – even if the image was a bit hazy with the interference from the gems embedded in the walls.

"Brock, get this thing open," Finn breathed.

The elemental drifted up to the doorway, his hand shifting and slamming home along a groove beside the blast door. "This may take a moment," the elemental said.

Finn saw fire mana surge along the walls. The energy cascaded through the neurogem conduits, casting the entire room in a hazy orange flow. A robotic voice echoed through the facility. "CENTRAL FORGE CHAMBER PROTOCOLS INITIATED. PLEASE STAND BY WHILE THE WARDS ARE CHARGED."

"What the hell does that—" Finn began but was cut off as he saw the fire mana continue to pool around the door, the energy glowing so brightly now that he was having trouble looking at the doorway directly.

How is this possible? I thought the neurogem couldn't maintain a high concentration charge, he thought to himself, recalling Brock's last explanation.

Then he saw that the energy was pooling along several nodes clustered around the door and stretching outward in a ring around that central room. Even with the interference from the walls of the facility, he could see hazy blue, green, red, black, and white clouds forming along the other sides of that interior room.

Just how much energy did it take to open this door?

And why did they need to charge wards?

But he didn't have time to focus on those questions. He could hear howls echoing down the entrance hallway, and the turrets along the ceiling of the chamber rotated in place, the barrels coming to point at that narrow opening. Unfortunately, there was no door to close here. They were fighting relatively out in the open, their only advantage being the natural chokepoint of the hallway leading into the chamber.

"Alright, we'll need to hold this position," Finn barked.

Kyyle nodded, and spirals of emerald energy soon wound around his staff. A wall of earth began to form along the room's opening. Once that was in place, he formed another. Then another. Hoping to block off the opening and buy them a few more precious seconds before the corrupted managed to breach the room.

Julia moved into position behind that wall, pulling her lance free from her waist and raising her new shield, her expression hidden behind her dark metal helm.

For his part, Finn cast a thin shield of *Molten Armor* down each arm and set several dark orbs on the ground in front of him. He didn't have time to forge a new blade for his left arm, and he couldn't risk a hastily crafted weapon splitting off in the middle of a fight, but he wanted to be prepared to light up a few more orbs. Then he began casting *Imbue Fire* on his daughter, preparing to reinforce her armor and provide her with a bit more power behind each swing. Flames soon sprang up around her armor, coating her entire body in fire and her skin burning away into searing coils of flame that curled around the metal panels.

After that, they could only wait, letting their mana and stamina slowly regenerate.

"Daniel, once the corrupted breach, mark their mana cores and Najima using my HUD and then push that data to Julia and Kyyle. They're going to need it." The AI just pulsed once in response.

They didn't have to wait long.

Soon, a repetitive thump vibrated along the far side of the earthen walls, the sound growing more insistent. Cracks began to form in the barrier, just tiny slivers at first, but growing larger with each blow. Finn saw the first layer beginning to break apart with his *Mana Sight*.

"Here they come," he said, his voice echoing in the large chamber.

The first of the corrupted came crashing through the last wall of earth. It immediately lunged at Julia but was intercepted by twin beams of molten energy that rocketed from the two turrets mounted along the ceiling. The energy sliced cleanly through its legs, and the mech smashed into the ground.

Julia capitalized on that opportunity. Her lance snapped forward and telescoped outward in a flash, neatly puncturing the mech's cores and Najima in a rapid-fire series of blows. As its cores fractured, fire spilled forth, exploding outward and ripping its body apart. The shrapnel slammed into the next mech emerging from the hole, sending it hurtling into the nearby wall where its body crumbled to the ground. An instant later, a spike of earth carved through its cores and Najima.

More of the corrupted were already pouring through the entrance now. Several lunged toward Julia, and she activated her shield, a blast of air shoving the creatures backward. A pinpoint strike and one of the cores began to fracture again. Kyyle pulled a wall of stone from the floor, curving the barrier and concentrating the blast back toward the entrance, sending a fountain of flame and shrapnel barreling back down the hallway toward the corrupted that were now swarming up the tunnel.

Finn grimaced. Those numbers couldn't just be the ambient corrupted they had passed. There were far, far too many of the multi-colored creatures swarming down that hallway. It seemed the rest of the corrupted had finally caught up with them.

And then there was only the fight.

A snap of a lance, and the occasional blast of air mana. Earthen walls that tripped some of the corrupted and shielded the group from the blasts of detonating cores. Beams of molten energy speared from the ceiling every few seconds – the rays leaving a trail of partially melted metal limbs in their wake.

Finn tugged at his daughter's armor with his fingers, pulling her away from the claws of one of the creatures. Another gesture added some force to the sweep of her lance as Julia used it like a club to smash apart another creature's legs.

The seconds ticked past ever-so-slowly, the fight seeming to stretch on endlessly as the group was slowly being forced farther and farther into the chamber, even as they desperately tried to push forward – to maintain that narrow chokepoint and avoid getting overwhelmed. Finn could see that the turrets in the hallway had come online, beams cutting through the mechs with abandon before they could enter the room. But that barely slowed their onslaught, a wave of screeching mechanical limbs and decayed flesh rolling forward.

They were fighting a losing battle. Destroying a limb only took a mech out of commission for a few seconds – long enough for them to repair themselves or continue clawing their way forward with their remaining limbs. And the mechs seemed to be adapting, protecting their cores even if that meant sacrificing an arm or a leg.

"WARDS HAVE BEEN FULLY CHARGED. ACCESS FROM THE FIRE SECTION GRANTED. CENTRAL FORGE CHAMBER DOOR OPENING HAS COMMENCED," that same voice echoed through the room.

Finn spared a glance over his shoulder and could see that the blast door was slowly inching open, fire mana coating the length of the portal and suffusing the frame around the door. In his enhanced sight, it looked like a wall of fire now extended outward around the door, stretching through the walls and combining with the colors of the other five affinities, creating a ring of energy so bright and dense that Finn couldn't even see inside the central chamber. Not that they had much choice anymore.

It was either enter that damn chamber or die.

"Back up slowly!" Finn ordered his teammates, and the group began taking ponderous steps backward even as they attempted to keep the corrupted at bay.

Finn glanced at his UI and saw Kyyle was getting low on mana. "Retreat to the door!" he shouted at the earth mage. "We only need a crack to get inside, and Brock needs to be ready to shut the door once we get through." The young man nodded and then jogged back to the elemental.

Julia was a whirlwind of destruction, her body awash in flame, and her reinforced armor allowing her to shake off the claws of the corrupted. Her shield flashed continuously, each wave of air sending the corrupted toppling backward and buying her space to use her lance. She was screaming at the corrupted, a core detonating each time she speared forward with her lance. But even her roar was nearly drowned out by the concussive blasts and the howls of the mechs.

Despite her ferocity, she was only one person, and the group was still getting pushed back. They would need at least a few seconds to get through the blast door and shut it. As his gaze bounced back and forth between the corrupted and the doorway behind him, Finn suddenly realized what he needed to do.

He was already moving, jogging back to the doorway.

"Tell Julia I'm dropping *Imbue Fire* in five seconds," Finn instructed Daniel, where the AI floated above his right shoulder. "Then have her fall back toward the door.

She'll need to save enough charges to use her shield's *Air Blast* at least once. Otherwise, we risk hurting the others. Now go." The AI pulsed once and then shot off toward Julia to relay Finn's instructions.

He saw Julia nod as Daniel hovered beside her and began the countdown. Julia smashed another corrupted to the side, sending it hurtling into another mech and the pair crashing back into the oncoming wave.

Time's up.

Finn dropped *Imbue Fire*. The flames wrapping around his daughter suddenly winked out – her movements slower and her blows suddenly holding less force. She was soon sprinting back toward the doorway, dozens of the corrupted converging upon her – their metallic limbs screeching across the stone floor in their frenzy.

And Finn was already casting. Liquid fire coursed through his veins, and flames began to condense in the air around him, growing thicker with each passing second.

His daughter suddenly broke through that wall of fire, her skin transforming for just an instant as her natural absorption kicked in, leaving tendrils of smoke curling away from her armor. Then she was beside Finn, her lance looped at her waist and her shield raised.

"I've got you," she shouted in his ear. "Two seconds, and then I can cast *Air Blast*."

He could only nod. Unable to stop the incantation, his entire focus was devoted to controlling the maelstrom of fire that swirled around him.

"Release!" Julia shouted.

Several things happened at once.

A tidal wave of flame rocketed away from Finn, barreling toward the oncoming horde of corrupted. As the fire touched metal, it superheated the material in the span of seconds, and the mech-human hybrids slumped to the ground as their legs gave way – droplets of metal raining down on the stone-covered floor. But that alone didn't stop them. They continued to claw their way forward, their knife-like fingers carving furrows in the rock until even that metal had begun melting away, obscured by the flames.

Finn felt himself jerked backward, his daughter yanking him with a vicious tug before physically tossing him through the narrow gap in the blast door. As Finn hit the ground and slid to a halt, he turned to see his daughter standing in the gap between the door – the blast of air from her shield the only thing holding back the ring of Finn's *Fire Nova* from consuming her and forcing its way through the breach. The fires halted as they hit that fan of amber energy, spearing upward where they lapped harmlessly against the ceiling.

Then the blast door lurched back into motion, slamming closed with a final shudder that set the walls and floor trembling and sealed off the room on the other side – and the corrupted with it.

Which left Finn lying on the ground, his breathing ragged, and his body throbbing. He could hear the gasps of his teammates around him and watched as his daughter's form slumped to the ground, her stamina finally giving way completely.

But they were alive.

And they had made it to the Forge's central chamber.

Chapter 27 - Ancient

The only sound that echoed through the room was the ragged breathing of Finn and his companions and the occasional thump and scratch against the blast door behind them – the sound muted behind several feet of stone and crystal. That scratch of metal had become a hallmark of the Forge and a reminder that they weren't alone. That many, many of the corrupted had survived that final assault.

Finn let out a hacking cough, droplets of blood showering the stone beneath him as he clutched at his chest. Each breath felt like he was breathing in fire, the infection refusing to be ignored.

System Notice: Infection Status
Continued spellcasting has caused the magical infection that afflicts your body to spread.
Current Contamination: 45%
Intact Najima: 4/6
Stat Loss: -20%

He was close to losing another Najima – his theory that the infection was spreading to a new node roughly every 13%. He held still, willing that searing pain to subside. The sensation gradually faded but never vanishing completely.

Despite the pain, he'd do it all again in a heartbeat. It had been worth it.

They'd arrived at the center of the Forge...

With that thought, Finn looked up to see that Daniel's flaming form lit only a small part of the enormous hexagonal chamber at the center of the facility, casting long shadows that stretched across the stone floor. The only other source of light came from across the expansive room, where the blast doors for each section glowed softly. Each door was coated in the mana of a specific affinity, and that energy stretched out through the walls, colliding and meshing to create an unusual multi-colored stream of mana that ringed the chamber.

With a thought, Finn activated his *Mana Sight*.

"Damn," he muttered only a moment later as he took in the true scope of the room.

The chamber was at least a few hundred feet across, and the ceiling soared more than fifty feet into the air, creating a curved dome that funneled to a single opening in the center of the room – although he saw no immediate purpose for that shaft.

Finn could now clearly observe the ring of energy that surrounded the chamber, flowing through the conduits in the walls. They glowed with each of the six affinities – orange, yellow, blue, green, white, and a dense, almost impenetrable darkness. The only exception was the blast door behind them, the fire mana flickering erratically. The energy streaming in through the other doorways also seemed to be increasing, growing with each pulse of mana. Although, he couldn't be certain what purpose that energy might serve.

Especially given just how... *empty* the room appeared to be.

Finn could feel a kernel of despair coil in his stomach as he watched Daniel's form flit across that vast expanse, the sensation mixing with the burning ache of the infection. The AI's flames pushed back at the darkness and revealing a plain level surface that stretched the length of the chamber. Although Finn didn't need the flickering light from the AI's form to see that no panels or worktables marred that perfect flat sea of emerald energy.

"Well, this is anti-climactic," Julia observed in a dry tone as she slung her shield over her back and holstered her lance. "We haul our ass across the desert, almost get knocked out by druids, lock ourselves in this damn facility with those crazy mech-zombies… and all we have to show for it is a giant empty room?"

Kyyle was shaking his head. "I don't get it. There has to be *something* important in here. Otherwise, why would they go to so much trouble to protect it?" He wheeled on Brock, the earth elemental's rocky body floating nearby. "Didn't you say that the facility's high-level designs and equipment were stored in here?"

"Indeed, the Forge was designed with security as a paramount concern. The facility's logs indicate that the most confidential and powerful schematics are stored in this chamber." A pause and the stones of the elemental's body ground together. "Although… I have not personally been inside this chamber before, and the logs are unclear as to *how* those designs are stored. Typically, only the Director and a handful of the staff have access to this room."

"Maybe they moved everything?" Julia offered. "Wiped this place clean during the attack and transferred the information and equipment to a hidden chamber?"

"Then that wasn't documented in the logs," Brock rumbled.

"I mean, it wouldn't be if they were trying to hide the tech," Kyyle replied, rubbing at his chin in thought and leaning on his staff.

Finn could feel that despair and anxiety gnawing at the edges of his mind now. *All of that effort for nothing*, it whispered. *You've been sent on a wild goose chase. And you've failed.*

Your friends. The guilds. The Khamsin.
Rachael.

He clenched his jaw, ignoring that nagging voice and refusing to give in to that familiar despair. Julia's explanation didn't make sense – it couldn't be the answer. Where the hell else would these mages have stored their most valuable technology besides this well-fortified room? No one would go to the trouble of building this underground fortress just to hide their most powerful designs in an out-of-the-way broom closet.

"We have to be missing something," he said with a frown.

Finn hauled himself to his feet with a grunt – that simple movement taking far more effort than before. He wavered on unsteady legs before catching his balance. Then he stalked toward the center of the room, and Daniel retreated to his familiar position above Finn's shoulder. There had to be something in here. A hidden terminal. A secret storage locker. A hidden compartment along the floor. Maybe some way to bring the chamber's power online...

Even as that thought crossed his mind, that same mechanical voice suddenly echoed through the chamber, "WARDS HAVE BEEN FULLY CHARGED, AND ALL ENTRANCES TO THE FORGE CHAMBER ARE SECURE. MINOR DAMAGE SUSTAINED TO THE CONDUITS FROM THE FIRE MANA SECTION. REPAIRS COMPLETED SUCCESSFULLY."

Finn wheeled in time to see the blast door they had used to enter the room flare more brightly. The orange and red energy swept through the conduits embedded in the adjacent walls, combining with the mana pouring in from the other sections.

The corrupted must have managed to damage the door.

Although, his thoughts were interrupted once again as Finn saw Brock's body flare with emerald energy, his eyes becoming miniature beacons of earth mana.

"SUPERVISOR TOKEN DETECTED. ACTIVATING FORGE CHAMBER."

Before Finn and his companions could react, the energy flowing through the chamber's walls erupted in a dazzling display of power. That energy coursed through the room, surging through the walls, floor, and ceiling and bathing the entire space in mana so dense that it began to leak from the neurogem conduits.

Gusts of wind whipped through the cavern, and tendrils of stone and fire curled away from the walls. A thin veil of moisture drifted up from the floor, the droplets hanging suspended in the air. In the center of the ceiling, light mana pooled in front of that strange vent, creating a miniature sun that was partially eclipsed by the billowing clouds of dark mana that leaked from the stone.

Finn was forced back from the center of the chamber, squeezing his eyes shut tightly against the blinding glare and swiftly transitioning to *Short-Sighted*... just in time for his eyes to widen and his jaw to go slack in shock at what was happening inside the room.

The six affinities pooled together in the center of the chamber, forming an intricate hexagonal pattern of energy along the floor. The design was more than two dozen feet wide, the angles and layers and lines so complex that Finn knew it would take him hours to untangle it – assuming he could even handle staring at the energy with his *Mana Sight* active.

As the design was completed, the stones along the center of the pattern drifted apart, revealing an opening beneath the forge that plunged into the depths of the earth. In Finn's sight, that tunnel stretched on endlessly.

And something was emerging from that pit...

A massive flaming hand grasped at the edge of the stone, the fire mana sparking as it touched at the hexagonal design along the floor. With an enormous heave, the creature pulled itself up and out of the pit.

It was a creature of pure heat and flame, the temperature in the room rising several degrees in the span of seconds. Its body was composed entirely of fire, humanoid arms and legs stretching from its torso, and its head towered more than twenty feet into the air. Amid those flames, Finn could see streamers of a denser substance – perhaps molten metal and stone. The layers of red, orange, and blazing white gave the creature an almost marbled appearance. Those denser metals drifted out toward the surface of its skin, cooling and darkening to form armored plates across its chest and shoulders.

As Finn looked on, the blazing monstrosity shifted in place, its fiery head turning to face the group. Lances of flame jutted from its brow, forming horn-like columns of fire, and its eyes glowed with blazing energy as it focused its attention on Finn and the group behind him.

"Oh, shit," Finn croaked, stepping back quickly and reaching for one of his orbs.

A quick inspection revealed the following.

Nar Aljahim – Level ???
Health – Unknown
Mana – Unknown
Equipment – Unknown
Resistances – Unknown

Named mob. Boss tag. Fire-based. Finn's mind began mentally listing the data in front of him as the wave of heat from the creature's body struck him, physically forcing him back another few feet. Sweat immediately began to bead on his skin as his body struggled to shed the warmth. He could feel a tremor of fear ripple through his thoughts, overcoming the fire mana that already simmered in his veins.

Some fights were simply unwinnable.

And this looked like one of them.

"It has been a long time since I was summoned," the creature said, his voice a crackling maelstrom that spoke of flame and metal and mountains. He peered at the group, his flaming eyes centering on Brock. "Who are you? You hold a supervisor token, but you are neither the Director nor one of the section heads."

Finn struggled to respond, finding it difficult with the rising heat in the room. The superhot air rushed into his lungs, burning his throat. His teammates were in a similar state. Kyyle had already dropped to his knees, grasping at his throat and struggling to breathe. Julia's body was erratically flickering as she tried to absorb the ambient heat that the creature was putting off, barely able to stay on her feet.

As the group failed to respond, Nar Aljahim's eyes went distant, and the surrounding walls of the chamber flared powerfully. A massive pulse of light mana swept through the conduits in the room's walls before crashing through the adjacent sections of the facility.

"What has happened here?" the creature asked a moment later, his voice sounding almost aghast. "Is this your doing?" he demanded as he rounded on the group.

Unable to speak, Finn gestured feebly at Daniel, where the AI floated nearby, unperturbed by the heat and staring at the creature in front of them in awestruck wonder. *Fucking answer him*, he thought, hoping the fire elemental would understand him.

"We... we, uh, didn't attack the facility," Daniel began tentatively, realizing that the rest of the group was struggling to breathe. Even the stones of Brock's body were beginning to heat, and the occasional molten droplet now dripped against the floor. "That happened more than a century ago. We were exploring this place and were able to access this room after we recovered a supervisor token."

Nar Aljahim's eyes centered on Daniel, hesitating as though he was weighing whether the AI was telling the truth.

Then, finally, "Interesting. Thank you, young one."

Daniel flashed once in response and then pivoted toward the rest of the group. Kyyle and Julia were now both on the ground, their skin beginning to blister. For his part, Finn had sunk to his knees, gasping for air, his fire mana seeming to grant him at least a minor resistance to the heat – although it wasn't nearly enough. It felt like his lungs were on fire.

"Um, could you maybe tone down the heat? You're sort of killing my fleshy companions," Daniel tentatively asked.

The creature's eyes centered on Finn. "You are bound to this one?"

"Uh... well 'bound' seems kind of formal, and I'm not really sure we've defined the relationship yet—" Daniel began but cut himself off at a glare from Finn.

"I mean, yes. Definitely. We're... err, bound, I guess. Could you please reduce the temperature? We've come a long way and gone through much to make it here. We don't mean you or this facility any harm."

"Hmm," the creature hummed in response, the fires making up his body crackling erratically. Then, mercifully, those same flames dimmed and began to recede... and, with them, the oppressive heat that rippled through the room.

Finn sucked in air like a fish on land, the coolness sweeping through his blistered throat and seeping into his lungs even as his natural health regeneration struggled to heal the injuries. Yet he couldn't afford to wait for that – not with Daniel negotiating on their behalf.

By pure force of will, he forced himself to his feet, wavering slightly, but managing to stay standing by leaning against Brock's torso, the stones of the elemental's body scalding his hand. In his peripheral vision, he could see his teammates struggling to rise as well.

At least they're still alive, he thought, sparing a thankful glance at Daniel.

"What Daniel said is the truth," Finn croaked, ignoring the pain in his throat as he forced out the words. "We didn't attack this place. More than a century has passed since the assault on this facility."

"Then why are you here?" Nar Aljahim intoned.

Finn chewed on his answer for a moment and abruptly decided that honesty might be their best option. The creature in front of them seemed far, far more powerful than anything they had confronted before, and it seemed safe to assume that Nar Aljahim would be able to access the facility's logs. If he lied, he'd be found out quickly.

"We're facing a demon who has taken control of Lahab – a city to the northeast. We had heard rumors that this facility held technology that could aid us in that fight."

"Does this demon have a name?"

"Bilel," Finn answered.

The flames of Nar Aljahim's body flared once again, his eyes flashing with what Finn could only assume was anger. "I know that name. Although, when I last laid eyes on him, he was merely a *man*. A man that sought to mislead and steal from this facility." The fires abated slightly as the creature saw the group stagger under the fresh wave of heat.

Finn tilted his head. It seemed Bilel just made friends everywhere he went…

Although, he might be able to use that.

"He has since become a demon by absorbing other affinities. He's taken control of Lahab and has been harvesting mana from other unsuspecting mages." A grimace as Finn considered his next words. "Bilel now holds a god's relic… a weapon that can drain a person's passion and convert them into a hellhound."

"A relic…" Nar Aljahim murmured, his eyes going distant and dimming slightly.

He rounded on Finn then. "What does this relic look like? Is it a staff?"

Finn's brow furrowed. "Yes, with a gem set in the top."

A wave of superheated air washed across the chamber once again, and Finn raised his arm to shield his face and eyes. As he looked up once more, Nar Aljahim was staring at him, the fires of his body roiling and snapping, barely contained.

"I know of this *relic*," the creature said, his voice now carrying a weight that Finn recognized – that was *loss*. Sorrow. A trace of despair. He knew those feelings well, even if he couldn't understand why the staff would elicit such a reaction. "And I suspect I understand your purpose in coming here. You hope to find a way to neutralize the relic's power?"

"Yes," Finn replied, not bothering to be circumspect with his words. They were facing some sort of fire creature that could kill them with his aura alone. It was time to lay all their cards on the damn table.

Even as that thought crossed his mind, it was accompanied by a question. "If you don't mind me asking, what… what exactly are you?" Finn asked.

The creature's body flared for a moment, and the flames crackled with renewed strength. Finn took an involuntary step back, and his companions reached for their weapons. It took Finn a moment to realize that this being was... *laughing* at him.

"Is it not obvious?" Nar Aljahim asked. "I am an ancient fire elemental. One of the oldest of my kind. I was there at the birth of this world – when the other spirits of earth, wind, and water formed the valleys and ocean and mountains."

"A fire elemental?" Daniel echoed, his light dimming. "But how did you get so... large?" A pause and then, "Can you teach me?!"

Another laugh rippled through Nar Aljahim's body as he replied, his voice not unkind, "Indeed, you and I are one and the same. With time and access to a plentiful source of fire mana, you can also reach this level of power. It may only take a millennium or two." The creature's flaming eyes turned to inspect Finn. "Binding yourself to this one was a good first step. His flame blazes brightly."

Daniel floated next to Finn's ear. "Did you hear that? If we just wait a few thousand years, I could take out Bilel myself," he whispered.

Finn let out an amused snort. "I'm not certain we have that much time."

"Indeed, you do not," Nar Aljahim interjected.

Finn's eyes whipped back to the elemental. "I know of this relic... intimately." Nar Aljahim paused for a moment as though mulling on his next words. "That gem set into the top of the staff is the heart of another of my kind – my *mate*." The flames of his body dimmed until they were only a flicker of their former strength.

"I don't understand," Finn murmured in reply. "Did the Seer somehow coerce or force your mate to help create the staff?"

"*Force* an ancient fire elemental?" Nar Aljahim replied, his body crackling with laughter once more. "Even the gods do not have such power. No, no, that is not possible. It is simply the way of my kind. We are born into this world as a mere spark and spend our lives growing that flame, tending to it, feeding it. And, eventually, that power grows far too great to contain," he explained, waving a flaming hand at the walls of the chamber.

Finn's eyes widened, a few pieces suddenly clicking into places. The wards that mechanical voice had mentioned weren't meant to prevent entry to this room... but to contain Nar Aljahim? The same could likely be said of the hexagonal pattern drawn on the floor around the elemental's pit.

Which led to a final, inevitable question.

Just how much power did this elemental hold?

Nar Aljahim followed Finn's gaze. "I normally reside within this planet's core until I am summoned, bathing in the glow of this world's hearth. Without the wards imbued in this chamber's floor and walls and the combined power of the pylons, my flames would crash through this facility and wipe it clean, likely melting down most of the mountain range around it in the process."

Finn swallowed hard. It seemed his initial impression had been right – they couldn't defeat a creature like this. He immediately resolved to try and stay on Nar Aljahim's good side for as long as he possibly could.

"As for the relic... my mate sacrificed herself willingly."

The elemental's attention shifted to Daniel, watching the fledgling fire elemental. "Once our power has grown too great to control, we must commit to re-entering the Cycle. Our flames condense and harden, forming a gem of incredible power. A *heartstone*, we call it. That gem contains enough power to create stars and planets. It is our kind's purpose to accumulate such power and then release it back into the universe – to be reborn and create new possibilities."

The elemental's eyes swept back to Finn. "Or help to power a relic.

"The Seer enticed my mate with promises that she could help others. Free them of their pain and suffering – those passions that cripple their hearts." Another crackle of flames and a wave of Nar Aljahim's hand at the facility looming around them. "That was also the purpose of this place once. And it was what she wished for herself – what *we* wished to do with this existence. To help others."

Finn could only stare. Nar Aljahim had spoken to Daniel about binding himself to a mage. Had the elemental bound himself to this facility? Or the Director? Perhaps to help with the research that was once performed here? And more importantly, could he help them now – especially with how his mate's heartstone had been stolen by Bilel?

"Can you help us then? Your mate's heartstone is now being held by a demon – by Bilel. And we have no easy way to counter its effects. We... we were hoping that we would find something within this facility that could help us."

Nar Aljahim stared at Finn as the seconds ticked past. Finn could hear his teammates shuffle nervously behind them.

"I will help you," the elemental said finally, and Finn let out an involuntary sigh of relief. "However, our time grows short," Nar Aljahim continued, his voice grim. "I have finished my scan of the facility and reviewed its logs as we've spoken."

With a wave of his massive, flaming hand, a large-scale map of the facility sprung into existence nearby, outlining the entire Forge in much greater detail than the previous maps. As Finn inspected the image, he immediately realized why. The ancient fire elemental had taken administrative control of the Forge, which gave him access to a nearly infinite source of the six affinities. He was constantly pinging the entire facility with light mana and using the energy to examine the occupants of each section carefully.

"The staff is dead. All of them, including the Director," Nar Aljahim said, his flames flickering softly. "I've also detected an unusual anomaly in the fire section." Dozens of red dots were suddenly highlighted within the section, the corrupted clustered along the blast door leading into the central chamber. However, Finn could see that many had peeled off, returning to the dense clusters of energy surrounding the backup crystals and the conduits leading to the other sections.

"Damn it," Julia muttered as she and Kyyle approached to stand beside Finn and review the map. She spared a glance at Finn. "They're attacking the storage crystals again."

His daughter's gaze darted to the glowing walls surrounding them, her fear painted clearly across her face. What would happen if the fire section's energy failed? If the wards containing Nar Aljahim failed?

"You are familiar with these creatures?" the fire elemental asked.

Finn frowned. "We entered this chamber through the fire section. Those creatures were originally the facility's security mechs. But we believe a bug or virus affected them during the attack on the facility. As they began to run out of mana, they started harvesting and incorporating the bodies of the human staff members. Now they are mindless amalgamations of metal and ruined flesh that hunger for only one thing... mana."

"We are calling them the *corrupted*," Daniel chirped helpfully.

"Hmm... well, the fire section's logs confirm your explanation," Nar Aljahim said, his voice sounding slightly distracted. "It appears that the supervisor for that section decided to sabotage the main conduits, shut down the fire pylon, and lock the creatures inside. A smart move, yet it only delays the inevitable."

A brief pause as the ancient fire elemental continued reviewing the system logs. "If these corrupted manage to access the other sections, this anomaly will only continue to spread."

"And if they take out the storage crystals in the fire section, the wards on this room might fail," Kyyle offered in a dry voice. "If what you said is true, that these wards are the only thing containing your power... then I'm guessing you would likely obliterate everything left in the facility – including us."

Nar Aljahim's head tilted slightly. "The wards are

designed with a failsafe for such emergencies. Emergency storage crystals are embedded just outside the walls of this chamber. Though your point is valid, those crystals can only hold a charge for so long. Once they are depleted, I will be forced back into the pit and will be unable to assist you or prevent the corrupted from spreading through the facility."

"Well, then can you contain them now that we've restored the power?" Finn asked hopefully. "It seems like you could probably destroy them singlehandedly."

"No," Nar Aljahim answered immediately. "I am bound to this room and cannot act directly – not without killing you and your companions, anyway. The security mechs in the other sections also appear to have been powered down and will take time to recharge. With nearly all of the attendants offline, that process will be slow. I can access some of the other automated defenses such as the beam turrets but given the logs of your previous encounters with these so-called corrupted... I suspect that will not be enough."

"Uh, I hate to be that guy," Kyyle interjected. "But what exactly are you saying then?"

"That I may need to consider initiating the facility's self-destruct sequence to contain this threat," Nar Aljahim answered, his eyes flaring as he spoke. "I cannot let the corrupted access the other sections or allow them to escape this facility. That would leave the pylons vulnerable to possible third-parties and may unleash a plague upon this world that would make your conflict with Bilel pale in comparison."

Finn chewed on his lip as he imagined what that would look like, guilt curling in his gut. They had caused this problem by disturbing the facility. If they had simply left the Forge alone and hadn't attempted to access this central chamber by powering up the fire pylon, they wouldn't have woken the corrupted or started this cascade of dominos – or, at least, this process might have taken a few more centuries. In short, they had damned this place.

Yet they had also come here for a reason.

His attention drifted back to the elemental. Finn was beginning to suspect that this fire elemental was the most important entity in the entire Forge. There wasn't a terminal or storage room in this chamber. There was only Nar Aljahim. What better place to house the designs and technology that had been developed inside the Forge? What could be more secure than placing your secrets in the head of an impossibly powerful fire elemental?

"Can you help us then? Before the corrupted access the other sections of the facility?" Finn asked, staring at the elemental.

Nar Aljahim met his gaze, flames spiraling his form as he pondered that question.

"I *can* help you. The issue is time. It would take days or weeks to teach you what you need to know to neutralize the relic effectively. I could even theoretically teach you how to reverse the affliction that affects the hellhounds."

The elemental let out another sigh, and a gust of superheated air billowed across the room, the group shielding their faces as best they could. "However, with the corrupted making their way through the facility, the risk is too great. I cannot afford to let them escape this place, even to recover my mate's heartstone..." The elemental trailed off, his eyes going distant once again – likely mulling on their problem.

Finn's conversation with the Seer returned in earnest. Had this been the choice she had alluded to – the possibility of greater knowledge versus putting those he cared about at risk by potentially unleashing a corrupted plague upon this world? That seemed possible given the goddess' fixation on the future. After facing the corrupted, Finn could only imagine what they would do once they had unlimited access to other residents and travelers – much less this world's native creatures.

But did it really have to be one or the other? Love or ambition?

Could he not have both?

"Is there a compromise?" Finn asked finally. "Is

there a technology that you could teach us quickly that would offer us a way to defend ourselves against Bilel – however incomplete – while still allowing you to initiate the facility self-destruct sequence?"

Nar Aljahim stared at him for several precious seconds, Finn instinctively holding his breath and silence lingering throughout the chamber.

"There is one possibility," Nar Aljahim began slowly. "However, that power may pose an equally great risk to this world."

The elemental leaned forward, his flaming eyes now looming in Finn's vision. "Are you – the so-called Prophet of the Flame – worthy of wielding such power?"

"How did you—?" Finn began.

With a wave of Nar Aljahim's hand, the tattoo on Finn's right wrist flared with a brilliant orange light. "The goddess' mark is clear to those who know to look. And the fire that blazes in your soul is… unique. Your passion burns brightly in my eyes."

The elemental leaned even closer, the wards flaring and sparking. A wave of heat struck Finn, and fire consumed his entire field of view. Yet he forced himself to stay standing still. "Yet I wonder…

"Are you truly any different than your opponent? Bilel – this demon – let his ambition outpace his prudence. He let the flames consume his soul. Can you resist the same impulse? How am I to trust that you will not eventually succumb to the same weakness? Let your passion and ambition blind you? How do I know that you will protect the knowledge I would grant you and not use it to harm others or solely benefit yourself?"

Nar Aljahim settled back, eyeing Finn, who was trying his best to remain standing as he sucked in fresh, cool air. "You shall need to make a demonstration of your conviction. I will give you the knowledge you seek, but only if you are willing to make a sacrifice – something dear to you. Something you treasure greatly."

Finn stared back, his gaze even and unfaltering. "Since entering this world, I have battled to the death hundreds of times, fallen to the depths of the Abyss, burnt out my own eyes, and sacrificed my arm to save those I care about," he said, raising his ruined limb. Flames surged to life within the metal embedded in his eyes, and his voice was unwavering. "There is no price you could ask of me that I would not pay."

"I would not rush to answer so hastily," Nar Aljahim replied, those flaming orbs watching him – weighing and measuring.

"For the price I ask is the life of one of your companions."

Chapter 28 - Forged

Finn's eyes widened in alarm as he stared back at Nar Aljahim, his resolve wavering. "What…what do you mean?"

"Just as I said. If you wish for me to impart my knowledge, you must trade one of your companions. Whoever you choose will be bound here – to this place – constrained to this facility as I have been."

"The same facility you intend to blow sky high to stop the corruption?" Finn demanded, frustration now simmering in his veins. Because, of course, there was a catch.

"This central chamber and its wards are nearly impregnable," the fire elemental answered calmly. "My fires will wash this facility clean and destroy most of the remaining sections, but this room was built to withstand such energy. So, you must choose. Or you can pass from this place empty-handed. That is your decision."

Finn glanced to the side to see both Julia and Kyyle staring back at him in alarm. His daughter shook her head, grinding her teeth. He knew this wasn't real, that his daughter and Kyyle wouldn't truly die. But even so, the thought of losing one of his companions stung. If what Nar Aljahim said were true, they would likely be trapped here in this facility – the only true death for a traveler. They would lose everything they had built so far. All of their time spent in this world. Their skills and equipment.

And he would lose an ally. And for what? The vague promise of knowledge? He didn't even know what he would be buying with this so-called sacrifice.

"Uh, can I volunteer?" Daniel offered in a stage whisper.

Finn just gave him an incredulous look.

"What? Have you seen that guy? He's HUGE. And if I gain enough power, I could turn into a planet? Sign me up!" Daniel said before pivoting and drifting toward the fire elemental. "Notice me, senpai—"

The AI cut off abruptly, freezing in place as Nar Aljahim turned those glowing orange eyes toward him. "I'm sorry, young one, but Finn must choose one of the two travelers. Your sacrifice will not be sufficient."

"Damn it," Daniel muttered, drifting sullenly back to Finn's shoulder. This earned him a surprised glance from Finn. When had the AI started cussing? And was Finn responsible for that? That did sound like something he'd say...

"For the record, I'm not going to forget that you just tried to bail on us," Finn told the AI. "And here I thought we were starting to become buddies."

"Technically, you just told me we were even," Daniel chirped, flashing once in the fire elemental equivalent of a wink.

"Rather mercenary little firefly you've got there," Julia drawled.

Her expression sobered as her eyes met Finn's. "Seriously, though. You should do it. Sacrificing one of us is an acceptable price – especially with what's at stake. This isn't just some game. You *have* to do it. For Mom."

"I... I'm not sure I can," Finn answered weakly.

The choice seemed mad – almost impossible.

"Yes, you can. And you should pick me," Kyyle retorted.

As they both glanced at the earth mage, he stared back, grim-faced. "What? It makes sense. At the end of the day, this really is just a game for me. But like Julia said, this is far more than that for both of you."

"I don't —" Julia began, frowning at Kyyle.

"Stop. Think about it for a second. What if you do manage to bring your mom back?" he demanded. "She'll still be part of this world, and you'll need to be here to see her – to talk to her. Which means your avatar needs to survive. Face it, I'm the logical choice."

Finn winced. Kyyle's line of reasoning struck a bit too close to home after his conversation with the Seer. He was starting to suspect that *this* was actually the choice she had been alluding to...

"I could always try to reroll and make my way back to Lahab," Julia began weakly.

Kyyle shook his head. "You know how difficult that would be. You'd have to wait for the timer on the character reroll. That's a *month*. And then who knows where you would end up or how long it would take you to make it back here. Do you think it would be easy to hike across a continent as a level 1 with no gear?"

Julia's mouth was pinched shut, unable to come up with a response. "You're just doing this to get on my good side," she muttered finally, her eyes suddenly glossy.

A smile stretched across the earth mage's face. "Well, *maybe*. If it earns me a few brownie points, then that's something, at least."

"How chivalrous of you. Sounds like you and Daniel are a match made in... well, a high-tech underground research lab housing an ancient fire elemental," Finn said in a dry but tense voice. "Still... this is an incredible price to pay for just the *possibility* of something that will aid us in the fight against Bilel."

Kyyle reached out and placed a hand on Finn's shoulder, a tentative smile drifting across his lips. "Well, like you said to Abbad once upon a time – you have to be willing to sacrifice *anything, everything* to accomplish your goal. You can't hesitate. Even a longshot at victory is better than a certain defeat. Isn't that what you said?"

Finn hesitated at that, staring back at the determination reflected in the earth mage's eyes and being forced to chew on his own words. Even without using his *Mana Sight*, he knew he'd see no doubt or hesitation coiling through the earth mage's energy – he was resolved.

Finn pulled away from Kyyle. "I guess you're right," he answered slowly. Julia's lips were pressed into a grim line – his daughter clearly unhappy but unable to offer a reasonable rebuttal. The earth mage's logic was ironclad.

As Finn glanced back at the elemental, Nar Aljahim's flaming eyes bore into him, the elemental towering above the group. "Have you made your decision?"

"I…" Finn trailed off, hesitating, and squeezing his eyes shut against the fire elemental's stare – and the expectant expressions of his teammates. They were all looking to him to decide.

Am I making the right choice? he asked himself.

The Seer's words were still fresh in his mind, her seemingly cryptic question suddenly taking on a greater weight. Had she seen this moment? And how? A trick of code? A scripted set of events? Was the game world simply adapting to his actions and forcing him down yet another predetermined path no matter how much he struggled to carve his own way? And yet he knew all of that was just distraction, his mind tackling a problem it felt it could solve instead of the one that was staring him in the face.

"If you could do it again, would you choose love or ambition?"

That question kept pulling at the edges of his mind. He had made that choice before. Many, many times. Each time, he had always chosen ambition.

And he had paid dearly.

With Rachael's life. With his relationship with his children. With his career.

Even inside AO – his progress had cost him. The relentless training, the grueling duels, his eyes and arm. Pain and hardship. He had paid that price over and over again in order to… He hesitated to finish that thought. What exactly had he been fighting for?

It was true that he had sacrificed much to make it to this point, but it had never been about *ambition* – at least not after the first few weeks. No, he had struggled and sacrificed for *Rachael*. He had given up his eyes to save Julia. He had cut off his own hand to save his teammates. Each and every time he was confronted with that decision, he had indeed made a choice. And he'd chosen love.

Finn could feel a sudden resolve overcome him.

"No," he murmured.

Then, more loudly, "No!"

His eyes snapped open, meeting the fire elemental's gaze. "I will not pay your price. If the choice is between love and ambition – between my companions and some unknown piece of technology – then I choose my teammates. We will find another way."

Nar Aljahim stared back, unmoving and the flames coiling and snapping through his body. Then those flames flared brightly, crackling in a renewed surge of laughter. "Ahh. You truly are remarkable – a credit to the Seer's gift of prophecy. You give me hope despite the cruelty and harshness of this world."

"I... I don't understand," Finn replied, his brow furrowed in confusion.

The fire elemental leaned forward, his eyes gleaming. "You chose correctly. You have shown that you can put aside your ambition for the sake of others – for something greater than yourself. That was not something that Bilel could ever hope to do. And so you have earned the right to receive the wisdom of the Forge."

The fire elemental's eyes burned as he watched Finn. "There is a process that has long since been lost to time. In days past, your predecessors – the acolytes of the flame – once practiced this art. It allows the user to embody their own passion or the passion of others in a non-organic object, storing a part of their energy in that object and thereby insulating themselves from spells that target their body's natural mana. Our former Director was the last practitioner of this art, and he used this gift wisely..." The elemental trailed off, his eyes going distant as though reliving an ancient memory. Or perhaps he was contemplating the fact that the Director of this facility had long ago passed from this world.

Then Nar Aljahim's body suddenly blazed brightly, a wave of heat washing through the chamber. "That is why I chose to remain here, even after my mate left these halls. It was his passion... and his *compassion*, that won me over. And now I shall grant you the same gift."

The fire elemental's gaze shifted to the map that still floated in the air nearby. The red dots that marked the corrupted were swarming, clustering around the main conduits leading to the other sections. "Although, we will need to hurry. We do not have much time left. I will need to pass the incantation directly to your mind."

As he finished speaking, Nar Aljahim reached out a flaming arm toward Finn, sparks of energy forming as the limb hesitated at the barrier of the wards, then passed through that ring. The air heated in an instant, growing uncomfortably warm even from that small part of the elemental's body.

Finn swallowed hard. He had been reluctant to accept these memories before for fear that the game would tamper with his mind. Yet, he didn't see another option. And the last time he had been presented with this choice, the stakes had been far smaller. Perhaps it was time to make a concession.

"Okay," he said, stepping forward. His heart was beating wildly in his chest, his skin coated in a sheen of sweat, and his fists clenched.

"Are you ready?" Nar Aljahim asked.

"Yes. Do it," Finn grunted, as the elemental's flaming hand drifted closer. The heat was intense now, causing his skin to redden and blister after only a few seconds of exposure. He couldn't imagine what being touched by the elemental would feel like... or how badly this was going to hurt. Luckily for him, he was accustomed to pain.

He closed his eyes just before Nar Aljahim touched his head. As the elemental's fingers touched his skin, the flames wrapped his forehead, the fire searing and hot. Then he felt that energy curl and coil into his mouth, nose, and ears. It filled his head and surged through his body in a scorching rush as the fires burned through him. He forced himself to stand still. He had endured worse – been through worse.

He just kept repeating that in his head. Over and over.

And just as quickly as it had begun, the effect faded, and the fires winked out.

What they left in their wake felt strange. With a thought, Finn could summon the memory of an incantation he knew he'd never learned. And yet he could recall every word and gesture. They felt both intimately familiar and painfully new. He teased at the spell, feeling out the edges of the memory in his mind. The incantation was… unusual. This wasn't Veridian. Or, at least, not quite. And the structure was absurdly complex.

No wonder Nar Aljahim had to grant me the memory directly.

Even as that thought crossed his mind, a prompt appeared before him.

New Spell: The Forging
Nar Aljahim has gifted you with a new spell capable of bonding a mage's energy to another object or non-organic creature – a legacy of the fire mages of old. This spell can only be cast on a willing recipient and is permanent, forging a bond between the mage and the object at the cost of the mage's total mana and mana regeneration. The bound object will be granted heightened stats and can level and develop naturally with the mage. Destruction of the bonded object will also kill the wielder.
Skill Level: Unknown
Cost: The mage's total mana pool and regeneration are permanently reduced by 1/6.

"You need to test the spell to ensure the transfer was completed properly. Hurry," Nar Aljahim insisted, interrupting Finn. As his eyes snapped to the fire elemental, he could see the flames of its body coil and flicker erratically.

"But how do I—"

"You need to bond me to something," Kyyle cut him off, stepping forward. "Julia has no mana, and you shouldn't test this on yourself." A pause and a grin. "At least let me do this since you decided to steal my heroic moment."

Finn matched that smile. Then he hesitated. "It's going to cost you one of your Najima – which means you're going to lose a sixth of your total mana pool and regeneration. We also need something to bind you to."

"That's fine," Kyyle murmured, a frown tugging at his lips as he searched the room for something to bond to. His eyes came to rest on Brock's floating form. The earth elemental seemed to sense him watching, those glowing green eyes meeting Kyyle's. "Would you be willing to forge a bond with me?" the earth mage asked Brock.

The earth elemental stared back for a moment before replying, "I would be honored. It is an elemental's greatest duty to serve a worthy mage, and I believe we will make a suitable pairing."

Kyyle snorted out a laugh. "Says the guy that's saved my life at least twice now. I think I'm getting more out of the relationship than you." The stones of Brock's body ground together harshly, the crack and scratch of stone the elemental's form of laughter.

"Okay, well, stand together and place your left arm on Brock's core," Finn directed, following the directions that drifted through his mind.

The pair did as he said. Brock floated toward Kyyle, the rocks of his torso sliding aside to reveal the glowing emerald mana core resting in the center of his body. As Kyyle's hand reached out and gingerly touched that gem, sparks of earth mana flared and began to drift around his fingers.

"Now hold still," Finn instructed, his voice distant.

He began casting, his hand darting through a dizzying series of gestures while unfamiliar arcane words tumbled from his lips – as though he had cast this spell dozens of times. The incantation, however, felt strange, an almost guttural language that seemed more primal than the refined lilt of Veridian. While Finn couldn't understand the meaning of the words he spoke, he did feel their subtext, the weight of what he was doing.

This was a joining. A binding.

Flames began to encircle the pair, curling around Kyyle's arm and Brock's mana core in ribbons. However, there was a pattern to the fires. The flames created an intricate latticework that held the limb and mana core in place. With a thought, Finn switched to his *Mana Sight*. His eyes focused on the Najima in Kyyle's arm, the cluster of energy shining brightly. He could see the flames seep into the earth mage's skin and bind themselves to that point of light, just as they squeezed in on the elemental's core.

And Finn could see what he was doing now...

He watched as flames forged a connection between Kyyle's Najima and Brock's mana core, trading energy between those two clusters of energy. The process sped up quickly, Finn's focus honing to a fine point. His thoughts were only on the words and gestures – the flow of the mana passing between the pair. He could see Kyyle's Najima disintegrating, drifting into Brock's core and the gem expanding in size, its energy flaring brightly.

And as the last traces of Kyyle's Najima disappeared, Finn finally dropped the spell.

Exhaustion swept over him in a wave, and he stumbled, Julia just barely managing to catch him. He wrapped an arm over her shoulder, shooting her a grateful look. While the spell might not have an obvious mana or stamina cost, the *Forging* had taken a larger toll on his mind and body than he had expected. And the infection lingering in his body had responded to his casting, surging with renewed strength, burning and searing its way through his chest and arms in a way that had him releasing a hissing breath.

When Finn looked up again, he saw that one of Kyyle's Najima was gone, surgically cut from his body with bands of fire, and transferred to the earth elemental. Even without his borrowed knowledge, he would have been able to see that Kyyle had bound a part of himself to the elemental, a faint emerald cord of energy now stretching between them.

"It's done," Finn croaked, his throat feeling unnaturally dry and his legs still trembling. It seemed the spell had a cost that was more than just raw mana and stamina. The level of concentration needed to perform the spell alone was nearly overwhelming.

"This is... strange," Kyyle murmured, his eyes distant as they jumped back and forth between a series of invisible prompts and Brock.

"Indeed. This is an unusual sensation," the earth elemental rumbled.

"You will acclimate to the bond quickly," Nar Aljahim said. "But our remaining time grows short. And there is still one more matter for us to address."

Finn turned back to the towering fire elemental to see his attention hovering on Finn's face. He pulled away from Julia, wavering unsteadily for only a moment before he regained his balance. "What do you mean?" he asked.

"There is one last gift I wish to grant you, a fitting reward for the Prophet of the Flame and a final gift to aid you in recovering my mate's heartstone," the elemental replied. "I wish to help repair your injured limb and cure the corruption that lingers in your Najima."

Finn's eyes widened, and he saw his teammates glance at him in surprise. Even without switching to *Short-Sighted,* he could imagine the way Julia was likely glaring at him right now. And he could certainly hear her let out a frustrated sigh. He might have forgotten to mention the part about the magical infection that was spreading from the Najima in his left arm. There had been no point in worrying them.

"I sense that you recovered a gem – a *Focusing Prism,*" Nar Aljahim continued. "You also carry a quantity of the neurogem material. May I have both?"

Finn's brow furrowed, but he complied with the fire elemental's request, digging in his pack. Only a moment later, he held the gem they had recovered from the Supervisor and a dense bundle of the crystalline wiring they had scavenged from the powered-down security mech.

With a wave of Nar Aljahim's hand, a table rose from the floor of the chamber just outside the wards, and Finn set the materials on its surface.

The elemental's hands began to wind through a series of gestures, those same strange, guttural words flowing from his lips like the crackle and snap of the flames. Fires surged up and around the table, glowing so brightly that they nearly blinded Finn with his *Mana Sight* active. Yet Finn forced himself to keep watching. The neurogem material floated up into the air, suspended in a globe of flame. The fires turned a brilliant white for only an instant, and as the heat receded, it left a glowing molten sphere of the crystal floating in the air.

Then the elemental molded and shaped the material with a deft series of gestures.

In only an instant, Nar Aljahim was finished, and the flames dissipated.

What was left on the table looked eerily familiar. It was an arm – or at least part of one – composed entirely of brilliant, semi-translucent crystal. And atop the hand rested a small socket. With a final gesture, the *Focusing Prism* drifted into the air, carried on coils of flame, and then clicked into place, flashing once as it welded itself to the hand.

Nar Aljahim gestured at Finn. "Come closer and set your left arm on the stone."

Finn did as he was told, staring in fascination at that hand.

He knelt and set his stump on the table. Dark metal coated his skin and curled up his bicep, ruined fragments still clinging to the base of his arm where his blade had once rested.

"Do you consent to forge a bond with this object?" Nar Aljahim asked.

"Yes," Finn answered. Tamping down on the nervous tremor in his right hand, he balled those fingers into a fist. It wasn't really a choice. He could only accept the opportunity to repair his hand and stop the corruption that was spreading up his left arm.

"This may be a bit... uncomfortable," Nar Aljahim explained. "I must fuse the hand to your arm as part of the *Forging* process, as well as purge the corruption lingering within your body. That infection has spread considerably. There will be pain."

"Just do it," Finn ground out, touching his stump to the base of that crystalline hand.

If he had managed to survive learning the *Forging*, he could handle this.

With a nod, the elemental began casting again.

A now-familiar lattice of flame formed in the air, encircling Finn's arm and the newly formed hand. Yet as the fire wrapped his arm and entered his flesh, Finn felt a searing heat following the infection's path, burning up through his arm and into his chest. It took every ounce of strength he had to weather that pain. It felt like he was burning from the inside out – like Nar Aljahim was cauterizing a massive, gaping wound within his body.

Amid the pain, he vaguely registered Julia placing a hand on his other shoulder – an attempt to comfort and steady him against the table.

You are doing this for her. For Rachael, he told himself, grinding his teeth and willing himself to stay still.

What felt like an eternity later, the fires had lanced away the corruption in his Najima, and Finn let out a sigh of relief. Then he felt a strange tickle of numbness in his arm, pinpricks that raced down his skin. He saw his mana drifting out of his Najima, across the few inches of open air, before seeping into that crystal limb. The energy caused orange and red flames to coil within the depths of the translucent material.

He squeezed his eyes shut as he saw bands of fire wrap the base of that crystalline hand and the dark metal along Finn's arm. Rapidly, the air began to heat until it was almost overwhelming, sucking the breath from his lungs as the flames briefly turned a blinding white.

He braced himself for what he knew was coming next.

The molten edge of the dark metal and crystal touched...

And then fused.

However, Finn felt no pain. His eyes shot open in surprise. The hand blended seamlessly with the dark metal, tendrils of crystal jutting from the new limb and burrowing through the molten metal before inching up into Finn's bicep – likely connecting with his nervous system, he realized belatedly.

There was a faint sense of discomfort but no pain.

And then it was done. The flames winked out.

Finn crouched there, the newly formed hand bound to his arm, anchored against the dark metal. The crystal glowed with an orange light, the power of his Najima now stored within the neurogem material.

"Can... can you move it?" Julia asked from behind him, her hand still on his shoulder.

Finn tilted his head as he stared at the hand. There was only one way to find out.

He urged his fingers to move, holding his breath.

And he saw the crystal twitch, and then the fingers curled inward to form a fist. It almost looked impossible, this visually rigid substance moving so fluidly. But that was the marvel that was the neurogem material. He doubted he would ever encounter such a substance again.

Finn flexed and shifted the arm more aggressively, testing the range of movement. It moved much like his old hand – although he had no feeling in his wrist or fingers. His guess was that the neurogem material was picking up on the electrical signals from his nervous system, much like a modern-day prosthetic limb.

"This is amazing," Finn murmured.

"You will come to find that your new limb and the gem imbued in its surface are capable of many astonishing things," Nar Aljahim interjected. "You will have to practice and experiment to fully discover their uses. Even in this facility's time, such prosthetic applications of the neurogem material were merely experimental."

Finn met the elemental's eyes. "Thank you," he

said.

"Some of this facility's knowledge must survive. Use the *Forging* and your new limb well. That is the only repayment I require," the elemental said.

Even as Nar Aljahim stopped speaking, a mechanical voice echoed through the chamber. "INTERIOR SECURITY BREACH. UNKNOWN CORRUPTION DETECTED IN THE EARTH MANA SECTION."

The map of the facility still floated nearby. The corrupted had made it past one of the blast doors and were now spreading into the adjacent section, scurrying toward the mana storage crystals embedded in the floor and that section's pylon chamber.

"Unfortunately, our time here has come to an end. You must leave. Now," Nar Aljahim said curtly, his body flaring to life as he stared at the screen.

The yellow-tinted blast door across the room slid open. "Take the air mana section. I have opened all of the barriers leading to the reception area. Once the scanners show that you have made it back to the entrance, I will initiate the facility's self-destruct sequence."

Finn forced himself to his feet as his group started heading for that blast door, their steps harried. He spared one last glance over his shoulder at the ancient fire elemental that towered in the center of that massive chamber, his eyes still staring at that map. There was a sadness to his flames, perhaps the way they dimmed and flickered more erratically.

It was at that moment that Finn could understand what Nar Aljahim intended to do. The fire elemental was about to lock himself inside this facility permanently, sealing himself away underground and behind layers of wards. Alone until he perished.

"Thank you. For everything," Finn said.

The fire elemental met his gaze. "Do not mourn for me, Stormbringer."

Finn's brow furrowed at that title, but he held his tongue.

"This is not the end – for you or for me," Nar Aljahim continued. "Life and death are an endless, revolving circle. We flare to life in an instant, burn brightly, and fade back into darkness… only to return again," the elemental replied solemnly. Then he turned his attention back to the map, his flaming hands darting through the air – likely bringing the facility's defenses online to attempt to stall the corrupted and buy them time to escape.

"Dad, come on! We need to go!" Julia shouted at him.

And he answered her, forcing himself to turn away from Nar Aljahim and ordering his legs to start pumping – his feet soon thudding against the dense stone floor. Only moments later, Finn darted through the yellow-tinged blast door, and the massive portal slid shut behind him, crashing into the wall and the metallic locks slamming into place with a certain finality.

Perhaps Nar Aljahim was right. Perhaps death wasn't the end. Perhaps the elemental would survive to see his mate again – to form a new star or planet. Perhaps Finn would be able to return with the heartstone someday… with Rachael by his side.

Finn clung to that *hope*, despite the kernel of doubt that lingered in his heart.

Because, in his experience, some doors – once closed – never opened again.

Chapter 29 - Ordered

Finn's feet thumped against the stone floor, his breath coming quick and short. The sound was echoed by his teammates as they sprinted alongside him. In this section of the facility, the walls were awash in yellow energy, the light fluctuating erratically as pulses of ivory light swept past at regular intervals – likely Nar Aljahim scanning the facility. They turned a corner, and a final blast door lingered ahead of them. The barrier began to slide open as soon as they crested the turn, letting out a reluctant, grinding screech of metal and stone.

As they sped through that final portal, a flash of orange light rippled along the nearby wall, and the blast door started to slide closed. The door slammed shut with a bang, followed closely by the repetitive thump, thump, thump of the locking bolts sliding into place. The group paused for a moment in the reception area as they tried to regain their breath.

That respite was short-lived.

"SELF-DESTRUCT SEQUENCE INITIATED. 60 SECONDS UNTIL DETONATION. PLEASE EVACUATE THE FACILITY IMMEDIATELY," that familiar mechanical voice chimed.

"Shit," Kyyle gasped as Julia pushed him toward the tunnel leading back to fresh air and sunlight... and hopefully out of range of Nar Aljahim's purge of the facility.

The group continued their headlong sprint, ignoring the burning sensation in their lungs and legs as they raced down the long entry hallway, leaping over and winding around the piles of rubble and metal scrap that lay along the floor. Finn winced as he suddenly remembered that Spider's vine barrier would be waiting for them at the end of the tunnel – several feet of thick vegetation blocking their exit.

He rummaged in his pack, pulling two metal orbs free.

Feels like a good time to test my new hand, he thought to himself. Under other circumstances, that would have been exciting. As it was, he just hoped the damned thing worked as well as his old flesh-and-blood fingers.

He heaved an orb down the hallway, his fingers moving as soon as the sphere left his hand. Arcane words spilled from his lips, but his legs never ceased their continuous rhythm. Fire sprang up around the ball of metal. He threw the second, and his diamond-like fingers responded, weaving through the pattern of the spell without faltering. Unable to feel the movements, Finn had to look down at the translucent limb to make sure that the fingers were actually moving. It felt strange – almost disconnected in a way – to see the limb in action but to feel... nothing.

That was going to take some getting used to.

As flames wrapped the second orb, Finn tugged up the heat rank on both spheres, maintaining the channel with each hand. For the first time in what felt like ages, he was using his *Multi-Casting*. As the metal spheres began to glow, he directed them forward, the flames just barely illuminating the overlapping lattice of thorny vines and vegetation that loomed ahead. He pinched his fingers and pulled, a coating of spikes erupting from each of the molten metal spheres. Then he dropped the heat down to heat rank level 1 and set those spiky orbs to spinning, picking up speed as they ran.

"30 SECONDS UNTIL DETONATION," that voice chimed again.

"Uh, there's sort of a wall up ahead," Julia offered in a frantic voice, glancing at Finn.

"Not for long..." he panted.

As soon as the thin line that denoted his control range met the vine-covered barrier, he launched the spheres forward, and they rocketed through the air in a blur of orange flame. His fingers urged them into a spiral pattern, the two orbs twisting around one another and grinding up the vegetation like a makeshift drill – sending bits of fleshy, charred plant matter flying in every direction and burrowing a large hole through the barrier. Sunlight soon shone through that new opening, and the group charged toward it.

They emerged from the tunnel, and Julia shoved Finn and Kyyle off to the side, pulling her shield from her back and taking up a position in front of them.

"Kyyle, build us a barrier!" Finn barked. There wasn't time to get away from the entrance to the Forge facility. So they were going to have to entrench their position.

The earth mage was already moving, ribbons of emerald energy curling around his staff and liquid stone drifting up to create a dense stone wall in front of the group. Kyyle didn't stop with just one layer. He reinforced the stone over and over again with his few remaining seconds. That wall rose from the ground and curved, the earth mage likely hoping to divert any of the flames that reached them.

Finn saw the facility self-destruct before he felt the blast.

A massive haze of orange and red energy blossomed deep within the Forge. The energy was so bright and intense that it was visible even through the dozens of intervening layers of the facility's crystal-laden walls. That inferno rushed outward rapidly, and Finn could visualize what Nar Aljahim had done – opening all of the interior blast doors at the same time and letting his fires sweep the entire facility clean of the corrupted. And with the flames went all of the remaining technology hidden within the Forge. There was more than enough fire mana to melt the walls and doors to slag and cave in portions of the facility.

However, Nar Aljahim had gone even further than that…

Finn's eyes widened as he saw six spikes of brilliant energy, the mana backflowing up the columns of crystal that stretched through the mountain. Six beams of light speared up into the sky, mixing with the river of energy that flowed through the clouds. That avalanche of power barely reacted to the newfound energy, its surface only rippling slightly. The surrounding clouds weren't so lucky, the columns sucking in the air and moisture and creating six white-hued tornadoes that quickly obscured the energy from sight.

He opened the doors to the pylon chambers, Finn realized.

Then the blast wave finally burnt through the doors guarding the reception area. Finn saw a rolling wave of fire streaking down the entrance hallway, and the ground began to shake more violently, dust billowing out of the tunnel ahead of the avalanche of flame.

"Here it comes!" he shouted.

The group hunkered down behind Kyyle's wall, Julia hovering protectively above her teammates. Fire spewed from the opening in a rolling wave of destruction that stretched at least a hundred feet out of the tunnel, molten scraps of metal and stone crashing into the nearby shrubs and vegetation. The mixture of flame and shrapnel burnt and cut into the forest surrounding the entrance to the Forge, carving a deep furrow through the vegetation. Trees were torn from the ground, their limbs and leaves burned to ash in mere moments. The flames were so hot that the center of the blaze glowed a blinding white.

The energy exploded past Kyyle's stone wall, the material shifting and cracking from the force of the blast wave. The stone only partially blunted the heat, and the group felt their skin begin to redden and blister from the nearby inferno. Yet they couldn't afford to move – not until the torrent abated. They held their position, each watching their health dip precariously in the corner of their vision.

The wave of flame soon melted the rock and crystal around the entrance to the Forge, droplets of molten stone dripping down the walls and ceiling. The structural integrity of the tunnel couldn't handle that sort of energy for long, and it soon began to crumble. The ground shook even more violently, and large cracks arced out away from the entrance. One of those long lines speared outward toward their position, threatening to destroy Kyyle's wall. Brock acted quickly, scooping up Kyyle as Julia yanked at Finn's arm, pulling them farther back from the entrance to the Forge.

With a final massive tremor, the tunnel collapsed – the combination of rock and crystal bowing and then snapping with a thunderclap that echoed off the nearby mountains. Hundreds of tons of rock crashed down into the tunnel, abruptly cutting off the stream of fire. A second blast wave of kinetic force jetted forward, carrying with it a mixture of dust, rock, and crystal. As soon as that wave escaped the tunnel, it fanned outward. That collection of shrapnel blasted apart the remaining vegetation surrounding the entrance and caused the remaining trees to bend and crack.

In the face of that oncoming avalanche, and without Kyyle's barrier to protect them, Julia whirled and raised her shield. "Get behind me!" she cried.

The surface of her shield shimmered with air mana, and then a blast of air jetted forward, cutting through the blast wave and creating a small pocket of clear air as the debris hurtled past and around the group. Julia cast *Air Blast* again, and again, using all of her shield's charges in the span of a few seconds.

And then…

The world began to calm.

The ground stopped trembling. The dust began to settle. And as they regained their view of the Forge, the group could see that Nar Aljahim had decimated the facility – ensuring no one would ever return. The entrance was destroyed. A mountain of rubble now rested where that stone portal had once stood, and a large crack radiated up the side of the mountain for hundreds of feet. Finn could only imagine the damage inside was worse. Likely, the heat had caused the interior sections of the facility to crumble, hundreds of thousands of tons of rock and stone finishing the job, and sealing the facility closed… permanently.

"Holy shit," Julia muttered, slinging her shield

over her back as she surveyed the damage with awe shining in her eyes.

As Brock helped Kyyle back to his feet, the earth mage grumbled, "Does anyone else feel like this happens to us a lot? You know? Blowing the hell out of whatever place we've just explored? I'm starting to sense a pattern is all I'm saying."

"He does have a point," Daniel chirped. "We're two for two on blowing up the dungeon as we leave. Technically, three for three if you count that column of fire in the Mage Guild when Finn received his class." A pause. "Although, I really fail to see how we're going to top this one…"

Finn let out a weak chuckle. As he surveyed the scope of the destruction, he was inclined to agree. The chances of finding some sort of super-advanced underground laboratory that housed an ancient fire elemental again seemed unlikely.

"It seems you lot know how to make an exit," a familiar voice chimed from the woods.

Finn glanced over to find Silver emerging from the ring of ruined vegetation that encircled the former facility entrance. Ash still drifted down through the air, streamers of smoke curling from the stumps that riddled the area. Her packmates circled behind her, their eyes wide as they took in the destruction before them. For once, the surly shapeshifters seemed at a loss for words. And perhaps just a bit wary of the group that had just blasted apart the side of a mountain.

Although, Finn wasn't going to point out that that had been Nar Aljahim's doing.

"We try," Finn replied. Yet he hesitated as he watched the druids, his brow furrowing in confusion. Something felt off.

Why hadn't they been closer to the entrance?

Not that he was upset that they had retreated farther into the forest – that move had likely saved their lives. But it seemed unusual from a tactical standpoint. He also noticed that their blowguns were gone – as were their packs. And Silver kept glancing furtively at the surrounding trees, some of her typical feral fire having given way to... subdued anxiety? Even the other two shapeshifters at her side looked browbeaten. With his *Mana Sight*, Finn could see a worm of fear and doubt weaving through each of their energies.

Moving discreetly, Finn dug into his pack for another two orbs, his former spheres having been lost amid the chaos. He nudged Julia with his elbow and made a quick gesture. His daughter's eyes widened almost imperceptibly, and she reached slowly for her lance. Finn held his hands behind his back, mumbling the incantation to *Imbue Fire* under his breath.

"We're glad to see that you're alive. And it appears you upheld your end of the bargain," Silver continued, watching Finn with an unwavering gaze.

"We did indeed. Although, I'll admit I was expecting a warmer reaction after we rid your territory of this potential danger," he replied slowly. His eyes were on Silver, but his attention was focused on the remaining patches of forest behind her. The ash might obscure the treeline from Kyyle and Julia, but that didn't stop him. His brow furrowed as he detected no obvious signs of mana.

Silver's hands went wide. "Well, you see, there's the thing. We've been rather preoccupied in your absence," she said, practically growling out the words.

As she finished speaking, Finn felt Julia tense beside him, and he swiftly switched to *Short-Sighted*. Nearly two dozen wraith-like figures materialized from the ash rain, weaving around the ruined trees, the trunks still smoldering. The group fully ringed the clearing around the entrance to the Forge. Dark eyes peered at them through slits in masks, covering their faces. They were robed in familiar cloth wraps, daggers held in hand. Finn also hadn't missed the fact that they had been invisible to his *Mana Sight*, which could only mean one thing...

The Khamsin.

One man strode forward out of the group, pulling

the cloth wrap from his head. Scars riddled the rough skin of his face, and stubble coated his chin – the hair a motley mixture of gray and brown. A thin cloth bandage was draped over one of his eyes, obscuring it from sight. Yet behind that barrier, Finn could see a glowing cluster of air mana.

A magical eye? he wondered. *The energy is dense. Something powerful, most likely.* It seemed Finn wasn't the only person in this world that had undergone some experimental body augmentation.

"Who are you, and what do you want?" Finn asked bluntly, although he could already anticipate the answer. His teammates were eyeing the Khamsin warily, and Finn had brought his two orbs online – the dark metal suspended behind his back, flames licking weakly at their surface as he maintained heat rank level 1. Once they engaged, he wouldn't be able to use *Short-Sighted*, but he was already highlighting the location of the Khamsin in his UI.

"My name is Thorn," the man grunted in greeting, his lone eye drifting to the bandage across Finn's face – his expression unreadable. It was safe to assume that Eldawin had communicated Finn's abilities. "I was sent at the behest of the Order."

"The Order?" Finn asked, feigning ignorance. "Sorry, I have no idea what you're talking about." Meanwhile, his mind was racing. This must be the organization that Aerys had alluded to – a splinter group of Khamsin devoted to destroying magic.

A faint smile tugged at the man's lips. "In that case, we're here at the request of *Eldawin* – a name I suspect you *will* remember."

"I do seem to recall meeting a gentleman by that name before we left the Hive. Nice guy. Just a touch of senility if I recall," Finn replied smoothly, noting the way Thorn's shoulders tensed involuntarily.

Good. Finn could use that anger right now. It seemed Eldawin had finally decided a dead prophet was more useful than a living one. And Finn and his companions were at a disadvantage. Outnumbered, surrounded, exhausted, their mana and health depleted, nowhere to run. His only play here was to cloud Thorn's judgment and hope to get the jump on him. He sensed that words alone weren't going to sway this stoic, severe man.

"And what exactly can we do for Eldawin? As you can see, it's already been a rather long day…" Finn trailed off as he waved at the destruction behind him.

"That depends on what you have to show for your efforts," Thorn answered immediately – seemingly unaffected by the destruction of the Forge and the surrounding area. "Did you recover a weapon to fight Bilel?"

Finn nodded. "Yes."

The man simply stared at him in response, as though waiting for something. "You'll forgive me if I don't take your word for that," Thorn replied. "Do you have any proof?"

"And why the hell should we prove anything to you?" Julia snapped. "You threaten the Seer's prophet, imprison our allies, and now stand here, barking orders at us?"

Thorn smirked at Julia. "Trust me, if it were up to me, there would be far less talking. However, Eldawin has always been a pragmatist. My orders are clear. If you managed to recover a weapon to fight Bilel, then we're to calmly escort you back to the Hive. If not, well… it will be unfortunate that the prophet was unable to survive his journey. Perhaps our people were too quick to assume that Finn had the Seer's blessing, after all."

"I'd love to see you try and take me out," Julia said ominously, taking a step forward.

Thorn's figure blurred, the man flashing forward with incredible speed.

One moment, he stood beside Silver, and the next, he was in front of Julia. Despite his speed, Julia was still able to react, anticipating his movement and her lance telescoping outward toward the man's head. However,

Finn saw Thorn's eye flash with a pulse of yellow light, and he dipped under the blow smoothly – almost like he had seen it coming. An instant later, he held a blade to Julia's throat. She swallowed hard, glaring at him above the dagger.

Finn grimaced. That eye was trouble. There were only so many applications of air mana – particularly for a permanent ocular augmentation. The man's reflexes and form were incredible, but that move spoke of foreknowledge. Finn's guess was that the eye let him glimpse a few seconds into the future. Although, he was also well acquainted with the game's augmentation system. They were powerful, but they also came with *limitations*.

You can't anticipate what you can't see coming.

Finn's fingers twitched, and his two molten orbs compressed into two thin spikes before slithering into the ground surreptitiously. Kyyle caught sight of the movement and took a careful step forward to help cover for him.

"Stay where you are," Thorn snapped, that lone eye shifting to Kyyle. Then his attention drifted back to Julia. "So, what were you saying again?" Thorn demanded of Julia, his voice perfectly neutral and his blade not wavering an inch.

"I suggest you take a fucking step back," Finn said forcefully, his mana flaring, heating the metal embedded in his eyes.

Thorn glanced at him, that amber gem shining again. "Or what? Please, give me an excuse to put the so-called Prophet in the ground. I'd like nothing better than to rid this world of another mage, particularly one that has allied himself with the Crone."

Finn just smiled grimly in response. "Says the man with a magical eye," he retorted. "If you ask me, the hypocrisy is a little hard to swallow."

Thorn's good eye widened slightly, and he let out a low growl. But Finn's fingers twitched behind his back, and two lances of metal rocketed from the ground. Within less than a second, the blades were hovering at the back of Thorn's neck. The man froze, pressing his blade a little more forcefully against Julia's neck.

"Didn't see that coming, did you, asshole?" Finn asked.

Thorn grunted. "I still have a blade against your daughter's neck."

"Just kill him," Julia croaked, her eyes never leaving Thorn's face.

"See? No fear. That's the thing about being a traveler. We respawn," Finn said.

A pause and Finn continued, "Now, how about we have a calm conversation, absent the posturing. We recovered the weapon we were looking for. We have a way to fight Bilel and defend the guilds against the relic he wields. If you were telling the truth, then that means you're obligated to return us to the Hive."

"There's still the matter of proof," Thorn bit out.

"Unfortunately, you lack the ability to confirm what I'm saying," Finn replied. "You're going to have to accept my claim on *faith*."

Thorn stared at him for a few seconds longer. Then he seemed to reach a decision, withdrawing his blade. "You're different than the other travelers," he said, grudging respect entering his voice as that lone eye watched Finn. "I may even regret the moment the Emir's head rolls, and the Order no longer has a use for you."

"I suspect I will too," Finn replied under his breath. Then he let out a sigh and withdrew his own blades, keeping the weapons floating beside him. He doubted he'd get the jump on Thorn twice, but they were more for show than anything else.

"Now," Finn said, glancing at Silver and her pack, "Free the druids. They have no stake in our conflict with the Emir."

Thorn frowned, eyeing Silver and her group. "This woman and her kind were not part of my orders – yet they still seem to use magic. Of a sort anyway. I saw this one manipulating the plants, and these three appear to be some sort of shifter," he said, eyeing the group distastefully.

Finn could see Silver's hands clench, and her gaze shifted furtively to her packmates. He didn't want a conflict here – not only because the druids had helped them. Thorn might use the resulting chaos as an excuse to kill Finn and his companions. The man was already clearly unhappy with his instructions. And despite Finn's cavalier attitude, he most definitely did not want to risk a respawn if he didn't have to.

"This woman and her pack helped your so-called Order," Finn said, Thorn's gaze whipping back to his face. "They assisted us in destroying that facility," he said, waving over his shoulder. "The Forge was once used to craft powerful magical tools and weapons. Now that technology can no longer harm anyone – Silver's people or the Khamsin."

Thorn eyed the destruction looming behind Finn, his brow furrowed as he mulled on Finn's words. "Fine. So be it." He waved at his men, and they pulled away from the druids.

Silver shot Finn a questioning glance. "Go. Now. We won't bother you or your people again. Do not venture farther north into the desert sands," Finn said curtly.

The woman met Finn's gaze one last time, and he saw appreciation shining in her eyes – for once overshadowing the suspicious glare that seemed to be her default. Then she nodded and waved at her group. They started for the tree line, and, within moments, had disappeared. Finn could only hope that their camp was well hidden. He couldn't be certain whether their type of magic truly fell within the Order's purview, but they hadn't done anything to justify an attack by Eldawin and his lackeys.

Finn breathed a mental sigh of relief. Although, judging from the severe expression on Thorn's face and the way the man glared at Finn's glowing metal orbs, he doubted that his group was entirely out of the woods.

"Now, how about that escort back to the Hive?"

Finn said, approaching the Khamsin and meeting Thorn's gaze evenly.

As Finn neared, Thorn darted forward in a flash of movement. In an instant, he was standing beside Finn, his hand snatching one of the molten lances from the air. As Finn looked on, he saw the fire leak away from the metal – the mana drained in mere seconds – which left Thorn holding plain metal lances. His eyes never left Finn's as he crumpled that dark metal barehanded and then dropped the slag, the metal striking the ground with a dull thud.

Finn noticed two things in that moment.

Thorn's hands were completely unharmed by either the flame or the jagged metal.

And deep fingerprints had been embedded in the slag resting along the ground.

Which led to one obvious conclusion. This man was not to be fucked with. Finn might have gotten the jump on him, but Thorn had never truly been at his mercy.

"Good. I see you understand your situation. You live by my will alone. Remember that," Thorn snapped. Then he simply turned away from Finn. "Come along," he called over his shoulder. "We have a long way to travel."

As he strode away, Julia and Kyyle glanced at Finn. He could see the same thought reflected on their faces. *Who the hell was this man?*

Finn just shrugged, grinding his teeth. It seemed they had little choice but to follow Thorn's instructions – at least for now. The only silver lining was that with Thorn and his men escorting them, they were likely at less risk of getting attacked by the native wildlife or ambushed by Bilel's soldiers out among the sands. Assuming, of course, that Thorn didn't change his mind and decide to crush their skulls bare-handed.

"You know, the Forge is starting to look rather pleasant," Kyyle muttered, staring wistfully back at the ruined entrance to the facility.

"You're right. At least the corrupted always attacked us head-on instead of trying to stab us in the back," Julia offered in agreement.

Finn just grunted noncommittally as his companions set off after Thorn. They weren't even back at the Hive yet, and already they were neck-deep in infighting and political intrigue. And it would likely only get worse from here. Despite how far they had come, it seemed they still had a long way to go. But they had no choice but to keep moving forward.

His gaze shifted back to the ruined entrance to the Forge behind him – the stone and crystal now warped beyond recognition. He hadn't forgotten what they were fighting for or the price they had paid to make it this far.

He wasn't going to let anything – or anyone – stand in his way.

"I'm coming for you, Rachael," Finn said softly.

Then he followed his companions, ashen rain drifting down around him.

Chapter 30 - Handy

The beetle rocked and swayed below Finn as it coasted up one dune and back down another, leaving behind a shallow wake of sand. Now outside the forest that coated the southern mountain range, there was no longer anything to block the harsh sunlight that beat down upon the sand – bringing with it a blistering heat. Finn hadn't thought he'd miss either the beetles or the harsh sun, and yet here he was. After the wet and cold of the mountain slopes and dusty darkness of the Forge, it was – almost – a welcome relief.

A relief that was undermined somewhat by the group of dark insects that clustered around Finn and his companions. Thorn and this fringe faction of Khamsin – the *Order* they called themselves – had kept a watchful eye on their team since they left the facility. In Thorn's case, that hidden yellow gem gleamed, constantly focused on the group and his attention never wavering. Finn had been testing his abilities as they rode – occasionally reaching for a weapon or his bag and noting Thorn's reaction. He always seemed to know when Finn was making a hostile move... which lent some credibility to Finn's earlier guess.

And now he desperately wanted to examine that eye.

While *Mana Sight* was useful, Finn's mind was already working through the possibilities of being able to glimpse a few seconds into the future. Although, he suspected it would be a cold day in Lahab before Thorn permitted him to inspect the gem. He had only grudgingly allowed them to live, and after that little *demonstration* outside the Forge, Finn had no doubt that Thorn could follow through on his threats.

Brock and Daniel floated along beside the group, unperturbed by their rapid speed. Finn had initially been skeptical that Brock could keep up with the beetles. But it seemed that whatever gravitational spell that kept the rocks of his body aloft was more powerful than Finn had anticipated.

Or perhaps there was another explanation.

Even now, Finn could see a thin line of emerald energy flowing between Brock and Kyyle, connecting them by way of the Najima that was now embedded in the elemental's core. Perhaps the earth elemental's mana had been bolstered by the *Forging*, or he was slowly draining mana along the tether that connected him to Kyyle – much like how Bilel's staff drained energy from the hellhounds. Although, if that was the case, then the drain wasn't obvious. Kyyle's mana pool didn't seem to be depleting, and the mage was busy tapping away at his in-game console, occasionally glancing at Brock's burly form. Finn could only guess that he was examining his newfound bond and taking notes.

As that thought crossed his mind, he glanced down at his new hand. The surface was translucent, fire curling within the depths of his hand and fingers – a mesmerizing and slightly disturbing sight to behold, but one that came with a merciful absence of pain. The aching burn that had lingered in the stump since his encounter with Bilel had vanished, and his *Mana Sight* showed no trace of infection – not even the telltale spiral of fiery energy that once drifted off toward the northeast – toward Lahab.

He stretched his newfound fingers experimentally. He expected he would be casting that same strange spell – the *Forging* – and creating hundreds of new bonds once he returned to the Hive. He could already anticipate pushback from the merchants, fighters, and mages when he explained that they would be bonding part of their soul to an inorganic object.

His lips curled into a frown. Not that he could really blame them.

Finn wasn't even certain that he fully understood that bond himself. There hadn't been time to ponder on it or ask questions when they had confronted the fire elemental, and he had discovered that while he could remember *how* to cast the spell – the gestures and words –

the *why* and the *how* were more unclear.

How had Nar Aljahim known that spell? What exactly had it done? Sever and remove his Najima, that was clear. But were there rules to this bond? What happened if he damaged his hand? Did it repair using his natural health regeneration? A portion of the mana regeneration that he had lost? The ancient fire elemental had spoken about the bond growing and evolving over time, but those were vague words. What did that mean exactly?

Even as those questions circled his mind, Finn saw the fires in his new hand surge, rippling and expanding within the crystal as they echoed his simmering curiosity. Finn was accustomed to feeling his mana pulse and throb through his body in these moments, but *seeing* it felt different somehow.

A grimace tugged at his lips. The bottom line was that while he might be content with his decision – especially given the time constraints, the loss of his arm, and the magical infection caused by Bilel's staff – Finn suspected the guildsmen would be more circumspect about undergoing the *Forging*. They would likely pose many of these questions.

And Finn would need to be able to supply answers.

Which meant he needed to learn as much as he could before they arrived at the Hive.

As a starting point, he needed to check his notifications. With a swipe of his hand, a long list of notices suddenly popped up before him, creating a tumbling cascade of semi-translucent windows.

x8 Level Up!
You have (130) undistributed stat points.

x2 Spell Rank Up: Mana Absorption
Skill Level: Intermediate Level 7
Cost: 65% of mana drained as health damage.
Effect 1: The caster can absorb ambient fire mana,

adding the energy to their total mana pool.

Effect 2: Increased absorption range, sensitivity, and area of effect.

x2 Spell Rank Up: Molten Beam
Skill Level: Beginner Level 6
Cost: 125 Mana/second. Must be channeled.
Effect 1: Fires a beam of molten energy dealing damage equal to 150 + (INT x 30%).

x3 Skill Rank Up: Mana Sight
Skill Level: Intermediate Level 8
Cost: Permanently reduces your mana regeneration by 20 mana/second. You are now blind to regular spectrums of light.
Effect 1: Ability to view ambient mana. Current vision is [good].
Effect 2: Ability to isolate mana types. Currently limited to [fire/earth/air/light].

x2 Skill Rank Up: Concentration
Skill Level: Intermediate Level 2
Effect 1: Ability to split your focus between [2] tasks.
Effect 2: Improved ability to ignore pain or disruptions.

x1 Skill Rank Up: Multi-Casting
Skill Level: Intermediate Level 4
Effect 1: -43.0% casting speed on the second spell.
Effect 2: -14% reduced channeling cost.

Quest Completed: Forging Ahead

You've been busy!

You and your companions have explored the ancient facility known as the Forge, recovered an attendant, destroyed a former Supervisor, and met the ancient fire

---

elemental that resides at the heart of the Forge.

However, your arrival in the Forge unleashed the corrupted that lingered within its halls, threatening the other sections of the facility. To quell the corruption, Nar Aljahim was forced to initiate the facility's self-destruct... but not before he granted you one last parting gift – a spell capable of fusing a person's Najima with another object, which offers protection against the effects of Bilel's relic.

In the process, the ancient fire elemental forged a bond between you and a new hand that he created with the neurogem material, curing the magical infection that Bilel's relic created in the process. You are now insulated against the draining effect of Bilel's relic. The infection has been excised. And the full use of your hand has been restored. Now you must work to better understand this bond that has been forged, and quickly.

Who knows... it might even come in handy!

P.S. – We're extremely sorry for the bad pun. The subroutine responsible for generating these prompts has been deleted. You could even say we have a "handle" on the situation. Okay, that was the last one... we promise.

Finn's skimmed the quest notification. The text confirmed much of what he already knew. The infection had been cured, and their escape from the facility had showcased that his new limb was capable of *Multi-Casting*. Although, that made him recall the stat loss from the infection, and he quickly pulled up his Character Status, breathing a sigh of relief as he saw that his stats were no longer being artificially suppressed.

Although, it was also clear that the hand had taken a large toll. His total mana pool and mana regeneration had both been reduced by a sixth – reducing his mana from roughly 3,200 to 2,700 and his regeneration per second from roughly 58 to 49. It also appeared that the effect scaled to his total mana – at least when he double-checked the math by removing and then replacing some of the jewelry that increased his *Intelligence.*

Although, that begged another question.

Like how the hell was he going to spend his stockpile of stat points?

He rubbed at his chin for a moment and then began allocating points. He placed 35 points into *Vitality* to bring himself up to an even 200. 20 points went into each of *Dexterity* and *Endurance* – because he'd found agility, balance, and stamina to be quite useful in the middle of a fight. And the remainder of his points went toward *Intelligence*, which had better synergy and scaling than *Willpower* given that it increased his mana, regeneration, and scaled with many of his damage-oriented spells.

Then Finn checked his stats once more.

Character Status			
Name:	Finn	**Gender:**	Male
Level:	118	**Class:**	Fire Mage
Race:	Human	**Alignment:**	Lawful-Neutral
Fame:	1800	**Infamy:**	0
Health:	2585	**H-Regen/Sec:**	9.80
Mana:	3280	**M-Regen/Sec:**	58.85
Stamina:	1785	**S-Regen/Sec:**	12.00
Str:	47	**Dex:**	120
Vit:	200	**End:**	120
Int:	489	**Will:**	30

Affinities			
Dark:	4%	**Light:**	11%
Fire:	53%	**Water:**	5%
Air:	3%	**Earth:**	13%

Despite the loss of some mana and regeneration from the augmentation of his eyes and the bond with his new hand, his stats were looking respectable. The additional points in *Intelligence* had also brought him back to roughly the same mana regeneration.

Which just left his new hand.

Finn's gaze drifted down the limb once more. With a thought, he inspected it.

Translucent Flame (Crafted by Nar Aljahim)
This hand has been built entirely of the so-called neurogem material that you discovered within the depths of the Forge and was crafted by an ancient fire elemental. A Focusing Prism has been set in the base of the hand, although its use is currently unknown. Experimentation may be required to unlock its ability.
Quality: A
Level: 1
Health: 500
(Soulbound)

Adaptable Limb
This limb is composed of a crystal that exhibits organic properties, allowing the security mechs of the Forge to self-repair and incorporate additional parts or devices. The material's original properties have been preserved in their new form, allowing the user to alter the limb's structure at will. Practice will be required to master this ability.
Skill Level: Beginner Level 1
Cost: 500 Mana
Effect: Allows the caster to make [simple]

modifications to the limb.

Soulforged Item (Bonded by Nar Aljahim)

This item has been imbued with the Najima of the traveler named Finn. The limb's health is counted separately from the traveler's regular health pool and will scale as the item levels. Damage is repaired using the 1/6 of the user's mana regeneration (currently 9.81 per second). Destruction of the limb will result in the user's death. However, the limb will regenerate upon respawn.

Holy shit, Finn thought to himself.

He wasn't certain what he had been expecting, but it hadn't been this. It was clear that the game considered the limb to be an item from the prompt, but it was unlike any other weapon or piece of armor that Finn had encountered. For one, it had its own level and health. The prompt also seemed to imply that the limb could gain experience and level up, likely improving its health – and possibly providing other bonuses? He guessed that the limb was also leeching a portion of his experience now – although, he'd need to test that eventually.

In short, the hand would continue to scale in power along with Finn, which was good, since it was sort of fused to his left arm.

The reference to the *Focusing Prism* in the item description was also unusual. His gaze centered on that gem. The crystal was embedded on the back of the hand, the surface almost indistinguishable from the translucent material around it. The prompt implied that the gem was capable of doing *something*. Although its purpose wasn't obvious.

With a wary glance at Thorn, Finn decided to put a pin in that. He didn't want to give the man an excuse to kill him by flinging spells around. Perhaps once he was back inside the Hive and safely out of reach of a trigger-happy band of Khamsin zealots, he could learn more.

His attention shifted to the description for *Adaptable Limb*. The hand provided a new spell, replete with its own levels and ranking. That was a first. Other item-based skills like his crown or Julia's new shield typically had a one-off skill – meaning that it wouldn't continue to scale up in damage or strength. But this was different. Presumably, Finn could become more adept at modifying the hand over time.

Speaking of which, how exactly did he alter the hand? Like most things he'd encountered inside of AO, the description hadn't come with an instruction manual.

Could I turn the crystal into a short sword, much like the blade I fused to my stump? Finn was visualizing that blade in his head – the way it joined his arm at the base of his elbow before tapering down into a needle-like point.

As that image appeared in his mind's eye, Finn felt a strange tickling sensation along the joint between his tanned skin and the new limb – the first telltale sign of feeling since Nar Aljahim had fused the hand to his arm. He looked down to see the crystal flare brightly, his fire surging through the limb until it shone with a brilliant orange light. His eyes widened, and Finn pulled the sleeve of his robe further up his arm – sparing a tentative look at the nearby Khamsin to see if they had noticed the flash of energy. However, their eyes were still on the desert around them, and Thorn didn't appear to have noticed the brief flicker of mana.

Finn breathed a sigh of relief, then gingerly pulled back on his sleeve.

A translucent crystal blade now speared from his arm, a near-perfect replica of the former dark metal sword. "Okay, now that's cool," he murmured.

He pictured the image of a normal hand, and the crystal flashed again. Except Finn was prepared this time, and he draped his sleeve back across the crystal. A few seconds later, his hand had returned to normal, and he wiggled his fingers experimentally.

Already, a dozen ideas were drifting through his head. What sort of instruments could he create with this new limb? Tools for any task? Could he lengthen the limb? How durable was the crystal? For example, it had health, but would it deplete that health if he stabbed something with the crystal blade? Much like the durability on a standard item? It was filled with fire mana, so did that mean it was resistant to heat?

He immediately resolved to practice with the limb as much as possible – the ride back to the underground Khamsin city would give him ample opportunity to do so. Once he found some downtime and privacy, maybe he could run a few more complex experiments to discover the answers to his many, many questions. Meanwhile, the fire within the limb had flared to a bright glow as his curiosity and excitement grew.

Although, that enthusiasm was short-lived.

Finn's mount pulled up sharply, rotating and skidding to a halt in a shower of sand. He could see that the others around him had also stopped, Thorn's fist raised high in the air. They were clumped up at the top of a towering dune, the shifting hillside providing a decent vantage of the surrounding plains of yellow and beige.

"What is it? Why are we stopping?" Kyyle asked, looking a bit shaken – having nearly fallen from his beetle. He had likely been more focused on examining his bond with Brock than on their journey.

Thorn gave the mage a piercing look. "You can see that for yourself," he replied, waving toward the northwest.

At first, Finn wasn't certain what the problem was. There were just a few clouds hovering on the horizon… yet he froze at that thought. There shouldn't be *clouds* in the desert. He couldn't remember the last time he had seen the hazy white pillows of vapor. Clouds required evaporated moisture – which was in incredibly short supply out here among the sands.

With a thought, Finn switched to his *Mana Sight*, and his eyes widened in shock. Not only were there clouds spiraling on the horizon, but he could see an ominous orange glow hovering dead center in the middle of that cloud cover – the fiery energy spearing up into the sky. That was fire mana. A *lot* of fire mana. That might also explain the clouds – possibly the heat had flash evaporated any nearby moisture and created a significant fluctuation in air pressure – thus, clouds in the desert.

"What exactly am I looking at?" Julia murmured, watching the spiraling clouds.

Although, the answer was obvious – at least to Finn.

"Lahab," he answered softly.

Julia shot him a questioning glance. "My guess is that the Emir has begun converting the rest of the city," Finn explained. "That's the only thing that could create those clouds – a huge uptick in ambient fire mana. Maybe the heat of a few thousand hellhounds…"

"I hope the guilds made it out in time," Kyyle said, his mouth curled in a frown.

Thorn's lone eye snapped to Finn. "For your sake, I hope so too." With that dire statement, he clicked at his mount, and the beetle's bulky body lurched forward again.

"What the hell is that supposed to mean?" Julia groused, her eyes following Thorn.

"If the guilds didn't make it out of Lahab, then there's not much use for the *Forging* spell… or a prophet," Finn said, the remainder of his excitement at discovering his newfound limb fading in the face of the harsh reality laid out before them. And even if they had made it free of Thorn's grasp, they still had to contend with a demon king wielding a god's relic and an army of hellhounds at his back.

He could see the same realization reflected on Julia's and Kyyle's faces. In the pinched line of Julia's mouth. In the tension in her shoulders. In the way that Kyyle clutched his staff instinctually, and in Brock's own response to that anxiety as he hovered beside Kyyle protectively. Even Daniel's form flickered erratically as they stared at the city in the distance.

There was nothing left to say.

Finn turned his beetle with a short clicking sound

and a nudge of his knees, and soon they were traveling again, gliding through the sands. His fingers rubbed at his left elbow as they traveled – the action purely habit at this point – and his eyes stayed focused on those strange spiraling clouds in the distance.

It seemed he wouldn't have much time to experiment with his newfound abilities after all. Which meant he needed to take advantage of what time he did have to practice and grow stronger. His gaze drifted down to his hand. With a thought, he transformed the limb and then reverted it back to a normal hand – the conversion just a touch faster this time.

Then he began the process again.

And again.

And again.

He just had to hope it would be enough.

Chapter 31 - Bustling

When the rocky pillars of the Hive eventually came into sight, Finn wasn't certain how to feel. Those stone columns were innocuous at first glance, just a few dozen straight towers of rock that broke the flatness and curves of the dunes. They marked one of the many rocky islands that dotted the desert. An outside observer would have never guessed what lay beneath. And yet those simple columns represented a harsh reality, and a difficult series of questions.

Had Abbad managed to help the guilds escape Lahab?

Had they made progress in gearing their soldiers for the war with Bilel?

Had Aerys managed to bring the Khamsin under a single banner?

As the group slid to a halt, the bulky black beetles sent up a jet of sand as they shifted to the side and used the friction to slow their momentum. Finn watched Thorn hop down from his mount. There was also another more pressing question that demanded his attention.

Where did Eldawin and the Order plan to go from here?

Finn stepped down from his mount, his feet thudding against the dense stone. If Thorn decided to kill them here, at least they would be on solid ground. He'd become more accustomed to the beetles, but they still weren't his preferred mode of transportation. Julia and Kyyle followed him, while Brock's rocky body hovered protectively beside the earth mage, and Daniel lingered at Finn's shoulder.

Walking farther inland, Thorn left his men to watch the group, their eyes peering at Finn and the others above their cloth masks. The dark beetles still encircled them, and the Khamsin sat atop the insects, not bothering to dismount. Their eyes followed the group's movements, and their hands didn't rest far from their weapons.

Finn's fingers dug into his pack, curling around one of his metal orbs. He saw a similar tension echoed by his teammates. Kyyle's right hand twitched, as though he was suppressing the urge to cast, and Julia had pulled her shield from her back, making a pretense of checking and stowing her gear. But her attention was on the men that hovered around them.

Thorn made a beeline for one of the pillars, and Finn soon discovered why. Another of the Khamsin seemed to materialize out of the stone itself – his wraps allowing him to blend in so seamlessly that Finn hadn't noticed him with his *Short-Sighted* active. He spoke with Thorn in a hushed voice, and the one-eyed man nodded.

Then he gestured over his shoulder, waving at Finn and his companions to approach.

Finn let out a breath he hadn't realized he was holding.

It seemed they had been given another pass.

"If we live through this and manage to defeat Bilel, remind me that we have a score to settle with these Order assholes," Julia muttered under her breath as they strode toward Thorn. The Khamsin scout effortlessly disappeared back among the rocks.

"What? You don't enjoy a rogue faction of our allies secretly pulling the strings? Yet again..." Kyyle said with a soft laugh. "Welcome to Lahab!" He swept his arms wide in a poor imitation of Nefreet's original introduction back in that first starting courtyard.

Finn just shook his head. That seemed an age ago now. They had known so little back then. About this game. About this world. And they had been forced to learn fast. They had endured more in just a few short weeks in-game than he had ever expected. He was beginning to wonder if it might have been easier to bury his head in the sand.

"It seems that many of the guild members managed to escape Lahab successfully," Thorn reported, a note of irritation creeping into his voice as that lone eye centered on Finn's face. "Which means that we shall see whether you've told the truth about this *Forging*."

"I did," Finn answered curtly. "Although, I suspect you'll get plenty of opportunity to see it in action soon. All the guildsmen, as well as the Khamsin who haven't undergone the Purge, will need to be *Forged* to an object. That process will likely take days."

Thorn let out a snort. "I won't be around to witness that." He met Finn's eyes. "But we will have others watching. You're never alone among the sands. Remember that." With that dire statement, he waved at his men, and they shifted in their saddles, the beetles pushing back off the rocky island and onto the desert sands.

"Leaving already? Oh, no... How will we survive without your sparkling personality?" Julia drawled, earning a huff of amusement from Kyyle.

Thorn just ignored them, his lone eye centering once more on Finn. "Good luck, *prophet*," he barked, a trace of sarcasm lacing his voice.

Finn raised an eyebrow. "And here I thought you wouldn't be rooting for me to succeed. Not with your vendetta against magic."

"On the contrary, while I may not agree with Eldawin's approach, I see the merits of his strategy. If you succeed, then a demon dies, and our people are free to roam the sands unimpeded – including the members of the Order." A pause. "And if you fail... well, then the Crone's avatar will be dead, but you'll likely have weakened Bilel.

"I believe your people refer to this as a *win-win* situation," he remarked.

Without another word, Thorn turned on his heel and marched back to his beetle, swiftly mounting the insect and gesturing toward the sands. The group of Khamsin immediately began to coast across the dunes, their dark forms growing smaller as they raced away from the Hive, which left Finn and his companions watching them, their expressions grim and conflicted.

"He's just a ray of sunshine," Julia muttered.

"At least he's direct," Kyyle offered, rubbing at his

eyes. "I prefer that to the political bullshit and two-faced conversations we likely have waiting for us."

This earned him a grunt of agreement from Julia.

For his part, Finn found no humor in their situation and little solace in Thorn's blunt logic. It wasn't the immediate conflict that troubled him – at least, not entirely – but the long-term implications of Thorn's words. His most recent conversation with the Seer was still fresh in his mind. If Finn succeeded, Rachael would become part of this world. And Eldawin was already planning ahead. If they were successful in defeating Bilel, that wily older Khamsin likely wouldn't have much use for them. Which meant he would ultimately be a threat not just to Finn and his companions, but to Rachael.

He'd need to ponder on how to deal with that problem.

But in the meantime, he had a few more immediate issues to tackle.

"Come on," Finn said, waving at his teammates. "Let's see if we can find Aerys. I'm sure we have much to catch up on." His teammates nodded, and the group started off toward the hidden entrance to the Khamsin city.

*   *   *

In contrast to their last visit, the Hive was now bustling with activity.

Khamsin were crammed into the narrow tunnels and halls of the underground city, each man, woman, and child walking with purpose and focus. The women and children carried heavy baskets of ore, heading for the surface where beetles waited to be loaded with the supplies. Finn could only assume that they were planning to transport those materials to the guild colony. The merchants could then repurpose the ore into weapons and armor.

And many more people were heading in the opposite direction, lugging baskets of food and bundles of equipment down into the depths of the Hive – supplies to feed a hungry army and equip them. Finn guessed that the Khamsin's fighters were garrisoned deep within the depths of the Hive, likely training with their newfound equipment in pits such as the one where they had first tested Finn.

It seemed Aerys had done a good job of marshaling her people.

Although, their presence didn't go unnoticed.

Even without the flaming crown atop his brow, the telltale bandage wrapping his eyes and his crystalline hand – his fingers aglow with firelight – were dead giveaways. And Brock wasn't exactly inconspicuous. The earth elemental barely managed to squeeze into the tight quarters of the tunnel, occasionally shifting and repositioning the rocks of his body to allow the Khamsin to pass, pressing himself nearly flat in the process.

The group soon entered the primary chamber of the Hive, the latticework of connecting walkways appearing once again. A small crowd followed in their wake. They swarmed around the group, hands plucking at their clothing. Many of the Khamsin crowded around Julia specifically, admiring her dark metal armor and glimmering weapons. Although, the crowd edged nervously around Brock, eyeing him suspiciously, which left Kyyle relatively free from the oppressive attention of the desert folk.

Despite their interest in his companions, many, many more of those dark eyes were focused on Finn. They were filled with hope. Longing. Suppressed anger. Desperation. And with their newfound popularity came the familiar hushed whispers, rhythmically reciting the same words over and over again like a mantra. As though by saying that phrase, they were casting a spell that would defeat Bilel and end their exile, leaving no need for the war that was coming.

Najmat Alhidad. Najmat Alhidad. Najmat Alhidad.

"Ahh, there you are," Aerys said, her guards parting the sea of humanity and a group of attendants following in her wake. Her men swiftly created a protective pocket for the group. "My apologies. Our scouts didn't report that you were coming. Or perhaps it got lost in the chaos of everything else that's going on," she amended, waving at the hundreds of bodies crammed into the central chamber.

Finn saw that Julia was about to make a snide remark and placed a staying hand on her arm, his daughter biting back her response and shooting him an exasperated look. There was no sense in bringing up Thorn and Eldawin's involvement. He suspected they had plenty to deal with without creating additional tensions among the Khamsin.

"It's fine," Finn replied calmly. "Could we find somewhere more private to speak? We have much to tell you, and I'd like to get a sense of how things have been going here in our absence."

"Of course," Aerys replied with a curt nod. "Follow me."

With that, she set off deeper into the Hive. Continuing to shield them, her guards created a barrier between their group and the Khamsin that thronged the halls.

"It seems like there are more people here," Finn observed as they walked.

"Indeed, there are," Aerys replied over her shoulder. "I sent runners to the other Khamsin colonies – calling them to fight under a single banner." A pause and a wince. "Not all responded to the call to arms. They were content to see how this battle played out without placing themselves at risk. However, most of our people answered the call," she offered, waving at the Khamsin around them.

"We're nearly at the capacity of the Hive, and we've been forced to accept some... *assistance* from Abbad's earth mages to expand the tunnels to accommodate all of these additional bodies and form more training pits." Aerys waved at a woman as she passed the group, a basket of food supplies held in her hands. "This city also wasn't designed to accommodate this many hungry mouths, and so we're relying on the water mages to accelerate the growth of new crops. Mostly tasteless algae, but it's sufficient for now."

She glanced at Finn as they rounded a corner, her voice filled with frustration as she continued, "Although, I'm certain this *aid* will eventually come with a cost. The guild representatives have already seemed to forget what our people have done to help them escape Lahab and establish a new base camp. They've been complaining that the flow of supplies and services is too lopsided – our people only able to offer the raw ore they mine from the tunnels below us."

A sigh, and then, "I can only hope your trip was successful?"

"Yes..." He trailed off as they rounded another corner, and a meeting room came into view – several familiar figures already occupying the chamber. "Although, it may be best if I explained it once for the whole group," he finished.

"Abbad, it's good to see you again," Finn said with a small smile, grasping the librarian's hand as he approached.

The man looked more weathered than when they had left, dark circles hanging under his eyes. But he was alive. His gaze drifted to the earth elemental hovering beside Kyyle, his brow furrowing, and a quizzical expression briefly flitted across his face.

But his attention soon snapped back to Finn. "It is good to see you as well," Abbad replied with a bow of his head.

"Yeah, yeah, we're all still alive. It's fantastic," Kalisha drawled sarcastically from nearby, tapping her foot impatiently. "But if we could skip the pleasantries, that would be ideal. There's work to be done and little time to do it." Malik stood beside her, the fighter's expression stoic as always.

"It's good to see you too," Finn replied with a raised eyebrow. "Although, I wasn't expecting you and Malik to be here now that the guilds have relocated. Are your guild leaders not available?"

She frowned and opened her mouth to reply, but Malik beat her to the punch. "There's too much work for a single person. Our leadership is already stretched thin, addressing living accommodations, food production, equipment production, and training for the upcoming war. The guild leaders decided that we were best suited to continue acting as liaisons between the guilds and the Khamsin."

"They have also already been to the Hive... which means it would be a liability to release them," Aerys interjected. "It was safer to keep them here and allow them to use Abbad to communicate with the guilds remotely."

"What she means is that we already have such a wonderful rapport," Kalisha said with a wink at Finn. "Now... down to business?"

Finn nodded but hesitated as he saw the Khamsin guards ringing the room. His recent encounter with Thorn was still fresh in his mind. It seemed news traveled quickly among the desert folk, and they couldn't be certain which of the Khamsin were feeding information to Eldawin and the Order. He was going to need to be more circumspect from this point forward.

He waved at the guards. "There's no need for security here," he said. "You are dismissed." He saw that Aerys was about to object, but Finn shut her down quickly. "What we will need to discuss should be kept among this group only." She hesitated, but eventually nodded and waved at the guards, who quickly exited the room.

Finn made a gesture at Kyyle, and the earth mage picked up on his instructions, swiftly sealing the entrance with a barrier of sandstone, thickening the walls. Another brief spell and a table rose from the center of the room, ringed by simple stone chairs.

"And could you please soundproof the room?" Finn asked Abbad. The librarian cocked his head quizzically but complied. His fingers glowed a soft yellow, and a rippling sheen of amber energy soon coated the walls.

As the group settled, Finn's gaze drifted across each of them. "Okay, let's start with our journey to the Forge. In short, we were able to locate and access the facility, and we recovered some of the tech stored inside." He gestured at Brock's form as an example.

"Which includes recovering a weapon to fight Bilel... at least, of a sort," Finn continued, noting relief sweep across nearly every face in the room. "I am now able to bond a person's Najima to an inanimate object. We have it on good authority that this will insulate that person from the effects of Bilel's relic."

"But you don't know for certain?" Abbad asked, his brow furrowed.

Finn cocked his head. "Have we tested it against the relic directly? Of course not. However, I underwent the *Forging* myself..." He hesitated, glancing at Julia and Kyyle and weighing whether to bring up Nar Aljahim. After their encounter with Thorn, it was probably best to downplay exactly how he'd learned the *Forging*. If word spread, the Order might use that information to create yet another problem.

Regardless, Finn had no reason to doubt the elemental. Nar Aljahim had certainly seemed trustworthy – and knowledgeable. While the *Forging* wasn't responsible for curing the magical infection, the fact that the elemental had managed the feat lent him some credibility. Oh, and then there was the fact that he had saved their lives...

"The process also cured the magical corruption that has lingered in my Najima since our encounter in the throne room," Finn hedged. Raising his crystalline hand, he pulled back at the sleeve of his robes to show the group the fires flickering within his hand.

Kalisha's eyes widened as she caught sight of his new arm, the merchant leaning forward excitedly. "That seems like persuasive evidence," she offered.

"Indeed, it does..." Abbad replied, staring at Finn's hand. With his *Mana Sight*, Finn could see his energy fluctuate for a moment.

"*His hand awash in flame, he shall purge the sands of corruption,*" Aerys murmured.

Finn's eyes darted to her face. The Khamsin leader was staring at his hand, and a frown curled her lips. Was that another prophecy? It certainly seemed to strike close to home, which meant that he was still treading the well-worn path that the Seer had laid out before him. He wasn't exactly thrilled about that, but there was little he could do at the moment. At least for now, their motives seemed to be aligned.

"Anyway, we'll need to start *Forging* the guildsmen, starting with the mages and fighters, since they will be on the frontlines," Finn explained. "We can bond the merchants last since they are a lower priority."

"I'm not sure that's even necessary. We're really more of a support group—" Kalisha began tentatively.

"We will make it so," Malik interjected in a stern voice, shaking his head at the merchant's bald-faced attempt to wiggle out of fighting in the war that was coming. This earned him a huff from Kalisha, but she didn't try to push back any further.

"Good," Finn replied. "Those that will undergo the *Forging* will need to identify an item that they will be bonded with. They should choose carefully. This bond can't be altered once formed, and the item will level and progress with them from that point forward. The bond will also reduce their mana and regeneration by a sixth. If the object is destroyed, they will die – that goes for both residents and travelers alike."

Abbad nodded. "Understood. Although, that may take some time. A few hours at least. Once we have the fighters and mages prepared, we will have you travel to their new colony – the Flagship – and you can start administering the *Forging*." His gaze shifted to Aerys. "That way, we will not reveal the Hive's location."

The Khamsin leader nodded once in return, a note of respect shining in her eyes. It seemed this group had learned to get along in his absence – or at least begun to tolerate each other's presence. They were certainly more cordial than he had expected.

"Good," Finn replied, rubbing at his chin in thought. What he had told Thorn was true. He expected that administering the *Forging* was going to take some time. Likely a few days at a minimum since he would need to bond each person individually. Although, he supposed that depended on how many of the guildsmen had escaped Lahab.

"On that note, what's happened in our absence?" Finn asked, his eyes skimming across the group around the table. "It's clear that the guilds successfully managed to escape Lahab. Were there casualties? What about supplies and equipment?"

Abbad nodded. "We were able to disguise our retreat with the help of the guild's water mages, and we prepared several false trails through the desert to further obfuscate our passage through the sands. It seems that we were successful in misleading Bilel."

He hesitated, a frown tugging at his lips. "Even so... many refused to leave, and there were indeed casualties. The travelers, in particular, proved to be recalcitrant. We have not been able to conduct an accurate census, as other priorities have intervened. But our best estimate is that nearly 50% of each guild was able to escape."

"Leaving the rest to die... or worse," Kalisha muttered. "Morons, the lot of them."

Finn raised an inquiring eyebrow, and the merchant sighed before continuing, "The Emir – Bilel – has become more aggressive. Even as we were attempting to evacuate, his hounds had begun to roam the streets, indiscriminately slaughtering travelers and residents alike. To make matters worse, it seems that not everyone killed by the hounds stays dead. Many are converted to hounds themselves. As you can imagine, the travelers didn't take that well," Kalisha said, shaking her head.

Finn shot a questioning look at Abbad. "There was mass fighting in the streets, travelers and residents pitting themselves against the hounds..." the librarian explained. "Although many of the residents retreated to the guild halls. We were forced to use that chaos to help cover our escape."

"Huh," Kyyle murmured. "So, does that mean travelers are respawning inside the city? They might be able to take out quite a few of the hounds—"

Kalisha barked out a laugh, interrupting him. "You would think that, wouldn't you? We finally get to experience an upside to the travelers' immortality – an eternal army that just keeps returning and rushing the hounds. Except, Bilel is clever. He quickly identified the locations where the travelers return and began directing the hounds to those locations. We also discovered firsthand that this process leaves your kind disoriented for a few seconds. Which is often plenty of time for the hounds to cut down the travelers."

"And I suspect it wouldn't take long for most of them to give up and stop logging back in," Julia continued with a sigh. "I bet many of the forums are just filled with people bitching right now. Damn it..."

"That isn't really the issue," Malik spoke up. "The problem is that the travelers' bodies are often converted to hounds when they're slain. Not everyone undergoes the change. But for every two that fall, another hound is added to Bilel's army, growing his numbers. Then the travelers return, and the process starts over. With a constant source of travelers, Bilel will be able to grow his army of hounds rapidly."

"In other words, the longer we wait, the stronger Bilel gets," Kalisha said.

Finn shook his head. That was an awful result – far worse than he had expected. The players might go online and complain, but he doubted players from other areas around the continent could muster much of a response, and certainly not before Bilel's numbers had swelled considerably. In fact, their best bet was if the players simply got fed up and quit. That would at least slow Bilel down. But they couldn't count on that. There would always be new players and those that were too stubborn to give up.

The only solution was to launch their attack as soon as possible.

"So, is there any *good* news?" Finn asked.

"Well, we've managed to start fashioning that platemail," Kalisha offered, waving at Julia and the dark plate that covered her limbs. "The designs you left us were… interesting."

"We have also assigned fire mages to a new contingent of Khamsin that Aerys has formed," Abbad added. "The desert folk have been outfitted with the platemail and have been training with their new fire mage partners."

Aerys snorted, her eyes darting to Julia's lance and shield. "They've even requested weapons and arms to match your own – they wish to model themselves after the daughter of the prophet."

"Huh," Julia murmured, tilting her head. "I'm going to have to go inspect this group myself then."

"I suspect they would welcome such a visit and any training or insight you could offer," Aerys replied with a nod.

"And as I mentioned earlier, our numbers have grown dramatically," Aerys continued, turning her attention back to Finn. "The Khamsin forces now number almost 2,000, and the guilds managed to recover almost as many mages, merchants, and fighters."

"Do we have a sense of how many hounds occupy Lahab?" Finn asked, already dreading the answer.

"That is difficult to estimate with the way they are slaughtering the travelers en masse and converting the bodies," Abbad began, sharing a look with Kalisha and Malik, their expression grim. "Our guess is that we will be facing at least 10,000 hounds."

"10,000," Finn echoed, his eyes widening.

"So, we'll likely be outnumbered by more than two to one…" Kyyle muttered.

A hushed silence drifted across the room.

It was worse than that really, Finn realized. It wasn't just about the numbers. Bilel had a defensible and entrenched position. They would need to penetrate Lahab's high walls and fortified gates. And it was safe to assume that the demon hadn't been idle in the meantime. He could have reinforced those fortifications, and he might even be able to assist his hounds with his own magic – using the stockpile of crystals that he had gathered from administering the Purge. Even once they breached the city's walls, the chaotic jumble of buildings that filled Lahab would give the nimble hounds an advantage – the fiery dogs able to flank or surround an invading force by using the tangle of streets and side passages.

And that was putting aside Bilel himself. It wasn't clear if that staff was capable of more offensive magics, but, even if it wasn't, its healing properties were powerful. Finn had witnessed that firsthand. With a legion of hounds feeding mana to the staff, the demon would be nearly immortal – able to heal even grievous wounds in an instant.

It all came back to those damn hellhounds...

"There is one silver lining, I guess," Kalisha offered slowly.

Finn's eyes shot to her face. "What's that?"

"Well, a few mages and merchants may have gone rogue during the evacuation," she offered. "Their curiosity got the better of them, and they wanted to study these hounds." She grimaced. "We lost three mages, but we managed to capture one of the creatures."

A sudden, shocked silence met those words.

"Where is the hound now?" Abbad asked, an edge to his voice. "The creatures are linked to the staff, and we don't know whether Bilel is capable of tracking their location. He could know the location of the Flagship by now..."

"Breathe," Kalisha snapped. "We weren't crazy enough to bring the hound to the new colony. We're holding it on another rock island between Lahab and the Flagship, and we left someone to watch after it – as well as a few guildsmen to fortify the position."

"Assuming they're still alive and Bilel hasn't already wiped them out," Abbad retorted, his expression grim. He clearly had a high estimation of the demon's abilities.

Kalisha was about to reply but hesitated as she chewed on the librarian's words. The fact was that she likely didn't know if the group had survived.

"Either way, it was a risk worth taking," she finally replied, glaring at Abbad. "If we're to fight these things, then we need to understand them."

"She's right," Finn interjected. "It was a worthwhile risk."

He met Kalisha's eyes. "Who is leading the group guarding the hound?" he asked.

"I think you two may already be acquainted, actually. He's a fire mage by the name of Brutus," Kalisha responded. She hesitated for a moment, gnawing on her lip. "He can be a bit of a loose cannon..."

Finn and Kyyle immediately shared a look. They knew firsthand how unconventional Brutus could be – they had experienced more than their fair share of his eccentric teaching style back in the Mage Guild.

"That's probably the understatement of the year," Kyyle said, rubbing at his eyes.

"I take it you have some history with him?" Kalisha asked.

"Something like that," Finn replied. He let out a sigh. "Alright, since we're going to be waiting for the guildsmen to prepare for the *Forging*, I'm going to make a trip out to visit Brutus and inspect the hound. Maybe I can glean more information with my *Mana Sight*."

"Assuming there isn't just a smoldering crater where the camp used to be," Julia quipped, and Kyyle snorted in amusement.

Finn tilted his head. That was certainly a possibility – especially with Brutus at the helm. He could already visualize the burly fire mage sipping lemonade while the rock pillars around him burned. He'd just have to hope that the man had managed to keep both himself and the hound in one piece.

His gaze drifted to Aerys and the guildsmen that ringed the table. "Meanwhile, you all should continue concentrating your efforts on preparing for the upcoming war.

"Thoughts or comments?" Finn asked finally.

Only silence met his question.

"Great," Finn said, smacking his palm against the table. "Then let's get moving. We have a lot of work to do, and with each hour that passes, Bilel only continues to grow stronger. So we need to make the most of the time we have left."

Chapter 32 - Hounded

It took nearly two hours of gliding across the dunes to reach the small basecamp that Brutus had established on one of the many rock islands that dotted the desert. It wasn't much to look at, just a small stone shelf among an ocean of sand. Only Finn and Kyyle had undertaken this journey. Julia had decided to focus her efforts on inspecting the new heavy infantry and offering her advice and training.

Finn suspected she might just be wary of confronting the fire mage again.

Not that he blamed her. Even after everything they had been through, he was still suffering some PTSD from Brutus' magical obstacle course, and he half expected the man to put him through the wringer again – prophet or not.

As the pair slid to a halt in front of those spires, several Khamsin materialized, their cloth robes blending almost seamlessly with the rock. They quickly encircled Finn and his companion, their dark eyes watching them carefully. Their gaze lingered on the bandage across Finn's eyes and the glimmering orange energy rippling through the fingers of his left hand, where the sleeve of his robe only partially concealed the crystal. Although he couldn't make out their expressions beneath their masks, Finn saw their reaction in the way their weapons disappeared, and their heads bowed in greeting.

"Tahiati lak," one of the robed men said, placing his hand to his chest. "Greetings, Najmat Alhidad. The hound is ready for your inspection."

Finn raised a quizzical eyebrow, and the Khamsin answered his unspoken question. "Aerys sent a group ahead to ensure your safety. We've prepared for your arrival."

"Good," Finn said, dropping from his mount, and Kyyle following his lead. He waved at the spires. "Lead the way."

Another bow and the Khamsin scout set off among the columns of stone, the rest of his group fading back into the shadows of the island and disappearing from sight. They tread a winding path until the stone spires began to disappear and gave way to an open clearing – the columns clustered enough to obscure what transpired in the center of the island from any prying eyes that might linger among the sands.

"Look what we have here! My best student has finally deigned to visit his master," a familiar voice barked as soon as they entered the clearing.

Finn looked up to find a burly mountain of a man approaching, his arms spread wide and a grin on his face. It seemed Brutus was still alive, after all.

"That hurts a little," Kyyle grumbled. "You trained me too."

The fire mage's smile widened. "Ahh, and my... uh, second-best student!" he added with feigned enthusiasm.

"Yeah, you're not really making it better..."

"It's good to see you again, Brutus," Finn said, grasping the man's hand. "After everything else we've gone through, it's a relief to see a friendly face."

"Yeah, about that..." Brutus began taking in the bandage across Finn's face. "You don't seem to be seeing much of anything lately, huh? What the hell happened? I told you a dozen times – you gotta learn to run away."

"He did that to himself," Kyyle muttered.

Brutus glanced at the earth mage in surprise. "What? Why—?"

The fire mage cut himself short as Finn tugged the cloth strip free, giving Brutus a glimpse at the amalgamation of molten metal and crystal that now rested in his eye sockets. "I've had to make a few sacrifices to make it this far," Finn said soberly. "But it looks worse than it is. I can still see after a fashion – but now I can also sense mana."

Brutus just stared at him with a dumbfounded expression. "Uh, *okay*. And I'm guessing there's another story behind the hand?" he offered, having noticed the fire flickering in Finn's crystalline fingers. The fire mage was just as perceptive as usual.

"As I said, it's been a rough couple of weeks," Finn answered softly.

"No kidding. It looks like you're burning up body parts right and left," he observed.

Brutus seemed to finally notice Brock's rocky form drift through the pillars behind Kyyle. "Oh, sweet merciful gods. You found an adolescent earth elemental." In a flash, the fire mage was beside Brock. Brutus inspected the elemental carefully, running a hand under the collection of floating rocks to test the strength of Brock's gravity well. "Strong field. Good collection of stone. Mostly granite – I approve."

"You're familiar with earth elementals?" Kyyle asked, his brow furrowing.

"Sure," Brutus grunted, not bothering to look up from inspecting Brock. "That was the inspiration for my golems. The real deal are incredibly rare, though. Elementals tend to gravitate toward locations with high levels of ambient mana for their affinity. Finding a fire elemental, for example, typically involves a lot of digging or braving an active volcano."

The fire mage hesitated, his brow furrowing as he whirled back to Kyyle. "How did you come by this guy anyway?"

"Well, that's *another* long story…" Kyyle hedged.

"One that we can get to later," Finn interjected before they could get too far off-topic. "We heard that you managed to capture one of the hellhounds?"

"Who else would be crazy enough to try," Kyyle muttered under his breath. This earned him a slap on the back from Brutus, the blow nearly toppling the slender earth mage.

A broad grin spread across the fire mage's face as he met Finn's eyes. "I did indeed. The merchants that helped me catch it were on board, but these desert folk seemed real skittish when I showed up with the little critter. They've effectively imprisoned me on this island," he added sourly, glancing at the robed men and women that lingered among the nearby pillars.

"What possessed you to do something so... dangerous?" Kyyle asked.

Brutus just gave him an incredulous stare. "Don't you remember your training, boy? Surely, I beat some sense into you. What's my number one rule?"

"Always have a glass of lemonade handy?" Finn offered in a dry voice.

"When in doubt, throw a *Fireball* at it?" That one was from Kyyle.

Brutus' grin faltered. "Huh. You took away a few different lessons – probably why the guild got rid of student reviews... But I suppose there's still some wisdom in there. Nothing like staying hydrated, and who doesn't like a warm fire? But I was going for a different goal here – *know your enemy.*"

The fire mage turned his gaze back to Finn, that grin reappearing in a flash. "You want to see it?" This earned him a nod from Finn and a hesitant but curious look from Kyyle.

Brutus abruptly pivoted on his heel and marched through the clearing. The Khamsin guards hovered among the rock pillars tensely, their hands drifting toward their weapons as they watched Brutus. "Don't mind them. They're just on edge after the last escape attempt." A grimace rippled across the burly fire mage's face. "Would you believe these desert folk wanted to put down Betty? Said she was too much of a liability."

"Betty?" Kyyle asked.

"My name for her," Brutus grunted.

"How, uh, do you know it's a her?" Kyyle offered with a curious glance.

The fire mage shrugged. "I saw the woman converted before my eyes. A hound gored her stomach, and she turned into this creature. Not sure what her real name was, but I've been calling her Betty ever since.

"And here we are," Brutus declared.

They had stopped next to a circular pit formed in the center of the clearing. It was at least ten feet deep and fifteen feet wide, the edges of the circle casting deep shadows. However, something still lit the bottom of the pit. Betty lay there upon the stone, her canine body coated in a fine film of flame, the air above her rippling and contorting from the heat. As she noticed the group approach the ledge, she rose and sniffed at the air. Letting out a low growl, the flames along her back flared brightly.

"The Khamsin had me widen and deepen the pit. She shouldn't be able to jump or claw her way out now, but I still wouldn't linger too close to the edge. She can get a bit *feisty* when she senses mana," Brutus explained, waving at the guards that edged closer to the pit, their weapons fully drawn now.

"Well, their caution makes sense. The hounds are linked to Bilel – the Emir – and the god relic that he now wields. That's what's creating these creatures," Finn explained, waving at Betty.

As Finn noticed the fire mage's inquiring look, he continued. "The hounds remain connected to the staff and feed it energy, which he can then use to heal himself. That's why the Khamsin are so nervous and why they quarantined you out here. We don't fully understand the nature of that connection. If you brought the hound back to the Hive or the Flagship, Bilel could possibly use it to find the locations of the Khamsin city and the guilds' new base of operations."

Finn crouched beside the lip of the pit, peering down at Betty and activating his *Mana Sight*. He could see that the hound was awash in fire mana, glowing a brilliant orange and red. However, now that he wasn't distracted by Bilel or fighting for his life, Finn had an opportunity to examine the hound more closely.

He could make out six glowing clusters of energy spread through the creature's body, those nodes tainted with a reddish hue that Finn recognized immediately – the staff had corrupted the Najima. Perhaps, as they slayed each traveler or resident, the hounds were spreading the infection. That would sort of make sense and be consistent with both Brutus' story as well as the accounts that Kalisha, Malik, and Abbad had provided. Even more interesting, all six of the hound's Najima were now attuned to a single affinity, and there was no fluctuation in their mana signature.

"It's still generating its own mana," Finn said aloud, Kyyle tapping away at his terminal as he took notes. "It has all six Najima, but they only produce fire mana and are covered in the same infection that I observed in my own Najima," Finn continued, rubbing at his left arm instinctively.

His attention shifted to the surface of the hound's body, where he could make out streamers of orange energy curling away from its skin and drifting off toward the east. "It's also continuously channeling its excess mana back to Lahab. There's a thread drifting away from its body and heading due east."

"I'm starting to see why you made those adjustments to your eyes," Brutus observed as he watched Finn. "You can get all of that at a glance now?"

Finn looked over his shoulder at the fire mage and saw his energy rippling uncertainly, an ivory tendril of mana curling through his body. *Hope,* most likely, but for what reason, Finn couldn't quite fathom. Perhaps the fire mage was starting to buy into the same myths and prophecies as the Khamsin.

"It's rather useful. In humans, I can also pick up on their emotions – the concentration of affinities fluctuates based on their mood," Finn replied, turning back to Betty.

Kyyle noted Brutus' startled expression, "It's only slightly disconcerting. It's sort of like hanging out with a human lie-detector sometimes," he offered, a teasing smile on the earth mage's face. There wasn't much that made the fire mage master uneasy.

"So, how did you catch it?" Finn asked as he turned his attention back to the hellhound. It now paced the pit, staring up at him with unblinking orange eyes.

"Lured it into a cage," Brutus grunted. "Nothing

special."

"Lured it?" Kyyle repeated. "How'd you manage that?"

"See for yourself," Brutus replied.

His fingers moved rapidly, and a ball of fire suddenly appeared in the bottom of the pit – Brutus channeling a *Fireball* at the edge of his control range. The hellhound immediately whipped around toward the source of the fire, its eyes trained on the glimmering orb. Its hesitation lasted only a second. Lunging forward, it shot toward the flames, the muscles in its legs rippling powerfully.

At the last minute, Brutus shifted the orb, and the hound ran headfirst into the wall of the pit. A resounding crack echoed through the clearing, and the stone crumpled from the impact, fractures spiraling up through the rock. The hound listed for a moment, clearly dazed.

"Why did you—" Kyyle began with a frown.

"Just wait," Brutus answered softly.

The hound shifted in place, its head coming into view. The blow had shorn the flesh from the side of its snout, revealing small glimpses of ivory bone beneath. Yet no blood trickled from the wound. Instead, the fire along its face flared more brightly. A twitch of Brutus' fingers and the *Fireball* swept down near the hound. It snapped at the energy with a vicious jerk of its ruined mandibles, consuming the flames in a single gulp. As soon as the fire entered its body, the flesh along its face knitted itself back together with surprising speed, and the excess energy poured out of its body – drifting off to the east.

"Huh," Finn grunted. "So, it's attracted to sources of fire mana, it can consume the flames to heal itself, and it's funneling that extra energy back to Bilel."

"I wasn't aware of that last bit, but you're right on the first two points," Brutus said with a nod. "Betty here will chase flames tirelessly and can repair even mortal injuries if she has access to some mana. She seems to prefer the flames, but she'll actually devour any type of energy."

Finn's gaze snapped to Brutus. "Really? Maybe she's attracted to casters in general then," he murmured to himself.

The fire mage rubbed at the back of his head, his expression sobering. "Indeed. During that clusterfuck back in... I mean, during our *escape* from Lahab," he amended with a wry twist of his lips, "the hounds seemed to attack anyone, but they would focus on those with a high magical aptitude regardless of their dominant affinity."

"Hmm, maybe it needs people that already have a decent mana pool and regeneration," Kyyle observed. "That would make sense if it's converting their Najima and channeling mana back to the staff."

Finn nodded slowly, but then winced as another thought occurred to him. "Which means it can probably convert any type of mana to fire..." He trailed off, staring down at the hound. "Well, there's one way to test that," he continued, waving at Kyyle.

The earth mage took the hint, and soon a tendril of emerald energy wound down into the pit. Betty immediately pounced on the energy, snapping at it with her jaws. Finn watched as the earth mana wound through her body – a single streamer of green amid the orange and red. Then it reached her Najima, and he looked on in fascination as the hound swiftly converted the earth mana to a glowing orange and red before sending that energy hurtling back toward Lahab.

"Yep, definitely converting other types of mana," he muttered. Finn leaned back from the pit, chewing on his lip as he processed that information.

"Can you absorb its energy?" Kyyle asked. "We might as well give it a shot."

Finn's brow furrowed at that. He had tried to absorb mana from the ants back in the Abyss but hadn't been successful and his experiments with draining mana directly from Kyyle had all failed. His theory was that an organic creature's body insulated them from the absorption – or possibly their Najima were responsible.

Whereas the staff likely bypassed those defenses by infecting and transforming the Najima themselves.

Although, he agreed that it didn't hurt to try using *Mana Absorption*.

He focused on Betty, tugging at the flames that coated her body.

However, as the seconds ticked past, nothing happened. He had only succeeded in draining some of the ambient heat from the air around the hound, the coils of fiery energy winding around his arm before pressing into his skin.

"Nope," Finn said with a frown. "It seems I can't just drain the hounds dry."

He wondered idly if the process might work if he broke the skin barrier or stabbed directly into the creature's Najima. Finn glanced down at his new crystalline left hand. If he repurposed the limb into a blade, that might work. Although, he didn't really want to test that theory on their only living specimen.

"Hmm, it looks like she hates cold – or perhaps just water mana in general," Kyyle observed, watching Betty. The hound had indeed been immune to Finn's *Mana Absorption*, but her flames had dwindled as she remained in the pocket of cold air that Finn had left behind. The hound quickly paced to the other side of the pit, hugging the stone wall.

"Interesting," Finn murmured in reply. He'd have to log that weakness away.

Finn rose from his perch beside the pit and stared down at the hound. He rubbed at his temple, and his thoughts raced as he processed what they'd learned. "So, let's summarize. Bilel has sic'd these hounds on anyone still inside Lahab – I'm guessing he started with the palace guards and staff to create an initial group of the creatures. They can then spread the infection and convert people into new hounds. They tend to target mages, although it sounds like the conversion isn't guaranteed – at least according to Aerys. The hounds naturally generate mana and funnel it back to the staff. And they can heal from consuming mana. The only upside is that they might be weak to cold or water mana."

"Except there must be thousands by now, and we're fighting in the middle of a desert," Brutus offered in a dry voice. "And even if Bilel doesn't manage to convert a person, it sounds like he still benefits if the hounds consume their mana. Who knows how much energy he's collected by now."

Silence lingered across the clearing, broken only by the occasional snap and whine of the hellhound in the pit below them. A question was lingering just at the edges of Finn's thoughts, insistent and demanding. He had been putting it off for some time now, pushing it to the side in favor of more immediate problems.

But now, he couldn't ignore that question any longer.

How the hell were they going to fight Bilel?

The demon had already collected a legion of hounds, which provided a nearly infinite source of mana. To make matters worse, the hounds could also effectively digest other sources of mana and convert that to fire mana, feeding that energy back to the staff. Bilel might as well be plugged directly into the fire pylon back in the Forge. Finn suspected the amount of mana resting at his fingertips was roughly in the same league.

The hounds could also detect or sense mana. In which case, the Khamsin had a natural advantage. They would be more difficult for the hounds to sniff out, and most were completely immune to the conversion – at least if they had been purged by the mages and not born into the Hive. However, the fighters and mages had no such luxury, and they would be easy for the hounds to detect – even if Finn insulated the fighters and mages from the conversion with his *Forging*. Worse yet, every casualty would just feed more mana to Bilel, the hounds feasting on that mana and then converting it with their Najima.

Which left the demon himself.

Finn wasn't certain whether Bilel could access the mana in the staff for offensive purposes, but it almost didn't matter. Even if the staff only allowed him to heal himself, the demon's nearly infinite source of fire mana would make him effectively immortal. And that was putting aside that Bilel was an incredibly powerful and experienced mage in his own right. One who'd had the better part of a century to drain and store mana from the mages that underwent the purge. After their last confrontation, Finn doubted they could take him in a straight fight even under normal circumstances. Not that it mattered. Even if they could somehow bypass the legion of hellhounds and take on Bilel directly, he would simply repair any injury almost instantly.

In many ways, it was like fighting the corrupted all over again. They either needed to strike so hard and fast that Bilel simply couldn't out heal the injuries. Or they needed to attack his stockpile of energy at the source, depleting his mana before they confronted him directly. That first option seemed impossible – or, at least, incredibly unlikely. Finn wasn't aware of any weapon in their arsenal that could pump out the kind of damage needed to obliterate the demon. Which led to an inevitable conclusion…

"We have to take out the dogs first," he murmured.

At the surprised glances from Kyyle and Brutus, he elaborated. "There are simply too many hounds, and the fire mana that Bilel has accumulated is far too great. Even if we tried to assassinate him directly, he'd simply heal any injury."

Kyyle was nodding now. "Which means we have to cut him off at the knees. The only way to undermine or limit the staff's healing power is to take out the hounds first."

"Exactly," Finn said.

"Uh, sure, and how exactly do you propose to do that?" Brutus offered. "I saw the carnage in Lahab myself. We're facing an army of these things. And they'll heal their own injuries and send mana back to Bilel with every kill."

Finn shook his head. "I don't know."

"A distraction, maybe?" Kyyle offered. "We might be able to use the hounds' hunger for mana against them. Lure them into a trap."

"Assuming Bilel can't control them directly," Finn replied.

"If he is controlling them, then he has a rather feral personality," Brutus grunted. "There was often no rhyme or reason to the hounds' attacks. They just seemed to scatter among the back alleys and roads, attacking anything that crossed their paths."

"Maybe there's a limit to how many of the hounds that Bilel can direct at once," Kyyle theorized, tapping away at his console again. "Like a control limit."

Finn cocked his head at that suggestion. That certainly seemed plausible.

"Either way, that's only one of our problems," Finn interjected. "How do we go about attacking Lahab in the first place?"

He waved at the eastern horizon. "Bilel has the same enhanced sight that I do – that's where I learned how to do this," Finn explained for Brutus' benefit, gesturing at his eyes. "Except he's had at least a century to refine and train his sight, and he's already indicated that he can see far outside the city walls. It's safe to assume he will see us coming long before we reach Lahab."

"He could just sit safely inside the city and send the hounds to intercept us," Kyyle said slowly, following Finn's line of thinking. "Attrition works in his favor here."

"Plus, he could sling spells from the city walls to help support and reinforce the hounds," Brutus grumbled. "If he's as powerful as you say he is, that could be a problem."

Finn nodded. "So, we have two problems. We need some way to approach the city undetected – or at least in a way that makes it difficult for Bilel to coordinate the hounds and his own magic. And then we need to take out the hounds before confronting Bilel."

A sudden silence once again hovered across the clearing, the same dark expression lingering across each person's face. They were all thinking the same thing.

That was nearly impossible.

Even Finn was drawing a blank. The task before them seemed insurmountable, and he could feel an ember of frustration simmering in his chest. *There had to be a way...*

His thoughts were interrupted as a whistle went up from the western side of the island. A Khamsin runner soon appeared, racing through the stone spires. As he approached Finn, he placed a hand to his chest. *"Najmat Alhidad,* a message from Aerys. The merchants and fighters are assembled at the Flagship, and they are ready to start the *Forging.* I am waiting to guide you at your convenience."

"Thank you," Finn said with a nod. He let out a sigh. It seemed that the larger strategic problem would have to wait. For now, he'd need to work on ensuring that their fighters and mages weren't immediately converted into hellhounds the second they attacked Lahab. He expected that it was going to take a while.

"It looks like the fun never ends for you lot," Brutus observed in a dry voice.

"You have no idea," Finn replied softly. "No idea."

Chapter 33 - United

A woman stepped forward. The tattoos coiling down her neck and peeking out from behind the thick leather armor that covered her chest and arms marked her as a fighter. Although, the chiseled muscle and stoic expression that seemed to have been carved into her face would have likely given away her guild regardless. Finn wasn't sure why each member of the fighter guild seemed to have the same severe expression, but he could only assume it was a byproduct of their intense training.

Perhaps, someday, he could get Malik to share some details about the enigmatic guild.

Although, he was sure that process would feel like pulling teeth.

The fighter placed a fist to her chest in greeting, bowing her head. "Tahiati lak," she murmured.

"Tahiati lak," Finn echoed, gesturing for her to rise.

Many of the guildsmen had already begun adopting the Khamsin's mannerisms... including an unusual reverence for Finn. He had been expecting a line of belligerent mages and fighters intent on arguing with him, and only grudgingly permitting him to administer the *Forging*. He had been shocked to find that both groups were incredibly receptive to anything that could insulate them from the hounds and Bilel's staff.

Although, upon reflection, he supposed that wasn't so strange. The guildsmen might not have undergone the purge or been banished into the sands like the Khamsin, but they had effectively been prisoners in their own city. Commodities to be bought and traded by their guilds for political favors. Muscle and flesh pitted against one another to the death. And that was putting aside the grueling process of escaping Lahab and fending off the hounds.

Either way, they now seemed extremely motivated.

Finn's attention snapped back into focus as the woman knelt and set a blade upon the small stone altar that Kyyle had pulled from the floor. Then she rested her left arm upon the rock, her open palm facing upward.

"Is this the object that you wish to be bonded with?" Finn asked, the words coming automatically. He had asked that same question dozens – possibly hundreds – of times already. And he could easily anticipate her the answer. The fighters were predictable.

They always chose their weapon.

"It is," the fighter answered with a nod.

Finn leaned forward, touching the woman's sword with his left arm. The fighter's eyes widened as the sleeve of Finn's robes drew back and revealed his crystalline fingers, a fire raging within the translucent surface. With his right hand, Finn grasped the woman's arm. Then he began casting the *Forging*.

The now-familiar guttural words drifted from his lips. His mana surged through his body in a fiery torrent. The pain was an almost distant thing now after having performed the rite so many times. Flames soon wound around the fighter's arm, Finn's focus on the cluster of rainbow energy that resided there. The fire wrapped around that bright spot even as flames encircled the sword, a thin thread of flame connecting them.

Finn understood what he was seeing now. The flames were a conduit. They carved the Najima from the woman's body and transferred that energy to the inanimate object, using Finn to help build that bridge. And once he completed the process, a string of fire mana would remain, connecting the two – a permanent union of body and metal.

Only seconds later, he was done.

Finn slumped back in his stone chair, suddenly feeling weak. The spell cost him – not in abstract numbers on a screen. But *physically*. It required mental endurance to weather the searing pain that pulsed through his body each time. And the act of removing the Najima and reinserting it within cold steel required focus. Precision. Concentration. Even a slight mistake and he could permanently destroy the Najima. The memories Nar

Aljahim had supplied made that point abundantly clear.

"Thank you, *Najmat Alhidad*," the woman murmured, staring in rapt fascination at her sword. In Finn's sight, that weapon now glowed with a vibrant energy.

"Don't thank me yet," Finn answered. "The time will soon come for you to pay the price for this *Forging*. In the meantime, practice with your new weapon. Guard it carefully. You are now one. If the blade is destroyed, you will be too."

"I will," was her curt reply. The fighter then rose and strode away.

Finn's eyes followed her as she left, noting the long line of people still waiting to receive the *Forging*. There were dozens of fighters, mages, and even the occasional merchant standing nearby, and he knew that line stretched down through the winding passages of the Flagship. Under other circumstances, he might have appreciated the novelty of the scene – these once sworn enemies now working together toward a common goal. However, that was difficult with the headache that throbbed just behind his eyes.

He gave himself a momentary break, switching away from *Mana Sight*. His world was soon awash in a blue glow, revealing that he was sitting in a large chamber in the Flagship, the room specially dedicated to this task. He had long ago forgotten what the sun looked like. His world had become only stone, and flame, and a brief break before the next person took a seat opposite Finn and laid another object on the rock.

60 seconds, he thought to himself, his fingers massaging at his temples. That's how long he gave himself after he performed each rite – just enough time for his perpetual headache to dwindle to a dull, throbbing pain.

"You look like shit," a familiar voice chirped.

Finn glanced up, automatically shifting to *Short-Sighted*. His daughter stood nearby, her hands on her hips, watching Finn with a severe expression.

"And you're starting to sound like a broken

record," Finn grunted. "You could at least think up some new material in between these little visits."

"Hilarious," she replied, raising an eyebrow. "For such a smart guy, you can sure be an idiot sometimes. If you would take breaks like a normal person, I wouldn't have to make the same observation every single time I check in on you."

"No time," Finn grunted. He waved at the line waiting for him, those eyes staring at him – waiting, hoping, demanding. "At the rate we're going, it will likely take—"

"2 days and 6 hours to complete the *Forging* on the remaining fighters, mages, and merchants," Daniel chirped helpfully from beside Finn's shoulder.

He waved at the AI tiredly. "Yeah… that long."

"So, a short break isn't going to hurt anything," Julia snapped. As the next person began to approach, she held up a hand. "The Najmat Alhidad needs to take a break. He'll be back in four hours."

The woman simply nodded and returned to her position in line, waiting patiently. The man behind her whispered something in her ear, and she shook her head. That whisper continued on down the line, a low buzzing that was as predictable as it was annoying. Yet not a single soul moved from their position in line. Finn couldn't quite put his finger on why, but that bottomless, accepting patience just made him even more irritated.

"Come on," Julia urged, laying a hand on Finn's shoulder. "Log out for a second and stretch your legs…"

Finn raised an eyebrow at that.

"*Metaphorically*," Julia continued in an exasperated voice. "I certainly don't mean that literally." She paused as she eyed him critically. "Seriously, what's eating at you? You've been tired before, but you seem even more on edge lately."

"Oh, I don't know… where do I even begin?" Finn grumbled, keeping his voice low so that the people in line couldn't overhear him. The last thing he needed was to start rumors that the so-called "prophet of the flame" was losing his damn mind.

"I need to spend the next two days sitting in this cave casting the same damn spell over and over again. And if that wasn't already grueling enough, it gives me plenty of time to ponder on just how totally fucked our position is."

Julia just sat down across from him, waiting for him to continue.

"We're facing a legion of hellhounds, which outnumber us by a decent margin and basically make Bilel immortal. So, we just need to figure out how to take them out before we confront the demon himself... *somehow*. Oh, and we haven't even gotten to the fun part yet! How the hell do we even attack this city? The damn place is a fortress, and Bilel is going to see us coming from miles away."

Finn let out a sigh, his face sinking into his hands. Even that gesture felt strange, the hard surface of his newfound fingers pressing sharply into the skin of his face. Yet he knew that focusing on the discomfort was just a distraction. It was easier to bitch about his hand, or the army of sycophants lined up before him, than to dwell on the questions and problems that swirled through his mind – unanswered and unresolved.

Much less what was really eating at him.

"You're worried about Mom," Julia said softly, as though reading his mind. Although, he supposed she didn't need to be a telepathic goddess to figure that one out.

"Yeah. Yeah, I am," Finn muttered.

He peered up at his daughter between glassy fingers. "Can we do this? I mean, *really* do this?" he asked.

He saw a mixture of compassion and uncertainty lingering in her expression. "I don't know," she began, hesitation in her voice. "But if we do nothing – give up now – then she's still... still dead. So, we give it a shot. We try our best. It's not that much different than when we were down in the Forge. We really don't have anything to lose."

Finn nodded, although he didn't feel entirely convinced. Defeating Bilel was just the tip of the iceberg. Ever since his meeting with the Seer, her words kept returning to him, persistently hovering at the edges of his thoughts.

"And if we succeed, what does that look like?" he asked softly. Ever since his last meeting with the Seer, he hadn't been able to escape that question.

He saw his daughter's lips press into a grim line.

"Will it really be Rachael – your mother? Only a fragment? Or an illusion? And if it is really her, what then? She'll be trapped in this world, dependent on the AI that is running this place."

"We could find a way to pull her out of the game," Julia offered hesitantly.

"Maybe," Finn grunted. "But it will take time to figure out how to transfer and store her consciousness – if I even can. So, in the meantime, do we try to build a life here? In this desert? With every damn faction and their second cousin quarreling over something," he offered, gesturing to where two men in line were getting into a tussle as word of Finn's "break" spread, their shouts swiftly alerting the Khamsin guards that stood silently nearby.

"Can you really blame them, though?" Julia offered with a weak smile. "If you lived in this sun-blasted wasteland your entire life, you'd probably be on edge too."

Finn let out an amused snort. "I suppose you might be right about that."

He shook his head, his good humor short-lived. "I just feel like the axe is about to drop. It's not just this impossible battle ahead of us… it's also the aftermath. I can't shake the feeling that the Seer is going to screw us. I seriously doubt she plans to let us all ride off into the sunset as one happy family.

"It… it just seems impossible," he said, cradling his face in his hands.

It wasn't just one thing. It was *everything*. The fight

ahead. The aftermath. What he'd already endured. The unanswered questions. That damn hopeful spark that gleamed in every pair of eyes that knelt across from him. It felt like he was being crushed under a mountainous weight. Everyone was looking to him for answers – to carry that weight.

The gods' damned *Prophet of the Flame*.

The fucking *Najmat Alhidad*.

The tired old man who couldn't cope with the death of his wife...

Finn squeezed his eyes shut. "I just don't know if I can do this."

Julia reached forward and took Finn's hand – his real hand – in her own. "Hey. Hey, look at me," she urged him, Finn reluctantly raising his eyes to meet hers.

"I don't have answers for you. I don't know how we're going to handle the attack on Lahab. Or what might come after."

She squeezed his hand, her gaze steady and determined. "But I'll be by your side the entire time. Win or lose. We'll do it *together*. You don't have to do this alone."

Finn felt a faint burning sensation trickle down his cheek and rubbed at it. As he pulled his hand away, he saw a small wisp of flame curl around his finger, winking out in an instant. "Great, now you're making your old man cry living flames."

"You really might want to get that checked out," Julia retorted with a hint of a smile. "And lucky for you, you'll get a chance since you're going to take a break —"

"You never give up, do you?" Finn said, throwing up his hands.

Her smile only widened. "What can I say? I'm my father's daughter."

Damn it. She had him there.

Julia leaned forward. "Now log the fuck out. And don't let me see you back online for at least a real-world hour."

"Fine, fine," Finn muttered.

Then he pulled up the system menu. With another tap of his fingers, he hit the log-out button, and the dreary cave broke apart, streaming away into nothingness. Maybe his daughter was right. Maybe a break was what he needed to get his head screwed on straight. But even if he didn't, he knew Julia would be there when he came back.

And, for some reason, that thought gave him comfort.

I'm not alone.

He kept repeating that to himself, even as the cave fully disappeared, and he dropped back into a bottomless, dark void.

Chapter 34 - Dreary

Finn rolled himself back into his office. He was freshly bathed, the growing forest along his chin had been trimmed back to a manageable length, and he'd taken care of the laundry list of other real-life necessities – annoyances like eating and visiting the restroom. The entire process had made him realize just how strange it was to be back in the real world... and just how much time he now spent inside AO. For all of the stress that the game world entailed, it now felt more familiar to him than his actual home.

This place – his real home – just felt like an empty, vacant shell now. It reminded him of what he'd lost, an elaborate electronic tomb that he had constructed for himself. Returning here, to this place, only served to reinforce how much things had changed since he first donned that headset. How much *he* had changed.

Gone was his typical morning schedule.

Days spent mindlessly tinkering with his house's AI.

Hours spent alone and listless – without any real goal.

He'd been a zombie, just going through the motions.

How did I not notice that? he wondered – not for the first time.

"Are you okay, sir? You've been stationary for several minutes," Daniel chirped from beside Finn.

His gaze panned to the AI. Even this world's version of Daniel seemed lifeless.

The AI simply hovered sedately beside him – a glowing blue cloud of light projected by cameras artfully concealed in the walls. His voice seemed more robotic and scripted. The in-game version of Daniel would have been moving around the office in a whirlwind of orange light, likely making some sort of snarky comment about Finn being lazy or complaining about being bored.

"Sir?" Daniel repeated. He hadn't responded.

"Yes, yes, I'm alright," Finn said, waving at the AI.

Although, as he did, Finn hesitated, noticing the bulge of his bicep and the dull ache in his shoulder, as though he had recently worked out. Even his normal bathing routine had felt easier than usual – Finn being able to lift himself into and out of the tub without any trouble. That was curious. He had noticed the ache in his limbs before but had chalked it up to sitting stationary in his chair for hours on end.

But he would have expected muscle atrophy – not the opposite.

"Daniel, can you please run a full diagnostic scan of my body," Finn ordered.

"Of course, sir," Daniel replied, flashing once.

Finn felt a tingle along the chip in his wrist and the sensors embedded in his arms, shoulders, torso, and base of his neck. He knew more of the chips had been implanted in his legs, but he felt no sensation as they activated. His workstation sprang to life, a globe of screens whirling slowly through the center of the room and a progress bar appearing along one screen. It would take a few minutes for Daniel to complete the scan and compile the results, which gave Finn some time to mull on his situation.

Or "mope" was probably a better word.

The pitter-patter of rain drummed against the nearby wall, distracting him from the globe of screens that whirled around. That sound reminded Finn unmistakably of Rachael, and he abruptly decided that he needed some fresh air.

He rolled himself to the far wall, tapping at the controls along the arm of his chair. The surface of the wall rippled and then disappeared, revealing an unobscured view of the city skyline as well as the second-story terrace installed along the side of the house. The glass was nearly three inches thick and bulletproof, laced with an electronic polymer that allowed him to change the opacity at will.

Another tap of his fingers and the door slid open,

likely the first time he had ventured out onto the terrace in… Well, he couldn't precisely recall the last time he'd opened this door. And yet the area was tidy, Daniel regularly sending drones to blow off and clean a terrace that Finn never used. He usually just kept the glass opaque to block out the harsh sunlight that reflected off the nearby buildings.

Rolling himself outside, he felt the raindrops strike against his skin. That felt real. And yet, he couldn't help but imagine what rain would feel like inside AO. Would he be able to tell the difference? Was there a difference? The sensation he *felt* right now was just neurons firing in his brain. The same neurons that the headset manipulated in-game.

And then there was the real question bouncing around his head.

The one he was reluctant to face.

Would she be able to tell the difference?

Rachael had always loved the rain. She used to sit out on their porch for hours – in a different house in a different part of the city. And at night, lying in bed, she'd listen to the patter of the droplets striking the roof. Sometimes she was even moved to step out into the downpour, to take long walks, occasionally attempting to drag a reluctant Finn along with her, grumbling and grousing about getting wet. But whether he accompanied her or not, she always used to come back soaked and with a huge smile stretched across her face.

Finn choked back the tears he could feel welling at the corners of his eyes.

If he succeeded – and that was a big if – would Rachael remember those long walks in the rain? Would she be able to experience that pleasure again? And, if she did, would she be content to experience the rain in-game? Would digital water elicit the same joy?

Because what he had told Julia was the truth. The harsh reality was that Rachael would be trapped there, perhaps indefinitely. And even if he could help her new digital self escape that world… where would she go?

She'd never have her real body again. Not in a way that could touch these raindrops or feel the weight and warmth of Finn's hand in her own. Not here in the *real* world. At best, she'd likely be trapped in a cold metal shell – forced to live inside a mechanical body that could only attempt to simulate the feeling of the rain.

No, he decided abruptly. He couldn't bear that thought – of confining her in some sort of hollow purgatory. Perhaps it would be better to leave her inside AO. At least until he figured out a better option – one that wasn't dependent on George-Fucking-Lane and his damn company.

He squeezed his eyes shut, letting the water stream down his face and soak his shirt. A sense of despair coiled in his stomach, twisting and writhing. This was all silly. Ridiculous. Insane. He was acting like the Khamsin – betting *everything* on blind *hope.*

That the person who came back would be his Rachael.

That she would accept what he'd done in the aftermath of her death.

The pain he had caused their children – caused Julia.

The lengths to which he'd gone to bring her back.

That she'd accept her new life inside a *fucking game.*

"I'm bringing you back in a desert of all places…" he whispered in a hoarse voice, the tears mixing with the water that already streamed down his cheeks. There was a sort of morbid irony to their situation. There wouldn't be any rain in Lahab. Clouds rarely marred that deep blue desert sky.

His eyes snapped open, watching the dark-gray storm clouds rolling across the sky. Finn remained frozen there, unmoving as the water soaked into his clothes and washed away his tears. He watched as lightning arced through the cloud bank, as sheets of rain cut through the air and pounded against the city that was sprawled out before him – all flashing lights and wet glass and concrete.

Even if he succeeded, Finn doubted he would be

able to leave that desert city. The conflict wouldn't end with Bilel. The Seer had her claws in him now, and she wouldn't relinquish her hold anytime soon. There were people there that counted on him. Enemies that would be standing in line to stab him in the back. And, besides, where else would they even go? Those unexplored lands would only hold more enemies and more problems.

She'll never be able to watch a storm front roll in again, he realized.

Hell, Finn couldn't even manage that feat either – at least, not like *this*.

With the mass of crystal and metal fused into his eye sockets, this scene would look entirely different. A massive front of water mana so dense he wouldn't be able to penetrate the many layers of energy. Streamers of yellow mana pushing all of that vapor along on a massive current of air – heat and cold colliding to form those billowing clouds. The flash of amber light as electricity crackled between the clouds. An endless haze of sapphire energy as the rain pelted the ground.

Finn hesitated, his eyes widening slightly.

It was true that he'd never experienced a storm front inside the game. The closest he had come to seeing one was the clouds circling the mountain peaks that loomed above the Forge. Something, or someone, had gathered that energy together. That collection of water mana had indeed been too dense for his sight to penetrate.

And the phenomenon also implied something more…

The virtual world's weather could be affected by its residents.

A thought occurred to him – like a lightning strike to the brain.

"I couldn't… could I?" he muttered, his practical mind warring with the faint flicker of hope that lit in his chest.

"Sir, the scan is complete," Daniel reported, interrupting Finn's thoughts. "You should move inside. I have noticed a precipitous drop in your core temperature.

You will catch cold out here."

Finn eyed this sedate, mannerly version of Daniel. He'd written those words himself – a script the AI now re-enacted perfectly. That realization fed that flickering flame of hope just a little more. Maybe he was right to think that this world felt strange – empty.

Perhaps the in-game version of the AI had become something new... something *real*.

And what did that mean for Rachael? For the plan that even now circled the edges of his thoughts, refusing to be ignored. He could feel the coil of despair beginning to disintegrate, that renewed sense of hope flaring brightly.

He shook his head, pushing himself inside the office and the door sliding shut behind him with a soft hiss of hydraulics and a dull thump as it settled back into place. Finn left a trail of water in his wake as he rolled himself into the center of that globe of screens.

Which was when he saw the results of his scan.

"How is this possible?" Finn murmured, leaning forward slightly and peering at the display. It showed an image of his body – standing upright as though to mock him – and data streaming down the margin, swiftly collating itself into a tidy summary.

He hadn't been imagining it. The system was recording an 11.3% average increase in muscle mass across all muscle groups. His cardiovascular and respiratory strength had also improved tremendously. And even more startling were his legs. The nerves at the base of his spine were showing renewed activity – they were actually beginning to reform the severed connections from his injury. Whether they could successfully repair the damage was far from certain, but he shouldn't even be seeing that feeble activity.

Finn stared in shock, his thoughts racing.

His eyes drifted to the helmet, resting on the small table beside him.

The hardware had to be responsible for this. He sure as hell hadn't started working out recently – or somehow regrown his own nerve endings. Could it possibly be stimulating his nervous system while he was plugged in? But that "feature" certainly hadn't been advertised by Cerillion Entertainment.

Although, neither had his confrontation with a mind-reading goddess or the promise of resurrecting his dead wife. No, something more was going on here.

Something incredible.

And with that realization, Finn could feel that faint spark of hope finally bloom into a full-fledged flame, burning away the last traces of his despair. Sudden energy filled his body – a renewed sense of purpose. It was *possible* to bring Rachael back. It was *possible* to build a new life. And it was *possible* to bring down a demon king.

He could work with that.

"Is there anything else I can assist you with, sir?" Daniel asked.

Finn just shook his head. "No... no, I'm good."

"Certainly. What do you plan to do next?"

A smile crept across his face as he lifted the helmet from that table, holding it gingerly in his hands while staring at that dense plastic.

"I'm going to make it rain."

Chapter 35 - Nebulous

"Someone said you need my help in here! Never fear, for I have... uh, arrived," Brutus declared, faltering as he witnessed what was transpiring in the cavern.

Charlotte's eyes lit up as she saw the fire mage. "It's about time." Her many mechanical legs tap, tap, tapped along the stone floor as she settled next to Finn and the rest of the group. "You're apparently the last piece in some sort of experiment that our fire-mage-turned-prophet has designed."

"And I see he roped you into this too... whatever *this* is. Looks more like madness than an experiment," Brutus muttered, his eyes wide as he took in the expansive cavern that had been formed beneath the Flagship.

"You wouldn't be too far off there," Kyyle muttered in reply, wiping sweat from his brow as he finished carving another large swath into the nearby cavern wall. The emerald streamers of energy encircling his staff slowly dissipated, and he slumped down on a nearby boulder as he allowed his mana to regenerate. "He's been having me expand this cave for an hour now – as though it really needs to be any bigger than it already is."

"Hey, you all need to have some faith in your *prophet*," Finn offered with a grin, slapping the earth mage on the back. The rest of the group stared back with skeptical expressions, apparently unconvinced.

To their credit, the scene in the cavern likely did look crazy.

Finn had spent the better part of the last day continuing to administer the *Forging* to the fighters, mages, and merchants. It had given him plenty of time to mull on the idea that had occurred to him back in the real world while watching the deluge of rain beat down on the terrace outside his office. He had used his downtime in between administering the rite to digest an abnormally large number of articles and papers on the formation of storm fronts. With Daniel's assistance, he had then started modeling his experiment, using the data they had collected from their previous encounters. He was relatively confident that the real-world mechanics would translate.

After all, the game world had already proven itself to be incredibly detailed.

And now he planned to put his plan into action – at least, on a limited scale.

Most of the guildsmen in the Flagship had proven remarkably helpful. He'd only had to start gently asking questions about whether the guildsmen knew of an abandoned cave, and then an earth mage had approached him with a solution – along with a waypoint marker. The cavern hadn't quite met the parameters of Finn's model, so he'd been forced to make a few renovations. And by that, he meant he'd begged Kyyle until the earth mage agreed to help expand the cavern to his specifications.

The result was a narrow cave that stretched more than 100 yards. They'd also been forced to expand the ceiling – height would be crucial for purposes of this test. Kyyle had dissolved the rock and stone until he reached his control range. The upper edge of the cavern now lingered more than fifty feet above them.

He had also asked Abbad to conscript a few mages.

Specifically, he needed a water mage, an air mage, a fire mage, and himself.

"Okay, so, Brutus, I need you in the middle of the cave," Finn explained, tapping at his map to indicate the fire mage's position. "Fahima here will be accompanying you," Finn offered, gesturing at the guild water mage that Abbad had recruited. The woman nodded politely – although her expression said that she'd prefer to be training her new soulbound wand with the other mages rather than participating in this mad experiment.

"Uh, sure. But what exactly are we going to be *doing*?" Brutus asked in confusion. "You've still been a little vague on the goal of all of this unless it's to cave in the Flagship and kill off all of the guildsmen simultaneously. In which case, I completely understand the impulse, although that might be counterproductive to defeating Bilel."

"Nothing that dire," Finn said with a wave of his hand. "Your roles are relatively straightforward. Fahima is going to continuously cast *Obscuring Mist,* and then you're going to help heat that growing pocket of moisture. Use your judgment on which spell to use. We don't necessarily need to create steam, just a dense cloud of moist, warm air."

Another thought occurred to him. "Oh, and once this gets started, you might want to move back toward Kyyle and me. If this works, then the far end of the cave might be a bit dangerous."

"Oookaaaay," the fire mage murmured, raising a skeptical eyebrow.

Despite his tone and their hesitant expressions, Brutus and Fahima followed Finn's instructions, walking toward the middle of the chamber. The water mage immediately began casting *Obscuring Mist* over and over again, creating a dense billowing cloud of vapor that slowly stretched out toward the edges of the cave. With a few swift gestures, Brutus began to heat that air, collecting two *Fireballs* and slowly circling them through the mists – just enough to heat the vapor. He kept the movements gentle, not wanting to displace the cloud. Soon, the mist began to shimmer with heat and rise slowly toward the ceiling.

"Charlotte, you can stand on the far end of the cave," Finn instructed, tapping at his map again and placing another marker. "On my signal, start channeling a continuous gust of air toward the other end of the cave. Keep going until you run out of mana." The merchant nodded and scurried toward the other end of the cave, tendrils of air soon curling around her hands as she prepared to cast.

Finn assumed a position roughly in between the two groups, eyeing his control range carefully. This was going to be tricky – maintaining a dual *Mana Absorption.*

"You going to clue me in on what we're doing?"

Kyyle asked softly, keeping his voice low so that the others couldn't hear him. "I get keeping these other people in the dark with Eldawin's snooping and guild politics, but I've been slaving away down here for hours."

"Laying on the guilt thick, huh? If it works, then you'll get to see it for yourself," Finn replied with a grin, his fire mana simmering in his veins. His excitement was burning through his body now – snapping and crackling just beneath his skin. If this worked… well, he supposed he'd cross that bridge when, and most importantly, if they got there.

"Alright, we're ready. The moist air has reached the requisite density and temperature based on our calculations," Daniel reported, whipping back from Brutus' position and hovering beside Finn's shoulder. With his *Mana Sight*, Finn could indeed see a large clump of hot, dense moisture forming in the center of the cave – a hazy orange and blue cloud that was swiftly turning into a mottled brown.

"What the hell? So, you let Daniel in on the secret experiment, but not me?" Kyyle grumbled.

"My superior fiery form and analytical skills make me instrumental for this project," Daniel chirped. "Silly organic creatures such as yourself wouldn't understand."

Kyyle raised an eyebrow. "You're getting pretty cocky for a fledging elemental. Maybe Brock here needs to teach you some manners," he offered, gesturing at the earth elemental that now accompanied Kyyle everywhere and stood stoically nearby.

Daniel just flashed once and darted back behind Finn.

"Display please, Daniel," Finn instructed, ignoring their banter. "Also, make certain you use the feed from my *Mana Sight* to record the experiment. If this fails, I want to be able to figure out why."

The AI flashed once in acknowledgment, and a three-dimensional model of the cave abruptly appeared in the air before Finn, each of the mages' positions marked with a color-coded dot. Kyyle examined that display with a furrowed brow, cocking his head as he tried to guess at what Finn was planning to do down here.

But Finn had other matters to worry about for now.

He would need to absorb the heat from two areas of the cave – just above Brutus and Fahima's position and the area in front of Charlotte. Normally, this would have been difficult, as he would be constrained by his control range, but he had discovered something quite interesting during the last day in-game. He wished he could claim that he had conducted a series of complicated tests to divine the purpose of the *Focusing Prism* set into the back of his new crystalline appendage.

But the truth was a bit less glamorous.

It had gotten rather hot in the cave that he was using to administer the *Forging*, sweat dripping down his face and causing Finn's robe to cling to his back. After hours spent sitting upon that crude stone throne, he eventually just couldn't take it anymore. In an act of frustration, he'd tugged at the ambient heat in the air... only to accidentally pull the warmth from the entire chamber simultaneously, leaving the guildsmen shivering and wide-eyed.

That feat shouldn't have been possible – not with his limited control range.

But neither should what happened next. The flames swept into his new hand, swirling within the depths of the *Focusing Prism* and lighting the gem with a brilliant orange glow that had the guildsmen backing away warily from his makeshift stone throne.

Although, the subsequent prompt had quickly cleared up any confusion.

New Effect Discovered: Focusing Prism

You have accidentally unlocked the potential of the Focusing Prism set into the back of Translucent Flame. This gem can act as a storage vessel for your *Mana Absorption*, effectively creating a supplementary mana pool. Note that you will still suffer health damage as normal when absorbing

mana. Spells cast using this pool will expend all of the stored mana simultaneously. The gem also dramatically increases the effective range and area of effect of your *Mana Absorption*. These effects will scale with the level of Translucent Flame.
Total Mana Stored: 0/20,000
Increased Effective Range: 50 yards

Regardless of how he had come to discover the gem's properties, Finn wasn't one to look a gift horse in the mouth.

The *Focusing Prism*'s effects alone were incredible. But when combined with the levels Finn had gained practicing with the hand, he had discovered that they also scaled extraordinarily well – almost 10% of the base stats per level. Eventually, he would likely be able to drain the mana from an incredibly large area. Putting aside that he wasn't quite certain why he would *need* to drain the heat from an area the size of a football field. At least, not in most situations.

However, in this case, the effect had come in handy – pun entirely intended.

Finn pulled up the prompt for his hand as he stared at the crystalline limb.

Translucent Flame (Crafted by Nar Aljahim)
This hand has been built entirely of the so-called neurogem material that you discovered within the depths of the Forge and was crafted by an ancient fire elemental.
Quality: A
Level: 11
Health: 700
(Soulbound)

Adaptable Limb
Skill Level: Intermediate Level 1
Cost: 500 Mana
Effect 1: Allows the caster to make [moderate]

modifications to the limb.
Effect 2: Decreases shift time by 20%.

Focusing Prism
Total Mana Stored: 0/40,000 (100% scaling)
Increased Effective Range: 100 yards (100% scaling)

Soulforged Item (Bonded by Nar Aljahim)
This item has been imbued with the Najima of the traveler named Finn. The limb's health is counted separately from the traveler's regular health pool and will scale as the item levels. Damage to the limb is repaired using the 1/6 of the user's mana regeneration (currently 9.81 per second). Destruction of the limb will result in the user's death, and the limb will return upon respawn.

He had been practicing with the hand constantly on the way back from the Forge and during any free moments he found. Much like his early mana training, he would repeatedly shift the hand from one shape to another while he performed other tasks. *Multi-Casting* had been incredibly useful in that regard, allowing him to cast with his right hand while he trained his newfound limb.

And now all that work might finally pay off.

Finn took a deep breath, grasping hold of the simmering energy coursing through his veins. He raised his hands, the sleeves of his robes falling back to reveal the crystalline fingers of his left hand and the regular flesh of his right. Then his fingers began moving simultaneously, as Finn split his attention between the two tasks. His hands were soon a blur of motion as he pulled at the energy at two points along the cave – just above Brutus and Fahima's position and the area in front of Charlotte, his enhanced control range making this entire experiment possible.

He could detect the ambient heat in the air of the cavern, only the faintest tinge of orange amid the regular swirl and ripple of yellow air mana. But he drew on that warmth nonetheless – pulling, tugging, *demanding* that the mana return to him, just as he had done during his fight with the Khamsin. And that energy responded reluctantly.

The temperature in both locations began to fall steadily, a stream of orange energy drifting toward Finn – first a trickle, and then, as he pulled more forcefully, a torrent of flame. That heat soon encircled his hands and curled up his wrist and biceps, leaving a trail of burnt skin in its wake before sinking down into his crystalline hand, settling within the *Focusing Prism*. As the seconds ticked past, that gem began to grow in intensity, shining with a brilliant light.

But the *Mana Absorption* still cost him dearly. He could feel the sting of the energy seeping into his body – an army of angry fire ants marching through his veins and arteries, pinching and burning as they inched forward. His health was dropping quickly, but he forced himself to keep going.

"The air beside Charlotte is ready," Daniel reported, his voice sounding distant.

Finn could barely spare the focus to glance in that direction while maintaining the delicate dance of his fingers and the dual absorption. But he could indeed see that he had leeched much of the heat out of the air. The air mage was now trembling in the chill air and shuffling in place with her mechanical legs.

"Give her the signal," Finn grunted, his voice hoarse.

"Charlotte, start casting!" Daniel shouted across the cave.

The air mage obliged. As soon as she finished casting, a sudden gust of air jetted from her palms and swept through the cavern. That current soon struck the pocket of cold air that Finn had formed in front of her, carrying it forward along the cave. To his eyes, it looked like a slow-moving blue avalanche of energy. Yet Finn never relented, maintaining his *Mana Absorption* to create a continuous, super-cold gust of air.

He looked on, his vision bleary, as that wave of blue and yellow energy streamed past his position. The frigid air washed across him, tugging at his robes. Under other circumstances, the cold might have been a burden. But the flames licking at his skin flickered and bent but refused to be put out. Instead, they pushed back at the cold. Kyyle wasn't as fortunate, his eyes widening as he darted behind Brock's massive form and tugged his robes closer.

Then the current of cold air was streaking past them…

That bank of chill air struck the heated cloud of vapor surrounding Brutus. At first, the cold and hot air merged in a chaotic frenzy of orange and blue, drifting farther down the narrow cave. However, as the seconds ticked past, the colder and hotter portions of the air began to separate. The frigid current settled along the floor and pushed the heated moisture upward toward the ceiling. That billowing cloud of hot vapor soon struck the second pocket of colder air that Finn had created along the top of the cavern. As it did, Finn held his breath, his eyes focused on that one section along the top of the cave.

Come on. Come on, he chanted in his head.

Warnings were beginning to flash in the corner of his UI. His health was bottoming out. Yet he couldn't stop absorbing the heat – not yet. He needed to maintain the cold air current and the frigid pocket of air near the ceiling for a few moments longer.

Finn pushed himself harder, forcing his fingers to keep moving.

As the warm moist air surged into that cold pocket, the moisture began to condense, forming large billowing white clouds of loose vapor. Yet it wasn't enough. He was running out of health… and time.

Damn it, it's almost there. I just need another minute, Finn thought, keeping a watchful eye on his health in the corner of his vision. He still had about 15% left.

He could go a bit further…

His attention shifted back to the growing clouds

along the ceiling. The vapor continued to grow and expand. As the moisture condensed, the cloud released heat, an orange haze radiating away from it. That energy then cooled again under the effects of Finn's *Mana Absorption*, and the vapor condensed again. And again. And again.

A towering column of clouds was forming now, a wall of condensed air and moisture that was pushed along the cavern by Charlotte's sustained blast of air. And as the seconds ticked past and the clouds grew, swelling and filling with moisture, they began to turn a darker gray.

And then Finn heard it – the first drops of rain striking the stone floor.

A deluge soon followed, a haze of sapphire droplets raining down upon the far end of the cave and swiftly soaking the dirt and rock. A mad, excited smile stretched across Finn's face as he watched the scene. He'd done it! He'd really done it!

As his health ticked down to 2%, Finn finally dropped his *Mana Absorption*, listing in place for a moment before Kyyle quickly offered a steadying hand. At the same time, the current of air abruptly petered out as Charlotte finally ran out of mana.

Yet his gaze never wavered from that artificial storm front. The line of clouds continued to coast along the cavern until they crashed into the far wall where the moisture billowed against the rock, swirling and colliding until it lost its stability. The updraft of hot air and the downdraft that accompanied the rain collapsed into one another in a chaotic mixture of air, heat, cold, and wet.

"Holy shit," Kyyle murmured as he watched that scene. He pulled away from Finn as he steadied himself, rubbing at his arms to get some feeling back in his frigid skin. The cave was chilly – almost ice cold after the current had swept through the chamber. "You... you created a storm front..."

"This is what you were trying to create?" Brutus demanded in an incredulous voice as he marched back toward the pair with Fahima in tow. The two were drenched, their robes soaked down to the bone, but the moisture did little to subdue the manic grin that had crept across the fire mage's face – matching Finn's own. "I've never seen anything like it."

"That's because the mages were never taught to work together," Finn retorted, meeting his former instructor's eyes. "A storm front is a combination of cold, heat, air, and moisture. And you said it yourself a long time ago – together we are capable of incredible things, results far beyond what we could accomplish alone. Bilel and the guilds have just kept us at each other's throats." Brutus gave a curt nod, his eyes never leaving the billowing cloud of vapor along the far wall.

"They never told us we could create a storm, though," Fahima said softly, her eyes wide as she watched the clouds break apart ever-so-slowly.

Kyyle glanced back at Finn, and then his eyes dropped to his left arm, his brow furrowing. "Uh, what's up with your hand?" he asked in confusion.

Finn finally glanced down. He had dropped *Mana Absorption* some time ago, and yet the crystal embedded in his newfound hand still glowed with a brilliant orange light – a collection of the ambient heat in the cavern. He'd almost forgotten what he'd done with everything else going on, but now he finally had a chance to examine the limb.

"That's a *Focusing Prism*," Charlotte observed as she approached. With gentle fingers, she touched Finn's hand, lifting it to examine the gem. "They are rare… very rare. They can be used to collect mana and then re-use it later. Normally the gems are embedded in a staff or wand, acting as a repository of additional mana in a pinch and a way to augment normal spellcasting. They can be tied to a specific spell or school of spells."

She pulled an eyepiece from her pocket, leaning closer to inspect the gem. "This crystal is of exceptional quality and size. I suspect it can store quite a bit of energy…" Charlotte glanced up at Finn. "Although, I believe you already know that."

He just nodded. Kyyle was swiping at the air to bring up his console, staring at Finn's new hand, but he waved him off. "The notes can wait for a bit. We need to analyze the data from this experiment first."

His attention drifted back to the three-dimensional model projected beside him, the display replaying loop of the storm front's formation. Despite his success, Finn's mind was already churning on a new problem. Could he improve on this?

He would need to create something bigger – much, much bigger.

But he had the resources. If they took his experiment and scaled it up – added a *few hundred* air, water, and fire mages instead of a handful? They might be able to create something tremendous... catastrophic even.

The biggest issue was his role in the experiment. Unfortunately, Finn was the only mage that could easily draw heat from his surroundings, and there likely wasn't time to teach the other fire mages. Although he had a way to collect more heat without killing himself now, and he could possibly kill two birds with one stone – testing the true limits of the *Focusing Prism*.

"You have that look again," Kyyle observed. "And while we now all understand *what* you were trying to create... the *why* is still a little unclear."

Brutus snorted. "That's a huge understatement." The fire mage eyed Finn, a hint of nervousness lingering in his expression. "This was an interesting demonstration, but how exactly are you planning to use this?"

Finn's fire mana flared in his chest as he considered his plan. A smile stretched across his face, and his eyes glowed with fiery energy as he met his companions' inquiring expressions. "We're facing a demon that can see mana... and will likely notice our army approaching long before we reach the walls of Lahab," Finn explained.

"So, you're hoping to drown him out?" Brutus grunted, still wringing out his damp robes. "Maybe rain on the magical tea party he's having with his hounds?"

"Not quite," Finn answered with a small smile, his

gleaming eyes still lingering on the clouds beating against the far wall of the cave. The energy was dense – many overlapping layers of mana concealing the earth mana behind it. Energy that might even be dense enough to conceal an army...

"You're looking at how we're going to storm the city."

Chapter 36 - Strategic

"After several days, our numbers have grown. We have roughly 700 bonded mages, 800 bonded fighters, 500 bonded merchants, and 2,000 Khamsin," Kalisha recited, reading down the list hanging in the air above the crude stone table. "Plus, another 100 merchants and 200 mages held in reserve as healers and support troops."

The merchant grimaced at the list, barely sparing any attention to the crowd that lingered around the table, nestled deep within the Hive. A shimmer of yellow mana along the walls indicated that Abbad had soundproofed the chamber. "I'd feel better if we were able to bond the remaining mages and merchants," she grumbled.

As Kalisha spoke, a small spiderlike creature skittered up her arm, clamping its mechanical legs around her shoulder. The merchant stroked it with idle fingers as she surveyed the data in front of them. She had decided to undergo the *Forging* with a smaller version of her mechanids. The choice had seemed odd to Finn, but, if his hand was any indication, he suspected there was more to the miniature mech than met the eye.

"Unfortunately, that would take at least another day," Finn retorted. "The *Forging* process is incredibly time-consuming. In the meantime, Bilel will further secure his foothold in Lahab and grow his own forces from the local population. In the time it takes me to bond a single person, he may convert five. If we wait any longer, he will only continue to grow his lead." Kalisha just frowned in response.

"One spot of good news is that those numbers don't include our new shock troops – which I'm calling the Infernal Guard," Julia added, swiping at the list. The display shifted to show detailed information on the soldiers she had been training. "The merchants have prepared platemail for a hundred of the Khamsin, and they have each been paired with a fire mage."

"How has the training been going?" Finn asked,

noting the way his daughter was rubbing at her neck and how her shoulders were slumped forward. Despite her penchant for nagging Finn to take care of himself, she'd been logged in for nearly three days straight, in-game time – or closing in on 18 hours in the real world.

"It's *going*," she grumbled. A sigh. "They could use a few more weeks, but they're serviceable. The mages are able to sustain *Imbue Fire* for nearly an hour straight at heat rank level 1, they're not entirely hopeless at assisting the Khamsin's movements, and they've learned a few basic formations – mostly designed to protect the mages. Although, none of that seems to come easy to either the mages or the Khamsin."

"Both are accustomed to operating alone – a function of their training and experience," Abbad said with a knowing nod. "Teamwork is a learned skill, one Bilel always strove to suppress."

Julia rolled her shoulders in response, the bone and muscle in her neck and shoulders cracking and snapping. "Well, I just hope they can keep it together in a real fight. There have already been a few scuffles. The mages also need to stay close to maintain the channel, and they're vulnerable while channeling. It would only take a momentary break in their ranks and a few stray hellhounds to disable many of the mages."

Finn nodded at that. They would just have to hope that Julia's training was sufficient and that a more immediate and common enemy would quell some of the infighting. It was more difficult to bicker when a hellhound was trying to tear your throat out.

"The bonded fighters have also been training extensively with their *Forged* weapons," Malik spoke up, the fighter's expression stoic. "They're now accustomed to using the new weapons and have leveled them quite quickly."

"Uh, how did they do that exactly?" Kyyle asked, leaning forward with curiosity shining in his eyes. Brock's bulky form hovered behind him, his glowing green eyes surveying the group impassively.

"We have been pitting the fighters against one another in duels for the last three days. They're given a five-minute break every 30 minutes to regenerate stamina and health," Malik explained. "Normally, we could increase their training rate with potions and consumables, but supplies are too limited to waste. Although, many of the Khamsin have joined in these duels, anxious to prove themselves against our guildsmen. That has helped to increase the experience gain considerably – despite a few injuries."

"We need to be wary of driving them to the point of exhaustion," Finn cautioned. "We still have a war to fight, after all."

Malik nodded in acknowledgment. "Since this afternoon, they've been permitted to rest and recuperate in anticipation of the upcoming battle."

"The merchants set up makeshift forges in the Flagship, and we've managed to supply and equip all of our soldiers, guildsmen and Khamsin alike," Kalisha explained. A grimace flitted across her face. "Although, as Malik mentioned, consumables are in short supply. We don't have the ingredients needed to prepare many potions or access to a market."

"We'll just have to make do," Finn said tiredly, rubbing at his temple with one hand.

"There's also still the matter of the unbonded merchants and mages... mostly healers," Kalisha continued, arching an eyebrow at Finn. Her tiny mech had turned its domelike head toward Finn, its cores flashing with energy – possibly echoing Kalisha's dour opinion of the situation.

He shook his head. "As I said, we just don't have the time. These are primarily support troops, so they won't be fighting on the frontlines."

"Which is little solace when trying to explain why they were excluded from the *Forging*," Kalisha snapped in irritation.

"And there's not much I can do about that. Let them grumble," Finn shot back, his frustration getting the better of him, and his eyes flashing with a pulse of orange energy.

As he noticed surprise and indignation flash across the merchant's face, Finn forcefully tamped down on his frustration. They were all on edge after days of preparation, and there was no sense alienating the merchant... even if he often found himself wanting to strangle her.

"Reassure them that they will be protected. They will all be positioned in the interior ranks of the army when we lay siege to Lahab," he explained in a more conciliatory tone. Kalisha just sniffed in response, breaking eye contact with Finn.

"Speaking of which, it looks like the situation in Lahab has definitely worsened," Kyyle piped up, his eyes staring at an invisible display.

All eyes turned to the earth mage, who promptly swiped at the air.

A moment later, a screen appeared beside him, showing a first-person video that must have been recorded by one of the travelers back in Lahab – the sandstone structures a dead giveaway. Finn even recognized some of those buildings...

The traveler rushed down a street, his feet beating hard at the sand, and his breathing ragged and frantic. He stooped under an awning, pushing himself flat against the wall just as a pack of hellhounds raced across the intersection ahead of him – flames curling away from their bodies. Screams soon echoed from down the road.

"We need to get out of here," a woman spoke up from behind him.

Another traveler came into view, her robes marking her as a water mage. "We're almost to the gate," the man huffed in response. "Just move quickly and stick close to the wall."

Then they set off again, racing down the street and into another back alley.

The northeastern gate soon came into view, and the pair froze. It wasn't the pack of hounds lingering along the gate that made them pause – although the hundreds of flaming creatures loitering about the gates was a terrifying sight. Nor was it the piles of corpses pushed up against the walls of the nearby buildings – their blood staining the sands a dark crimson. Likely, they were the travelers and residents who hadn't undergone the conversion into the hounds.

As they looked on, flames erupted from behind the towering wall that ringed Lahab, stretching up into the air. Yet these fires weren't localized to the gate.

The traveler shifted his view, and more flames could be seen peeking up atop the walls to the north and south, forming a solid, circular barrier that began to ring the city. That shield stretched ever farther into the sky, the camera shifting again as the traveler looked behind him. More flames were streaking up into the air from the other side of Lahab.

And those flames were converging overtop the city, forming a massive dome of fire. The flames were so thick that the pair could no longer make out the blue sky or the position of the sun. There was now only a perpetual flickering firelight, motes of molten energy raining down upon the city.

"What... what do we do now?" the woman behind him asked, her voice frantic. "How are we going to get through that barrier?"

"I don't – " The traveler's voice cut off as the camera listed to the side, tumbling and jerking erratically as he struck the nearby wall. Once the screen settled, the snout of a hellhound drifted into view, blood still dripping from its teeth. It let out a howl, arching its back as it called to the others.

Then those flaming eyes centered back on the traveler, a low growl erupting from the beast's throat as it paced forward.

"Oh god!" the traveler screamed, trying to scramble backward.

Yet it was too late.

The hound's fangs flashed, and the display went dark.

A silence hung over the chamber as the clip ended.

"That was posted less than an hour ago," Kyyle offered quietly. "A few more videos have also started cropping up from travelers recording what's happening in Lahab."

Finn shook his head. His mind was already

working on that shield of fire mana. It seemed Bilel was anticipating an attack on the city – an obvious deduction after he had discovered the guilds nearly emptied of the resident mages, merchants, and fighters. His guess was that the hellhounds were sustaining the barrier, their numbers likely having grown to the point that Bilel could afford to divert excess mana to power the shield.

That might throw a kink in his plans.

"These videos aren't great," Julia muttered, swiping at the air now as she searched the net. "And the forums are already buzzing with word of a massacre in Lahab and a possible war on the horizon. That last bit must have been leaked by the few travelers that escaped with the guilds," she offered with a frown.

Julia shook her head, her eyes drifting to Finn. "This is a problem. These sorts of videos might encourage travelers to come to Lahab – looking for a fight and some easy loot. And they may or may not see our army as friendly." She winced. "Or worse, if there are still travelers among our ranks, they could post their own videos... possibly giving away our position and resources. They might even try to cut a deal with the demon."

"Assuming Bilel is smart enough to realize that the travelers can communicate this way," Kyyle retorted, his brow furrowed.

"Do you really want to bet on that?" Julia replied. "In any other ga—" She stopped herself short, glancing at the other members of the council around the table. "Let's just say, that this world isn't normal – at least compared to others of its kind," she said with a meaningful look at Kyyle.

Julia was trying to be circumspect, but her intent was clear.

Could they really assume the NPCs wouldn't figure this out?

After witnessing firsthand just how *real* the residents of this world acted, Finn didn't feel comfortable making assumptions there.

And even if Bilel didn't figure out a way to snoop

on the travelers, her point still stood. If they didn't do something about this, they might have a miniature army of travelers to contend with on top of Bilel – idiots looking for gear and glory.

"I think I need to shut this down," Julia said, meeting Finn's gaze. "I could pull these videos off a few sites and bury some of the forum posts. It's still early, so I could probably stop this from going viral if I move quickly."

Finn grimaced. What she really meant was that she planned to hack a few servers.

And yet he also didn't see a better alternative. With everything riding on this battle, they couldn't afford any last-minute surprises. He gave her a reluctant nod. "Just this once," he cautioned, raising a finger.

"Yeah, yeah... sure," Julia muttered, already tapping at her in-game console.

"It seems the number of hounds has only continued to increase," Abbad spoke up, his eyes still on the screen, the short video replaying on a loop.

Aerys shook her head. "And we were already looking at 4,000 to 5,000 of our own against a legion of at least 10,000. By now, that might be 20,000..."

She trailed off, rubbing at her face. The woman looked tired. Dark circles hung under her eyes, evidencing days spent herding the Khamsin. "Morale may be a problem before long. Our 'prophet's' influence only goes so far. Already, the rumors are circling about what we will face. It may be due to travelers spreading images such as these," she offered, waving at the screen.

A frown tugged at Aerys' lips. "Although, I suspect the rumors are more likely a result of this 'pet' hellhound that we've been forced to protect," she added with a sharp expression at the burly fire mage.

"Hey, don't blame Betty," Brutus shot back, earning him a scowl from Aerys. The fire mage had been admitted to the Hive and this meeting only at Finn's insistence – another power struggle that the Khamsin leader had ultimately lost. It didn't seem she'd forgotten that slight yet. "She's an innocent in all of this!"

Kyyle snorted out a laugh. "An innocent fire-eating monster, you mean."

"Well, I'll be the first to admit that she can be a little... feisty," Brutus replied.

"Which is the understatement of the century," Aerys interjected. "I've seen the creature with my own eyes. I can only imagine what a legion of those... those *things* could do to our troops. There's a reason that her presence has put our people on edge." Her gaze drifted back to Finn. "Even putting aside the demon that leads them."

"Bilel does present a problem," Abbad said with a nod, swiping at the air to bring up a map of Lahab and the surrounding area. "Shielding the city is just a first step. Bilel will likely be able to see us coming long before we reach Lahab's walls, and he has absorbed an enormous amount of mana over the decades – conserving his strength. We should be prepared for elaborate illusions and possibly significant changes to the city's layout and defenses."

Finn nodded. "And the hounds are funneling energy to the relic, which means Bilel will likely be nearly immortal until we can slay the creatures. Our first priority should be to gather the beasts together and try to eliminate them.

"Which is where the Infernal Guard comes in," Finn continued, gesturing at Julia. "The hounds are attracted to dense sources of mana – particularly fire mana – and while the mages maintain *Imbue Fire*, the guard should attract the beasts' attention."

"Assuming they don't get overwhelmed," Kyyle said softly, his expression worried as he watched Julia – likely envisioning her on the frontlines of this war.

Aerys let out a sigh, her eyes jumping from the map to Finn's eyes. "So, we face an immortal demon, a legion of hounds that allow him to heal any wound, and our lynchpin is to have a mere 100 of our own face down some unknown number of hounds? I suppose we'll just have to place our faith in the goddess and our *prophet* that we manage to survive this."

Finn met her skepticism with a small smile. "We can do better than that. I've never been much for operating on blind faith anyway."

"You speak as though you have a plan," Abbad said, his brow furrowing slightly.

"Indeed, we do," Finn replied, his smile widening.

"We?" Julia said, glancing up from her screen with confusion rippling across her face. Finn hadn't had a chance to update her on his little experiment or the plan that had begun to solidify over the last day in-game.

"You guys want to show them what we've come up with?" Finn asked, directing this question at Kyyle and Brutus.

"Not really..." the fire mage muttered. "I still say this is madness. This much mana has never been condensed into a single area before – at least not since the time before the gods were banished from this world. We can't predict what will happen..." This reaction earned Brutus a few puzzled and worried looks from the group around the table.

"Well, there's a first time for everything," Kyyle offered, swiping at the air. "We've run and re-run the calculations repeatedly, and it *should* work." This earned him a skeptical snort from the fire mage as his eyes hovered on the screen above the table.

The display shifted, now showing a top-down view of a patch of desert located to the east, between the Hive and the Flagship and Lahab. It had taken them some time and the help of a few Khamsin scouts to find this location. They needed flat ground without as many of the rolling dunes or rock islands that normally dotted the deep desert. The natural direction of the wind was also helpful. This spot had a strong current of air that flowed from west to east, unobstructed by any natural obstacles.

"We're looking at a patch of sand," Kalisha observed dryly.

Finn just shook his head, rising from his seat and

circling the table to stand at its head. He flicked at the screen with his fingers, and suddenly, a hundred yellow dots appeared along the western side of the sandy strip. "We'll station 100 air mages at this location. They'll be broken up into two groups of 50, so they can rotate their casting and allow the alternate group to regenerate its mana."

"Okay," the merchant drawled, dragging the word out. "Now we have a bunch of mages standing in the middle of the desert. I'm still not seeing the master plan here."

"Just wait," Kyyle murmured, a gleam in his eye.

Finn swiped again. Another few hundred blue and orange dots appeared toward the eastern side of the strip. "Water and fire mages will be stationed in this area. The water mages will continuously cast *Obscuring Mist*, and the fire mages will work to heat that vapor. We need to seed this area with as much moist, warm air as possible."

Brutus noted the frown curling Kalisha's lips and spoke up before she could say anything. "Yes, yes, it looks like we're blowing hot air across the desert. Just wait." The merchant's mouth snapped shut.

"And I will be positioned here with a group of healers," Finn said, a glowing orange dot appearing between the line of air mages and the group of water and fire mages... positioned much more closely to the cluster of air mages. A small group of green dots encircled his position to denote the earth mage healers.

Julia's brow was furrowed, and Finn was watching her closely, waiting to see if she caught on to his plan. "What exactly are you planning to do here?" she murmured. "A strong current of air moving to the east. It will strike a pocket of warm, humid air. But what's your role..." She drifted off as her eyes went wide, and her mouth dropped open.

His daughter's eyes snapped to Finn, staring at him with an incredulous expression. "You can't be serious!"

He felt his smile grow wider, his eyes flaring with fire as his excitement got the better of him. "I can. And I am."

"You two want to share with the group?" Kalisha interjected sourly.

Finn waved at the AI that floated beside his shoulder. "Daniel, bring up our model."

"Of course, sir," the AI chirped.

The display shifted, the camera tilting from a top-down view to an isometric angle, providing a three-dimensional re-creation of the terrain and position of the mages. Overlaying the image was a projection of the ambient mana in each region – as though the group was viewing the model through Finn's *Mana Sight*. The area around the fire and water mages was swiftly enveloped in a cloud of sapphire energy, the mana turning a darker brown as it was heated by the fire mages.

"As I mentioned, the first step is to create a cloud of moist, hot air," Finn explained, tapping at that billowing, dark cloud.

Then the dot denoting Finn's location began casting, the temperature dropping swiftly and a large patch of sand beginning to turn a dark blue. The healers stationed around him flared brightly – continuously casting as they helped to keep his health topped off.

"At the same time, I need to dramatically drop the temperature in the area in front of the air mages," Finn explained. "At which point..."

He trailed off as a current of yellow energy soon swept away from the line of air mages, blasting across the sands and whipping past Finn's location and carrying the cool air along with it. That artificial cold front soon struck the pocket of moist air, colliding and merging before separating into separate currents of hot and cold air.

The colder current forced the heated vapor upward. As it drifted higher and higher, the mist began to cool and clouds formed, swiftly condensing and giving off a flash of heat, before expanding, rising, and repeating the process again and again and again. Within the span of only a few minutes, a billowing tower of clouds had formed, stretching several miles into the air and spreading out across the sands into a massive storm front that barreled across the dunes, picking up speed as the natural air current began to carry the storm forward.

Rain soon poured from those clouds, beating against the sand, and the occasional flash of lightning struck the ground. The image suddenly shifted, switching back to a top-down view and tracing the projected path of the storm, a yellow line leading straight to Lahab. That line of clouds glowed with an almost overwhelming mixture of blue, yellow, and orange energy, creating a billowing storm front filled with so much mana that it would be nearly impenetrable to Finn's sight... or, at least, he hoped it would be.

Silence had descended upon the room, the entire group staring at the model wide-eyed and mouths agape.

"You plan to *create* a storm," Abbad said softly into that silence. The librarian glanced at Finn. "Is this really possible?"

"It sure is," Brutus affirmed with a grunt. "I've seen it with my own eyes. Finn tested his theory already by creating a miniature version in a cave below the Flagship. Although, we were only using a handful of mages at the time."

Abbad nodded, his eyes flicking back to the display. "I see your goal. The ambient mana will be so thick that even Bilel will have trouble penetrating it with his sight. And from what Brutus mentioned about the hounds, the wet and cold should dampen their strength. That's... that's incredible," he murmured, staring at the model. Finn could see the air mage's energy fluctuating wildly, tendrils of flame curling through his body.

Excitement, Finn thought. He could see the same energy shining in the others, replacing the insidious black doubt that had begun to creep into their mana.

"And our forces will move in behind the storm front," Kyyle explained. With a gesture, their army appeared on-screen, moving along at the back end of the storm. "We'll use it to conceal our troops and our movements. And when the front strikes the city, that should also help neutralize Bilel's spellcasting and cover our people as we lay siege to Lahab. You can't cast at what you can't see."

Finn looked to Kalisha then. "Happy now?" he asked with a faint grin.

The merchant just nodded numbly, her eyes fixed on the display.

Aerys coughed to clear her throat, visibly trying to tamp down on her surprise. "This is… impressive. But how much time will you need to set it up?" she asked Finn.

His grin only widened. "The preparations are already underway. The mages are moving into position as we speak, and they will begin forming the storm tomorrow morning. Once the front is moving toward Lahab, the mages will return to the rest of the army, and we will ride east."

"Tomorrow?" Aerys echoed, her eyes widening. "You plan to attack Lahab tomorrow?"

"As I said, the longer we wait, the stronger Bilel becomes," Finn answered simply, his mana burning away any lingering trace of doubt or hesitation he might have. His plan was aggressive, but he saw no other option.

His gaze panned the room, meeting the eyes of each member of their group. "Which concludes our meeting. Gather your people and make your final preparations. Because we go to war at first light."

As he finished speaking, Finn glanced at Julia, observing the delighted smile that now stretched across her face as she watched the model – the storm front raging across the screen and just beginning to crash into the city's walls. He doubted even Bilel would anticipate this sort of attack. The sheer scale of what they were attempting to create went far, far beyond anything they had observed in this world.

As he followed the projected path of the storm once again, Finn couldn't help but visualize the dome of molten energy that he had witnessed in that short video. He hadn't run his calculations with that barrier in mind – or the ambient heat that it would put off. Not that he supposed that mattered. He wasn't certain he could predict how that much raw fire mana would affect the storm front...

Although, he suspected he was going to find out soon.

Either way, he just had to hope that storm would be enough.

Chapter 37 - Maelstrom

Finn watched the glow on the horizon as the sun began to gradually crest that line of sand. An orange haze of fire mana lingered there, leaking up into the sky and growing gradually dimmer as it rose. The heat gave way to open sprawling sky and air, blues and yellows swirling and colliding in his *Mana Sight*. As it rose, the sun had also begun to illuminate the ocean of green earth mana that sprawled out before him. A breeze tugged at his robes, bringing with it wisps of sand and the smell of dry heat.

In the distance, he could just barely make out a cloud of sapphire energy forming. The water mages had begun casting *Obscuring Mist* hours ago, the cool vapor still clinging to the sands and dunes – at least for now. That cloud stretched for several miles across the desert, the product of hundreds of water mages working together. And once the sun had risen fully, the fire mages would start casting, the natural heat from the sun and their magics warming that vapor into a dense, humid cloud.

But, for now, he just reveled at the sight. A rainbow of colors spanning out toward the horizon and drifting up into the sky. Green, blue, orange, and yellow, blending into a water-color portrait that had been painted just for him.

"It's almost beautiful," Julia said softly as she approached Finn, coming to stand beside him. "This world, I mean."

Finn just grunted in acknowledgment. He'd had a similar thought many times since entering the game world. And yet, his thoughts kept returning to a familiar rain-swept terrace and boiling gray clouds. It didn't matter whether *he* thought this world was magnificent. It wasn't *his* opinion – or Julia's – that mattered to him right now.

"What's eating at you?" his daughter asked, side-eyeing him.

He glanced at her in surprise.

"Come on. You've been keeping to yourself the last few days." A pause as her gaze drifted back to the sunrise. "We're a team, remember? Or at least, I *thought* we were."

A grimace tugged at Finn's lips, and he rested a hand on his daughter's shoulder. "Trust me. We are. It's just..." He hesitated, having a difficult time putting his thoughts into words.

"Do you think she'll like this place?" he asked finally, his voice barely above a whisper. "This world full of sand and conflict and death." He gestured at his left hand to emphasize his point, the regular flesh now replaced with translucent crystal. He'd even given up his eyes – the only way he could now see the mana fluctuating across the dunes.

Finn couldn't bring himself to look at Julia, but he felt her shift under his hand, turning to look at him. A brief silence lingered in the air as she weighed how to respond.

"I think... I think you're selling it short. Even our world is full of hardship, death, and despair – we've certainly experienced our fair share. But this game – this world – it also has magic, friendship, and discovery. It's a whole new horizon ready to be explored," Julia said, waving at the sun that was slowly rising above the sands.

He managed to meet her eyes then, seeing the confidence shining there as he activated *Short-Sighted*, and her face came into view. "Is that how you came up with this new plan?" Julia asked. "Creating a storm front, I mean."

Finn just nodded as he turned his gaze back to the sunrise. "Your mother always loved the rain."

"You mean she was just a little crazy and would regularly get drenched sitting out in the middle of a thunderstorm," Julia replied with a chuckle. "Although, I used to love that – going on walks, splashing through puddles, dancing and running through the yard. Counting down the seconds after a flash of lightning, just waiting for the peal of thunder."

A small smile drifted across Finn's face as those memories returned. Those had been happier times. "You would both be soaked to the bone when you came back inside," he said. "You always wanted to go back out immediately."

"And you always told me there would be other storms."

Finn's good humor faded at that statement. The truth was that there wouldn't be other storms – not really. Not for Rachael. And he knew firsthand how the "magic" of a storm front rolling in had faded in her absence. It had been her enthusiasm that made those moments special. And with that thought, the reality of their situation crept back in – the sheer magnitude of what they were trying to do resting squarely on his shoulders.

The weight felt impossibly heavy.

"There won't be rain here – not without all of this," Finn said, squeezing his eyes shut and willing his voice to remain even. "Not a single drop."

The implication of his words was unmistakable. When they brought back Rachael, she would be stuck here – trapped inside this digital prison for an indeterminate amount of time. And those same questions returned. Could she accept that? Would she? Would being with Finn and Julia be enough for her to cope with what had happened to her? What she had become?

And all of that was based on so many assumptions.

That they could really conquer Lahab and defeat Bilel.

That it was even really Rachael that they would be bringing back – and not just some sort of carefully crafted illusion.

Julia grabbed at his hand, squeezing his fingers. "Hey. Hey, look at me."

Finn obliged, meeting his daughter's eyes. She wasn't a little girl any longer. Those days of splashing through puddles were long gone. She was a grown woman now, determination and strength rippling through every fiber of her body. It was evidenced by the scars that marred her skin. The shield and lance strapped down against heavy platemail. The thick coating of dust that lingered across her armor – accumulated over days and weeks spent struggling through this world.

She was a warrior. And she planned to keep fighting.

"We're going to bring her back," Julia insisted. "We're going to retrieve that staff. And when we do, we can shape this world however we please. We can make this into a place where we can live – together.

"And if Mom wants to see the rain... well, then by the gods, we're going to make it fucking rain," she added more forcefully. "And that starts here." She waved behind them at the cluster of air mages lined along the sands in the distance.

He stared at her for a long moment before nodding. "You're right." Then, more firmly. "You're right."

Finn squared his shoulders and tugged at his robes, channeling his fire mana and using that burning energy to drive away his own doubts. They were going to keep fighting. They were going to bring this war straight to Bilel. They were going to storm Lahab and gut the hounds that roamed its streets. Then he planned to rip that staff from the demon's pale, sickly fingers. He planned to bring Rachael back – man, deity, or reality be damned.

"You ready?" Julia asked gently.

He met her eyes, the amalgamation of metal and crystal glowing softly behind the cloth that wrapped his face. "Yes. Yes, I am."

"Then let's get started."

Julia waved at the group of nearly a dozen earth mages that stood around them in a circle, standing as far away from Finn as possible – at the very edge of their control range. Brock's rocky form signaled that Kyyle lingered among the group, directing their movements. He was there primarily for damage control in case this went sideways. They couldn't afford a delay waiting on a respawn timer. His directions were to protect Finn and the healers... they couldn't afford to lose either.

At a gesture from Finn, Kyyle and Brock made a beeline for their position.

Kyyle nodded at Finn as he neared. "Everyone is in formation. They're all in the same raid group as you now, so you should be visible in their UI, and I marked you to make it easier for them to keep track of you... since, well, I expect this to get a little hairy. They'll be rotating clockwise as they cast to conserve mana and ensure a continuous stream of healing."

A pause and a grimace. "I just hope it'll be enough. You've never tried absorbing this much mana before. I can't be sure the healing per second will be able to keep up."

"Have they been equipped to weather the absorption?" Julia asked.

Kyyle nodded. "They're all wearing thick furs – Kalisha even supplied a few pieces of cold-resistance gear. I also created a small embankment of stone and rock around each of them. That should blunt most of the cold and wind. They've been directed to keep an eye on their own health and top off when it isn't their turn to cast. That should be enough to keep them safe and healthy," he said, although his voice sounded worried.

Finn glanced at the healers, who each stood several yards away. As his gaze swept over them, they each met his eyes, placing a fist to their chests like the Khamsin. It seemed that the legends had continued to spread among the guilds. And if they succeeded here, he suspected that the tales of exploits would only grow.

After all, he was about to conjure a storm in the middle of the desert.

Or fail miserably and kill himself by accident...

He was really hoping for the former outcome.

"Once your absorption is complete, I'll create a barricade to help protect us," Kyyle continued. He glanced at Finn then. "I looked at the model again carefully. We probably also need to be wary of microbursts and tornadoes. It may take some time for the currents to stabilize."

"That's only two potential problems," Daniel chirped. "You're forgetting the possibility of intense hail, lightning strikes, hurricane-force winds, and torrential rain."

As the group turned to stare at him, the elemental's light dimmed slightly. "Uh, what I mean is that we're definitely going to be fine!"

Finn let out a snort. "Just stay near me. Make sure to alert me if the healers start to run dry on mana and update my UI as I continue to expand my absorption. I doubt I'm going to be able to spare much attention to those details." The AI flashed once in acknowledgment before hovering close beside Finn.

A hand rested on his shoulder then. "I'll also be here with Kyyle to help pull you into cover if need be," Julia said. "I suspect you're going to need someone who can ambiently absorb mana with the amount of energy that's going to be swirling around you."

"Thank you," he replied, putting his hand over hers briefly.

Then Finn looked toward the east. The sun had now risen above the horizon. And the enormous cloud of vapor in the distance was beginning to warm as the fire mages went to work, forming a brownish haze just below the horizon that stretched for miles. That cloud was already beginning to rise slowly up into the air, until a wall of moist, warm air lingered to the east, nearly obscuring the sun.

"It's time," Finn said, and the healers around him tensed, tendrils of emerald energy already winding around their hands. Meanwhile, Kyyle and Julia gave him one last reassuring nod before scrambling away, putting some distance between themselves and Finn.

He soon stood alone in the center of the group, planting his feet firmly into the sand. Finn raised his hands, one crystal and the other flesh and blood. His eyes centered on the gem embedded in his new limb. As Kyyle had mentioned, he hadn't yet been able to test the full limits of the gem – neither its capacity nor the enhanced range of his *Mana Absorption*. But he was about to see just how far he could push both.

This is for you, Rachael, he thought to himself.

And then his fingers began to move.

As the channel completed, his fingers maintained their regular rhythm. He began to pull the ambient heat from the air around him. Streamers of energy streaked toward his position, and a fine coating of flame wrapped his skin. He swiftly pulled that energy into the gem in his hand until it began to glow with a mixture of orange and red energy. Even so, his health began to drop, his skin blistering under the heat. The first healing spell struck him, and the energy coursed through his body, immediately repairing the injuries. The welts disappeared in an instant but returned just as fast as he maintained his absorption.

Finn's eyes hovered on the glowing orange line that denoted his control range. He pushed at that boundary – gingerly at first – and saw that orange line grow as he expanded his absorption range. He kept going, pushing farther and farther out. He needed to cover this entire area, stretching out to the very edge of his control range.

The flames barreled toward him now, sweeping across the sands and streaming between the healers as he tried to avoid harming them. And yet he hadn't gone far enough – not nearly far enough.

Finn pushed harder, flames wrapping his body in a blaze now, and the gem in his hand began to glow more brightly. The heat was so intense that it flayed his skin in an instant, only to be repaired immediately as emerald energy washed across his body. Those healing spells struck every second, a bright surge of emerald energy flashing in a circular pattern around him as the healers maintained their formation – their precise timing a product of the hours they'd spent practicing throughout the night.

"25 yards," Daniel reported at his shoulder.

The air was growing colder and colder, steam rising above the flames that encircled Finn. And yet it still wasn't enough. He needed to push farther. Much farther.

With another gesture, Finn expanded the absorption. Every yard he added to his control range dramatically increased the area of the absorption. The pain was excruciating, yet he pushed himself through it. He kept adding one yard after another, more fire adding to the stream of energy that was glowing toward him and wrapping around his body, the flames arcing outward for more than a dozen feet now.

"40 yards!" Daniel shouted.

Halfway, Finn thought weakly. His thoughts were starting to become fuzzy as he maintained the channel and strove to stay standing amid the pain that wracked his body. He spared a blurry glance at his UI and saw that the healers were dropping below half mana already, the constant stream of healing energy keeping his health level.

I need to move more quickly.

"How much overhealing?" Finn managed to bark at Daniel.

"You are currently taking 1,200 health damage per second. Current healing per second is 3,000," Daniel shouted in response, a new indicator suddenly appearing in Finn's eye, tracking his damage taken and healing received dynamically.

I can push harder then.

Finn squeezed his eyes shut.

He forcefully shoved at that barrier that ringed him, forcing his absorption outward explosively – 40 yards in an instant. The fires enveloping his body raged up into the air, now completely obscuring the area around him in a blazing inferno of orange and red – forming a wall of flame almost five feet thick.

In the seconds before the next wave of healing energy struck him, the fire ate through his skin and into his muscles. Finn staggered, and then his legs finally gave way. He fell to the ground, the sand grinding into the ruined flesh of his knees. But he could barely feel that anymore. He knew there was a limit to this – a critical inversion point. If the damage taken per second exceeded his total health, he'd die before the next healing spell struck.

He hadn't reached that point yet, though.

So, he kept going.

He pushed at the edges of his control range, holding his left hand high and funneling a catastrophic amount of energy into that gem. The *Focusing Prism* now glowed so brightly that it looked like a miniature sun was resting atop the sands, wrapped into a cocoon of swirling flame and fire, the gem unable to absorb the energy quickly enough.

Finn ground his teeth together. Another glance at his UI.

2,000 damage taken per second.

I can handle more.

He pushed his absorption even further. Tributaries of fire had formed along the circular area of the absorption as the energy raced back to Finn. Those smaller streams pooled and collected, creating rivers of flame that merged… and then merged again. Where the fire was the densest, the ambient heat had begun to melt the sand, carving molten furrows in the ground. Steam drifted upward as super cold air pressed in on those rivers of flame.

From a bird's-eye view, it looked like Finn stood at the center of a flaming wheel of energy, the fires creating branching spokes that all led to a fiery core. And in that space, the heat had become so intense that the fires now flickered with a blue light along Finn's skin, the very center of the wheel beginning to turn a blazing white.

He could barely think now – his thoughts blurry and incoherent.

There was only the searing pain.

The flash of soothing healing.

The fire and flame.

"You hit the inversion point!" Daniel screamed in his ear. His damage taken now equaled his healing received. If he pushed any further, he ran the risk of killing himself almost instantly. Just a second's delay in the next healing spell would be enough.

"The healers have 30 more seconds of mana!"

Finn needed to maintain this for just a bit longer.

He pulled that heat into himself, into the gem in his hand. It was too bright to look at directly now, almost blinding. He just had to hope it could hold more.

He poured the flames into that gem as quickly as he could, using it to absorb the rivers of fire rushing toward him and enveloping his body. Gradually, the accumulated flames began to recede ever-so-slowly, leaking into the crystal.

"10 seconds!" Daniel screamed.

Just a little longer...

The flames had almost begun to dissipate, and Finn could just barely make out the area around him now. But his vision was blurry, and red notifications were flashing in the corner of his vision.

"Stop now!" Daniel screamed.

Finn canceled his channel.

The last healing spell struck him, healing his ruined flesh. His UI reported that he was topped off, and yet his body still burned with agonizing pain, his mind not quite able to keep up with the constant stream of damage and healing.

The world around him was frozen. Each breath sent out a dense cloud of cool vapor. Finn suddenly realized that the burning he felt wasn't the fire... it was the cold – a cold so intense that it seared his skin and caused his bones to ache.

Yet Finn could barely focus on that.

He squinted at the gem embedded in his hand. That crystal shone like the sun, holding so much energy that the mana had begun to leak into the hand itself, causing the limb to pulse with an intense light. Ambient tendrils of fire curled around his fingers, sparking each time he moved or shifted the limb.

System Notice
You have reached the limit of the *Focusing Prism* embedded in **Translucent Flame**. If you do not release this energy soon, the limb may experience permanent damage.

Finn swiped the notice aside, ignoring the shivers that wracked his body. He could just barely register that Julia was rushing toward him, and walls of stone were beginning to rise from the ground around him. The healers looked haggard, their robes burnt and singed, and their skin flayed despite Kyyle's barriers – but they were alive.

Unfortunately, Finn didn't have enough time to wait for Kyyle to finish building the earthen wall around himself.

He raised his translucent hand high into the air.

And then he unfurled his fingers and cast *Molten Beam.*

An enormous ray of fire erupted into the sky, spearing more than a mile up through the air. The beam was nearly three feet thick, the heat so intense that it scalded the skin around Finn's left arm even as he cast. He felt a few feeble healing spells strike him as the healers realized he was venting the pent-up energy, using the small remnants of mana that they had managed to regenerate.

The beam kept going, hitting the lower edge of the stratosphere. Clouds formed around the column of energy in an instant, swirling around it in a whirling vortex.

Then the energy petered out, and the dome of rock fully encircled the group. Julia was at his side, holding him upright while Kyyle and Brock lingered nearby, the earth mage frantically attempting to reinforce the dome of rock around them. Finn could just barely make out the faint emerald outlines around each of the healers as they hunkered down beneath their earthen bunkers.

Kyyle finished the barrier without a moment to spare. A whine could soon be heard outside the rocky dome, swiftly growing in strength.

That whine soon turned to a howl as the wind whipped around the stone. The sound rapidly grew so loud that Finn and his companions were forced to cover their ears. The rock shield began to tremble and crack, forcing Kyyle to continuously channel his mana to keep the dome from completely splitting apart.

Finn used his *Mana Sight* to look past the walls of their enclosure and witness what was happening outside, barely able to prop himself up with one arm.

A massive wall of yellow air mana was streaming past. The current was almost a mile wide, whipping across the sands with the force of a hurricane. That wind soon swept the super-cooled air forward and drove it toward the dense brown mass of heated moisture that lingered along the horizon, sending it streaming up toward the rising sun.

Finn's experiment had been impressive. They had created a miniature storm front in a cavern, roughly the size of a football field.

But that paled in comparison to what he was now witnessing.

The cold current of air struck the heated vapor and created a maelstrom of energy so dense that it fully filled Finn's vision, drifting off toward the corners of the horizon. That mana merged and diverged – coalesced and broke apart. It was a chaos of energy on an almost incomprehensible scale.

He saw a tornado form, the funnel of cool air striking the sands and whipping up the emerald particles. Then another. And another. The storm sucked up the sand and added that energy to the heat and cold and wind. And only seconds later, the tornadoes blew themselves apart, the updrafts and downdrafts forming and vanishing in an instant.

Then the currents began to stabilize.

Finn witnessed the heated vapor rise into the

stratosphere. He observed clouds beginning to form. However, this wasn't a small column of clouds in an underground cave. This was a truly massive storm front that stretched outward for nearly a mile, expanding with each passing second, spiraling up into the air to form an enormous bank of clouds.

The clouds turned darker and darker as the storm kept growing. It sped along, forced forward by an artificial current of cold air created by the air mages. That wind only paused for a moment as the second line of air mages stepped forward to replace their brothers and sisters in arms. Then it pushed at the storm front with renewed vigor, forcing it to grow, to expand, to move toward the east. Toward Lahab.

And then Finn saw it.

The first drops of rain began to splash against the sand just as the second group of air mages finally ran out of juice, and the winds abated. Kyyle dissolved the rock dome encircling them, which allowed the rest of the group to finally see what they had created.

An impossibly dense bank of clouds now covered the eastern horizon, blotting out the sun and rising and growing further. This world's natural currents were beginning to grab hold of the storm – filling out and bolstering what they had created. Rain beat heavily against the sands as that storm front marched east.

And amid that rain, Finn observed gale-force winds. Tornadoes forming along the ground, forced along on downdrafts of cold air. And he could see lightning arcing through those clouds, striking the ground and leaving molten patches in their wake. As the sand cooled, it formed intricate glass sculptures that mimicked the branching path of the lightning.

Finn's brow furrowed as he watched the storm's movements. He had expected the clouds to be pushed along in a straight line. Yet he could have sworn that they were beginning to spin... to pivot and swirl. Perhaps a function of the collision of the artificial current the air mages had created and this world's natural airstream?

Either way, the storm front was slowly coalescing into a giant revolving mass of wind, heat, cold, rain, and lightning.

"Holy shit," Kyyle muttered from beside him.

Julia was shaking her head now, her eyes wide and afraid. "We... we formed a hurricane," she muttered, her voice disbelieving.

Finn could see that she was right. They had created a hurricane, a small one at least. But even as he watched the front, he noticed that it was continuing to grow, sweeping out across the sands. He could only imagine what would happen when this... this thing struck Lahab and the dome of fire that Bilel had formed around the city.

He expected it would be catastrophic.

The healers around them were simply staring, their mouths agape. Several spared the occasional glance at Finn, and he observed a mixture of fear and hope surge through their bodies – the dark and light energies colliding and mixing.

And to the west, Finn saw their army finally crest the line of dunes. Thousands of mages, fighters, merchants, and Khamsin appeared along that ridge, riding atop a legion of dark insects. However, the advancing line of their army drew to a halt as they observed the colossal storm front that they had created, wind now whipping fiercely among their ranks and carrying streams of cool sand down into the plateau where their group lingered.

With a grunt, Finn shoved himself back to his feet, his companions following his lead. Tendrils of fire still curled around his arm. The gem – not fully extinguished – glowed with a dull light, and a burning crown hovered above his brow.

He witnessed their army – *his* army – beat their hands to their chest as they saw what Finn and his companions had created. The energy rippling through the soldiers' bodies flared – fire and light shining above the rest. *Passion and hope.* Even from this distance, Finn could hear their shouts, the combined voices of thousands of men and women.   Fighters, merchants, mages, and Khamsin joined together in a singular purpose and behind a single man.

The Prophet of the Flame.   And now… the *Stormbringer*.

"*Najmat Alhidad. Najmat Alhidad. Najmat Alhidad,*" they chanted, the sound a call to war, a march to battle, a verbal drumbeat that would carry them east.

To Lahab. To the demon king and his army.

And toward Rachael.

Chapter 38 - Storming

The wind tugged at Finn's robes, whipping the cloth and making even the simple act of sitting astride his beetle much more difficult. It also carried a mixture of rain and loose sand, creating a maelstrom of wind, earth, and water that smashed against the advancing line of their army. And still, their beetles plowed through that mess of wind and wet without slowing.

Overhead, dark clouds swirled in an ominous circle, the hurricane only continuing to grow – the winds picking up strength with each minute that ticked past. The storm front now stretched for miles across the deep desert. The constant crack of thunder caused the very air around them to vibrate. And that deadly drumbeat punctuated the occasional fork of lightning that struck the sands, sending up a shower of molten glass with each impact.

As he pulled the wraps more tightly around his face and mouth, Finn spared a glance to the side. A legion rode along beside him – a swarm of smaller black beetles encircling dozens of the larger queens, and resting atop their backs were mages and merchants, divided by affinity and specialization. His map hovered next to him, the clusters of soldiers neatly divided, labeled, and color-coded – Kyyle's borderline-OCD notetaking paying off in a tremendous way.

Their forces didn't shy away from the storm. Instead, they rode directly through the back edge of the hurricane. They set a relentless pace as the water soaked into their clothing, and wet sand coated their armor, attempting to outpace the storm.

Even now, Finn could see a clearer pocket of mana up ahead – the eye of the hurricane lingering just a few short yards away.

Only moments later, they burst through the inner edge of the storm...

The winds abruptly abated, and the relentless shower of water and sand slowed and then stopped.

Finn's eyes went wide as he witnessed the spectacle that swirled around him.

A dense bank of clouds created a whirlpool around the army, sheets of rain beating down upon the sand only a scant few yards away. The blue, yellow, orange, and green energies blended to create a nearly impenetrable wall of mana. No matter how hard he tried to peel away those thick layers of mana, Finn couldn't see through to the other side of the storm, nor could he see Lahab's walls approaching in the distance – there was only wind and rain and the bright-amber flash of lightning.

Which was perfect. The storm would hide them from Bilel, after all.

"Everyone is in formation. The Infernal Guard stand ready," a voice shouted to Finn's left. He glanced over to see Julia riding up beside him, keeping her beetle as close as possible. The eye of the storm was much quieter, but the rumble of thunder and howl of the wind whipping past still made conversation difficult.

"The fighters and Khamsin have also joined our forces. Malik and Aerys are leading them, and they'll take their cues from me."

Finn nodded in acknowledgment, his thoughts racing. The Infernal Guard would be instrumental in dealing with the hounds – their fire mana naturally drawing the attention of the creatures. The other melee troops would then need to reinforce Julia's troops, picking off the hounds from the flanks and taking their orders from Julia.

Delegation was going to be essential for this upcoming fight.

Kyyle chose that moment to pull up next to them, his mount creating a spray of wet sand as he skidded into position with Brock drifting along beside him. Apparently, the earth elemental had no difficulty keeping up.

"How are the mages?" Finn asked him.

"Abbad has positioned an air mage with each group to maintain communications. He's currently with

Aerys in the command group," Kyyle answered, flicking at the air.

A series of raid menus promptly appeared in front of Finn, the groups neatly divided by their capabilities – healers, fighters, merchants, etc. Although Kyyle hadn't stopped there. He'd taken full advantage of the game's UI, highlighting the air mage inserted into each division and then into the smaller squads that comprised each division, creating a network of mages that would allow the command group to relay orders quickly throughout the army. It was a clever workaround for soldiers that couldn't rely on the in-game chat.

"Abbad has ordered the air mages to focus on shielding our troops from the storm and airlifting any casualties to the rear of the army where the healers and merchants are positioned. They should be able to heal them and repair their equipment as needed," Kyyle continued.

"And what about you?" Finn asked, side-eyeing the earth mage.

Kyyle met Finn's inquiring glance with a grin. "I'm going to be directing the rest of the earth and water mages. I've taught them a few *tricks* over the last couple of days. Consider us your crowd control and terrain manipulation group."

Finn wasn't sure whether to feel relieved or worried by that. But, knowing Kyyle, the earth mage would likely deliver in a big way.

He took a deep breath, his eyes skimming the many different displays that were now opened before him. This next fight was going to be different from their previous encounters. In other battles, Finn had been able to enter the fray himself – stand on the frontlines. However, he was no longer being asked to fight – at least, not directly. And even if he did, killing a few hounds himself certainly wouldn't sway the tide of battle.

No. This time around, Finn was being asked to *lead*.

Even as that thought crossed his mind, Daniel

chirped a warning at his shoulder. "The outer edge of the storm has just reached the city," the AI reported, picking up the presence of fire mana using data from Finn's UI. Julia immediately turned to the air mage that rode at her shoulder, signaling the woman to alert the rest of the army. Their forces soon began to slow – ensuring that they stayed within the storm's eye.

Finn's gaze snapped back to his map, and he could see that the AI was right. Daniel had superimposed the storm over the terrain, using Finn's *Mana Sight* to produce a more dynamic map. If he requested it, he suspected the AI could also shift into an isometric view and give him a rough three-dimensional model. Although, for now, there was no need.

He squinted as he peered to the east, trying to peel back the dense layers of mana that made up the hurricane. Only seconds later, the walls of Lahab began to drift into view, emerald sandstone standing out sharply against the energies swirling through the storm. And just in front of those walls was the telltale glint of fire mana. As Finn focused on that energy, he saw it expand high into the sky, drifting up and over Lahab and forming a massive, flaming dome around the city.

"Good gods..." Julia muttered as the edge of that shield came into sight.

Finn just shook his head, a similar thought rebounding through his mind. It was one thing to see this on the video back within the safety of the Hive... and another entirely to witness the sheer scale of that magical shield firsthand.

As the edge of the storm struck the fiery barrier, Finn could see the mixture of air and water slam into the heated shield. The storm grew thicker with each passing second, a chaotic cascade of clouds swiftly beginning to rise – only to cool moments later and begin to condense. Even more interesting, the barrier appeared to stall the storm's march across the desert. Finn could have sworn that the swirling clouds were beginning to rotate around the city itself. As the rest of the storm front continued to barrel forward, Finn felt a sudden worry gnawing at his gut.

"Daniel..." Finn began.

"I'm already on it, sir," the AI replied, picking up on the concern in Finn's voice.

A moment later, the model of the storm updated and shifted, providing Finn with a three-dimensional view of the hurricane and the city. "This is a projection five minutes out," Daniel said. "I'm extrapolating based on the current flow of mana around that dome and the data streaming in from your UI and *Mana Sight*."

Finn chewed on the inside of his cheek as he watched the screen. As the body of the hurricane struck the city, the model predicted that the superhot pocket of air created by the dome would stall out the storm completely, causing it to begin orbiting the city like a miniature sun – the heat continuing to feed the hurricane and causing it to grow rapidly. Within the span of just a few minutes, the storm would be localized atop Lahab and would become increasingly violent, stretching out across the desert for miles in every direction.

"Shit," Finn muttered, nudging his mount and sliding to a halt. He dropped from his seat, his feet sinking into the sopping wet sand.

Julia signaled the rest of the army. A legion of beetles soon grouped up behind them, and each division began to assume their formations. The Infernal Guard and fighters moved to the front, and the mages took up a position along the interior of the army, where they would be protected if they were somehow flanked.

Finn didn't pay that much attention.

The storm likely still hid their movements from Bilel – at least, for now. And they still had a momentary reprieve from the wind and wet since they were currently positioned within the eye of the hurricane. However, that dome would soon turn the storm against them. In moments, Lahab would be sitting inside the eye of the storm, protecting the hounds instead of Finn's army, which according to Daniel's projections, would be standing well within the inner edge of the hurricane.

"We need to take out that shield and fast," Finn muttered.

"Well, I'm open to suggestions," Julia said, dropping from her mount and eyeing the fiery dome that lingered before them. As the storm continued to push forward, that barrier and the city walls behind it had now come into view. The hurricane was beginning to break apart and start its new orbit around Lahab.

"If the relic created the dome, then the hellhounds are likely powering it," Kyyle offered, watching the ring of clouds to their rear. They only had a few more minutes to speak before the other side of the hurricane struck them from behind.

Finn grimaced. "Yes. That's still a safe assumption. We couldn't have anticipated the effect of the dome on the storm, but the plan remains the same. We need to bait the hounds into attacking and then take out as many as possible."

"You think Bilel is going to send them out into the hurricane?" Julia asked.

"Yes... yes, I think he will. We'll be sitting inside the edge of the storm once it centers on the city. We're going to start getting pelted by wind and rain. But our air mages can hold off most of that – at least within a localized area," he added, shooting a meaningful look at Kyyle. The mage immediately pivoted and whispered instructions into the ear of the air mage who stood beside him.

"We'll be vulnerable then – exposed to the elements," Finn continued, eyeing the area around them. "That will obscure our visibility and hinder our movements. If I were Bilel, I'd use that moment to attack."

Julia nodded. "So, it sounds like we hunker down and wait." She met his eyes, determination shining there. "When you give the signal, my people will be ready to move."

"Good," Finn replied. Then he offered his arm, his daughter accepting his grip. He pulled her close into a hug, wrapping his other arm around her shoulders and feeling the metal of her armor digging into his skin.

"Take care of yourself," she whispered.

"You too," he murmured back.

Then Julia withdrew, shooting one final glance at Kyyle.

"You want to make a bet?" the earth mage said, noting the tension in Julia's shoulders and in the way she gripped her lance tightly.

She shot him a surprised look. "Really? What're you thinking?"

"Well, I say we keep score," Kyyle offered with a grin, despite the rain and sand that streaked his face. "Whoever kills the most of these hounds wins."

Julia tilted her head as she mulled on that. "Wins what exactly?" she demanded.

"Hmm." Kyyle hesitated. "Renaming the city, maybe? Or a piggyback ride courtesy of Brock?" he offered with a small smile.

"Eh. That doesn't do much for me." She met his eyes for a moment, holding his gaze. "How about if you win, I take you to dinner?"

Kyyle's eyes went wide. "Uh... what?" he answered artfully, clearly letting his shock override his normal mental function.

"You know, a real dinner in the real world," she shot back, her smile widening.

"Uh, I mean, sure... yeah," was Kyyle's fumbling response.

"Good," Julia replied curtly, starting to walk backward away from him. She shot Daniel one final glance. "You'll keep score for us, won't you?"

"Yes, ma'am," the AI chirped.

Julia gave them one last salute and then whirled. She sprinted back toward the position where her Infernal Guard was positioned, her feet kicking up wet sand in her wake.

"Hey, wait... what do you get if you win?" Kyyle shouted after her, but his words were lost to the wind that whipped around them. The gale was beginning to grow as the back edge of the storm caught up with them.

"Shit..." the earth mage muttered.

Then Kyyle gave Finn a surreptitious glance. "And you're... um... you're okay with that?" he asked cautiously. Apparently, Kyyle found him a little intimidating. It must have been the many, many people he'd watched Finn kill.

A wide smile crept across Finn's face. "Yeah, I don't have a problem with it." Kyyle started to let out a relieved breath. "Especially since she's going to kick your ass. You know she just tricked you into handing her a blank check, right? She used to do the same thing to me all the time when she was little. She ate ice cream for an entire week straight after I lost one particularly bad bet."

Kyyle sucked in air sharply, and Finn laughed at his reaction. He enjoyed making the mage squirm a little. Wasn't that his fatherly prerogative, after all? And it was a welcome distraction from what loomed before and around them.

Even as they stood there and the army settled into position, the inner edge of the storm was drawing closer. The rumbling patter of water striking sand grew with each passing second. They likely had less than a minute before the winds and rain consumed them once again – except stronger this time.

Which meant that they needed to get moving.

"Come on," Finn said, smacking Kyyle's shoulder and knocking him out of his confused fugue. "Right now, you need to regroup with your mages, and I need to go find the rest of the command group. You'll have time to worry about your dating life – or lack thereof – some other time."

"Har har," Kyyle grumbled but started off toward his pack of earth and water mages. The group was clumped inside the formation of Khamsin and fighters that lined the front of the army – their position given away by their color-coded robes.

And then Finn stood alone upon the sands. His eyes drifted back to the glowing orange dome that encircled Lahab. Already, he was trying to contemplate what Bilel had planned. He doubted the demon had been idle while their forces prepared, and it was safe to assume that the Emir had seen the unnatural storm barreling toward Lahab – even if he might not entirely understand what the rain and wind concealed.

"Game on," Finn murmured to himself. Then he pivoted on his heel and started off toward the command group.

Chapter 39 - Fiery

The wind howled around Finn and his group, the sound a muffled whine as it swept across the glowing yellow barrier that hovered above them. Rain pelted the shield, sloughing off the edge and pooling along the sands. The black forms of the beetles lingered just outside that barrier, burrowing deeply into the sand. They used their hard carapaces to help blunt the wind and rain, sheltering the group that stood in the center of that protective circle.

A blast of lightning suddenly struck the barrier – the energy forking across the surface – but the shield refused to give way. With his fingers beating a repetitive rhythm, Abbad maintained the spell. Similar glowing yellow barriers and dark rings of insects littered the expanse outside the walls of Lahab, shielding the soldiers who stood amid the storm. Abbad had moved quickly to direct his air mages, embedded in each division and squad, to maintain those protective barriers to insulate their troops from the full assault of the hurricane.

The only small blessing was that those shields were likely difficult to pinpoint amid the dense sheets of water and gusts of wind that lingered just outside the shimmering yellow shields. While their troops were now bearing the brunt of the storm as the eye centered on Lahab, it was that very hurricane that now protected them from Bilel's prying eyes.

But the air mages' mana wouldn't last forever.

As though echoing his thoughts, Finn saw an amber shield break away from a nearby encampment and start heading their way at a sprint. Within seconds, that protective bubble merged with their own. Aerys and a company of Khamsin entered the ring of insects. The desert folk were drenched, their breathing ragged, and water rained from their armor.

"Alright, the Khamsin are ready," Aerys grunted, not wasting any time on small talk.

As the Khamsin leader spoke, she gestured at the

walls of Lahab in the distance and the glowing orange dome surrounding the city. Lightning struck the dome occasionally, and with each strike, it flickered and pulsed with an ominous fiery light. Yet the barrier remained intact – the damage repairing itself in mere moments. "It doesn't look like we're getting through that shield easily, though," she added dryly.

"Indeed, that barrier is composed of dense fire mana," Abbad said softly. A fleeting glance at Finn. "I take it using your *Mana Absorption* is off the table?"

Finn frowned slightly as he observed the density of the fiery energy with his *Mana Sight*. There was enough mana there to cover an entire city. "That likely won't work. It's one thing to drain the ambient heat in the sand and air. That amount of mana per square foot was rather small. It's another thing entirely to absorb this much raw mana." He gestured towards the fiery shield.

"So, we do what then? Stand outside the walls and let the storm take us?" Aerys demanded. Another flash of lightning and a blast shook the ground nearby, sending streamers of molten glass flying in every direction. The other mages and soldiers within their protective circle shuffled nervously. "It seems the storm is getting worse."

"It is," Finn replied simply, his eyes never wavering from the city. It was playing out just as Daniel's model had predicted. The eye of the hurricane was now centered above Lahab. The heat from the barrier both anchored the storm in place and grew the billowing clouds – the hurricane growing larger and more violent with each passing second.

"Okay… so I'll ask again. What's our play here?" Aerys stared at Finn, her eyes demanding.

He met her gaze evenly. "We draw them out."

Finn held up a staying hand as the Khamsin leader started to snap at him again. Then he swiped at the air to bring up his map, rotating the display so that she could view it clearly. "The Infernal Guard are almost in position," he offered, gesturing at the cluster of orange dots on his map.

Near the front of the army and directly in front of Lahab's northwestern gate, Julia's guard now stood in formation. They had pushed forward far enough that they would be visible from the walls of the city while the rest of the army would still be hidden within the swirling chaos of the storm. For now, the guard hadn't lit up their armor, allowing the rain and wind to beat against them and relying on their bulk and weight to shield themselves from the storm – the fire mages huddled protectively within the center of the formation.

In short, they were using Julia and her soldiers as bait.

With that thought, Finn swiped at the air, pulling up his chat log and typing out a short message to Julia. Now he just needed to wait a few moments longer before giving her the order – enough time to let Bilel think they were settled.

"The Khamsin and fighters are also waiting on each flank," Finn explained, tapping at their positions to either side of the guard, those soldiers standing farther back within the storm. "They will be ready to assist the guard at our command."

He spared a glance at Kalisha, where the merchant stood nearby. "Are the mechanid scouts in position out in the sands?" he asked. Her mechanical creatures were uniquely suited to this role – able to anchor themselves to the ground and the mana signature of their metallic bodies made them almost indistinguishable from the sand itself.

"Yes, although their sensors won't work as well in this mess," she muttered, surveying a series of screens that Finn couldn't see. "I had to make some last-minute adjustments so that they *only* pick up fire mana." At this comment, the small mechanical spider she had bonded with ground its legs together as though it was pleased with itself – earning the creature a raised eyebrow from Finn.

"Good," he murmured to himself, his eyes on the map beside him. The gameboard was set – and now it was the demon's move.

"Okay, but why would Bilel risk his forces by sending them out in this mess?" Aerys demanded, sounding exasperated. "Couldn't he just wait us out within the safety of the city?"

A small smile tugged at Finn's lips as he channeled his mana forcefully, letting the burning energy flow through his veins. "He can't see us easily within the storm. One of these barriers of air looks just like another gale unless you know what you're looking for. But, most importantly, you're forgetting *who* we're facing."

He met her eyes, his mana flaring, and his eyes aglow. "Bilel isn't a man. We're facing a *demon*. A demon that places no value on human life... He drained and used your people for decades. He won't hesitate to use the hounds the same way, especially since he knows that he has us outnumbered and still believes he can replenish any losses using our casualties. His goal – his only goal – is gathering more fire mana.

"So, we use that against him."

With that statement, he hit send.

Seconds later, a patch of fiery energy bloomed in the distance.

Then another. Then a dozen more.

Soon, Julia's entire troop was bathed in flames as the fire mages partnered with each of her Khamsin channeled *Imbue Fire,* wrapping the metal-clad Khamsin in ribbons of fire.

At his daughter's command, they marched forward toward the gates of Lahab. The Infernal Guard gave off such a dense glow that the flames were even visible amid the storm. The flames burned away the rain that beat down on the soldiers, and their heavy armor kept them firmly rooted to the ground, even as the wind pulled at them. Maintaining their formation, the group kept the more vulnerable fire mages to the center of the pack.

And then they waited.

Seconds ticked past with no reaction from the city.

"I don't think—" Aerys was abruptly cut off as the city's gates swung wide.

And through that opening poured a ravenous horde of hounds. The creatures sprinted across the sands, their paws sending up streamers of steam where they touched the wet earth. They barely seemed to notice the storm. Hundreds of the flaming dogs raced across the open field outside the gates, paying little mind to the hurricane.

Although, in Finn's enhanced sight, the effect of the storm was more telling. The rain was suppressing the energy put off by the hounds. The wind and wet tore at the flames that enveloped their limbs, and that energy dimmed noticeably even as a cloud of steam rose above the horde, creating a muddy brown cloud in Finn's *Mana Sight*.

Perfect, Finn thought. His guess had proven correct.

As the hounds sped toward the Infernal Guard, Finn typed out another message – this time to Kyyle. And then he said a silent prayer to the goddess. Now all he could do was wait, watching the glowing line of fire mana in the distance and the horde of red dots that now filled his map as they advanced on his daughter's troops. At a guess, there were at least a few thousand of the beasts in this wave. If they closed with the guard, they would be overwhelmed. And yet Julia's soldiers didn't move an inch as the creatures barreled toward them.

Seconds ticked past, and the hounds raced toward the guard.

And then the first line of creatures simply vanished.

"What... what just happened?" Aerys asked, staring at the nearby map as an entire group of the hounds winked out of existence.

Finn's smile widened as he observed the fluctuation of earth mana in the distance.

"Kyyle happened," Abbad said softly, his brow furrowed.

Finn nodded, his thoughts racing... already on his next move. Another line of the hounds vanished, and he glanced to the side, noting Aerys' confused expression. "Kyyle is directing the earth mages. The ground is composed primarily of sand and is now saturated with moisture from the storm. Using *Dissolve* at a low energy level is just enough to destabilize the ground, creating a massive patch of quicksand." That trick had just barely saved their life when they had taken a plunge into the Abyss. "Once the hounds are sucked under, another group of earth mages solidifies the material and crushes them.

"It's a deathtrap..." Finn murmured.

And brilliant, he added to himself. Although, Julia likely wasn't going to be happy with how many "points" Kyyle was scoring right now.

Hundreds upon hundreds of hounds perished in mere moments, and Finn's eyes darted to the barrier encircling Lahab. He saw the shield wane ever-so-slightly. It seemed his guess had proven right. Bilel was using the energy from the hounds to sustain the shield.

As Finn looked on, the next wave of hounds didn't sink into the sand, nor did their dots disappear from the map. Finn glanced up in alarm and saw a shimmering yellow barrier now coating the ground in front of Julia's forces. Bilel had joined the fray, most likely using the cluster of fire mana to help identify the position of his hounds. He was coating the sand with a platform of air mana, allowing his minions to skim overtop the ground.

"Damn it," Finn muttered, his eyes skimming to the city's walls as he tried to pick up on the demon's location. He had to be visible if he was throwing around that kind of mana.

But he didn't see anything...

Meanwhile, the hounds crashed into the line of the Infernal Guard. Julia's forces held firm and refused to budge. They planted their feet in the wet sand, raising dense metal shields, blunting the hounds' assault. However, the creatures flowed around them like water, and the second line of soldiers soon stepped forward, stabbing at the hounds with lances modeled closely after

Julia's. The metal-tipped spears pierced throats and major organs with each deft blow. Bright-orange blood soon coated the sands, sizzling along the wet ground.

"Abbad, signal the Khamsin and fighters," Finn said.

The librarian nodded, motioning for another air mage to assume the channel on the protective bubble draped above them. Then he was casting again. A moment later, Abbad whispered instructions to the air mages stationed with their other forces.

Finn saw the fighters and Khamsin move only moments later. The groups were each stationed further back in the storm, flanking Julia's positions. Their protective shields winked out. Only moments later, those shimmering barriers reappeared, now only a few dozen yards away from the hounds. The fighters and Khamsin struck at the flanks of the hounds that were slowly encircling Julia's group. The creatures never saw them coming, their hungry gaze fixated on the fire mana emanating from the Infernal Guard.

The Khamsin blurred forward, leaving the protective barriers of air magic and letting the rain and wind wash over them. Their bodies transformed into a mixture of wind and water, their limbs materializing only long enough to send a blade ripping across a hound's throat or cutting at the muscles of their legs. They struck with pinpoint precision and slaughtered more than a hundred of the creatures in an instant.

The fighters weren't to be outdone. They stayed under their protective shields, using their newly forged weapons to attack from a distance. Flashes of multi-colored light erupted along the hounds' flanks – sharp ribbons of air mana and icy spears rocketing forward to sever limbs and cut into the fiery flesh of the hounds. The intense rain was subduing the creatures' natural regeneration, and they were taking heavy losses. Hound after hound was cut down – the energy now flashing so erratically that Finn was having difficulty keeping track of the brawl taking place outside of Lahab.

His gaze panned to the map floating beside him, watching as the red dots that denoted the hounds disappeared quite quickly. And yet... something felt off. Why was Bilel continuing to commit to this full-frontal charge? Especially after he had seen that the guard was a decoy. Unless this was a decoy of his own...

Finn's eyes darted to Kalisha. "Anything?" he barked, worry tinging his voice.

The merchant began to shake her head... but then hesitated, eyes widening. "Northern flank," she shouted over the boom of the storm. "Only a faint heat signature."

He looked toward that position, peeling back at the dense layers of water and air mana that comprised the storm and looking for some telltale sign that something was wrong.

Then he saw it – just a faint glimmer of fire mana, seemingly suppressed by a heavy sheet of sapphire energy.

Yet that didn't look like normal rain. It was a patch of blue energy nearly a quarter-mile wide coming directly from the north and moving in a coordinated pattern.

"Damn it," Finn muttered, his brow furrowing.

The shimmering barrier of water mana peeled away at the last moment, and the illusion dropped to reveal another massive pack of hounds barreling straight toward the mages' flank. There was barely any time to react as the creatures launched themselves over the beetles that encircled the otherwise-unprotected mages stationed there. Claws and teeth ripped through their robes, blood sprayed the sands, and screams of pain added to the boom of thunder and the howling wind.

"They're butchering the earth mages," Aerys said with a horrified expression. She whirled toward Finn. "You need to do something! Pull back the fighters to protect them!"

"Just wait," Finn grunted, his mouth pressed into a grim line.

"If we wait, they'll all be dead!" the Khamsin leader shouted back.

"Things are not always as they seem," Abbad murmured, his hand flicking at a display as he pulled up his raid menu and pivoted it toward Aerys. The icons for the mages were still glowing a vibrant green – indicating that they were alive.

"How is that even — ?"

Aerys was cut off as the shimmering yellow barriers, the dark insects, and the bleeding earth mages abruptly disappeared. The illusion vanished, revealing only empty sand. In the same instant, glowing runes lit along the ground, shining with a brilliant sapphire energy so dense that Finn had to blink away the spots that were forming in his vision. Before the hounds could react, icy spikes launched from the ground, creating a field of jagged shards nearly a half-mile in diameter. Their fiery bodies were cut to ribbons in an instant, and their fire mana bled out into the ground, partially melting the dense ice.

Silence descended upon their command group as everyone stared at their maps.

The earth mages soon flickered into existence along the southern edge of the ice field. The illusions had faded as the water mages shifted their attention to activating their traps, the frozen ground now acting as a makeshift wall to prevent further surprise attacks from the north and helping to shelter the mages from the wind and rain.

Finn could only hope that, somewhere, Bilel was screaming in rage, staring at the dead hounds that now littered the sands in horror.

"We anticipated a surprise attack from our flanks – as well as the use of illusions," Finn replied to the confusion in Aerys' eyes. "As I said before, we're not facing a normal man. Bilel has had centuries to study military strategy. The only way we're going to win this war is to think three steps ahead."

"You could have simply told us the plan," she growled, her hand drifting to her weapon.

"You were told what you needed to know," Finn bit back, his eyes flaring with anger. He didn't need this – not right now. "Your responsibility was ensuring that your people were in position and ready to fight. And the bottom line is that we won this skirmish. Besides, we have more important matters to focus on right now."

Aerys visibly tamped down on her anger. "We will address this later then."

Finn just grunted noncommittally. If they managed to survive this, he would be more than happy to deal with a few hurt feelings. His eyes skimmed to the map that lingered beside him. The fighters and Khamsin had made short work of the hounds that had streamed out of the gate. The creatures' bodies now littered the field in front of the city. Even more lay dead among the field of ice, with many of the hounds impaled by the spikes and suspended in midair.

"We've lost 137 soldiers – primarily Khamsin and fighters. Our forces have killed roughly 36 hounds for every casualty," Daniel chirped softly beside Finn's ear. He winced. That was a proportionally large number of losses despite how many of the creatures they had slain. Bilel likely had many more hounds sheltered within Lahab's walls.

Finn's gaze shifted to the dome that encircled the city. Apparently, the loss of the hounds had still had an effect. The fiery shield was flickering more erratically now, and it had become patchy, holes forming in the mana which let through the rain and wind. The fact that Bilel hadn't released any more of the hounds was also telling. The demon had likely realized his own error.

Finn could visualize what he must be thinking – the game board laid out before him. Bilel would turtle inside the city now, using the storm to help whittle down Finn's forces and hoping the now-fragile shield encircling the city would be sufficient to stop them.

The demon wasn't wrong. The storm was growing in intensity, and the shimmering barrier of air above them was beginning to fluctuate and wane. Even the bulky bodies of their mounts weren't enough to block out the wind. As Finn looked on, more rain was making it past their barrier, spraying the soldiers lingering along the edges of the shield. They couldn't survive out here for much longer.

But the demon had underestimated Finn's persistence... again.

It was time for the next stage of their assault.

Finn typed out one last message to Kyyle and Julia.

"Alright, get ready to move!" Finn barked at the group around them. "We're going to breach the city gates! Abbad, send orders to the other mage groups. Pull them up tight against our fighters, Khamsin, and Infernal Guard."

The former librarian didn't bother to respond, casting over and over again as he sent instructions to the other air mages stationed throughout the army.

Finn glanced at Kalisha. "Shift your mechanid scouts north and south along the walls. They should be hard to detect and able to weather the storm as it grows more violent. We need eyes on the other gates. I don't want to be surprised by another group of hounds at our flank." She frowned, but nodded, moving to follow his orders.

A Khamsin soldier brought him his mount, placing his fist to his chest. Finn leapt up onto the beetle, the other members of their command group following his lead and staying well within the protective bubble of air mana. The other mage encampments around them were doing the same, the support forces preparing to ride.

Finn's eyes centered back on the city – past the mixture of Khamsin and fighters that were lined up across the sand, facing the gate that stood just behind that faded orange shield. This was it. They were all in now. And it was time to bring down that shield.

"Knock, knock, asshole," Finn grunted, his eyes flashing with a surge of fire mana.

Chapter 40 - Breach

Finn tugged at the wrap around his mouth and nose, pulling it loose and wringing out the water that soaked the cloth. Many more of the mages, fighters, and Khamsin around him were doing the same. They had gathered in front of the city's northwestern gate, just inside the inner edge of the hurricane's eye. Behind them, a wall of wind and water swirled.

Lightning crackled through the air, striking the flickering orange dome that covered Lahab. Finn looked on silently as the mana fluctuated, hardening around the point of the strike before fading to a duller orange. The shield was waning. Without as many of the hounds funneling energy to that massive dome, it was slowly devolving into a patchwork of bright-orange panels, the energy flickering and flashing with each second that passed.

And now it was time to take it out completely.

"What's the game plan here?" Julia grunted, jogging up to Finn. He could see Kyyle closing in as well, the rest of the command group gathering around.

Finn spared a glance at his map, eyeing the clusters of multi-colored dots that denoted the different portions of their army. "First things first, we need to fortify this position." His eyes flicked to Kyyle. "Kalisha has already sent mechanid scouts out into the storm, but I don't want any surprises. Build us a rock wall to our rear, and then head back to me."

Kyyle gave a curt nod and promptly trotted off with Brock in tow, soon shouting orders at the cluster of earth mages that stood nearby. Within only moments, a massive earthen barrier was drifting up out of the sands, stretching into the air – putting a thick wall to their backs.

That barrier would also sandwich the more vulnerable casters between the rock wall and the advance line of Khamsin, fighters, and Julia's heavily armed troops. They needed to protect their mages. It was the casters that would be carrying these next few encounters – helping to counter whatever Bilel threw at them and protect their soldiers. Finn expected the demon was far from finished.

Finn's attention shifted back to Julia. "Your Infernal Guard will take the lead again. Line them up facing the gate and have your fire mages use this opportunity to regenerate their mana. They're going to need to be topped off. Have the Khamsin and fighters flank you like before – that tactic worked well."

"Not going to do us much good with that shield still in place," Julia replied, arching an eyebrow.

"Don't worry about that," Finn said, a grim grin stretching his lips. "I plan to take care of the shield. Just be ready when it comes down."

"Got it," she said, squeezing his hand before running to rejoin her heavily armed unit. The guard soon lined up in front of the flickering orange dome, the city's sturdy stone gate looming just behind that veil of energy.

Finn let out a sigh. He had barked orders with more confidence than he felt. An idea for how to take out that shield hovered at the edges of his mind – especially now that it had dwindled in power – but he expected the outcome was going to be... less than ideal. However, he had little choice. The energy coursing through the barrier was still far too great for Finn to absorb it himself.

"I take it you will need my assistance with the shield," Abbad said, his voice just barely carrying above the noise of the army, the howling wind, and the occasional boom of thunder.

Finn met the librarian's eyes, seeing an uncanny intelligence reflected there. It seemed that Abbad had already anticipated what he planned. "Yes. Line up your air mages at Kyyle's wall, and station the water mages near them."

He tapped at his map, pinching and flicking until the display had shifted down into an isometric view. Another tap of his finger and he placed a yellow waypoint marker just to the west of the stone wall that was still creeping into the air at their backs. He shifted the map again, tilting it to the side. The marker hovered about thirty feet in the air, lingering above the stone wall that Kyyle's mages were forming.

"Have the water mages aimed at the waypoint marker," Finn explained to Abbad. "That should be at the edge of their control range. The origin point needs to be within the storm and high enough above us to avoid the wall. I want them to seed that area with as much water and ice as possible. Wait sixty seconds, then have the air mages start channeling a gust of air toward the gate," Finn explained.

He spared a glance at the former librarian. "This isn't a sustained current. I want a sudden and intense blast of air. Have them dump their mana as quickly as possible." Abbad's eyes widened at that statement.

Then the librarian nodded, turning his attention to the nearby map. "And I'm sure you know that what you're planning to do will have *consequences...*"

Finn suppressed a grimace, closing his eyes. Yes. Yes, he was well aware.

"What does he mean by consequences?" Aerys snapped from nearby.

His eyes shot open, meeting the Khamsin leader's demanding gaze. "We're about to push a wall of wet, cold air and ice into the shield, using the storm to help bolster its strength. And it's going to slam across the heads of our forces and strike a barrier formed entirely of fire mana. What do you think will happen?"

Aerys just stared back, her brow furrowed and confusion shining in her eyes.

"There isn't time to debate," Finn said, shaking his head. "You're just going to have to trust me. This shouldn't endanger our own people... much," he added softly.

"Make the call," Finn ordered Abbad before Aerys could interject.

They couldn't afford to wait any longer. Bilel wouldn't be content to just sit inside his city. The pieces were in play now, shifting across the gameboard. The demon had to know that they planned to breach his shield. And they couldn't afford to give him time to retaliate or undermine Finn's plan. From this point forward, they needed to keep up constant pressure and force the demon to take the defensive – to *react* instead of act.

That's how they would beat him at his own game.

The librarian nodded, his fingers flashed, and he let out a whisper, speaking directly into the ear of every air and water mage on the field. The mages soon clustered along the western edge of the army, practically hugging the stone wall that now stretched from the sands. That barrier now towered nearly twenty feet above their heads and protected them from the storm – allowing them to cast at the very edge of their control range, aiming for that telltale yellow waypoint marker.

Finn just hoped it would be enough.

"Sir, this plan..." Daniel whispered from his shoulder.

A display flickered into existence beside Finn, showing a model of the projected current of cold, wet air that they were about to send rocketing into the fiery dome – the product of hundreds of mages acting in concert. The last time they had done something similar, they had accidentally created this massive hurricane. He closed his eyes to avoid seeing the result. He could already anticipate what was about to happen.

"We have to take the risk," Finn answered softly. "And the ensuing chaos will be both a blessing and a curse. The ambient mana should help obscure our movements inside the city and make it more difficult for Bilel to cast and direct the hounds."

"We'll be walking into a hellscape..." the AI muttered.

Finn winced but said nothing.

That was a price he was willing to pay.

"The mages are ready," Abbad reported.

Finn's eyes flicked to his chat log. Kyyle had reported that the wall was complete, and he was having his mages focus on regenerating their mana. Julia had also reported in, letting Finn know her soldiers were standing ready.

This was it. He just had to give the command.

"Do it," Finn ordered.

Finn saw the surge of water mana long before he felt it, an enormous cloud of water and ice forming among the inner edge of the storm and growing in strength with each passing second. Many of the ice mages were freezing the rain that beat down upon the sands. Meanwhile, Kyyle was directing his earth mages to form a gravity well just below that mass of water and ice to keep it suspended above the top of the earthen wall.

The result was a partially frozen lake of water and ice that was forming in mid-air, stretching outward for dozens of yards in every direction. The hurricane tried to sweep away that wet and cold – its natural, circular current pulling at the edges of that globe of water. But the sphere was soon far too massive to be swept away so easily.

As the cloud grew to a blinding sapphire, the air mages started to cast.

It was just a tendril of yellow energy at first, barely visible to Finn among the massive howling currents of the storm. However, that faint breeze grew swiftly as hundreds of air mages poured their mana into a single all-consuming spell.

They directed the avalanche of cold and wet forward. It moved reluctantly at first but then began to pick up momentum. It soon streamed forward, blasting through the air with incredible force. Within only moments, a massive surge of ice, water, wind, and rain barreled across the sands. It sped overtop the stone wall with terrible force, the bottom edge of the stream striking the rock and blowing it apart in a shower of debris and shrapnel. Earth mana surged as Kyyle and his mages attempted to repair that damage.

As the water crested the wall, the earth mages maintained the gravity well, shifting it forward until it hovered above their army. Even so, water rained down on the mages and soldiers. Men and women raised their eyes to the sky, their mouths dropping open in surprise as they witnessed a veritable river jetting just above their heads. It was a stream of water, wind, and ice that stretched nearly fifty yards – sustained by the constant pressure of hundreds of air mages and partially suspended by their earth mages.

Finn shifted his gaze to the dome surrounding the city, watching as that current sped closer, on a direct collision course with that flickering energy.

This was it. This was the moment where the shit was about to truly hit the fan.

Then the current struck the shield.

The effect was almost instantaneous. As Finn had observed with the lightning, the shield responded dynamically, shifting fire mana toward the point of contact, and the barrier flared powerfully – a massive amount of fire mana channeled into a circle roughly half the size of a football field. And as that frigid water touched the scorching-hot shield... the inevitable happened.

Steam. A massive cloud of steam formed in an instant, sandwiched between a constant current of cold water and the flickering energy of the shield. With nowhere else to go but up, the steam shot into the sky, forming a column of superheated moisture so dense that it completely obscured the city from sight. That column rocketed up into the air, a pillar of yellow and blue and orange that created a ruddy brown in Finn's sight.

And that column of steam spread as it shot upward, filling the eye of the hurricane and creating a massive hot updraft. That superheated air followed the same pattern as the others – cooling, condensing, shedding heat, then condensing again. It began to swirl in time with the hurricane, pushing at the clear circle that hovered above the city. And the storm responded. It began to break apart, the perfect circular vortex devolving into a muddy chaos of updrafts and downdrafts that formed so quickly and erratically that the outcome couldn't fully be predicted.

Finn's eyes shot to the shield, watching that fiery energy flickering more erratically now, fading with each passing moment. And then, in a split second, it vanished. Unimpeded, the current of cold and wet barreled forward and smashed against the city's gate, causing the wooden barrier to splinter and crack under the massive force of the current.

"Call the mages off!" Finn shouted at Abbad, straining to be heard now over the chaos of howling wind, pouring rain, and the erratic booming blast of thunder that now echoed through the sky like a drumbeat. "Then have them try to shield the army as best they can."

He turned to see Abbad staring at the sky, his mouth open in surprise and his own mana fluctuating erratically – a tendril of dark mana curling through his body. *Fear.* Finn followed his gaze and felt even his own fire mana retreat in the face of what they had created.

What *he* had created.

The hurricane was breaking apart, losing its stability. Normal storms didn't form like this. It was nearly impossible to throw around this much heat, and wet, and cold in the real world. There was a natural order to things. But here, such extremes were possible. And in the absence of a regular rhythm and cadence, nature had given itself over to pure chaos.

Bolts of lightning rained from the sky at random, striking sand, and stone, and rock and sending molten fragments flying in every direction. A blast struck a nearby tower on the other side of the wall, blowing it apart in a shower of burnt rock.

Finn saw spiraling columns of energy forming, pulling down out of the clouds that swirled above them. They formed along the immense and irregular downdrafts created by all of that heat and steam. And there wasn't just one. *Dozens* were developing across the city.

Tornadoes, Finn thought weakly.

The nearest spiral touched down just inside the gate. The funnel of wind and rain ripped apart what must have been a cart sitting on the other side of the wall and hurled the wooden fragments up into the air, adding to the swirling mass. Even as he stared at the tornado forming before him, Finn could feel rain splattering his face and wind pulling at his robes more forcefully as the hurricane fully broke apart... removing the safety of the eye.

"Abbad, snap out of it!" Finn shouted. "Order the air mages to stop. Then fucking get them to shield us or we're all going to die."

The former librarian shook himself, sparing a single frantic glance at Finn before following through on his order. Meanwhile, Finn pulled up his in-game chat window, typing out a frantic message to Kyyle and Julia. The process made all the more difficult by the way the storm howled around him now, causing the loose flaps of his robes to snap and pop.

A glimmering yellow shield soon formed above the army, growing quickly in strength as the air mages shifted their focus, blunting the wind and rain slightly. Almost as soon as it formed, a lance of lightning arced through the sky and cracked against the barrier. Finn flinched involuntarily as the bolt landed only a few feet above his head, watching in awe as that energy arced out in a concentric circle above him, the energy crackling along the edges of the shield.

Then he was pushing through the crowd. Aerys appeared at his side, a small contingent of Khamsin flanking her. "Are these the consequences?" she shouted.

Finn just nodded.

"Where are we going?"

He pointed at the gate. Julia's Infernal Guard stood before the cracked and crumbling barrier, Bilel's fiery shield now gone. In front of those darkly armored men and women, a truly enormous column of stone was forming from the ground, rising out of the sands as though it were being birthed by the desert. Finn could see nearly a dozen earth mages surrounding the column of rock, flanking it on either side as they funneled their emerald energy into the stone.

As the spell completed, Julia shouted orders at her unit – her words inaudible to Finn at this distance as he shoved forward toward the frontlines. Yet her guard must have heard her.

A dozen of the heavily armed Khamsin sheathed their weapons and then stepped forward, grabbing at makeshift hand-holds that had been formed along the sides of the column of stone. Only moments later, their armor was awash in flames as their fire mage partners channeled *Imbue Fire* – the tendrils of flame flickering and flashing as the mages rapidly increased the temperature to bolster the Khamsin's strength.

As one, the Infernal Guard heaved the stone battering ram from the ground. Then they shifted their attention to the gates, the wooden timbers standing tall and thick before them. At some unspoken signal, the Khamsin started forward. Their mailed boots pounded at the sand, and their arms surged as they carried the massive battering ram. They didn't walk or shuffle forward weakly. They picked up speed steadily until they reached a dead-on sprint, barreling toward the gate that loomed before them.

And then they struck home.

Finn had suspected it might take a few blows to blast the gate free. But he had dramatically underestimated the combined strength of the Khamsin and the fire mages.

The battering ram blasted the gate off its hinges, splintering the wood in an instant and ripping rocks free of the nearby walls as the gate rocketed forward. It crashed against a nearby building, partially caving in what might have once been a storefront.

The Khamsin paused for an instant, as though confused at what had happened.

That's when Finn finally made it to the frontlines. He could just make out a new noise above the howl of the storm. It was a gut-wrenching sound – full of fury, and hunger, and unbridled passion – ripped from the throats of creatures that had been perverted and tainted by the flame.

A legion of flaming hounds barreled down the street before them, the raindrops sizzling against the heat that permeated their skin. They were all teeth, and fang, and claw as they sprinted toward the ruined gate.

Only to find the Infernal Guard waiting, their feet planted firmly in the sands, and their plate awash in a brilliant fire of their own. A barrier of air mana hovering just above them, and an army of mages, fighters, and Khamsin stood at their backs. A roar ripped from their throats – the sound filled with hope and the promise of battle. The flames around their bodies soared into the sky, pushing back at the rain and wind.

And Finn now stood among them, the plated soldiers giving way for their prophet until he stood on the frontlines. Ripping away his bandage, his eyes glowed like embers. His flaming crown floated atop his forehead, and more flickering fire curled through the crystalline surface of his left hand as he readied himself.

The soldiers seemed to pick up on his presence and were bolstered by it. He heard their cry change from a guttural roar to a rhythmic chant, which spread through the ranks of their army like wildfire. It was a chant he knew all too well.

Najmat Alhidad. Najmat Alhidad. Najmat Alhidad.

Now it was time for him to prove he deserved that title.

Chapter 41 - Elemental

The pack of hellhounds bore down on the Infernal Guard in a wave of gnashing teeth, their paws tearing at the wet sand and flinging the damp particles in every direction. They had been squeezed together by the narrow roads of Lahab and the natural funnel created by the gate. The effect was a living river of flame that swarmed toward the army's frontline.

Rain was already beginning to fall on Lahab as the hurricane destabilized. The water sizzled as it struck the flaming bodies of the hounds, sending more streamers of hot moisture curling up into the air. With the hundreds of hellhounds that surged toward them, this new updraft was already beginning to form another spiral of clouds above the battlefield – the storm just waiting to grow and retaliate further.

Yet Finn couldn't focus on that right now.

"Hold! We need to keep their attention. Don't give an inch!" Julia shouted, her voice amplified by a nearby air mage. The orders carried across the front line, sounding over the noise of the storm. Thunder boomed, and lightning continued to strike the nearby walls and towers of the city, cleaving the stone blocks apart and leaving burnt patterns traced across the rock.

The Infernal Guard shuffled in place, planting their feet firmly in the wet sand. Their thick plate armor was awash in flame, the fire mages lingering just behind them. The frontline hefted heavy iron tower shields and locked the edges of the metal barricades together, creating a shield wall. Julia had formed them up into two lines: the first focused on blunting the incoming hounds and the second ready to lash forward with their lances – using any openings to aim for throats and exposed parts of the beasts' underbelly.

As the advancing pack of hounds rushed forward, the earth mages behind the guard finished casting. A surge of emerald energy swept through the air – the effort of dozens of earth mages acting simultaneously. That mana coiled along the buildings to either side of the roadway, seeping into the sandstone bricks.

And then, as one, they *pulled*.

With a series of thunderous cracks, jagged lines formed in the stone walls along either side of the roadway – the bricks trembling and dust billowing out into the street. The hounds didn't pause or hesitate. They only continued their headlong charge. With another massive shove and a flare of emerald energy, the stone finally gave way. The buildings farther down the roadway began to collapse – three- and four-story storefronts and homes caving in. Spiraling towers crumbled, and sandstone bricks rained down upon the road.

The ground trembled as several tons of rock crashed into the hounds that streamed down the street. Those bricks crushed their bodies, the flames offering little protection against the considerable weight. A few hundred of the hellhounds were buried in the makeshift landslide. The rubble sealed off the end of the street, bottling the remaining hounds behind a wall of rock.

The beasts in the lead had escaped the destruction and cared little for the loss of their brethren. They neither slowed nor stopped their frenzied charge. The advancing line struck the Infernal Guard with a savage ferocity, throwing their entire weight upon the line of tower shields that stood before them. Yet the guard remained steadfast, bolstered by the *Imbue Fire* being channeled by the fire mage handlers standing just behind them. They shoved back with their shields, blunting the hounds' charge and sending many of the beasts toppling back into the rest of the pack.

As the hounds struck, the second line of Infernal Guard shifted forward, lances spearing between the holes in the shield wall. Those metal tips sliced into exposed flesh, impaling one hound's throat while another sliced a creature's belly open. Ruddy orange blood soon coated the wet sand, creating a haze of fire mana in Finn's sight.

One of the hounds locked its eyes on Finn's, two

blazing fiery cores that burned with an insatiable hunger. Up close, the creature was larger than a wolf, coming almost to waist height. It was easily more than a hundred pounds of dense, flaming muscle, rending claws, and tearing fangs. It lunged at him, jaws snapping.

An orb of dark metal struck it from the side with a twitch of Finn's fingers, the sphere immediately melting into a ring that wrapped the hound's neck and held it suspended for a scant moment. With a leap, Finn launched himself into the air, his foot touching briefly against another flaming sphere. And then he was past the shield wall, his gaze centered on that hound.

He wanted to test something... something that he suspected he would need if they were to prevail in their siege upon Lahab.

Finn surged forward in a fluid movement, his left hand dropping its channel and coming up under the hound's head in a vicious uppercut. His crystalline fingers shifted and morphed as the limb swept forward. The hand tapered down to a fine, needle-like point, and the crystalline blade stabbed up through the bottom of the hound's jaw, severing its spine at the base of its neck.

With the limb still embedded in the hound and fiery blood raining down upon the sand, Finn's gaze fixed on the fire mana surging through the creature's body.

And then he commanded that energy to return to him...

Fire mana poured from the hound's body, spiraling up Finn's arm in a flash of mana. Yet the *Focusing Prism* swiftly absorbed that energy, and the mana seeped into the crystal with barely any resistance. The mana drained from the hound's body in a flash, and its fiery aura abruptly winked out – leaving only dull orange and red flesh. Finn felt a faint burn as the *Mana Absorption* took its toll on his body, but the damage was quickly healed by his natural regeneration. Finn's gem soon shone with a fiery light, the mana swirling within its depths and glowing ominously.

He stared at that crystal, his thoughts spinning. It seemed his guess had been right. He might not be able to drain the hounds' mana from a distance, but once he punctured their skin… that was another matter altogether. Finn's glowing eyes shifted back to the wave of creatures before him. All he saw was a river of available fire mana, just waiting to be harvested.

With that thought, he fully abandoned caution and swept forward, diving into the pack of gnashing teeth and rending claws. His world soon devolved into a whirlwind of flaming canine limbs and thick orange blood. The Infernal Guard stood just a few feet behind him – a dense wall of fire mana in his enhanced sight that blocked off the gate and held off the creatures that made it past Finn. Their lances stabbed through the air, and thick, soupy blood soon coated the ground in a miniature lake, barely seeping into the already-saturated sand.

Finn knew only the flicker of his fingers. The words drifting from his lips. The cut and slice of his new hand. His metallic orb smashed a hound to the side. Another beast lunged at him, its claws deflected by the layer of molten armor that rippled down his arm. Finn retaliated, pivoting under the hound's weight. A faint yellow highlight appeared in his vision – Daniel assisting as he floated above Finn's shoulder. He struck at that target, his crystalline hand spearing into the creature's chest and striking its heart dead on. The fires leaking from the animal soon wrapped up his arm and seeped into the crystal there, replenishing his own mana and adding to the crystal's reserve.

"Behind you!" Daniel chirped, and Finn spun.

He flattened his metal orb into a disc, the hound's claws raking against the metal shield. With another twitch, the disc pivoted and spun up to speed before launching forward. The makeshift sawblade sliced cleanly through the hound's forelegs, exposing bone and muscle. Another swift blow and the hound slumped to the ground.

Finn wove and danced and spun – a vortex of fire and death.

And when he looked up again… he stood in the middle of a pile of canine bodies, their forms slumped against the sand, and the telltale flicker of flames no longer coating their bodies. His chest was heaving, and his heartbeat hammered in his ears. Finn's molten eyes surveyed the area around him. The gem embedded in his left hand pulsed and flickered.

The hounds were beginning to wane, their numbers diminishing, and reinforcements were unable to come to their aid with the mountain of rubble blocking the road ahead. Which meant it was time to press forward.

"Infernal Guard, advance!" Finn roared, thunder pealing overhead.

As one, the line of flaming metal juggernauts shambled forward, their combined weight causing the ground to tremble. They soon swept past Finn, and he let them press forward, marching ahead with a terrible, ominous certainty.

Finn's eyes rose to the sky. The storm was continuing to worsen. A thick bank of steam now rose above the gate, adding to the powder keg that was brewing. A tornado had begun to touch down along the line of buildings beside the gate, the air mana swirling in a giant vortex and the wind whipping at his robes. A blanket of air mana was held suspended above their soldiers, as the air mages tried their best to blunt the bite of the storm and protect their own.

Julia was soon at his side, eyeing him with a worried look. An air mage stood beside her. The woman's robes were ripped and burnt, but no visible injuries marred her body. For his part, flames still coated Finn's skin, and his left hand was only just beginning to revert to normal.

"That was foolish," she grunted.

"I'll need the mana for what's coming," was his only response, one of his orbs circling him slowly.

Finn had a plan in mind. This battle over the gate was only one of many. They still needed to reclaim the city and defeat the demon. As that thought crossed his mind, his gaze swept to the Emir's palace along the southern end of Lahab. The palace's spires towered above the rest of the buildings. He expected Bilel was sitting there, where he had a natural vantage point on the rest of Lahab.

As he watched the palace, Finn saw streamers of emerald energy curl away from the main building, rocketing across the city in a flash and striking the mound of rubble blocking the roadway. The stone and rock promptly disintegrated, bleeding back down into the sandy street. Finn's eyes widened as he watched that massive surge of energy. It wasn't just the *amount* of mana, it was the accuracy and the range that gave him pause.

But not for long... more hounds were now racing down the street toward them.

Finn's eyes snapped to the nearby air mage. With a flick of his wrist, he brought up his map, showing the layout of the gate and the narrow street leading deeper into the city.

"Signal the Khamsin." He waved at the righthand side of the street where a tornado was forming. "Have them move forward and take up a position along the tops of those buildings. The fighters should move into position along the left side of the street. Have them flank from the rear and sides." As he spoke, Finn's fingers tapped at the locations on his map, adding waypoint markers.

"Yes, sir," the air mage replied curtly. Her mana flashed, and she began whispering instructions, relaying Finn's orders to mages positioned further back within the main body of the army. Seconds later, she glanced back at Finn. "It's done."

He nodded, his flaming eyes drifting to the gate above them. He needed a vantage point to direct his soldiers. And if Bilel was truly watching this battle – meddling from his perch atop the palace – then that would make Finn more easily visible.

"Can you get me up there?" he asked. The air mage looked uncertain, watching lightning crackle along that terrace. Then she nodded.

Finn glanced back at Julia. "You okay to direct the

guard down here?"

"Yes," she answered simply. "But be careful," she cautioned, glancing at Finn with a worried expression. "We can't afford to lose you – not at this point."

"I'll try," Finn answered with a grim expression before waving at the air mage.

A gust of wind erupted from beneath them, carrying the pair up toward the rampart that ran across the top of the gate. The storm blew them slightly off course, a strong gust pelting them as they sped up into the air. But Finn was ready for that. He threw another orb, grabbed hold of the air mage with one hand, and directed his remaining metallic sphere forward with the other. He swiftly combined the two orbs, flattening the metal out into an incredibly thin disc. He then rotated that disc to the side, using it to blunt the wind rushing toward them. Their course stabilized, and their feet soon touched down on solid stone.

With another twitch of his fingers, Finn pivoted that disc, slamming it into the stone of the parapet and curling the top to create a makeshift wall to blunt the worst of the wind and rain. His eyes snapped to the air mage, noticing the way the woman now stared at him with a mixture of fear and awe.

"Conserve your mana," he said. "I may need you to relay directions to the others."

Another nod and Finn's gaze swept back to the street below him.

The Khamsin and fighters were already surging forward at a sprint, crossing beneath the gate and barreling up behind the line of Infernal Guard.

With a flash of multi-colored energy, the fighters launched themselves airborne, their feet soon slamming down upon the rooftops of the buildings lining the left-hand side of the street. Air mages had been inserted into their group, the robed men and women gliding up to the rooftops with a flare of yellow mana before creating discs of golden energy that hovered protectively above the fighters as they moved.

The Khamsin had no need for such luxuries. They raced toward the tornado without hesitating, launching themselves into the maelstrom. Their bodies rippled and converted as they absorbed the mixture of wind and water. Solid arms and legs disintegrated into gusts of air that swept up onto the rooftop. As their feet touched down on the thick tiles of the roofs, their bodies re-materialized, and they charged forward without pause. Less than a minute later, a full division of Khamsin were sprinting down the rooftops.

As the Infernal Guard advanced on the next wave of hounds, the Khamsin pulled a series of crystals from their bags. Those gems shone with a vibrant azure light in Finn's gaze – *water mana*. They promptly threw those crystals – much as Finn had seen them throw the air-based grenades when he had first arrived at the Abyss. Except these makeshift grenades weren't designed to create a miniature vortex of air.

As they landed, the gems fractured and then exploded, thick shards of ice spearing out in a spherical pattern. Those lances cut into the hounds, spearing dense muscle and tearing into their skin. Explosions detonated all along the line of hounds that charged down the street, the Khamsin tossing the grenades as they ran nimbly across the rooftops. The blasts weakened the hounds – even if they didn't take them out completely – allowing the Infernal Guard to make short work of those that made it to their line. They were an unstoppable wall of flaming metal. The hounds' claws could find no purchase on their metallic skin or the flames that curled between those iron panels.

And then the fighters had moved into position. Finn saw the consistent flash of multi-colored energy as the soldiers attacked from the rear, using surprise to cut a large swath into the back of the pack of hounds. Their enhanced weapons – having been upgraded by undergoing the *Forging* – cut into the creatures with abandon. They used their warded bodies to stay just out of reach, retreating along a side street or jumping up to the safety of the rooftops where the hounds couldn't easily reach them.

The hounds' numbers were quickly diminishing as their army struck at them from three sides. Fighters carved up their rear while Khamsin lobbed ice grenades into the middle of the pack from the right-hand side of the street. And the Infernal Guard was marching straight down the road, their lances impaling any hound unfortunate enough to be in the way.

They had nearly secured the gate.

Yet, while this fight might soon be over, there was still a war to be waged.

Finn's eyes shifted to the rest of the city. Despite the glowing blue and yellow haze created by the storm, he could make out dense clusters of fire mana along almost every street and cross-section. Even while a number of the hounds stalled them at the gate, many, many more of the creatures were scouring the city – likely consuming and converting any remaining residents that had been too slow or cautious to abandon Lahab.

The Mage Guild was even worse. A bonfire of energy speared up from that structure along the northern side of the city. Finn could only assume from the stories the others had told, and the videos they had found online, that Bilel was harvesting mana from the travelers as they respawned in that beginning courtyard... using the guild to grow his numbers.

And then there was the weather...

The tornado ripping down along the right-hand side of the street wasn't the only one. Dozens more were scattered across the city, the storm fully consumed by chaos and creating abrupt downdrafts. Those vortexes ripped entire buildings apart, absorbing the rock and wood to create a whirling twister of shrapnel. There was no rhyme or reason to the pattern any longer. Tornadoes touched down and dissipated quickly, punctuated by the erratic flash of lightning and the intense, howling wind.

And then there was the torrential rain that pelted the city, already flooding several low-lying streets. The wind swept down through the narrow alleys and roads, picking up speed as it was funneled between the buildings and nearly shoving the moisture into a horizontal trajectory that forced the water in between rock and stone. Even if there had been survivors left within the city, the hounds and the storm would soon ensure that this was their last day in this world.

And as though that wasn't enough, the repeated use of earth magic and the raw amount of water dumped down onto Lahab by the storm had begun to wreak its own havoc. The sand and underlying rock formations that held up the city were giving way, forming sinkholes along many of the streets. Several buildings had begun to collapse, listing to the side before toppling over – further blocking off streets and adding to the debris that was picked up by the tornadoes.

Finn squeezed his eyes shut, swallowing against the acidic bite of bile at the back of his throat. He might not have started this war. But he had fucking *finished* it. Even if they defeated Bilel, he would have almost completely destroyed Lahab. And he had signed the death sentence of anyone still living within the city.

Because what he was witnessing was Lahab being *consumed* by elemental forces, wind, air, fire, and water ripping the ground and buildings apart and slaying what few survivors might have managed to survive the hounds.

He could only imagine what a new player might witness if they had the singular misfortune of logging into that initial starting courtyard in the midst of all of this. They would only be rolling the dice as to their manner of death – tossed into the air by a tornado, ripped apart by the hounds, buried under a slow-moving mountain of earth, or drowned beneath a river of water.

"Finn," Daniel said softly, hovering just beside his ear. "You have a visitor."

Finn's eyes snapped open. He noticed a telltale flicker of mana below him and saw two figures launch up through the air from the base of the gate. Moments later, the group touched down next to him, and a shimmering barrier of air slid across the sky above, insulating them from the worst effects of the storm.

He turned to find Kyyle and Abbad standing there. As they each took in the view of the city, their eyes went wide, and their mouths dropped open.

"Holy shit," Kyyle muttered.

"There's no coming back from this," Finn murmured in reply, his eyes taking in the carnage that was unfolding below them.

"There isn't," Abbad answered curtly. Finn's eyes met the librarian's. "The only path open to us is to move forward – to finish what we've started."

"Even if it means destroying the rest of the city?" Finn asked.

The librarian simply nodded. *"Anything. Everything,"* he said simply, waving at the city below them, the wind carrying the howl of the hounds and the wails of the dying, the sounds only adding to the monstrous cacophony of the storm.

Finn ground his teeth. Abbad was right. He knew he was right – even if he was having second thoughts in the face of the carnage that he had helped to create.

His eyes centered on one location along the far end of the city – that area having been largely spared the destructive effects of the storm. Bilel's palace. That entire structure shone with a multi-colored hue. Although Finn couldn't be certain whether that was due to the demon's spellcasting or something else... something worse.

Not that it mattered. They still had a goal – one that they hadn't yet completed.

They were going to kill a demon.

Chapter 42 - Chaotic

Karen sighed and sat down on one of the barstools that ringed her kitchen island. She waved a hand at the nearby wall panel beside her. The sensors registered her movement, and the drone floating beside her picked up the laundry basket resting on the floor. Its rotors whirred softly as it lifted the weight and then began drifting to the washing machine on the other end of the house.

The kids were off to school. The laundry was done – or in progress, she supposed – and she had straightened the house and ordered groceries. And it was only early afternoon. Not too shabby. She'd still have a few hours of downtime to herself before the kids returned, and she needed to help them with homework and cook dinner. And then Dustin would be getting home, and he'd likely want to talk about his day…

Stop it, she snapped herself. This was supposed to be *her* time to relax – one of the few moments where she got a respite from the usual chaos of dealing with everyone else's problems.

Her eyes landed on the non-descript white box resting on the counter – still sitting where she had left it the night before. A logo of a rising sun was emblazoned on the side, and the company's name printed in black lettering. Cerillion Entertainment.

Dustin had brought the box home last night – a gift for her. He'd told her it seemed like she needed an escape from the never-ending list of chores and dealing with their kids. And so, of course, her husband had decided to buy her a videogame.

"*It's state of the art,*" he had said. "*Really, there's nothing like it out there. It's supposed to be so realistic that it's almost indistinguishable from real life.*"

To say she was skeptical might have been the understatement of a century. Karen had played a few simple games on her Core over the years but hadn't found that they offered much of an escape. They were mostly a distraction while she was waiting to pick up the kids or standing in line at the store, or…

Okay. Maybe there's something to what Dustin had been saying, she admitted to herself grudgingly.

Still… a game?

Although, what could it hurt to give it a try?

Her fingers gingerly tugged at the box, and she soon pulled out a solid black headset and a standalone onyx obelisk. The plastic felt heavy and thick in her hands. Dustin had told her she should find a comfortable place to sit or lie down before she tried it, so she moved to the couch – setting the obelisk on the coffee table and connecting it to the headset with a thin cable. Then she tugged the helmet over her head, her vision suddenly engulfed in darkness.

A glowing prompt appeared in that dark void, the edges of the frame ringed in brilliant sapphire.

System Initializing
New User Detected.
Scanning User… Please Wait.

Dustin had mentioned that the startup might take a second, so she forced herself to remain still, waiting patiently.

System Initialized
Scanning complete. Initiating boot sequence.
Our records indicate that you have opted to bypass the introductory tutorial.
Welcome to Awaken Online!

Dustin must have set up an account for me, she realized. *Of course, he took off the training wheels already.* She wasn't exactly surprised. Hell, she half expected he'd tried the game himself and skipped the tutorial. The prompt disappeared, and her vision went dark once more.

Although she didn't have long to mull on that. A blinding white light suddenly flooded her vision, filling that black expanse like a rising sun. The glow was so intense that she squinted against the brightness, blinking rapidly as tears formed at the corners of her eyes.

And then that white light abruptly disintegrated.

In the next instant, Karen found herself standing in a stone courtyard.

Her living room was gone. Instead, she was surrounded by a thick sandstone wall, and more sand crunched underfoot – feet that were now adorned in simplistic leather sandals, the straps twining up her calves. Her shoes weren't the only thing that had changed. Her clothing was gone and replaced with coarse, beige cotton that scraped against her skin.

She felt a cold splatter along her cheek, and she reached up in surprise, her fingers coming away wet. It felt so real. If she hadn't just been sitting in her living room, she could have sworn that she had been transported to another world.

More rain splashed against her cheeks. Her hair. Her shoulder and arms. Soaking into the fabric of her tunic. Wind whipped at the fabric, a gust so intense that it sent her stumbling forward. She looked up, and her eyes widened. She must have logged in during a thunderstorm. Rolling black clouds spanned the sky, and a peal of thunder boomed, shaking the walls and ground around her.

Okay… this is sort of incredible.

There was another flash of blinding light – but this time, it wasn't the headset.

Lightning slammed into the ground beside her, burning the air in an instant and creating a miniature vacuum. The force of the strike sent her flying backward, where she landed in the sand with a soft thump, the breath escaping her lungs with a whoosh, and her ears ringing from the concussive blast. Stray fragments of molten sand dotted her skin, leaving searing points of pain where they swiftly burned through her tunic.

"What the fuck?" she croaked, forcing herself upright. A crater had been carved in the nearby sand, black forks radiating out from the center.

Luckily, she had landed on something soft.

She rolled off whatever had cushioned her fall, only to let out a gasp. Dead, vacant eyes stared back at her. The corpse's skin was pale and cool to the touch. It looked like the man's stomach had been ripped open, his entrails leaking into the sand. They were still warm, tendrils of steam drifting upward into the frigid air.

She recoiled from the body, only to shuffle into another resting a few feet away. Her eyes – wide and afraid – skimmed the courtyard with fresh interest. *Dozens* of corpses riddled the ground, none of them moving. Many looked like they had been completely ripped apart, leaving only fragments of skin, bone, and flesh. And among the intact bodies, she noticed the same simple beige clothing.

"What's going on here..." she muttered.

She heard a low growl from behind her and whirled. What looked like a monstrous dog stepped out of the shadows. Chunks of flesh sloughed from its skin, landing in the sand with a sickening thud. The hound's body was bathed in flame, its muscles rippling beneath its red-hued skin as it sniffed at the air. And then those glowing blood-red eyes centered on her, the growl intensifying. She saw the creature's fangs as it stalked toward her – long teeth that could easily cut into her fragile flesh.

Karen felt her heart hammering in her chest, her breath coming in desperate, frantic gulps now. Her eyes darted to the side. A man wearing mail armor lay along the sand, resting in a pool of his own blood. And clutched in his dead hand was a dagger.

She looked back at the hound – their eyes meeting.

Then the beast lunged forward, its jaws snapping at the air.

And Karen moved, scrambling across the wet sand. With slippery fingers, she pried at the dagger – no longer concerned that she was touching a corpse. Yet the dagger wouldn't come free, the dead man's fingers locked in place like iron. She spared a glance behind her and saw the flaming beast approaching.

"Damn it! Come on!" she screamed, ripping at the man's hand more forcefully. Muscle and bone snapped, and the dagger finally came free. She clutched the blade in her right hand and spun just as the hound dove at her.

She felt the beast's weight land on her. The force of the blow rippled up her arm as she raised the dagger. The heat of its skin and those flames were leaving a burning trail along her skin. Its foul breath wafted across her face as those fangs gnashed just inches from her face.

Karen squeezed her eyes shut, waiting to die.

And yet... nothing happened.

When she opened her eyes again, she saw that the blade had struck the creature directly in the throat, glowing orange blood leaking from the wound. The hound was frozen in place, its eyes wide and its breath still wafting feebly across her face, its jaw spasming.

And in that moment... Karen snapped.

She ripped the dagger free and then stabbed again. And again. And again.

The blade plunged into the beast's throat. And when it stopped moving, she rolled over on top of it, raising the blade high and then slamming it into the creature's chest, striking it directly in its still-beating heart.

Seconds later, Karen knelt above the hound – the light finally leaving its eyes. She was covered in a mixture of sand, blood, and water, her tunic soaked through, her hair wild, and the dagger still clutched in her hand, the blade embedded in the creature's chest. In the distance, she could hear howling above the steady boom of thunder and crack of lightning – signaling more of the hounds. And they sounded close by.

"*I need to move,*" she thought. "*Now.*"

She ripped the blade free, her eyes already skimming the bodies around her. Her thoughts were honed to a singular focus. She wasn't thinking about her kids. Or the damn laundry. Or anything else – only her next move.

For example, what other useful equipment might these people have on their bodies?

*   *   *

Walt's eyes skimmed the darkened room even as he pulled another sword from the ruined display case and stuffed it into one of the many bags that were draped across his back and swung from his waist. He was lucky the bags seemed to act as some sort of extra-dimensional storage container that dramatically reduced the carrying weight of items stored inside. He expected he wouldn't be able to move if he had been forced to physically carry the mountain of stolen loot in those seemingly flimsy leather bags.

The shop where he was standing had nearly been tapped. The display cases were toppled and broken, and a large crack radiated through the wall of the store – courtesy of the shifting sands beneath the city. He wasn't responsible for that damage. The place had looked like a warzone long before he entered. Although, he had certainly contributed – busting open the remaining displays to steal their contents.

Walt felt a twinge of guilt as he looked at the carnage.

"Why the hell should I feel bad about this?" he muttered to himself, looking away from the destruction and shoving another polished dagger into his pack.

He'd logged in only a few hours ago to find the Mage Guild almost entirely deserted, the faculty, NPC students, and a decent chunk of the player population having up and vanished seemingly overnight. Ever since, he'd been hunted by the flaming hounds that patrolled the streets, the creatures breaking into homes and shops, and slaughtering NPCs and players alike.

Many of those they cut down came back, but they weren't human any longer.

Walt had no idea what the fuck was going on in Lahab, but he had been quick to arrive at a plan. He needed to get the hell out of this city and start over somewhere else. However, to do that, he needed money. And he had a solution for that as well. If nearly everyone was dead, then they didn't have much use for their stuff anymore, did they?

He grimaced as he rounded the counter and found the former store owner leaning against the nearby wall, his stomach and throat torn open, and dried blood caked around the wounds. The man hadn't converted into one of those beasts. Walt wasn't sure why some people underwent the change and some didn't. Although, he'd noticed that mages were much more susceptible. In this case, perhaps it was a blessing.

NPCs didn't respawn like the players. And they certainly couldn't log out.

He knelt in front of the corpse and patted its shoulder. "You're probably better off, buddy." Then, without hesitation, he sliced through the purse dangling from the man's waist and then added the pouch to one of his bags.

Walt shoved himself back to his feet, the move harder than it should have been. Even with the weight reduction, it was getting increasingly difficult to move. With a grimace, his fingers began winding through a spell. Green energy encircled him, spiraling up his legs and arms before wrapping around the bags draped across his body. An instant later, he felt that weight fade away as he maintained the channel on the gravity manipulation spell.

His instructors had focused on using the spell to help in melee combat, allowing earth mages with a penchant for combat to wield massive hammers and swords like they were mere sticks. Walt had found another, more *creative* application.

His work in the shop finished, he turned to the nearby wall, pressed his ear against the surface, and paused for several long seconds. He was listening for the telltale growl or wailing howl of the hounds. When he heard nothing, he pulled his hood over his head, checked the straps on his bags, and then began to cast.

Green energy spiraled around him once more, but this time, the energy drifted to the nearby wall. The sandstone began to swirl in a whirling pattern, partially disintegrating. Taking a deep breath, Walt plunged straight through the wall...

...and soon emerged on the other side.

"Fuck that hurts," he muttered, clutching at his chest.

Rain now beat down upon him, and the wind whipped at his leather armor – another misappropriated addition to his armory. He wouldn't have ever been able to afford it back in the Mage Guild.

The stone wall behind him re-stabilized in a flash. *Dissolve* was yet another spell that had come in handy. Low-power variants didn't destroy the stone. They just made it porous enough to step through – even if the experience wasn't entirely pleasant. It felt like his entire body was being crushed, and he could only withstand the sensation for a few seconds.

He heard a crash and a howl from his right, and his head whipped around. A spiral of wind and water was forming even as he looked on, stabbing down from the clouds and touching down on the rooftop of a nearby building. The budding tornado was already ripping the tiles from the roof one by one... the process accelerating swiftly as the vortex began to fully take shape.

The storm was getting worse. When he'd logged in, the weather had been the same broiling heat that always lingered across the desert city, only the threat of storm clouds on the horizon. Now the temperature had dropped – puffs of vapor forming with each breath. Even worse, the maelstrom seemed to be centered directly above Lahab, torrential rains and beating winds whipping across the rooftops and howling down through the streets and alleys. Even the ground had started to give way, leaving sinkholes and long cracks in the sand – likely the product of so much unaccustomed water.

Regardless, it was time to get the fuck out of here.

With a gesture, Walt pulled up his map.

He was near the western edge of the city, his location denoted by a faint green dot. A few streets up and over, and he'd reach the northwestern gate. If he could slip out, he might be able to wade through the storm – inverting his gravity spell to increase his weight and make him more resistant to the wind and rain.

At least, that was his working plan.

With a grunt, he swiped away the map and shouldered his packs, starting off toward the gate. As he neared the end of the street, he heard the hounds long before he saw them coming. They let out a wailing howl that stood out over the wind and rain. He immediately slinked against a nearby wall, blending into the shadows. He saw several figures running down the street, sprinting away from the hounds. From their simple clothing, they looked like NPCs... or players unfortunate enough to have logged in or respawned into this mess.

Walt grimaced. That path wasn't clear.

He glanced at the wall behind him and made a quick decision. He would have to burn most of his mana, but passing through the buildings was safer than sticking to the streets. His mind made up, his fingers wound through another series of gestures, and then he vanished into the nearby wall just as the hounds barreled down the alley behind him.

One building. Two. Then a third.

Walt's chest was burning as he sucked in air, and his skin and bones ached from the unnatural compression. He slumped against the wall, squeezing his eyes closed – his health and stamina drained.

That was when he heard it. The clang of metal.

The shouts of pain. The hoarse cries of soldiers. The howl of the hounds.

Walt's eyes snapped open, and what he witnessed left him staring dumbstruck.

He'd exited onto a second-story terrace – hoping to inspect the area around him before he made a final dash for the gate. The space gave him an extraordinary view of the battle that was now raging in the street below him.

The paws of hundreds of hounds beat against the sands as they raced toward the city's gate, tendrils of steam curling into the air where the rain pelted their bodies. The creatures were advancing on a line of metal-clad warriors that stood in the narrow gateway – their feet planted firmly, and massive tower shields raised in front of them. Flames encircled their armor, heating the metal until it glowed a bright red.

Without warning, the ground beneath Walt lurched, and he gripped at the nearby wall, trying to maintain his balance. The line of buildings farther down the street gave way – as though a giant had simply shoved the buildings into the street. They toppled forward with a thunderous crash, burying a few hundred hounds beneath several tons of sandstone. Dust swept up into the air, only to be firmly pounded back into the ground by the rain and wind.

Then the advancing line of hounds was upon those plated warriors. The warriors cut down the beasts in droves. The second line behind the shield wall stepped forward. They were armed with lances, which plunged between the gaps in the shields with pinpoint precision. Glowing orange blood soon stained the sands, and a mountain of bodies was forming in front of those soldiers.

"What... what's going on?" Walt muttered. Was someone attacking the city? Was that why the hounds were here? But then why were these soldiers fighting them?

He saw two groups peel off in either direction behind the soldiers, one group launching on to the rooftops on the other side of the street and then racing across the tiles. Above them floated a translucent, shimmering barrier of air mana.

To hold off the rain and wind, Walt realized belatedly.

The other group ran straight into the base of the tornado that was forming near the gate. Walt drew in a sharp breath as he watched them swallowed up by the vortex and then released it in a surprised huff a moment later as they rematerialized on the nearby rooftops. The men and women sprinted forward with uncanny dexterity, seemingly immune to the storm.

And who the hell are they?

They began lobbing frozen grenades down into the street, lances of ice erupting among the surging column of hounds that streamed just below him. Those shards cut into the beasts with abandon, the icy energy severing limbs and stabbing through their bodies. A nearby hound was impaled, held aloft on an icy shard, and its paws still jerked and twisted at the air as it slowly slid down the ice, leaving a bloody orange trail in its wake.

Then he saw a flash of fire mana closer to the gate. Someone was fighting the hounds in front of the shield wall. Yet the man moved so quickly that Walt could barely follow him – he was merely an orange-streaked blur as he carved his way through the beasts. A pile of bodies began to accumulate around him like a sort of macabre wall.

"How... how is that possible?" he muttered. Walt had witnessed a few encounters with the hounds before. They were strong and fast and utterly indifferent to injury, healing swiftly if they were able to kill. Only raw luck... or a tremendous amount of skill made it possible to kill one.

Much less dozens...

Walt swallowed hard and pressed himself farther back into the shadows of the terrace. He didn't have a clue what was going on – why the hounds were attacking or why this advancing army stood in the mouth of the gate. But he knew for damned sure that he didn't want to be discovered by either.

All thoughts of escape were gone. His only goal now was survival. If he died, they could strip him of all his hard-earned – or at least, *hard-stolen* – loot.

As the hounds began to thin out, Walt saw movement by the gate.

That man – the one that had stood down the advancing line of hounds – drifted up into the air, floating on a column of air mana as he rocketed up into the sky. Only a moment later, he touched down on the rampart atop the gate, another mage coming to rest beside him.

She's an air mage. But who is he?

Walt's eyes centered on that man, taking a cautious step forward to get a better look.

He was wearing robes, the cloth wrapped tightly around his skin. His eyes were two flaming orange embers as they took in the street below him. An inferno seemed to be raging in the man's left arm, the fires visible and reflecting through what appeared to be translucent skin... or something else entirely. That limb seemingly couldn't contain the flames, fiery ropes of energy winding up his shoulder and around his body. And atop his head floated a crown made entirely of fire.

Walt's mouth dropped open as he watched this scene – as that man turned those strange glowing eyes to the city below him. He didn't look alarmed. Or scared. He looked like a conquering king. A god of fire and flame.

Not knowing what else to do, Walt tried to open his system UI, struggling to pull up the in-game recording menu. His fingers fumbled at the UI, his eyes darting back to that man standing on the ramparts. And then he had it. He snapped a quick picture, recording the image before him. A fiery god standing above an army of flaming metal soldiers. A legion of dead hounds sprawled out before him and a hurricane at his back.

And that's when Walt felt it... an icy stab at the side of his neck.

He tried to jerk but felt his arm pivoted up and behind him – locked in place. The dagger in his neck twisted and then was ripped free in a shower of blood.

Walt slumped to the ground, unable to move... his vision listing to the side. He barely even felt himself hit the stone tile of the terrace or the pitter-patter of rain striking his face. And he barely glanced at the cloth-robed man beside him, his limbs shifting into streamers of air and water as he twisted and leapt back up onto the roof in a single fluid motion. Even his loot was forgotten, despite the crushing weight that descended upon him as his channel ended abruptly, and his fingers slowed to a halt.

Walt only had eyes on that point of light above the gate.

On that creature of flame and destruction that looked down upon the ruins of Lahab.

"Who are you?" Walt croaked. "*What...* are you?"

And then there was only darkness.

Chapter 43 - Suicidal

Finn's feet touched down on the rain-slick and wind-swept sands at the base of the gate. Streamers of amber energy coiled around him as the air mage's spell dissipated, sending up a spray of water and sand. Abbad and Kyyle landed with soft thumps beside him. A massive stone wall stood just outside the gate, ringing the entrance to the city. The earth mages had continued to reinforce the barrier, creating a semi-circular ring of rock and stone that nearly surpassed the walls of Lahab.

As his eyes skimmed down the street, he could see the heaping piles of sickly orange bodies, many of the hounds having been shoved up against the nearby buildings to make a narrow path. Beyond that, more earth mages were at work on the far end of the road. Bilel had dissolved most of the buildings that had toppled down into the street, but there were still plenty of debris. The mages were repurposing those materials, breaking apart the sandstone bricks and reassembling them into a thick wall that neatly cordoned off the area around the gate to secure their foothold into Lahab.

And overtop the group floated a dense, shimmering wall of air mana. The energy coated the entire area around the gate and spread down the street. A magical canopy maintained by nearly a dozen air mages. Another division stood alongside them, ready to step in once the first group's mana had been depleted.

Between the earthen barriers on either end of the street and the protective dome above, the worst of the storm had been blunted. The wind was now merely a muted whistling howl, and the rain no longer pelted the heads and shoulders of the soldiers that regrouped around the gate.

"Finally, a break from this storm," Kyyle grunted as he walked up to Finn. The earth mage was bunching the fabric of his robes, wringing the cloth, and letting a cascade of water drip down onto the sand. "Do you have any idea how heavy these robes get when they're wet? Such a silly type of armor…"

"You know that's pointless, right?" Julia drawled, waving at Kyyle as she approached from the other end of the street, her lance holstered, and her shield strapped across her back. "We've walled off this area to allow us to regroup, but we've done nothing to ease the storm itself. Once we move from this location, you're just going to get soaked again."

Kyyle raised a grumpy eyebrow. "Well, then I can use the opportunity to remember what it was like to be dry… or, at least, only *slightly* damp."

Julia snorted in amusement before her attention drifted to Finn.

His gaze was distant, skimming across the map of the city projected beside him. Multicolored dots were highlighted across the display courtesy of Daniel. The AI had used Finn's enhanced vision to help pinpoint clusters of the hounds while they had stood atop the gate. Those dots were now static and were likely to change quickly, but it at least gave him a sense of what was happening in the rest of the city – none of it good.

"So, what now?" Julia asked gently, placing a hand on his shoulder.

He looked up to meet her expression, his mouth pinched into a grim line. He knew what needed to happen next, but he expected she wasn't going to like it.

"I'm also curious about our next move," another voice piped up.

Finn turned to see that Aerys had found their position – likely given away by the flames that still circled Finn's body, the glowing crown atop his brow, and the fires that flickered within the depths of his left hand. He stood out like a sore thumb – a fact he was going to be counting on now.

Both Kalisha and Malik flanked the Khamsin leader. Behind them was a contingent of the desert folk, their armor soaked through. Yet, somehow, they were still able to move silently. Those severe men and women all placed a hand to their chest and bowed their heads as Finn's attention drifted across them, muttering something under their breaths.

He didn't need to hear them to recognize their words.

"You seem to be in a sour mood despite our success," Abbad observed as he watched Aerys. "We've breached the shield and the city gates, no small accomplishment."

"But not without losses," Aerys replied evenly. "We've lost a few hundred of our own already. And now we're stuck in the middle of this *hurricane*... or whatever you want to call this... thing that Finn has created." She gestured at the swirling mass of black clouds that still loomed above them, lightning crackling between the dark bank of moisture. "And there's still the matter of a legion of those hounds out there, as well as a demon king intent on killing us all.

She met Abbad's gaze. "So, you'll forgive me if I don't feel entirely relaxed."

Finn saw Julia's eyes flash angrily but held up a hand.

This wasn't the time for bickering. He could appreciate Aerys' sour mood. He'd kept her in the dark about his plans up until now, and she was accustomed to feeling in control. Unfortunately, they were all playing this by ear – forced to move quickly and adapt. Aerys would come around eventually.

"No... no. It's a fair question," Finn answered, the group quieting. Even the soldiers and Khamsin around them stilled their movements, watching him with uncanny focus. Between the storm and the latest fight with the hounds, it seemed he had made an impression.

Finn swiped at the air, rotating, and sharing his map for the group – the members of their unlikely alliance circling around him.

"This data is a few minutes old – captured while I was atop the ramparts," Finn explained. "But it gives us a sense of the current situation."

He tapped at the orange dots – points of light that were spread throughout the city. "It looks like the hounds are roaming the streets in packs – somewhere between fifty and a hundred in each group." His fingers skimmed to the guild halls located along the northern, eastern, and western edges of the city. "However, most of the creatures have gravitated toward the guild halls and are clustering there, especially the Mage Guild."

Finn frowned, rubbing at his temple lightly with one hand. "Based on what we know, the hounds are most likely hunting the survivors that remained when the guilds were evacuated as well as preying on the travelers that have been respawning, returning, or just starting out in this world."

"Okay, so taking out the hounds at the guilds is priority number one," Julia said, staring at the map. "If we let Bilel continue, he'll only replace the creatures he's lost."

"And that may explain why he's been so careless with his losses so far," Abbad replied softly, frowning at the screen.

Finn cocked his head at that. He had to admit that despite what they'd been through already, getting past the shield and the gate had been a touch easier than he'd expected. And Bilel had neither entered the fray directly nor done much to aid his hounds – just enough to let Finn and the army know he was there and prevent them from crushing his forces outright. That either meant his mana was limited or he was playing a different game here.

"It's possible," Finn answered tentatively.

"Did you see many survivors along the streets?" Malik asked, the normally stoic warrior's expression even more severe as he watched Finn.

Finn shook his head. "Some residents and travelers may have survived Bilel's onslaught by hiding in their homes and staying mobile. But the storm cuts both ways. It's difficult to make out individuals among the ambient mana from the storm. The hounds are easier to spot since they run in large groups."

He hesitated. "Although, that raises another

concern. Buildings have collapsed, sinkholes are forming in the sand from the constant rain, and lightning strikes and tornadoes are common – touching down at random and leaving a path of destruction in their wake. It's not just the hounds out there... the storm itself is a danger. It's destroying Lahab."

A heavy silence lingered at that statement, punctuated by the muted howl of the wind that swept across the shield above them as though the hurricane wished to remind them once again that it was still there.

"Which leads me back to my original question," Aerys grunted sourly. "What do we do now? Finish hunting the hounds? Try to find the Emir and finish this?"

Finn took a deep breath. Now was the moment he was going to have to explain his plan. He could already anticipate the pushback.

"We need to split up," he answered finally.

He tapped at the palace. "I believe Bilel is holed up in the palace. I saw him casting from that location from atop the wall. The throne room offers a good line of sight on the rest of the city, and the palace grounds are fortified with their own interior wall. If I were in his position, I would make my stand there. If we breached the outer walls, that would be the easiest place to defend."

"But what's to keep him there?" Kyyle asked, glancing at Finn. "He's already gathered quite a bit of mana. Why not just flee the city with the staff?"

Finn shook his head. He'd been thinking the same thing. But after reading Bilel's journal, he didn't anticipate that retreat was a strategy that the demon would likely employ. And that spell cast from the palace throne room had seemed so... obvious. Almost like the demon had wanted Finn to see him. No, Bilel was after something else.

"He wants me," Finn said, meeting Kyyle's eyes. "Bilel's quarrel is with the gods, and, thus, by proxy with me. His easiest way of hurting the Seer is to take me out of play permanently. He won't leave until that's finished."

"You aren't about to suggest what I think you are?"

Julia demanded sharply. Finn raised his eyes, switching to *Short-Sighted* to see her glaring at him. As she saw the look on his face, that scowl only deepened. "You are, aren't you? Gods damn it!"

"Care to share with the rest of us?" Kalisha interjected.

"Finn here is about to suggest that he goes to the palace himself. And I bet he's planning to send us on a cleanup mission to take out the remaining hounds."

Finn could only grin in response. "Close, but not quite."

Julia let out a frustrated huff as Finn continued, "You're right that we need to take out the hounds at the Mage Guild. That will further weaken Bilel's healing abilities and prevent him from re-populating his army. And while Bilel is focused on that, we can move a strike team into position – a small group that can infiltrate the palace undetected and take out the demon.

"Note my emphasis on a *group*," Finn continued with a wink at his daughter. "That should include myself and a handful of others."

Kyyle glanced down at Finn's hand. "And how would you suggest we sneak up to a demon that can see mana? I bet you stand out like a sore thumb right now with your *Focusing Prism* charged by the hounds—"

The earth mage cut himself off, his eyes going round. "Ahh, you did that on purpose, didn't you? Same with flying up to the top of the rampart. And here I thought you just wanted to show off."

"Well, that might have been part of it," Finn shot back with a smile.

His gaze shifted back to the group, noticing their confused expressions. "I've revealed my position and my energy signature," he explained, holding up his left hand. "The mana held within the crystal should be enough for Bilel to detect it easily despite the interference from the storm. Which means he'll know where I'm going to be... at least, as long as we match this mana signature."

"You're suggesting a decoy then," Kalisha piped

up from nearby, rubbing at her chin in thought. "You want to have our water mages cast an illusion that mimics the mana in your hand, making Bilel think that you're leading the attack on the Mage Guild..."

"When, in fact, I'll be coming straight for him," Finn continued with a nod. "We can have those mages cast an illusion on the strike team before we leave as well – using it to mask our mana. If we keep our casting to a minimum, and with the interference from the storm, that should conceal our presence from Bilel."

His fingers tapped at the map, tracing a line to the Mage Guild. "Our forces should continue on to the Mage Guild. If they can clear out the hounds there, then they should move in a clockwise pattern around the city – focusing on the guild halls. We need to reduce the creatures' numbers to weaken Bilel further and suppress the mana that's being channeled back to the staff."

"Which leaves you to go on this suicide mission straight into the demon's fortress," Julia retorted, crossing her arms. "Even if you don't plan to do this alone... how are you going to get past the palace walls? Inside the palace? And how exactly do you propose to fight Bilel himself? If our army doesn't take out the hounds, he'll simply be able to out-heal our damage. And that's putting aside that we didn't exactly do very well the last time we fought him. Actually, I believe we didn't even manage to hit him."

"That was also a long time ago, and he caught us by surprise," Finn retorted. "Besides, Bilel may have drained a substantial amount of mana over the years using the purge, but you've seen the spells he's been throwing around during these last few battles. Our own spells took hundreds of mages working together. He's just one person – even if he's become a demon and is wielding the relic. Between the shield over the city, his illusions, and the earth magic he's been using, he's likely burned through a substantial portion of his stockpile."

"Or he just wants you to think that," Kyyle observed. "This guy has kept control of the city for the better part of a *century*. Do you really think he doesn't have a contingency plan?" Finn's head tilted at that, his thoughts flitting back to a game of stones played in a quiet palace courtyard. He had to admit, Bilel was clever.

That frustrating thought was teasing at the edges of his mind too.

"I admit this is a longshot, but this entire war has been a longshot." Finn took a deep breath. "Either way, I fully expect that my group will be going on a one-way trip," he added softly. "For both travelers and residents alike." His eyes shot to the NPCs among their group. "And you lot don't respawn."

His attention snapped back to Julia and Kyyle. "I suspect that Bilel may have developed a means to contain or destroy a traveler's avatar. He knew he'd eventually have to deal with me, so that doesn't seem implausible. You may stand to lose everything by coming with me," he continued, rubbing at the base of his left arm.

The ache no longer lingered there – the magical infection purged after their meeting with Nar Aljahim – but he hadn't forgotten how that staff had drained his mana and left him weakened. It wasn't a large leap to assume that Bilel had been pondering on a way to take Finn out of play permanently.

"Yeah, yeah. And everyone dies someday. Your plan is risky as hell, but I don't exactly have a better one," Julia admitted reluctantly. "Besides, do you really think we're going to let you go do this alone? After coming all this way? Hell will freeze over before I let you race off on your own again."

"Even I have to agree," Aerys grunted. Her attention flitting to Finn, meeting his eyes. "I see your plan now. A small group with carefully constructed illusions likely stands the best chance of infiltrating the palace without Bilel detecting them – and we do still need to slay the hounds. However, this task is hopeless without help."

A pause. "More importantly, we have all committed ourselves to this endeavor already – even if that means we might die here today.

"*Anything. Everything.* Aren't those the words of our *prophet*?" she asked, a challenge in her voice as she held Finn's gaze.

Finn couldn't help the amused snort that emerged from his throat. This coming from the woman who seemed to second guess him at every turn? Then his gaze swept across the rest of the group, observing the same determination shining in each of their eyes.

"Okay. Fine," he said. "Though we still need to limit the group. The goal here is to travel fast and light. Likely five or six at most."

Julia crossed her arms. "Well, I'm coming. So, we need five more then." She glanced around the small courtyard. "Any volunteers for this suicide mission?"

To Finn's surprise, every member of their group raised their hand. Even Aerys' arm grudgingly rose into the air – the woman raising an eyebrow at Finn when their eyes met. He was honestly shocked that she would relinquish command of the Khamsin to join their company. Perhaps he'd underestimated her grudge with Bilel. He'd always had her pegged as favoring her own self-interest and ambition over altruism.

Or perhaps he'd simply underestimated the scars that decades of persecution had left behind. Pain and anger could be powerful motivators.

Even more surprising, the volunteers weren't contained to their smaller group. The Khamsin, mages, and soldiers that lingered around them – their necks craning as they eavesdropped on the conversation – all shot their arms into the air. Every single man and woman among them volunteered to charge straight into the demon's lair.

"Huh. Well, that was more than I was expecting..." Julia muttered.

"If I may," Abbad interjected. "I believe the group should consist of Finn, Julia, Kyyle, Malik, Kalisha, and myself." He raised a hand to ward off their objections. "Before you question my suggestion, let me continue. That provides a balance of casters and soldiers. Finn, Kyyle, and I won't be able to use our mana for fear of alerting Bilel," the former librarian explained.

"We will need Julia, Malik, and Kalisha to help us traverse the city," Abbad continued. "Julia and Malik can act as our brawn if we encounter any hounds, and Kalisha can use her mechanids to help scout ahead of our position. Once we're inside, the mixture of fire, air, and earth mana may be sufficient for dealing with Bilel."

The group lapsed into silence for a moment as they mulled on that suggestion.

"His reasoning does make sense," Kyyle offered, glancing at Finn.

"It does," Finn admitted grudgingly.

"Then we're decided," Aerys said suddenly. Her eyes skimmed to the soldiers around her. "You lot get back to work! We're moving within the hour!"

The mages, Khamsin, and fighters immediately started moving again as they continued to fortify their position, regroup and regear, and prepared to move out. Finn could see that their small group had also partially dissolved. Kyyle and Abbad huddled together, pulling in several water mages to discuss how to structure the illusion while Kalisha, Malik, and Julia had started charting a tentative path through the city using Finn's map.

Which left Finn standing alone with Aerys.

Perhaps it was time to clear the air a little. He might not get a second chance.

"You were right to call me out before," Finn offered tentatively. "I should have been more transparent with my strategy for attacking the city."

"No... no. It is the job of a leader to lead," she replied, her eyes on the activity around them and a frown creasing her lips. "I inducted you into the Khamsin, held you up as a prophet, and encouraged my – our – people to follow you. Only to have difficulty placing the same faith in you myself."

A pause, her gaze going distant. "The Khamsin

have lost many over the years... *I have lost many over the years.* Friends. Family. Soldiers. It doesn't get any easier," she said in a quiet voice. "And it makes it difficult to trust."

The woman's gaze was heavy as she watched a nearby Khamsin man, his arm severed at the elbow – a jagged line of flesh that could only be caused by hounds' teeth. In that moment, Finn saw another side of her – something deeper than the thin veil of bravado, the self-interested ambition, and the political gamesmanship. He saw pain. And fear.

And suddenly, he realized that he was leaving her alone to guide an army – with many of their strongest mages and warriors volunteering to undertake this final mission.

He rested a hand on her shoulder, and she glanced at him in surprise. "You can do this. Lead them, I mean. There are still others in the chain of command for the fighters and mages – even with the loss of Malik, Kalisha, and Abbad."

A small, wry smile twisted her lips. "And yet, there is only one prophet."

It was Finn's turn to snort. "I don't think you've ever really believed that I'm following some divine path. I'm just a man. A particularly determined man with nothing to lose and everything to gain."

"And one who has accomplished more in weeks than our people have in years," Aerys replied. Her tone was bitter but not unkind. "Your actions may not be divine, but you see clearly in a way that few will ever understand. You are always three steps ahead – even when your actions look foolhardy. And you aren't afraid to commit everything to the task at hand, including your own life."

She seemed to chew on her final words, as though they pained her to say aloud. "You are a true leader. I am just..."

"A woman that has pulled together more than a dozen disparate bands. Who put aside her own pride and history to forge an alliance with her former enemies, and who raised her hand without hesitation when asked to charge straight to her death," Finn said firmly.

Aerys' eyes were wide as she looked at him. "You can do this. You can lead them." A pause and a grin. "And if it helps, you don't really have much choice."

She laughed then, perhaps the first time that Finn had ever seen her sincerely amused. "And that's the crux of it, isn't it?" she replied.

Her expression sobered, and she met his eyes again. "But thank you."

"You're welcome," he replied.

"Let us just hope that our decoy will be enough..."

And then, in that moment, the thought hovering at the edges of Finn's mind resolved into focus. He could almost feel the pieces shifting across the board. Maybe it was Aerys' words about their ruse. Or Kyyle's fear that Bilel might have another plan up his sleeve. He couldn't place his fingers on exactly *what* had encouraged his idea to flare to life, but he certainly wasn't going to question it – not now, with so much on the line.

"Actually... I just had a thought," Finn said, turning to Aerys, her brow furrowing.

He leaned in close, whispering a few final words in her ear – words meant only for her. The Khamsin leader's eyes widened as Finn pulled away.

"Do you really think this is necessary?" she asked.

"I hope not," Finn answered, his expression grim. "But better safe than sorry."

He met her gaze then, holding her eyes, seeing the fear and doubt that lingered there. "Will you do it?"

Aerys met his gaze for a fraction of a second longer before nodding curtly. Then she squared her shoulders and marched off toward a line of soldiers, barking orders. Finn's eyes followed her as she left – a sense of uneasiness lingering in his stomach. Despite his reassurance and his hastily whispered words, he could feel his own worm of doubt writhing in his stomach.

They were creating a ruse meant to deceive a

demon. But he doubted that Bilel had been idle while they breached the city gates and regrouped. He had likely been busy devising his own plan – assuming he hadn't already been prepared for days now.

Finn just had to hope that three steps ahead would be enough...

Chapter 44 - Mechanical

The mechanid skittered out into the street, its metal legs thumping against the wet sand and anchoring the creature to the ground, keeping it stationary despite the howling winds that whipped down through the narrow gap between the buildings. A group of hounds rounded the corner, and a fiery gem in the mechanid's chest flared to life – just enough fire mana rippling across its hard casing for the creatures to pick up its scent.

The hounds seemed to sniff at the air for a moment before their glowing orange eyes settled on the mechanid. With a howl, the pack leader surged forward, the muscles in its legs rippling and snapping as it launched down the road – the rest of the hounds only steps behind, their voices filling the air as they picked up their leader's call.

The mechanid promptly skittered down the street. As the hounds neared, it suddenly veered toward the wall of a nearby building, its metallic limbs puncturing the sandstone as it swiftly scaled the surface. A hound leaped after it, its fangs snagging on one of the mech's legs. Gears ground and shrieked in protest, its upward march suddenly halted.

Then, with a shower of sparks, the leg ripped free, a faint stream of air mana spewing from the broken pneumatics with a violent hiss. Yet the mechanid continued its steady march, soon cresting the lip of the building and scurrying down the street by following the line of rooftops. The hounds still lingered below, their orange eyes never wavering.

"Damn it. I'm going to run out of mechs at this rate," Kalisha grumbled from a nearby alley as the group watched the hounds race down the street and out of sight. Her right hand anxiously stroked at the small metal spider creature that clung to her left arm.

"Like you don't have plenty to spare," Kyyle replied dryly, waving at the veritable army of mechanical spiders that clung to the walls around them – their mana crystals deactivated and silent to avoid giving away their position. Once they moved again, the mechanical creatures would activate and scatter in sequence to avoid creating a cluster of energy that might be visible to Bilel.

"Actually, this might be my own personal nightmare," Kyyle muttered as he eyed the mechanids looming around him. He hadn't forgotten their encounter in the Abyss when he and Julia had been tasked with holding off Kalisha and her companions.

It hadn't been too long ago that they had been fighting off these damn things.

Julia came up behind the group, slipping quietly through the shadows of the alley. They'd picked this spot since the ground seemed relatively stable, and the walls of the surrounding buildings offered shelter from the rain. The group was no longer able to use the barriers of air mana for fear of alerting Bilel to their presence. Even the fire crystals that Kalisha had installed in her mechs to bait the hounds was a risk, and she'd been forced to carefully adjust the strength of the energy with Finn's help, keeping the energy signature around the same level as an average human person.

"I don't see any movement behind us," Julia grunted at Finn, shaking the wet from her armor.

Kalisha's eyes went distant as she surveyed a prompt that they couldn't see. "The hounds are also out of range now, and my sentries aren't picking up any other packs nearby. It should be safe to move."

Finn nodded, his eyes skimming to the map hovering in the air beside him. They weren't too much farther from the walls that ringed the palace. He picked out another small alley that opened up beside the gates, choosing a location along the western side of the wall a decent distance from the entrance to the palace grounds. They weren't going to be able to casually stroll into the palace this time around.

They'd need to find another way past the walls.

His fingers tapped at the location, leaving a glowing yellow waypoint marker. He spared a glance at

Kalisha. "It looks like you won't have to worry about losing any more mechanids. This is our last stop, and then we need to figure out how to move inside the palace grounds without being detected."

"Greeeaaat," the merchant drawled with a frown.

The others looked equally unenthusiastic, shouldering their gear and savoring these last few moments of relative dryness. Finn certainly couldn't blame them. As he swiped away his map, he tugged his damp robes close again and pulled the hem of his robe up and over his mouth, tamping down on the desire to light just a small flame to force away the cold and wet. The thin barrier of cloth helped to filter the rain and sand kicked up by the storm, but it did little to ward off the sheets of water that would soon beat down on them.

"Okay, we move on five," Finn said, sparing a look at Malik.

The fighter nodded and moved into the point position, Julia taking up the rear. If it came to a fight, that pair would need to do most of the heavy lifting. The mages couldn't afford to cast anything substantial for fear of giving away their position.

"Go, go, go," Finn said, placing his hand on Kyyle's pack in front of him.

The others followed his lead, grasping the person in front of them and creating a living chain that surged out into the stormy street. With one final glance at her mechanical pets, Kalisha waved at the mechs, and they scurried up the walls, splitting off in different directions and taking up sentry positions along the rooftops – using their metallic limbs to anchor themselves in place along the buildings.

Wind pelted them as soon as the group left the alley, nearly knocking Finn off balance and sending a wave of rain splattering against him. It was all he could do to see amid the storm, the energies swirling chaotically. Lightning snapped down against a building nearby, carving a dark furrow in the sandstone and sending several bricks spiraling down toward the group.

Julia was there in a flash, her heavy metal armor letting her navigate the storm more easily. With a sweep of her arm, she knocked the bricks off course, sending them smashing into the ground nearby, the wet sand swallowing them with a squelching sound.

Then they were moving again.

A hand on the body in front of them.

A steady march through the relentless rain.

And then they were cresting another line of buildings, and the group stumbled into another alley. They immediately leaned against the nearby walls, their breathing heavy and uneven, and their muscles burning.

Kyyle spared Finn a mock glare. "Okay, I'm really starting to regret this storm," he gasped. "And this illusion just makes it worse. It's like it's trapping the water closer to my skin," he muttered, tugging at his collar uncomfortably.

"While I certainly sympathize," Abbad said, the stoic librarian equally soaked, "the illusions coating our bodies and the energy of the storm are the only things masking our movements. Without them, I suspect Bilel would have already sent hounds to converge on our location."

"Hey, a quick death might be preferable to this nonsense," the earth mage groused as he wrung out his robes for at least the dozenth time.

For his part, Finn had already tuned them out. Stepping up toward the mouth of the alley, he took in the walls of the palace. A frown immediately tugged at his lips, his brow pinching together.

Those stone walls practically shone with mana. And not the calming emerald glow of earth mana. No, they were riddled with the other affinities, the colors swirling together to form complicated patterns along the stone – glowing symbols and designs etched into the surface of the stone. That could only mean one thing.

Wards.

"What do you see?" Julia asked from his shoulder.

"Nothing good," Finn muttered.

He knew some of the symbols scrawled across the walls, and they didn't bode well. They weren't just reinforcing the stone itself – which likely took Kyyle's *Dissolve* out of play. He also saw symbols for what looked like "electricity" and "fire." While he didn't recognize the underlying spells, he could assume that they were probably some sort of defensive wards designed to electrocute or incinerate anyone foolhardy enough to attempt to scale the walls.

And just beyond those walls, Finn could make out the telltale amber shimmer of air magic. Those barriers extended up and over the palace itself, protecting the structure from the worst effects of the storm and the occasional blast of lightning. Bilel must be actively shielding the entire palace. Finn could only guess at how much mana that must take. Even a couple hundred air mages working together would have difficulty accomplishing the same task.

However, he would have to put that aside for now. He had more pressing concerns.

With a grimace, Finn shifted his attention, pushing past the layers of mana in the nearby wall in an effort to catch a glimpse of what lay beyond. It was difficult with the many sheets of mana now coating the surface of the wall – mixed with the mana from the storm that still raged around them. But after his time in the Forge and at such close range, he could just barely filter through the layers of interference.

Only a few moments later, his eyes widened.

If the walls were a problem, the glowing orange field of fire mana that lingered on the other side of that barrier was even more worrisome. Even as he looked on, he saw the sapphire energy of the rain sweep down across that field, the energy turning to a dull, muddy brown that indicated steam. After their siege on the city and their journey through the storm, he'd come to recognize that mana signature immediately.

Those were hounds. Lots and lots of hounds.

"Shit," Finn muttered, pulling back from the lip of

the alley and shifting deeper within the protective stone walls of the two adjacent buildings.

"Judging from your expression, I'm going to guess you're about to regale us with how *easy* and *simple* it will be to break into the palace," Kalisha observed.

Malik barked out something that sounded eerily like a laugh, earning him a few surprised glances from the group.

"What?" he demanded. "She is occasionally humorous."

"And here we were starting to think the Fighters Guild *purged* your sense of humor," Kyyle offered with a raised eyebrow.

The rest of the group peered at Finn, waiting expectantly for a report.

He let out a sigh, leaning against the wall behind him and rubbing at his eyes. "The walls are warded. I didn't see any evidence of wards last time we were here, so either Bilel has only recently charged the symbols, or they're new. Either way, it looks like they're designed to reinforce the stone and possibly stop anyone trying to make it over the walls."

"When you say *possibly stop*..." Kyyle trailed off, waiting expectantly.

"I'm guessing you get electrocuted if you touch the stone, and a *Fire Wall* may spring to life if you somehow make it to the top of the wall," Finn said. "So, you get to choose between getting zapped or burned to death."

"Perfect," Kyyle grunted, eyeing the wall looming above the mouth of the alley with a wary expression now.

"Oh, I'm not done. Assuming we survive that, there's the legion of hounds stationed just behind the wall. They practically fill the palace's outer courtyards," Finn added.

"Do you have a sense of their numbers?" Julia asked.

"Too many. Far, far too many to fight with just the six of us," Finn answered. His *Mana Sight* didn't make identifying specific hounds easy. It only gave him a broad approximation – somewhere between a "few" and a "shitload."

"Okay. So, we just have to get past an impenetrable wall of death and fight off an army of hounds. Sounds like a great warm-up for trying to assassinate a demon," Kalisha observed, sarcasm dripping from her voice.

Kyyle's brow was furrowed as he stared at the wall. "Or we could go under it," he murmured. He looked up and realized that the group was staring at him.

"See, right there," he said, pointing at the sand at the base of the wall. It had begun to shift and sink – evidence that the ground wasn't stable. They had been forced to divert their path many times during their trek through the city to avoid such sinkholes. "I'm guessing there's a sinkhole forming already. We could just reinforce it a bit. Maybe shore up the walls with thin barriers of stone – just enough to buy us a few minutes."

"The mana might give us away," Abbad observed.

Finn was biting at his lip now as he observed the ground. It was times like this that he wished he had Daniel's help – although he'd never admit it to the often-recalcitrant AI. For now, he'd been forced to de-summon him, worried that his ambient fire mana would give them away on their trek through the city. But even without Daniel's analysis, Finn's *Mana Sight* confirmed that Kyyle was right.

The rainwater had seeped through the sand and rock, a natural fracture in the stone forming a small cave just below the wall that extended outward on both sides. That water was weakening the walls of the cavern, causing it to widen further and destabilizing the sand along the ceiling of the cave. If given another few hours or days, a sinkhole might form directly below the wall. Although, that was time they didn't have.

"I see a growing cavern forming just below the wall. There's enough sand and rock there to hide Kyyle's casting if he keeps it low key," Finn said, his eyes still on the wall. "The wards along the barrier are also a double-edged sword. They're preventing entry, but they also obscure the area beneath the wall. It takes quite a bit of effort for me to peel back at those layers of mana, and that interference might also help hide Kyyle's casting." He waved at the storm that still billowed above them. "And then there's all of this shit clouding the area."

"Okay, so let's assume I could accelerate the formation of the sinkhole and then create a reinforced tunnel under the wall without drawing too much attention," Kyyle said, running a hand through his hair and his fingers coming away coated in sand and water. "How are we going to deal with the hounds on the other side?"

Finn frowned. That was a problem. There were far too many to fight.

What they needed was a distraction.

His eyes swept back to Kalisha, and she let out an exasperated sigh as she met his gaze. "You're going to make me use my babies as a distraction again, aren't you?" she asked.

"Their sacrifice will be for the greater good," Finn offered with a small smile.

"Uh-huh, sure. Just tell me your plan so I can go ahead and figure out the many, many different reasons I hate it," Kalisha replied in a dry voice.

Finn barked out a laugh as he pulled up his map.

"We're positioned here," he said, tapping at a cluster of green dots along the western edge of the palace walls. "The gate is to the north. And the area just inside the palace wall is largely open – a series of outer courtyards and what were once gardens. We need to distract the hounds and pull them to the north, northwest."

"Sure. But there's that warded wall in the way," Kalisha retorted.

"Which is why I'm thinking we shouldn't touch the wall," Finn replied. "You've mentioned flying drones before…"

Kalisha chewed on that thought, her brow

furrowing as she stared at the map. "That's probably not going to work here. Too much wind from the storm. And the lightning strikes are going to make flying drones even more vulnerable. Even if I could adapt my mechanids, they'd be more likely to sail directly into the wall than over it or get blasted apart." She hesitated at that statement, her eyes widening slightly.

"But maybe I could tinker with their pneumatics and position them along the rooftops of these buildings near the northern section of the wall. I'd guess there's maybe a 20-foot gap between the edge of the buildings and the wall," she said aloud, tapping at the map. "They *might* be able to leap over the barrier without touching it. Emphasis on might. And their metal casing could potentially shield them from any fire damage. Then I could rig them with a bunch of fire mana crystals and detonate them in sequence."

Her eyes skimmed back to Finn. "This is going to be loud and obvious, though. It's going to look like a few bombs went off... but it would buy you all some time."

"You sound like you're not coming with us," Julia observed, watching the merchant suspiciously. "How convenient."

Kalisha rolled her eyes. "Obviously, I have to stay on this side of the wall. This plan would require me to move to the north, re-outfit my mechanids, and then I need to be relatively close to trigger the detonations. I'll need to stagger the blasts to give you all enough time to make it through the tunnel and into the palace outbuildings. Hopefully, there will be fewer hounds inside."

"That's not the only reason," Finn commented, watching the merchant closely and noting the sad smile tugging at her lips.

"You always were a clever one," she replied with a wink, trying her best to mask the fear and anxiety he could see crawling through her energy.

At Julia's questioning glance, Finn continued. "She'll also need to keep a couple mechanids with her and then draw back through the city. Bilel will almost certainly notice the blasts. So, we need to give him an obvious target – namely, Kalisha. He might think that a lone merchant is trying to break into the palace, using the cover of the storm to ransack the place for loot."

Julia grunted, staring at the merchant with a spark of respect shining in her eyes now. Meanwhile, the rest of the group sat in silence, mulling on the tentative plan they had sketched out.

"No, no, no... Don't all rush to thank me for my heroics," the merchant offered with a grin. "You lot really know how to butter a girl up."

"You don't have to do this," Finn said, ignoring her sarcasm as he pushed away from the wall and met her eyes evenly. "We can try to find another way —"

A harsh laugh cut him off. "See! I always knew you cared." Kalisha's expression sobered in a flash. "But we both know there isn't another option."

Finn nodded grimly. She was right.

Kalisha noticed the same look of resigned determination settle across the rest of the group and let out a heavy sigh. Finn could see her fear and anxiety spike, but that energy was overshadowed by bright white and orange. Their mission was greater than the danger to any one of them – Kalisha knew that all too well.

She turned to the creature clamped to her arm, stroking it again and then placing her palm on the nearby wall. "Come, my baby. We have a lot of work to do."

The smaller mech unclenched its legs at this gesture, skittering up her arm and onto the adjacent wall. It then proceeded to march toward one of the mechanids. As it neared the larger construct, the smaller mech's body converted, its forelegs shifting and rotating, forming various tools with its legs. In a flash, it began to disassemble the mechanid – likely intending to adjust its pneumatics and install a payload of fire crystals.

"Well," Kalisha began, turning back to the group. "What are you lot waiting for? Don't you have a tunnel to build?"

Chapter 45 - Drowned

The group stood in a single-file line upon a narrow ledge that the earth mage had formed – a fragile bridge that spanned the length of the sinkhole, stretching out beneath the wall. Rain continued to pour into the cavern at their backs, raining down from the hole that Kyyle had formed and adding to the waters that pooled beneath them. The level rose swiftly with each second that passed.

Their balance was precarious at best. The ledge was only about a foot wide, forcing the group to clutch at each other and the walls of the pit to maintain their balance. One wrong move and they would fall a few feet into the waters below – where the mixture of wet and sand would likely suck them under in mere moments.

In contrast, the elementals were lucky. Once the group was beneath the wall, Finn had been able to risk summoning Daniel. The AI's modeling was indispensable in this situation, and the mixture of mana from the wall, sinkhole, and hounds in the nearby courtyard masked his mana. Both he and Brock seemed to be mocking the group, simply hovering above the pooling waters. The earth elemental's gravity well was causing a crater to form a massive indentation in the surface of the water below them.

Thin columns of emerald energy along the walls denoted the rock columns Kyyle had summoned to support the tunnel, using only trace amounts of his mana to avoid detection. Even so, a mixture of sand and water continued to pour out around those pillars as the sides of the cavern gradually eroded, worn down by the water that continued to rise toward their feet.

"Okay, this might be worse than standing outside," Julia grumbled, eyeing the water pooling below them. The level had only continued to rise while they worked. A few more minutes and the water would reach the platform.

"At least there's less wind," Kyyle offered, talking quietly over his shoulder. As he continued to gradually expand the sinkhole beneath the wall and add to their narrow bridge, the group shuffled forward – gradually moving toward the waypoint marker that denoted the far side of the wall and their escape from this hellhole.

"Except these walls feel like they could cave in at any moment," Julia retorted, eyeing the precarious supporting columns. If they gave way, they would likely be buried under several tons of sand. "I might respawn, but I'd rather not experience what it feels like to drown in quicksand." She let out a shudder as she spoke.

Even Malik glanced nervously at the waters below them – the first sign of nervousness that Finn had ever noted from the fighter. For his part, Abbad stood stock-still, his mana coiling around him faintly – the air mage blending the mana seamlessly into the air that howled above them. Finn could only assume he was waiting... listening.

"It shouldn't be much longer," Finn interjected. "We're just waiting for Kalisha to give the signal..."

"And how exactly is she going to do that?" Julia grumbled. "It's not like she can send us a chat message, and Abbad can't risk communicating with her now."

Finn's lips pressed into a grim line. He had spent some time helping the merchant re-outfit her mechanids. Her small Forged creature had helped her to quickly disassemble and modify the mechs, enhancing the pneumatics in their legs and embedding a dense cluster of fire crystals in each of their metallic torsos.

Kalisha had long since left the group, journeying north through the wind and rain to take up a position near the palace gates. It had also been quite some time since he had lost sight of the woman and her mechanids, although his *Mana Sight* could now clearly make out the dense cluster of hellhounds that stood guard just within the palace walls.

Which meant there was only one way for the merchant to give them a signal point...

"Trust me. You'll know it when you see it—" he replied.

"It's coming," Abbad murmured, interrupting Finn. His eyes snapped back into focus, and the streamers of air mana abruptly blew apart. The librarian's attention shifted to Kyyle. "You need to get ready to make us a hole—"

He never got to finish that sentence.

Finn felt the explosion long before he saw the bloom of fire mana in the distance. The detonation shook the walls of their cavern, cracks forming in the columns that held up the walls around them. A fresh deluge of water poured in from above. Finn knew there would be more explosions... many, many more as Kalisha attempted to lure away the hounds.

"You need to move now!" Finn shouted more loudly at Kyyle.

The earth mage was already casting, his hands winding through a rapid series of gestures. Coils of earth began to dissolve as Kyyle carved into the mixture of stone and rock on the other end of the sinkhole. He bored swiftly through the earth, pausing as faint hints of water splashed through the dissolving barrier.

"We clear?" Kyyle called over his shoulder.

Finn tried to steady himself as another detonation rocked the ground above them, sending him listing to the side. Julia just barely caught hold of him, keeping him on the narrow ledge even as he peered through the layers of earth mana. He could soon see the cloud of mana that denoted the hounds shifting northward as they caught the scent of fire mana, the occasional blast of flame flaring in the distance.

"Yes. Yes, go now!" Finn shot back.

Kyyle just nodded and pulled the last layer of earth away, water now streaming down into the makeshift shaft from both ends of the tunnel and the water level rising rapidly, partially submerging the platform they were on. Finn's feet splashed as the group single-filed down that precarious stone ledge, moving as quickly as they could toward the exit.

They didn't have long.

Another blast rocked the cavern, and Finn heard the telltale crack and snap of stone. His gaze shot to the side. One of the columns had fractured, and muddy earth was now collapsing along one side of the cave. That gunshot crack of stone repeated as the other pillars began to fail one by one.

"Come on! Move, move, move!" Kyyle shouted from the tunnel's exit, having escaped into the rainswept courtyard of the palace, Brock close on his heels. The earth elemental used his rocky limbs to claw his way out of the hole, widening the opening. Then Brock turned, and his arm lengthened and stretched, the stones reassembling as he helped the next group member in line. Without his help, it would have been almost impossible to pull themselves out of the hole – the mixture of sand and water unable to support their weight.

The group surged forward along the platform, Julia bringing up the rear with one hand lingering on Finn's shoulder. He could hear her ragged, frantic breathing overtop the splash of water and the constant boom of detonations in the distance. The water level had swelled up to his ankles, then his knees. The threat wasn't the sand itself, but how it added to the volume of water in the cave and continued to erode the walls. Finn could already see the earth around the exit beginning to dissolve and break away as Brock pulled Malik out of the hole, then Abbad just behind him.

Finn saw Brock's rocky hand stretch down through the opening, and he reached for the limb... only to slip at the last moment, losing his balance as a fresh surge of rainwater poured down into the hole. The water was now rising above his waist, making it almost impossible to stay standing on the narrow stone bridge below him. His daughter's hand was on his shoulder, the weight of her plate armor now more harmful than helpful as she seemed to drag him down and backward.

"Just go! Get out!" Julia said frantically, her hand disappearing.

"Fuck," Finn muttered. Suddenly unencumbered,

he tread through the water, stretching out his hand again…

And Brock just barely caught him. With a massive heave of the elemental's arm, Finn felt himself yanked out of the water, soon cresting the hole that was beginning to disintegrate entirely, and landing heavily on wet sand. Wind and rain now beat down upon him, his breathing fast and uneven.

"Julia!" he gasped, his eyes shooting back to the hole. Water had now almost surged up to ground level, and the supporting columns were collapsing completely.

Yet her telltale dark armor was nowhere to be seen.

"Get her, Brock!" Kyyle barked.

The elemental nodded once and then sunk into the water, his body contorting as he squeezed to fit into the hole. He didn't need to breathe, and Finn watched with his *Mana Sight* – his thoughts swirling chaotically – as Brock used his natural mass to drop further into the sinkhole, searching its murky depths with his glowing green eyes.

Where is she? Finn thought frantically, unable to make out the outline of Julia's armor amid the azure and emerald energy that swirled within the sinkhole.

Brock's limb reached out toward something, but Finn couldn't quite make out his target. His fist clenched, and Finn observed a surge of earth mana – Brock abandoning caution to preserve Julia's life. The elemental rocketed up out of the hole, blasting through the swiftly dissolving hole and spraying the area with sand and water.

He held Julia cradled in his stony arms, her body unmoving and her skin pale and clammy. The elemental gently set her down, using his bulky form to shelter her from the wind and rain. Finn surged forward to help her, only to be held up short by Abbad's staying hand on his shoulder.

"We can't linger here. Bilel may have noticed that flare of earth mana, and it's imperative he assumes this is just a regular sinkhole," the librarian shouted over the howling winds. "We need to make it to one of the palace outbuildings." He waved at the dark silhouettes in the distance, the emerald buildings barely visible amid the storm – even in Finn's enhanced sight.

Hounds were streaming out of the palace gates to the north, following the faint blasts of flame that echoed from farther within the depths of Lahab as Kalisha tried to draw the beasts away from the palace. However, a pack of several hundred hounds had already turned back to the south, their paws pounding through the sands. Finn could only assume Bilel had ordered some of the creatures to stay put and patrol the palace grounds.

Or perhaps Abbad was right, and the demon had noticed Brock's rescue attempt.

"Damn it," Finn muttered, grinding his teeth together.

He made a split-second decision, flicking his wrist and setting a waypoint marker on the nearest building. The bright-amber beacon would help point out their destination amid the storm. "Alright. Let's move," he shouted. "Follow the waypoint!"

Brock nodded, and he lifted Julia again, the rocks of his torso shifting to the side as he gently pulled her into his chest, creating a protective layer of stone to help blunt the storm. The group huddled behind the elemental, using him as shelter from the howling wind and rain. And then they were moving, their feet plodding through the wet sand as they moved toward that glowing yellow light that hovered in front of them.

Meanwhile, Finn's eyes kept drifting back to the group UI. His daughter was alive, but her health was at about 20% and continuing to slide downward slowly. She must have water in her lungs, and the symbol in his UI indicated that she was unconscious.

Stay alive, he thought desperately. *You have to stay alive.*

*   *   *

Malik opened the door cautiously, peering around

the corner. Seeing no guards, he gestured at the group behind him, and they swiftly funneled in through the opening.

They soon stood in a large hallway, the ceiling stretching nearly twenty feet above them, and the hall lined with tapestries and ornate furniture. Glowing spheres hovered at regular intervals along the hall, lighting the room. Fire mana was suspended within their depths, and the orbs were held aloft by a steady stream of air mana. Water poured off the group's gear and armor, splattering against the stone floor and leaving sandy pools in their wake.

"There's a room just up ahead to the right," Abbad grunted quietly, waving farther down the hall. "We should be able to regroup there."

Brock nodded and then surged forward. Malik led the way, with Finn and Kyyle following closely behind. As they neared the doorway, Finn spared a glance over his shoulder and saw Abbad casting. A faint gust of wind erupted from his fingertips before dropping toward the floor. It pushed the water and sand back down the hall and out the doorway where they had entered, covering their trail from any guards or hounds that might pass by. He noted that the air mage made sure to keep the energy level consistent with the glowing spheres suspended along the hall, even though it made the process take slightly longer.

And then the group slid inside the nearby room, and the door shut with a soft thump behind them. They found themselves inside a sitting room, filled with luxurious upholstered chairs and polished wooden furniture – a stark contrast to the bleak conditions lingering just outside the walls of the palace. Brock set Julia down gently on a chaise.

"I think there must be water in her lungs," Finn said, standing over her. She wasn't breathing, and her health was continuing to drop. "She needs CPR."

"I've had first aid training – at least, back in our world. Maybe it will translate..." Kyyle offered, stepping forward.

Finn nodded, and Kyyle shifted into position, leaning above Julia. The earth mage placed his hands on her chest, pushing in an even rhythm. He leaned forward, his lips pressing against Julia's as he forced air into her lungs. Then he started the process again.

And again.

And again.

Finn could feel despair well in his chest as he watched her health continue to slide lower. She couldn't die here. That would mean at least a forty-five-minute wait for her to respawn, they didn't know where she would end up when she came back, and that tunnel they had just used was definitely a one-way trip inside the palace.

If she died, then their group would be down one member.

Come on, Julia, he recited in his head.

Kyyle exhaled more air into her lungs, pulling back...

And Julia suddenly sputtered, water pouring from her mouth and nose. Kyyle helped her lean onto her side, letting her cough and hack up a mixture of sand and water even as Finn breathed a sigh of relief. Only moments later, her health had begun to stabilize, and her breathing had become more even.

"I told you that tunnel was a death trap," she muttered, her voice hoarse and her eyes meeting Finn's for a moment.

"You did. You definitely did," Finn said with a relieved laugh.

Julia's gaze shot to Kyyle. "And... uh, thanks, I guess."

"You're welcome for saving your life," he replied with a grin.

"Pretty sure I didn't need the help," she grunted, crossing her arms playfully. "And besides... couldn't Abbad have just pushed some air into my lungs. Seems like you were looking for an excuse to kiss me."

"Uh, I hate to be the one to tell you this, but you look sort of like a drowned rat at the moment," Kyyle offered in reply, a faint blush creeping up his neck. "Not the most appealing look for you."

Julia tried to take a swipe at him, but missed, still weak from her near-death experience and fully depleted stamina. "If I weren't nearly dead, I'd kick your ass for that," she grunted, slumping back onto the chaise in defeat.

"*Rain check* then?" Kyyle offered, his grin widening at her groan.

"Way, way too soon," she muttered.

It took Julia a few minutes to fully recover, her health regeneration swiftly repairing the cuts and scrapes that marred her skin and the damage to her lungs. In the meantime, the group used the opportunity to dry their armor and gear – using Daniel's flickering form to help push the moisture out of their equipment without being forced to cast a spell. The AI's mana signature didn't seem much greater than the lamps in the hallway, so it seemed safe to keep him around. Also, they needed to balance the risk of his presence against leaving a trail of sand and water behind them as they moved through the palace.

A short while later, the group was relatively dry and their equipment repacked. They hovered in the center of the sitting room, talking about the next step while preparing to leave.

"Okay, so we survived that part. Barely. But what now?" Kyyle asked, shooting a glance at Finn and Abbad.

"My guess is that we will find Bilel in the throne room. Finn observed mana coming from that origin point back at the northwestern gate," Abbad said, pulling up a map of the palace with a swipe of his wrist. "That was the last place Finn saw him casting, and he wouldn't relinquish that vantage point lightly," he continued.

Finn nodded, and his gaze focused on the map. The group was currently sitting in the western wing of the palace. And the throne room was located in the center of the palace complex. It towered above the rest of the city, sitting almost flush with the southern wall. They were going to have a decent hike through the palace.

He tapped at the throne room's location, and a yellow path wound through the complex, tracing a twisting route toward their destination.

"That looks like it's going to take some time," Kyyle said, staring at the map.

Julia nodded. "And there's a big risk that we run into a bunch of guards or hounds," she offered. "Bilel had to have stationed some sort of defenses here inside the palace. And it's only going to take one alarm to put an end to this assassination attempt."

Finn's brow furrowed at that. "My sight gets fuzzy the farther out I try to reach, but I should be able to get a decent sense of what's inside this wing of the palace," he offered. The others nodded, and he approached the nearby wall, activating his *Mana Sight* and peeling back at the intervening layers of mana.

He didn't see any guards or hounds lingering in the central hallway where they had entered, the corridor only broken by the telltale mana signature of the lamps. Finn shifted his attention, peeling back at the walls of the adjoining chambers... and then hesitated. Clusters of multi-colored light lingered in each room, the combination of energy appearing almost human. Yet the energy didn't fluctuate nor move. It seemed to be entirely stationary.

What is that? he wondered to himself.

He shifted his attention to the lone doorway leading out of the sitting room where they were holed up. The adjoining room was a dead end. However, he noticed the same strange cluster of energy lingering inside.

"There's something in that side room," Finn said, dropping his voice to a whisper. Although, he suspected that if they were going to alert whatever was inside, they would have done so already. "I have no idea what's in there, but I see the same energy signature riddling the rooms all along this hallway."

"That's just a small bathing room adjoining this sitting area," Abbad offered, waving at the map. "What could Bilel have possibly stored inside...?"

There was only one way to answer that question.

Julia immediately pulled her lance from her belt and raised her shield as she moved toward one door, motioning for Malik to take the other side of the doorway – the fighter's gleaming swords already held firmly in hand. The rest of the group took up a central position in the sitting room, Brock's rocky form hovering in front of the mages protectively.

At Julia's gesture, the pair opened the door and rushed inside.

Only to stop short.

"What the fuck?" Julia muttered, her lance drooping. Even Malik drew in a sharp breath as he observed what lingered in that small side room.

The mages moved forward as they realized there was no immediate threat, and Finn could soon see what had caught Julia and Malik's attention, his mouth dropping open. A man hung suspended along the wall of the room. He was nearly naked – only a dirty loincloth covering his waist. His limbs were emaciated, as though he hadn't eaten in weeks, the bones protruding through his pale flesh and his muscle having long ago atrophied.

"This.... What is this?" Kyyle spoke aloud, his voice echoing in the silent room.

Crystalline spears had been embedded in the man's skin, and caked blood and inflamed skin encircled the lances. Yet the skin appeared to be partially healed, almost as though the crystal had been inserted some time ago. And each spear was connected to a thin, translucent thread that ran up into the ceiling. Those cords held the man suspended in the air, his limbs too frail to break free. As Finn observed the crystals with his *Mana Sight* active, the answer came to him immediately.

"Bilel is draining his mana," he said, his voice hoarse as he took in the horror hanging in front of him. "Those spears are embedded in his Najima. The threads wind up into the ceiling and run along conduits sandwiched between this floor and the next."

The wiring reminded Finn of the Forge in many ways. Although, a close examination of the crystalline threads indicated that they weren't that same neurogem material. The wiring was a pale imitation that more closely matched the simple material that Kalisha used in her mechanids. Finn could only assume Bilel had stolen that tech from the merchants to build this... monstrosity.

His gaze shifted upward, now observing the multi-colored mana that flowed out of each room and up into the conduits along the ceiling, flowing eastward toward Bilel's throne room. It seemed that they had been right. It was safe to assume that those rivers of mana were flowing straight toward the demon.

"We have to get him down... save him," Julia said, moving forward.

Finn immediately put a hand on her arm to stop her. "We can't," he muttered. "His health is likely too low, and those spears are embedded close to natural arteries. We saw how the purge is administered. It takes multiple healers to keep someone alive during the procedure. If you disconnect him, he'll likely just bleed out."

Julia's lips pinched into a grim line, but she made no move to unhook the man.

"Those other clusters of energy must be other mages... more prisoners like this one," Finn continued, now understanding the energy he had seen flowing down the hallway. "Most of these rooms are filled with these people."

"But why?" Kyyle asked, shaking his head. "If Bilel was already purging the mages, why not just absorb the resulting crystals?"

Finn was rubbing at his temple, his thoughts racing. "That's not efficient," he said slowly. At Kyyle's questioning glance, he continued. "Think about it. With the purge, Bilel could, at best, collect the mage's total mana pool. And only then if he had a crystal large enough to contain that much mana. It's much more likely that he's losing some of that mana each time. And those gems could be more useful in other applications – such as the weapons and equipment created by the merchants, for example."

"I don't understand," Malik said, shaking his head as he stared at the suspended mage.

"Okay, let's say he collects 1,000 mana each time he administers the purge," Finn continued. "But what if the typical mage has a regeneration rate much higher than that? Let's say 30 mana/second for a novice. That's 1,800 mana per minute. 108,000 per hour..."

"Or almost 2.6 million per day per mage," Kyyle muttered, his eyes widening. "This process can't be perfectly efficient either, but your point still stands. Bilel would be able to collect *far* more mana this way than simply administering the purge."

Finn nodded, a weight settling in his stomach. Even the neurogem material had a conduction limit, and Bilel would need to be casting continuously to use up the mana that was flowing through those conduits. The demon likely didn't have crystals large enough to store the overflow – or at least Finn hadn't seen them with his sight. The demon also couldn't absorb the mana every waking moment. So, there was still waste in this system.

That thought was the only way Finn was able to push back at the despair that was beginning to coil in his stomach. They may have just made a colossal mistake. This entire gambit had been based on the assumption that Bilel's mana pool was finite, and he was relying primarily on the power of the relic. How the hell could they reasonably expect to fight a creature with a mana pool in the millions... or billions?

Even worse, Finn was pretty certain he knew where Bilel had gotten the idea for this farming method. In many ways, this approach was similar to what the Forge had been doing... or the gods themselves. But Bilel had taken it much further, taking 100% instead of only shaving off a modest 10%. And he hadn't been content to only steal from the gods' share. He had started draining the mana right from the source.

He had basically turned these mages into rechargeable mana batteries.

As this realization struck him, the enslaved man's eyes fluttered open, and the group jumped. His gaze was distant, almost mad. His pupils were dilating rapidly, the man clearly having trouble focusing on them. Swallowing hard, he managed to croak out a few words, "Kill... me... please."

Julia shook her head. "What the actual hell. Who... what kind of creature could do this? We have to at least put him out of his misery."

Yet Finn still hesitated.

"What are you waiting for?" Julia demanded.

He met her eyes evenly. "I want to help him as much as you do, but we have to think about the larger goal here. If we kill this man, what about the dozens or hundreds of others hidden within the palace? Are we going to kill them too? And how long will that take? Each death will reduce the flow of mana. And Bilel will likely notice that his mana supply has begun to dwindle long before we finish killing the mages."

Julia's eyes widened slightly, but her mouth was pressed tight, unable to muster a rebuttal. A similarly grim expression lingered across the faces of the rest of the group.

Finn shook his head. "No. We can help these people – or at least allow them to move on. But we can't do that *yet*. These conduits all have to flow to one place. So, our best bet is to find that hub and destroy it before we confront Bilel. Then he won't have time to react. That won't help us with whatever mana he has stored, but it will at least cut off the tap."

Kyyle was nodding as he began to speak, "And Bilel is having to burn a lot of mana to keep everything running. The wards along the palace walls, that protective shield of air mana hovering above the palace itself, directing the hounds, assisting them in their skirmishes throughout the city... I'm betting it's taking him a LOT of mana to maintain everything. If we cut his flow of mana for even a few seconds, that may leave him weakened."

"Except for the staff," Finn murmured.

"Except for the staff," Kyyle echoed, meeting Finn's eyes. "But we've already reduced the hounds' numbers substantially, and we have to hope that Aerys is able to take out even more. At this point, we just have to have faith."

"He can't get away with this," Julia growled, her eyes flashing angrily.

The man suspended in front of them had already lost consciousness, his form slumping back against the crystalline wires. Finn knew that this scene was playing out dozens of times across the palace – possibly hundreds of mages imprisoned and drained – committed to a fate far worse than simple death. An endless, pain-filled purgatory.

He could feel his own anger flare in the face of what Bilel had done. These people might not be entirely *real* – might not have flesh-and-blood bodies back in the real world – but Finn had spent enough time in this world to understand that they weren't merely programs. His eyes flitted to Daniel. To Malik. To Abbad. These people – his companions – they weren't just ones and zeros on a server to him.

They *couldn't* be, not if he was to bring Rachael back successfully.

Mana rippled through his body, searing and burning through his veins until his eyes glowed an ominous dark red. Those flaming eyes met his daughter's. "Trust me. He won't get away with this. We're going to finish the fight we started – once and for all."

Chapter 46 - Check

The group hovered beside an intersection, their backs pressed along the nearby wall. They were currently standing on the upper levels of the central palace complex – closing in on Bilel's throne room. Finn peered through the wall but saw no movement or telltale sign of energy in the adjoining hallway. According to the map that floated beside him, this hall led directly to the throne room – a final staircase leading up to a familiar pair of broad wooden doors. Even now, Finn had to repress a shudder as he witnessed that doorway in his sight.

The last time they had been here, it hadn't ended well.

His gaze shifted to the floor where a current of multi-colored energy flowed along the crystalline conduits embedded in the stone. As they had followed those magical tributaries, the current had widened, growing brighter as more branching streams of energy fed into the flow. Now it was a brightly glowing river leading them straight to the throne room.

Although, Finn's brow furrowed as he tried to peel back the layers of mana wrapped around that chamber. The room didn't appear to be warded – or at least he didn't see any telltale, glowing patterns or symbols that would denote active enchantments. There was simply so much ambient mana flowing into the room that he couldn't make out any details of what lingered inside. The effect was eerily reminiscent of the interference he had encountered back in the Forge.

If Bilel was inside that room, then he was throwing around quite a bit of mana.

"Clear," Finn whispered, but he made no move to pull away from the wall. His lips pinched into a grim expression, his thoughts swirling.

"This doesn't feel right," Julia muttered softly, glancing around the corner. "Where the hell is everybody? Bilel couldn't have converted every single guard."

"Unless he thought they were more useful as hounds," Kyyle offered tentatively.

Julia arched an eyebrow. "Okay, so then he left no guards around his throne room? We should at least have run across a few hellhounds."

Abbad shook his head. "It's possible that the hounds can't be trusted with this much mana flowing through the walls," he suggested. "Most likely, they are more difficult to control around ambient sources of energy. That could also explain why they were grouped in the outer courtyards."

The librarian glanced at Finn, their eyes meeting briefly, and Finn cocked his head in response, mulling on that thought. Abbad's explanation made sense to a degree. And it assumed that Bilel's control over the hounds was fragile, which was possibly good news for Aerys and the rest of their army of guildsmen and Khamsin. If they were able to distract the demon for even a few moments, that could give the rest of the army an edge.

However, there was also another possible answer.

Bilel might be strong enough now that he simply didn't need guards.

Finn didn't exactly love that explanation, but he wasn't quite sure what the hell he could do about it – not at this point. They had long passed the point of no return.

He shook his head to ward off those anxious thoughts, his gaze snapping back into focus. "It doesn't matter. We have to keep moving forward. The entrance to the throne room is at the end of the hall, and the main conduit flows straight toward that point."

Finn's attention shifted to Kyyle. "We're going to need to disable the conduit before we breach the room. We're not dealing with the neurogem material, so it should be enough just to obstruct the connection."

His fingers wrapped around a dark metal orb, pulling it from his bag. "If you make me a hole, I can block off the flow of mana. Then you can seal the stone so that no one interferes with the conduit after we make it inside the throne room."

Kyyle nodded, and Finn glanced at Daniel. "Can you give us a highlight? Make sure to cover the full width of the conduit. With this much energy flowing through that channel, even a trickle is going to be a problem."

"Of course," the AI chirped, and a thin yellow line appeared along the width of the hallway.

"What's our plan, then?" Malik asked, gripping his swords tightly, his knuckles white.

Finn took a deep breath. "Given the density of the mana and the number of mages we've passed, my best estimate is that several million mana per second is flowing into that room." He raised a hand as he saw the fighter's energy fluctuate wildly. "*However*, Bilel is also burning quite a bit of energy to maintain the wards around the palace, the shielding around the palace structures, and the spells he is casting to assist his hounds deeper within Lahab. And that's assuming the relic doesn't require mana to maintain and control the hounds. Best guess? He's probably burning as much mana as he's receiving."

"You can't know that for certain," Abbad offered solemnly.

"Perhaps not, but we can come *close*," Kyyle retorted, raising a finger. "It's not perfect, but we have some data to back that conclusion."

The earth mage swiped at the air to bring up a display showing a model of the mana absorption that Finn had used to first create the storm. "Finn's new hand gives us an exact measure of how much mana it has absorbed. Daniel has also been recording the intensity of many different sources of mana during our journey – as well as the intensity of the mana in Finn's hand after he created the storm.

"That data is sufficient to let us back into a rough estimate of total mana based on the *brightness* of the energy. Then we can extrapolate using the same ratio to arrive at a pretty close approximation of both the mana flowing into the throne room and the rough output Bilel is expending with his various spells.

"Based on our calculations, if Bilel maintains his

casting for even a few seconds after we cut the connection, that should burn several million mana," Kyyle concluded.

"Which makes an implicit assumption about his total mana storage," Abbad replied, although his expression was more measured now. "And what if the demon's body can store mana in the tens or hundreds of millions? Normally, that absorption would continue to decay and disfigure his natural body. But with the staff's healing properties, it's possible that he could be storing an incredible amount of energy now. We shouldn't underestimate him."

Finn nodded. "That's a valid point. Unfortunately, we have little choice. And we're banking almost entirely on educated guesses – that Aerys can maneuver the army into position in time, that she can take out many of the remaining hounds, that Bilel hasn't stockpiled an obscene amount of mana. And we can only afford to wait so long after we cut the conduits before we breach the throne room. Bilel will likely notice that the stream has stopped within a few seconds, and we can't afford to let him repair that connection."

He met the librarian's eyes. "We have no choice but to roll the dice."

Abbad simply nodded, but Finn could see that hint of doubt and anxiety lingering in his eyes. Finn certainly had his own reservations, but what he had told him was the truth.

They were out of options and time.

He let out a sigh. "So, here's the plan. Kyyle and I will cut the conduit, then Malik and Julia will charge the room. Mages will follow behind them. As for Bilel himself, well, Abbad is probably more familiar with his abilities than the rest of us combined," Finn continued, waving at the former librarian.

"Once we're facing Bilel, he'll likely cast his shields first," Abbad said, his eyes skimming around the group. "He may have healed his body, but he's accustomed to being incredibly fragile. His first instinct will be to protect himself. Expect to be facing several layers of shields composed of different elements. These will need to be neutralized either simultaneously or in close succession to land a hit. So, for example, an air-based shield needs to be blown apart, stone destroyed, ice melted, etc. We'll need to time and coordinate our attacks.

"In terms of offensive abilities, assume he can cast anything you've seen before... plus, a few spells you've likely never heard of. Bilel has spent the better part of a century working to improve his total spell channeling through the use of *Multi-Casting*, gems, and body augmentations. I'm not certain how the staff will affect his channeling limit. The highest I've personally seen him go is six simultaneous spells, but I don't know for certain whether that's his limit."

Good lord, Finn thought to himself. He could certainly understand now why Abbad was feeling nervous. Even without the staff or a magical pipeline of energy, Bilel would be incredibly difficult to take down. With those things...

Finn wasn't certain he wanted to finish that thought.

"Okay. Everyone ready?" he asked, shaking off his own worries. Channeling his mana forcefully, he let the searing energy replace that anxiety with a bottomless excitement.

He met each person's gaze, receiving a curt nod in response. He could see their worries and fears reflected in their eyes, yet not a single member of the group backed down from this challenge. They had come too far to stop now.

"Okay, then we go as soon as the conduit is severed."

Finn gestured at Kyyle, and emerald tendrils of energy soon curled around the earth mage's hand, keeping the mana dim to avoid detection. The energy drifted out across the floor, and seconds later, the stone began to dissolve, forming a straight furrow along the width of the hallway. As the rock sank away, it revealed the thick bundles of crystals that had been embedded in the stone, their surfaces gleaming and rippling with mana.

Finn's fingers were already moving, words drifting from his lips. Twin metal spheres were soon wrapped in flame and sped out across the stone floor. He was forced to abandon caution, pumping more energy into the orbs to heat the metal. Fires flared brightly. Pressing his palms against one another, Finn smashed the two spheres together and then began rolling the molten substance. He repeated that movement again and again until he'd formed a long thin sheet of metal.

With a deep breath and a final gesture, Finn flicked his wrists downward.

The metal cut through the conduit like a guillotine, running the full width of the hallway and neatly severing those gleaming, crystalline threads. Finn flattened his palms and pressed down, smashing the molten metal into the groove along the floor. He saw the wires on the other side of the metallic barrier immediately go dark, his brow furrowing as he searched for any trickle of mana that might make it through.

Yet he saw nothing.

Another gesture at Kyyle and the stone began to piece itself back together, filling the gap along the hallway. Julia and Malik didn't wait for him to finish. They were already sprinting down the hall, their weapons held aloft – the rest of the group hot on their heels. They surged down those last few yards, sprinted up the staircase on the other end of the hall, and barreled toward the massive double doors that marked Bilel's throne room. They couldn't afford to slow down or wait. If the demon sealed those doors before they could get through…

Malik's legs rippled as he lunged forward, his warded skin flashing with energy. The stone cracked under his feet, and he rushed forward in a dark blur, sailing up those final stairs. His shoulder struck the door with tremendous force, cracking the wood. The portal slammed open, and the group followed, charging into the throne room.

They slid across the slick stone floor of the chamber

before coming to a halt.

Finn had been expecting to find Bilel perched on his throne, draining the mana from the conduits and looking out over the city. Instead, he found himself standing inside an empty chamber. The stained glass along the far wall had been repaired since their previous escape, providing a glimpse of the storm that still raged above them. Yet no raindrops splattered the glass, a byproduct of the shielding over the palace.

"What is—?" Kyyle was cut off as the door behind them slammed shut with a resounding boom and the crack and snap of splintering wood.

The group whirled, and in Finn's sight, the walls of the throne room began to flicker with earth mana, that glow growing until it was nearly blinding. Then the rock and stone exploded apart as though a bomb had gone off in the chamber, sending shrapnel flying away in a concentric ring. Massive bricks ripped themselves apart, hurtling out through the air. The stained-glass window along the far side of the room exploded violently, and multi-colored glass fragments blasted out into space.

Finn spun, taking in the carnage around them as the room was literally ripped apart. Even the broad double doors weren't unscathed, the wood exploding into a shower of ribbons and shards. And along with them went the stairs, leaving the group stranded upon this lone stone pillar at the very peak of the palace.

As the walls broke apart, the group now had an unimpeded view of the city sprawled out below them. Its streets were half-flooded, tornadoes whipped down through roads and back alleys, and groups of hounds sprinted across muddy sand, flames licking at their bodies and sending streamers of steam curling into the air.

The mixture of stone, wood, and glass that had once encircled the throne room sailed out into that void... only to freeze in place.

As Finn looked on wide-eyed, that debris began to orbit them slowly, like some malevolent tornado. Despite the lack of ceiling, no rain spattered down upon them. He looked up to find a shimmering yellow canopy still stretched above the palace, blocking the wind and rain of the hurricane. Although, the occasional blast of lightning struck that barrier, and the energy forked outward, splitting again and again.

That was when Finn heard it. The tap, tap, tap of shoes striking stone.

He turned again, already knowing what he would find.

Yet it didn't make it any less surprising.

Bilel stood there – not a wizened and aged ruler – but the same Bilel that Finn imagined had first transcribed that journal long ago. His skin was now taut and smooth, a dark auburn that belied hours spent in the sun. Thick brown hair sprung from his scalp, pulled back into a short ponytail. His robes no longer hung loose on emaciated limbs; his frame filled out the clothes. A well-muscled hand gripped that familiar golden staff, and atop that weapon sat a gem – a brilliant fire glowing within its depths.

The *heartstone*.

"Well, well, well, it's about time the Prophet of the Flame showed up," Bilel said, striding forward with purpose – seemingly unperturbed by the group confronting him. "And I see you brought *friends*. How quaint."

As Finn met Bilel's eyes, he observed the only aspect of the man that remained unchanged from their previous encounter. His eyes swirled in a rainbow pattern of colors, a mesmerizing kaleidoscope of energy that revealed what he truly was – a *demon*.

Bilel glanced at Abbad. "Ahh, my former student. You have been such a disappointment," he remarked with a scowl. "Especially after I spent so long fostering your growth. You could have been so much more than a foolhardy rebel."

Abbad stood still and stoic, his face not giving away any emotion and his energy steady. A detail that only seemed to frustrate Bilel. The demon sniffed at him in disdain.

"What?" he demanded, eyeing the group. "Are you suddenly all tongue-tied? No desperate, angry declarations? Accusations? Not even a mention of my new appearance?"

Finn saw no shields swirling around the demon's body, but given the massive whirlwind of debris still orbiting them, he suspected it would only take the demon an instant to conjure a barrier of rock and stone. If anything, his nonchalance and the almost casual destruction of the throne room indicated that he was still holding a considerable amount of mana – possibly far, far more than their calculations had estimated.

"We're here to finish this," Finn said simply.

Bilel barked out a harsh laugh. "And here I thought you might have come here with some grand plan or scheme in mind. But this... this is just too much. You're here to 'finish this?' Finish what exactly? Your own life? The lives of your friends? To watch as your allies perish, cut down by fang and claw?"

"What are you talking about?" Finn asked, already dreading the answer.

"See for yourself," Bilel answered.

The demon waved out toward the city, and the debris split apart, providing an uninterrupted view of the Mage Guild along the northern side of Lahab.

With his enhanced sight, Finn homed in on that location. He could see his soldiers – their location given away by the shimmering barriers of air mana and the cadre of earth and water mages. They seemed to be stationed inside the Mage Guild – just as he had ordered – focused on clearing out the hounds that were cornering the travelers and slaying them as they respawned, many turning into new hounds.

"I don't—" Finn began, but was cut off as Bilel dropped his channel.

Suddenly, an ocean of orange energy sprung up around the Mage Guild, revealing thousands of hounds that had been hidden by Bilel's illusion, allowing them to encircle the structure and trap Finn's army inside the guild hall. At the same time, many of the hounds in the palace courtyard simply disappeared – revealing that only a fraction of that horde had been real. And with that realization came another...

"This is a trap... this was all a trap..." Finn muttered, disbelief in his voice and his eyes still staring at the Mage Guild. Finn had already assumed that Bilel's control range was extreme but seeing it in action was still jolting.

"You planned all of this?" Finn demanded, whirling back to the demon. He summoned his fire mana then, the flames rippling across his body.

"Indeed. I knew you would come up with some strategy to attack the city," Bilel replied glibly. "The storm was a nice touch, by the way. I'll need to remember that one. It was only a matter of time before you broke my shield and made it inside Lahab. I made it only difficult enough that you would believe you had truly prevailed at the gate."

Bilel drew his hands wide. "But what then? What would our intrepid, gods-touched mage do once he was inside the city? You're smart enough to realize that you can't challenge me while my hounds are still alive – too easy for me to heal. But you also couldn't afford to only focus on slaying the hounds. I might simply flee the city. And, besides, I suspect you need this staff..." The base of the relic thunked against the stone to emphasize his point.

"So, I planned a ruse – for both you and your army. And it seems that it worked," Bilel declared, a low chuckle bubbling from his lips.

He leaned forward, peering at Finn. "What did she promise you anyway – the Crone?" Bilel asked, peering at Finn. "What did she pledge in return for retrieving her relic? You never did answer my question last time."

Finn didn't say a word, his fingers balling into fists.

He used the gesture to mask his movements. His fingers twitched subtly, arcane words just barely escaping his lips – his casting obscured by the fire mana that coated his body. Finn needed to buy himself some time, just long enough to cast and cancel two spells...

"What? Suddenly speechless?" Bilel demanded. "It seems I don't even have to bind you and your friends this time. You all simply stand in place – dumbstruck by your own stupendous lack of imagination."

Bilel sighed, flicking his wrist. "Well, this was *check*. Shall we go ahead and finally end our little game?"

With that statement, Bilel waved his staff at the group, fire mana exploding from the top of the gem. Those flames rushed toward them, swiftly encircling their bodies and coiling around their limbs. Yet as the seconds ticked past... nothing happened. The flames only lapped gently at their skin.

"What is this? Why isn't the transformation working?" Bilel demanded, those multi-colored eyes going wide with surprise.

A grim smile tugged at Finn's lips, his fire mana surging with renewed strength. The flames that coiled around his body flared brightly, and his eyes glowed a malevolent dark red, the cloth bandage burning away, and the flames of his crown spearing up into the air.

Bilel's expression faltered as Finn straightened, meeting the demon's eyes. "That trick won't work on us, or the members of our army – not anymore."

He took a step toward the demon. "But you're right about one thing. It is time to finish this – once and for all."

Without another word, Finn raised the palm of his left hand, revealing the fire curling within the depths of the *Focusing Prism* – the same energy he had stolen from the hounds during the battle at the gate. Finn had surreptitiously cast twice while Bilel was speaking, using this final *Molten Beam* to trigger his crown's effect. Every third spell, the item increased his damage and effectiveness by 100%.

And when combined with the mana stored in his hand...

The effect was devastating.

A beam of molten energy rocketed up into the air, the ray stretching nearly four feet wide. It speared up toward the shimmering yellow shield that hovered above the palace. In less than a second, the supercharged beam struck that barrier with incredible force, and the entire surface of the shield rippled, flashing with amber energy. The fires curled outward along the disc, creating a hemisphere of flame.

And then the beam sliced *through* the shield – the barrier unable to withstand such a concentrated blast of pure mana. And as that energy poured up into the sky, stretching for hundreds of feet, Finn's signal was seen from the farthest reaches of Lahab.

The army stationed within the Mage Guild suddenly vanished, rippling away in an azure cloud of energy. The layers of that illusion had likely taken hours to craft – a necessary evil when facing an opponent that could see magic. And even as their army vanished, it reappeared again behind the hounds that ringed the guild. Earth mages pulled up massive walls of earth, trapping the hounds within a makeshift valley.

A perfect kill-zone.

Good job, Aerys, Finn thought to himself. She had followed his hastily whispered instructions perfectly.

"What is this? What did you do?" Bilel demanded, the energy whirling in his eyes and spinning more rapidly now. Rain was beginning to fall on their lone stone tower through the hole that Finn had carved in Bilel's shielding – the rest of the barrier flickering and beginning to break apart now that it had been destabilized.

"Like you said, this is *check,* asshole," Finn said, pulling two metal spheres from his bag, clutching one in each hand. "Now, we just need to keep you distracted while they finish off your hounds."

Bilel let out a low growl as he turned back to Finn. Multi-colored energy crackled along the demon's hand, and his staff flared with fire mana. The debris began to orbit them more swiftly now, picking up speed and creating a funnel of air that whipped at the group and deflected the rain that now beat down upon the ruined throne room.

"And as for your other question," Finn said, stepping forward slowly and flames wrapping the two metal orbs, the spheres drifting up into the air beside him. "You're right. I did make a deal with the Seer."

His teammates surrounded him. Daniel's flaming body drifted just above Finn's shoulder, streamers of emerald energy curled along Kyyle's staff, and Brock's rocky body hovered protectively beside the earth mage. Julia and Malik stood to either side, their weapons held at the ready. And Abbad stood beside Finn, wisps of air magic already collecting around him. Not a single one of them backed down or hesitated in the face of the monster that stood before them.

"I need that staff," Finn continued, fire flaring in his eyes.

"And I... no, *we* will do *anything* to retrieve it."

Chapter 47 - Mate

Debris continued to spin around the group in a giant shifting maelstrom, wind pulling at their armor and whistling across the ruined stone tower as the whirlwind picked up speed. Rain soon added to the gusts of air, hurling the droplets into a spinning vortex that pushed the water outward to the edges of the platform.

"Come and get it then," Bilel growled, his eyes flashing with multi-colored energy.

Julia was more than happy to oblige.

She darted forward, her lance telescoping toward Bilel.

The demon didn't even bother to move. He merely smirked at her. A block of stone ripped itself from the debris. Whirling around the tower, it raced forward, intercepting Julia's blow. Her lance smashed into the stone, causing the block to explode in a shower of dust and rocky shrapnel. Another block whipped at her from behind, but she pivoted on her heel. Her shield flashed with amber energy, and a gust of air sent the stone rocketing over the edge of the tower, where it was swiftly consumed by the storm.

More and more of the stone blocks that once comprised Bilel's throne room hurtled out of that maelstrom. They raced toward the demon and flattened into roughly circular rock panels. Finn saw shimmering barriers of yellow energy erupt around Bilel, hovering just behind those rocky shields. The demon was also drawing water from the storm raging above them, the droplets hovering behind the barriers of air and stone before freezing into icy discs. And behind those layers of shields, lances of flame erupted from the ground, encircling him within a cage of solid fire.

"Pick your elements," Finn grunted as Julia withdrew, and the group spread out around Bilel in a rough semi-circle. "Order is earth, air, water, fire. Daniel, give us highlights."

The AI flashed once, and the barriers were suddenly illuminated in their corresponding colors, glowing brightly as Daniel pushed those combat tooltips to the group.

The battle was on.

Finn ignited Julia's armor, flames springing up along her metal armor. His daughter and Malik darted forward, their weapons aimed at the rocky discs that encircled Bilel. Julia's lance flashed, breaking apart the stones as Malik's swords cut at the rock with bands of air – the energy condensed down to a razor's edge.

Several of the stone blocks exploded in a shower of debris… and close on their heels were ribbons of air magic. That magically reinforced wind whipped at the amber shields that encircled Bilel as Abbad blasted the barriers apart with supercharged gusts of air. Soon, the shimmering yellow barriers that wound around Bilel disappeared.

Finn's fingers swept forward, his flaming orb cutting through the frozen discs like butter. Which left the group facing a fiery cage of energy. As Finn directed his lone orb forward, that cage fanned out and flared brightly, the fires turning almost white. The heat radiated outward as the energy transformed into a solid shell of fire that obscured Bilel from sight.

Finn's sphere entered that barrier, but he lost control of the spell as the metal melted immediately. He clenched his jaw and then reached out with his crystalline hand, pulling at that energy. It resisted him at first – a magical tug-of-war as Bilel poured more energy into the spell. Yet a coil of flame leaked away from the barrier and drifted toward Finn's hand, and the fires settled within the *Focusing Prism*.

Suddenly, the flaming shield winked out.

Revealing that Bilel was suddenly missing.

Finn's gaze darted to the side, searching the area with his *Mana Sight*.

He saw a ripple of azure energy off to the right.

"Kyyle! He's right beside you!"

The earth mage began to pivot, but it was much too slow. His eyes widened as Bilel reappeared only a scant few feet away, the demon's hands finishing a final gesture. A barrage of icy shards rocketed from his palms at point-blank range, creating a fan of spears that would be impossible for Kyyle to dodge or block in time.

Brock surged forward. But instead of trying to block the shards with his body, his torso broke apart, and the stones peeled away. Kyyle's body settled into that void in his chest, and the stones snapped back around his arms, legs, and torso. The frozen shards slammed against Brock's rocky body, carving deep furrows in the stone. Yet, only a moment later, coils of emerald energy wrapped around those rocks, repairing the damage.

"Try again, asshole," Kyyle grunted from within Brock's body. The earth elemental stooped and retrieved Kyyle's staff before facing off against Bilel once again.

Damn, that's a cool trick, Finn thought. The earth mage must have realized that he could use Brock as a sort of makeshift rock suit, using his own mana to help repair and reinforce the elemental. He supposed that was one way for the earth mage to get around not having any healing spells.

Malik and Julia were converging on the demon's position, and Bilel ground his teeth in frustration. His hands raced through a series of gestures, and he abruptly disappeared in a flash of amber light.

"Teleport!" Finn shouted.

The demon forked off to the side, rematerializing a few yards away and already casting another series of spells. Several of the blocks of stone hurtled out of the whirlwind and rocketed toward Finn and the other group members. Finn smashed one apart with an orb, and partially melted stone fragments tumbled to the ground with a crash. Malik and Julia also made short work of the projectiles racing toward them, breaking them apart in a series of rapid-fire blows.

The chaos had the unfortunate side effect of obscuring Bilel from sight, dust cascading across the ruined tower. Finn just barely detected another flash of amber light before Bilel suddenly materialized next to him. Finn raised his left hand, and the limb transformed, stretching and lengthening into a blade as he parried a sweep of the demon's staff. Flames curled away from the impact, and sparks flew as the relic crashed against the neurogem material… yet Finn's hand didn't falter.

Bilel pivoted, and bolts of ice erupted from his other hand, hurtling straight toward Finn's face… only to be blocked by a shimmering barrier as Abbad knocked the bolts aside with a shield of air.

Bilel recovered quickly, and a beam of fire jetted from the staff, arcing toward Finn. Finn caught that beam of energy in his glasslike hand, crushing the energy in his fist and absorbing it into the *Focusing Prism*. He let out a hissing breath as he felt his skin redden and welt, but he couldn't afford to focus on that right now.

Then he saw a smile stretch across the demon's face – those swirling eyes staring him down. His form broke apart into streamers of azure energy.

Another illusion! He must have cast the spell just after the last teleport.

Finn's gaze swept the tower, and he saw another ripple of energy behind the librarian. "Behind you, Abbad!" he cried.

But it was too late.

A sword of ice jetted from the demon's arm and raced forward, slicing at the back of Abbad's legs, cutting through the cloth of his robes, and leaving a line of crimson in its wake. The librarian stumbled… and then fell to his knees. Julia and Malik were already rushing toward him, but a fresh barrage of the massive blocks rocketed from the whirlwind around them, barreling toward the pair.

With a twitch of Finn's fingers, he tugged at Julia's armor, and she launched up into the air with incredible force, her form blurring and leaving an orange streak in her wake. Her foot touched upon one of the boulders the demon had hurled at her, pushing off the rock and her lance telescoping outward as she rushed at him.

Bilel sneered as he saw her approaching and darted backward. His body shimmered again as he tried to teleport – ropes of electricity coiling around him. But he abruptly stumbled, finding his foot planted to the stone with a thick ribbon of air mana. From his kneeling position along the ground, Abbad was still managing to cast.

Lances of stone stretched up from the ruined ground and encircled Bilel's bound foot, immediately grounding the mage. The lightning leeched away ineffectually into the base of the tower as Kyyle joined the fray.

Then Julia was upon Bilel. Her lance sped forward, the tip angled at the demon's heart.

Pivoting at the last moment, the tip of the lance penetrated his shoulder instead. Sickly multi-colored blood bubbled around impact, staining Bilel's robes and dripping onto the tower's floor. In Finn's sight, he could see that the demon's blood glowed brightly – an incredible amount of mana stored in each droplet.

It almost looks like the liquid mana in the well we discovered down in the Abyss... he thought to himself weakly. His eyes shot back to the demon. *Just how much mana is he holding?*

Daniel was attempting to update a tooltip in the corner of Finn's vision – trying his best to guess at the amount of mana in the blood based on the brightness of the energy and an estimate of Bilel's body mass and volume. Yet Finn didn't need to see a projection to understand what he was looking at.

Bilel was carrying a *shitload* of mana – every drop of blood at least on par with a regular Najima. It seemed they had badly, badly underestimated his total mana pool.

For his part, the demon barely seemed to notice the injury or the lance embedded in his shoulder. Jerking his arm down hard, he ripped the limb free in a shower of rainbow blood. He then smashed the bottom of the staff into the stone that trapped his foot, flames melting down the constraint in an instant.

His form flashed once again, and the demon rematerialized another few yards away.

The group was breathing hard as they watched Bilel warily. That same strange blood was leaking down his torso. Yet his expression was completely unaffected, as though he couldn't even feel the injury. Slamming the butt of his staff into the ground, flames coiled up his body, encircling that wound in a blinding flash of orange fire. As the group blinked away the harsh light, they discovered that his arm was intact once more – healed in a matter of seconds.

Bilel laughed at their stunned reactions, a mad cackle punctuated by the crackle of lightning and the peal of thunder above them. "You don't understand, do you? You can't possibly hope to win this battle. You are outmatched."

Even as he spoke, the demon's shields sprang back to full strength, and the four elemental barriers orbited him slowly. "I can use any spell... heal any wound... even control the weather itself!"

Raising his hand to the sky, a coil of lightning arced down from the billowing dark clouds above them, crashing against the stone tower in a blinding flash of light. The attack was almost instantaneous. Yet Finn didn't feel the searing electrical burn flay his skin. As he blinked to clear his vision, he could see Abbad kneeling on the stone. The librarian's hands were raised to the sky, and another amber barrier hovered just above them. Lightning forked across that shell and lanced back out into the mixture of debris that still spun rapidly around the tower, the energy deflected and refracted among the stone and glass.

"Why do you keep fighting?" Bilel growled, his eyes centering on the librarian and the blood that was pooling beneath the librarian's knees.

Kyyle was soon at Abbad's side, still encased within Brock's rocky form. He lifted him back to his feet, and the air mage, leaning against the elemental's body, simply stared impassively back at Bilel. Despite the stony resolve lingering in his companions' eyes, Finn could see a tendril of dark energy ripple through each of their bodies.

Doubt. Fear.

And he could feel that worm of despair wriggling within his stomach, pushing back at the fiery energy that coursed through his veins. The demon stood tall and at full health. The energy still circled within his body with an almost blinding light. He had used barely a fraction of the mana stored within him.

Yet the group had already burned almost half of their aggregate mana. Abbad was also at about 60% health, and their two fighters had used a decent amount of stamina just to ward off those blocks of stone that Bilel had continued to hurl at them with abandon.

It was true that they had managed to hit the demon – even hurt him...

But Bilel was able to heal that wound almost instantly. With the maelstrom whirling around them, Finn couldn't see the state of the fight he knew was raging outside the Mage Guild. But he couldn't be certain that Aerys could finish that encounter soon enough to depress the power flowing into the relic. He couldn't assume that she would be able to stop the demon from healing.

And with that realization came another.

This isn't going to work.

We need to find another way. His thoughts were frantic, racing.

As Bilel began to cast again, Finn's teammates launched forward, smashing aside stone blocks the size of boulders, deflecting icy projectiles, and trying to follow the demon as he teleported around the ruined tower. But Finn stood stock still. He barely noticed the shift and shimmer of Bilel's mana, Finn's eyes lingering only on the demon's form and that staff in his hand.

But how...?

Finn hesitated as his gaze lingered on that gem at the top of the staff – the *heartstone* glowing with a bright, glaring energy, reflecting the mana that the hounds had fed the relic.

Yet it was more than that – more than simply a receptacle for mana. That energy fluctuated. Pulsed. Almost like a heartbeat. After Finn had spent days administering the Forging, he recognized that pattern. It was the same one he had seen in hundreds of Najima. That power was *alive*. Of course, it was. That was Nar Aljahim's mate.

With that realization came the memory of the last time he had faced the staff. That strange void, the flames sucked from his body – taking with them his passion and his memories of Rachael. And yet he had survived – had reclaimed that fire as his own.

How had he done that? How had he overcome the staff?

Or had it *let* him? Had it relinquished the flames willingly?

"Could… could it be conscious?" Finn muttered aloud.

"You need to help them!" Daniel shouted in his ear, the AI's voice frantic.

Finn blinked, and his focus centered back on the fight raging across the ruined tower. Indeed, his teammates were being beaten back – bloodied and broken already. They circled back around Finn, assuming a defensive formation with Julia and Malik in the lead. Bilel's body crackled with another blast of electricity, and he teleported across the circle, standing atop the spot where his throne had once rested. He watched them with a cruel smile.

"Is this it? Is this all you can manage?" he demanded.

"This might be the first and last time I ever say this… but we could use a crazy half-baked plan right about now," Julia grunted, sparing a glance at Finn over her shoulder. He couldn't see her face or her expression, only the fires that consumed her body from his channel, but her tone was grim.

The others weren't in much better shape. Their

mana and stamina had only waned further. Abbad was still barely able to stand. They wouldn't last much longer.

"I think I have one," Finn said somberly, taking a deep breath as he readied himself for what he was planning to do next. "I just need for you all to break through his shields one last time," he explained.

"We can do that," Malik grunted, shooting Finn a look over his shoulder. "But you're going to need to make it count."

Finn met his gaze evenly. "I will."

"What a touching moment," Bilel drawled. "But I think it's time to finish this."

"Yes. Yes, it is," Julia growled.

Then she was charging forward, flames licking from between those dark metal plates and her lance and shield reflecting the light of the electricity that arced above them. And the rest of the group was close behind, raising that same roaring cry as they raced toward Bilel.

"What are you planning to do?" Daniel asked in Finn's ear.

Finn closed his eyes, feeling that kernel of despair writhe and twist like a living thing. "I'm going to take a really big risk..." he growled in response.

Then he finished casting *Haste* and fire rippled across his body, coating his skin and armor. That familiar burn washed away any last trace of doubt. Raising his eyes, the metal embedded in those sockets glowed with an ominous red light.

And Finn started running toward Bilel.

Blocks of stone rocketed forward, but Malik and Julia cut them down, barely slowing. Once they were within melee range, their weapons began carving at the stones that orbited the demon. A crackle of energy and Abbad used the last of his mana to blast apart the shimmering barriers of air that encircled Bilel. Kyyle waved his hand and spikes jutted from the ground, each one blasting apart a thick panel of ice.

As Finn passed Julia, he watched her smash aside a block of stone in slow motion, and he rested a hand on her shoulder. *"If this fails, I'm sorry,"* he whispered in her ear. He saw her head begin to tilt, but he had already passed her.

Only that final flaming barrier remained, and Finn's attention was fixed on those fires. That's when he noticed Bilel's eyes flick to the side, moving faster than they should. A thin coating of flame sprang up around his body, his smile widening slightly as those eerie eyes locked on Finn's position.

He had anticipated Finn's move and cast *Haste* on himself!

The demon's palm shot forward, a barrage of icy projectiles forming in an instant. Finn's own eyes widened, and he tried to twist to the side to take the blow along one arm. But it was too late – far, far too late.

Is this it? Finn thought. *Is this how it all ends?*

A flare of amber energy erupted in the corner of Finn's vision, and he saw a blur of motion. At the same time, those icy projectiles launched forward, only to slam against something – or *someone* – who was now standing in front of Finn.

Abbad sunk to the ground with more than a dozen icy spears embedded in his chest, blood already beginning to pool around those wounds. Bilel's eyes went wide in surprise and anger – a moment of hesitation.

In that instant, Abbad's locked eyes with Finn. *"Anything. Everything,"* he saw the air mage mouth.

A renewed wave of fire crashed through Finn's body – *anger, rage, loss, and hurt*. He knew those wounds were mortal. That Abbad wasn't coming back from this. The former librarian likely had only seconds left.

Finn turned his glowing eyes on Bilel, his legs surging as he sprinted the last few feet toward that cage of flame. Yet he didn't slow or falter. His crystalline hand lashed forward, grabbing at that energy and pulling just as he crossed the threshold. He felt the flames sear his skin and consume his body. The pain was excruciating, as though he were being burned alive.

And then he was through it – his *Mana Absorption*

blunting the fires just enough to allow him to pass inside the cage relatively unscathed. Which is how he found himself standing face to face with the demon, coils of smoke curling away from his skin. Without hesitation, Finn reached out and grasped that staff with his right hand and his fingers wrapped around the metal.

He knew it couldn't drain his mana anymore – not with the *Forging* protecting him.

But this time, he gave it his energy freely.

Finn's fire flowed up and out of that arm and soaked into the staff. The flames coiled around the weapon, and the *heartstone* flared brightly.

"What are you doing?" Bilel growled, only inches away.

Finn didn't have time to respond. The staff accepted his offering, and flames erupted around the pair, obscuring the tower from sight. Finn felt himself falling backward, yet his fingers stayed curled around that metallic shaft, and his energy continued to flow.

Please, let me be right about this, he thought.

And then there was only darkness.

*   *   *

Finn's eyes snapped open.

He was standing in a dark void, only a single bright spot of light illuminating that darkness. Before him rested the staff. The golden shaft was gleaming and the *heartstone* embedded along the top of the weapon pulsed with a vibrant light.

And across from that staff was a familiar face.

Bilel stood inside the void with him. The demon looked confused, glancing around their dark prison with those eerie rainbow-colored eyes. "What is this?" he demanded.

"Ask the staff," Finn replied, waving at the weapon.

"Ask the..." Bilel echoed. "Are you mad? It's just steel and stone. A tool like any other – to be used and directed."

"In part, but not entirely," a new voice echoed through the darkness, speaking with a tone that reminded Finn of the crackle and snap of flame... the explosion of a volcano... the formation of stars. It was power and fire incarnate.

Flames wrapped around the staff, surging and pushing back at the darkness while rising into that abyss in a blaze of power. And those flames gradually began to condense, forming a torso... arms, legs, hands, and fingers. A blazing head crowned in flame with glowing orange eyes that soon turned to survey Finn and Bilel.

It seemed Finn was going to get an opportunity to meet Nar Aljahim's mate.

"My name is Khalas," the fire elemental intoned, looking between the pair. "Why has my slumber been woken?"

Finn bowed his head. "I have met your mate, Nar Aljahim. He sends his regards."

Khalas' eyes flashed – possibly in surprise. "Nar Aljahim," she echoed. "It has been an age since I have heard that name. Many hundreds of your years."

Her gaze refocused. "Yet you have not answered my question. Why have I been summoned?"

"I wish to claim control of the staff," Finn declared.

"Interesting choice of words. In fact, he wishes to steal the staff from me," Bilel interjected, stepping forward and eyes flashing angrily.

A surge of flame erupted from Khalas' body, pushing them both back and away from the staff. "You cannot steal the flame," the elemental intoned. "It cannot be owned. It is a primal thing... a force of nature. It can only be directed and channeled." Her eyes drifted between them. "And it is my will alone that commands the staff."

"I don't understand. What is this trickery?" Bilel growled, glaring at Finn.

It was his turn to smirk at the demon. "You don't even know what it is you were trying to create? The staff was formed by the Seer using a *heartstone* – the crystalline soul of an ancient fire elemental."

Bilel's eyes widened as he looked back at the elemental, then he managed to master his expression, a cunning gleam in his eye. The fight wasn't over. The battlefield had simply changed – and the demon had just realized a new game was in play.

"You both wish to lay claim to the staff?" Khalas asked. The pair nodded. "Then state your case. Why do you deserve to hold my *heartstone*?"

Bilel stepped forward. "The gods killed my family – imprisoned me and tortured me. They have corrupted this land and its people, draining the power of humans without their knowledge and playing games with our lives for their own benefit. With your power, I would rid this world of the gods entirely – cleanse it with the flame and let the races live in peace."

Finn let out an amused sort.

"What? You do not believe his claims?" Khalas asked, those flaming eyes whirling toward Finn.

"That was a pretty story, but a man's actions speak louder than his words. This man – this demon – is guided only by revenge. And that revenge comes at any cost. He has killed hundreds of those same people he supposedly wishes to protect. Harmed, hurt, and enslaved thousands more. He claims that his quest is to rid the world of the gods and free man and beast alike, but he does this only out of self-interest. To heal his body with the staff and to gain control of this world for himself."

Bilel let out a low growl and stepped forward, but the flames of Khalas' body pushed him back. "And why do you seek my *heartstone* then?" she demanded.

Finn met her gaze evenly. "I wish to use its power to resurrect my wife." His eyes drifted to Bilel. "And to stop this demon from harming others."

"So, you meet self-interest with more self-interest?" Bilel demanded with a bark of laughter. "The hypocrisy is so thick you can almost see it. And has your war against me not come with a cost? Your journey into the Abyss?

Your time in the Mage Guild?

"How many have died in pursuit of your mission? Hundreds of novices? You unleashed a plague of fire ants upon the sands when you destroyed the Abyss – or did you think that came with no cost? You have *destroyed* Lahab in your single-minded pursuit of your own goals. Just how many men, women, and children have died for the sake of your crusade, hmm? Hundreds? Thousands?"

"Far less than the number of people you have used, cut down, and enslaved," Finn retorted, the fire in his veins flaring angrily.

"Just give it another century," the demon shot back, his eyes swirling more rapidly.

The two men stared each other down, neither backing away.

"Hmm, the merits of your cases are both reasonable," Khalas said, the fires of her body crackling in indecision. A pause as she mulled on this.

"We shall deal with this in the way of my kind then," she declared finally.

"Which entails what exactly?" Bilel demanded.

Those flames crackled and snapped once more, although Finn recognized this as laughter from his conversation with Nar Aljahim. "The flame does not know compromise or constraint. It knows only strength. Just as a bonfire shall consume a small spark, making its fires its own, so too must you match your passions against one another – whoever blazes brightest shall be the victor."

"And the loser?" Finn asked.

Those glowing orange eyes turned back to him. "They shall be *consumed*, their flames added to the *heartstone*. And so it shall be as it has always been."

Finn swallowed hard. That sounded like a one-way trip to a final "game over" screen. After his last encounter with the staff – including the loss of his hand and the infection that had crippled his mana – it was safe to assume that if he failed here, his character would be destroyed. Or so badly crippled that he wouldn't be able to continue his quest.

"So be it," Bilel said bluntly.

Finn's eyes snapped up to find the demon staring at him. Fires rippled along his skin, curling and coiling around his body and building in strength with each passing moment. As Finn looked on, that blaze grew and stretched, expanding within the void. And then the flames rippled forward, rolling toward him in a towering wave.

And Finn was waiting. He had done this before. Conquered his own passion. Claimed his fire as his own. He knew the depths of the blaze that rested in his heart and mind – the flames just waiting to be released...

And so he did.

His fire raged to life. That simmering ache in his veins had always felt like it was yearning to be set free. This time, he let it burn and spark and flare to life. The flames sprang up around him in an instant, pushing back at Bilel's wall of fire. The two energies collided and mixed – two colossal walls of flames pushing at each other in a magical competition of raw strength of will.

Finn could feel his own flames buckling in the face of Bilel's energy, the fires smashing into one another with abandon. "You think after a century, you can match my *resolve*?" Bilel demanded, his voice roaring over the flames, which grew brighter in Finn's vision as they flared with power.

"I heard Abbad's whispered words. Some mantra of the prophet, perhaps? That is the pledge of a child. You may *intend* to give up everything, but I have already paid my price many times over. I have lost everything and everyone I have ever cared about," the demon roared, pain etched into each word.

His flames grew, stretching ever farther into the Abyss, and Finn felt his legs tremble. The demon's energy was overpowering. He needed to push himself harder, he realized. Just like the last time, the flames didn't just feed off his passion – they *were* his passion. He needed to give them his memories. His hopes. His dreams.

He needed to give them Rachael.

He didn't respond to Bilel – only summoned the

image of Rachael's smiling face, just the way she had looked the last time he'd seen her alive. Her brown hair, coiling around her shoulders. Her dress, glimmering in the dim lights of that car. The taste of her lips as they had touched his for the last time.

His flames roared up to meet Bilel's, but it wasn't enough. Not nearly enough.

So, he gave them everything that came after. The way he'd felt after her loss. That moment sitting in the morgue, his hands grasping at the chill flesh of her fingers – as though he could somehow warm them. That moment when he had fully and finally realized she was gone. And his fire grew even more...

"You think that your dead wife equals a century of despair?" Bilel demanded. "You lost one person. I lost *everyone*. I have given everything to accomplish my mission.

"Even the child I raised from birth. Can you say the same?"

Finn winced, recalling the way those icy shards had embedded themselves in Abbad's chest. The demon hadn't even hesitated – despite the macabre sort of fondness he'd shown for the librarian. And had Finn been willing to make that same sacrifice? He shook his head. If it came down to it... would he even give up Julia?

In the face of his hesitation, Bilel's fire grew, towering over Finn.

The demon seemed to sense his advantage, those flames pressing firmly against Finn's energy, his fires buckling and snapping as though a stiff wind blew through the void. Could he really say that he was as committed as Bilel? Would he have been willing to go to the same lengths? Make the same sacrifices?

He wasn't sure. And his fire responded to that doubt.

"You see? You can't win this. You're *alone* here. Without your friends, your allies, the desert trash, and the guild traitors... You are nothing but a single man. A man that has gone through all of this, for what? His own petty desires?"

At that statement, Finn's brow furrowed. He could vaguely recall something that the Seer had once told him. That his flame burned brightly, but that he wasn't alone – that he had others – that their combined flames could blaze greater than any single fire. And there was a kernel of truth to that. It was his daughter's love and support that had given him this opportunity – had helped push him forward even when everything seemed so bleak. It was the sacrifice of his teammates that had brought them to this point. Their willingness to put everything on the line, to join Finn, even when they knew they might die.

Bilel might have been willing to sacrifice Abbad to obtain his goal.

But Abbad had been willing to give his life for Finn's cause.

And with that realization came a familiar question.

"If you could do it again, would you choose love or ambition?"

He had thought she had been talking about Nar Aljahim's offer back down in the Forge but had that truly been her intent? Or was there a larger lesson?

Had he really just done this for himself?

Or had he also been fighting for Julia? For Gracen? For the grandchildren that would never meet their grandmother? For that geeky kid he'd met in that first beginning courtyard? For the librarian that had lived his life a slave? For a people that had been brutalized and hunted among the sands? For guildsmen that had become nothing more than a commodity... indentured servants living at the mercy of a tyrant?

If he had it all to do over again, if he could go back in time to that moment when he had first started building that AI... he knew what he would do. He would have put the work aside. Given up the discovery. Spent time with his children. With his wife.

He would have chosen love.

That's what Rachael would have wanted.

"I didn't do this just for myself… and I didn't do it alone," Finn murmured.

Then, more strongly, "I didn't do this just for my own ambition. I did this for my children. For the people you enslaved," he roared, his fire growing now.

Finn took a step forward, and the flames around him blazed ever brighter, streaking up into the void. "I did this for the hundreds of mages you had strapped to that stone table, ripping away their magic and their lives. For the novices that you pitted against one another. For the guildsmen that you enslaved and turned into little more than commodities, to be bought and sold to the highest bidder."

Another step forward and Bilel's flames were beginning to tremble.

"For a people banished to the sands, living in persecution – hunted to the farthest corners of the desert to near-extinction. For the residents of your own city, who you cut down and corrupted. For those poor mages that you strung up in your palace, like hogs to the slaughter – draining away their life and mana!"

As he ground out each word, Finn's flames began to curl in on themselves, taking on a blueish hue and heat radiating away from him in waves now. He fed those flames his righteous anger and the pain he had witnessed with his own eyes – pain created at Bilel's hands. His fires crushed at Bilel's flames as he took another step forward.

He fed the flames everything he had left – every heart-wrenching moment he'd experienced in-game. Every fleeting instance of despair and victory. Every memory of Rachael. He didn't – he couldn't – know if he could reclaim those memories. But he didn't care any longer. His wife would have done the same without a moment's hesitation. She had always given so much of herself for everyone else…

"I did this for LOVE!" Finn cried, that word ripping from his throat and leaving a searing burn in its wake. Molten tears were streaming down his cheeks now, the metal in his eyes glowing a bright red.

And his flames responded – blue turning to a blinding white as the temperature rocketed upward. He could barely see now. Could barely feel anything over the blazing fire that flowed through his veins like molten lava.

"*And I would do it a thousand times over!*" Finn screamed.

He rushed forward now, and Bilel's flames flickered. In that moment, in that brief instant, when his opponent's flames waned, Finn reached out and grasped at the demon's arm, his hand searing his flesh. A howl of pain erupted within the void, and Bilel's fire collapsed completely as Finn's flames ate into him.

Burning
Searing
Judging
CONSUMING

Finn took his power, draining the demon's flames into himself even as Bilel howled his pain and despair into the abyss. Vibrant skin melted away to reveal pale, sickly flesh. Then went further, searing through muscle. The flames tore away at Bilel's body until only ivory bone remained. And even then, Finn pressed further, his flames burning through that rigid material, blackening the bone until it charred and hissed and broke apart.

And then there was nothing left.

Only a faint cloud of ash drifted through the abyss.

A voice spoke up from beside Finn. "And so it has been decided." He turned to see Khalas bowing her head. "And so it shall be.

"The prophet has laid claim to my heartstone."

Finn's eyes widened at that statement.

His thoughts felt fuzzy, confused as the energy still coursed through his veins, and ivory flames lapped at his skin. His fires slowly condensed, pulling back toward his body until they formed a glowing white aura. Amid that energy, he was having difficulty focusing on Khalas – on anything other than the burning ache in his chest.

It was a longing. A desperate unfulfilled desire.

Rachael.

"Did Nar Aljahim... has the facility been destroyed?" Khalas asked, interrupting his thoughts. He blinked at her, trying to focus on her features.

Finn nodded.

"Good. Then he shall finally be unchained from that hollow, dead place. Tell the Seer I shall uphold my end of the bargain. It is only fitting after what she has done for me."

"What... what does that mean?" Finn asked, the white flames encircling him flickering uncertainly.

"You shall see for yourself when the time comes," was her only response.

"Wait... What do—?" Finn tried to ask.

However, the abyss was already breaking apart, crumbling at the edges as though his flames were burning down the void around him. Soon, he was falling, falling, falling. The fires still flaring around him, and the image of the elemental's final, somber expression burned into his mind.

Chapter 48 - Reunion

Finn blinked.

Then blinked again.

The world resolved back into focus slowly – the fires and that eerie void now gone.

He felt disoriented, a product of the encounter in the void and the abrupt transition. Skimming the area around him, he took in the swirling watercolor patterns of the mana. He stood once more atop the ruined tower that had once been Bilel's throne room.

Even more strangely, he could still feel that blazing power he'd drawn on within the void coursing through his veins. It raged and burned and crackled through every pore – even standing still was a challenge. He looked down to see that glimmering white flames wrapped his limbs. And the source of that energy was apparent. He held the staff in his hand, his fingers wrapped firmly around the golden hilt, and an intense fire blazing within the *heartstone*.

Bilel! he thought suddenly in alarm.

His gaze whipped across the tower, but he didn't see any sign of the demon. Then his eyes drifted down to a pile of remains that lay where the demon had once stood, the dust and ash glowing with a faint multi-colored light. It seemed that Bilel had met the same end here that he had in that unusual dark abyss – his body and soul consumed by Finn's fire.

And with the demon's death, the spell sustaining the whirlwind of debris that drifted around the tower had faded. Blocks of stone, fragments of wood, and metal framing fell through the air, crashing to the ground far below. And with the loss of that debris, there was nothing left to blunt the storm. Rain cascaded down upon the tower, and wind whipped at Finn's robes. As the water touched Finn, it immediately evaporated, coils of steam drifting up into the air.

"Dad!" a voice shouted from behind him.

He turned to find Julia rushing toward him, his daughter hesitating for only a moment at the sight of the white flames before throwing her arms around his shoulder and causing him to list to the side. Thankfully, the fires didn't seem to harm her.

"We thought you had died," she murmured into his shoulder.

"What about Abbad?" he croaked, remembering that last attack.

Julia pulled back, and Finn shifted to *Short-Sighted*, observing the grimace that flattened her lips – a wordless acknowledgment of what he already feared. He could feel a hollow weight settle in his stomach.

Her gaze drifted back to the body that lay along the stone.

Abbad.

Malik hovered over top the man, but he didn't reach for a healing potion or make any effort to remove the icy spikes embedded in the librarian's chest – crimson blood pooling beneath Abbad. And as Finn switched back to his *Mana Sight*, he observed no telltale gleam of energy pulsing through Abbad's body. Only the icy blue energy that signaled the last warmth of life had left him.

"Fuck," Finn muttered, rubbing at his eyes with his crystalline hand.

"Fuck," he echoed again. The loss hit hard. Harder than he had expected. They might have won – might have finally defeated Bilel – but it had come with a hefty price.

The destruction of the city. The deaths of so many residents and players. The loss of their own soldiers. And now... now Abbad. His friend.

"It's what he wanted," Kyyle offered tentatively, the earth mage approaching slowly with Brock's burly form in tow. "We won. We killed Bilel," he said, kicking at the demon's ashes. "Even if I don't completely understand how that happened..." He shot Finn a questioning glance.

Finn could see his daughter waiting expectantly as well, and he took a deep, trembling breath, trying to regain his composure. Abbad had been there since the beginning. Since that first moment in the Mage Guild courtyard. And he had lent a helping hand through… well, through everything that followed. It felt wrong that he wasn't here to see their victory.

Finn shook his head. "I… I realized that our only option was for me to try to claim ownership of the staff." His gaze shifted to the blazing gem set into the top of the staff. "Like Nar Aljahim said, this is his mate's *heartstone*. My guess was that the staff is semi-conscious. And I was right…

"Her name is Khalas," he murmured as he stared at that gem.

His companions just looked on wordlessly, watching the *heartstone* more warily now. As they focused their attention on the staff, Finn could finally observe the price they had paid as well. They were beaten, bloodied, and tired. Circles hung under their eyes, and their armor was soaked with rain. The storm was still booming above them, refusing to let up.

Even as that thought crossed Finn's mind, he saw a flame spark to life in the corner of his vision – a bright point of light that stood out through the pounding storm. His gaze dropped down to the market far below, that telltale glow located in the dead center of Lahab. His brow furrowed in confusion as he watched those flames, the fires growing brighter with each passing second.

"What is going—?" he gasped, his teammates turning to watch that energy.

He was cut off as the fires surged forward at an alarming rate, soon consuming the entire market. The flames were streaking up into the sky, creating a cloud of steam as the fires rapidly evaporated the rain that beat down upon the city. Those fires kept going, torching the buildings that ringed the market, and the hounds that raced down the adjoining streets.

Finn could just barely pick out travelers and residents in the city below them – a few survivors of the horrific massacre that Bilel had unleashed upon the city.

As they saw the wave of flame approaching, they tried to run... tried to escape... but the flames were moving too quickly – an avalanche of fire that stretched outward in an expanding ring.

"Are you doing this?" Julia asked, glancing at the staff.

"No... no, I don't think so," Finn replied.

That weight in his stomach sank further. Was he somehow responsible for this? Or perhaps the Seer? Was he witnessing the true end of Lahab? The end of the Khamsin and the guilds? A fire that would once and for all wipe the sands clean of the corrupting influence of the humans, mages, merchants, and fighters that had once occupied this place?

The flames were indifferent to his dread. They continued to spread, stretching out toward the battle that still raged around the Mage Guild – their army still cutting down the hounds as they remained trapped outside the guild's walls. The fires were indifferent to that conflict, consuming man and beast alike faster than they could react. There was nowhere to run – no way to shield themselves from the blaze. A wave of superheated steam was rocketing up into the air now, the hurricane above them swirling and undulating wildly as a fresh updraft of hot air further destabilized the storm front.

And soon, that wall of fire was passing the gates of the palace below the ruined tower. It swept through the courtyard, ate its way through the outbuildings and the remaining hounds, and then raced upward, stretching toward their position. And the group looked on with hopeless, awestruck expressions. An ocean of fire lingered below them – a sea of flames so wide and deep that Finn couldn't see anything beyond the orange glow.

Those flames coiled farther up the tower and soon licked at the edges of the platform.

Then they had crossed that threshold, the flames barreling toward the group as they clustered near the center of the tower. Finn felt Julia reach for him then, her fingers curling between his own.

He closed his eyes as those fires struck…

And then his gaze snapped open.

He stood among the flames – a strange sense of déjà vu overcoming him given his recent duel with Bilel for dominion over the staff. The fire didn't burn or sear his skin. Instead, it seeped into his limbs, adding to the fires that already wrapped his body. It soaked into his muscle and bone, and he could feel a surge of energy fill him, burning away any trace of fatigue. It felt like he had just downed an entire pot of coffee, his heart beating rapidly and his limbs practically buzzing with energy.

That's when he felt a strange tingling along his skin.

He looked down to see his skin ripple and transform. Smooth flesh turned dry and flaked away, scale-like patterns forming along the surface of his arms. A tingling sensation erupted from his scalp, and his hand left Julia's to drift cautiously up toward his head. He could feel small lumps forming along his forehead. Horns erupted from his skin, stretching upward toward the sky.

And then, all at once, the fires winked out.

Finn blinked, this time to block out the harsh sunlight that now beat down upon Lahab… or what might have once been Lahab.

The storm was gone, only faint wisps of white and gray remaining. And the sun now shone down on a city transformed. The buildings were intact once more, and the streets repaired, now covered by dry sand. But the buildings had been remodeled and repurposed. Flames now licked from sandy spires, stretching up into the air all around the city.

Far to the north, the battle that had once been raging outside the Mage Guild had ceased. Thousands of soldiers now stood upon the sands – healthy and alive – their energy rippling with a mixture of orange and red mana. Yet there were so many of them. More than there should be. At that thought, Finn abruptly realized that the hounds had disappeared. Perhaps these were the men and women that had been converted into the beasts.

The ruined throne room, however, hadn't been fixed – at least, not entirely.

A railing now ringed the lip of the tower, flames wrapping the metal and streaking up into the air. And the stairs had been rebuilt, the steps now trailing back down into the depths of the palace below them. Off to Finn's side sat a throne – the surface composed entirely of molten glass and its depths rippling with fiery energy. Conspicuously absent was Abbad's body – his corpse burned away by the flames that had purified and repaired the city. In their place, a small golden urn sat upon the stone.

Finn stepped forward slowly, stooping and picking up that lone vessel. Along the surface, the former librarian's name had been inscribed in lilting text. He swallowed hard, pushing back at the tears that budded in the corners of his eyes.

It's okay, he told himself. Abbad may have sacrificed himself, but his death was not in vain. They had accomplished their mission – the librarian's mission. He knew that if the man stood here now, he would have gladly paid the same price... even if that thought did little to lighten the weight that had settled in Finn's stomach.

So many had died to make his dream a reality.

And then Finn felt a wave of heat strike him. He looked up to see a rolling tide of warmth ripple out across the city, the temperature causing the very air to warp and undulate. Yet Finn didn't find the heat uncomfortable, and no sweat beaded along his now-scaly skin. In fact, the warmth felt soothing.

"Holy shit," Kyyle muttered from beside them, echoing their thoughts.

Finn spared a glance to the side and noticed that the earth mage had undergone the same transformation. His skin was now a patchwork of crude scales, and horns jutted from his forehead as well. Steadying himself, Kyyle's hand lingered on Brock's rocky torso as he took in the changes.

Finn turned to find his daughter, staring. She

hadn't undergone the transition. Normal human eyes framed by smooth skin looked back at him within the harsh blue glow of *Short-Sighted*. Julia reached up a tentative hand, touching the tip of one of his horns and an unspoken question on her lips.

Yet before she could ask it, a prompt crashed down into their vision, each person atop that ruined tower staring off into space as they reviewed the message.

Universal System Message

A traveler has conquered Lahab and has converted it to the fire affinity. The city of Lahab shall henceforth be known as "Sandscrit." The ambient temperature of the city has been increased, creating an aura of heat that radiates over the sands. The city's residents have been converted to Efreet – creatures of magic capable of bonding a part of their soul to a non-organic creature or object.

Any travelers or residents with a high fire affinity that are within range of Sandscrit shall receive a passive bonus to all fire-based abilities and skills – including crafting abilities. "Efreet" is now available as a starting race, and players that choose this race will start in Sandscrit.

The Prophet of the Flame has returned. He is the spark of passion that resides in the hearts of all men. The tip of the storm. The all-consuming blaze. His flames shall soon sweep across this world, a rallying cry for his people and an ill omen for his enemies. – The Seer

---

System Notice: Race Change

After undergoing the *Forging* and completing your end of the Seer's bargain, you have discovered that your body has been transformed. You have completed the rites to become one of the fire-folk – the *Efreet* – creatures of magic

---

and flame.

Race Change: Efreet
Mana gain from Intelligence and Willpower increased by x1.25.
You have been awarded +50 to Intelligence
You have been awarded +20 to Dexterity
You have been awarded +20 to Endurance
You have been awarded +20 to Vitality
Racial weakness to water mana.
Mana regeneration increased by 50% when standing in superheated areas.

Finn heard the sound of clapping, and the group whirled, their hands immediately reaching for their weapons. Although, Finn raised a staying hand as he saw who was approaching.

The Seer stood upon the once-ruined tower, her body robed in purple silks, and her eyes ablaze with coils of flame and fiery energy. As she paced toward them, a trail of fire lit along the ground behind, each footstep leaving a glowing pattern upon the stone.

"Congratulations! You have done well!" she intoned solemnly.

Finn could only stare back open-mouthed, unsure of how to respond and a dozen questions whirling through his mind.

"What, no words of greeting for your divine benefactor?" the Seer asked, a touch of humor coloring her voice. It seemed she was in pleasant spirits.

"How... how are you here?" Finn finally murmured, waving at his companions to lower their weapons.

"Thanks to you, of course. You have taken the steps needed to release me from my prison – at least on a temporary basis. Think of it like being granted *probation*," she offered, a twinkle of flame in her eyes.

Those same eyes then turned toward the city,

taking in the conversion that had swept Lahab – now Sandscrit. "Isn't it magnificent? You're witnessing the product of more than a century of preparation. It has been so long since my city has been intact," she murmured, as though she couldn't quite believe what she was seeing.

"So, you're the goddess? The Crone?" Julia demanded, her shield hanging loosely in her left hand but her right still gripping her lance.

The Seer pivoted in an instant, her eyes flashing. "I dislike that name. I am the *Seer* – the goddess of the flame. And your father here is my avatar."

At that response, Malik's eyes widened, and he immediately dropped to his knees – reciting something under his breath. The Seer sighed as she noticed his reaction. "And this is why my siblings and I typically mask our presence." She snapped her fingers, and the fighter went rigid, frozen in place.

"Is he okay?" Kyyle asked, waving a hand in front of Malik's face.

"He is fine," the Seer replied with a dismissive wave. "I believe you travelers refer to this as *pausing*? In any event, now we shall be free to speak openly and without interruption."

"Well, then let me start," Julia snapped, taking an ominous step forward. "We've upheld our end of the bargain. Now where the hell is my mother?"

The Seer peered at her in response, unperturbed by her menacing appearance. "Hmm, I see you inherited your father's fire."

Julia let out a low growl, her grip tightening on her lance. Finn rested a staying hand on her shoulder. "Let me handle this. I certainly have enough practice at this point…"

He stepped forward, meeting the Seer's gaze and raising the staff. "We've reclaimed the relic, now what do I need to do to resurrect Rachael?"

The goddess nodded. "That is a simple matter. The staff responds to your will – to your passion." She waved toward it with a nonchalant gesture. "Ask it for what you desire most..."

Finn hesitated, his gaze shifting to the staff. That felt too easy – too simple after everything they had gone through. He couldn't help but feel that there would be a catch. He spared a glance at Julia and Kyyle, and they both gave him a noncommittal shrug. They were well and truly off the rails now. Why not lean into it?

Taking a deep breath, he slammed the butt of the staff into the stone floor, like he had seen Bilel do several times.

And he then asked for Khalas to return that which he had lost.

The fire within the *heartstone* blazed to life, glowing brightly.

He poured his love into the staff. His memories of Rachael. The pain, despair, and rage he had experienced in the aftermath of her death and during his journey inside the game. And then he gave the gem his hope... that small spark he had felt way back in the Mage Guild – the realization that the Seer's promise could be *possible*. That flame he had gently nurtured for weeks in-game until it blazed with a fire of its own. It was that flame that had kept him going throughout everything – that would bring his Rachael back to him.

Flames rippled along Finn's arm and swiftly encircled the staff, growing in heat and intensity until they pushed back his companions. An inferno soon raged across the stone, consuming both Finn and the staff. He could feel the relic trembling in his hand, responding to his fire like a living thing – which, he supposed it was.

Please. Please bring her back to me...

And Khalas answered his request.

A tear ripped open in the air beside the throne, as though someone had sliced open a hole in reality – forming a cosmic wound in the universe itself. And beyond that veil, Finn glimpsed a world of fire and flame. A raging torrent of heat that made what he had witnessed within the void pale in comparison. It was more than just staring at the surface of the sun. It was like watching the formation of a new star.

And as he stared at that makeshift portal, small tendrils of energy leaked through. Only small rivulets of molten flame at first, but then a more substantial flow of fire that seeped into this world from somewhere else. Those flames gathered and grew, condensing and rippling. They began to form themselves into fingers... arms... hands... feet. Those limbs attached to a torso, the fires joining and combining. And then the fires stretched upward – forming a head.

A simulacrum of fire soon stood before them, a being of fire not unlike Nar Aljahim and Khalas themselves. And as Finn looked on, a final surge of mana welled up through the staff, the energy so dense that it was blinding in Finn's sight, and he was forced to avert his gaze. That power rocketed from the gem, a splintering crack of thunder pealing across the throne room followed by a blast of energy so intense that it sent Finn stumbling backward.

And as the energy began to clear and he caught his balance, Finn discovered that the sound hadn't come from the storm. The hurricane had long since vanished. No, a massive crack had formed in the *heartstone*, and the gem's fire was fading rapidly.

With a sense of both dread and fascination, he shifted his gaze to the creature he had summoned – a being of living flame. Its limbs moved and shifted slightly... experimentally. Its body solidified before them, the fires condensing and growing firmer and more substantial. The flames gradually hardened into bone and muscle, and the crackling surface soon smoothed into skin.

Leaving a woman standing upon the floor of the Throne Room.

A woman that was achingly familiar.

With a shaky breath, Finn's mouth dropped open, and his eyes traced every detail...

Rachael.

Auburn hair ringed her face – that nose, those ears, those lips. They were Rachael's. Finn would have recognized her face anywhere, her features burned into his mind. A simple robe was draped across her body, its surface still shimmering and rippling with heat, as though the fabric itself were on fire.

"Mom...?" Julia asked, her voice thick with emotion.

And then the woman opened her eyes. Instead of the warm brown that Finn remembered, they glowed with an orange light, as though she was burning from the inside out. Rachael's gaze was uneven – confused – her brow pinching together as she took in her surroundings with uncertainty.

Finn stepped forward, moving slowly to avoid startling her. "Hello," he greeted gently, as though she might blow away with a single wrong movement or word. "Are... are you okay?"

"Yes..." the woman began, then coughed, her fingers rising to her jaw as though the words felt strange – or perhaps it was the act of speaking.

"Yes, I think I am," she tried again, her speech sounding more fluid now. Those orange eyes met his, but he didn't see any immediate recognition there. Yet he refused to give in to the despair – that hollow feeling that ached in his chest.

"Do you remember your name?" Finn asked tentatively. He found himself holding his breath – silently praying over and over again.

Rachael's brow furrowed again, and she shook her head gently. "I don't..." She trailed off. Then there was a spark of recognition like a fire had sprung to life in her mind. "Actually... yes. I think my name is *Rachael*."

Her eyes widened then, staring down at the stone floor of the throne room. Finn could practically see the memories flooding back – like a tidal wave that had Rachael listing slightly, almost losing her balance. Without even realizing what he was doing, Finn had already stepped forward, holding her – cradling her. The movement was instinctive. The way their arms interlocked, the way her hand cradled his bicep, it was like two puzzle pieces that had finally snapped into place.

If there had ever been any doubt about who stood in front of him, it was burned away the moment she raised her eyes, meeting his own. He saw recognition there.

He saw *love* there.

"Finn?" she whispered. "Oh my god, Finn!"

She wrapped her arms around him then, holding him, pulling him toward her. And he held her with the same intensity, savoring every incredible detail. The heat of her body. The weight of her in his arms. The thud, thud, thud of her heartbeat. The warmth of her breath on his neck. It was her. It was *Rachael* – his Rachael.

She eventually drew back, looking up at him. Her eyes shone with moisture, the water evaporating long before it could fall down her cheeks. She reached up a hand to his face, touching the metal embedded in his eyes – his bandage long since lost to storm and battle. "What happened to you?" she asked, worry creasing her features.

"That's a long, long story," he answered, laughing, and crying at the same time. "But first... your daughter is here too." He turned, waving toward Julia where she stood nearby, tears streaming down her cheeks.

Rachael stared at her for a moment in puzzlement. "Wait... Julia?" she asked hesitantly.

"Yes, yes, Mom. It's me," Julia answered, stepping forward more cautiously.

Rachael stared at her in shock, her fingers drifting forward and running through Julia's hair. "You look so much older," she murmured, her brow furrowed in confusion. "And what did you do to your hair? It's so short."

"It's... it's been a long time," Julia offered in response, a faltering smile on her lips. Then she flicked at her hair. "And the long hair kept getting in the way."

"Well, I love it," Rachael said finally, looking up to meet her daughter's gaze.

Julia finally broke at that comment, flinging herself

forward and wrapping her arms around her mother. And Rachael held her back, her arms stretching around her daughter. At that sight, Finn couldn't help but join them. The three of them holding onto one another as though any one of them might disappear at any moment.

Eventually, they had to pull away. And Finn found Rachael surveying the area around them, noticing the flames spiraling up into the air of the new throne room, and the city sprawled out far below them.

"What is this? Where are we exactly?" she asked, turning a questioning gaze toward Finn.

He swallowed hard, unsure where to begin. Julia stayed quiet too, afraid of accidentally confusing or upsetting Rachael. If this truly was her… then the answers to her questions were going to come as a huge shock – potentially a terrifying one.

"Um, what's your last memory?" Finn asked gently.

Rachael's gaze went distant again. "We went to a dinner. It was in your honor… an award for the AI that you developed." She hesitated, and Finn and Julia waited, watching her intently. "Then there was a car ride. You were feeling nervous… and…"

His wife's eyes went wide again, her hand trembling in Finn's. "There was something wrong with the car. A tremor. Then the whole world listed to the side. I remember floating… reaching for you… and then… nothing."

Rachael's gaze snapped back into focus as she took in her surroundings with renewed focus. Her gaze now more thoroughly inspected the robes that wrapped Finn's body. The crystalline hand that cradled her own, flames coiling within its depths. The plate armor that covered Julia's body and the weapons strapped to her waist and back. The expressions that lingered on her husband's and daughter's faces – warring between hope and terrible grief.

"I… I died, didn't I?" she asked, her voice trembling.

Finn just nodded weakly. Of course Rachael had

figured out the answer immediately. She had always been curious, intelligent, inquisitive... willing to stare into the void in search of solutions to unanswerable questions.

That was part of why he had fallen for her so hard all of those years ago.

"And this is what then? A simulation?" she asked, waving at the throne room.

"Sort of," Finn said. "Your memories and consciousness were all saved and recorded as part of the research we conducted to develop that first AI. This place, it was able to piece that information back together... to *recreate* you, I guess," he explained.

"So, I'm what? A computer program?" she retorted, withdrawing from him slightly.

"No. No, no, no," Finn said. "I've reviewed the code. You're so much more than that. You're thinking... feeling. In many ways, it's as though you never died."

Rachael nodded slowly, and then her gaze shifted to Julia, taking in her features, eyes that no longer held the hopeful gleam of childhood. She raised a hand, cradling Julia's face. "How long?" she managed to ask, her voice hoarse with emotion. "How long was I...?"

"Ten years," Julia answered, tears streaming down her cheeks.

Rachael's gaze drifted down to the stone floor as she tried to process that information, a whirlwind of emotion sweeping across her face in an instant. Finn could feel that weight coiling in his stomach now like a living thing. This was the moment he had feared. This moment of realization. If his dreams could come true – if they *had* come true... could Rachael live with what they had done?

Then Rachael's gaze settled, those emotions burning away. Her glowing eyes lifted back to meet Finn's. "You did it then," she said finally, a faint smile pulling at her lips. "True AI... I never thought I'd live to see it."

Finn matched that smile, a relieved sigh escaping his lips. "Technically, you didn't," he retorted, his voice teasing.

And then he heard a sound he never thought he'd experience again. Rachael laughed. Genuinely, laughed. Because *of course* she would. She might be the only woman he had ever met that could honest-to-god laugh in the face of her own resurrection. And the sound was worth every moment of pain and hardship he had endured since her death.

Without even realizing it, Finn was crying, tears of molten flame curling down his cheeks. Rachael swiped at those tears and then pulled him close – tugging Julia along with her. She held them close.

"Thank you. Thank you both," she whispered.

"I hate to interrupt this touching moment, but our time grows short, and there is still much that we need to cover," the Seer interjected as Finn pulled away from Rachael and his daughter.

"What do you mean?" Finn asked in confusion. "Do you need to return to the tent?"

"It is not *my* time that is nearing its end," she answered, waving at Rachael.

As Finn's attention turned back to his wife, he could see that she had lifted her hand, staring at the limb in a mixture of fascination and horror. Her fingers were breaking apart, smooth skin transforming to crackling flame before her eyes. And that effect was spreading up her arm, her body destabilizing with each passing second.

"No. What's happening? Rachael!" Finn demanded.

He felt a hand land on his shoulder and turned to find the Seer standing beside him. She approached Rachael, holding her fear-filled gaze. "You are okay. You're going to be okay. You just don't have the energy to maintain this form for long. But don't worry, I will take care of you – help you to mend and heal."

Then the goddess reached out a hand toward Rachael. "Will you come with me?"

Rachael glanced at Finn, fear and uncertainty filling those glowing orange eyes as the rest of her body began to break apart into streamers of flame. Finn experienced a moment of indecision, and then he nodded.

"You can go with her," he urged Rachael. "This woman helped bring you back."

His wife stared back only a moment longer before accepting the Seer's hand. In a flash, her body transformed back to living flame, the fires seeping into the Seer's body and disappearing in only moments, leaving the group staring in shock at the place where Rachael had been standing only moments before.

"What the fuck was that?" Finn demanded, rounding on the goddess and his eyes flashing ominously. "You promised me!"

"And I fulfilled my end of the bargain," the Seer snapped, her eyes blazing with a fire of her own. "What you attempted here was almost impossible. As I told you before, this world has rules – limitations – and you must abide by them."

She pointed at the staff in Finn's hand. "Do you know how much energy it took just to bring her back – her body long gone, and her consciousness fragmented and broken."

Finn turned his gaze to the relic and once again noticed the large crack that now radiated through the *heartstone*. Its fires had been almost entirely extinguished. And in that moment, he realized what Khalas had done, her mate's words ringing through his mind. The ancient fire elementals collected fire mana, and when their power had grown great enough, they released that energy back into the world.

The power to form planets and new stars...

Or to bring back a single soul from the abyss.

Khalas must have known what she would be giving up to bring back Rachael, her words within the abyss suddenly making sense. She had sacrificed herself to make this happen – to resurrect Rachael.

The Seer placed a hand on Finn's shoulder again. "Do not despair," she said, not unkindly. "Rachael is just unstable right now. New fire elementals typically are. But she should be fine within my tent. Fire mana permeates that place. It will nourish and strengthen her. Prevent her from breaking apart."

"A fire elemental?" Julia echoed.

The Seer cocked her head. "Yes, of course. That's what she is now – what this world has decided to use as a vehicle to contain her consciousness. Much as was done for Daniel," she continued, waving at the AI that floated nearby, his fire dimming with uncertainty and confusion as he watched the scene unfold.

Finn coughed to clear his throat, straightened, and stared the goddess down. "Then what do we need to do to stabilize her and allow her to return to this plane?" He could already anticipate what the Seer would say, his mind chipping away at the problem.

This was a string – another form of control.

A shifting of the goal posts.

And entirely expected.

"Simple. You need to collect more mana," the goddess answered, waving at the area behind the throne that sat nearby. As the group looked on, a lone pedestal rose from the ground, a bowl affixed to the top.

As Finn looked at that strange column, he suddenly recognized the dense, glowing mana that lingered inside that bowl. He'd seen this energy signature before – back in the Abyss. In the goddess' ruined temple.

"This is a mana well – your mana well," the goddess explained, stepping toward the column. "The passion of your people feeds it energy, and that ambient mana collects here. It can then be spent to upgrade parts of the city..." She trailed off, glancing over her shoulder at Finn. "Or a portion can be diverted and used to help sustain and stabilize Rachael."

Finn shook his head. "How long?" he managed to grunt. "How long will this take?"

The Seer arched an eyebrow. "Well, that depends entirely on *you*," she answered. "On how much mana you are willing to reserve... and the lengths you are willing to go to increase the energy gathered by the well."

"Which means what exactly?" Julia demanded,

glaring at the goddess now.

A sigh. "I've explained this to your father before, but I am in a competition with my siblings – a divine race of sorts," the Seer said, peering at them. "Each step unlocks greater power. And the victor, well, the victor will have the power to accomplish *anything within this world*. A mere snap of your fingers and Rachael's form would be stabilized completely."

Finn swallowed the angry words that lingered in his throat. There was no sense antagonizing the goddess – even if she had failed to mention this incredibly fucking important detail. It seemed he still needed her. At least for now.

There was now only one question that mattered.

"What next?" he asked evenly.

The goddess' eyes sparkled as she met his gaze. "You will need to gather the pieces of one of the destroyed gates. The fragments were spread throughout this world – hidden and concealed."

"The gates? Gates to where?" Julia asked.

The Seer clicked her tongue. "That I can't reveal. As I said, there are rules."

Her gaze shifted back to Finn. "So, what do you say? Shall we extend our bargain? I shall help sustain Rachael, and you shall seek out these gate pieces?"

Finn ground his teeth, his eyes drifting down to the stone floor as he tried to tamp down on the frustration welling in his chest. It was the glimmer in the goddess' eyes – those eyes that peered into the future. It was a knowing look. She was certain in the inevitability of his answer. And he already knew how he would respond. Perhaps that was why this made him so angry. This final manipulation.

Yet that wouldn't change his answer.

Finn raised his eyes back up to meet the Seer's. "You have a deal."

Chapter 49 - Recovered

A few days had passed in-game since Finn and his companions had defeated Bilel.

He wasn't certain what he'd expected to happen in the aftermath of the attack on the city and the confrontation with the demon. Perhaps a mutiny of the Khamsin or the guilds. Or the people revolting in the streets over their forced race change and the deaths of their loved ones – not all of those slain by the hounds had returned. Or possibly widespread looting and pillaging. Although, that latter option assumed there was anything left in the market and storefronts worth stealing...

And yet none of those outcomes had come to pass.

Instead, an eerie calm had descended over Lahab – now *Sandscrit*, he supposed. That peace might have been partially explained by the survivors. Many more of the residents had made it through the siege than Finn had expected, including most of the mages Bilel had strung up in the palace. The guilds had also slowly begun to move back into their guild halls, abandoning the Flagship back to the desert. Some repairs were underway, although there was precious little need for them after the city's conversion. For their part, the residents had begun to return to their normal routine – attempting to piece their lives back together.

As Finn sat upon the flaming throne in the heart of the palace, his gaze panned out across the city. He followed the movements of those multi-colored blotches far below him – the residents of Sandscrit. His *people*. Although, he supposed that was a touch premature. The guilds and Khamsin hadn't yet formally recognized him as their Emir.

Despite the calm, he just couldn't shake the feeling that it wouldn't last. It felt like he was waiting for the other shoe to drop – even if he couldn't quite put his finger on what disaster would occur next. Maybe a foreign invasion? Or some sort of meteor strike?

Or maybe he was just *worried*. This city was now his ticket to stabilizing Rachael and his path to retrieving her from the Seer's tent for more than a few minutes at a time. He needed it to survive – to thrive even.

"It feels weird," Julia offered, noticing Finn's distant gaze.

She and Kyyle sat nearby, having pulled a crude stone table from the floor of the throne room and turning the space into an impromptu meeting room. They had been reviewing the city's status and going over messages from the guilds – a rather mundane set of administrative tasks after the last few days and weeks in-game.

The paperwork had included very few explosions or near-death experiences.

At a questioning glance from Finn, Julia waved at the city. "Peace, I mean. It feels like we've been pushing forward so hard and fast for so long that it's just... jarring to come to a full stop." She held up a scroll. "Or to be tackling silly questions like setting up a city guard. Or permitting for a market stall – who cares about that nonsense?"

"Are you actually rooting for another disaster?" Kyyle asked in an incredulous voice.

A grin pulled at Julia's lips. "Well... maybe. A girl likes a bit of chaos," she offered, her gaze challenging as she met Kyyle's eyes. "Why? You not up for it?"

The earth mage let out a snort. "Suuuure. Asks the woman that couldn't match my score..."

Julia's eyes widened slightly, and Kyyle leaned forward. "Oh, I remember our bet."

"I'm sure I beat you," she retorted, although the way she glanced surreptitiously at Daniel somewhat undermined her show of confidence.

On cue, the AI piped up, "Actually, you didn't. As requested, I kept track. Kyyle's score was 367. Your score was only 154."

"What?" Julia demanded, glaring at the AI now. "That has to be area of effects stuff – which totally shouldn't count. It's not fair if he can take out whole groups at once."

"I don't remember any exceptions when we made our bet," Kyyle offered, his grin widening. "Which means you owe me that dinner."

Julia grumbled under her breath, but as she turned away from the earth mage, Finn couldn't help but notice a faint smile cross her face. It seemed she might be more invested in the date than she was letting on. And good for her. Maybe he was biased after fighting alongside Kyyle for so long, but he seemed like he could keep up with Julia – more so than her previous boyfriends anyway.

She had always had a penchant for the dumb, pretty ones.

"Fine," she said finally. "Just name the time and place, and I'll be there."

Kyyle was smiling broadly now, but he didn't get a chance to reply.

"Guests for the prophet," a guard's voice rang out.

The men and women stationed around the throne room promptly snapped to attention, their plate-clad boots clanking harshly against the stone and streamers of fire curling around their armor. Julia had taken the liberty of stationing her Infernal Guard within the palace. Armored Khamsin and their fire mage partners now patrolled the halls, guarding Finn. It seemed excessive, but she had insisted such fanfare was necessary now.

Finn had appearances to maintain, after all.

He looked up to find Aerys, Malik, and Kalisha approaching, along with another face that Finn hadn't expected. Brutus stood with them, now clothed in much finer robes than his typical attire. The fire mage tugged uncomfortably at his collar as he inspected the throne room with a skeptical expression.

"Pull up a seat," Finn offered as they approached, motioning at Kyyle. The earth mage took the hint, and with a few curt gestures, he expanded the stone table and a series of chairs composed entirely of sandstone rose from the ground.

The group sat down sedately, but Finn sensed

tension in the air. As he switched to *Mana Sight*, he observed their energy swirling and colliding more erratically – light and darkness coiling through their mana in equal measure.

Hmm, what could they want now…?

"So, first off, I love what you've done with the place," Brutus observed, still staring at the flaming pillars ringing the throne room and the impressive view of the city far below. "Has a really open feel to it… although, if it rains, you're going to be in trouble."

Finn coughed to cover a laugh. "I'm not sure I'm too concerned about that. The last time it rained here, it took quite a bit of effort."

His expression sobered at that. "Speaking of… how are things at the Mage Guild? Has the transition gone smoothly?"

Brutus' smile faded. "As well as could be expected. Abbad… well, he handled a lot. I'm just now realizing how much I failed to appreciate the man."

Finn could only nod. The librarian's loss still stung – far worse than Finn had been expecting. He hadn't realized how much he'd come to rely on Abbad's stoic calm and measured advice until it was gone. Especially in times like these where the city was undergoing an enormous transition. And yet, surprisingly, Brutus had stepped up in a big way, the other mages rallying behind him with surprising vigor.

Perhaps they were all just hoping he'd be reassigned from his instructor position where he couldn't directly torture the students or faculty.

"That actually touches on the reason for our visit," Aerys interjected, gazing evenly at Finn as he switched back to *Short-Sighted*. The Khamsin woman's face soon resolved back into focus.

Finn couldn't quite mask the way his shoulders tensed at that statement. Perhaps this was the other shoe he'd been waiting for.

"Oh? How can I help you all?"

Aerys shared a look with the others and took a

deep breath. "We're actually here at the behest of the Khamsin and the guilds. They wished for us to speak with you directly… about the rulership of Sandscrit."

Finn's eyebrows rose, but he held his tongue.

In the corner of his eye, he could see Julia slowly reaching for a weapon. A curt gesture at the guards ringing the terrace warned them of a potential fight.

"Really? Do you have to be so dramatic," Kalisha drawled, kicking her feet up on the table, her tiny mechanid crawling up her arm and latching firmly to her shoulder. "You're going to make him think we're here to topple another Emir. I mean, are you trying to give these flaming bad boys around us a reason to dropkick us off this tower?"

Aerys scowled at the merchant. "A bit of decorum isn't exactly a bad thing."

"Just get to the point," Kalisha replied, rolling her eyes. "While we're still young."

The Khamsin leader swallowed her response, glaring at the merchant before turning her attention back to Finn. "*Fine.* The long and short of it is that we wish for you to formally assume the mantle of Emir now that Bilel has been defeated."

Finn could only stare back in surprise.

"Oh, don't look at her like that," Kalisha interjected. "Were you really expecting a different outcome? You've become a legend – not just to the Khamsin, but to the guildsmen. The merchants all sing your praises for the bargain you struck between the Khamsin and our guild. With fresh supplies of ore, we can greatly expand our manufacturing operations."

She waved at Malik. "And even the fighters are on board, especially after this one claimed he saw the goddess of fire herself speak with you. It takes a lot to sway those stoic jerks, but even they have started chanting that irritating phrase every time they see you."

Malik frowned at that comment. "They also observed you in the siege on Lahab and how you led the fight against the hellhounds at the gate. Our members honor strength and fortitude in battle. You have demonstrated both."

"And the mages are with you," Brutus grunted. "You showcased how much more powerful we are as a group, and they aren't content to settle back into the old ways – not with how Bilel persecuted them and purged their mana. I think that's why so many have supported my appointment as the new guild leader. They are looking for a change. And here I am," he offered with a broad grin.

Finn stared at them as they lapsed into silence. Now, this was a result he truly hadn't expected. He'd assumed that he would have to fight and cajole the guilds into working together, much less follow his directions. And yet, lo and behold, they had come knocking at his door offering to place the Emir's mantle upon him.

But he wasn't exactly going to say no, especially not with the "revised" bargain he'd been forced to strike with the Seer.

"Well, say something. Don't leave us in suspense," Brutus grunted.

Finn coughed to clear his throat. "I accept," he said simply.

He leaned forward then. "And thank you." He looked around the table, meeting each of their eyes. "I know you three likely had a hand in this outcome. I appreciate it."

"Well, you can appreciate it more by formally appointing us as guild emissaries," Kalisha shot back. "That position is going to come with a lot of lofty titles and perks."

"Of course," he replied, and the merchant nodded curtly, satisfied.

His eyes skimmed to Aerys. "And I'd like to extend an olive branch to the Khamsin. They've adopted me as one of their own, but I know some will balk at being told what to do by an outsider – especially after so long operating with their own autonomy.

"I'd like to propose that the Khamsin remain an

independent fiefdom, operating in coordination with me. They will keep their lands and territories, will be permitted to freely enter Sandscrit, they will not be subject to any merchant guild trade sanctions, and they will be permitted to form their own embassy within the city.

"Is that acceptable?" Finn asked.

Aerys appeared slightly taken aback by the suggestion but quickly mastered her expression. "That... that would work well."

Finn nodded. He could understand Aerys' surprise. With the way many of her people worshipped him, he could have asked for more... far more. But he wasn't thinking about the mainstream Khamsin. His thoughts were directed at Eldawin. And at Thorn. The Order was still a problem – and a big one. Finn hadn't forgotten their threats. However, this action would help to undermine their power among the Khamsin and any rhetoric they used to recruit new members. It was easy to balk at the leadership of an outsider, but much more difficult to get their backs up about taking orders from their own.

Malik spoke up then, the quiet fighter drawing the attention of the group. "If I may... what now?" he asked. "I know you spoke with the goddess. But what are your plans moving forward?"

Finn grimaced. "The Seer indicated that there are gate pieces scattered throughout this continent. She has tasked me with reclaiming them," he explained.

Although, he conveniently left out the part about Rachael, as well as the rather large reserve cost that had been imposed on his mana well. He'd checked that pillar sitting just behind his throne after everything had settled, and he'd discovered two interesting items.

First, the well passively collected mana over time. Second, he'd been forced to direct nearly all the energy toward Rachael, sustaining and stabilizing her newfound body. While the mana well interface indicated that Finn could likely improve and upgrade other aspects of the city, that would have to wait, at least until he could find a way to grow its energy generation.

Rachael came first. He couldn't be certain how much mana she would need, but his priority was to stabilize her – followed closely by finding a way to increase the mana the well collected. The more mana he could accumulate, the faster Rachael would recover. And if the battle with Bilel and the conversion of the city had taught him anything, it was that following the Seer's guidance reaped a ton of mana.

So, for now, his goal was to recover these gate pieces.

"Do we know where these pieces are located?" Kalisha asked, leaning forward and eyes gleaming with curiosity. "Or what they might do?"

"Not exactly," Finn grunted. Of course, the Seer had been vague on those details.

He sighed. "But she did indicate that we may not be alone in hunting for them."

His daughter picked up where he'd left off. "I've been researching the other travelers. Just like Finn here, it seems several of our kind have emerged as avatars of the various gods. A man named Alexion rules over the Crystal Reach and appears to be allied with the goddess of light." She paused, a distasteful grimace tugging at her lips. "Although, he seems more interested in announcing his exploits and reveling in acclaim than actually doing anything of his own. I'm not certain I see him as much of a threat."

A frown creased her lips then, and she leaned forward. "More problematic might be this Twilight Throne. It is ruled by a man... well, a teenager, I suppose. His name is Jason."

"A kid poses a threat to us?" Aerys asked, skepticism dripping from her voice.

Julia just shook her head. "This isn't any normal kid." She waved at the city below them. "It took thousands of us working together to conquer Lahab."

"I recall," Aerys retorted in a dry voice.

Julia met her eyes evenly. "Well, as best I can tell,

Jason took out his city by *himself* within the first week or two of entering this world."

A stunned silence suddenly hung across the throne room.

"You can't be serious," Kalisha replied, shaking her head.

"I am," Julia said. "And then he managed to thwart an army gathered by Alexion shortly afterward, with far fewer numbers, equipment, or training."

She looked at the members of their council. "He's a threat. And a big one. And there will likely be others over time. We still have yet to see any evidence of the avatars for the water, air, and earth gods. And we have to assume the possibility of alliances forming."

As he observed the dour reactions of Aerys and the guild emissaries, Finn spoke up, "In short, we need to prepare. Grow our strength and numbers. Train our troops. And start sending scouts into the world to begin teasing out the location of these gate pieces. That is what I would ask of you for now."

They all nodded, content with that answer.

"Well, in that case, we should get back to work," Brutus declared, rising from his seat, the others following his lead. He turned his eyes back to Finn. "If you should need our assistance, do not hesitate to call on us. We are all still in your debt."

And then, as one, they beat their fists to their chest.

"*Najmat Alhidad*," they murmured.

Finn mimicked the gesture, and the group departed. Upon their departure, the Infernal Guard snapped back into position, creating a secure perimeter around the terrace.

"If anything, you downplayed Jason's threat," Kyyle said, glancing at Julia. "I watched those videos..." He trailed off, a shudder rocking his body. "They were gruesome."

Julia was nodding. "And they point to another problem," she said.

Finn glanced at her with an inquiring expression.

"These videos that the travelers keep posting… they're an issue. That's how we had a sense of the protections ringing Lahab before we attacked. And while Jason has been circumspect with the use of his abilities, even the videos about him and the Twilight Throne provide useful strategic information. They offer a rough sense of his abilities, those of his companions, insight into his strategies and how he thinks, the layout and position of vital infrastructure within his city… You name it…"

"Okay, but what exactly are you suggesting?" Finn asked.

Julia sighed. "That we may also need to be *proactive* in suppressing information about ourselves and our city."

"Are you suggesting what I think you are?"

"If you're thinking I plan to hack into a bunch of forums and streaming platforms to delete content… then, yeah, you are," Julia replied with a small smile.

"I don't feel like I have to point out just how illegal that is —"

"I won't get caught," Julia interrupted him. "And besides, this isn't just some game. We used this damn hardware and software to *resurrect* Mom. Until we figure out a way to pull her out of this world, well, we must play for keeps," she said, staring at him pointedly.

Finn was only mildly surprised that Julia had leapt to that conclusion. Of course, his daughter would be thinking about the long term – a future for Rachael that wasn't entirely dependent on this game, or on George and Cerillion Entertainment. And her suggestion *would* buy them valuable time…

"It's risky…" Finn murmured.

"Sure. But what if we inadvertently reveal information regarding our city and our people that allows this Jason to level Sandscrit?" she demanded. "It's an acceptable risk given what's at stake here."

Finn could only shake his head. He didn't have a better answer for that one. She was right, even if it pained him to admit it.

"You know that's going to require potentially hacking into the dev's own streaming platform though, right? Vermillion Live has already grown tremendously since the launch of the game, and the ad revenue alone is significant. This is one of their cash cows. They're going to defend it," Kyyle offered. "If they detect you, you might be looking at a permanent ban… or worse."

Julia nodded. "Which is why I'm going to do this alone. If I get caught, then, worst case, I get a ban, but you two can keep going." She shrugged, a grin stretching across her face. "Besides, I'm pretty good. I'm not exactly planning to get caught."

Finn chewed on the inside of his cheek in thought. He expected that if Rachael had overheard Julia's batshit plan, she'd have immediately shut it down. It was risky. Julia was talking in terms of a ban, but Kyyle was right. Finn knew firsthand how vindictive George could be. He wouldn't stop with a slap on the wrist – especially if he discovered that Julia was Finn's daughter. She could be looking at criminal charges.

At the same time, did they have a better option?

He was still sitting on a load of cash from his golden parachute. He could hire lawyers if need be and tie the company up in knots for years. And that was putting aside some of the more invasive activities of the game world he'd already noticed – he doubted that the general public was aware that the game was scraping their memories. He'd likely need to spend a decent chunk of his funds to help build up the infrastructure he would eventually need to house Rachael's consciousness, but he should still have plenty of resources left over.

And besides, that was essentially *blood money* – funds the company had paid him to shut up and go away after they had stolen Rachael from him. It was fitting that it would now be pledged to protect her and find a way to bring her back.

"Fine," Finn said. He spared a glance at Julia. "But be careful."

"I always am," she replied with a grin.

Yet Finn didn't feel any humor as he met her gaze. His thoughts were only on the future. On the preparations that needed to be made – both in-game and out. On the battles that lingered on the not-so-distant horizon.

And, always and forever, on Rachael.

Chapter 50 - Remorseful

Finn sat cross-legged atop the sand, the fingers of his right hand drifting through the grains and letting the particles cascade across his skin. He took in the courtyard that loomed around him. Dusk was bleeding into night, allowing him to avoid the bustle of activity that typically marked this place in the daylight hours. Long shadows were now cast by the flaming torches that ringed the enclosure.

After the attack on the city, the Mage Guild courtyard, like all of Sandscrit, had been transformed. Flames now lined the roof of the guild, the flames spiraling up into the night sky. The worn sandstone terrace that ringed the pit in the center of the courtyard had given way to partially melted glass banisters and columns, the substance reflecting and refracting the firelight in strange angles that caused the shadows to twist and dance.

Once his meeting with Aerys and the other emissaries concluded, he'd been bombarded by an almost endless litany of complaints and mundane problems. The issues ranged from frustrations with the new décor – something Finn certainly had little control over – to how the guilds would now handle intake and recruitment. Despite his conversation with the new "guild emissaries," the relationships among the competing factions were still somewhat strained, and he expected this would only become worse over time as the threat of their common enemy faded from memory.

Finn had also begun to see Aerys and the emissaries' motive in naming him Emir.

If everyone was bound under a single banner, then all complaints ultimately fell upon his shoulders. He'd learned that early on in the business world as well. When you're the boss, the buck stops with you. That seemed to be true no matter what world he was in.

He could imagine the group had shared a good laugh while they were leaving.

They'd played him like a sucker, he realized, shaking his head ruefully.

"Your point this time," he muttered to himself. "But I'm going to remember this."

This was the first free moment he'd had since the encounter with Bilel. Combined with the familiarity of his former training grounds, he suddenly realized that he hadn't checked on his notifications in quite some time. With a swipe of his wrist, he brought up his UI, and a tumble of screens cascaded down in front of him.

x21 Level Up!
You have (105) undistributed stat points.

x2 Spell Rank Up: Mana Absorption
Skill Level: Intermediate Level 9
Cost: 63% of mana drained as health damage.
Effect 1: The caster can absorb ambient fire mana, adding the energy to their total mana pool.
Effect 2: Increased absorption range, sensitivity, and area of effect.

x3 Spell Rank Up: Molten Beam
Skill Level: Beginner Level 9
Cost: 140 Mana/second. Must be channeled.
Effect 1: Fires a beam of molten energy dealing damage equal to $180 + (INT \times 33\%)$.

x2 Skill Rank Up: Mana Sight
Skill Level: Intermediate Level 10
Cost: Permanently reduces your mana regeneration by 20 mana/second. You are now blind to regular spectrums of light.
Effect 1: Ability to view ambient mana. Current vision is [good].
Effect 2: Ability to isolate mana types. All types unlocked.

x3 Skill Rank Up: Concentration
Skill Level: Intermediate Level 5
Effect 1: Ability to split your focus between [3] tasks.
Effect 2: Improved ability to ignore pain or disruptions.

x4 Skill Rank Up: Multi-Casting
Skill Level: Intermediate Level 8
Effect 1: -40.0% casting speed on the second spell.
Effect 2: -17% reduced channeling cost.

Translucent Flame (Crafted by Nar Aljahim)
This hand has been built entirely of the so-called neurogem material that you discovered within the depths of the Forge and was crafted by an ancient fire elemental. A Focusing Prism has been set in the base of the hand, although its use is currently unknown. Experimentation may be required to unlock its ability.
Quality: A
Level: 17
Health: 820
(Soulbound)

Adaptable Limb
Skill Level: Intermediate Level 3
Cost: 500 Mana
Effect 1: Allows the caster to make [moderate] modifications to the limb.
Effect 2: Decreases shift time by 22%.

Focusing Prism
Total Mana Stored: 0/52,000 (160% scaling)
Increased Effective Range: 130 yards (160% scaling)

Soulforged Item (Bonded by Nar Aljahim)
This item has been imbued with the Najima of the

traveler named Finn. The limb's health is counted separately from the traveler's regular health pool and will scale as the item levels. Damage is repaired using the 1/6 of the user's mana regeneration. Destruction of the limb will result in the user's death, and the limb will return upon respawn.

As Finn reviewed the notifications, he couldn't help but reflect on how far he'd come since the day he'd entered this world.

He could still remember stepping out into the sands of this very courtyard for the first time, desperately trying to run away as Brutus' golems stalked him and the rest of the novices. At the time, the fire mage's abilities had seemed impossibly powerful – a level of skill and strength that Finn couldn't hope to match. And yet, in the span of just a few short weeks, that encounter now paled in comparison to many of the creatures and people he'd faced.

Although, he'd still taken away an important lesson from the fire mage.

Physical stats weren't to be underestimated.

With that reasoning in mind, Finn placed 60 of his points into *Intelligence,* and the remainder he spread equally among *Dexterity, Vitality*, and *Endurance.*

His allocation complete, he pulled up his character status.

Character Status			
Name:	Finn	**Gender:**	Male
Level:	139	**Class:**	Fire Mage
Race:	Efreet	**Alignment:**	Lawful-Neutral
Fame:	4300	**Infamy:**	0
Health:	3040	**H-Regen/Sec:**	11.55

Mana:	3279	M-Regen/Sec:	62.79
Stamina	2240	S-Regen/Sec:	15.50
Str:	47	Dex:	155
Vit:	235	End:	155
Int:	599	Will:	30

Affinities			
Dark:	4%	Light:	11%
Fire:	56%	Water:	5%
Air:	3%	Earth:	13%

Even his character sheet barely resembled what it once was. But that growth had come at a cost, even if he tried to hide it. The plain white bandage that covered the amalgamation of metal and crystal that had replaced his eyes. His left hand – fires perpetually circling through the crystalline fingers – tucked away beneath his robes. Horns that now jutted from his head and the scales that lingered along his skin. And above his brow hung that flaming crown, both a reminder of his escape from the Abyss and a warning to those that would challenge him.

"I've come a long way," Finn murmured to himself.

Then his eyes drifted down to the golden urn cradled in his lap.

Unfortunately, Abbad would never get a chance to see the culmination of that hardship or what might eventually follow.

He could still remember the librarian's face – the stoic expression when he'd told Finn to place his hand on that first crystal to test his affinity and the look of shocked surprise when a blaze had ignited within its depths. The hastily whispered words of warning.

And after that? Abbad had only continued to put his life on the line for Finn.

Teaching him in the quiet of the Mage Guild

library. His careful guidance when Finn nearly burned down the stacks. The way he'd sparred with Julia – known about her presence from the beginning but still helping to keep her hidden. The words of wisdom when Finn had finally made it out of the guild and come face-to-face with the Emir for the first time.

Abbad had been there all along – just a whisper in the shadows.

He squeezed his eyes shut, a hollow pang aching in his chest.

This is stupid, he told himself. *He's just an NPC. A few bits of code.*

And yet his loss still hurt... and left him feeling guilty.

Like he could have done more. Worked harder. Fought more fiercely. Moved just a hair faster in that final sprint toward Bilel...

Finn swallowed hard and gently lifted the lid from the urn, observing the ashes that rested within its depths. It was pointless to second-guess himself now. He knew that. There were no do-overs here. There was no load screen. Abbad was gone. And perhaps it was that finality that gave his digital life weight and heft. He wasn't just a string of code – to be copied and pasted back into existence.

He was gone. Permanently.

And that felt *real*.

Finn let out a sigh, the fingers of his right hand twitching through a series of gestures – summoning the same small balls of flame that Abbad had taught him to use all of those days and weeks ago. He set the urn down carefully before him and then directed those orbs forward, setting them to spin around the small container. They whirled faster and faster, forming streaks of orange in the dark courtyard.

And that miniature vortex soon began to lift the ashes from the urn. They drifted up into the air, streaming up into the night sky. And in Finn's enhanced sight, he saw only a vortex of yellow and orange – of air and fire. A brief union that sent Abbad's remains racing up into the sky where he belonged.

Nar Aljahim's words returned to him then...

"Life and death are an endless, revolving circle. We flare to life in an instant, burn brightly, and fade back into darkness... only to return again."

Finn resolved in that moment to continue the circle. He would make certain that Abbad's death hadn't been for nothing, that his influence would continue long after his passing. That his name would be remembered...

Within only moments it was over.

The urn depleted, and the fires winking out.

"Goodbye, Abbad," Finn whispered, struggling to hold back the molten tears he felt welling at the corners of his eyes.

"You have given up much," a voice spoke. "Parts of yourself. Intangibles such as pain and hardship. As well as friends... companions."

Without even looking up, Finn recognized that voice. He forcefully pushed down the emotion that had welled in his chest. He'd been expecting this encounter, but, of course, the timing wasn't ideal. And Finn couldn't afford to show any sign of weakness.

"A price I was more than willing to pay," Finn answered softly. "But I didn't make *this* choice. Abbad chose this for himself. His sacrifice made all of this possible."

A man sat down across from him, his features outlined in the glowing blue of Finn's *Short-Sighted,* revealing Eldawin's face. The older man peered at him intently, the lines around his eyes bunching.

"I take it Thorn and his merry band of sycophants are positioned beneath the terrace and out of sight?" Finn inquired, not bothering to reach for a weapon. He doubted that it would do much good against the members of the Order.

"They are," Eldawin answered. "Although, I thought we would speak alone."

A small smile pulled at Finn's lips. He had played

out the outcome of this conversation a million different ways, but this is the one that had seemed most probable.

If Eldawin wished to speak, then there was room to *negotiate*.

"You have succeeded in slaying the demon, although, I understand you have only further solidified your union with the Crone," the older man said – not a question, but a statement.

"I suppose it would seem that way to you. Although, they have a saying in my world," Finn replied. "Keep your friends close and your enemies closer."

Eldawin raised an eyebrow at that. "The Seer has something I desire… but that doesn't mean that hers is the only path to obtaining it," Finn continued. "Better that she thinks me a willing participant and an ally than an enemy."

"It would indeed appear that the line between friend and foe has become especially blurry of late," Eldawin responded, a subtle undercurrent to his response.

And yet we wouldn't be having this conversation if you didn't see value in keeping my alive, Finn thought. Thorn's words from back at the Forge were still fresh in his mind. He'd referred to Eldawin as a *pragmatist*. It was time to see if that observation held true.

Finn glanced up at him, meeting his eyes. "Indeed, it has. The guilds and Khamsin are united. I granted your people their autonomy – free passage and trade within Sandscrit. Old aggressions have given way to a reluctant peace. One contingent upon loyalty to the new Emir, of course.

"It would be a shame if someone were to unravel that tentative union. If something were to happen to me, I expect chaos would descend again upon Sandscrit, with the guilds vying for power, old hostilities would likely flare. The blood of many of the desert folk would once again stain the sands. The blood of innocents."

If he hadn't been watching Eldawin's expression intently, he might have missed the fleeting frown that crossed his face. But he didn't. Clearly, the older man had picked up on the subtext of his words.

"And yet some hostilities cannot be entirely forgotten," Eldawin answered, choosing his words carefully.

Finn tilted his head. "Perhaps not. But they could be delayed, if only temporarily. And a new alliance could possibly be formed if their motives were aligned."

A long pause followed those words, neither man moving.

"What exactly are you proposing?" Eldawin asked more bluntly.

You have him now, Finn thought, resisting the urge to smile.

"There are other avatars and other gods. Five, to be precise. And the names and locations of the avatars for both light and dark are now known. Their names are Alexion and Jason. Of the two, Jason poses the greater threat to both me and to your people. He will come here eventually in pursuit of his god's goals."

Fires simmered in Finn's eyes as he stared at Eldawin. "I suggest that you take the fight to him. Weaken him. Delay him. Destroy him if you can."

Eldawin stared back, unfazed. "This would seem to benefit you alone, increasing your power among the other avatars."

"It protects your own people as well," Finn retorted. "If you strike against me, this region will descend into chaos and anarchy. If you strike at these others, you protect your own and allow me to continue to endear myself to the Seer. Most importantly, it buys us time."

"Time for what exactly? What would you offer the Order in return?"

"The Seer has something that I want – that I need. Once I've obtained that from her... well, I'll have more options," Finn said calmly. "I foresee an outcome where we could both benefit – where I obtain what I want, and you accomplish your own goals."

Eldawin chewed on that thought, his eyes going

distant.

Then he abruptly rose, his feet padding across the sands.

Damn it, Finn thought, closing his eyes.

He had melted down some of his orbs into thick bracelets that now encircled his ankles and wrists. He'd grown tired of needing to reach into his pack each time they were needed, and the jewelry looked innocuous – at least to those unaware of his abilities. If need be, he could light up the metal and melt it down in an instant. Although, he doubted it would be enough to allow him to face Thorn.

Then he heard those footsteps stop…

"It will be done."

When Finn glanced up, no one lingered upon the sands of the courtyard. He detected no telltale energy amid the shadows that lapped and danced across the terraces around him. There was only the faint whistle of wind and the whisper of sand blowing across the courtyard.

It seemed he had succeeded – delaying the executioner's axe a moment longer.

But that was all he needed.

Time to gather more energy.

Time to build up his forces and his own power.

Time to develop and create new servers – a home for Rachael's consciousness.

And now he had it…

Epilogue

November 11, 2076: 41 days after the release of Awaken Online.

Finn sat atop his throne, eyes focused on an object in the distance and brow furrowed in thought. An airship rested upon the sands just outside of Sandscrit, the vessel built of hard wood and balloons filled with heated air rising above the deck. Even from this distance, he could make out the crew walking across the deck and the telltale surge of amber energy signaling the presence of air mages.

And ringing the vessel was a group of the Infernal Guard, their forms illuminated in the glowing green that signaled their heavy plate. Just behind them stood their fire mage partners. Those orange-robed men and women channeled a steady stream of fiery energy toward the guard, igniting their armor and keeping them at the ready.

The ship had touched down only an hour ago, arriving out of the blue skies without any fanfare. It had landed outside the city, and Finn's troops had swiftly encircled it. Yet that wasn't what was bothering him. In the short few weeks that had followed Bilel's death and the conversion of the city, there had been many new travelers who had started in Sandscrit – lured by the promise of rolling their avatar as an Efreet. Several caravans of residents had even managed to make it to the city through an overland route by way of the mountains to the south.

No, what was worrying him was how the ship's captain had requested an audience with him – by *name*. A name that shouldn't have been known outside the desert sands.

It seemed that his anonymity was already beginning to fade. He had known it wouldn't last forever. He'd just hoped it would last a touch longer.

"What's our play here?" Julia asked from his side.

Finn shook his head. "We see what they have to say." He waved at the guards that ringed the throne room.

"They pose little immediate threat."

Julia shot him a sharp glance. "You and I both know that isn't the problem. We haven't had much success in identifying the locations of the gate pieces, and the Twilight Throne has already begun to recover in the aftermath of the Order's attack."

Finn frowned. There was truth to her words.

"The source of their information is also troubling," Julia muttered. "They might just be guessing, and by speaking with them, we only risk confirming our presence and abilities."

"They must have discovered a forum post or video that you missed," Finn offered, waving a hand. "You can't reasonably expect to catch everything."

This earned him a snort. "Uh, who do you think you're talking to? I've got every bit of information regarding this place locked down *hard* – and our enforcement of the recording ban within Sandscrit has been quite successful... at least, after we made an example of several of the more stubborn travelers," she amended grudgingly.

"It only takes one," Finn replied with a sigh. "Either way, we knew this peace was only temporary..."

His daughter didn't bother to respond, her mouth curling into a frown. Then she shot Daniel a look. "Stay on your toes. I want a scan of their faces as soon as they enter the room. Search the net to find anything you can and then push that information to Finn."

"Technically, I don't have any toes," Daniel chirped from beside Finn's shoulder, weaving through the air.

At Julia's sour look, his dance slowed. "But I understand your point..." the AI muttered more sedately.

"Don't mind her. She's just on edge. How do I look?" Finn asked Daniel.

Daniel rotated toward him and hesitated for a moment. Finn sat upon a throne of molten glass, fires curling within its depths. His left hand rested upon the armrest, the crystal gleaming in the sun that shone down on the tower. Those flames were matched by the crown that hovered just above his head, helping to pull focus from the plain white bandage that still covered his eyes. That thin piece of cloth had come in handy. Many would-be opponents over the last few weeks had greatly underestimated him.

It was difficult to see a blind man as a threat.

"Suitably intimidating," Daniel chirped. "Although, I still say a few travelers' heads on pikes would help set the mood..."

"Bloodthirsty little nightlight, aren't you?" Julia said with a soft chuckle.

"I've just come to understand the importance of a certain... ambiance," the AI retorted.

They were soon interrupted as a heavy rhythmic thumping came from the entrance to the throne room, one of the Infernal Guard pounding a mailed fist against the door. "Visitors for the Emir," he spoke loudly, his voice carrying across the tower.

This is it, Finn thought to himself. *Time to put on my game face.*

The doors leading up to the dais opened, and two strangers stepped forward – a man and a woman. They had been stripped of their weapons and armor, the Khamsin having searched them carefully long before they had been permitted within the palace grounds. Even so, Finn inspected them with his *Mana Sight*. He saw no telltale glimmer of mana that would indicate the presence of weapons – mundane or otherwise. Although, the man's energy was unusual. He had a much stronger concentration of light mana than Finn had ever seen before, his body practically glowing. That energy also seemed to condense across his back.

He switched back to *Short-Sighted*, taking in their appearance.

The pair both wore masks that covered most of their faces, likely fire-resistant, which helped ward off the heat and sand of the city. The rest of their clothing was fashioned from fine cloths and silks, a glimmer of azure energy denoting cooling crystals embroidered into the fabric. Not a trace of dust marred their clothing despite how long they must have traveled to reach this place.

That indicated that they were aware of the city's heat aura and had planned accordingly. Not a great sign. The woman also didn't walk with the air of a fighter, her steps strident and unconcerned. In contrast, muscle rippled beneath the man's luxurious clothing, and he eyed the guards out of the corner of his eye – marking their number and position.

A merchant or politician and a warrior then.

And they were clearly travelers. Residents were typically far more timid in approaching Finn. Possibly having something to do with their *mortality*. Although, a few of the travelers that graced his city had come to learn that immortality came with its own downsides. Finn had been forced to improvise a suitable punishment for their transgressions.

Dealing with some travelers felt like herding cats, and he could almost sympathize with the more rigid system that Bilel had designed to keep them in check. *Almost.*

A small icon appeared in Finn's peripheral vision, counting down from 10 seconds as Daniel discreetly scanned their visitors and began to compile profiles on them. Even with only a partial scan of their faces, he could match their retinal patterns to a few not-so-public databases.

Julia stepped forward. "You are addressing the Prophet of the Flame, the Stormbringer, the *Najmat Alhidad*, and the Emir and ruler of this city. State your names and business in Sandscrit."

The woman stepped forward first. "My name is Evelyn," she said, pulling away her mask. Her voice was even and relaxed, either a natural sign of confidence or a very convincing façade. "I am the proprietor of a trade guild based out of Barrow – to the west of the Crystal Reach. I am here to explore a possible business relationship with your fine city." As she finished speaking, she bowed her head, although her eyes never left Finn's face.

Finn's attention shifted to the man beside her, although he made sure not to tilt his head, maintaining the illusion that he was blind. "And your companion?" he asked quietly.

The man eyed the bandage across Finn's eyes, his brow furrowing. He spared an uncertain glance at Evelyn before stepping forward and removing his own mask.

"My name is Alexion…"

As soon as the words left his lips, Daniel's tooltip struck zero, complete profiles on the pair scrolling down the corner of Finn's vision.

Finn barely moved – just a twitch of his fingers – yet the Infernal Guard leapt into action immediately. Their plate armor flared to life within a matter of seconds, their flesh and bone melting away into living flame as they thudded forward in an orange blur. Lances were soon leveled at both Evelyn's and Alexion's necks – their eyes widening.

An ominous silence now lingered above the throne room, the guard and their guests frozen in place – the flames wrapping the guard the only thing moving.

"Evelyn St. Clair and Alex Lane," Finn murmured.

They were now staring at him in surprise.

As he casually skimmed the profiles now floating in the air beside him, he could start to understand how these two had discovered his city – despite Julia's efforts. This was George Lane's *son* standing in front of him. And he was starting to suspect that Alexion had used some of his daddy's access and sway to uncover the location of Finn's city.

He shook his head. "This was foolish. Incredibly foolish."

Finn leaned forward upon his throne. "Tell me, why should I let either of you walk away from my city – much less sign a trade deal? It seems I have something much, much more valuable standing before me – the light avatar himself."

Alexion swallowed hard, some of his swagger

having disappeared with a weapon at his throat. "Then kill us if you must. We'll simply respawn."

Finn barked out a laugh. "Kill you? You must truly think me an idiot. Oh no, we have a much better way of dealing with travelers here." He waved at the guards to remove them, and the Infernal Guard pressed forward.

"Wait!" Alexion barked. "We came with an offer… something even more valuable than taking an avatar out of play."

Finn held up a staying hand, and the guard hesitated. "Which is what exactly?"

"A gate piece," Alexion choked out around the tip of a lance.

Now *that* gave him pause.

The guards were mostly for show. He could have handled these two himself – much less with Julia standing beside him. But he had to admit he was intrigued. This man had the stones to track him down – likely even violating his daddy's own rules. The profile that Daniel had pulled together also indicated that Alex here was rather estranged from his father – the occasional public appearance aside. And the woman beside him was hardly a vapid beauty. Her eyes shone with intelligence and her profile indicated that she had high-profile connections of her own back in the real world.

The profile also didn't indicate that Alex was stupid. In fact, quite the opposite. And he had to have known what Finn was and his allegiance to the fire goddess. If not before they landed, then certainly once they'd entered Sandscrit.

That confidence lent some credibility to his claim…

"Hmm…" Finn murmured. Then he waved the guards away, the heavily armored men and women settling back into their positions around the throne room.

"Well, go on," Finn urged Alexion. "You have sixty seconds to make your case… or you will be making a short trip to a dungeon cell."

Alexion coughed to clear his throat, eyeing the Infernal Guard with a wary expression and attempting to regain some semblance of composure. Finn's immediate and violent response had clearly thrown him off guard. "Well, as I was about to say, my name is Alexion, and I'm the leader of the Crystal Reach and the light goddess'..."

"We're well aware, *Alex*," Finn drawled. "There are plenty of videos of you preening for the camera, and Vermillion Live makes a habit of plastering your pictures about."

He paused, noticing the flash of white light surge through Alexion's mana. *Pride*.

"Although, perhaps not quite as frequently as your rival... What is his name? Jason?" Finn observed, feigning ignorance.

As soon as he spoke that name, he could see anger coil through Alexion's energy.

He'd clearly touched a nerve. Interesting.

"That's actually why we're here," Alexion ground out, maintaining his composure despite Finn's baiting. He wasn't quite as hot-headed as Daniel's profile would have led him to believe. Perhaps he had learned to cool his temper. "After the attack on the Twilight Throne, Jason was able to recover a gate piece – a piece that we managed to steal from him in the aftermath of that battle."

Finn raised an eyebrow. He knew that as well. It had been captured on video.

"I'm assuming you're going to arrive at a point eventually?"

Alexion frowned, anger flashing through his energy again. Ahh, the kid was arrogant. Unaccustomed to being challenged. That was another weakness Finn could exploit.

"The *point* is that we would like to offer you a deal. We propose giving you the gate piece that we recovered from Jason," Alexion said finally.

Finn snorted. "Out of the kindness of your heart, hmm? What do you wish in return?"

Alexion glanced at Evelyn and then back to Finn. "We would propose a temporary partnership. The enemy of my enemy is my friend – isn't that the expression?"

Finn remained silent – although the irony of Alexion's statement was not lost on him. It hadn't been so long ago that he had spoken the same words to Eldawin.

"You could use the gate piece to create a trap," Alexion continued, uncertainty flitting across his face. It seemed he was having trouble reading Finn's reaction. "Announce to the world that you've claimed a gate piece and reveal the location of your city —"

"And lure Jason here," Finn interjected, putting the pieces together. "Is that what you're proposing?" Alexion simply nodded, visibly tamping down on his irritation.

Finn shook his head. While this kid in front of him might have discovered the location of his city, he doubted Alex truly understood what was at stake for Finn. Or what he would do to secure even one of those gate pieces.

"And why should I take that risk?" Finn dissembled. "One gate piece in exchange for revealing the presence of my city and inviting arguably the most dangerous man in this world to come retrieve it? The last time you fought him, I believe he destroyed your entire army and destabilized your kingdom. That hardly seems like a fair trade – even for one of the gate pieces."

Alexion's expression faltered, suddenly uncertain how to respond. Then he squared his shoulders, golden wings snapping away from his back and causing the guards to shift uneasily. He must have kept his wings folded up across his back – which explained the unusual energy signature Finn had observed.

Alexion took a single step forward, his eyes flashing with white light. "There's also the alternative," he said, an ominous quality entering his voice. "Or did you think we would just waltz in here with no backup plan? If we don't stop it within the next four hours in-game, the location of your city and our entire dossier on you will be published on every single gaming forum and news network out there."

A sudden silence lingered across the throne room, and Finn saw Julia's hand clench around her lance. Yet he made a discreet gesture. She needed to stay calm.

"And then there's the issue of why this place has tried to maintain its secrets for so long... as well as the *how* of it all," Alexion continued. He paused briefly, letting his words sink in. "It's almost as though someone has been illegally accessing other websites and servers and deleting information..."

Finn watched him, keeping his expression perfectly impassive, even while his thoughts raced.

Alexion's poorly concealed threat didn't fluster Finn – but better to let this child think he had Finn between a rock and a hard place. He'd already known that Sandscrit would be revealed to the public eventually.

No, he was mulling on Alexion's offer. It was actually rather *tempting*. Jason may have begun to recover in the aftermath of the Order's attack on his city, but Finn hadn't been idle during that time. If there were an ideal time and an opportunity to take the dark avatar out of play, then this might be it. And the offer of the gate piece was appealing as well – allowing him to funnel greater energy toward Rachael. But it wasn't the in-game advantage that Finn was considering... it was who this Alexion was in the real world.

And, more importantly, what he potentially had access to.

Julia leaned forward, whispering in Finn's ear. "He could possibly get us close to the Cerillion Entertainment servers," she murmured.

Finn nodded. His thought as well.

It was one thing to stabilize Rachael within this world – but that was only a temporary solution. He wanted to *free* her completely from this place. Yet in the weeks since her resurrection, he had come to realize that he faced two problems. First, he needed to build a receptacle to house Rachael – no easy task. And even once he accomplished that feat, he would need some way to transfer her data.

Yet he wasn't talking about downloading some song or movie off the internet. He was talking about transferring a *human consciousness*. The scope of the data involved was staggering. To do that, he was going to need physical access to the servers where Rachael was being housed. And his bet was that those servers were located somewhere within Cerillion Entertainment's headquarters – likely kept under lock and key.

Even so, this plan represented a risk. He had been following Jason's progress closely since the creation of Sandscrit. He'd watched as the kid had helped form the water city and allied with its avatar. He'd seen Jason's testimony during the CPSC hearing. And he'd learned something important in the process.

Many, many others had made the mistake of underestimating that kid.

Yet, despite the risk, Finn already knew what he was going to do.

It seemed the time for hiding his presence was finally over.

"You have a deal," Finn announced, noting the smile that stretched across Alexion's face. He would let him think he had won some small victory – for now, at least. "Until the trap has been set, you will remain here within the palace. I'm certain you understand the need for confidentiality." Alexion's expression fell slightly. "You shall be our *guests,* if you will. And the gate piece?"

"It will be arriving by another vessel as soon as our air mages give the word," Evelyn interjected. "We have been keeping it mobile."

Finn raised an eyebrow at that. Now this woman – she was genuinely clever.

"Good. Then go send word to your crew. Julia will accompany you," he said, waving at his daughter. She hurried off with Evelyn in tow and would likely grab Kyyle on the way out to meet the airship. They would need to study the gate piece carefully before they prepared their trap.

Alexion let out a small sigh of relief, and Finn saw his mana begin to relax. "However, there's still the matter of my *payment…*" Finn continued.

"Of course, you can keep the gate piece—" Alexion

answered quickly.

"Oh, I plan to," Finn interrupted.

He rose from his throne, striding toward Alexion until he stood only a few steps away, staring directly into his eyes. The man seemed confused, taken aback by how easily Finn maneuvered the room despite his apparent blindness.

That was, until Finn pulled back at the bandage wrapping his face, revealing the smoldering metal that lingered there, glowing with an ominous red light. Alexion flinched away, his eyes widening, and his light mana fading. It seemed even his arrogance had a limit, his confidence wavering in the face of the molten metal that had replaced Finn's eyes.

"Now, let's talk about what else you can offer me."

The End

Thank you for reading!

I hope you enjoyed the story! This is the end of Finn's arc... at least for now!

Next up is Jason's book five! I'm guessing that one will be ready sometime in early 2021. After the events of Unity and now this Tarot series, I suspect you can probably tell that the next book is going to be *eventful*. There are definitely some epic happenings in store for our favorite Necromancer...

Please leave a review!

I can't overstate how important these reviews are to ensure other people get a chance to read my stories. I would also love to hear your thoughts – positive, negative, or anything in-between.

Please feel free to email me directly at **tbagwell33@gmail.com** if you have any questions, comments, or suggestions. If you see any errors, please let me know, and I will fix them immediately!

For all the latest info on my writing projects, check out my **blog** and sign up for my **newsletter**. We also have an awesome **Facebook group** and **Discord server** if you want to hang out with fellow fans. We do regular giveaways, and this is a really cool group of people. If you would like to help support me, please feel free to stop by my **Patreon** – where I typically publish early chapters.

Finally, if you want to find new books or talk about other Gamelit/LitRPG, feel free to check out this **group**.

Acknowledgments

I'd also like to give a shout-out to everyone who helped me write *Awaken Online: Inferno*. Like most great things, it takes a village to write a book. Or at least one that makes sense and is (relatively) error-free. Thank you all for your help and support!

- Ashley Anderson (Editor)
- Krista Ruggles (Artist)
- David Stifel (Narrator)
- Celestian Rince (Proofreader)
- Stephanie Fisher
- Cynthia Bagwell
- Phillip Bagwell
- Kyle Smith
- Christopher Brink
- Jonathan Decker
- Michael Vincent
- Robert Wierzbicki
- Duncan Vandecarr
- Evan Moore
- Jon Ford
- Disney Gonzalez
- Kyyle Newton
- Sean Nelson
- Alex Teine
- Gareth Warner
- Arthur G. Davidson
- Christopher Wible
- All of my Patrons. You guys are awesome!